"Rebecca York's writing is fast-paced, suspenseful,
and loaded with tension."
—Jayne Ann Krentz

"York delivers page-turning suspense."
—Nora Roberts

PRAISE FOR

EDGE OF THE MOON

"York has penned a convincing and sensual paranormal romance,
and readers who fell in love with the characters in her last book,
Killing Moon, will be glad to meet them again.   —*Booklist*

"She writes a fast-paced, satisfying thriller."   —UPI

"High sensuality and suspense . . . enticing."   —*Huntress Reviews*

"An enchanting trip."   —*Midwest Book Review*

"Clever and a great read. I can't wait to read the final book in this
wonderful series."   —*Paranormal Romance Reviews*

KILLING MOON

"Mesmerizing action and passions that leap from the pages with
the power of a wolf's coiled spring."   —*Bookpage*

continued . . .

"A delightful supernatural." —*Midwest Book Review*

"If you like romantic suspense . . . if you're a fan of paranormals [or if] you're fond of both genres, then *Killing Moon* has your name written all over it." —*All About Romance*

WITCHING MOON

"York's colorful characterizations, mood-setting sentences . . . and flair for details make this paranormal romance a compulsive read." —*Publishers Weekly*

CRIMSON MOON

"Once again, York delivers an exciting and suspenseful romance with paranormal themes that she gets just right." —*Booklist*

FULL
MOON

REBECCA YORK

BERKLEY SENSATION, NEW YORK

THE BERKLEY PUBLISHING GROUP
Published by the Penguin Group
Penguin Group (USA) Inc.
375 Hudson Street, New York, New York 10014, USA
Penguin Group (Canada), 90 Eglinton Avenue East, Suite 700, Toronto, Ontario M4P 2Y3, Canada
(a division of Pearson Penguin Canada Inc.)
Penguin Books Ltd., 80 Strand, London WC2R 0RL, England
Penguin Group Ireland, 25 St. Stephen's Green, Dublin 2, Ireland (a division of Penguin Books Ltd.)
Penguin Group (Australia), 250 Camberwell Road, Camberwell, Victoria 3124, Australia
(a division of Pearson Australia Group Pty. Ltd.)
Penguin Books India Pvt. Ltd., 11 Community Centre, Panchsheel Park, New Delhi—110 017, India
Penguin Group (NZ), Cnr. Airborne and Rosedale Roads, Albany, Auckland 1310, New Zealand
(a division of Pearson New Zealand Ltd.)
Penguin Books (South Africa) (Pty.) Ltd., 24 Sturdee Avenue, Rosebank, Johannesburg 2196,
South Africa

Penguin Books Ltd., Registered Offices: 80 Strand, London WC2R 0RL, England

This is a work of fiction. Names, characters, places, and incidents either are the product of the author's imagination or are used fictitiously, and any resemblance to actual persons, living or dead, business establishments, events, or locales is entirely coincidental. The publisher does not have any control over and does not assume any responsibility for author or third-party websites or their content.

FULL MOON

PRINTING HISTORY
Killing Moon: Berkley Sensation mass market edition / June 2003
Edge of the Moon: Berkley Sensation mass market edition / August 2003
Berkley Sensation trade paperback omnibus edition / February 2006

Berkley Sensation trade paperback ISBN: 0-425-20776-5

This title has been registered with the Library of Congress.

PRINTED IN THE UNITED STATES OF AMERICA

10 9 8 7 6 5 4 3 2 1

CONTENTS

KILLING
MOON

1

ROSS Marshall was dressed for stealth. Black knit shirt, comfortable black pants, black running shoes.

Just before sunset he pulled under the sheltering foliage of a low-growing maple and cut the truck's engine. After rolling down the window, he sat motionless behind the wheel of the Jeep Grand Cherokee, his dark eyes scanning his surroundings, his ears pricked for telltale warning sounds in the depths of the forest.

His senses were only those of a man. Still, he had trained himself to watch and listen with as much skill as a human could acquire. In the branches above him a few birds still chirped and rustled. And he saw a doe and a fawn come through the woods on the far side of the road. She stopped, sniffed the air, and tensed, then turned and bounded back the way she'd come, taking her offspring with her. He was sorry he had frightened her. Yet her instincts had been right.

As the gray of twilight edged into the darkness of night, he grabbed the knapsack from the seat beside him and exited the truck, uncoiling his six-foot-plus frame and brushing back the mahogany hair that fell across his forehead. For a moment he stood breathing in the scents floating on the spring air. Tipping his head up, he looked toward the heavens, toward the pinpoints of light winking to life in the black velvet of the sky.

As he focused upward, a vision stirred in his brain, and he imagined his long-ago ancestor standing in a sacred grove and asking the gods for powers beyond those of mortal men. His request had been granted. By the gods, or fate, or some cosmic jester. It had been granted for his sons, as well, and their sons after them, down through the generations.

Fingers of wind shaking the branches above his head brought Ross's mind back to the present. The world was different than it had been for his ancestors, yet some things never changed. Men still reached for the forbidden—and suffered the consequences.

His face set in hard lines, he hoisted his knapsack over a muscular shoulder and set off, blending into the shadows of the forest.

With an eagerness for the hunt, he quickened his steps, his running shoes crunching the brown leaves that still lay on the ground. The chain-link fence topped with razor wire was a hundred yards ahead. When he reached it, he squatted, opened his pack, and pulled out the wire cutters he'd brought. The pack contained other tools, as well. It would be too damn bad if he needed them later.

After laying his pack on a pile of leaves, he cut the links, and pulled the edges of the fence apart, making a hole wide enough to accommodate a low, lithe body. Then he quickly stood to pull the knit shirt over his head and toss it on top of the pack.

Pants and shoes followed. He hadn't bothered with underwear. The air was cold on his bare skin, but he stripped to the buff.

Closing his dark eyes, he called on ancient knowledge, ancient ritual, ancient deities as he gathered his inner strength, steeling himself for the feeling of disorientation, even as he said the words that he had learned on his sixteenth birthday.

"Taranis, Epona, Cerridwen," he intoned, then repeated the same phrase and went on to another.

"*Gá. Feart. Cleas. Duais. Aithriocht. Go gcumhdaí is dtreoraí na déithe thú.*"

The words and the blinding pain that came immediately after them had been the death of his older brother. Ross had had more luck. At least that was what he thought at the time, when he'd still been giddy with relief at his own survival. It was only later that he'd understood that he'd given up as much as he'd gained.

On that night so long ago, the words had helped him through the agony of transformation, opened his mind, freed him from the bonds of the human shape. He had tried more than once to watch in a mirror, but his vision had blurred as if his own consciousness rejected that which was beyond a man's comprehension.

But comprehension was apparently unnecessary for reality. Even as the human part of his mind screamed in protest, he felt his jaw elongate, his teeth sharpen, his body contort as muscles and limbs changed into a different shape.

The first few times he'd done it had been a nightmare of torture and terror. But once he'd understood what to expect, he'd learned to ride above the physical sensations of bones crunching, muscles jerking, cells transforming from one shape to another.

Thick gray hair formed along his flanks, covering his body in a silver-tipped pelt. The color—the very structure—of his eyes changed as he dropped to all fours, no longer a man but an animal far more suited to the forest around him.

A wolf.

A surge of freedom rippled through him, and he pawed the ground with the joy of a creature totally at one with nature. Raising his head, he sucked in a draft of air, his lungs expanding as his nose drank in the rich scents that were suddenly part of the landscape.

His body quivered. The blood sang in his veins. He wanted to throw back his head and howl for the sheer joy of it. But he checked the impulse, because the mind inside his skull still held his human intelligence. And the man understood the need for stealth tonight.

An owl screeched above him, flapped away into the night, and he saw the wings beat the dark air—saw the grace and power of the bird as it went in search of prey.

His own prey was on the other side of the fence. He pressed low to the ground, slithered through the hole he'd cut, then shook the dead leaves from his thick fur. Sniffing the wind again to get his bearings, he trotted into the woods. He knew that a house lay to his right, hidden by a dense stand of trees. Instinctively the wolf gave the place a wide berth—avoiding the evil that lurked there.

Eyes and ears tuned to his surroundings, he noted the rustling sounds of small animals scurrying to get out of his way. But he wasn't here to hunt the creatures of the forest tonight.

He had come to this tract of land for evidence that would satisfy human laws.

Scent was his most important sense, but his eyes were sharp, too, helping to guide him through the inky darkness under the trees. A quarter mile from his point of entry, he was stopped short by the thick, sickening odor of decaying flesh—too faint for a man to catch. Cautiously he approached a mound of newly turned earth where someone had dug in the forest floor, then piled the dirt back into place. The grave hadn't been there long. Only a thin layer of leaves and other debris had fallen to cover the fresh scar on the land.

He circled the mound, fighting the cloying scent, then pawed at the loose dirt, carefully removing the top layer of soil, and more. Less than a foot below the surface he discovered what he had been certain he would find—the partially decomposed remains of a woman's body, the flesh marred by stab wounds. Backing away, he scratched in the leaves to clean the tainted dirt from his claws.

Penny Delano, he thought. Or maybe Charlotte Lawrence. Both of them had been missing for months. Both of them, he was certain, had ended their young lives on this piece of property. Alone, except for their torturer. A son of a bitch named Donald Arnott.

It was Penny's parents who had hired him to find their daughter—and his investigation had led him to this grave in the woods. He had hoped that perhaps he was wrong, but now there was little doubt where their daughter was buried.

He was too focused on the grim pictures in his mind, too sickened by his discovery, to hear the crackle of dry leaves, the stealthy crunch of human footsteps.

The sound of a rifle shot and a bullet plowing into a tree trunk inches from his head brought his mind zinging back to his own present danger.

He was already sprinting into the cover of the forest before the next slug splatted into the ground behind him.

But he wasn't fast enough. The third shot caught him in the right hind quarter, sending a shaft of fire through the leg.

He didn't let it slow him down. Mind clenched against the pain, he put on a burst of speed, zigzagging through the woods, even as the sound of more bullets echoed behind him. Despite the fire in his leg, he was faster than any man as he circled into the forest, then headed back toward the opening he'd made in the fence, his ears tuned to sounds of pursuit.

Breathing hard, he reached the fence and flattened his body to the ground, his right hind leg in agony as he clawed his way toward freedom. Relief surged through him once he was on the other side.

Panting, he stood on wobbly legs, staring at the knapsack and pile of clothing he'd left on the ground.

If he changed back to human form, he could pick up his belongings, carry them away. But transforming now, when Arnott was closing in on him, was too dangerous. The shock of changing with a bullet in his body might knock him out cold.

When his wolf ears picked up the crunch of leaves in the distance, he was forced to make a decision. Snatching up his trousers in his teeth, he left everything else where it lay and headed toward the truck.

Arnott's own fence would stop him for the time being. He wouldn't be able to wiggle through the wolf-size opening—not without enlarging the hole. And the tools for doing that were on the other side.

Dragging the trousers along the ground, the wolf made it back to the truck and stood with his sides heaving.

As a wolf he was unable to utter the words of transformation aloud. But the silent chant echoed in his mind as muscle and ligament, skin and bone transmuted themselves once again—this time from wolf shape to human.

A cold sheen of sweat filmed his skin, but there was nothing he could do about the bullet torturing his flesh except grit his teeth and push past the agony. In the end, the effort was too much.

He realized he'd lost consciousness when he woke up on the ground beside the vehicle. He was still naked and now shivering with cold. His head was cradled in a pile of leaves and his leg was lying in a pool of blood.

Muzzy-headed, vision wavering, he longed to simply lie there on the cool ground and close his eyes again, but giving in to that impulse was a death sentence.

Summoning all his remaining strength, he pushed himself to a sitting position and grabbed his trousers, fumbling in the pocket for his keys. Thank God they hadn't fallen out during his wild dash to the truck.

Crawling toward the driver's door, he pulled himself up and managed to get the key in the lock. There was no point in wasting energy getting dressed. He simply tossed the pants onto the floor of the passenger side, wincing as his leg hit the console.

For a moment he sat gripping the steering wheel to keep from passing out again. Then he reached for the bottle of water he'd left on the passenger seat. Fumbling off the cap, he took a long swig, spilling some down his chest and belly.

With clumsy fingers he reached into the glove compartment and pulled out a first-aid kit. Unwrapping a bandage, he wound it around his thigh, stanching the flow of blood.

He held back a groan as he turned the ignition key, then pressed on the accelerator, wondering if he could stay conscious long enough to make it home. He'd made a mistake tonight by underestimating the man who'd dug the grave. Or maybe it had only been bad luck that he'd been discovered.

But it didn't matter what had gone wrong. Either way, he was in a hell of a mess.

DONALD Arnott stood with the rifle pointed toward the ground as he stared at the hole someone had cut in his fence.

Playing the flashlight beam over the forest floor on the other side of the chain links, he could see a trail of blood leading toward the road. The dog was hurt, all right. Maybe it was bleeding too bad to get much farther.

He swept the beam in an arc. When the yellow light struck a knapsack and a pile of clothing, he went rigid, then charged toward the fence, his fingers gripping the cold metal links as he stared in disbelief.

Holy shit!

He'd expected to come upon the big dog dazed and wounded—cowering against the barrier—waiting helplessly for the kill shot.

Instead he'd found someone had cut a damn hole in his fence. A hole large enough for the dog to squeeze through.

Turning, he trotted back to the house, where he quickly exchanged the rifle for a Beretta and grabbed a plastic trash bag. Then he jumped in his Land Rover and sped toward the gate.

Jesus. What if he hadn't come outside tonight?

He'd been walking through the woods—the need for another woman building in his gut like gas expanding through a rotting body. It had been weeks since he'd finished with Charlotte. And the memories of the things he'd done to her no longer had the power to bring him to hard, aching arousal.

After the first little blond bitch he'd taken, he'd waited almost a year before daring to repeat the delicious adventure. Last time, he'd been able to hold off for only a few months.

He made a guttural sound in his throat. Charlotte had been too weak, given up too easily. And he hadn't gotten the full measure of gratification he craved. That's why he'd been so restless tonight. But he was thankful now that he'd been out of the house because he'd heard the animal digging, taken aim, and scored a shot.

He screeched to a halt at the gate, jumped out of the SUV, and worked the combination on the padlock. After driving to the other side, he carefully relocked the barrier before barreling down the driveway and turning right, heading for the spot on the road parallel to where the knapsack was lying.

Was the man coming back for his stuff? Unlikely. Probably he'd gotten the hell out of the area while the getting was good, with or without the dog.

He found the knapsack and the clothing easily enough. Squatting, he stared at the abandoned possessions, wondering if this were some kind of trap. Like what? A bomb stuffed into a shoe?

With a snort, he pawed through the knapsack, finding a collection of tools. Then he picked up a shirt and shoes. Only the trousers and underwear were missing.

Touching the discarded clothing sent a shiver of dread slithering down his spine. Thrusting the feeling aside, he stuffed everything into the plastic bag he'd brought, hoping the guy had been stupid enough to have put an ID tag on the knapsack.

That would make things easier, although it wasn't essential. Someone had sent a dog to his private graveyard tonight—and he had to assume that it wasn't a random act of bad luck. Some bastard had discovered what he was doing and had come after him with a bloodhound. No, not a hound. Something with thicker, shaggier fur. Maybe a shepherd mix.

His hand clamped around the butt of the gun, the cold metal digging into his flesh.

He was going to find out who it was—because failure was not an option, not when failure meant the end of everything. Life. Freedom. And the sexual satisfaction he needed to exist.

2

MEGAN Sheridan folded her arms across her chest, rubbing briskly at the sleeves of her lab coat.

She'd already tried to turn up the heat, but a newly installed plastic box covering the thermostat made it impossible to change the setting without a key. One more Monday morning surprise at Bio Gen Labs.

"Is Walter trying to freeze off our fingers, then collect on the insurance?" she muttered under her breath.

Her coworker Hank Lancaster gave a sharp laugh and handed her a hot mug of coffee. The mug was a freebie from a drug company pushing a new diuretic, and the picture emblazoned on the side of the bright yellow ceramic showed a pair of kidneys.

"Here, maybe this will help. And don't let him hear you. He may think it's a good idea."

Megan rolled her blue eyes as she cupped her hands around the mug's warmth. Two years ago, after her medical internship at Johns Hopkins and a year of postdoc work, she'd had her pick of job offers from the biogenetic laboratories clustered around the Washington-Baltimore area.

She'd gone with Bio Gen because the CEO, Walter Galveston, had sold her on the potential of his up-and-coming company. Now in his early forties, Walter had learned the ropes at several area labs, then gone out on his own. After telling her he was looking for projects that would bring in money as well as scientific prestige, he'd listened attentively to her proposal for using gene therapy to treat Myer's disease, an inherited form of macular degeneration that struck in young adulthood. Walter had given the project priority at Bio Gen until some of the well-publicized deaths caused by gene therapy had hit the news.

Now he was holding up her clinical trials until she dotted every "i" and crossed every "t" in her proposal. Not only that, but in the past four months, she'd watched Walter shift her hours away from her project to routine paternity testing, chromosome studies, and genetic profiles—jobs that paid nice fees in the short run but contributed nothing to the basic genetic research that fired her enthusiasm.

From where she stood, it looked like Bio Gen had a cash flow problem. Only Walter hadn't bothered to share the information with his employees. And he hadn't bothered to come in on time this morning, either, Megan thought with a snort—then suffered a pang of guilt for her mutinous attitude. Bitching behind her boss's back made her feel uncomfortable. Yet sharing her frustration with her coworker was turning into a ritual, probably because their research goals were so similar.

She and Hank were both in their early thirties, both highly educated, both dedicated to their research projects. She'd gotten her MD, then realized it was impossible to keep her distance from her patients. She cared too much, was affected too much by their suffering and their deaths. And so she'd withdrawn to a safer venue—where she could impose the veil of lab procedures between herself and flesh-and-blood patients.

Hank had gone a different route—earning a Ph.D. in biology before coming to Bio Gen. He was different, too, in his feelings about people. While she appreciated the unique human qualities of each individual, he was the kind of man who classified everyone he met according to IQ. The smarter they were, the more he respected them.

She watched him walk down the hall to the front office, pause for a brief conversation with the receptionist, Betty Daniels, then return with a clipboard in his hand and a carefully bland expression on his face.

The feigned nonchalance didn't fool her. Sweeping back a lock of dark blond hair that had fallen across her eyes, she said, "You might as well hit me with the bad news."

He gave an upward thrust to the clipboard, managing to make it look like an obscene gesture. "We've got eighteen paternity cases this week. And almost as many clients who want genetic profiling before they consider having children."

Megan did a rapid calculation. That was going to suck up most of the workweek. Which meant that if she were going to do anything with her own project, she would be doing it after hours. Damn, what was wrong with Walter? Didn't he know that if she succeeded in her treatment protocol, Bio Gen would have plenty of money? Not to mention credit for a major medical breakthrough?

Hank rolled back the top sheet of paper and stabbed his long finger at a line on the second page. "There's a notation on this one—about a client who lives in Lisbon. Apparently he wants someone from the lab to go out there and get a blood sample."

"Lisbon, Howard County? Or Lisbon, Portugal?"

He laughed, apparently giving her points for the quick comeback. "Howard County."

"That's an hour's ride from here."

"Maybe he's got some nasty genetic defect that causes warts all over his body, so he doesn't go out in public."

"Sure."

"Or he could have a sick kid who can't be left alone."

Megan felt her stomach clench in that old familiar way. She didn't even know the man, but she could imagine what his life might be like. If he were taking care of a critically ill youngster with a serious genetic defect, he might well have trouble getting to the lab.

"Whatever it is, you can bet Walter is charging him through the nose for the house call." Hank let the top sheet fall back into place, set down the clipboard on the edge of her desk, and pulled a quarter out of his pocket. "I'll flip you for it."

"Sure. Why not?" she agreed, wishing she could be as blasé as he was. She called heads. And lost, of course. Her luck hadn't been particularly good lately.

"I'll cover the next house call," Hank offered as he took in her gloomy expression.

"Like we're going to get another one anytime soon," Megan answered, picking up the clipboard.

The conversation came to a halt when the outer door slammed open with enough force to shake the walls.

"What the hell was that?" Hank muttered as they exchanged glances.

In the reception area, a man was bellowing at Betty.

The administrative assistant's voice was unnaturally high as she responded—and hardly anything usually disturbed her equanimity. She was a veteran office manager whom Walter had enticed away from NIH. He liked having her in the front office for the combination of motherly warmth and polished efficiency she projected. And her word processing skills were nothing to sneeze at, either.

By unspoken mutual agreement, Megan and Hank started down the hall, bent on rescuing the poor woman.

They both stopped dead when they saw that the person bellowing at Betty was Walter Galveston. Ordinarily their boss looked like he'd just sauntered out of a photo session for *GQ*. This morning, his charcoal gray suit was rumpled, his expensively cut hair was mussed, and Megan thought his face appeared to have aged five years since she'd seen him Friday afternoon.

Her own features contorted. "Walter, what is it? What's wrong?"

He flapped his arm in an angry gesture. "Some bastard ran me off the road on the way here. Then he sped away before I could get his license number."

"Oh, my God. Are you all right? What about your car?"

His jaw trembled with emotion. "I'm just shaken up. But there's a gouge on the side of the Mercedes where I sideswiped a traffic barrier."

"Did you see what kind of car it was?" Hank asked.

Walter shook his head. "It all happened too fast, and I was busy staying out of that ditch where they're laying sewer pipes on Montrose Road."

Megan pictured the intersection he meant. "Were there any witnesses?"

"Probably, but everybody just kept driving by. You know—the usual behavior these days. People don't want to get involved. And no wonder. If you stop to break up an argument between two motorists, you could get your head blown off."

As she nodded in agreement, Hank asked, "What exactly happened?"

"The car came up behind me, nudged me to the side, then sped away."

"You think it was an accident?" Hank asked. "Or road rage? Did you do something to yank his chain? Cut him off or something?"

A guarded expression crossed Walter's sharp features. "I don't know."

Megan wondered if he *had* cut the other guy off—or done something else he wasn't going to admit.

Before they could ask any more questions, he was shoving open the front door. "Come see what the bastard did to me."

Bio Gen was in an industrial park, near the end of a one-story building of buff-colored brick strung out along a parking lot. Separating the entrance and the paved area was a five-foot strip of crabgrass. Walter's only concession to charm was a couple of conical evergreens in fancy cement pots on either side of the front door.

As Megan and Hank followed Walter down the short sidewalk and across the blacktop to the parking spaces, she braced against the late March wind. Betty trailed behind them, clutching a baby blue cardigan closed across her ample breasts.

Walter's gold Mercedes was parked in a reserved spot next to the handicapped space.

Her lab coat whipping around her legs, Megan followed Walter's gesturing hand and squinted, trying to locate the damage to the vehicle. Finally her gaze lit upon a hardly noticeable scrape in the gold metallic paint.

Behind Walter's back, Hank raised his eyes toward the heavens. "It shouldn't take too much to fix that," he commented.

"Yeah, well, it's not just the paint. There's a dent underneath you can feel if you run your hand along it. I'm going to start making calls to body shops right now."

As he strode back inside the building, his bemused audience followed.

Walter paused to grab a phone book from the drawer in Betty's desk and then stalked down the hall to his plush, private office, leaving his three employees in the reception area.

Standing with the others, Megan felt the awkwardness of the moment. Obviously nobody knew what to say about the boss's uncharacteristic behavior. The clipboard was still in Megan's hand. To give herself something to do, she looked at the name and the phone number of the guy in Lisbon. "Ross Marshall," she murmured. .

Betty responded almost instantly. "The guy who doesn't want to come in to the lab."

"Right. I guess you talked to him."

"Uh-huh." She paused for a moment, taking a pencil from the holder on her desk and fiddling with it. "He's got a very . . . compelling voice."

Perhaps Hank was worried that the Ross Marshall job was still up for discussion, because he turned and hurried out of the room.

Megan stood where she was, studying the secretary's unfocused expression and the fingers she ran up and down the pencil shaft. It wasn't like Betty to react to clients in anything but a professional way.

"Walter confirmed an appointment for this afternoon," the assistant informed her. "Mr. Marshall said he'd be home. So you or Hank just need to set the time."

"I'm doing it."

"I keep wondering what he looks like. Since I'm not going to see him, I expect a full report."

Megan blinked. "Okay," she agreed, as much to end the conversation as anything else.

Her curiosity piqued, she returned to her desk and dialed the phone number on the sheet. On the fifth ring, an answering machine picked up. Five seconds into the recorded message, she understood what Betty had been reacting to in the man's voice. It was assured, compellingly masculine. But there was something more. An inviting quality that set off a subtle vibration deep within her.

"This is Ross Marshall. I'm out of the office right now. Please leave your name and number, and I'll get back to you as soon as possible."

When he finished speaking, she looked again at the sheet in front of her. According to the notation, she was supposed to be calling a home number. Well, maybe the guy worked from home.

She'd hoped to get directions to his place. So she asked if he'd call her back, then added that she planned to be at his house around four-thirty. What she didn't say was that she was going to be really pissed off if she drove all the way to western Howard County for nothing.

A couple of miles away at the Second District police station, Detective Jack Thornton stared down at the thick file in front of him as he rubbed his thumb against his lean jaw.

Inside the file was a name he hadn't expected to encounter: Ross Marshall. One of his most useful contacts.

He'd met Marshall three years ago. Jack had just been promoted to detective and was working a seemingly unsolvable homicide case. A woman named Helen Dawson had disappeared from a car later found pulled into a patch of weeds along Falls Road. There were no suspects—except the estranged husband who was the beneficiary of an insurance policy that the woman had neglected to alter when they'd separated. The man had an alibi, though, that stood up to extensive investigation.

With no police leads, the woman's distraught parents had hired Marshall to find out what happened to their daughter. A week later, the PI contacted the department, saying he had some pertinent information. Jack had been skeptical at first, but he'd agreed to a meeting with Marshall at a coffee shop on Rockville Pike.

He remembered their first encounter with vivid clarity. The PI had been tall, athletic, intelligent looking, and reserved in a way that made it hard to get a handle on him.

Telling himself not to make any judgments until he heard the whole story, Jack had listened to the tale Marshall had to tell: that Dawson had been abducted, raped, and killed by a man named Billy Preston, a mechanic who had done some work on her car several weeks before and who had become obsessed with her. When she'd stopped for gas on the night she'd disappeared, Preston had asked for a ride to a nearby shopping center. But they had never reached that destination.

Jack remembered asking Marshall how he'd come up with that kind of detailed scenario. The PI had declined to reveal his methods, but the look on his face dared Jack to ignore the information. Still figuring it was a long shot, he had pursued the lead, using an outstanding traffic violation as an excuse to search Preston's car. He'd hit pay dirt when he'd found Dawson's bloodstained sweater stuffed in a gym bag.

Marshall never had explained how he'd fingered Preston, but the Dawson case had been the start of a working relationship between the two of them. On his end of it, Jack ran license plates for Ross, checked outstanding warrants, and meted out inside information available only to the department. In exchange, Ross provided leads that could have been obtained only by illegal means—or magic.

Jack didn't believe in methods impossible to verify. Which meant that Ross was collecting information through clandestine searches and other questionable procedures. The assumption put a barrier between him and the PI, a barrier that neither one of them had been able to breach.

Yet Ross kept coming to him when he had something he thought the police department could use. Although Jack admitted to himself that he still had suspicions about the guy, he continued to accept his help.

He stared across the squad room, his blue eyes unfocused. Then the phone rang on a nearby desk, and his attention snapped back to the file on his blotter—a five-year-old missing persons case, a man named Edward Crawford.

There was more in the folder than simply information on Crawford's disappearance. The man had been a suspect in the killings of several young women from the Baltimore-Washington corridor. Then his sister had reported him missing—and the murders had stopped.

That was the end of it—a Stone Who Done It. An unsolvable case. Until three weeks ago when torrential rains had washed a skeleton out of the ground in a rural area near Sugarloaf Mountain. It had been identified by dental records as Crawford.

It hadn't been Jack's problem five years ago. The dead man's folder had ended up on his desk because the primary investigator, Ken Winston, was now retired.

Jack had started by going over everything in the file: pages from Ken's notebook, a couple of Post-it notes, an old envelope with the sister's address, a couple of business cards, and neatly typed official paperwork.

One of the notebook entries had yielded a very interesting piece of information. A private detective named Ross Marshall had been hired to find out who murdered one of the missing women, Lisa Blake.

Jack paged to the medical examiner's report. Because of the deterioration of Crawford's body, the cause of death was undetermined. If the man had been shot, the bullet hadn't shattered any bones. If he'd been strangled, the hyoid bone hadn't been crushed. And there was no skull-crushing trauma to the head.

But a soil sample estimating the decay placed the burial at about the time of Crawford's disappearance.

The Frederick County officers who'd been called to the scene had searched for evidence. Things like old cigarette butts, a lighter, buttons—anything that might provide clues. But there was nothing useful. Either physical evidence had been covered by falling leaves, or someone had carefully cleaned up the burial site.

Next Jack studied the pictures of the grave, then of the skeleton, along with a few shreds of clothing that still remained. Also included was a close-up that showed the victim's neck and one shoulder. Accompanying text noted that these areas had been gnawed by a predator. And there had been some dog hairs near the body.

As he looked at the photo, an unaccustomed sensation of cold traveled across his skin. He had certainly seen far more gruesome bodies— like jerks who went up in the attic in the middle of summer to hang themselves and weren't discovered until several days later. So he wasn't sure why he was having such a reaction to the pictures of Crawford's remains.

Still, he had learned to pay attention to his hunches, and he had the feeling that Ross Marshall could tell him something about this case.

He went back to the folder, spreading out several sheets of Ken Winston's cramped handwriting. One cited a meeting requested by PI Ross Marshall to talk about Lisa Blake. Marshall had pointed the finger at Crawford, but Winston hadn't followed up on the tip. Well, that fit what Jack remembered about Winston, a tight-assed type unlikely to act on information he couldn't verify for himself.

A week after the meeting, another woman had been found murdered, although, again, there was no proof to link her to Crawford. Two days after that, the man had vanished off the face of the earth.

Winston had gone back to Marshall with some questions. Ross had no alibi. He'd been home alone in his house in Lisbon, he said. But there was no evidence that linked him to Crawford's disappearance, and Winston had been forced to give up on that angle.

Yet as Jack sat at his desk now, he couldn't stop his mind from playing out an interesting scenario:

Marshall goes to Detective Winston with evidence he's sure will nail Crawford. When Winston presses him for details on his sources, Marshall clams up. So Winston blows him off. Marshall stews over the lack of police cooperation. Then Crawford kills again, and Marshall takes the law into his own hands.

Jack thought it a fascinating line of speculation, even if he did say so himself, but it didn't fit with the Ross Marshall he knew. Marshall was calm, controlled. Had he been a hotdog five years ago? Angry and outraged enough at another woman's death to put Crawford away?

Jack drummed the blunt-cut nails of his left hand against the papers.

There were no other leads in the case besides the tie-in to Ross Marshall. If the media had known Crawford was a murder suspect, then the families of the victims might be possibilities. But the investigation hadn't gotten far enough to go public.

Which led him back to Marshall.

He'd never run a background investigation on the PI beyond checking to see that he didn't have a police record and that he wasn't a former cop who'd washed out and had to settle for the next best thing. Thinking about it, he realized how little he knew about the man—and how little he'd wanted to know. Because Ross had been a good contact, he hadn't wanted to rock the boat.

That might have been a mistake.

He'd gotten the impression from the Jeep Grand Cherokee Laredo Sport that Ross drove and his clothing that he lived a reasonably upscale life. And from their talks, he'd assumed he was a serious, career PI.

But working as a private investigator didn't usually bring in big bucks. Was freelance investigation Ross's main source of income? Was there something hiding in his background? A child custody battle? A lawsuit?

Mentally Jack checked off other sources of information. Utility bills. Cable and phone company records. The man's credit report.

Then, flipping open a notebook, he reached for the phone.

ROSS'S body was burning up. His mouth felt like a desert wasteland. And it took a major effort of will to distinguish reality from the fevered imaginings swirling in his brain.

Crawford. Arnott. His family. Father, mother, brothers—and all the children who had never had a chance.

In his lucid moments, he knew that if he didn't get to the bottle of antibiotics in the kitchen cabinet, he was going to die from the infection spreading from his leg to the rest of his body.

He'd arrived home yesterday—or was it the day before? He wasn't sure anymore because the hours had blended into each other like watercolor paint splotched by an unexpected spill.

He remembered sitting in the truck, gathering his strength for the drive home. He remembered the pain in his leg when he'd pressed on the accelerator. The rest of the trip came to him in nightmare snatches. Then he'd staggered into the house and down the hall to the bathroom, where he'd dug the bullet out, working in the oversize bathtub so that he could wash the blood down the drain. And he'd sloshed antiseptic onto the wound before tying on another bandage. If he'd been thinking more clearly, he'd have started antibiotics, too.

Too bad the disinfectant hadn't done the trick. Or perhaps the infection was just more of the bad luck dogging the Crawford case.

No. Not Crawford. Arnott.

Keep them straight, he ordered himself.

Crawford had died a long time ago. Or maybe he was coming back to get him. In his present condition Ross wasn't sure.

Yet he knew he needed to get out of bed, get to the antibiotics. Because an enemy might come charging through the door. And he suspected the pain of trying to change to wolf form now might finish him off. So he pulled open the drawer in the bedside table, got out his Sig .40, and slid in a clip.

Wrapping his hand in a death grip around the weapon, he heaved himself off the mattress and stood swaying on his feet, gritting his teeth with the effort to remain erect. By the time he reached the hall, his vision was blurring. Moving to the wall, he slid his shoulder against the vertical surface, willing himself to stay erect.

Every step was agony, but he pushed himself along, even when his muzzy brain forgot where he was going and why.

Blackness gathered at the edges of his vision. He made it as far as the rug in front of the sofa before he went down, first to his knees, then flat on his face—consciousness slipping from his brain even as he tried to struggle to his feet again.

3

MEGAN braked the car and stared through the windshield at the sign tacked to the gray bark of an oak tree at the foot of Ross Marshall's driveway.

NO TRESPASSING. THAT MEANS YOU.

The black letters were faded, and the white background had taken on a dirty gray tinge. But the aging appearance did nothing to diffuse the potency of the warning.

Marshall's voice might sound inviting, but the man didn't have the welcome mat out for company.

She felt her neck muscles tightening, felt the stirrings of pain at her temples, and made a deliberate effort to relax. She'd been stressed out almost from the moment she got to work that morning. No—stressed out since last night, since the phone call from Dory. Her sister had been drunk. Abusive. Angry.

And Megan had hung there on the end of the line, taking it. More than taking it. Abandoning her previous resolve, she'd ended up promising to write a check to cover Dory's rent so she wouldn't get kicked out of her apartment.

Megan stared unseeing at the dappled sunlight filtering through the trees. She and Dory both had inherited two hundred and fifty thousand dollars from their parents, a mind-boggling amount in light of their father's frugality. Megan had used part of her share on a down payment for a house. The rest was still in the bank.

Dory had gone through the money like a plague of locusts chomping through a wheat field.

Broke again inside of a year, she'd started working on her sister's feeling of guilt, and there was plenty of that. Enough so that this morning, even with time for second thoughts, Megan had put a check for nine hundred dollars in the mail.

Partial payment for sins she hadn't known she was committing.

She squeezed her eyes shut, struggling to push the painful memories out of her mind. Life had been tough for the Sheridan women—not because Dad had been into physical abuse. He'd known how to be careful of the law and nosy social service workers, how to deal out punishment that for the most part wouldn't leave any physical marks. Most of the damage had been psychological, and each of the Sheridan women had handled the pain differently. Mom had turned into a Stepford wife, terrified to do anything to set off her husband's derisive outbursts. To an outside observer, Megan admitted, her own demeanor must have appeared similar to her mother's. Being a good little girl was the easiest way to keep from setting off the man who seemingly lived to criticize and humiliate the women in his family.

But the surface had given no clue to what was inside her. Secretly she'd vowed to make something of herself—to prove to the tyrant who alternately belittled and lashed out in anger that she wasn't the fucked-up mess he wanted her to be.

Not like Dory—who had gone out of her way to prove the accusations true. Rotten grades. Shoplifting. Joyriding in stolen cars. A pregnancy when she was sixteen—ending in an abortion at Dad's insistence.

Last night, Dory had come back to a familiar theme—accusing Megan of abandoning her. And in a way it was true. A long time ago, she'd turned her back on everything familiar. Moved from Boston to Baltimore when she was still in college, because she'd had the strength to save only one person—herself.

Now it was too late for her to help her sister. About all she could do was try to stanch a bleeding artery with a Band-Aid.

Megan slumped down and rested her head against the steering wheel until a sudden puff of wind shook the leaves overhead and buffeted the car, bringing her back to present reality.

It was like some cosmic hand shaking her out of her lethargy. Raising her head, she looked around, then reminded herself that she couldn't afford the luxury of sitting here feeling sorry for herself—or anyone else.

She'd already wasted twenty minutes backtracking down Route 99 when her computer-generated directions had erroneously indicated a right turn instead of a left. On the other hand, now that she was finally at the entrance to Ross Marshall's property, she couldn't help wondering if this harebrained assignment from Walter was going to get her shot.

Thumbing through her purse, she pulled out the number she'd copied down that morning and reached for the phone she kept in the closed compartment below the dashboard. It was a portable phone—not attached to the car. But she wasn't the kind of dork who sat in a restaurant or strolled down the walkways of a mall while carrying on a loud private conversation that was going to annoy everybody within fifty feet of her. The car was where she was most likely to use the phone, so that was where she kept it, not weighing down her pocketbook.

After punching in the number, she listened to the ringing on the other end of the line, then the same recorded message she'd heard that morning.

"Mr. Marshall?" she asked, unable to keep her frustration from creeping into her voice. "Are you there? I'm at the end of your driveway. If you're home, pick up the phone."

Her plea met with silence, and she felt her anxiety level crank up a notch. Where was he? Hadn't he gotten her message? Or was something very wrong at the Marshall house?

She was normally a calm person. Methodical. Careful. And she ordered herself to settle down and think with the logical mind she knew she possessed. She was already late because of the map problem. What if Marshall had come outside to wait for her—and that's why he wasn't answering?

Or what if he'd called the lab after she'd left and canceled the appointment?

Clicking on the phone again, she dialed the Bio Gen number. Betty answered.

"Hi. It's Megan. I'm out on that house call. Did Mr. Marshall by any chance phone to say he wasn't going to be home?"

"I haven't heard from him. Isn't he there?"

"I don't know. I'm at the bottom of his driveway, facing a No Trespassing sign."

"Oh, dear."

There was no point in asking Betty what to do. She couldn't make a good judgment from her desk in Bethesda.

"Okay. I'll go on up there. But if you don't hear from me tomorrow, send the police," Megan quipped, speaking only half in jest.

Betty laughed nervously.

"Just kidding. I'll see you in the morning."

"Oh—before you hang up, I have a message for you from Dr. Stillwell."

Megan made a face, glad that Betty couldn't see her expression. "What did he want?" As if she didn't know.

"He wants to discuss that plan of action he proposed."

"Well, I can't do anything about it now. I'll have to call him later." Or never, she thought as she got off the line.

Carter Stillwell was turning into a nuisance. She'd been introduced to him at a medical conference in September by one of her fellow Hopkins interns. He'd invited her for a drink and questioned her about her research, then told her that he knew someone at NIH who could get her funding to work on Myer's disease without the backing of Bio Gen. At first she'd been interested in at least pursuing the alternative. But as she'd gotten to know him better, she'd decided that he was all talk and no action. At least on the medical front. Personally, there was too much action. He was the kind of guy who stood too close, touched too much. He made her uncomfortable, and she'd been trying to stay away from him for the past few months. But he wasn't taking the hint.

With a sigh, she put away the phone, eased her foot onto the accelerator again, and started up the narrow drive. It looked like the access road had once been covered by gravel, but most of the chippings had been ground into the dirt or washed away, leaving large ruts that practically swallowed the wheels of her Toyota. How did Marshall get up and down here? she wondered. In a tank? Or one of those SUVs that guys seemed to love?

The road wound uphill, through light forest, where the first delicate green buds of spring leaves were visible on the dark branches. A number of the tree trunks were adorned with signs similar to the one near the entrance, just in case she hadn't gotten the original message.

She left them behind, then crossed a creaking wooden bridge spanning a stream where dark water tumbled over rounded rocks. Along the banks, delicate pink flowers carpeted the forest floor. It was a beautiful little surprise. Captivated, she swept her eyes over the gurgling water and the pink blossoms, caught by the aura of the place. It was a magical spot. And if at that moment some mythical creature—an elf or a fairy—had come wandering out of the woods, she wouldn't have been shocked.

Blinking, she shook off the fantasy. Elves and fairies! Really. She had work to do.

The scenery changed abruptly just a dozen feet on the far side of the bridge. The woods ended in a small glade warmed by the late-afternoon sun. Diagonally across the clearing was a stunning one-story wood and stone house, so cleverly sited on the property that it almost looked like a natural feature of the landscape. It wasn't large, probably two or three bedrooms, she judged.

At the edge of the woods, on a three-foot-tall post, was another sign. Braking to look at it, she saw it was also white, also faded. It said DÍTHREABH.

She struggled with the unfamiliar syllables, carefully pronouncing the word aloud. Was it "No Trespassing" in some foreign language? Or maybe the name of the house?

Shaking her head, she drove toward the building, emerging into the sunshine. A Jeep Grand Cherokee was parked close to the front door. Apparently she'd guessed right about Marshall's choice of transportation.

Glad that she hadn't turned around prematurely, she parked, picked up the kit she'd brought to collect a blood sample, and stepped into the late-afternoon sunshine. Immediately she was struck by the isolation of the place. No traffic noises drifted up from the road, but the woods seemed alive with the sound of birds.

She had started up the walk to the front door when she stopped short as she spotted a trail of red droplets spattering the stone walkway. Stooping to get a better look, she decided they were dried blood.

Immediately all sorts of dire possibilities leaped into her mind.

But she shut off the speculation. Whatever had happened, she'd find out pretty quickly. Raising her hand, she knocked on a varnished panel of the front door.

There was no answer. After waiting a full minute, she closed her fingers around the knob and turned, feeling the latch click.

Long ago her family had been in an automobile accident, hit from the rear at a red light by a driver whose brakes had failed. She'd been in the backseat with Dory, and when the car had slammed into their vehicle, she'd felt herself being thrown forward, then yanked backward as the seat belt had caught and held her. The crash must have taken place in mere seconds. But time had slowed at the moment of impact—making her feel as if she'd stepped outside herself and was watching the action in a slow-motion film.

She felt that way now—as if she'd stepped out of ordinary time into a separate reality. In the long-ago accident, she'd been helpless to change the outcome of events. This time, though, she had the power to make a choice. She could turn around and back away. Or she could push the door open.

If she did the latter, some sixth sense told her that her life would never be the same again. On the face of it, that was a ludicrous notion. Still, the impulse to turn and run for the safety of her car almost overwhelmed her. Backing away from the door, she decided to hedge her bets.

The living room windows were huge. Surely she could find out what waited for her inside the house.

Stepping off the walk, she waded through the bushes that flanked the front of the house. They were low hollies, and the sharp leaves raked her stockings, pulling at the delicate nylon.

Suppressing a wince, she cupped her hands around her eyes to cut the glare, brought her face to the glass, and peered inside.

It took a moment for her vision to adjust to the dimmer interior light. She was looking into a large, comfortable room—a great room, she supposed it would be called—with furniture of leather and rich wood, a massive stone fireplace along the far wall, and a floor of wide planking covered in several places by wool scatter rugs.

It was expensively done. Nothing looked out of the ordinary—aside from the man lying sprawled on his stomach across one of the throw rugs. He was naked except for a blood-soaked bandage wrapped around his right thigh.

All thoughts of flight vanished from her mind. Tearing back

through the bushes, heedless of the thorny leaves, Megan leaped to the front door, turned the knob again, and plowed inside.

"Mr. Marshall?"

"Wha . . . ?" The word sighed out of him, a shadow of the deep, rich tone he'd used on the answering machine, yet just as compelling in its own way.

Hunkering down, she touched his shoulder. Though his skin was hot and clammy, the feel of his naked flesh under her fingers sent a sudden and totally unexpected electric buzz through her hand and up her arm.

With a small involuntary sound, she snatched her hand back, even as impressions assaulted her. The stale sickroom smell. The barely conscious man—his physical perfection like the work of a Renaissance sculptor. He lay facing the door, one hand flung out to the side and hidden under the edge of the couch.

She stared down at his unclothed body, remembering her conversation with Hank. Both of them had assumed that some debilitating genetic illness had kept the client from coming to the lab. If so, the defect wasn't anything obvious. His arms and legs were muscular. His shoulders were broad, his hips narrow. Firm buttocks. Olive skin that was flawless, except where it was marred by several scars—the one on his shoulder quite recent.

He conveyed an impression of healthy, lean strength—but for the oozing bandage on his right thigh. The skin at the edge of the bloodstained gauze was an angry red. She was sure that if she removed the bandage, she would find an infected wound.

Megan felt her heartbeat quicken. She was a physician, but a physician who hadn't treated a sick patient in over three years.

Still, old lessons and the old sense of involvement came flooding back. She felt for the pulse at his neck, counted the beats. It was fast and rapid. Did he have a thermometer in the bathroom?

God, what did it matter? She could tell he had a raging fever just by touching his skin.

She started to stand, intent on looking for medical supplies, when he made a low moaning sound.

One moment he was motionless. In the next, he had lifted his head, pushed himself up on one elbow. As she watched, mesmerized, sooty black lashes fluttered against his cheeks. Then his lids snapped fully open, and his midnight gaze zeroed in on her. No, not on her. She was pretty certain he wasn't seeing Megan Sheridan, that his gaze had pierced through present reality to some other scene.

"Mr. Marshall. What happened to you?"

A harsh, guttural word welled in his throat. *"Namhaid."*

She had no idea what it meant or even what language he spoke.

Before she could ask what the strange-sounding word meant, the hand that was hidden under the sofa emerged. Holding a gun. Pointed in the general direction of her stomach.

Her gasp of fear was followed by a quick plea. "Don't shoot me!"

His eyes were bloodshot, haunted as they bored into her—or was it through her?

"Crawford." He spat out the word as if it were a curse.

"No." Violently she shook her head.

Marshall ignored the protest. "Did you come back to even the score?" he demanded, struggling to push himself up farther and flopping down again with what must have been a painful thunk. But the weapon was still in his hand, the muzzle only a foot from her body.

God, if his finger twitched on the trigger, she was a dead woman.

She wanted to back away. Run. But instinct told her that was exactly the wrong thing to do. "Put the gun down before it goes off," she ordered, amazed that her voice held steady.

The weapon wavered, then came back with unerring accuracy to the center of her stomach.

"Crawford," he said again, then dragged a labored breath into his lungs.

"No. My name is Megan Sheridan," she answered in a kind of daze, wishing she'd had the sense to get off his property before she looked in the window. "Please, don't shoot," she begged. "You don't even know me."

He stared at her with narrowed, red-rimmed eyes that struggled to focus on her face. *"Namhaid,"* he said again, though this time he sounded less certain. "Enemy."

"I'm Megan Sheridan," she repeated desperately, wondering if he could hear her through his delirium. Apparently he had no idea who was in the room with him. Which would make no difference when he blew a hole in her abdomen.

He made a kind of growling noise in his throat that stirred the hairs on the back of her neck.

Then his body went slack, and the hand with the gun fell to the floor, the weapon clanking against the bare wood, as though holding it up had simply become too much effort.

Without giving herself time to think about the danger, she sprang forward, grabbed his wrist, and pushed the gun barrel away from both of them as she struggled to pry his fingers off the weapon.

He tried to hold on to the gun, to wrest his hand from her grip, but he was too weak to fight her. She got control of the pistol, scrambled to her feet, and backed away, setting the weapon on a low chest at the other side of the room.

God, now what?

Fear urged her to keep on going out the door, to get as far from this man as humanly possible. She made it to her car in a blur of motion, her lungs burning from lack of oxygen. She had to get out of here before she ended up dead. Or worse.

She couldn't say where that last thought had come from. She had no idea what worse might be. Just a sense of foreboding that was impossible to shake.

Locking the car doors on the chance that he'd come staggering naked from the house, she scrabbled in her purse for her keys.

But even as she reached toward the ignition, an invisible force seemed to stay her hand.

She might be frightened. He might be dangerous. But she couldn't leave an injured man who was burning up with fever. Couldn't leave *this* man.

Call 911. Get out of here while the getting's good.

Intelligent advice. She closed her eyes and pressed her fingers against her temples, suddenly aware that the pain she'd been trying to fight off all day had mushroomed into a full-blown headache.

Not just from the personal confrontation with Marshall, although that had been bad enough. The encounter with him had brought long-suppressed turmoil bubbling to the surface of her mind. Treating patients on a daily basis had been too emotionally draining for her to endure. Yet quitting the medical profession would have been an admission of failure—an admission that her father had won in the end. That he'd been right about her all along. So she'd made a compromise and found a more detached way to practice medicine.

Within the space of seconds, detachment had vaporized like early morning fog burning off in bright sunlight.

If she'd ever known anything in her life, she knew that Ross Mar-

shall needed her. She couldn't simply walk away from him. Not and
live with herself. Not now.

Maybe when she got him stabilized. But certainly not when his life
might depend on what she did in the next few minutes.

Still, her heart threatened to pound its way through the wall of her
chest as she marched back into the house.

4

MARSHALL lay where she'd abandoned him, but he'd pushed himself
onto his back.

He was a large man. Over six feet. Long limbed. With impressive
male equipment.

Chagrined that she was staring at his genitals, she dragged her eyes
upward to his face. The features were very masculine. A classic nose, a
strong jaw. But purple smudges almost like bruises marred the skin below his closed eyes, and a sheen of moisture coated his broad brow. "Mr.
Marshall? Ross?"

His mouth tightened when she called his name, but he made no
other response. And she was painfully aware of his stillness, aside from
the labored sound of his breathing. As she watched him struggle to fill
his lungs, she felt a thick pain in her own chest.

The sensation was more than physical. The man, the wound, the
strange circumstances made her feel as if she'd suddenly stepped into
another world where the laws of the universe were different from her
own. Where anything she could imagine might come to pass. The notion caught her, held her the way the fantasy and science-fiction stories
she'd read as a teenager had transported her away from her oppressive
Boston existence. Only now it wasn't a story. It was real life. And she
couldn't step away from the scary part by closing a book.

She shivered, then with an effort of will shook off the fanciful notion. She was in the home of a man who desperately needed her help,
and she was wasting time. Lips compressed, she started making a mental list of what she needed to do.

There was a well-worn quilt draped over the back of the sofa. Unfolding it, she laid it over him. When she spotted the gun still lying on the chest, she grimaced. It was sitting out in full view. What in the world was wrong with her?

After shoving the weapon into a drawer, she returned to the unconscious man. Gingerly she knelt beside him—ready to spring back at the first sign of another attack. "Mr. Marshall? Ross?"

One moment, his face was immobile as granite. Then his eyes blinked open, fixing her with the intensity of a laser beam. She cringed as she remembered his delirium. But this time was different. This time she was sure he saw her—Megan Sheridan—not some phantom enemy springing up from his subconscious to trigger his aggressive instincts.

His dark gaze pinned her, making escape impossible. The breath stilled in her lungs as she felt the two of them make a sort of wordless contact—communication on some deep level that she only dimly understood.

For long seconds, she was incapable of speech, incapable of movement.

His voice broke through the spell. It was raspy now, the richness eroded by the ravages of pain he must be suffering. "Who are you? What are you doing here?"

"I'm Megan Sheridan. From Bio Gen Labs. You called us to make an appointment."

He closed his eyes, then opened them again.

"You called Bio Gen Labs," she repeated.

His head gave an almost imperceptible nod of understanding.

"What happened to you?"

He made a sound halfway between a laugh and a groan. "I was dumb enough to get shot."

"Shot? You have a bullet in your leg?"

"I dug it out. It was a flesh wound."

Lord, what kind of man could dig a bullet out of his own leg? When she tried to imagine inflicting that kind of torture on herself, a shudder went through her. "You should be in the hospital. I'll call an ambulance."

His fingers closed around her wrist, and his dark eyes focused on hers with a sudden fierceness that made her throat constrict. "Please . . . no hospital . . . no doctor."

"Why not?"

He heaved a deep sigh, seemed to gather his strength. "They'd have to . . . report it. Can't talk about what happened . . . with them. Have to talk to . . . Thornton."

"Who's Thornton?"

"The police."

"I don't understand."

He sucked in air, his gaze holding her again, and she decided his eyes were the most compelling she had ever seen. Dark and bottomless, full of depth that drew her toward him as no other man had ever drawn her. "I'm a private detective. . . ." he wheezed, then paused to take in more air. "Investigating . . . murders. Of . . . women. But . . . can't prove anything . . . yet. Can't risk a bunch of questions."

The short speech exhausted him, and he went limp against the rug.

"You'd risk your life for an investigation?"

The eyes hardened. "To put Crawford away." He stopped, blinked, began again. "To put Arnott away . . . yes."

"You won't put him away if you're dead."

He grimaced. "I won't be. I just need . . . antibiotics."

She opened her mouth to say he needed around the clock nursing care.

Before she could deliver the advice, he started speaking again, his words tumbling forth as if he were afraid that his stamina would give out before he delivered the message. "Keflex. In . . . kitchen cabinet nearest the door . . ."

The drug was probably the right choice. Where had he gotten it?

"Please."

The plea tore at her, partly because she sensed that he wasn't a man who needed to beg for anything under normal circumstances. He was a man who took charge of situations. Even wounded and half out of his head, he'd instinctively defended himself. He'd probably dragged himself out of bed to get the medicine. His iron will had carried him this far, but now he was at the end of his strength.

"Just get me . . . Keflex. Then you can go."

His lids drifted closed, and he lay very still, probably at the end of his strength.

She stared at his unmoving form, thinking that the biggest favor she could do him was call an ambulance and get him to the hospital. It was the logical thing to do. The right thing. Medically.

Emotionally, it felt more like betrayal. Because he'd trusted her to keep his gunshot wound between the two of them.

Hardly understanding her own motivation, she realized she'd made a decision. Standing, she looked around. The kitchen was on her immediate right.

To the left of the sink she found a mostly empty cabinet that held the plastic container of blue caplets. The prescription was eight months old. There were only six caplets, apparently left over from some other illness. She knew from her training that taking leftover antibiotics was a bad idea, but the medication hadn't reached its expiration date, and the supply in the bottle would be enough to get him started.

After filling a glass with water, she retraced her steps.

Marshall was lying where she'd left him. She thought he'd drifted into a fevered sleep, but his lids flicked open when he heard her footsteps approaching across the wood floor. She froze when she encountered the same dangerous glint in his eye that she'd seen just before he pulled the gun from beneath the edge of the couch.

God, was she a fool, spending another minute with a man who'd proven that he was dangerous?

"I'm Megan Sheridan from Bio Gen Labs." She repeated what she'd told him earlier, her fingers tightening on the glass of water, ready to throw it at him if she had to. "Do you remember? I'm here to help you."

He considered the question, the cloudy look in his eyes fading as he studied her. "Are you a doctor?"

"Yes."

"But you won't report you're treating a patient who's been shot?" he asked, his voice tense.

She gave a small laugh. "I'm treating you without a license. I think we're even."

He took that for agreement, and she set the water on the floor so she could open the medicine bottle. "Can you sit up?"

He tried, giving the project considerable attention, the strong muscles of his arms and chest straining with effort. When he couldn't raise himself enough to drink the water, she came down beside him and helped him up, propping his back against the base of the sofa. Then she handed him the caplet and the glass.

He managed to get the blue pill into his mouth, then grimaced as the bitter medication hit his tongue. With a jerky motion, he lifted the glass to his lips and gulped water, some of it spilling down his chest.

Before he could drench himself, she took the glass from his hand and eased him back against the rug.

"The bandage you wrapped around your leg probably needs changing."

"Yeah," he wheezed. "First-aid stuff . . . bathroom. Antiseptic. More bandages."

She might have told him to wait right there, but she knew he wasn't going anywhere.

UNTIL he'd found that big dog pawing at Charlotte's grave, Donald Arnott had thought he was safe.

The moment of discovery had sent terror shooting through him like the shaft of an arrow.

But his confidence hadn't been punctured for long. He had been scooping up women and doing what he wanted with them for the past eight years. And he was damned if some snoop with a dog was going to fuck him up.

Since he'd shot at the dog, he'd been too busy to worry. He had dug up Charlotte's body, and the rest of them, then taken the evidence to the mountains, where nobody would connect the dead women with him.

When the bodies were out of the way, he'd used a rototiller on the fresh earth and visited a garden center, buying twenty shrubs to landscape the newly plowed areas. Spring was supposed to be a good time to plant bushes. And he'd made it look like he was into a massive home improvement effort. That took care of the burial ground on his property.

The underground room wasn't a problem. He'd built it like a bunker, with a steel door hidden under what appeared to be the ruins of an old barn. Nobody was going to find it.

The morning after the break-in, he'd driven down to the road, checking out the area that was closest to his fence. There had been fresh tire tracks in the dirt beside the shoulder. From a pickup truck or an SUV, he judged, noting the size of the tires and the space between the wheels. Unfortunately, the information did him little good.

But he was absolutely safe for the moment, he told himself firmly. He'd shot the dog, scared the man away, and let him know that Donald Arnott was a formidable enemy.

Everything he'd picked up beside the fence was in a plastic storage box he'd bought at Kmart. Opening the door to his workshop, he lifted the box off a shelf and set it in the middle of the table.

In the merciless glow from the fluorescent light, he examined the contents once more, looking for something he had missed when he'd first inspected the haul.

Again he picked up the wire cutters. The adjustable wrench, the set of Craftsman screwdrivers. The flashlight that looked like it had come from Sunny's Surplus. And a pair of Bausch & Lomb binoculars that must have cost the earth.

He turned them over in his hand. They were lightweight but powerful—with 200mm lenses. Setting them down, he picked up a running shoe, examined the treads, then fingered the soft fabric of the shirt.

Who the hell was this guy? Not a cop. The cops didn't have a clue about him. He'd been too careful for that. Still, he'd been going over and over it in his mind, and he couldn't come up with a scenario to explain why some guy would be sneaking around in the woods less than half dressed.

Unless he was some kind of pervert.

That brought a bark of laugher to his lips. A pervert stalking a pervert. Nice.

At least that was how the world would think of him. He preferred to style himself as a man whose level of existence was so far above the petty lives of normal human beings that he functioned like a god. A god with the privileges and obligations of ruling over ordinary mortals.

At least the women. They were all sluts. Like his mother. And that gave him the right to decide which of them would live, which would die, and which would gratify his sexual desires.

But he hadn't anticipated some guy interfering in his chosen pursuits. A man with a dog. A man who had cut his fence and then sent his dog searching for evidence. Because that was the only scenario that fit.

A sudden surge of anger flared inside him like hot lava shooting from a volcano. Picking up the wrench, he slammed it against the workbench, the thunk of metal against wood sending a shockwave up his arm.

The pain sobered him, set his mind working again. Because the worst thing he could do now was let this throw him off his stride.

He had to find the guy. Maybe the way to do it was through the dog. It had been injured. Shot high up in the right leg. Christ, the bullet should have slowed the beast down. But he'd kept running with a strength and speed that Donald would have admired—if the two of them hadn't been mortal enemies.

Still, the animal would need to be treated. And the bullet wound was something he could use to his advantage—the centerpiece of a story he could tell the local vets.

He chuckled as he imagined the conversation. *Have you found an injured dog? I saw somebody shoot it, but it ran away before I could catch it, and I'm worried about the animal.*

Yeah, that would work.

Methodically he replaced the man's possessions in the box, stowed it on the shelf, and then went in search of the telephone book.

MEGAN went looking for first-aid supplies and found them on the bathroom counter where Marshall had tossed them. Before returning to her patient, she wet a clean washcloth with warm water. After laying the cloth on a towel, she knelt beside Marshall again, fighting the unaccustomed sense of unreality that had crept up on her earlier.

His eyes were closed once more, and for a long moment she stared down at him, struck by the notion that there was something remarkable about this man. Something she didn't quite understand.

His voice had been compelling when she'd heard it on his answering machine. Even in his weakened state, his physical presence added to the impression of strength and power. Not just physical strength. Something more. Charisma? That didn't seem to be the right word. Cutting off the speculation, she bent to her task.

He was still covered by the quilt. With a firm hand, she moved it away from the right side of his long-limbed body. When she connected with his thigh, her fingers felt icy against his hot flesh.

Calling on rusty skills, she assessed the wound. The hole in his leg was red and oozing, ragged around the edges where he'd dug out the bullet. The surrounding skin was hot and swollen.

He groaned as she began to clean it, groaned again as she sloshed on antiseptic.

Next she replaced the bandage, praying that the antibiotic was going to take care of the infection. Otherwise they were looking at blood poisoning.

She sat there beside him, feeling overwhelmed. Then she shook herself, because she couldn't leave him on the floor.

Unfortunately, there wasn't a chance in hell that she could carry him to bed. What was the alternative? Getting a sheet under him and pulling him along the floorboards?

Grimacing at the prospect, she pushed herself up and retraced her steps down the hall—this time entering his bedroom. As she'd anticipated, the linens were stained with blood. First she stripped the bed and remade it with fresh sheets and pillowcases she found in the closet. After bundling the soiled laundry into the hamper in the bathroom, she returned to the man on the floor.

"I have to get you into bed. Can you help me?" she murmured, not really expecting an answer.

"Yeah."

She jumped, wondering how long he'd been with her again.

"Did I hurt you when I changed the dressing?"

"No."

She was sure he was lying.

Then he asked a question of his own. "Did I threaten you with a gun?"

"You remember that?"

"Well, it has a . . . dreamlike quality." Regret etched his chiseled features. "Sorry."

"You were pretty out of it."

"I'm . . . not in the habit of shooting visitors."

She nodded tightly. "Can you walk?"

"I hope so."

"How do I get you on your feet?" she asked, turning the problem over to him.

He thought about it for a moment. "Need to sit up." After taking several breaths, he heaved his torso to a vertical position, sweat breaking out on his forehead from the exertion. Moving close to him, she squatted and draped her arm around his waist, holding him up.

He took several more breaths, then said, "You . . . count to three. Then . . . I'll push . . . you lift."

"Wait." Realizing that he was going to be naked again when he got to his feet, she tugged at the edge of the quilt, pulled it away from his legs, and tucked the fabric over his shoulder like a sort of toga.

Then she started to count. As she reached three, she felt his muscles strain. She was pretty sure he couldn't have stood on his own, but working together—pushing and pulling—they managed to get him erect, where he stood swaying on his feet, leaning on her shoulder. She knew they weren't home free yet, and she wanted to urge him to hurry before he toppled back to the floor. His progress down the hall was painfully slow, with his weight on her shoulder increasing and the quilt slipping immodestly off his body as they moved. Finally, when she thought one of them might trip over it, she kicked it away.

By the time they reached the bedroom, he was naked again, and they were both panting from the exertion of moving him thirty feet.

She eased him down onto the mattress, pulling the top sheet out of the way as he collapsed with a groan. When he was horizontal, she pulled the sheet back into place, covering the lower half of his body.

The trip down the hall had provided a fresh assessment of his condition—and of her ability to take care of him. "You should be in the hospital," she said again.

"No. I'm tough."

She didn't bother to argue, because she knew that much was true. Partly because she wasn't sure how a man in his condition had dragged himself down the hall before she'd arrived, and partly because she was sure that few men in his shape would have made it back to the bed on their own feet—even with help.

"More water," he said.

She left him, went back for the glass, and topped it off at the kitchen sink.

It seemed he was out of energy. Although he gave it a good try, he couldn't push himself up again, and she sat down beside him on the bed, lifting his shoulders, cradling his back against her front, feeling like she was invading his privacy as she felt his body trembling against her.

She wanted to tell him there was nothing humiliating in being weak from a high fever. She was pretty sure he wouldn't agree. So she simply held him as he took several swallows of water.

"Enough?"

"Yes." His voice was barely audible now.

She helped him lie back on the mattress, and he sank into sleep within seconds of his head coming down on the pillow. Instead of getting up, she remained beside him on the bed. With a tissue from the nightstand, she gently wiped the sweat from his brow, then brushed back a strand of his dark, wavy hair. It was fine textured and seemed to twine around her fingers of its own accord.

Her touch must have startled him, because those fathomless eyes blinked open again. Feeling as if she'd been caught doing something illegal, she scrambled for something to say.

"You need to sleep."

"You need to leave."

"I can't leave you like this. You and I both know you should be in the hospital."

"No hospital. I'm used to . . . being alone," he said through gritted teeth.

"Not in this condition."

"You . . . clear out."

She sensed danger in his dark eyes now. Danger to her, on some hidden level that she hardly understood. Yet he couldn't be a physical threat—not when he could hardly hold his head up.

Still, as she stood up, she knew it would be a good idea to take his advice. Clear out of his house before something happened—although she couldn't say what.

A sudden image flashed in her mind. The two of them. Herself and Marshall on the bed, their naked bodies tangled together, their breath coming in sharp gasps as searing heat swirled through every one of her nerve endings.

Momentarily dizzy, she swayed on her feet, her heart pounding and her breath rushing in and out of her lungs. She must have made some sound, because his eyes shot to her face, and she had the sudden conviction that he'd seen the same image as she. That they had unaccountably shared the same heated vision.

"No," he said thickly. "Get out of here."

"All right," she breathed, and this time she took a step back.

His features relaxed, and she turned and bolted from the room.

Standing in the dimly lit hallway, she felt her mind clear, her heart rate and breathing returning to normal. Resisting the impulse to look back over her shoulder, she wondered what had happened to her. The vision had been like a prophecy. A promise. A promise that she longed to keep.

Teeth clenched, she shook off the notion. God, had she ever been so unprofessional with a patient? Well, it certainly wasn't going to happen again.

The bottom line was, she needed to stay. To give him medical attention because she'd promised not to call an ambulance.

Deep within herself, though, she knew that she wasn't being entirely honest. There were other reasons for her reluctance to leave, reasons that had nothing to do with logic and everything to do with the way this enigmatic stranger made her feel.

5

JACK finished the note he was writing on Marshall, then rocked back in his chair, feeling a little surge of excitement flare in his chest. It was the old hunting instinct, he supposed. Not the primitive hunt of a man in the woods, stalking game with spear or a gun. But the modern variety—following a paper trail, adding bits and pieces of information until you had enough to take the measure of the man you were investigating.

He was still waiting for utility records, a credit report, and tax information. But he'd found out some fascinating—and unexpected—stuff as a result of checking through motor vehicles.

Not the two speeding tickets Marshall had acquired over the past five years. No, his interest had pricked up when he'd seen the long string of address changes, going back to when the PI was eighteen and had moved out of his parents' home.

Jack looked down at his notes on his interview with Rosa Lantana, who'd lived a couple of doors down from the Marshall family in Parkville, a working-class neighborhood north of Baltimore.

"I'm doing a credit check on Victor Marshall, and I was wondering if you're acquainted with the Marshall family," he'd begun.

"Is that no-good son of a bitch in trouble again?"

"I'm not at liberty to say."

That had led to an earful about the family. The senior Marshall was an auto mechanic by trade and a belligerent individual who had alienated everyone in the neighborhood. He'd also beat the hell out of his sons and finally driven them away—including the middle one, Ross.

"Alice, she's a saint," Lantana went on. "He kept her pregnant and barefoot until she got too old to have any more of his children."

"There are a lot of children in the family?"

"No. Most of them were stillborn. Let's see. There were four or five boys who lived into their teens. I think there are only two who are still alive. None of them are at home anymore. Troy got himself killed in a bar fight. Adam is out west somewhere. Ross is still in the area. I know 'cause he visits his mother sometimes when the old man isn't home."

Mrs. Lantana rambled on.

Two boys had keeled over from mysterious causes in their teens. Personally, she thought the old man had beaten them to death, although there was never any evidence against him.

She painted a picture of a classic dysfunctional family, if there was such a thing. And she also put forth the theory that the senior Marshall supplemented his mechanic's income through some kind of illegal means.

Long after they'd dispensed with any material that would be relevant to a credit check, he kept digging for information, recognizing pay dirt when he encountered it.

"Did Ross get in any trouble that you know of?"

"That boy? Oh my, no. I never saw a youngster more determined to make something of himself. Starting when he was fifteen, he worked as a carpenter's helper in the summers and after school. Then he started doing, you know, handyman projects on his own. He built the shelves under my stairs. And . . . let's see. He practically rebuilt my falling-down shed out back. He was in college—the University of Maryland—on a scholarship, when he bought a row house in the city. His mother told me. You should have seen her face; she was so proud of him."

Instantly alert, Jack asked, "Where did he get that kind of money?"

"I don't know. But I can tell you he came by it honestly. That boy was a real straight arrow. Not like his good-for-nothing father. He sold that first house he fixed up. And he bought another one. And then did it again."

Well, that accounted for the string of addresses in progressively more affluent neighborhoods around Baltimore and D.C. Apparently he'd made a career out of buying distressed properties, whipping them into shape, and investing the profits in more real estate.

Jack slipped the notes from Mrs. Lantana into the folder. It wasn't what he'd expected to find out about Ross. A young man from a troubled family who'd made good in the eyes of the world. It sounded like a real success story. Except for the violence factor. The father had pounded on his sons, taught them that might makes right. Had Ross learned that lesson too well? Or had he escaped that part of his heritage?

Standing, Jack went to the computer room to put Victor Marshall's name into the database and see what he got.

*   *   *

MEGAN headed down the hall to the bathroom, leaving the bedroom door ajar so she could hear her patient if he needed anything. She'd been in a hurry when she'd stuffed the dirty sheets in the hamper and collected medical supplies. Now she had time to look around.

The room had obviously been remodeled—with a greenhouse wall totally exposed to the woods. There were no blinds and no screening, except for the lush-looking ferns hanging in the window over the large spa tub. At least the toilet was behind a half wall, giving some privacy. The remainder of the area was dominated by the tub and the curving window wall. The open vista and the indoor greenery gave the room the effect of being in the middle of the woods.

After using the facilities, she washed her hands, then cupped her palms under the faucet, scooped up some cold water, and gulped it down.

She made her way back to the great room—and another bank of windows.

The house was as open to the natural environment as it could be and still keep out the elements, she thought as she stared at the meadow and the forest beyond, the leaves taking on a golden hue where they caught the last rays of the sun.

Then the sun disappeared, and darkness began to swallow up the landscape, blurring the shapes of the bushes and the trees.

When she'd stopped at the wooden bridge over the stream, she'd imagined cunning little fairies and elves gamboling among the ferns and flowers. Now the images that came to her were much darker: creatures of the night, monsters you wouldn't want to meet in this isolated location—or any other.

She stifled a nervous laugh. All kinds of amazing images had been popping into her head since she arrived here.

Not just images, she reminded herself. There had been one strikingly memorable incident, too. When Marshall had pulled that gun on her.

Perhaps it would be smart to take his advice and get out while the getting was good. Forget about imaginary monsters in the woods. She was focusing her fears in the wrong direction—like the heroine of a horror movie who goes around locking all the doors and windows only to find that the real threat is inside the house. It was folly to stay here with a man she didn't know. A man who had already proved himself to be dangerous. And who'd chosen to live in as secluded a spot as you could find in the Baltimore-Washington corridor.

She had told him she would leave.

On the other hand, she had also told him she wouldn't call an ambulance. And she couldn't possibly do both those things. So she chose to stay and make sure he didn't die.

As soon as she knew everything was all right, she would go home and stop obsessing about Ross Marshall. That was a promise she was making to herself.

She told herself she'd been acting in a perfectly rational manner since arriving here. And the decision to clear out as soon as it was safe to leave her patient lifted a weight off her shoulders. Feeling lighter, she moved around the living area, turning on lamps, the yellow pools of light shutting out the darkness beyond the windows.

The room had been made for nighttime. In the lamplight, the leather upholstery took on a soft, inviting patina, and the wood floor gleamed.

The massive stone fireplace was set about two feet from the floor, with a neat stack of wood piled underneath. It was an appealing, cozy environment, and she thought for a moment how nicely a roaring fire would chase away the evening's chill. Unfortunately, she had little experience with building fires. And trying to learn the skill with someone else's fireplace smacked too much of taking liberties.

Instead she drifted toward the custom-made bookcases that took up the rest of the fireplace wall. Reading had been a part of her life since she'd gotten old enough to ride her bike to the library on Saturdays to bring back a stack of books. Novels. Nonfiction. Her own parents hadn't been readers. In fact Dad had jeered at her for having her "nose stuck in a book" instead of doing something constructive. But reading had opened up a world for her that reached far beyond the confines of her middle-class Boston neighborhood. And she'd come to the conclusion that you could tell a lot about people by the kind of libraries they owned.

One thing she knew about Marshall: he was a collector. Books lined the wall from a foot above the floor to several feet above her head, with two wheeled ladders attached to tracks along the shelves giving access to the upper volumes.

She learned more as she began to study the titles—like the fact that Ross Marshall was a very organized man who arranged his books by subject matter and then alphabetically by author. With such a well-ordered collection, it was easy to see that his interests were wide, ranging from philosophy and psychology to genetic diseases and criminal investigation and animal husbandry.

Apparently he liked poetry. Particularly e. e. cummings, Emily Dickinson, and T. S. Eliot. Unusual reading material for a man who made his living as a detective. Well, it was more than simply making a living, she amended. When he'd spoken about investigating a killer, she'd caught a fervor in his voice that revealed he was on a personal mission to wipe a demon from the face of the earth.

Lord, what kind of man was he? she wondered. Dangerous. Powerful in ways she didn't understand. Idealistic. Intelligent. Stubborn. Macho. Sexy. *Let's not forget sexy.*

Resolutely pulling her mind away from that direction, she returned her attention to the bookcase.

He had a large section on mysticism, ancient history, early Christianity, and pagan religions—the biggest portion of which was on the Druids of pre-Roman Britain. He also had not one but three Gaelic-English dictionaries.

And his taste in fiction ranged from Mary Renault and C. S. Lewis to Robert Heinlein and E. B. White.

His fantasy collection was particularly impressive. She smiled when she saw the complete set of Lewis's Narnia books, her first foray into fantasy after a favorite teacher had lent her the first book in the series. Along with the Narnia books were Grimm's Fairy Tales and all sorts of stories of the supernatural—tales of witches, ghosts, vampires, and werewolves.

Dracula, Frankenstein, The Turn of the Screw, the complete works of Edgar Allan Poe, *Rosemary's Baby, The Exorcist.*

Her hand was drawn to a volume in that section that had obviously been read many times, judging from the condition of the dust jacket. It was called *Darker than You Think* by a writer named Jack Williamson—a tale of werewolves who preyed on the human race, she gathered from the cover copy.

The grim subject matter brought a tightness to her chest, and she quickly replaced the book in the shelves, lining it up with the volumes on either side so that he wouldn't know she'd taken it down.

When she realized what she was doing, she gave a tiny laugh. What did it matter if he found out she'd been thumbing through the volumes on his shelves? Except perhaps that he'd know she'd been poking through his stuff—after he'd told her to leave.

Well, she'd found out he had eclectic tastes in reading—much broader than her own. After her science fiction and fantasy phase, she'd consumed a lot of literary fiction and poetry in college. But these days her recreational reading was mostly confined to easily accessible fiction. When she came home from the lab, she was too worn out for anything taxing.

In truth, she was worn out now. And the panty hose she'd been wearing all day were starting to bind.

In the trunk of her car were a clean T-shirt and sweatpants that she'd been planning to wear to the gym that evening, although it looked like she wasn't going to manage to get there, again. Despite the extenuating circumstances, she felt a stab of guilt. Going to the gym was supposed to be one of her priorities. Like cooking dinner instead of grabbing something already prepared from Sutton Place Gourmet or Fresh Fields on the way home. Every morning she got up promising that she'd do forty minutes on the weight machines after work. But somehow those sessions got pushed back when she had too much to finish at the lab.

Well, putting the gym clothes on now would make sense, if she was planning to stay. Even for a little while.

Flipping on the porch light, she took a tentative step outside. Immediately she was struck by the quiet and the solitude. There wasn't another house in sight—or even a light winking through the trees. Again she noted that even the traffic sounds from the road were nonexistent up here on Marshall's hill. She could be in the middle of the Maine woods.

Shivering in the evening chill, she hurried through the darkness to retrieve her gym bag, her eyes scanning the woods even as she told herself it was childish to be afraid of the dark. Still, she was back inside in under a minute and locked the door behind her with a firm click.

After changing in the bathroom, she folded up her skirt and blouse, stuffed them in the bag, and headed into the kitchen to see what she could discover for dinner.

The freezer was stocked with steaks and chops. And there were few canned goods. The closest thing she found to fast food was a can of beef and barley soup. Warming that up shouldn't be too difficult, she decided as she eyed the microwave over the stove.

While the soup heated, she tiptoed down the hall and looked in on her patient. He seemed to be resting peacefully, so she didn't go in to pull up the sheet, which had slipped midway down his lean hips.

She also peeked behind the other doors along the hall. Next to the bathroom, there was a room set up as a home office with a desk, computer, and filing cabinet. Behind another door was a rack of barbells and one of those universal home gyms where you could do fifty different strength-training exercises. But she didn't see any aerobic equipment. Maybe Marshall was a runner or a jogger.

Another thing she didn't see was a guest bedroom.

Well, he'd said he was used to being alone. Apparently that meant he didn't encourage overnight company.

As she sat at the kitchen table sipping her soup, she pulled out the small writing tablet she always carried in her purse. She was a researcher, and she'd found she never knew when documentation was going to come in handy.

On a clean page she labeled "Ross Marshall" at the top, she began to write up detailed notes on what had happened so far, editing out the fact that the wound had come from a bullet.

In the middle of her case study, she found herself yawning. Maybe she'd better set a timer to make sure she gave Marshall his next dose of Keflex, she thought as she moved to the couch in the great room.

She knew she should keep her eyes open. But closing them was simply too tempting. And once she'd blocked out the world, she drifted into a light sleep—until a sound from somewhere nearby made her sit bolt upright.

She was still trying to figure out where it had come from when a low groan from the back of the house told her it was Marshall—and that he was in trouble.

He cried out again, the sound more like that of an animal in pain than a man.

Pushing herself up, she went running barefoot down the hall to the bedroom.

Marshall was thrashing around on the bed, the covers on the floor and his body glistening with a sheen of perspiration.

"Ross," she called, crossing to him, then jumping back as his arm flailed, barely missing her leg.

Even semiconscious he was dangerous. Especially semiconscious.

"Ross, don't. It's Megan Sheridan. Remember?"

He didn't respond, and she sat down on the bed so that the flailing arm was trapped between his side and her hip. Leaning over, she pressed her hand to his reddened cheek. As she'd known it would be, his skin was hot and damp. Without a thermometer, she'd guess that his temperature was at least a hundred and five. Much too high.

His head rolled back and forth on the pillow, his dark hair plastered to his forehead.

"It's all right. You're going to be all right. The antibiotics will start working soon."

His eyes were closed. His fingers dug into the bottom sheet. Then his lips moved, shaping syllables she couldn't catch. The words were low, in some foreign language that had nothing in common with English.

At first she couldn't even distinguish the syllables sliding from his lips. Then his tone changed, becoming sharper, more distinct. More urgent.

"Taranis, Epona, Cerridwen," he intoned, then repeated the same phrase and went on to another.

"Gá. Feart. Cleas. Duais. Aithriocht. Go gcumhdaí is dtreoraí na déithe thú."

The low grating tone of his voice and the strange words raised goose bumps on her arms and stirred a deep primal fear in the marrow of her bones. The words were like nothing she had ever heard—a throwback to a time before written history, when the world was a savage place. They sounded like a chant or a prayer—incredibly ancient syllables passed down through the ages without benefit of written language. They roared through her, rooted her to the spot where she sat as surely as if Ross Marshall had reached out and circled her wrist with one of his strong hands.

She stared down at him, unable to take her eyes away. Unable to move or even speak.

The strange, sharp sounds echoed in her brain, rising and falling, distorting her senses so that all she heard now was a ringing in her ears that was below the level of perceived sound. And something was happening to her vision, as well.

For a moment out of time she could no longer clearly discern the man on the bed. His skin seemed to go a shade darker, grayer, the texture changing to something she couldn't name. And the very shape of his face and of his body wavered dangerously in her vision, turning fluid like a movie image of one familiar object morphing into another.

The rational part of her brain simply wasn't capable of dealing with what she was seeing. But the deep, primitive part responded, a stab of fear like the blade of an ancient dagger piercing through her chest. She wanted to run from him, run for her life. Run for her sanity. But she couldn't move, because she was caught in the grip of some terrible magic spell. It held her—and the man, too. Only he was the one doing it. He was the master magician working the transformation.

There was no way she could articulate what she was feeling. But a sound she hardly recognized welled in her throat. A sound that was part mind-numbing fear, part protest that came from the depths of her soul

His body stiffened. The outlines snapped back into his familiar male shape. And in the space of a heartbeat, the spell was broken.

She stared down at him, her eyes and her brain telling her that she had only imagined what she thought she saw. Her groggy mind had been playing tricks.

Somehow she had been in the grip of a weird hallucination, as if she were the one with the high fever and he were only a silent witness to the delusions wafting through her mind. Because that was the only way she dared explain to herself what had happened.

His eyes blinked open, focused on her. And a deep shudder went through him.

His lips moved. "No."

"What happened?" she gasped out.

"Nothing."

She waited for him to say more, to admit that he understood what she was talking about, but he only closed his eyes with profound weariness.

Caught in a tide of emotion she couldn't understand, she reached to cup his shoulder. As she did, she was jolted by the terrible heat radiating from his body. God, he was burning up. And she was sitting here like a dummy when the first priority was to bring his fever down. The best thing would be to get him into a cool bath. But she had no illusions about her ability to carry him down the hall. And she was pretty sure he'd gone past the point of being able to make it under his own power.

Instead she dashed to the bathroom, threw open the medicine cabinet, and sighed in relief when she found an almost full bottle of denatured alcohol.

On her way back to the bedroom, she grabbed a washcloth from the linen closet.

Her patient lay very still now, so still that her stomach twisted as she eased onto the bed beside him.

Quickly she poured alcohol onto the washcloth, then began to rub the pungent liquid on his face, his neck, his chest.

He coughed from the strong scent rising toward his nostrils. "Don't," he choked out, turning his head and trying to push her hand away.

It was obvious that the smell bothered him. But she ignored the protest, catching his arm as she had before and wedging it between her body and his. Then she poured more of the alcohol directly on his chest, feeling his strong muscles ripple beneath the cloth and sweeping dark hair first one way and then the other as she tried to cool him down.

He coughed again. "Are you trying to kill me?"

"I'm trying to bring down your fever."

His body jerked, but she held him in place with one hand while she used her other to rub him with the damp cloth.

When he began to shiver, she breathed out a little sigh, relieved that the rapidly evaporating liquid was doing its work.

Reaching down, she pulled the sheet up to his waist, covering him again. When she looked up, his eyes were open, fever bright, their intensity pinning her anew.

"What's wrong with me?" he asked in a low voice that was almost a growl.

"You got shot. The wound is infected. I'm trying to get your temperature down," she told him, repeating earlier exchanges of information.

She watched his expression change as he looked down toward the bandage on his leg. Experimentally he flexed the leg, grimacing from the pain.

"Can you tell me why someone shot you?" she asked.

"I found . . . one of the graves."

"What grave?"

"Of one of the women Crawford killed." He stopped, blinked. "Not Crawford. Crawford's dead."

She shuddered.

He had been speaking almost to himself. He focused on her again, looking startled, as if he had just realized she was in the room with him. "You can't stay here."

"Somebody has to take care of you."

"Not you."

"You think I don't know what I'm doing?"

He closed his eyes, lay motionless for several moments as though gathering enough energy for a long speech. Still, his next words, when they came, were so low that she had to lean closer to hear him.

"I know you don't. Or you'd have the sense to get out."

The way he questioned her competence had her lifting her chin and glaring down at him—a tough combination to manage, but she did it. "I have a medical degree. I may not have treated a patient in several years, but believe me, I know the right things to do for you."

He made a low, dismissive sound more animal than human. "I'm not talking about your medical degree. . . . You and me. Not good."

"We don't even know each other."

"We know enough."

"I don't understand what you mean."

His eyes snapped open, drilled into her. "Don't lie to me." He dragged in a ragged breath and let it out slowly. "I wasn't going to let this happen. It can't happen." Agony mingled with a sense of purpose in his voice.

She leaned toward him, wanting him to explain. But his eyes took on a shuttered expression. "I called the lab, and they sent *you*. Jesus!"

She didn't understand what was upsetting him. Didn't understand what he meant.

She might have kept asking questions, but the exchange seemed to have used up all his energy. His eyelids fluttered closed, and the regular rise and fall of his chest told her he had sunk back into sleep. Leaving her with more questions than he had answered.

6

ROSS drifted in and out of sleep, ambushed by nightmares that gripped his fevered imagination, scenes following one another in a jumbled order that made no sense in the way they filtered up from deep within his subconscious.

First he was in the kitchen at home, looking at his hollow-eyed mother, listening to her tell him about his father's latest scrape with the law. She looked so old and tired and worn out from years of living with Vic Marshall that he felt his heart turn over.

"Leave the bastard," he urged.

"Don't call him that. He's your father."

"Leave him."

"Where would I go?"

"You can live with me."

She snorted. "Live with you! He'll come to get me, and one of you will kill the other."

It was an old argument. One he had never won, and his hands squeezed in frustration.

Then he heard the sound of footsteps crossing the floor.

The Big Bad Wolf. Christ, if his father found he'd dared to come here, they were in for a hell of a fight.

Adrenaline surged through his body. Fight or flight, and he was spoiling for a brawl. His mother's pleading eyes stopped him.

He wanted to tell her he was sorry—for the things his father had done and for the grief he'd given her.

Before he could get the words out, the scene shifted abruptly. He was no longer in the house. Now he was a wolf, running through the woods, tree trunks rushing past him. Brambles reaching out to grab at his gray coat. But he kept moving, fleeing the footsteps behind him.

He dared not look to see who was back there. But he knew the pursuer was a blond, blue-eyed woman, her body naked, lithe, sexy, shimmering in the moonlight. Blood pounded in his veins. He wanted her with a strength that bordered on madness, yet he fled from what he wanted most. Because if she caught him, he would turn her into something sad and pitiful, old before her time. Like his mother.

So he kept running, each breath a sharp stab in his lungs, and finally she was no longer behind him. Instead he was the pursuer, chasing a demon named Crawford through a nighttime landscape thick with trees and rich with the new life of spring.

Energy flowed through his body. He felt the blood pumping in his arteries. Felt his own power.

The breeze riffled his thick coat, his predator's eyes pierced the moonless night, and he drank in the scent of his quarry. The scent of man. The scent of fear.

Crawford, ahead of him in the darkness. Running for his life. Stumbling over a tree root in his terror. Splashing through a stream, hoping to throw his pursuer off the trail.

But there was no shaking the chimera behind him, no escape from the yellow eyes and white fangs of the beast.

Because the wolf was on a sacred mission.

Now, in his dream, a hot fire sluiced through him as he followed the trail that his quarry was helpless to hide. This was no rabbit, no fox, no animal using instinct and cunning in a desperate attempt to escape. This was a man—a man with a gun.

It was a fair contest, Ross told himself as he deliberately closed the distance between them.

Crawford had stopped in a small clearing, gasping for breath, spinning in a circle as he pointed the gun first in one direction, then in another—unable to spot the enemy.

The wolf padded to a halt behind a tree, his body quivering, a low growl gathering in his throat.

Then he sprang.

Crawford fired at the gray shape—once, twice—but Ross dodged the deadly projectiles with canine grace, then leaped for the kill, sinking his fangs into the man's neck, cracking his larynx, gnawing through his carotid artery.

He was a hunter, and blood was a familiar taste in his mouth. Animal blood. But this liquid was different. It gushed over his muzzle and down his throat in a hot torrent, pumping through his brain with a white heat that made him dizzy. Licking his lips, he lifted his head and howled his triumph into the darkness.

In the dream he was human again, feeling a sense of horror sweep over him. Staring down at the chewed remains of his victim, he was struck by a sickening truth: He was no better than the killer he had stalked and slain.

He woke from the nightmare, drenched with sweat, feeling blood pounding in his ears like the thrumming of a primitive drum.

His body braced for an attack, he lay on the tangled sheets in darkness, struggling to draw in a full breath. But it was impossible to fill his lungs. The air around him was too hot and thick.

He had dreamed of Crawford. And before that? The first part was hazy in his mind. He remembered only the lust for blood. Remembered his vow five years ago—that the intoxicating pleasure of the manhunt and the kill were too dangerous to repeat.

It took several moments for him to comprehend that he was in his own bed. He felt the raw pain in his thigh and remembered the bullet.

Retribution, he thought. If he died from this wound, it would be justice coming full circle.

He had ripped out Crawford's throat. And Arnott had shot him.

Part of him welcomed the pain. He deserved the punishment. Yet in the end, he couldn't let the killer win. He had to stop him, and he had to do it through the rules of law, not the rules of the jungle. Because if he sank to that animal level, he would lose what humanity he could still claim.

A sound outside the bedroom made his throat tighten with tension. Then a light snapped on in the hallway, and every muscle of his body went rigid as he prepared to spring from the bed. His mind mixing reality with nightmare, he imagined Crawford or Arnott walking through the door. *Namhaid.* The enemy.

He needed his gun. He would fight with the weapons of a man. Not teeth and claws.

Where was his gun? he wondered as he felt frantically over the sheets.

Then he saw the figure in the doorway and recognized the woman. The woman who had come to take care of him, her hands moving over his body with a familiarity that he should never have permitted.

He knew the consequences of her touch.

As he stared at her, another part of the dream leaped back into his mind, and he felt a pulse jump in his belly.

He wanted to call to her, reach for her, pull her down to the bed with him. But he kept his hands locked at his sides.

In the dream she had been naked, moonlight washing over her skin. Now she was wearing a T-shirt and sweatpants. The knit clothing clung to her shape, molded her breasts as though forcing his attention to center there.

Desperately his mind struggled to separate reality from fantasy. She had been in his house. Ministered to him. Spoken to him. And he thought he had ordered her to leave. Apparently she hadn't followed directions.

The light from the hall illuminated her shoulder-length blond hair. Her delicate features were hidden from his view, but he remembered them with vivid clarity. The wide-set blue eyes, the dainty nose, the full, sensual lower lip. Even in his man shape he caught the delicate scent that clung to her. Lemon and soap and woman. And a thousand dreams he had never dared to bring into the light.

Her nighttime voice was soft and seductive. "You're awake."

"What are you doing here?"

"It's time for your medicine."

He summoned strength he didn't know he possessed. "I told you to go."

"You're sick. You need me."

Part of him knew it was already too late. "Don't you know that a wolf mates for life?" he asked, wondering if he meant the words as a warning or an invitation. A warning, surely.

She cocked her head to one side as though considering the pronouncement, and he cursed himself for saying what had leaped into his mind.

Bending over him, she set a glass of water on the bedside table, then pressed her hand against his forehead. "You're still feverish."

"I think you woke me out of a nightmare."

"About wolves?"

"Yes," he answered, hoping that neither one of them would remember this encounter in the morning.

At least she took him at his word. Then she asked, "Can you sit up?"

Pride wouldn't allow him to say no. Gritting his teeth, he pushed himself erect, and she shook a caplet into his hand. When he'd put it in his mouth, the sharp taste made him shudder.

Seeing his reaction, she quickly offered him the glass of water. He remembered sloshing the cold liquid down his chest when he'd taken the medication earlier. Now he took care not to spill any as he gulped several swallows, washing down the medicine and moistening his dry mouth and throat.

When he finished, she took the glass, and he felt a small shock as her hand brushed his. He knew she felt it, too, by the way she snatched the glass away and set it down with a thunk on the nightstand.

"I need to check your wound," she said, her voice businesslike now.

Silently, he slid down against the pillows. Getting prone was easier than sitting up.

The mattress shifted as she lowered herself to the edge of the bed. "I'm going to turn on the light."

Appreciating the warning, he closed his eyes against the sudden flare of brightness, then watched through his lashes as she eased the sheet away from his leg, being careful to uncover only as much of his flesh as she needed to see.

As she removed the bandage, her fingers on his thigh, he struggled not to react to the pressure of her hands on his flesh. She worked quickly and efficiently, yet he sensed she was fighting the same pull as he—that the intimate touch was binding him to her in ways he couldn't explain on any conscious level. And binding her to him.

Years ago, his father had told him what it would be like to be drawn to a woman by powers beyond his control. The need of the werewolf to take a mate—to perpetuate his kind.

Vic Marshall's crude, mocking words came back to him now. "You think you're better than me. Well, the same thing that happened to me will happen to you. Around when you turn thirty, sonny. Whether you like it or not. You'll see her. You'll know she's the one you've got to fuck or die. And when you touch each other, you'll be a goner, and so will she. She'll give herself to you on every possible level. Sexual, mental, emotional."

Like the way his mother had given herself to his father, and now she was trapped with a man who used her as he wanted. A man who didn't know the meaning of love.

"No!"

"Ross, are you all right?"

He blinked, realized he'd spoken aloud.

If he could have heaved himself off the bed, he would have jerked away from her—away from the intimacy binding them together as closely as a vine twined around the trunk of a tree.

The image in his mind sharpened. The vine covering the tree, sucking the life from the living plant even as the tree gave it a refuge.

Or perhaps it was all in his imagination—blown out of proportion by his fever. Nothing serious had happened, and nothing *would* happen because he wouldn't allow it.

He'd always known women were attracted to him, that he could have almost any one he wanted if he put out a little effort. Maybe that was part of the werewolf aura. A scent that drew the opposite sex? A fortuitous combination of physical characteristics? It wasn't something he'd tried to analyze.

But it had made him cautious.

He'd never allowed a woman to work her way past the defenses he'd built up. Never allowed his own control to slip.

Tonight he felt as if all choices had been yanked away from him by some ancient cosmic jester who had been waiting for aeons to spring this trap.

Striving for detachment, he watched his beautiful blond doctor replace the gauze. "How is it?" he asked, hearing the thickness in his voice.

"A little better."

"Turn off the light."

She did as he asked, and he felt more comfortable in the darkness, where it was easier to hide. It had been a long time since he'd been in a bedroom with a woman. And never here. He had never brought a sexual partner to his lair.

Before he could stop himself he reached for her wrist, circling it with his thumb and index finger.

There was no strength in his grip. And he knew she could have pulled away. Instead she simply sucked in a sharp breath, her hand resting in his grasp.

He stroked a finger over her knuckles, testing the feminine skin, then pressed his thumb to the pulse point at her wrist, feeling her heart rate accelerate. And his. Hearing a sound like wind roaring in his ears, he closed his eyes, the only contact point his hand on her wrist. A slender connection, yet it sent blood pounding through his veins.

"Did you help yourself to some of my clothes?" he asked imagining one of his T-shirts covering the soft swell of her breasts like a lover's palm, his pants cupping her feminine bottom—before he stripped the clothing off her and pulled her naked body beneath his on the bed.

It was only a fantasy. He was too weak to make it reality. But the very weakness drew him further into the tantalizing reverie.

Maybe she was following the direction of his thoughts. "They're my gym clothes. I keep them in the trunk," she hastened to inform him, tripping over the words as if she were having trouble controlling her tongue and lips. Snatching her hand away, she was off the bed in seconds, out of the room before he could catch his breath.

Maybe now she would take his advice and leave. If it wasn't already too late.

DONALD Arnott was awake, restless and on edge. He needed a woman. But he couldn't take one. Not until he learned the identity of the man who was stalking him and got rid of the bastard.

Heaving his body out of bed, he stood naked in the darkness, feeling blood swelling his cock. Still naked, he strode to the back door of his house and stepped outside. The night air was cold on his fevered skin as he made his way down the familiar path to the ruined barn.

Shoving aside hay bales, he heaved open the trapdoor, then switched on the overhead light as he descended into the underground chamber.

He stood in the middle of the brightly lit room, his breath quickening as he stroked the stained wooden table, the leather restraining cuffs, feeling his erection grow harder. By the time he ran his fingers across the metal instruments neatly arranged in racks along the wall, he was aching.

The videotapes were on shelves along the opposite wall. He walked past the camera on its tripod and read the titles on the neatly labeled boxes. Penny Delano. Charlotte Lawrence. Cindy Hamilton. Mary Beth Nixon. And half a dozen more.

He went back to Cindy. One of his old favorites. A plump girl with big breasts and a thatch of silky pubic hair he had shaved off with a dull razor.

Sliding the tape into the machine, he took the remote control and relaxed into the easy chair in front of the large-screen TV.

He skipped the first part of the tape where he was showing her his knives and got right to the good part, stroking his cock as he watched himself work her over, climaxing with a hot shudder of pleasure as she begged him to let her go.

The second climax wasn't quite as good. It never was, not when he was alone. When he had a woman down here, he could come over and over from the strength of his response to her pain and fear. Only part of what he needed came through on the tape. But the self-gratification calmed him so that he was actually whistling a jaunty tune as he made his way back to the house and started getting ready for work.

He was on the ten-to-six shift this week, at Westfield Shoppingtown Montgomery, although nobody ever called the place anything besides its former name, Montgomery Mall. He'd worked there as a security guard for the past year. Before that, he'd been living in Pennsylvania and working at King of Prussia Mall.

A mall was a good place to meet women—sort of like combining work and play. But he couldn't stay too long in any one location, because it was imperative that he not establish a pattern that the police could pick up.

The last thought made his features contort and his hands squeeze so hard that his nails dug into his palms. A man with a dog had picked up on what he was doing. And he was going to either obliterate the bastard—or obliterate all evidence of this room, sell the property, and move on.

7

"WHEN Ken said he was going to retire, I told him I didn't care how he spent his days, just so he was out of the house from nine to five," Mildred Winston had told Jack when he'd called and asked to speak to her husband. "There's no phone in the workshop," she continued. "If you want to talk to him, you can come over, or wait until lunchtime."

Jack elected to drop by around ten. Following Mildred's directions, he parked in the driveway behind a Chevy Suburban, bypassed the house, and took the gravel path around to the small, shingled workshop at the back of the property.

The sound of a power saw sliced through the morning quiet as Jack stepped onto the porch, and he waited until the cut was finished before knocking on the door.

Ken Winston, gray-haired and potbellied, was holding up a small pine rectangle, inspecting the cut he'd made.

"Hey, Jack!" he said, setting down the piece of wood and switching off the power on the saw. "What brings you around?"

"I wanted to get some input on one of your old cases."

The retired detective wiped his hands on the sides of his blue overalls. "You want some coffee? Coke? I got all the comforts of home out here. I only have to go inside when I need to take a leak."

Jack opted for coffee—black. As Winston poured them both a mugful, Jack looked around the workshop. On the shelves lining the wall were fifteen or twenty precisely made, identical bird feeders.

"You going into the bird feeder business?" he asked.

"Nope. They're for the PTA fair at my grandson's school."

"Nice job."

Ken beamed. "Thanks. I like it. You can see what you're doing. Get the same results every time. I got the design and the measurements down pat now. So what case did you want to talk about?"

Jack took a sip of coffee. "Edward Crawford."

Winston thought for a moment. "The murder suspect who disappeared?"

"Um-hum. His body—well, his skeleton—turned up at Sugarloaf Mountain."

"Cause of death?"

"Undetermined."

"Yeah, well, I wasn't too broken up when the guy evaporated. He probably abducted and murdered five or six women."

Jack set down his coffee mug on the worktable and slipped his hands into his pants pockets. "It says in the case file that you were working with a PI named Ross Marshall."

The older man's eyes narrowed. "That slippery bastard still around?"

"You didn't like him?"

Winston's jaw tightened. "He came to me with some cock-and-bull story about Crawford's hanging around across the street from the Damascus High School campus where that girl Cherry Phelps went to school. When I asked him where he got his information, he clammed up, wouldn't tell me a damn thing."

"Maybe he saw him there."

"How'd he know to look?" Winston demanded, obviously reliving his reaction at the time. "Nobody else saw anybody who fit Crawford's description."

"He could have been in disguise."

"Then how did Marshall figure out it was him? All I wanted was a simple answer to my questions about his investigative techniques, and he got this closed look on his face. Just acted superior, like he knew things I didn't."

Jack wouldn't have put it quite that way. Ross was secretive, but he didn't act superior. At least with him.

"The guy wanted me to feel like I wasn't doing my job. Then the next thing you know, Crawford vanishes," the older man was saying. "And you better believe I pushed Marshall on that. He was real hostile. Guilty acting. You know what I mean? But I couldn't prove he'd been anywhere near the guy."

Jack didn't point out that another victim had been taken between the time Ross had tried to give information to Ken and Crawford's disappearance. What was the point?

It was obvious that Ken Winston and Ross Marshall hadn't hit it off—on a professional or a private level. And it was obvious that Winston was unable to deal with tips that he couldn't verify by other means.

"Anyway," Jack said, "the mystery of what happened to Crawford is solved."

"But we don't know who did it." Winston raised his voice. "I still like that Marshall guy. Why don't you see how he reacts when you tell him you found the body?"

"I might do that."

Winston shoved his hands into his overalls pockets, as he studied Jack. "I heard you were working with him on some stuff."

"Where'd you hear that?"

"Around. You trust his information?"

"He's given me some good leads. Helped me clear some cases."

Winston nodded tightly. "And what about that violent streak of his?"

"What violent streak?"

"Don't tell me you can't see it below the surface. That guy is a pressure cooker. And maybe the lid blew off with Crawford."

Jack sucked in a breath, held it in his lungs before exhaling. "He doesn't have a rap sheet."

"Yeah. So he's been lucky."

Jack nodded without bothering to add that he'd checked out the father, Vic Marshall, and found that he'd been arrested and convicted of a number of minor offenses—disorderly conduct, simple assault, battery. If a guy was prone to violence, you'd expect that kind of thing on his record. But, unlike his old man, Ross was clean.

Jack shifted his weight from one foot to the other. "Well, I appreciate the insights. It's always good to get the perspective of a guy with thirty years on the force."

Winston looked somewhat mollified. "Um. Right. But I should get back to work. The PTA is expecting me to deliver twenty-five of these feeders by the end of the month."

After an awkward exchange of good-byes, Jack left, knowing why Winston hadn't accepted any help from Ross Marshall. It had as much to do with his own prejudices as any vibes he'd picked up from Ross.

Still, Jack was thinking about violence as he climbed back in his car. That hadn't been something he'd personally seen in Ross, and he considered himself pretty good at reading people. But there was the abusive background.

Had the man been different five years ago? Changed himself? Or was there really something below the surface ready to break out and strike again? Something dangerous that a police detective would be remiss if he ignored?

*   *   *

MEGAN stood with her shoulder propped against the doorjamb of the bedroom, looking at the sleeping man, studying his features—the slightly parted lips, the three days' growth of beard darkening the lower half of his face. She reached out a hand toward him, then let it fall back to her side, dropping her gaze to the steady rise and fall of his broad chest. The covers had slipped almost to his waist, exposing dark hair spread in a circular pattern around his flat nipples.

One foot splayed to the side, peeking out from the edge of the sheet, and she could see his toenails, blunt cut across long toes.

She had no excuse for standing here watching him sleep, yet she remained where she was, looking her fill.

She'd been in his room several times during the night, drawn by her need to take care of her patient—and by something more, some deeply buried compulsion that she was powerless to describe.

In the hours after the sun had set, she'd felt an invisible force gathering in the room around them, drawing them to each other on levels that existed below conscious thought.

Then, afterward, she couldn't be sure that anything had really happened.

Suddenly she found herself fighting the impulse to wake him and demand that he tell her if he'd felt the same disturbing pull. But she wasn't selfish enough to interrupt his rest. And she wasn't crazy enough to ask about feelings she couldn't articulate—feelings that she might have conjured up from some self-conscious need of her own.

Perhaps she was simply reacting the same way she had to previous patients—getting involved with them on a level beyond the professional. Getting her emotions mixed up with Marshall's. And the problem was worse than usual because she'd avoided this kind of situation for so long that her nurturing instincts were working overtime.

She folded her arms across her chest, reassured by rationalizations as she struggled to view her patient with professional detachment.

He had been sleeping for the past four hours, and he'd barely awakened when she'd changed his bandage again and given him another Keflex. But it seemed to be a normal sleep, not a fevered stupor.

Sometime during the night he'd dragged himself out of bed, put on a pair of white undershorts, and somehow made it to the bathroom without her help. She knew that because she'd been startled to find the toilet seat up in the morning.

She couldn't imagine how he'd managed to stagger down the hall— not in his condition. Apparently his determination and his stubbornness were formidable. Which meant he'd probably set his recovery back. The assumption gave her a good excuse for staying. That was better than admitting she was in the grip of a compulsion she couldn't explain—as if leaving had become somehow unthinkable.

And even if he'd heaved himself out of bed during the night, he wasn't going to be cooking any food. Or driving his car to the pharmacy. He was down to his last caplet, and he needed a lot more to finish the course of the medication.

Again she walked through the house, this time searching for the telephone she knew he owned, since she'd left a message on his answering machine.

She didn't find the machine. So he was probably using the phone company's answering service.

But where the heck was the phone that went with it? All she found was the charger for his portable.

Finally, she went outside, intending to use the one in her car. But she stopped to look around first, picking up details that she hadn't noticed on her way into the house the day before or in the dark.

Near the front door and extending along the side walls were natural looking plantings of ferns, violets, and other woodland vegetation that she couldn't identify this early in the season. Interspersed among them were bright blue, yellow, and red primroses, some of the earliest spring flowers. The plants could have grown there by accident, she supposed, but the arrangement was a little too artful to be accidental.

Apparently Ross Marshall was a talented gardener as well as a private detective. A strange combination. Thinking that the man was full of surprises, she walked around the side of the house, noting the way the garden blended with the edge of the woodland. After staring at it appreciatively for a while, she went back to her car.

Knowing she was stalling, she clasped her hands and stared at the compartment below the dashboard where she kept her portable phone.

She'd never bothered to get a license to practice medicine in Maryland, so she needed Walter to write Ross a prescription for Keflex. Still, she knew instinctively that telling her boss a lot about Ross would be a mistake. Prevarication wasn't her strong suit. After hesitating for several more moments, she picked up the phone and switched it on.

The Bio Gen receptionist, Betty Daniels, answered.

"Can I speak to Walter?"

"Who's calling, please?" Megan asked.

"This is Megan Sheridan."

"Oh, Dr. Sheridan. I'm sorry I didn't recognize your voice. Where are you? We called your house, but nobody answered. We were starting to get worried."

"I'm fine. I'm with a client."

"You are? You don't mean the one from yesterday? Ross Marshall?"

"Yes."

"Oh, my. What are you still doing there? Was he as . . . sexy as he sounded over the phone?"

Megan blinked. For Betty, interjecting *that* into the conversation was definitely out of character.

Ignoring the question, she said in a no-nonsense voice, "Mr. Marshall is sick. I've got the situation under control. But I need to speak to Dr. Galveston."

"Uh, you had a couple of other calls. One from Dr. Stillwell again. He says he needs to talk to you."

"Oh, shit," she blurted, and immediately wished she'd kept the reaction to herself.

"What?"

"Betty, I'm sorry. I don't want what Stillwell's selling."

"And your sister called."

"Dory called me at work?"

Betty made a throat-clearing noise. "She was quite . . . uh . . . forceful. She says you owe her a check."

Megan struggled to control her anger. She wanted to protest that she didn't owe her sister anything. Instead she said, "It's in the mail. You can tell her that if she calls again. And please put me through to Dr. Galveston."

"Certainly. Just a moment."

Walter came on the line, his voice querulous. "Megan, where are you?"

"With that client. Ross Marshall."

"I thought you went out there yesterday afternoon. What's going on?" he demanded.

"I did come out here yesterday. He's sick. I stayed to take care of him."

"That's not your job."

"Well, if he dies, you won't get a fee out of him."

"He's dying? What the hell is wrong with him?"

"He has an infection. He had some leftover Keflex. I gave that to him last night and early this morning. But he needs more."

"What's he got, some sort of immune deficiency that makes him susceptible to opportunistic infections?"

That was the last thing she'd ascribe to Ross Marshall, but she hedged. "I don't know. He hasn't been in shape to tell me much."

"How long are you going to be out there?" Walter demanded.

Megan closed her eyes, picturing her boss's stormy expression. Walter didn't like surprises, and he wouldn't like having to juggle the workload. Maybe he'd even have to do some of the lab tests himself. Too damn bad.

"Until tomorrow, at least," she answered.

"Well, if you're taking care of him like a private duty nurse, charge him at that rate. What is it, fifty dollars an hour? Seventy-five?"

"Walter . . ."

"Either charge him, or come back to town."

She sighed. "Okay."

"Okay what?"

"I'll charge him," she answered grudgingly, knowing that she was lying. It was getting to be a bad habit. "But I can't write a prescription. I need you to order him some more Keflex. He got the last bottle at the Giant Pharmacy in Lisbon," she added, giving Walter the phone number.

He asked more questions. She answered with evasions. And when she hung up, mission accomplished, she was shaking. Yet she found it impossible to share anything with Walter beyond the bare essentials. She'd been angry when she'd had to drop her work and come out here. Now her feelings had changed, although she wasn't willing to go into the reasons too deeply.

ROSS listened for the sound of her moving around the house. She'd been in his room earlier and thankfully hadn't come over to put her hands on him again. Now she was gone. He hoped she'd left. He should get up. Eat some meat. But he was too weary to move.

He dozed, then slipped deeper into sleep. As another dream dug its claws into his mind, a moan rose in his throat.

When he realized he was back in the terrible summer of his fourteenth year, his whole body began to shake. It was late at night in the room he shared with his brother, sixteen-year-old Michael. A deep fear clogged his chest, making it almost impossible to breathe.

He and Michael had always been best friends. Troy was older. He'd moved out of the house two years ago. Adam was five years younger—a pest. But he and Michael had stuck together. They'd played cops and robbers. Sat next to each other at the dinner table. Climbed the fence at the rich kids' pool and gone for a midnight swim. Gotten sick trying cigarettes. And run away together—staying in the woods half the night until the Big Bad Wolf had sniffed them out and nipped their flesh all the way home.

Michael was the one who helped him with his math homework. The one who had kept Thad Stevenson from beating the crap out of him on the way home from school.

But after tonight they were going to be separated forever—one way or the other.

Michael's body was making the change from boy to man. And with that change came another demanded of the werewolf species. A demand that could not be denied.

His time had come. Tomorrow night he was going to the forest alone with Dad for the ancient ceremony. No one else could be there. Michael would say the chant he had learned. And he would transform to a wolf for the first time. Or he would die.

The scared, sick feeling in Ross's chest threatened to overwhelm him. With every scrap of self-control he could muster, he struggled to keep it from showing in his voice as he and Michael talked long into the night.

They wouldn't have dared to stay up so late if Dad had been in the house. But he was out, getting money. Stealing money, although nobody was allowed to talk about that secret. But Mom knew. And the boys knew.

"Are you worried about tomorrow night?" Ross whispered.

"No."

Ross didn't believe the emphatic denial. And his stomach clenched painfully when Michael continued, "I've got fifty dollars saved. In the bottom drawer of my dresser. I want you to have it . . . if, you know . . ."

"You're gonna be fine!"

"I know. I memorized the words and all. And Dad coached me how to . . ." He swallowed. "How to ride above the pain. But just in case. Don't let Dad get his hands on the money. It's mine. I saved it up."

"I won't. I promise, Michael. I promise."

Desperation rose in his soul as he fought the need to climb out of bed, throw his arms around his brother, and hold on tight. But that would have embarrassed both of them, so he stayed where he was, because if he hugged his brother, then he might start to cry. And if Michael could be strong, then he could be, too.

In the way of dreams, the scene changed. Time compressed. He was standing at the front door in the twilight, feeling small and alone—watching Michael and Dad get into the car, seeing the rigid lines of his brother's face and knowing he was terrified.

And then, in the blink of an eye, the car was coming back. Not their real car but a long black hearse. Pulling slowly into the driveway.

Panic stabbed a dozen knives into his chest, choked off his breath.

Michael. Where was Michael?

Then his father was standing at the back door, holding Michael's body in his arms.

His mother was falling to her knees, weeping. And his father was staring at him over Michael's body—telling him with his eyes that it was his turn next.

WHEN Jack got back to the squad room, most of the reports he'd requested on Ross Marshall were sitting on his desk. The PI's credit record, his phone company records, his credit card statements. He didn't have cable TV out where he lived in Howard County. Or a satellite dish, for that matter, so he apparently didn't watch much TV. He also didn't have a wife or an ex. Or any children that he acknowledged.

Ross's credit rating was excellent. He paid his mortgage on time every month, and he owned only the one piece of property—a twenty-four-acre plot off Route 99.

He kept a minimum credit card balance. Most of his purchases weren't extravagant, except for big orders of expensive meat from a place called Omaha Steaks. Apparently the man liked his beef.

In the past six months he'd acquired a state-of-the-art digital camera and a pair of expensive binoculars, both of which he undoubtedly used for surveillance. He'd bought ammunition for a .40-caliber gun a couple of months ago. And he had a license to carry a concealed weapon.

Interestingly, he didn't seem to own many of the other fancy toys Jack had expected a PI to acquire—nightscopes, listening devices, recorders, transponders—unless he'd bought the stuff several years ago. But then why hadn't he updated his equipment, when technology was changing so fast? Either he couldn't afford the newest and best—which the credit report belied—or he'd decided he didn't need all that fancy stuff.

So how did he come up with his amazing leads? Jack had the sudden image of a comic book superhero endowed with powers beyond those of mortal men. Ross Marshall could make himself invisible at will. Or he could see through walls.

With a shake of his head, Jack dismissed the absurd notions and shuffled the reports into the folder. Ross was the only lead in a case that had gone cold five years ago. But Jack had done his homework on the PI and couldn't find any evidence of criminal activity.

So why did he still have the feeling that there was something missing from the picture? Something he could figure out if he fit the pieces of the Ross Marshall puzzle together correctly.

8

BUSINESS clothing was an important part of the self-image Megan had created for herself over the years—another proof that she wasn't the "slob" Ray Sheridan had raised. This morning, however, she'd decided she'd look more presentable in her sweat clothes than her rumpled skirt and blouse from the night before.

But as soon as she stepped into the Giant Food outlet in Lisbon, she felt uncomfortable about appearing in public in sweats.

At the pharmacy counter, she struggled not to squirm under the clerk's scrutiny.

"Ross Marshall," the petite redhead behind the counter repeated, looking Megan up and down as she glanced from her to the name on the prescription Walter had called in.

The redhead flicked a glance at her left hand—which was absent of rings.

Megan could almost read her thoughts. *Who is this woman picking up medicine for Ross Marshall? His girlfriend? A nurse?*

Well, Lisbon was a small town. And Ross Marshall was a good-looking guy. So it wasn't strange that the women around here had noticed him—and would notice a woman who was doing errands for him.

Still, her relationship with Ross was none of the clerk's business.

Although words of explanation bubbled at the back of her throat, she kept her lips pressed together as she waited while the woman searched through the box of medications that were ready to be picked up.

"Does he have an insurance card registered?" the clerk asked.

"I don't know."

The woman went to a computer, called up a file. "Yes. He owes a ten-dollar copayment."

Megan had intended to pay for the antibiotics with a credit card. Instead she pulled a twenty-dollar bill from her wallet and waited for change.

Stuffing the envelope with the prescription bottle into her purse, she fled into the grocery aisles. She might have left the store at once, but there was hardly any food at Marshall's house. So she grabbed some chicken soup off the shelves, then bought eggs, milk, bread, and a few other staples. Because this was one of those big stores where you could buy almost anything except a hunting rifle, she put a three-pack of panties into her shopping cart and an orange-and-black Baltimore Orioles T-shirt. Then she went back to one of the drugstore aisles and grabbed a toothbrush.

She didn't have enough cash to pay for the groceries and other purchases. At the checkout counter, she was forced to fork over her credit card, repressing the urge to look over her shoulder to see if the pharmacy clerk was watching the transaction.

She was fully aware that she was acting paranoid. And out of character. What did it matter if the clerks at the grocery store knew the name of the woman who had come in to get medicine for Ross Marshall?

It didn't matter at all—unless her own emotional investment in the man was making her jumpy as a cat on thin ice.

Maybe it was hormonal, she told herself with a disgusted shake of her head as she clenched her hand around the strap of her purse. It had been a long time since she'd gone out with a man she was attracted to—let alone made love with anyone. That long dry spell had made her susceptible to Ross Marshall, and now she was feeling things that she had told herself could stay on hold until she met the right guy.

Her mind switched gears again. Did that mean Ross Marshall was the right guy?

It hardly seemed likely, yet from the moment she'd found him lying on the floor, she'd been on an emotional roller coaster.

So if the women in the Lisbon Giant Food store were looking at her speculatively, it was really no more speculatively than she was looking at herself.

Making a rapid exit from the store, she plucked the two bags from her shopping cart and headed for her car.

It had been sunny when she'd left in the morning. As she got into her car, she saw that heavy gray clouds had begun to gather in the sky. By the time she crossed the bridge leading to the meadow, the atmosphere had darkened, making her feel like the sky was pressing down on her shoulders.

Braking at the edge of the meadow, she stared at the sign she'd seen the first day. Not the ones that said NO TRESPASSING. The one that said DÍTHREABH. This time she pulled out her notebook and copied it down.

Inside, the house was dark. After stopping to turn on a lamp in the great room, she set the bags of groceries in the kitchen, then tiptoed down the hall to her patient's room.

Marshall was still sleeping, or perhaps he was feigning sleep to avoid interacting with her. She might have let him slumber, but she needed to assess his condition.

Gently she touched his shoulder, and his eyes snapped open, regarding her with the intensity that had unnerved her the night before.

"How do you feel?" she asked, hearing the husky note in her voice as she set a glass of water down on the bedside table.

His gaze turned inward as if he were taking an inventory of muscle and sinew. "Better," he finally answered without elaborating.

"You got out of bed last night."

"Early in the morning."

"You should have asked me to help you."

"I made it down the hall and back again on my own."

"If you'd fallen, it wouldn't have been good for the wound."

"I didn't."

His clipped answers told her that the conversation was an imposition, and she felt a stab of disappointment tighten her chest.

With an inward sigh she acknowledged she'd been hoping that things would be different when he started getting better. That their communications would normalize.

Now, as she remembered her thoughts at the grocery store, she felt her face flush. As far as he was concerned, this was simply a doctor-patient relationship—and not a very cordial one, at that.

Cutting her losses, she changed the subject. "It's time for your medicine."

He pushed himself up and reached for the bottle she'd set on the night table, shaking out a caplet into his hand. When he picked up the water, she saw he was able to hold the glass steady. He was definitely getting better—and asserting his independence.

But there were still things he needed from her.

"I should check the wound," she reminded him.

Without commenting, he slid back to a prone position. As quickly as possible, she changed the dressing, more aware than ever of her hands on his flesh, aware that he was watching her from under his long, dark lashes.

"How is it?" he asked.

"Healing."

He accepted the information without comment.

"Do you think you could eat something?"

He reached for the second pillow on the bed, propped it behind his back. "There's meat in the freezer."

Her response to that suggestion was instantaneous. "You can't handle meat. You're still too sick."

He looked like he was about to argue, then shrugged. "What do you suggest?"

"Chicken soup is more like it."

He sniffed the air, looked puzzled. "I don't smell any."

His quizzical look made her laugh. "I'm not the domestic type. You have a choice of Campbell's Chicken Rice or Lipton's Chicken Noodle."

He debated, apparently weighing the merits of each. "Lipton's, I guess," he answered, sounding less than enthusiastic. "With lots of noodles."

She retreated to the kitchen and concentrated on fixing the soup, telling herself that investing any kind of emotional energy in the man was a mistake. When she returned to the bedroom, she saw he'd straightened the covers. His head was turned, and he was staring out the window.

She was pretty sure he knew she was standing in the doorway, yet he kept his gaze focused on the swaying tree branches thirty feet away.

The blur of motion brought back memories from her childhood— images that she'd thought she'd outgrown.

"Do you see animal shapes moving in the leaves?" she asked in a low voice.

"Do you?"

"Yes. I'd look out my window when I was a little girl and see them. They scared me."

"Do they still?"

She managed a laugh. "Unfortunately, yes."

He gave her a considering look. "It just means you're imaginative."

"Scientists aren't imaginative."

"Don't duck away from a compliment. Of course you are."

Before she could think of how to answer, his gaze moved back to the window, and he looked like he wanted to climb out of bed and disappear into the foliage.

"I'm sorry. It's going to be a few days before you can get out of the house."

"I need . . ."

"What?"

"Fresh air. Going outside won't hurt me. It will help me get better."

"You can barely walk."

"I'm at home in the woods."

She wasn't going to waste his strength arguing about it. Realizing she was still holding the mug of soup, she set it on the nightstand, along with some plain soda crackers she'd purchased at the grocery store.

He gave the meal a wry look. "Is this what the doctor ordered?"

"Yes."

He thought for a moment. "My memory's a little vague about the past couple of days."

"That's nothing to worry about. You were pretty sick."

"Yeah, well, did you tell me you were a doctor? That you work for Bio Gen?"

She nodded, wondering exactly how much of their previous exchanges he recalled. The words they'd spoken. And all the rest of it. Her holding him while he drank. Her looking at his naked body. His trapping her wrist in the circle of his thumb and finger. The sense of connection that defied explanation.

She felt her face warm and was glad he had turned to reach for the soup. Picking up the mug, he blew on the hot liquid, then took a cautious sip.

After several swallows, he raised his head, looking at her with his unnerving dark gaze. "I should thank you," he said grudgingly. "I don't mean just for the soup. If you hadn't come along when you did, I would have been in trouble."

"Then I guess I should say you're welcome."

"Tell me you would have done it for anyone."

"Why?"

"Then it's nothing personal."

The curt observation stung. She was about to back out of the room when he asked, "Would you open a window so I can at least smell the outside?"

That was an odd way to put it, she thought. With a tight nod, she crossed to the window wall, which featured an enormous middle glass panel that was fixed in place. There were two side units, however, that could slide open and closed. She pushed open the one on the left, then watched as he dragged in a deep lungful of air and let it out as he relaxed against the pillows.

She stood there regarding him, her own breath quickening as she tried to understand what he was experiencing.

"Thank you," he said, his eyes fixed on the woods. He said nothing else, ignoring her as if she were no longer in the room. The night before, he'd ordered her to leave. This morning he was using a different tactic.

She opened her mouth to point that out, then closed it again. Wondering why she was staying to take care of a man who so obviously wished her out of his house, she exited the bedroom.

Her car was outside. She could collect the blood sample she needed for the genetic test he'd requested and clear out, but she couldn't bring herself to abandon him. Or to go back into the bedroom and confront him again, either.

After standing uncertainly in the hallway for several moments, she strode into the bathroom and locked the door. Again she hesitated, staring nervously at the expanse of unbroken glass and the windblown trees beyond.

Then, telling herself that no one would dare spy on Ross Marshall's house, she ripped her gaze away, turned her back, and pulled off her clothes. After she took a quick shower, she changed into the T-shirt and underpants she'd bought, using one of the plastic grocery bags for her dirty clothes. Too bad she didn't have another pair of sweatpants, too. But she wasn't about to borrow any of his.

In the great room she stood staring at the furniture, then the bookcases, finally focusing on the Gaelic dictionaries. With an odd sense of anticipation, she crossed the room and reached for the largest one, turning to the *D*'s.

The word *díthreabh* was there. It meant "wilderness, hermitage, isolated place of safety away from other human beings."

So that was how he thought of this property—this house. As his refuge. And she had invaded his territory. No wonder he wanted to get rid of her.

Yet he was attracted to her. All the feelings experienced over the time she'd been here had not been one-sided. She couldn't believe that. He might be fighting the pull, pretending it didn't exist, but he felt it, too.

That was *why* he was fighting it, she thought with sudden insight. Because he sensed what was happening, and he feared the intimacy.

Because of his illness? Not from the gunshot but the genetic problem that had caused him to call Bio Gen Labs in the first place. Despite his apparent physical health, there was something wrong with him. Some inherited defect he didn't want to discuss—and perhaps didn't plan to pass on to the next generation.

When she considered his situation in those terms, his reserve made perfect sense. Maybe he'd gotten close to a woman before. And maybe she'd run in the other direction because she'd decided the risk of bearing his children was simply too great.

Megan pressed her fist against her mouth, feeling a stab of anguish for him as she imagined that kind of rejection. Whatever he'd called the lab about wouldn't be something he'd want to reveal on the first date. But she was in a unique position. She already knew there was some genetic problem in his background. That was something to consider carefully before she got in any deeper.

Good advice. But was she capable of taking it?

After putting the dictionary back, Megan flopped onto the sofa and stared into space. Finally she pulled out her tablet and started to add to the notes she'd written the night before, intent on documenting how quickly her patient was recovering.

But fatigue pressed against her chest, her limbs. Succumbing to an unaccustomed lethargy, she swung her legs onto the couch, propped a cushion behind her head, and let her mind drift. For months she'd been working at breakneck speed, trying to make some progress on her gene therapy treatment for Myer's disease while getting through the increasingly heavy workload that Walter was demanding. Now her routine was totally disrupted. She had nothing to do, and the feeling was unsettling.

She intended to close her eyes for only a few moments.

Hours later, she woke with a start, disoriented and immediately on edge. When she realized where she was, her gaze flew to the window. The sky had been gunmetal gray when she'd fallen asleep. Now the sun had set.

Which meant that Marshall had missed a dose of medicine, unless he'd gotten it himself. A lot of good she was doing him, insisting on staying here.

Standing too quickly, she wobbled on her feet and reached out a hand to steady herself against the sofa back. Then she made her way down the darkened hallway to the bedroom.

The door was closed. She knocked. "Ross?"

No answer.

"Ross?"

A sensation of cold scraped at the back of her neck. Clenching the doorknob, she tried to make it turn. But it was locked from the inside.

"Ross. Are you all right in there?"

No answer.

"Ross, open the door."

Flicking on the hall light switch, she bent to examine the lock. It was similar to the ones in the house where she'd grown up, and she knew that if she found something slender enough to penetrate the small hole in the center of the knob, she could spring the locking mechanism.

An unbent hairpin was about the right size. But she didn't have a hairpin.

Again she rattled the knob. "Ross! Let me in."

When he failed to acknowledge her demand, she ran down the hall to the kitchen and started opening drawers. There was nothing she could use.

God, what if he'd had a relapse? What if some problem related to his genetic makeup had kicked in?

Frustrated and frightened, she pulled open the door to the utility room and looked wildly around. One wall housed a washer and dryer flanked by shelves of laundry supplies. The rest of the room appeared to be a well-stocked workshop. There was a large workbench, a table saw, and lumber neatly stacked in racks along the wall. Shelves held hand and power tools. On other shelves were cases of small plastic drawers containing various items such as washers, nails, and screws. All of them were too large in diameter to fit the hole in the doorknob. But she found a piece of wire that looked like it might do.

Back at the door of the bedroom, she called to her patient one more time. "Ross, if you can hear me, open up!"

When he still didn't answer, she unwound the coiled wire and pushed the slender tip into the hole in the knob. After wiggling it around, she finally heard a soft click.

"I'm coming in," she informed him as she pushed the door open and charged into the room, almost tripping over something on the floor as she skidded to a stop beside the bed.

It appeared to be empty.

Lunging back to the door, she switched on the light so that she could see better.

There was still no one in the room, but she discovered what she had tripped over. The shorts Ross had been wearing lay on the floor beside the bed. She also saw that the side window panel she'd pushed partway up was fully open.

She stood there breathing hard, a combination of fear and anger making her stomach churn. Then, unable to cope with the empty room, she ran down the hall to the bathroom, hoping she'd find him there. But that room was empty, too.

The bedroom had been locked from the inside. But her brain didn't seem capable of processing the information. In a rising state of hysteria, she ran through the rest of the house, switching on lights, calling his name, thinking she was going to discover him sprawled on the floor the way he'd been yesterday afternoon. But there was no answer. And no body.

Nearly defeated, she made her way back to the bedroom, pulled open the closet door, and swept her hand behind the clothing hanging in a neat row. But he wasn't hiding there like a kid afraid of the dark.

Finally, inevitably, she switched off the light and moved to the window. Because if Ross wasn't in the house, the only place he could be was outside.

Staring into the gathering darkness, she strained her eyes for the sight of a naked man moving among the trees or spread-eagled and unconscious on the ground.

She saw branches swaying, heard the sighing of the wind, smelled the earthy scent of trees and soil, but she saw no one. She knew he had to be out there. And she had to bring him back.

The idea of leaving the house sent a wave of cold sweeping over her skin. But there seemed to be no other choice. Not when he had been burning up with fever the day before. Not when this stunt was going to set his recovery back days.

God, was the man crazy?

Her mouth compressed into a thin line, she eyed the window, picturing herself climbing out. But the opening was several feet from the floor, and her legs were not as long as her patient's. Retracing her steps down the hall, she crossed the great room, switched on the porch light, and opened the front door.

Silently she stepped out into the night and stood with her arms wrapped around her shoulders.

Although the sky had been overcast early in the evening, the clouds had blown away, making way for the radiance of a three-quarters-full moon. It bathed the meadow in cold light that did nothing to banish the goose bumps rising on her skin.

"Ross?" she called, feeling the wind take the word and hurl it from her.

She had never felt comfortable in the dark. But when Ross didn't answer, she stepped off the pad of cement at the front door and began to circle the house, keeping the solid bulk of the structure to her back and her gaze to the ground as she searched for his limp body.

She was facing the woods when a sudden burst of wind swished through the trees. In the light filtering like ghostly ribbons through the swaying branches, she saw a gray shape prowling the forest, its head bent to something on the ground.

For a moment she told herself it was simply her childhood fantasy of shapes moving in the trees. Then she sucked in a sharp breath as she saw it really was an animal.

A large dog. Maybe a German shepherd—or a husky-shepherd mix. But somewhere in the deep, primitive part of her mind she knew it was a true creature of the forest. A wolf.

As soon as the thought surfaced, she rejected it as impossible. There were no wolves in Maryland. At least she had never heard of any.

Yet her mind continued to shout the word *wolf*.

She stared at him. Him.

From where she was standing, she couldn't see the sex. But she had the absolute conviction he was a male from the way he held himself, his posture dangerous and aggressive. He was standing in the moonlight as if he had owned this patch of woodland since before man had tread upon the continent.

As she watched, he raised his head, surveyed his forest.

Details came to her with striking clarity. His pelt was silver gray. His ears alert, edged with black. His tail full and held at a downward angle, except where the black tip curved upward.

The bottom half of the face was light gray, in sharp contrast to the shiny black nose.

His eyes were his most striking feature. They were yellow—and glowing with an intelligence that seemed impossible for an animal to possess.

He bent again, and she saw what she hadn't noticed before—a limp furry form on the ground in front of him.

His teeth flashed. When she realized what he was doing, she made a small sound of protest in her throat. It looked like he had caught a small animal and was tearing at its bloody flesh with his sharp teeth.

The wolf must have heard her. Or more likely he had known she was there all along and had finally decided to acknowledge her presence.

Lifting his head, he pinned her with his gaze, a low warning growl drifting to her on the wind. It was a sound that gave meaning to an old cliché—the feel of icy fingers walking themselves down her spine.

She had never known the sensation before. She felt it now, the quivers starting at the base of her spine and traveling to every nerve ending of her body. She wanted to run back the way she'd come, around the house and through the front door. But her legs refused to cooperate. Immobilized, she watched the animal abandon its prey and move toward her. His gaze burning into her, he closed the distance between them until he was standing a mere ten feet away and she could see the blood staining the fur of his muzzle.

Her heart was pounding so hard in her chest that she could barely draw in a full breath as she stood there, exposed and vulnerable, sure that his brilliant yellow eyes might be the last thing she saw on earth—before he ripped her throat out.

The wolf regarded her with a stare that seemed to penetrate to the depths of her soul. Then his lips pulled back over sharp white teeth.

She waited for him to spring, braced for the impact of his body slamming against hers, knocking her to the ground. Instead some emotion she couldn't read gathered in his face. For heartbeats she and the creature of the night stood facing each other. Then, as if he'd changed his mind about tearing her limb from limb, he turned abruptly and trotted into the woods, disappearing into the darkness under the trees.

Released from his spell, she sagged back against the wall of the house, breathing in jagged gasps, feeling as if she'd made a miraculous escape. Not just from physical danger. From something more basic that she was helpless to name.

Pushing herself up straighter, she made an effort to collect her scattered thoughts—then suddenly remembered why she had come out here in the first place.

"Ross! For God's sake, Ross," she croaked, her voice barely carrying above the sound of the wind.

She had come looking for him. But she was too terrified to continue now. When he didn't answer, she turned and dashed for safety, slamming the door behind her.

Closing her eyes against the sudden light, she leaned against the solid barrier of the closed door, trying to stop shaking.

When she was able to move again, she ran back to the bedroom, staring at the empty bed, the open window.

"Ross!" she called once more, her voice high and desperate.

She pushed the window closed far enough so that she was sure a wolf couldn't slither through. Then she dragged the heavy easy chair partway to the window and sat, staring out into the night, her eyes trying to penetrate the darkness under the trees.

But the wolf had vanished. And now that she was alone and safe in the house, she wasn't even sure whether she had imagined the whole strange incident.

She cursed Ross for going outside into the night. Cursed her own cowardice. Her only comfort was what he'd told her earlier. He was at home in the woods. He craved the outdoors. And maybe he and the animal out there had reached some kind of accommodation.

He must know it lived in his woods. He wouldn't have left the house if it was a danger to him.

Her numbed mind tried to go back over the conversation they'd had earlier in the day. Had he been warning her that he was going out? Preparing her without raising an alarm? Asking her not to worry? She clutched at that, telling herself that he would be back soon. And if he wasn't, it would eventually be light and she'd go looking for him.

Because there was simply no way she could go out into the darkness again and face the creature with the yellow eyes and the sharp teeth.

9

THE wolf was as shaken by the midnight encounter as the woman. In the shadows under the trees, he stood with blood roaring in his ears.

Trying to cope with the human and animal emotions clashing inside him, he finally turned away from the house and prowled deeper into the woods. When he caught the scent of another rabbit, he gave chase, bringing down the creature and eating like a starving cur. He *was* starving—for protein. Raw and as close to its natural state as possible. His system demanded fresh meat to heal itself. One more wolf trait he was powerless to deny.

But even the urgency of the hunt couldn't stop his mind from circling back and back, frantically turning one way and then the other like a wounded animal trying to outrun its pain.

When he'd seen Megan come out of the house, a shockwave had rolled through him as he pictured the scene as she must—a wolf tearing his prey apart. The horror of it had seized him by the throat—even as he made the decision to stand his ground, to let her see what he really was. Then the fear in her eyes had slashed through him, the pain as hot and intense as the bullet that had mutilated his flesh.

Long after he was dizzy with fatigue, he stayed away from the house, afraid of what he would find when he went inside. Afraid to put a name to the emotions roiling inside him.

But finally there was nowhere else to go but home to Díthreabh. His refuge, until the woman with the silky blond hair and the wide blue eyes had stolen it from him.

When he saw her car still in the driveway, relief surged through him. It was followed quickly by regret. If she'd only taken his warning to heart and cleared out, he'd be free of her by now.

Still in the shadow of the woods, he changed back into human form, then propped his shoulders against a tree, gathering the strength to limp across the stretch of grass between the woods and the house. When he discovered the front door was locked, he retrieved the spare house key hidden under a rock and slipped back inside.

An almost frantic need grabbed him as he stepped across the threshold. Where was she? How was she?

On shaky legs, he made his way down the hall and found her slumped in a chair by the window—no doubt exhausted by the silent confrontation with the wolf and by the toll the past few days had taken on her. He wanted to go to her. Hunker down beside her. Touch her. Wake her. But he turned away lest she see the blood on his face and hands.

After grabbing a pair of jeans and a T-shirt from the laundry room, he stepped into a hot shower, washing away the evidence of the night's activities. Afterward, too exhausted for anything besides sleep, he went into the great room and collapsed on the sofa.

The first rays of the sun striking the windowpanes woke him. For long minutes, he lay with his eyes closed, his thoughts focused on the woman who had driven him from his bedroom.

Dreading what might come next, yet helpless to stop himself, he tiptoed down the hall, gritting his teeth against the pain in his leg.

Megan was still sleeping, sprawled against the corduroy chair cushions. On bare feet, he moved closer, stopping eight feet away, caught and held by the delicious scent of her body. Soap and woman and something personal that he couldn't name. But he would always know it was her scent, always react.

He stood in the early morning light, cataloguing physical details. Her legs were drawn up, her hair like spun gold was spread out around her face, and her head was tipped back. Her slightly parted lips gave her the look of a child who had begged to stay up late on New Year's Eve and had fallen asleep before the magic stroke of midnight.

But she was no child. He had learned over the past few days that she was a very resourceful, very stubborn, very appealing woman. Testing his reaction to her, he let his gaze slide over her face—the brows several shades darker than her hair, the high cheekbones, the small chin. From there it was a natural drop to the slender column of her throat, then lower to her breasts—small but tempting mounds, high and firm-looking, hidden by the barrier of her T-shirt.

She was wearing a shirt with a picture of the Baltimore Orioles mascot. And he caught himself watching the bird's beak move back and forth across the tip of one nipple as her chest rose and fell with each breath. It wasn't difficult to picture his finger there instead of the bird's rigid beak, caressing that delicate peak, bringing it to arousal with his touch. Tightening his jaw, he forbade his body to react. He reminded himself that he had been close to death two days ago. He was still weak. Yet it was impossible not to respond to her.

He told himself it was because he hadn't had a woman in a long time. Only half believing it, he clenched his teeth against the physiological response. When he found he had no control over the hot blood pooling in the lower part of his body, he whirled—welcoming the stab of pain in his injured leg as he strode back down the hall to the bathroom.

Naked, aroused, he turned on the water, adjusted the temperature to cold this time, and stepped into the shower enclosure. The needle-sharp spray cooled his hot skin.

He stayed there for a long time, leaning against the shower wall to steady his still-weakened leg. Cutting off the water, he shook droplets from his dark hair, then reached for the towel.

After shaving off four days' growth of beard, he pulled on his jeans and black T-shirt.

Finally, when he could no longer postpone the confrontation, he opened the door and started for his room, trying not to limp. He'd left Megan sleeping. Now she was staring fixedly toward the hallway, apparently having heard him approaching.

"You're awake," he said, feeling his voice clog. Remaining in the doorway where he could prop his weight on his good leg, he slipped his hands into the pockets of his jeans as he watched her eyes flash with a mixture of anger and something else. Relief?

Would she tell him about the wolf? What would she say? What would he answer? He waited, his breath shallow in his chest. He could force the issue, here and now. Tell her he was the animal she had seen outside. Send her screaming from the house.

Because there were only two possibilities he could imagine. She would understand that he was a monster, and leave. Or she would think that he was a dangerous lunatic—and leave.

He found he could face neither of those. So he stood very still, waiting.

She raised her chin. "What are you? Self-destructive? Going outside in your condition . . . I came in to check on you yesterday evening. You weren't in your bed. You weren't anywhere in the house. You think you're in shape to go tramping off into the woods?"

He had never been in quite this situation, and he wasn't sure what he was going to say until words came from his lips. "I'm not used to explaining my thinking . . . or my actions." By an effort of will, he kept the hands in his pockets from clenching. "But, okay, I'll give you a little pertinent background. My ancestors were Druid priests. For me, going into the woods—making myself one with nature—is part of the healing process," he said, managing to keep a straight face as he mouthed the touchy-feely explanation.

"You need to go outside in the dark, naked—"

"To revive my body and my spirit, yes," he finished calmly, omitting the part about needing to hunt for fresh meat.

He would have liked to stay where he was—twelve feet from the woman in the chair. A safe distance. But he didn't have the energy to stay on his feet much longer, so he moved into the room and lowered himself to the edge of the bed.

She looked torn between telling him that his explanation was bullshit and respecting his pagan beliefs.

"Nothing happened. I'm fine."

She sucked in a sharp breath and let it out in a rush. "I saw a . . . a big dog out there. It threatened me. It could have attacked you."

"That's not going to happen."

"How do you know?"

He pretended utter innocence. "Are you sure of what you saw?"

"I . . ." She looked uncertain, then lowered her gaze to the hands clasped in her lap. "I don't know."

"Are you sure it was a dog?"

"I . . . don't know," she said again, this time more uncertain.

"Well then," he answered mildly.

The wolf had confronted her, intent on burning the encounter into her brain—and chasing her away. But she was still here. And the man was thankful that she wasn't ready to cope with the implications of the late-night meeting. He might have been surprised by her morning-after reality check, but he'd seen the phenomenon before. Human eyes saw a large menacing animal where no animal should be. And the mind behind those eyes turned away from the evidence because it was too disturbing to be real.

He helped along the process of denial—gave her a couple of other alternatives. "I take it you were pretty upset. Maybe you saw . . . what did you call them? Animal shapes in the leaves? Or maybe it was just a bad dream. A very vivid dream—brought on by the stress of the last few days."

He saw her swallow. "Maybe," she said in a doubtful voice. "But why would stress make me see a wolf?"

"A wolf? I thought you said you saw a large dog."

She closed her eyes for a moment, pressed her hand against her mouth. "I . . . don't think there are any wolves in Maryland. But it looked like a wolf."

"Have you ever seen one before?"

"I don't think so."

"Well, all the more reason why it must have been a dream." Before she could take away control of the conversation, he said, "You came here to get a blood sample. You can do it now."

She looked startled, as if she'd forgotten all about the original purpose of her visit. Then she rallied. "Yes. Right. But first I'm going to take a shower and brush my teeth, if you don't mind."

Ross was left staring at the swaying rear end of his uninvited guest. He'd thought he could get her out of the house immediately. But she'd just worked her way around his resolve. Cursing under his breath, he pushed himself off the bed and winced as his foot hit the floor. Still, he walked rapidly past the closed bathroom door so he didn't have to imagine any intimate details as he heard the water come on in the shower.

In the kitchen, he pulled one of his expensive shrink-wrapped steaks out of the freezer. After sticking the package in a pan of tepid water to thaw, he propped his hips against the counter and looked down the hall toward the bathroom, where he could hear water running.

MEGAN turned up the hot water a notch, tipping her face into the shower spray, then let it play over the tense muscles of her back and shoulders while she tried to sort through her memories of the night before.

What exactly had happened last night?

For starters, she had panicked when she'd found Ross's door locked. She'd torn through the house looking for him. And when she'd satisfied herself that he was absent, she'd gone outside.

That's what she remembered. Until Ross had questioned her memory.

Her jaw started to tremble. Gritting her teeth, she directed her mind back to the conversation they'd just had. When she'd confronted Ross, he hadn't denied going outside. So that made the first part real.

Didn't it?

Sometime during the night, she'd fallen asleep in the chair. She knew that much for sure. At least that was where she'd woken up when she'd heard the shower running this morning.

But the rest of it . . . *Could* it have been a dream?

As she stood under the water, clenching and unclenching her hands, a long-forgotten memory came surging back.

When she'd been a powerless little girl, afraid of Daddy, she'd invented a magic bear who would growl at her father when he got too mean.

That bear had been very real to her—a necessary ingredient in her young existence. She'd named him Mergatroid. He'd been her protector and her friend. And she'd fallen asleep every night, imagining he was crouched beside her bed as she whispered to him in the dark, telling him about her hopes and fears.

The memory had been buried for a long time. Now it was so vivid that she could clearly picture the large brown animal dressed in the checked vest he always wore. Back then when she'd needed emotional support, she might have mixed up dreams and reality, she silently conceded.

What if it was happening again?

What if she'd gone outside, seen something frightening that she couldn't explain—something so disturbing that she couldn't cope with it—and translated it into the scene with the wolf?

Another memory bobbed to the surface. This time it was from a book she'd read in her abnormal psychology class in college, *I Never Promised You a Rose Garden*. It was written by a former mental patient, a woman who had invented an imaginary land where she took refuge from the things in the world that disturbed and frightened her. At first her private refuge had been inhabited by friendly people, but gradually the land had taken on a life beyond her control. The population had turned nasty and started to dominate her—and she'd been helpless to escape. Finally she'd ended up in a mental hospital where a psychiatrist had helped her sort through fantasy and reality.

Was that happening now? Megan wondered with a shudder. To her? God, after two days and nights of private nursing duty, was she losing her mind?

The hot water turned gradually cold, and she started to shiver. Not just from the temperature—from her unwanted thoughts. Reluctantly she turned off the shower and reached for a towel, rubbing briskly. But the cold went deeper than her skin.

She'd told herself from the first that she should get out of Ross Marshall's house as fast as she could. Then he'd warned her to leave. Too bad she hadn't taken either her own or his advice.

With a grimace she looked at the clothes she'd worn the day before—and then slept in. And too bad she hadn't thought about borrowing Marshall's washer and dryer. Just another example of how she wasn't thinking too clearly—on a lot of fronts.

ROSS had slapped the steak onto the stove-top grill when Megan came into the kitchen, her hair towel-dried but still damp.

He didn't look directly at her as he pretended to contemplate the meat. She seemed shaken, more fragile than she had been at any time since she'd arrived, even when he'd pulled that stunt with the wolf—and then given her reasons to question whether the whole episode had been a bad dream.

At the moment he was regretting his impulses. He wanted to apologize for frightening her and making her doubt her own senses. He wanted to reach out and catch her shoulder, pull her toward him and fold his arms around her, knowing the comfort would be as much for him as for her. But he sternly clamped down on the desire because he knew that touching her was a bad idea. For both of them.

She seemed to be working at control as much as he. Her pale lips were pressed together, and the skin around her eyes looked pinched. When she briskly filled the kettle at the sink and set it on a burner, he relaxed a fraction.

As she turned on the gas flame, she said in a slightly breathy voice, "I couldn't find any coffee yesterday."

"I don't drink it."

"Do you mind if I fix some instant I picked up at the grocery store when I filled your prescription?"

Caffeine had always made him sick. Just the smell of coffee was enough to make him a little queasy, which was probably a good thing today since he was trying to keep his hands off the woman standing two feet away. So he shrugged and got down two mugs. For himself, he also pulled out a packet of wild berry tea.

He and Megan moved stiffly around each other in the kitchen, he forking up the steak and turning it over, she waiting for the kettle to boil. As he watched her from the corner of his eye, he was vividly aware that no woman had had breakfast here.

"You take this nature stuff seriously," she said, eyeing the box of herbal tea.

He shrugged again, backed away from the pungent aroma that rose from her mug as she stirred hot water into the coffee crystals. While she poured milk into the coffee, he started steeping the tea bag.

The steak had a thin layer of brown on both sides, enough for cosmetic purposes, he decided. Transferring it to a plate, he took it to the table, sat down, and began to eat, aware that he was being rude.

"I bought some eggs at the store yesterday. Do you mind if I scramble a couple?"

He chewed and swallowed the piece of steak in his mouth. "There's a pan in the lower cabinet next to the stove."

"Do you want some?"

"The steak is enough for me."

As he ate, he watched her cracking eggs into a small bowl, stirring in a little milk, melting butter in the pan. For an unguarded moment he found himself fantasizing about having her here every morning.

When he realized what he was doing, he slammed the door on the pleasant mental picture and focused on the smell of the sizzling fat.

Clearing his throat, he said, "I wouldn't mind a couple of eggs."

She added two more to the bowl and stirred them in, along with more milk, salt, and pepper. Then she transferred everything to the pan.

As she watched the eggs cook, she said, "I realize you're anxious for me to collect my sample and clear out of your house."

He managed a little shrug.

"I'll get this over with as fast as I can. But when a client calls for a genetic workup, we need to get some background information."

He shifted in his chair. "Like what?"

"You told our secretary that you have a genetic disease in your family."

Was that what he'd said? He didn't remember being that direct.

"Have you had the condition evaluated?" she asked.

"No."

"Then how do you know it's a genetic disorder?" she asked.

"I know what happens to the children born in my family. Not just to my parents. My grandparents. Further back."

"Can you be more specific?" she asked, moving the eggs around in the pan.

He could be specific as hell. All he said in a clipped voice was "The girl babies die shortly after birth. The males hang on until puberty, at which time about half of them join their sisters. I'm one of the lucky survivors."

10

HE saw something flash across her face. Pity? He didn't want pity from her or anybody else.

"Genetic disorders are my specialty. And I've never heard of anything like that," she said as she quickly scooped eggs onto two plates. "Has this disease ever been diagnosed?"

He cut a piece of meat, and chewed and swallowed as though he were enjoying the food, although the ability to taste anything other than his own tension had suddenly deserted him.

"It hasn't been diagnosed, because nobody's talked about it in public. It's been treated like a shameful family secret. But the evidence is there. For as many generations back as we have family records." *And further than that,* he silently added. *Back into the mists of antiquity.* Female babies died. Teenage boys died.

She kept her features neutral as she brought the plates of eggs to the table, along with a fork for herself.

"You're sure *all* girls die? And half the boys die in their teens?"

"Yes."

"For the boys, is it a degenerative process?"

"No."

"What then?"

"I don't know. It's a sudden event. A stroke maybe," he answered in a low voice, remembering the terrible burst of pain in his own head when he'd first changed. It had felt like a thousand daggers piercing his brain tissue, and he'd thought it was going to kill him. But somehow he'd conquered the pain.

He stole a quick glance at her to see if he'd given too much away. Her vision was turned inward, her eggs forgotten, cooling in front of her on the table.

"What you're describing—a sex-linked disease—sounds like it would have to be passed on through a recessive gene. In other words, a child would have to receive a defective copy from both the mother and the father."

"No, this is passed on only through the males. They're the only ones who survive."

"How do you know that for sure?"

"I can document it for four generations. My great-grandmother had twelve children," he recited in a flat voice. "Six girls died at birth. Four boys died before their sixteenth year. Two boys survived into adulthood. My grandmother had fifteen children. Eight girls died at birth. Four boys died in adolescence. Three boys survived—including my father. My own mother had nine children. Four girls died at birth. She was lucky with the boys. Three survived into adulthood. Including me. I think you can see the pattern."

"Yes. But it could still be a recessive gene."

He shook his head. "That's not what's happening."

"How do you know?"

"The men in my family share certain . . . characteristics that aren't found in the general population."

"What?"

He shifted in his chair. "The reason that I didn't come to the lab in the first place was that I didn't want to discuss it."

He saw her swallow, hesitate. "You seem perfectly healthy—apart from your recent infected wound. Which is healing faster than expected. Do the men have some defect that only shows up later in life? Have you heard of Huntington's disease? Is it something like that?"

"I've read about it. It's not like that."

She pushed a portion of egg around on the plate. "It would be helpful if you could tell me a little more."

Below the level of the table, he clenched his hands. He'd wanted to avoid this, although he hadn't really understood how painful it would be. "It's not an illness, but there are physical changes in the men who survive. Under certain circumstances I have heightened sensory perceptions. And you've already seen that my body has unusual recuperative powers." He sighed. "And there are some . . . social consequences. When the men in my family reach maturity, they find it impossible to live in any kind of proximity to one another. I have a brother who's a forest ranger in Texas. I haven't seen him since he left home ten years ago. I wouldn't try to stay in the same room with my father for more than half an hour. We'd end up slugging it out."

He watched her staring at him, waiting for more information. He had never spoken of these things with anyone, not even his mother, and it was agony to continue. But he forced the words out of his mouth.

"This is something that's been in my family forever. In the past, it was accepted as a curse or a blessing—depending on whether you were one of the ones who beat the odds. But with modern gene technology, I think there's a chance to change the outcome."

"You're looking for a cure?"

"I didn't ask for genetic testing because I thought it would solve any problems I have." He stopped, then forced himself to continue, speaking to her more directly than she probably realized. "I don't intend to put an innocent woman through the hell that was my mother's life. Bearing child after child. Knowing the girls will die at birth. Waiting to find out if the boys will survive beyond the age of fifteen or sixteen—then having them move away because they couldn't stay in the same room with their father. I've read about gene therapy. I've heard about using transfusions of fetal blood to cure sickle-cell anemia. I'm hoping there's a therapy that will do the same thing for my children. If not, then I won't be responsible for passing this genetic curse on to another generation." He sat there, amazed that he had said so much—and to this particular woman sitting across the breakfast table.

She looked shocked, and yet there was a kind of excitement glowing in her eyes. "All right. Yes. The first thing I want to do is a karyotype—a profile of your chromosomes. If I do an analysis of your DNA, I'd want to test your parents, too—and some of the other men in your family."

He gave a grim laugh. "My father would run you off with a shotgun if you came near him to try to get a blood sample." *Metaphorically speaking. More likely with his fangs. The way I tried to do last night. Only he won't hold anything back.*

"Do you ever go home?"

"Only when the Big—" He stopped abruptly, rephrased the answer. "Only when the old man isn't around."

"I don't need blood. I could use hair from his comb."

"I suppose I could get my mother to get some for me."

"You said two brothers lived into adulthood."

So she'd been paying attention to the details. "Yeah, well, getting into dangerous situations is one of our characteristics, I'm afraid. One of my brothers died as the result of a, uh, barroom brawl."

"I'm sorry."

He gave a small shrug.

"And you've channeled your aggressions into detective work?"

"Yeah. It's an excellent outlet."

When he didn't elaborate, she nodded. "Because of the family sensory talents you spoke of?"

"Yes."

Her expression had grown thoughtful. "There's something I was curious about. You work out of the office down the hall?"

He nodded, wondering where the conversation was going now.

"I left a message on your answering machine. Then when I saw all the No Trespassing signs along your driveway, I called you again. I assume you didn't get the message."

"No. I was too sick to call in for my messages."

"When I needed to get a prescription for more Keflex, I couldn't find your telephone."

"I don't have a hardwired phone. I use a cell phone. Part of the package is the answering service." As he listened to his own words, his mind streaked back to four nights ago when he'd grabbed his pants in his teeth and run like hell from Arnott.

As the scene leaped into his mind, a sudden feeling of panic crawled through his gut. "I'll be right back," he told her, pushing his chair away from the table and lurching to his feet.

Limping down the hall as fast as he could move, he surged into the bedroom and picked up the pants from where he'd kicked them into the corner. With icy fingers, he reached into the right front pocket. His keys were there, but no telephone. His wallet was in the back left pocket where he'd left it. There were a couple of pieces of loose change on the right.

Carefully he went through all of the pockets again. No telephone. Jesus!

He felt the hair on the back of his neck stir as he bent to search under the bed, under the dresser. Looking up, he saw Megan watching him.

"You're trying to find the phone?"

"Yes."

"Can I help?"

"It isn't in here!"

"In some other room? The office?"

"No. I came straight to the bedroom, took off my clothes, and fell into bed. When I felt like I could get up, I went into the bathroom, climbed into the tub, and cut out the bullet."

She winced, then came back with another suggestion. "Maybe the phone is in your SUV."

"Yeah." Hoping against hope, he reached for the running shoes under the bed and jammed his feet into them. Then he brushed past his guest and sprinted for the car, ignoring the throbbing in his leg.

A pool of dried blood had soaked into the driver's seat and dripped onto the floor mat. He ignored the mess and checked under the front seat, then wedged his fingers into the cracks where the seat cushions and backs met. Megan pulled open the rear door on the other side of the SUV and methodically went over the back, even feeling around under the front seat.

He followed suit on his side, pulling up the floor mat, sweeping his hand under the seat. The only things he found were a quarter and the ice scraper he hadn't used since February.

"It's not here," she said, her voice strained, her face reflecting the tension he felt.

He nodded tightly, knowing there was only one place where he could have dropped the damn thing. In the woods outside a serial killer's chain-link fence. Too bad he'd been too busy running for his life to check his pants pockets.

Straightening, he slammed the car door, feeling his facial muscles tighten.

"What?" she asked, closing the opposite door and coming around to his side of the vehicle.

"You have to get out of here," he said.

She raised her eyes to his. "You said that a number of times when you were sick."

"Yeah, and now I know the reason why. The guy I was investigating knows I was on his property. If he finds that phone, he can figure out who I am. And if he does, it's dangerous for you to be here."

Megan didn't move. "If it's dangerous for me, it's dangerous for you, too."

"I can handle him."

She cocked her head to one side, gave him a long look before speaking again. "I hate to contradict. But didn't he shoot you in the leg?"

His gaze drilled into her. He was accustomed to making men back off by giving them that look. But she stood her ground. And when he took a step forward, she stayed where she was, her hands clenched in front of her. He couldn't repress a flash of admiration, but standing her ground wasn't going to change anything.

"If he comes looking for me, he'll be on my turf. And I'm not going to discuss my plans with you. What you're going to do is clear out so I don't have to worry about defending you as well as myself," he said, punching out the words for emphasis.

She gave him a small nod, then reminded him they still had unfinished business. "Before or after I take the blood sample I came to collect?"

11

MEGAN watched Ross flap his hand in exasperation. "Take the damn sample. Then get out of here before we're both sorry."

"Okay. My kit's inside."

In the kitchen, she cleared the table and washed the white Formica surface with a soapy dishcloth because she was too obsessive a technician to work with half-eaten plates of food sitting in front of her. But there was another reason, too. She needed to give her hands enough time to stop shaking before she tried sticking a needle into Ross Marshall's vein.

He'd told her he'd dropped the phone at the house of the killer he was investigating and that the man might come after him. And he was ordering her to leave so she wouldn't get caught in the cross fire. If there was going to be any cross fire.

Calmly she dried the table with a paper towel, watching the smooth motion of her hand sweeping across the flat surface.

God—he was asking her to just walk away when he might be in danger. She didn't like what he'd told her about the phone. She hated the idea of leaving him alone, yet she was pretty sure she didn't have a choice. She'd known from the beginning that he would have kicked her out if he'd had the strength. Now that he was capable of doing it, she wasn't going to make him waste his strength on her.

"You need to sit down," she said around the clogged feeling in her throat.

He sat, and she washed her hands at the sink. Then, turning back to the table, she opened her kit and took out a hypodermic, a Venoject tube with lithium heparin, and a piece of rubber tubing to wrap around his arm.

"Turn your arm over."

He obeyed, and she tapped the veins, finding one that looked promising.

After cutting off his circulation with the tubing, she swabbed his flesh with alcohol, watching his nose wrinkle.

"I guess you hate the smell of this stuff."

"Yeah."

"Then why did I find a bottle in your medicine cabinet?"

"Because when it stings, I know it's working."

"You like to punish yourself."

"No. I like to know the wound's being disinfected."

"You hurt yourself often?" she asked, aware that her shaky nerves were making her chatter.

"Yeah."

He was back in his laconic mode, so she cut her losses and concentrated on the procedure.

Some patients looked away before she pierced their flesh. He kept his gaze fixed on what she was doing.

She'd touched him far more intimately when she'd changed the dressing on his thigh. But he'd been half out of it then. Now she sensed that he was fully aware of her fingers sliding against his skin, of her hand releasing the rubber tubing.

She knew he was concentrating on staying very still as she took about eight milliliters of blood, withdrew the needle, and pressed a sterile piece of gauze to his arm.

Methodically she pushed the green stopper into the tube's mouth and then wrote his name on the label.

He watched her work. And when she lifted her eyes, their gazes collided.

For a charged moment, neither of them spoke. Then she cleared her throat, thinking she had nothing to lose by telling him what was on her mind. "If you were anybody else, I'd order you to bed. But I guess I've figured out that I can't order you to do anything."

"That's right. But you don't have to worry."

She knew he was saying the last part with as much reassurance as he could project, but she wasn't going to let him off that easily. "Tell me what you're going to do about the phone."

Sighing, he answered. "When it gets dark, I'll go back and look for it. If I find it, the problem's solved."

"And if you don't find it?"

"I'll cross that bridge when I have to."

She heard herself asking, "Will you call me—tell me what happened?"

She half expected him to refuse. Instead he nodded.

"Thank you." Reaching into her purse, she brought out a business card, then wrote on the back. "This is my home number. Call me as soon as you know anything."

He stood up. "In the middle of the night?"

She turned to him, raising her face to his. "I don't think I'll be able to sleep until I know you're okay."

When he didn't answer, she added softly, "You hate that, don't you? Someone staying up late at night, worrying about you."

She'd been here for two days, feeling like an intruder, feeling his resistance to any meaningful exchange of emotions between them. The barriers were still in place. His barriers. And she understood the reason—at least part of it.

But now that she was leaving, she was damned if she was going to let it end without some measure of honesty—on her part if not his.

The tight, warning expression on his face only spurred her on. She'd never been an impulsive woman. And her childhood had made her wary of men who took control of situations like a storm front blowing away all thought of opposition. Despite all logic, she found herself moving forward quickly, before she could change her mind. She saw his eyes darken, saw him glance behind himself and find that he was blocked from escape by the edge of the table.

Opening her arms, she reached for him, clasped her hands behind his back. For an instant he went rigid. Then she felt as well as heard the breath hiss out of his lungs. Her own breath was frozen inside her as she absorbed the impact of her body pressed to his. The contact was as potent as she'd known it would be. No, far more potent.

Stunned, she clung to him, knowing full well that he was strong enough to break her hold, wrench himself from her grasp. Instead she felt his arms rise, circle her shoulders, tighten, wedge her body more firmly to the length of his.

"Ross."

Earlier this morning she'd been badly off balance—torn between doubting her encounter with the wolf and doubting her own sanity. In his arms, she felt centered, secure. Eyes squeezed shut, she laid her cheek against his broad chest, drawing strength from him even as she felt him leaning into her.

She breathed in the fresh-washed scent of his skin and, below that, his unique scent, something like the tang of rain on the wind. Greedy for more, she moved her hands over the hard muscles of his back, pressed her face more tightly to his chest, feeling the deep steady thrumming of his heart beneath her cheek. He might be holding himself still, but she knew she was affecting him as powerfully as he was affecting her.

She had tried to deny the deep sense of connection to this man, but that had suddenly become impossible. Her heart leaped as she felt his hands move over her. He pulled her closer, aligning her body more perfectly with his, and she felt a tide of heat sweep across her skin, sink into her flesh, burn its way to the marrow of her bones. It felt good, right. It felt like something she had secretly craved for a long time, yet the need hadn't been there until she'd met him.

"Ross." She said his name again, lifted her face, and saw his eyes burning hot and bright. Time had stopped. The world had contracted to the circle of his arms clasping her to him. For a charged moment, she stared up at him, as though the two of them were shipwreck survivors who had miraculously washed up on the same beach after fearing each other lost. Her mouth opened slightly, anticipating the feel of his lips coming down on hers. Anticipating the jolt of heat.

But it didn't happen.

Gently but firmly he cupped his hands on her shoulders, moved her body back and away from his.

She felt abashed. Light-headed. Confused.

And the look on his face told her he was experiencing all those things, too.

"Are you feeling sorry for me?" he asked, his voice gritty.

"No."

"Then what?"

She struggled for honesty. "I . . . I like you."

"Didn't you listen to anything I told you?" he asked, his voice thick.

"I listened to everything."

"Then you know the consequences of getting mixed up with me."

"Is hugging a man getting mixed up with him?" she asked quickly.

"You can't argue it both ways."

"I—"

"If you're smart, you'll back off before . . ."

"Before what?"

He didn't answer. But the image she'd had that first evening—the image of the two of them naked on a bed, hot and wanting—came back to her. The bed down the hall.

In her mind she understood that he was little more than a stranger. A man with secrets and sorrows. Yet the feelings building inside her defied logic. As she stood there staring at him, she knew that she longed to feel connected to him. Physically, emotionally.

Before she could tell him what was in her heart, he turned away and rested his elbows on the counter, and she knew he was calling on more strength than she possessed at the moment. She saw it in the rigid set of his shoulders, heard it in the rasp of his breath.

He uttered a fierce oath, then said, "You'd better go."

Torn, she stood beside him for seconds that felt like an eternity. Every female impulse inside her urged her to reach out and touch him. If she did, he would turn. He would take her in his arms again. It was what they both wanted. But she understood that this was the wrong time. Because he had asked her to do it, she backed away. Perhaps that was the only thing she could do for him now.

Later was another matter.

But she didn't allow herself to think about later.

Turning, she grabbed up the kit with the blood sample and her purse and fled the house.

She was in the car when she saw him stride outside.

Feeling a reckless surge of hope, she rolled down the window as he came toward her, anxious to hear what he had to say.

It was, "Where's my gun?"

She struggled to keep hurt and disappointment out of her eyes. "In the chest near the front door."

He nodded and turned, and she watched the door close behind him with a sense of defeat.

In the car, driving home, she had ample time to reflect on the pain and confusion she was feeling.

She had always been cautious with the opposite sex. It took a long time before she let herself risk getting close. And she'd always picked men who weren't like her father—men who weren't harsh, dominating, aggressive, strong. In the two days she'd known Ross Marshall, he'd been all those things. And yet she'd put her arms around him and held him close as though he were precious to her.

A shiver rippled across her skin. She was attracted to him on some deep level where no man had ever moved her before. Yet at the same time she was afraid of him. A little while ago she had blocked the latter out. Now she didn't know what to do about it—or the attraction.

Always before, relationships with men had been on her terms. And they went no further than she wanted them to go. She had been to bed with a few of the men she'd dated and enjoyed the experience on a superficial level. But she knew that with Ross Marshall making love would be different. More powerful. More meaningful.

She blinked, brought herself up short. She was still thinking about making love with the man. And he had done everything possible to put distance between them—until this morning when she'd forced him to confront the powerful emotions building between them.

Even then he had been compelled to fight the attraction. Earlier she'd wondered if his genetic problem was the reason he was putting up barriers between them. After what he'd told her this morning, she was sure it was the case. That and his tragic family background. He hadn't spelled out that last part. But it didn't take much imagination to picture the grief his mother had gone through—losing so many daughters at birth, then half her sons.

God, what a sad life. Why was she even thinking about getting mixed up with a man who had told her his heritage was grief and suffering?

By the time she reached her house, she had made what she considered a smart decision. She would turn the blood sample over to Hank and let him proceed with the tests.

By the time she'd discarded her sweat clothes and put on a crisp skirt and blouse, she had changed her mind. As she put on lipstick and a bit of blusher, she told herself she wasn't going to take the coward's route. She would do the tests herself, report back to Ross on what she found, and see where things went from there.

WHEN she arrived at the lab, however, she abruptly abandoned all work plans. Betty was sitting at the reception desk, looking distraught. And Walter, his face pinched and his skin gray, was talking to a couple of uniformed police officers who had apparently been there for a while. Barlow and Sandler, their name tags said.

Completely disoriented, she stared at the unaccustomed scene. For a terrible moment, her mind leaped to the conclusion that this had to do with Ross—with the lost phone. The killer had found it, come after him. And now the police were at the lab to tell them that their client was in the hospital—or worse.

"What happened?" she wheezed, reaching out a hand to steady her-self against the wall.

"A burglary," Betty said.

It took another moment for the words to sink in. "A break-in? Where?"

It was Walter who stepped away from the cops to answer. "Here. Somebody forced the lock on the door early this morning. Betty found the door open when she came to work. She was afraid to go inside so she left a note on the door and went to call the police. We all stayed outside for over an hour, waiting for the police to come," he said, an accusing note in his voice as he glanced toward the two detectives.

Megan took in the overview, then zeroed in on the personal ramifi-cations. "My project," she gasped, and dashed into the lab area. Quickly she inspected her laminar flow hoods, her virus cultures. Her genetic material.

The officer named Sandler followed her. "You're Dr. Sheridan?"

"Yes."

"Was your work disturbed?"

She did a more careful inspection, then breathed out a small sigh. "Not as far as I can see."

He wrote that down in a notebook. When the microphone clipped to his collar sputtered, he pressed a button and conferred with some un-seen dispatcher. After completing the call, Sandler turned back to Megan. "Would you take a look at your desk area?"

She retraced her steps and walked into the office she shared with Hank, who had evidently gotten the assignment to check the file drawers.

He glanced up when she entered and rolled his eyes. "Welcome back. Your timing is impeccable."

"Right." She sank into her desk chair, opened drawers, shuffled through the contents. Nothing seemed to be disturbed. Then she booted up her computer and brought up her main directory, scanning the entries.

There was no problem accessing her directories. And when she opened some of her files at random, the information was intact.

"I'm not finding anything missing," she reported.

Sandler asked, "Can you tell me where you were this morning?"

She might have taken offense, but she realized he probably had asked everyone the same question.

"Getting a blood sample from a client of the lab," she answered. "You can check with him if you like."

"His name?"

"Ross Marshall," she answered, then fumbled in her purse for the slip of paper with his address, which she read off to the detective.

Sandler copied it down before returning to the hall, where Walter was still standing, giving his report to Barlow. When her boss finally wound down, the officer handed him a business card.

"If you have anything else to report, give me a call," he said.

When they had departed, she joined a scowling Dr. Galveston in the hall. "Yeah, and if we do think of something, good luck in getting you to call back," he muttered.

"Did anything turn up missing?" Megan asked.

"It looks like the alarm scared them off. But the officers took some fingerprints from the door."

"It's strange that someone went to the trouble of breaking in, then took off," she mused.

Walter's expression turned darker.

"What?" she asked.

"Nothing."

"Something's bothering you."

His mouth tightened. "Maybe there's a pattern here."

"A pattern of what? Did you tell that to the police?" When he didn't reply, she prompted, "Walter?"

He glanced toward the office, where Hank was still thumbing through files, then lowered his voice before saying, "Let's go where we can talk."

Wondering what he wanted to keep so close to his vest, she followed him to his office, a room that was twice the size of the area where she and Hank worked. He pulled the door shut, then rounded his oversized rosewood desk and lowered himself into the executive leather chair.

Uneasily she took one of the comfortable guest chairs, waiting for him to speak.

When he finally did, his voice was pitched low. "Six months ago, there was an incident."

"What kind of incident?"

"A couple came in for genetic testing. It turned out that the test results were erroneous."

The word hung between them.

As the implications sank in, a wave of cold swept over her skin. "A test I did? Is that why you called me in here?"

"I think it was one of Hank's."

"You don't know for sure?"

"The records have disappeared."

She stared at him. "Disappeared? How?"

He shrugged.

"You've spoken to Hank?"

"No. And I don't want you to, either. Anyone can make a mistake." He looked down at his desk blotter, then up again. "Or maybe what I'm trying to say is that it was really my fault. I'd piled too much work on him, and he was rushed."

"You're piling too much work on both of us," she answered, then wondered why she couldn't simply keep her mouth shut. But this time he was the one who'd brought it up. Maybe he was feeling guilty.

She saw him swallow hard and glance toward the closed door. "I got an angry call from the client threatening me. That was several weeks ago and nothing happened, so I figured the guy was just blowing off steam. Then there was the incident Monday on the way to work."

She was thrown completely off track. So much had happened since Monday morning that it took several moments for her to recall what he was talking about. When she remembered the way he'd come in all upset, her eyes widened.

"You said somebody ran you off the road."

"Yes. And I thought I recognized the guy."

"You didn't mention that!"

"I was hoping I was wrong. Then this morning, after I discovered the break-in, I checked my case files. Some of them are gone."

"Did you tell that to the police?"

"No."

"You have to."

"And have an article impugning the reputation of the lab in the *Washington Post* tomorrow? No thank you. I don't need news like that spread across the headlines. Not when I'm expecting a big contract to come through."

"What contract?"

"That's confidential information."

"But, Walter, you're already giving me confidential information," she argued.

He glared at her, then made an effort to relax his features. "Let's wait and see what happens. Waiting a few days isn't going to hurt anything."

"You're not thinking this through logically."

"I want to handle it in my own way."

"Walter—"

"I'm trusting you to let me deal with the problem. And to keep this conversation between the two of us. Do I have your word on that?"

"I guess so," she answered reluctantly.

"I need to know you won't blab to Hank or Betty."

"All right."

"Thank you."

"Why are you telling *me*?"

"I just want you to know the background, in case something happens to me."

"And then what?"

"Then you can tell the police. Until then, I expect you to keep your mouth shut."

12

SINCE there didn't seem to be anything more to say, Megan got up and started down the hall to her own office. But she stopped short before she reached the door. Hank was probably there, and she couldn't face him after Walter's accusation, so she switched directions and stepped into the ladies' room. Locking herself in one of the stalls she sat down on the closed toilet seat and pressed her palms against her forehead, trying to dispel the sudden throbbing in her temples.

God, what a mess. Walter was telling her the lab was under attack from a crazed client. And that it was Hank's fault. Or was that really true?

She pressed harder as the pain in her head reached Anvil Chorus proportions.

Could Walter have done something he wasn't prepared to talk about? And was now blaming it on Hank?

She and Hank had a good, solid working relationship. She wanted to ask him if he remembered the test. But she'd promised Walter she'd keep the information confidential.

Damn him. He'd boxed her into a corner. The way Ross Marshall had boxed her into a corner.

Two different men, with two completely different styles, and they both had her flummoxed.

A year ago, when her parents had died, she'd made the mistake of mentioning her inheritance to Walter, and he'd urged her to invest in the lab. It was a topic he brought up every few months—but so far the money she hadn't used for a down payment on her house was still in the bank.

Now she was grateful that she hadn't leaped to invest in Bio Gen. Because it looked like the business was falling apart in front of her eyes.

The idea of bailing out was becoming more appealing by the minute. But if she found another job, would she be able to take her research with her? Or would her boss claim it was the property of the lab?

She sat there for a long time, wondering what the hell she was going to do.

Since she couldn't come up with a long-term answer, she decided to start the test on Ross Marshall's cells.

ROSS sat with three pillows propped behind his back, his notes on Donald Arnott spread across his lap and on the bed. His eyes were fixed on a line of type. But his mind was far away. Megan had said she wanted samples of genetic material from his parents. And he pictured himself standing in the house where he'd grown up, broaching the subject to his mother.

Only he wasn't seeing himself as the Ross Marshall of today. He was an eighteen-year-old kid, home from his freshman year of college, leaning against the cracked and stained kitchen counter.

He'd been telling Mom he could replace the work surface for her. Replace the cabinets.

Apparently his dad had been standing in the dining room listening, for he'd come charging into the kitchen, his eyes blazing.

"So you think you're better than me, because you've got a big-deal scholarship to the University of Maryland and you've got some money saved from your pissing little construction jobs."

"No," he answered automatically as his mother slipped out of the room.

"Don't lie to me, sonny. You blame me for the tragedy of your mother's life. 'Cause I picked her for my mate. And now you're gonna make everything nice for her."

He'd started to turn away, but his father's words held him, words he'd heard in some form or another many times before.

"You dare to blame me, you shit-head moron? Wait till it happens to you. They call it chemistry." His father gave a harsh laugh. "They hardly understand the meaning of the word. They don't know the burning need. The lust. The pain. Wait until you're old enough to start searching for a mate. When you meet her, you'll *know*. Fucking her once won't get her out of your system. Because a wolf mates for life, sonny.

"The good part is that she'll want to fuck you as much as you want to fuck her. When you catch her scent, when you touch her, you'll understand what it's like for one of us, you sanctimonious bastard. So if you want to have some fun with the gals, do it now. 'Cause when you meet your mate, your cock just won't go in any other hole."

He'd heard it all before, more times than he could count. This time his hands balled into fists, and he struck out, caught his father on the chin. One minute they were standing; the next minute they were rolling on the worn vinyl tile, snarling, hands at each other's throats.

It was his mother who had dashed back into the kitchen and stopped the fight by dousing them with a pan of cold water. It was his mother who had fixed the cut on his cheek, hugged him fiercely, and said he'd better leave. She'd tried to give him money. He told her he didn't need it, but he'd promised to call her when he found a place to live. He'd clung to her for long moments, the way he had when he was a little boy and he'd scraped the skin off his knee. Then he'd gone, because he knew what would happen if he stayed. But his father's words were still ringing in his ears.

He'd studied genetics and social biology, and he knew that bonding with one female was counter to the usual male survival tactic. In most species, the male scattered his seed as far and wide as possible. He'd come to the conclusion that the male werewolf needed to be around for the transition of his sons from boy to wolf. He needed to teach them the ritual and coach them on surviving the pain of transition.

The werewolf was unique in that. And unique among wolves, too.

Ross had also studied wolf behavior and had learned that in a wolf pack, there was only one alpha male, and all the others were subservient to him. Apparently werewolves didn't conform to the same social order. Every adult male was an alpha male. And if they stayed in one another's company for long, they would fight for supremacy. He'd explained that to Megan this morning, but not in such concrete terms.

Once again, he found his thoughts wandering to her. Cursing under his breath, he pulled his attention back to the notes spread across his lap. His life depended on thinking through his options, on not making another mistake with Arnott tonight. And instead of planning his return to the scene of the disaster, he was thinking about Megan and his father.

Of course, it didn't take a genius to figure out why. He was scared shitless. Not about Arnott. About what had already happened with Megan in the two days she'd been here.

He wanted her—wanted her in a way he had never wanted another woman. Wanted her with a bone-deep hunger that clawed at his insides. And in the kitchen this morning she'd let him know in no uncertain terms that the feelings weren't all one-sided.

Squeezing his eyes shut, he shook his head in denial. He wasn't going to let hormones or chemistry or genes rule his life. He wasn't Vic Marshall. He was in control of himself.

He wasn't a selfish bastard like his father, incapable of real love, only interested in fulfilling his own needs—and to hell with anyone else he hurt in the process.

He wasn't a hostage to his genetic heritage. He—

Another scene leaped into his mind. The woods at night. Crawford. The wolf following the scent of his prey. The blood lust of the kill. It had been the night of the full moon. Was that a coincidence? Or did the moon really affect werewolves—the way the old myths said?

He made a strangled sound in his throat. When he realized he was mangling the sheet of paper in his hand, he loosened his grip.

He had been younger then. Unaware of the danger that came from within. But he'd learned to handle his aggressions, channel them in an acceptable direction. And now he was damn well in control of himself. Ross Marshall, private eye.

Who had dropped his phone in the woods where a serial killer could find it. And if he wanted to stay healthy, he had better get that phone back.

Then there was the rest of the stuff he'd abandoned beside the fence. His brain had been too muzzy to think about that earlier. Now he closed his eyes, picturing the knapsack. He hadn't been stupid enough to stick a name tag on it, of course. Inside he'd stowed his wire cutters, the adjustable wrench, the set of Craftsman screwdrivers. The flashlight. And the big-ticket item: a top of the line pair of B & L binoculars.

Arnott had probably pored over the contents, trying to figure out who had lost the pack. But there was nothing to tie any of that to a PI named Ross Marshall.

The phone was another matter.

A knock on Megan's office door had her looking up. She was startled to see Dr. Carter Stillwell standing there.

She stared at his thin face, mop of curly hair, and deep-set brown eyes. When they'd first met, she'd thought he was handsome. Then she'd stopped liking the way the pieces fit together. Now she saw he was working to keep his features composed.

"Carter?"

He stepped into the room, glided toward her desk on silent feet. "I was in the neighborhood. Since I don't seem to be able to get you on the phone, I was hoping to catch you in."

"I've been out of the office for a few days. I'm just getting back. And we had some problems here this morning. A break-in."

He kept his unnerving gaze fixed on her. "The secretary gave me an earful."

"We're all kind of upset."

He waited a beat, then lowered his voice before saying, "I've got some new information that could be very helpful to you on your gene therapy project. Get you funding that won't have to rely on . . . a boss who's lost interest in your research."

It was so completely inappropriate for him to be saying that *here,* she felt her jaw drop. Recovering, she said, "Carter, I'm afraid . . . I'm too busy right now. I've got a whole bunch of work to catch up on."

His eyes narrowed. "I was hoping we could get together to discuss it. But you seem to be too busy all of the time lately."

"What can I say?"

"Really, Megan, it's a mistake to brush me off like this."

"I'm not."

"Then when can we talk? What about lunch today?"

"I, uh—"

Before she could finish, Walter stepped into the room.

A few minutes ago, he had put her on the spot. Now relief flooded through her. "Uh . . . Walter. This is Carter Stillwell. Carter, this is my boss, Walter Galveston."

They shook hands stiffly, made the appropriate noises.

"Megan and I have a meeting," Walter said. "I was just coming to look for her."

She glanced down at her hands to hide the expression on her face, since this was the first she'd heard of any meeting.

"Well, then, I'll get out of your way." Stillwell pushed past the other man and exited the room.

"Thanks for rescuing me," Megan breathed.

"I could see you wanted to get rid of him. Who is he?"

She thought about how to answer, then settled on, "I met him at a convention. He keeps making up excuses to get together with me."

Walter looked down the hallway. "He has some nerve barging in here." Turning, he left Megan sitting at her desk. She stayed there for several moments, collecting herself, then pushed away from the desk and headed for the lab. After donning a white lab coat and rubber gloves, she reached into the refrigerator and pulled out the tube with Ross's blood.

No, not Ross's blood. It was the wrong sample, she realized with a start as she stared at the label. Putting it back, she carefully retrieved the correct tube. She'd done hundreds of karyotypes and couldn't remember making a mistake like that before, yet this time she felt a sense of personal involvement that had always been missing in the past. Lord, was she trying to prove there was nothing wrong with him by testing the wrong sample?

Don't think about the man, she ordered herself. It was impossible to completely shut him out of her mind. Still, the scientist in her was able to focus on the tasks she had to accomplish. The first step was to break apart the double strands of Ross's DNA and the probe DNA being used by heating them in a solution of formamide at seventy degrees Celsius so that they could bind to each other.

Working on autopilot, she finished the procedure, then placed the sample on a glass slide, set a cover slip on top, and sealed the edges. Next the slide went into an incubator at thirty-seven degrees Celsius, where it would have to remain overnight for the probe to hybridize with the sample chromosomes.

Wishing she could go on to the next steps right away, she stared at the incubator. But there was no way to speed up the process. So she went back to the load of tests their boss had piled on her and Hank. Hank had already completed some of the procedures. She started on the next one, glancing over at his work area, wondering if he were making some vital mistake that was going to get them in trouble.

But that didn't sound like Hank. He was always meticulous in the lab. In fact, the way things were going today, *she* was more likely to screw something up, since only half her mind was on what she was supposed to be doing.

When she looked up and found Walter standing beside her workstation, she jumped.

"Sorry," he apologized. "Do you have a minute?"

Since the automatic equipment was now handling a polymerase chain reaction test, she nodded and stepped to the door.

"In all the excitement, I forgot to ask you about that guy out in Lisbon. Ross Marshall. I thought you said he was really sick and you wanted to stay with him."

"He got better pretty quickly."

Her boss raised a questioning eyebrow.

"Apparently he has remarkable recuperative powers."

Walter's eyes flashed with interest. "I thought he had some sort of genetic defect. Is it something that affects him personally, or is he a carrier?"

"He didn't want to give me much information."

"This isn't supposed to be a guessing game. Have you started any tests on him yet?"

Megan could have kicked herself as she recognized the eager look in his eyes. If she'd been less distracted, she would have thought of something more noncommittal. "I've started the karyotyping," she answered.

"Well, let me know what you find."

"You really want a report on a routine case?"

"From the way he approached us—and from what you're telling me—it doesn't sound routine."

She shrugged, trying to look casual though her heart had started pounding like a trip-hammer inside her chest. She didn't want to discuss Ross Marshall with Dr. Galveston. She didn't want her boss poking into his business. But she forced a light tone into her voice when she said, "I'll let you know if I find anything interesting."

* * *

ROSS washed the bloodstains out of the car seat as best he could, threw away the floor mat, then ate a couple of raw steaks for lunch. Pulling the blackout draperies in the bedroom, he slept until eleven-thirty that night and woke feeling almost normal. After warming up and doing a half hour of weights, he showered and dressed in a black sweatshirt and pants. He was out of the house by twelve-thirty, hoping the late hour would provide some protection from Arnott. His *namhaid*, he thought, using the ancient Gaelic word.

He had studied the language. He could probably hold a conversation in ancient Gaelic. If there was anyone to speak it with. Certainly not with his father. Vic Marshall had laughed at him when he'd first caught him studying a book on the ancient Druids, called it crap. He'd been interested in present results. Not his ancient heritage.

Amadán. Fool, he warned himself.

Keep your mind focused on the killer. But as he took the back roads to upper Montgomery County, he realized he was thinking about his own life. How it had worked out since the day he'd left home and never returned, except for brief visits to his mother when he knew the Big Bad Wolf was out of the house.

He'd found himself a cheap room to rent in Cheverly, not too far from the university. Found a construction job for the summer, and lucked into his first detective case. The owner of the construction company, Phil Laniard, had been losing materials from one of his building sites. And Ross had said he could tell him who was doing it, if Laniard seeded a delivery of new lumber with wintergreen oil.

The boss had been skeptical. But he was willing to give anything a try. Two days later, Ross led him to a garage in Dundalk where the lumber was being stored.

That earned him a five-hundred-dollar bonus. And a referral to a guy who thought his wife was having an affair with one of their friends, only he didn't know which one.

That time, Ross had negotiated a two-thousand-dollar fee—and earned it within the week.

Other jobs had followed with increasing regularity as it became known that the Marshall boy could find missing objects and track people with uncanny accuracy.

He'd banked as much of his earnings as he could spare all through college. Before he graduated, he had enough for a down payment on a run-down row house in the city. The bank had only been willing to give him a short-term loan. But that didn't matter. With his construction skills, he'd rehabbed it himself, sold it at a nice profit, and picked up another property in Ellicott City. All the time continuing his detective work.

The two sources of income had allowed him to sock away enough to buy a twenty-four-acre tract in western Howard County with a house he could remodel to his liking.

He'd been satisfied with his life. Until Arnott had shot him in the leg and Megan Sheridan had found him lying naked on the living room floor.

Megan. Inevitably his thoughts had circled back to her. He tried to wrench his mind away. Tried not to think of her in the same breath with the crude language his father had used when he talked about the werewolf and his mate. But Ross was under no illusions about what he wanted to do with Megan.

He didn't know how much of what his father had said to him over the years was true. Some of it, certainly, although he'd learned the bastard was capable of lying for effect.

But he'd taken the warning to heart. His sexual partners had been few and far between. He'd never stayed with anyone long enough to get attached. And as he'd gotten closer to the age at which his father had married his mother, he'd stayed away from sexual liaisons altogether. Which was probably why he'd reacted like a stallion scenting a mare in heat when he'd encountered Megan. It was a plausible explanation. He wanted it to be true.

More than that, he wanted her to stop haunting him. Her face, the touch of her hands, the way her breasts filled out the front of her T-shirt. Her sweet feminine scent, like a meadow in the sunshine.

As the memory of her essence flooded his senses, he found himself hard and aching for her again.

Cursing, he deliberately turned his mind to graves and bullets and the hot pain in his leg that had almost led to his death. The effect was sobering enough to drive thoughts of sex from his mind for the time being.

After passing the spot where he'd parked last time, he drifted farther down the road, pulled onto the shoulder, and eased the SUV under some low-hanging tree branches.

The last time he'd been here, he'd been energized—eager for the hunt. Tonight he felt subdued as he walked two dozen yards into the woods, where a thick tangle of brambles hid him from any motorists who might happen to pass by at this late hour.

Discarding his clothing, he stood in the darkness, naked, mentally preparing himself for the pain that always came with transformation— and thinking about the words he was about to speak.

He knew the meaning of them all. Taranis, the Lord of Thunder. Cerridwen, the Goddess of Darkness. Epona, the Goddess of Horses. Although the texts didn't say so, he was sure her influence extended to other animals as well.

The familiar syllables flowed from his mouth.

"Taranis, Epona, Cerridwen," he intoned, then repeated the same phrase and went on to another.

"Gá. Feart. Cleas. Duais. Aithriocht. Go gcumhdaí is dtreoraí na déithe thú."

His damn ancestor had asked for a miracle, a great feat of prowess, a gift from the gods. And he'd even dared to be specific—to ask for the power to change his shape.

Ross repeated the words, felt the change—felt his jaw elongate, his teeth sharpen, his body contort as muscles and limbs transformed into the shape of his other self. Dropping to all fours, he endured the sensations of bones crunching, muscles jerking, fur sprouting from naked skin.

In seconds it was over, and the world was a different place—rich with promise. A shiver of anticipation rippled through him as he breathed in the odors of the night. Damp soil. Rotting leaves. Insects. Tree bark. A rabbit in its burrow. All of it coming to him in layers, each scent separate and distinct and exciting.

As always, he wanted to throw back his head and howl for the pleasure of it. But his human brain kept the words locked in his throat— kept him focused on the night's purpose.

Ignoring the tantalizing rustling sounds in the underbrush and the scents of the animals around him, he trotted through the woods, heading for the place where he'd cut the fence.

As he drew closer, he breathed in his own scent from four days earlier. It was still clinging to leaves and the debris on the ground but overpowered by the stench of another man, stronger, more recent, more pervasive. It could only be Arnott's. He must have come out here more than once, compulsively searching the woods for something besides the knapsack.

Had he found the phone? Ross didn't allow himself to contemplate the possibility as he padded through the darkness.

He was so intent on his purpose that he didn't see the glint of metal until almost too late.

Recognition filtered into his brain; and he pulled back his right front paw. Hair rose along his spine as he stared down into the jagged teeth of the animal trap that had almost closed around his leg.

A deep animal growl of anger welled in his throat.

Arnott had been doing more out here than looking. He'd been busy setting traps for the animal he'd shot. The animal that had gotten away.

For a split second, it flashed into his mind that somehow Arnott had figured out what kind of creature was stalking him. Then he dismissed the notion as beyond the realm of possibility. The killer had shot at and wounded a large dog, maybe even a wolf. Then he'd found a knapsack and clothing. That added up to a man and an animal. A K-9 unit.

Sternly he reminded himself of what kind of man he was dealing with. Arnott fantasized about the brutal acts he wanted to carry out on the bodies of young women—and followed through with the scenario. But his type didn't go around imagining paranormal creatures in his backyard.

Still, that didn't mean the danger was less. He knew Arnott was deadly and resourceful. The trap was only another demonstration of his ingenuity.

All Ross's senses were on alert as he padded past oaks and poplars, wild cherry and dogwood, their newly budded branches swaying slightly as the wind picked up. He was a hundred yards closer to the fence when a more disturbing thought slammed into him.

If Arnott had gone to the trouble of setting out traps, he could also have set out alarms—which had already been tripped. If so, the bastard could be on his way out here, with an Uzi instead of the hunting rifle he'd been armed with four nights ago.

The wolf's mouth drew back in a snarl. He had his animal senses. The hunter had modern technology on his side.

Yeah, modern technology. He was sure he hadn't left the phone on. But all he needed now was for the damn thing to somehow ring. Then he'd be in big trouble.

DONALD woke to the sound of a bell ringing. For a moment he was disoriented, thinking it was the phone, blinking as he stared at the green numbers on the alarm clock.

One-twenty in the morning.

Who the hell was calling him in the middle of the night?

Anger warred with a flash of fear as he snatched the receiver from the cradle—and heard nothing but a dial tone. But the ringing persisted. Then he realized it was the alarm system he'd installed the day before.

Jesus Christ. He'd hit pay dirt. Already.

Leaping out of bed, he pulled on his clothes, grabbed some serious firepower, and pounded down to the gate.

His fingers were clumsy on the lock, and he cursed as he forced himself to slow down, get the numbers of the combination right.

The lock clicked, and he snapped it open, slipping outside into the night, the excitement of the hunt pumping through his veins. This time the bastard wasn't going to take him by surprise. This time when he saw the damn dog, he was gonna be ready. Or maybe it wasn't the dog—maybe it was the man. Well, that was even better.

THE need for caution warring with the need for speed, Ross continued on a course through the darkened woods that would take him near the spot where he'd dropped the knapsack. He kept his nose to the ground and all his senses tuned for trouble. His bad leg was throbbing dully now, but he ignored the pain.

To his right was another trap. Then another on the left, the metal cold and deadly in the darkness. How many of the fucking things did Arnott think he needed? He'd spent a lot of money on setting out a defensive perimeter. That was one more indication that the bastard wasn't living on his salary as a security guard.

The wolf paused, sucked in a deep breath. The scent of the killer was stronger here. But so was the Ross Marshall scent.

MEGAN stared at the clock on the bedside table. One-thirty in the morning. Ross had promised to call and tell her he was all right. But she hadn't heard from him, and she'd been lying in bed, feeling her pulse pounding in her temples, thinking that her blood pressure had probably climbed to one-fifty over ninety as she waited to hear from him.

More and more edgy by the minute, she slapped her fist against her palm. Damn Ross Marshall for making her care about him! Was he home safely? Had something bad happened?

Or was he even going to bother with a call?

Plumping up the pillow behind her head, she made an effort to relax. But it was impossible to let go of the tension.

Then, because she couldn't stand to lie in the dark another minute, she heaved herself out of bed, turned on the hall light, and padded down the hall to the kitchen. Picking up her purse from a chair where she'd set it when she brought in groceries, she opened the side compartment and felt for the slip of paper that had Ross's phone number. In the light from the hall, she read the numbers.

Again she glanced at the clock. One forty-five. By now he was probably home, fast asleep in his wide bed, while she was standing here in the kitchen with her teeth on edge.

The image of him lying in his bed made her fingers crumple the piece of paper. Carefully she smoothed it out again.

Damn him for doing this to her. Damn him for making her crazy with worry. Well, she knew how to pay him back.

Crossing to the counter, she lifted the receiver of the wall phone and reached toward the keypad.

THE wolf moved more slowly now, closing in on the strongest source of the Ross Marshall scent. When he came to a swirl of fallen leaves, he was sure that was the place. Although he couldn't see the phone, he could detect it nonetheless—either the instrument or something else he had carried close to his body. He was darting forward, ready to snatch it from the leaves, when he heard the sound of booted feet crunching on the dry ground. Coming toward him fast and eager.

Animal instinct briefly took over. Coherent thought fled from his brain. There was only fear. And searing pain—the remembered pain of the rifle bullet tearing into his flesh.

His breath was coming in sharp pants. The animal part of him wanted to turn and run for his life. The part that was human forced him to stay where he was, pawing at the leaves, struggling not to work too fast and screw it up.

The scent grew stronger. Then a slender rectangle of black plastic appeared among the leaves—a man-made intrusion on the forest floor. He lowered his mouth, caught the object in his teeth, then bolted for safety as a spray of bullets hit a tree trunk inches from his body.

Changing directions, he twisted through a tangle of wild roses and blackberries, lowering his head to avoid the sharp thorns. The man couldn't follow without getting badly scratched, but he sprayed the thicket with a hail of bullets.

The frightened animal part of him would have dashed straight for the safety of the truck. The human part knew that would be a fatal mistake. Making a wide circle around the vehicle, he ducked through more brambles and emerged, breathing hard.

He was in no shape to run for his life. But he had no choice, so he sprang ahead, outdistancing the man with the gun. Behind him, he could hear Arnott pelting through the forest, but he sensed he was out of danger now. The man could never catch him.

He slowed his pace as a tantalizing thought wafted into his mind. He could circle back, get behind the man, spring on his shoulders, and bring him down before he even knew what had hit him.

On a surge of adrenaline, he imagined pinning his quarry to the ground, sinking his fangs into the column of the neck.

The sweet, hot taste of blood welled in him, and a vivid image of the kill filled his mind like a bright light that blotted out all conscious human thought.

He was pure animal now as he turned and raised his head, sniffing the air, drinking in the scent of the man with the gun.

Body quivering with renewed purpose, he started back the way he'd come, eager for the feel of his teeth punching through soft tissue, crunching through bone.

13

THE wind sang a hunting song in his blood. A song without words. A song that drew him forward, primed him for the kill.

But he had taken only a few eager steps when the screech of an owl above the treetops broke the stillness of the night. The bird dived toward some small animal on the ground. In that instant, reason came flooding back through the wolf's brain cells, and he stopped in his tracks.

His jaw snapped around the phone he still carried in his mouth, and his right front foot pawed the ground. For long moments he stood with his body trembling and his breath rushing hotly in and out of his lungs as he forced himself to stand in place. Forced himself to forgo the unholy pleasure of showing his enemy who was hunter and who was prey. Of wreaking vengeance for the bullet that had almost killed him.

Silent, subdued, he turned and started for the place where he'd left the truck.

Minutes later he had transformed to human shape, welcoming the pain that came with the change. Dressing quickly in his pants and shirt, shoving his feet into his shoes, he climbed behind the wheel. His skin was covered by a film of perspiration from the pain in his leg and from the effort of controlling his instincts. His motions were jerky as he started the engine and pulled off the shoulder of the road, his back wheels spinning on gravel as he roared away into the night, the beat of his pulse drumming in his temples.

DONALD heard the car engine and sprinted toward the road, heedless of the brambles tearing at his pants legs. Breathing hard, he broke through the cover of trees and saw the bulk of a large vehicle—an SUV moving rapidly away. Red taillights mocked him. He zeroed in on the pool of light between them where the license plate rode low over the bumper.

Straining his eyes, he picked up the first two letters—DE. But that was all he could get. And he couldn't see the color or figure out the model in the dark. He was aiming at the bastard when headlights came blazing around a curve in the road, and he froze, a stream of curses tumbling from his mouth. He couldn't risk a shot, not when he might hit another vehicle. He waited until the other car had passed. Then, in frustration, he lifted the Uzi and squeezed the trigger, letting loose a hail of bullets into the trunk of an oak tree, bark flying as the projectiles hit.

His finger didn't loosen until the clip was empty.

"Fucker," he spat. "Fucker."

He was talking about the man, not the big dog he'd shot at again. The man had been back here in the SUV, waiting for the animal—ready to peel rubber the moment the animal appeared.

He stared in the direction in which the vehicle had disappeared. DE. How many license plates began with those letters? A couple of thousand, he was sure.

Anger bubbling inside him, he walked slowly back through the woods, kicking at debris on the ground. But he didn't let his anger get the better of him. Methodically he illuminated the path in front of him, being careful not to step in any of the steel-jawed traps he'd set out.

The dog had been lucky. Or smart. Or something. An involuntary shiver traveled down his spine, and for a moment he allowed his brain to conjure up an image of a devil dog. Satan's spawn. Come to punish him on earth for his sins.

He shook off the ridiculous notion. That dog out there was no supernatural apparition. It had come in a truck with its master. And it was just a very well-trained animal. He'd shot it, hadn't he? And followed a trail of its blood.

Shot it four nights ago, he realized with a start.

Shit, he hadn't even been able to locate the vet that had treated it. And now it seemed to be good as new.

Well, animals healed faster than people, didn't they? Or maybe it was another dog. Maybe the fucker stalking him had a whole kennel full of the yapping bastards primed and ready to go. Maybe he was some kind of K-9 nut.

Still cursing, he started off again in the direction of the gate, swinging the light in an arc across the forest floor. When he hit a spot where the ground covering had been disturbed, he paused and squatted down.

It looked like the animal had pawed into the leaves.

Jesus. Had the man dropped something else, something besides the knapsack and his clothes? He sifted his fingers through the ground cover, feeling nothing. Standing again, he gave a savage kick at the dirt, imagining he was kicking the man in the head or the guts, thinking about all the things he was going to do to the guy when he finally caught up with him.

DRENCHED in sweat, Ross drove as if furies were pursuing him. Tonight he'd almost done it again. He'd almost lost control and ripped out his enemy's throat. At the last minute, sanity had returned.

Human sanity. Not the primitive instincts that ruled the wolf.

Those instincts had almost overwhelmed him. Yet somehow intellect had won out tonight.

Was it only the screech of the owl that had saved him? Or would he have stopped himself before he leaped for the man's throat, jaws snapping?

He didn't know. But he wasn't going to give himself the benefit of the doubt. Not when he remembered the hot joy of the hunt.

He felt a tight, choking sensation in his throat. Pushing the accelerator to the floor, he tried to outrun the wolf. But the creature kept pace with him—a part of himself that he could never cast away. The dangerous, primitive part that most men never encountered on a conscious level.

It was different for him. But he had never been under the illusion that he was like most men. He was the outsider. The man who could never completely trust the humans around him—because they would turn against him if they learned his secret. Even Jack Thornton, his friend. Or as close to a friend as he'd ever hoped to have. After Michael had died, Adam had tried to get close to him. But he hadn't responded to his younger brother's overtures. He'd been too depressed, he realized now. Then he'd decided that there was no use in establishing a relationship, when one or both of them was likely to die.

He thought of his father. Another loner, hiding his true self from the world. Was the need for secrecy what had transformed Vic Marshall into a hard, cynical man focused on his own needs and his own pleasure?

In all the years that Ross had hated the man, he'd never thought of his father in those terms. Never felt any sympathy for him. Now he wondered if his judgment had been too harsh. He'd taken care of his own—his wife and his children—in his fashion. He'd even let the boys stay home until they got old enough to challenge his authority, Ross thought with a snort, remembering Troy's and his own battles with the Big Bad Wolf.

His mind scrambled to escape from the thought of his home—lost to him forever—and came winging back to Megan.

He'd promised to call her.

His eyes flicked to the clock on the dashboard. Two-thirty. She couldn't be up now, waiting to hear from him. Could she?

She'd forced the promise from him at a vulnerable moment. Which canceled out any obligation, as far as he was concerned.

Pulling to a stop in front of his house, he cut the engine and sat in the darkness, staring out at the familiar landscape. His home.

He had named it Díthreabh. His refuge. As a wolf he could roam his property, letting go of all the human problems that plagued him.

Tonight he had already prowled through the woods—hunting for human prey. And the outcome had brought him to the brink of disaster.

Moving slowly, his body worn out from the physical and emotional turmoil of the night, he limped into the house and found himself gravitating toward the kitchen counter, where he'd tossed Megan's business card. He stared at the white rectangle, remembering the way they'd stood in the kitchen early this morning. She'd hastened across the floor toward him, and he'd taken her in his arms. She'd wanted to kiss him. And more. He had seen it in her eyes, felt it in his blood.

An hour ago he had felt something else in his blood. The killer lust of the wolf. The animal that lived in the same body with the rational man. He'd sworn to control the animal, keep it on a tight leash. Tonight it had broken that leash—leaped out of control with a savage fury that had frightened him to the depths of his soul. If he had a soul.

Was he human—or animal?

Despair choked him, cutting off his breath. He didn't know how to find his humanity. Not tonight.

Not tonight. When he felt as if he were standing alone on a desert island in the middle of an endless ocean.

Then, from somewhere in the depths of his consciousness, an old Simon and Garfunkel song floated into his mind: "Bridge over Troubled Water." He thought of the words, then thought of that bridge—stretching, stretching across a wind-tossed ocean to the lonely island where he stood alone. Megan was on that bridge, running toward him the way she'd come to him in the kitchen, her eyes so large and beautiful, looking at him. Ross Marshall.

She'd reached for him, and he'd clasped her in his arms. A man holding a woman. As simple as that.

With a sound of pain that rose from deep inside him, he snatched up the card, then pulled the phone from his pocket. Feeling a need, a desperation that was almost beyond control, he lifted the receiver to his ear and punched the On button.

After four days of lying in a pile of leaves in the woods, the phone was stone-cold dead, and a curse rose to his lips.

Striding down the hall to the office, he dropped into the desk chair and reached for the charger—with its extra battery. When his fingers closed around the spare, he breathed a sigh of relief. Inserting it into the phone, he listened for the dial tone, then punched in Megan's number. After switching the light off again, he leaned back in the comfortable chair and closed his eyes.

She answered on the first ring, and a feeling of warmth and gratitude flooded through him when he heard her voice. "Ross. Thank God."

She sounded relieved, the relief tinged with other emotions that brought a painful pressure to the region of his heart. She was worried and angry, and he longed to soothe her. "How did you know it was me?" he asked softly.

"Who else would keep me awake, waiting for him, until . . . almost three in the morning?"

"You're angry."

A breath sighed out of her. "Well, I was worried. I thought of calling you. Then I realized that would be a bad idea."

The way she said it increased the painful pressure in his chest. "I just got back. I told you I was going to be late."

"Did you run into a problem?" she asked anxiously.

"No," he lied, because he hadn't called to worry her. He had called because she was the only person in the world who could ease the aching knot of tension in his chest.

"You have the phone? You're all right?"

"Fine," he answered automatically. He was far from fine, on a number of different counts, but he wasn't going in to them. "You should get some sleep."

"I'm okay."

He'd fulfilled his obligation. He ought to let her go to bed. Instead he sat there, his hand tightening around the phone, held captive by his own blind, selfish needs. He couldn't hang up. And he couldn't handle the depths of his feelings, either. So he pretended to himself that the needs he felt were on some safe, superficial level. The same needs he'd felt with other women. "What are you wearing?" he heard himself asking.

"What?"

"Never mind." Bad idea.

"A T-shirt and . . . panties."

"I was picturing you in a gown. Something sexy," he said into the darkness of his familiar surroundings. He was miles away from her. That made this conversation okay. There was no harm in staying on the line. At least that was what he told himself. "Are you in bed?"

"No, I'm in the living room. On the couch. Where are you?"

"In my office. Are you lying down or sitting up?"

"Lying down."

He imagined the knit fabric stretched across her breasts, her long legs bare and smooth. He didn't know why he was torturing himself with the vivid picture. Again he started to speak before his brain had a chance to consider the consequences. "I wanted to kiss you this morning in the kitchen."

"Yes. It was in your eyes." Her voice hitched. "Then you turned away from me—and I felt . . . desolate."

He made a low, incoherent sound, the words and her voice tearing at him.

For long moments there was only silence on the phone line. He pictured her now. And pictured the look on her face when she'd been standing there with her lips parted. Suddenly being separated from her was more than he could bear. He wanted to touch her. Wanted to hold her. Wanted to get as close to her as possible.

Eyes closed, he pressed his fingers to his mouth, the touch sending tingling sensations through his body as he imagined the sweetness of kissing her. "Do something for me now. Touch your fingers to your lips. Rub them for me," he asked, his voice thickening even as he wondered if she would do it.

On the other end of the phone line, he heard her breathing accelerate. Or maybe it was his own breath rasping in and out of his throat. After several endless seconds he asked, "Did you do it?"

"Yes."

"Your soft lips," he murmured, imagining the feel of them against his.

She gave a shaky laugh. "Not soft. Chapped."

Her laugh only increased the tension coursing through him. He had told himself he needed to feel connected to her. He was feeling that, all right.

"If I touch my lips, you have to do that, too," she whispered.

"I already did."

"Oh!" Then, "Did it feel good?"

"Yes." He drew in a gasp of air, let it out in a rush. It felt intoxicating. So much better than the pain he'd felt earlier in the evening.

"Is this something you like to do with women? I mean have phone conversations like this?" she questioned, her tone a bit shaky.

"I've never had a phone conversation like this."

"Neither have I."

"Good. That's good."

"You have a very sexy voice."

"Do I?"

"Don't you know? Your voice turned the fifty-year-old administrative assistant at Bio Gen into a quivering mass of marshmallow cream."

He laughed.

Silence stretched again. Then she asked, "Ross, what are we doing, exactly?"

He considered the question. "Getting as close as we can to each other without being together. Don't try to distract me with the fifty-year-old secretary at Bio Gen. Are your eyes opened or closed?"

"Closed," she whispered.

The image in his mind had changed. Now her neck was arched up, pale and vulnerable for his pleasure. "If I were there, I would nibble my way along your jaw, your neck."

"Oh."

"Nip you with my sharp teeth," he said in a low growl, waiting to hear her response. She drew in her breath, quick and piercing.

His voice turned to honey in the darkness. "Touch your fingers there for me—stroke your neck."

"Oh!" she said again, this time with more force.

"You like that?"

"Yes."

He was reckless now. Somewhere along the line, the conversation had gone out of control like a train with no brakes speeding down the tracks. "I want to touch your breasts. I want to cup them. Feel their weight in my hands." Again her little gasp egged him on. "I want to rub my hands back and forth across your nipples. Make them hard so that they stab against my palms," he said, his body clenching from the intensely tactile images he'd painted.

He heard a high sound escape from her, part arousal, part protest. "I shouldn't be letting you do this."

"Do what?"

"You know what you're doing to me."

"Do I? Tell me."

"No."

"Arousing you?"

"You know the answer to that."

Unable to stop, he pushed a little further. "I want to touch you, but I can't. You have to do the touching for me."

"Don't ask me to do that."

"Why not?"

"It's indecent," she said in a whispery voice that feathered along his nerve endings like fire.

"You've never touched your own breasts? I mean, because it felt good?"

Her voice quavered. "Don't ask questions like that. And don't ask me to do anything else now."

"Are you embarrassed that I'm turning you on like this?"

"Yes."

The admission fueled his reckless need. Heedless of the consequences, he demanded more from her. "All right, but I don't have to ask, do I? You can feel it anyway. In your breasts. Between your legs."

"Please . . ." He heard a desperate note in the plea.

"What do you want? Do you want me inside you?"

He needed to hear her say it. Needed to know she was as hot and wanting as he.

She made a strangled sound. He heard her suck in a shaky breath, then let it out in a rush. "You have to stop."

"Say it."

"Ross, I can't handle this."

He blew out air, shifted in the chair, trying to ease the ache in his groin as he imagined his body covering hers, imagined himself plunging into her.

There was a roaring in his ears—the sound of her breath coming hard and fast, matching his.

When she spoke again, her voice was low, barely above a whisper. "Why did you start this?"

Because I'm frightened of what I might do to Arnott. Because I'd rather play games with you than think about wanting to rip his throat out.

"Because it feels good," he growled.

"Yes. But it's . . . bad."

"Does it feel bad?"

"It feels wicked."

"No."

She was silent for several moments; when she spoke again, there was a measure of control in her voice. "You said what we were doing was getting close."

"Um-hum."

"You meant you wanted to create physical sensations. You didn't mean you were going to tell me any more about yourself than you already had."

It was his turn for silence. She was right. He hadn't been thinking in terms of revealing his secrets. He had only thought about how talking intimately to her on the phone had eased his pain. Turned his thoughts away from the fears that haunted him.

"Ross?"

"I shouldn't have started this."

"All you want from me is sex?"

"Yes," he lied, closing his fingers around the phone so hard that the knuckles whitened. He refused to let her glimpse his vulnerability, but he couldn't stop his mind from spinning back to what he'd been feeling when he'd dialed her number.

"Then I'm going to hang up now."

"Wait." The plea rose to his lips before he could call it back.

He heard silence on the other end of the line and felt a stark panic at the thought of her severing the connection. "Are you there?"

"Yes."

Relief sighed out of him.

"Tell me something about Ross Marshall."

He held back a laugh, knowing she would run screaming in the other direction if he gave her what she thought she wanted. Still, he scrambled for something to say, something that would keep her on the line without giving too much of himself away. "I make my living as a private detective."

"I know that. Are you the one who remodeled your house?"

"What makes you think so?"

"I was in your workroom when I was looking for something to unlock the bedroom door. I saw all your tools. And a lot of wood and stuff."

"Okay, yeah. I remodeled the house."

Her voice turned warm. "I love what you did with it. The bookshelves in the great room are wonderful. Do you call it a great room?"

"Yes."

"And the kitchen. I love the kitchen."

"Thanks."

"The bathroom is the only thing I'd change."

He gave a small laugh. "You don't like soaking tubs?"

"Those big windows with no shades are a little disconcerting."

"I like soaking in the tub and looking out at the woods."

"Are you the one who plants the flowers? Or do you have a gardener?"

"You noticed a lot of stuff."

"Um-hum."

"I do it. It relaxes me." Then, "Now I get to ask some questions. How did you get into medical research?"

"I found out I'm not all that good with patients."

"You were good with me."

She hesitated for a moment. "I get too . . . involved."

"Like with me."

"No. With you it was something more."

She was giving him an opportunity to take the conversation in a different direction. Instead he asked, "Where did you grow up?"

"I grew up in Boston. My sister still lives there."

"What about your folks?"

"My parents were killed in a car crash about a year ago."

"I'm sorry."

"I miss Mom."

"But not your dad?"

"He was the kind of guy who had to get his way." She paused, then went on. "And when the least little thing was out of his control, he . . . made life hell for Mom."

He sucked in a breath. "That sounds like my old man."

"Does it?"

"Yeah. I warned you to stay away from me."

"You're not your father," she murmured.

"I'm more like him than I want to be," he admitted in the darkness.

"Don't beat yourself up."

"Why not? I came within a hairbreadth of . . ."

"Of what?"

"Killing the bastard who was shooting at me again," he admitted.

"He was shooting at you! Oh, God, Ross. You said you didn't have any problems."

"Well, I was lying. I almost killed him."

"In self-defense."

He sighed, feeling as if he were back where he'd started. "We'd better hang up. You have to go to work in the morning."

"Ross . . ."

"What?"

"You're a good man."

He gave a hollow laugh. "You don't know me."

"I learned a lot about you in the past few days."

"Didn't I pull a gun on you five minutes after we met?"

She came back with an immediate excuse. "You were delirious."

"Okay. Right. See what happens when I can't control my impulses?"

"You risked your life tonight going after a very bad man."

"How do you know he's so bad?"

"He runs around shooting people. And you told me he's murdered women."

"Did I?"

"Yes."

"What else did I say?"

"Nothing."

He wondered if she was telling the truth. He might have pressed her, but the emotions churning inside him had become too raw for him to continue the conversation. "You need to get some sleep."

"I don't want to get off."

The way she said it started an ache deep in the pit of his stomach. "Get some sleep," he repeated, then said, "Good night, Megan." Before she could answer, he broke the connection. For the second time tonight, he'd been out of control.

The first time the sound of an owl screeching had snatched him back to sanity. The second time . . .

The second time, it was Megan who had taken control.

14

WHEN the alarm buzzed at seven, Megan turned it off and gave herself an extra half hour to doze, then lay in the gray light of morning, taking a physical and mental inventory.

Physically she felt better than she had any right to feel after staying up so late and worrying. Mentally, she wasn't so sure.

In the smug little world she'd occupied until a few days ago, she'd never understood why people would engage in phone sex. The idea had always seemed perverted. But she'd certainly let Ross turn her on over the phone. Maybe because she'd allowed physical attraction to a man she didn't really know overwhelm her. A man who was as mysterious and frightening as he was sexy. A man who had told her he thought he had some strange genetic disease that she suspected she wasn't going to find in the medical books.

That alone should send her running in the other direction. But she'd found running away wasn't as easy as it should have been. Whether either one of them wanted to admit it or not, they were involved. On a level that was more intimate than anything she'd felt before.

That was scary. Pulling back from the thought, she deliberately started thinking about the blood sample that she'd been incubating overnight. This afternoon she could get to the next phase of the test—looking at his chromosomes, she thought with a mixture of anticipation and dread.

She was glad that Walter wasn't around when she arrived at the lab, glad that she had routine stuff to do until she could get to the next step in the karyotype.

JACK was working his way through a stack of reports when the phone on his desk rang.

"Thornton," he answered.

"This is Ross Marshall."

"How's it going?" he asked, feeling a small pang of guilt. He'd been investigating the man all week and now knew a great deal more about him than he had the last time they'd talked.

"I'd like to meet you for lunch."

Interesting. Marshall hadn't contacted him in at least six weeks. Now, in the middle of the Crawford investigation, the PI was making a point of getting in touch. Of course, unless Marshall was clairvoyant or had some hidden source of information in the department, there was no way he could know about the body that had washed out of the ground up at Sugarloaf Mountain.

"Sure. Where and when?"

"How about that Middle Eastern restaurant where we met last time? Across from Congressional Plaza."

He remembered the place. Not one of the glitzy eateries that paid for an address on Rockville Pike but a more modest establishment where the decor ran to travel posters from Jordan. But the food was plentiful and good.

"Sure. I can be there at twelve-thirty."

In fact, he made a point of arriving early and settling himself in a booth at the back of the smoking section where he could study Marshall as he arrived. Outwardly, he was confident that he looked relaxed. But his nerves were jumping.

The PI walked into the restaurant at the appointed time, wearing jeans, a dark T-shirt, a leather jacket, and a tight look around his eyes and mouth. He was limping slightly, too.

He spotted Jack and started toward him, favoring his right leg. Before he'd taken ten steps, he stopped and rubbed his eyes. By the time he drew abreast of the table Jack had taken, he was coughing.

Casting a glance at a guy two tables away who had left a cigarette smoldering in an ashtray while he ate his baba ganoush, Ross asked, "Do you mind changing tables?"

"Right. You're allergic to smoke," Jack said, as if he'd forgotten. The choice of tables had been deliberate, since he'd wanted to watch the effect of a little stress on Marshall. Sliding out of the booth, he pointed toward a corner table on the opposite side of the room. "What about over there?"

"Fine."

When they were settled, he gave his luncheon companion a closer look. In addition to the red eyes, the limp, and the tight features, his complexion was pale.

"You okay?"

"I picked up something on an investigation—in the woods at night. How are you?"

"Good. Haven't heard from you in a while," he answered conversationally.

"I've been busy."

Jack didn't bother to ask for clarification. He'd learned long ago that Marshall only gave out the information he chose to share.

"So what have *you* been up to?" the PI asked.

"Well, you remember the case of the hidden video-camera in the ladies' dressing room at the YMCA? A couple of county councilwomen use the place, so we've had a lot of R, J, and F A on that one." R, J, and F A was running, jumping, and fucking around. In other words, outward signs of great activity where nothing is really accomplished.

Marshall laughed. "Yeah. I was feeling sorry for you when that hit the papers. I take it you haven't caught the enterprising voyeur?"

"Well, we figure the camera was installed when the building was remodeled. There were workmen and contractors in and out for nine months. So we've narrowed it down to about three hundred suspects."

Marshall shook his head, then opened his menu and studied the selections. When the waiter came over, he ordered a combination lamb and chicken shish kebab, rare, with rice pilaf.

Jack ordered a beef kebab, medium, still thinking about how to play the interview. The element of calculation made him feel guilty. He hated wondering if Marshall had had something to do with the death of a scumbag serial killer five years ago. What did it matter how Crawford had died, really? Eliminating him had been a public service.

Still, there was a nagging voice in the back of his mind as he took a sip of water. The file had landed on his desk. And his job was to close as many cases as possible.

Marshall glanced up and caught Jack's speculative gaze. His shoulders tightened. "What?" he asked.

"I was just thinking that whatever you picked up on that investigation must have been a doozy."

"Yeah, it's hanging on."

Jack shifted in his seat. "You've got something for me?"

Before Marshall could answer, the waiter brought their food, and they were both silent until the man had left them alone again.

Marshall cut a piece of rare, marinated lamb in half and forked up a piece.

Jack tucked into his own meal.

After finishing several pieces of meat, Marshall reached into his jacket pocket, brought out a folded piece of paper, and pushed it across the table.

When Jack unfolded it, he found a man's name at the top.

Donald Arnott, 5962 Newcut Road. Security guard, Montgomery Mall. White male. Thirty-five. Brown and brown. Five eleven. One hundred seventy-five pounds. Owns several guns, including a hunting rifle and a compact machine gun.

Underneath Arnott's description were the names of five women. Two, Penny Delano and Charlotte Lawrence, he recognized as missing persons cases. One recent, another from about five months back. The three others were unfamiliar. Lisa Patterson. Cindy Hamilton. Mary Beth Nixon.

"Arnott moved here about eight months ago," Marshall said. "Before that, he was living in Paoli, Pennsylvania. You'll find missing persons reports on three of the victims up there. There are probably others."

"You're telling me Arnott is responsible for Delano and Lawrence?"

"Yeah."

"But you can't prove it?"

"I was on his property a few nights ago. There were shallow graves. They're probably gone by now."

"He spotted you prowling around?" Jack asked, his cop's mind making rapid connections. Marshall was limping. He said he'd caught something on an investigation. The implication was that he'd caught a cold or the flu. But what if he'd caught a bullet and managed to patch himself up without medical attention? Was that what had happened? A bullet in the leg? A shot low on the body. Maybe Arnott had come upon him down on the ground, digging for evidence. And somehow he'd gotten away. As he debated proffering the hypothesis, Marshall started speaking again, his voice hard.

"He knows somebody's on to him. Which is why you have to act quickly, before he decides to pull up stakes and try his luck somewhere else."

"You've got a personal interest in this?"

"I was hired to find one of the women, Penny Delano. When the police drew a blank."

"She disappeared after work at Montgomery Mall one evening. Nobody saw her leave. There was no evidence to go on. She'd broken up with her boyfriend a few weeks earlier, but he had a rock solid alibi for that night. And we don't have any other leads."

"Arnott is a security guard at Montgomery Mall. I know she was in his vehicle."

"How?"

"I have my methods."

"Which you aren't going to share."

"I don't have the same constraints that you do. He's got a Land Rover with a ring bolted to the back of a fold-down rear seat. My guess is that he uses it to restrain his victims when he carts them home. He's probably got handcuffs to go with it."

Jack winced. "We can't search without probable cause."

"I know. I'm hoping that if you tail him, you'll come up with something. I'm also hoping you can stop him before he does it again."

"Not like Edward Crawford." Until the moment he mentioned the man's name, he hadn't been sure he was going to bring up the unsolved murder.

Marshall didn't move, but the blood drained from his face. "What about Edward Crawford?"

"You were investigating him five years ago."

"What about him?" Marshall repeated.

"His body turned up at Sugarloaf Mountain."

The PI shifted his legs under the table. "I always wondered what happened to that bastard. What was the cause of death?"

"Undetermined."

Marshall nodded.

"You gave Ken Winston some information—but he didn't use it. Then another woman was killed. That must have been frustrating."

"Winston made it clear he didn't want any help from me."

"So what would you do if I didn't act on this tip you're giving me now?"

"I'd be disappointed, because I think we have a good working relationship. And I'd be angry when Arnott took another victim."

"Will he?"

"You know he will."

"You told me you're not bound by the same rules I am. Would you try to stop him if I can't?"

"If you mean, would I try to get evidence that you can use, the answer is yes. If you mean, would I kill him to stop him, the answer is no, because that would put me on his level," Marshall said, his voice low and firm. His eyes bored into Jack's as he sat there on the other side of the table, waiting for the next question.

Jack elected not to ask it, and Marshall picked up his knife and fork and cut another piece of marinated lamb.

After he'd chewed and swallowed, he came back with a question of his own. "So what kind of condition was the body in?"

"Skeletal remains. Apparently mauled by some large animal."

"How long has he been dead?"

"The ME thinks about five years."

"So he died right after he disappeared."

"Yeah."

Marshall leaned back in his chair. "Interesting," he said, both his tone and his hand steady as he took a drink of water.

MEGAN'S hand shook slightly as she washed the slide of Ross's tissue with a salt-detergent solution.

Get a grip, she ordered herself. *You've done this a hundred times.* But she hadn't done this analysis on genetic material from someone she'd gotten to know personally, someone whose deep, sexy voice had aroused her over the phone the night before.

Someone she would be speaking to again after she finished this analysis—unless she chickened out and gave the job to Hank.

Lips pressed together, she added a series of dyes designed to make the details of each chromosome stand out. There were two basic classes of chromosome aberrations, numerical and structural, one or the other found in association with many abnormalities of development: Turner's syndrome, Klinefelter's syndrome, fragile X syndrome, complex malformation syndromes.

With the advent of chromosome banding techniques in the 1970s, it was possible to identify with certainty all chromosome pairs and to characterize more accurately abnormalities of number and structure. She was looking for either or both, although Ross had told her she wasn't going to find anything that had already been described. But she'd check that out for herself.

While the traditional method of analysis was very labor intensive, she had access to an automated system that used an interferometer similar to ones employed by astronomers for measuring light spectra emitted by stars, with the results analyzed by a computer program and displayed on a monitor.

Afraid of what she was going to find, she waited for the computer to complete the analysis, then looked at the screen, prepared to settle down to the process of checking for any of the known abnormalities. What she saw made her jaw drop open.

After glancing over her shoulder to make sure nobody was standing behind her, she looked at the screen again, touching each set of chromosomes with her finger, counting carefully to verify what she thought she was viewing. The correct number of human chromosome pairs was twenty-three. Ross Marshall had an extra twenty-fourth chromosome. Impossible.

Yet there it was on the monitor. Once more, she made sure that her eyes weren't playing tricks on her. But the results were the same. No mistake in her counting.

Had the computer program made some kind of error? Carefully she went through the steps of the procedure again, waiting with her pulse pounding in her temples for the analysis to finish. The picture on the screen was the same one she'd viewed a few minutes earlier.

She knew of abnormalities caused by an extra chromosome, but the anomaly was always an extra one of the known chromosomes, like the extra Y chromosome responsible for a documented type of violent-aggressive male personality. She had never heard of a case of a totally undocumented twenty-fourth chromosome.

After saving the analysis onto a disk, she exited the program, went back to her desk, and sat down. Glancing at Hank, she saw he was bent over his computer. Ordinarily she wouldn't hesitate to confide in her colleague when she found something as startling as what she'd just seen. But this was different. Walter had given her reason to worry about Hank's research skills. And even if he hadn't, what she'd found out about Ross was something she didn't want to advertise.

Still, she needed confirmation that her results weren't out of whack. "Can I ask you a question?"

Hank looked up, blinked as though coming out of a fog.

"Sorry to interrupt you."

"It's okay. What do you need?"

"The cytogenetic analysis equipment—have you used it this morning?"

"Yeah. I did a couple of workups."

"And you didn't have any difficulties with the computer system?"

"Uh-uh. You got problems?"

"Not really. I was just checking," she said lamely.

He gave her a considering look, and she thought he was going back to his work. Instead he said, "Are you mad at me or something?"

"What?"

"You've kind of been avoiding me since yesterday."

"Have I?"

"We usually joke around about stuff. You've been . . ." He shrugged. "I don't know. It's like you've withdrawn or something."

He was right, of course. But she didn't know what to say—couldn't tell him that Walter's accusation had tainted her image of him.

"I'm sorry," she murmured. "I guess I'm kind of preoccupied with some personal stuff."

He nodded, stared at her for a few more seconds, then went back to his computer. She looked at the phone, thinking that her next step was to call Ross. But not in front of Hank. She'd wait until he left for lunch.

ROSS slid behind the wheel of his Grand Cherokee, turned the key in the ignition, and looked behind him before easing out of his parking space. His movements were slow and careful, as if he were afraid that he would make a mistake and Jack Thornton would come running out of the restaurant to give him a traffic ticket.

Thornton was still inside. In the men's room. And Ross was making his escape.

There hadn't been a great deal of conversation after the detective had asked how far Ross might go in his quest to stop a man like Arnott—or Crawford. Somehow Ross had forced himself to keep sitting in his chair and calmly finish his lunch—while he felt the walls of the restaurant close in on him.

Now that he was outside, he was feeling a bit less claustrophobic, but the lunch he'd eaten was as heavy as a bag of sand in his stomach. He'd told Thornton in no uncertain terms that he wasn't going to kill Arnott to put a stop to his activities. But he'd come within a hairbreadth of doing just that last night.

And if he'd come that close, well . . .

Ignoring the pain in his gut, he deliberately went back to the conversation with Thornton—the other part, about Crawford.

With as much objectivity as he could manage, he analyzed the exchange of information and the probable consequences. The detective had let him know that Crawford had died five years ago, that his body had been found, that the cause of death was unknown—and then watched him for reactions.

After that, the police detective had answered questions about the body and the crime scene. The killer's flesh had decomposed, so there was no evidence that his throat had been ripped out. No fiber or trace evidence on the body, if there ever had been any. That is, if Thornton was telling the truth. Which he might not be. Because when a cop was interrogating a suspect, he was likely to lie like hell.

But what would knowing the cause of death prove? Only that a large animal with sharp teeth had killed Crawford. Not a man.

And not a man who could change himself into a wolf. Because any police detective who tried to pin the crime on a werewolf was in for a long session with the department shrink.

The chain of logic made Ross relax a little. Finally able to think of something else besides the meeting with Thornton, he reached into the pocket of his jacket, took out the phone that he'd turned off before going into the restaurant, and checked for messages.

There was one. From Arthur Delano, Penny Delano's father—the man who'd hired him to find his daughter. What timing!

"I don't want to keep pestering you," the man had told the answering machine. "But I haven't heard from you in a couple of weeks, and my wife and I were wondering if you've found out anything new about our daughter. So if you could give me a call, I'd appreciate it. Our phone number is 301-555-4976."

He stabbed the brake pedal, pulling up short at a red light. He was sure Penny was dead. But there was no proof yet, and he didn't want to give the parents that kind of news without being positive. Confirmation would have to come from Thornton—if he trusted the information Ross had given him.

He scrubbed his hand over his face, then punched in the numbers.

Arthur Delano answered immediately. "Hello?"

"This is Ross Marshall. I have a message to call you."

"Thank you for getting back to me. At least you return phone calls."

Hating to leave the man twisting in the wind, he said, "I'm sorry that I don't have any definite information for you, sir."

"Definite information?"

Ross sighed. "I'm hoping to have something for you in the next few weeks."

"We've already been waiting weeks."

"I know. And I wish I could alleviate your anxiety." The words sounded hollow in own ears. He wanted to do something more for this man, but his hands were tied.

"We were assured that if anyone could find our daughter, you were the one. I guess we were being optimistic when we hired you."

A horn honked behind him, and he jerked across the intersection. "I've been working on the case. I've given information to the police that I hope will have some positive results. If you'd like, I can return the retainer you've given me."

Delano thought it over for several seconds. "No. You might as well keep the money. You might as well keep working for us."

"I'm sorry, sir. I wish I had more I could give you at this time."

There was another hesitation on the other end of the line. "Will you just tell me one thing? Please? Do you think there's any chance that Penny will be found alive?"

Ross debated for a moment, then answered, "Honestly, no."

"I won't tell that to my wife. But I appreciate your being straight with me."

"I wish I could give you better news."

"Please tell us the moment you know anything definite."

"I will, sir."

He hung up, driving automatically. When he almost smashed into

the back of the Honda in front of him, he decided it was time to get off
the road. Pulling into one of the shopping centers that lined the pike,
he found a parking space and sat with his eyes fixed on a furniture display window.

Christ, there were things about this job that he utterly detested. It
was gratifying when you could come back to a family with the good
news that you'd located their missing relative. It was hell when the
only thing you could give them was confirmation of a death. Which
was what he was going to have to give the Delanos eventually—but not
until Jack came through for him.

While he was still sitting in the parking lot, the phone rang again.
Pushing the Receive button, he found himself talking to Megan.

All she had to do was say his name in a slightly breathy voice and
he felt his heart speed up as he remembered the previous night's conversation.

"What can I do for you?" he managed.

"I need to talk to you about the chromosome analysis."

Of course. There'd been so much else on his mind that he hadn't
been thinking about that at all.

"You've got some information for me?" he asked, striving to mask
his sudden tension.

"I'd rather not go into it over the phone. Uh . . . could we talk in
person? Can you meet me at the lab?"

He felt a fine sheen of perspiration bloom on his skin. "You remember I didn't want to come to the lab in the first place?"

"Right." She was silent for several seconds. "Uh . . . my house?"

That wasn't a great alternative. But where? Not a public place like
the restaurant where he'd just talked to Thornton. Not when she had
some very personal information.

"The lab's better," he answered grudgingly. "But could we make it
after hours?"

"All right. What about six o'clock?"

"Okay."

They hung up, and he sat there, feeling a pulse pounding in his
temple. She'd found something. Something abnormal.

But why was he surprised? He'd known that all along, hadn't he?

15

NERVOUSLY Megan checked her hair in the ladies' room mirror, then applied a touch of lipstick, powder, and blusher.

Peering at her reflection, she saw the brightness of her eyes, the slight flush of her skin.

Despite what she might have told herself in the morning, she was excited about seeing Ross Marshall again. And worried. Partly because their relationship was strangely tangled on a personal and professional level, and partly because she wondered how he would react to the news she had to give him. Would he tell her any more about the effect of the syndrome or the men in his family? Or was he going to clam up?

And why should she care so much?

Opening the door to the ladies' room, she stepped into the hall and started decisively toward her office. Before she'd taken half a dozen steps, she heard the drumming of rain on the roof of the building. And suddenly she remembered stopping to fill the car with gas on the way to work, spilling some on the pavement, and tracking it into the car. She'd rolled the window on the passenger side partway down to get rid of the smell. And she was pretty sure she hadn't remembered to roll it back up again.

Damn.

It wasn't supposed to rain today. Just her luck.

She took a quick look at her watch. Ross wasn't due for another ten minutes. She probably had time to dash outside and close the window before he came.

The rain was coming down pretty fast, and thunder rumbled in the distance. Stepping into the lounge, she snatched up the umbrella that she'd forgotten to take home the week before.

The front door was still unlocked, and as she turned the knob, the wind snatched the door away from her and flung it wide.

The lights in the parking lot must be out, she thought, fumbling with the umbrella as she stood in the doorway, the rain coming down in sheets so thick that she couldn't see more than a couple of feet in front of her face.

She was considering going back for the flashlight on her desk when a dart of movement caught her eye. Turning her head, she saw a man materialize out of the rain and darkness—a man hurtling purposefully toward her.

There was hardly any warning before he crashed into her, almost knocking her to the wet ground. The still-unopened umbrella sailed out of her hand and onto the grass, and she gasped, stumbling on the water-slick sidewalk, numb with shock as arms fastened around her body, pulling her close in a parody of an embrace.

He was taller than she, and too close for her to see anything. But she felt him, solid and menacing in the darkness.

Rain pelted against them, drenching her hair before he pushed her against the wall where the overhang gave some protection from the torrent of water.

She began to pound at him with her fists, trying to make him loosen his hold. But he was wearing something slick like shiny rubber or plastic so that her hands slid off of him, unable to get a grip on the wet surface.

When she finally landed a heavy blow, he grunted. Raising her hands, she tried to claw at his face, his eyes, but his head was covered by some sort of knit fabric—a ski mask, from the feel of it.

He had deliberately hidden his face, and that simple fact spurred her terror. Sensing there was no point in wasting her breath on pleading with him, she simply fought him as he wrestled her to the wet pavement.

Desperately her fingers scrabbled under the edge of the ski mask, and she raked her nails across his neck.

With an angry roar, he slapped a hand across her face so hard her ears rang. Coming down on top of her, he tore at her clothing, his hands on her body in intimate places—high up on her legs, her breasts.

And the scream that had been frozen inside her tore from her throat.

A woman's scream pierced the downpour. Ross had been sitting behind the steering wheel of his car, eyes closed as he waited for the rain to let up enough so that he could dash to the door of the lab. He was still tired from the night before, still weak from the leg wound, and he was half dozing, lulled by the drumming of the rain on the roof of the SUV.

But the scream snapped him to instant attention.

Megan. God, that was Megan. In trouble.

He didn't stop to think, because thought had become impossible. He was already kicking off his shoes, tearing off his jacket and shirt and throwing them onto the seat of the car. Then, leaping onto the rain-slick pavement, he pulled his pants and underwear off and kicked them under the car even as the words of transformation rose in his throat.

"Taranis, Epona, Cerridwen. *Gá. Feart. Cleas. Duais. Aithriocht. Go gcumhdaí is dtreoraí na déithe thú,*" he shouted into the deluge then repeated the phrase.

He could see nothing through the driving rain. But the wolf would know. The wolf would find her.

He had never felt this urgency, never tried to hurry the transformation. But tonight he pushed the process, the pain searing him as he forced muscle and sinew to respond to his commands.

He picked up Megan's scent even before he was down on all fours and streaking across the strip of blacktop.

MEGAN fought as the assailant dragged her skirt over her hips and clawed at her panty hose.

Dimly, in the back of her mind, she thought she heard the sound of a car door opening and strange words drifting toward her above the pounding rain.

She couldn't understand them, and yet she had the feeling she'd heard them before.

Thunder rumbled in the distance as if nature were providing background music for the attack. The next sound that reached her ears was an animal snarl, deep and dangerous in the darkness. It sent a jolt of awareness through her system, and all she could think was that a hound from hell had come to tear her to pieces.

The attacker must have heard it, too, because his whole body stiffened.

Claws clicked against the pavement. She could still see nothing through the pouring rain, nothing from her position on the ground. But she felt a heavy body crashing into the man on top of her—heard more growling, snapping, snarling, the scraping of claws.

MEGAN'S scent had led him to the struggling figures. She was on the ground. A man was on top of her. Rage coursing through his mind and body, the wolf leaped onto the man's back, jaws snapping, claws digging through slick vinyl to contact flesh.

The assailant gave a cry of pain and terror and sprang away from Megan, his face strange and grotesque in the darkness.

Not a human face at all.

Before the wolf could puzzle it out, the man raised his hand to protect his eyes as he skittered away across the wet pavement.

With a growl the wolf started to leap after him—to finish him off.

Then the woman on the ground moaned, and he knew his first thought must be of her.

Words clawed their way to the surface of his brain. But there was no way to force them from his mouth.

Megan. Talk to me.

Are you all right?

He couldn't speak, couldn't ask the question. He could only stand there in the rain, staring down at her with anxious eyes as she pushed herself up and cringed away from him.

A car door slammed, an engine started, and a car skidded off through the pelting rain. Dimly he realized that he had let the man escape. But that was good, wasn't it? He hadn't killed him. He had gone to Megan instead.

He stood for a moment, choked with a swirl of emotions. Then, backing away, he turned and fled to his own vehicle, shielding himself behind the open door as the words of transformation echoed in his head again. Once more he pushed the process. Once more he intensified the pain, his head spinning with it, his vision blurring.

Then he was standing on two feet—a man, naked in the slackening rain. Reaching under the car, he found his jeans and shoved his legs into them before grabbing his shirt and pulling it over his head.

DIZZY, disoriented, Megan scooted back under the shelter of the roof overhang, out of the rain, her hand grasping at the rough surface of the brick wall. Her mind was focused on standing—running. But when she tried to shove herself up, her legs were like rubber, and she flopped back to the pavement with a sob of frustration.

She was making another attempt to coordinate her limbs and her brain when the light in the reception area snapped on, casting a dim glow into the rain and darkness. It was enough for her to see a man's shape filling the doorway.

"No." The cry tore from her throat just as the man came down beside her on the pavement, looming over her.

She was still cringing away when the sound of his voice, his words, penetrated her fear.

"Megan. Megan, are you all right? Megan," he said over and over.

When she realized who it was, a sob welled in her throat. "Ross?"

"Yes. I'm here. I'll take care of you."

She pressed against him, and he scooped her up, carrying her inside the building. Leaning back against the wall, he set her gently down, but he didn't let her go. His arms embraced her, cradling her close, protective and possessive. She burrowed into his warmth, the familiar scent of him, the strength.

"God, Ross," she gasped out, clinging to him, her face burried in his shoulder.

He moved them to the reception room couch, holding her on his lap, stroking the wet hair out of her face. Then his hand touched the sleeve of her blouse, and she realized it was ripped.

"Did he hurt you?" he asked, his voice hoarse.

"No. The dog stopped him. Or was it the wolf?" Unable to meet his gaze, she kept her face pressed against his chest as she asked, "Did I dream that, too?"

She heard him make a low sound in his throat. "Do you want it to be a dream?"

"Yes."

"Then it is."

The confirmation soothed her. Something had happened. Something strange that she had no way to explain. But she didn't want to think about the details. They were far too threatening.

Instead she nestled closer to him. Ross. Ross was here. Not the wolf. Seeming to know exactly what she needed, he rocked her in his arms, leaning back so that her body rested against his. She felt his lips skim her damp hair.

"He was on top of me, tearing at my clothes," she said, gulping.

"He won't hurt you. He's gone," he said, repeating the reassurance, probably because he knew she needed to hear it again.

She nodded, but the thought of what had almost happened stabbed at her, and she made a small sound of protest.

As Ross's arms tightened around her, she lifted her face, stared up into his dark eyes. She could lose herself in those eyes, she thought. Lose herself in him.

For long moments, he didn't move, didn't speak. Then he cleared his throat. "We have to call the police."

She started to protest that she didn't want to talk about it with the police, then realized he was right. "You'll stay with me?"

"Of course."

Pushing herself up, she tried to straighten her clothing and found that the front of her blouse was hopelessly torn and her skirt was sopping. Quickly she walked to the lab and grabbed a white coat and a pair of scrub pants that she sometimes wore when she was working with chemicals that might ruin her clothing.

Ross stood guard at the door, then escorted her to the ladies' room where she changed into the coat and pants and stuffed her ruined clothing inside a plastic bag from the supply closet.

When she came out, he was there, although she'd thought she heard him run down the hall while she was in the bathroom. He stayed beside her as she returned to Betty's desk and stared at the phone, her hand suddenly shaking.

"You want me to do it?" he asked.

"Would you?"

He picked up the receiver, made the call to 911.

"A patrol car is on the way," he said after he hung up.

She nodded, then thought about Walter. "I should call my boss."

"I can take care of it."

She pictured Walter's reaction to yet another disturbance in his ordered way of life. "No. It's better if I do it."

Ross handed her the phone, and she struggled to control her trembling fingers as she punched in Walter's number.

She got his answering machine and was relieved that she wouldn't have to talk to him right away. Instead, she left a message saying that there had been another incident at the lab and to call her as soon as he could.

As she sat on the couch in the reception area, her eyes lifted to Ross, who was pacing back and forth.

She studied him, thinking that he'd been barefoot when they'd first come in. Or was she remembering that right? Because now he was wearing his shoes again.

Her eyes flicked to his jeans and shirt. His clothing was damp, but not as wet as hers had been.

Why not? she wondered, an uneasy feeling gathering in the pit of her stomach.

"What should I tell the police when they get here?" she asked.

"Tell them what happened."

"That you chased him away?"

She saw him swallow. "Yes."

Even as she nodded her agreement, some part of her knew that she was treading on dangerous ground. Unstable ground that could open up and swallow her whole. Instinct urged her to back away, back to where the surface under her feet was firmer.

The wolf . . . .

He had stood there, staring at her.

No. *Forget the wolf,* her mind ordered. *You were scared spitless, and you made him up. That's all.* It had to be all, because there was no other way her mind could cope.

ROSS forced himself to stop pacing, forced himself to sit quietly on the couch in the reception area with his arm around Megan. While she'd been in the bathroom, he'd retrieved his shoes from where he'd dropped them before he changed. The underwear he'd shucked off was in the pocket of his coat. Presumably the police weren't going to search him, so there'd be no reason to explain why his underclothes were in his pocket instead of covering his butt.

Now that he had time to think things through, he knew that he'd had no real reason to change into a wolf. Private detective Ross Marshall could have gone after the man who'd attacked Megan. But when he'd heard her scream, animal instinct had taken over. He'd torn off his clothing, changed into wolf form, and leaped on top of the bastard.

Instinct again. The curse of the werewolf. And now he had to deal with the consequences—whatever they were going to be.

At least he hadn't ripped out the man's throat. That was something.

Before he could wander any further down that line of thinking, two uniforms came through the door, introduced themselves as Officer Brant and Officer Martinez, and began taking information from Megan.

They were in the middle of taking her initial statement when a detective joined the proceedings. It was Jack Thornton, and Ross's first thought was *Oh, shit.*

16

JACK stared at the bedraggled couple sitting on the sofa in the reception area, Ross Marshall and a woman who had apparently been assaulted outside her office. He was wearing rain-spattered jeans, his leather jacket, and a shirt—the same clothes he'd had on earlier in the day. Her hair was wet and mussed, and she was clutching the front of a white lab coat.

He'd responded to the call because he was working the late shift. From the expression on the PI's face, it looked like he wasn't pleased to see Detective Thornton.

After telling the uniforms they could leave, he studied the couple's posture. Marshall had his arm around her. And she was leaning into him as though she were seeking comfort and protection. Maybe more than that, he thought with sudden insight.

He introduced himself to the woman. "I'm Detective Jack Thornton,"

"Dr. Megan Sheridan," she replied. "And this is Ross Marshall."

"We know each other," Ross interjected.

She looked from one of them to the other. "Professionally?"

"Yeah," Marshall answered.

Jack cleared his throat, addressed her again. "You work here?"

"Yes."

"You're a medical doctor?"

"Yes, but I don't treat patients. My job is research oriented."

"You want to tell me what happened?"

"No. But I will." She pressed closer to Marshall, and his arm tightened around her. "I was working after hours. When I realized the window of my car was open—" She stopped, made a face. "It's still open! Anyway, I got an umbrella and went outside."

"You're not wearing the clothes you had on during the attack?"

She looked down at the lab coat. "No. I put this on because my blouse was torn and my skirt was wet."

"Where are they?"

"In my office."

"I'd like to send them to the lab."

"For what?"

"Trace evidence. Hair. Fibers. Something to help us identify the guy."

She got up, swaying a little on her feet. Marshall was about to jump up and steady her when she lurched away and walked stiffly down the hall.

Jack watched Marshall keep his eyes trained on her until she disappeared through a doorway. "How is she?"

"Shaken up. Not hurt," the PI answered.

Before he could ask about Marshall's role in the incident, she was back carrying a plastic bag, which she set down beside Jack.

"Okay. Sorry for the interruption," he said. "You grabbed an umbrella and went outside."

"Yes, I opened the front door, and it was raining really hard. I couldn't see more than a couple of feet in front of me. I was thinking about getting a flashlight when a man came out of the darkness and attacked me."

"What did he do exactly?"

She shivered, and Marshall stroked his hand up and down her arm. "He grabbed me, threw me to the ground, and started ripping at my clothes." She stopped, glanced at Marshall, and a look passed between them that Jack wished he could read. "Then Ross got the guy off me."

"Did you pursue him?" Jack asked Marshall.

"He got away."

"Were you in the building?"

Marshall shook his head. "No. I was in the parking lot and heard Megan scream. I came running toward the door, and I could dimly see her struggling with someone on the pavement outside."

"You pulled the guy off of her?"

Marshall's mouth tightened. "Yes."

There was something odd about Marshall's answers. Something that he wanted to understand. But he decided to come back to that later. "Can either of you tell me anything more about the man?"

"He had a ski mask over his face," Dr. Sheridan said. "I know because I tried to claw him, and my hand hit the fabric."

"It was dark. I can't give you many details," Marshall added. "I guess he was something over medium height. Medium weight. I couldn't see his features, of course."

Jack wrote it down, then asked, "What kind of work does Bio Gen do?"

Dr. Sheridan replied, "Genetic testing—mostly for couples who want to know if planning a family is a good idea. Also testing in paternity cases. And I have my own research."

"On what?"

"Myer's disease, a genetic form of macular degeneration that strikes certain individuals in their thirties. The macula is the part of the eye where the vision is sharpest. I'm working on a gene therapy that I hope will arrest further deterioration."

"Gene therapy? Isn't that dangerous?"

"It's gotten some bad press. But what I'm doing is different. I'm using an adenovirus—a modified cold virus—to deliver a normal copy of the gene to the back of the eye. But I haven't gotten to clinical trials, if you're thinking that someone I damaged with my wild experiments came after me."

Again her expression shifted subtly. He waited for her to elaborate, but she apparently didn't have any more to say on the subject.

He turned to Marshall, "And what were you doing at the lab?"

"I was here to meet Megan," the PI answered.

"You mean, for a date?"

"Business."

"Which was?"

"Why is that relevant?"

"Everything's relevant."

"I had asked the lab for genetic testing."

Jack stared at the arm that Marshall kept firmly around the woman's shoulder. "And you and Dr. Sheridan have gotten to know each other well during the course of your professional relationship?"

Marshall was silent.

Sheridan answered. "He and I have gotten close."

Jack burned to explore that simple statement, since he'd doubted that Ross Marshall was close to anyone. It was another thread he had to drop for the moment. "What kind of genetic testing?"

Marshall hesitated, then answered in a low voice. "A family trait that causes high infant mortality."

"And you recently got the test results?"

"No. That was why I came over here."

So was that why he'd been uptight at lunch? Jack wondered, suddenly revising his assessment of their recent conversation. Marshall had been anticipating some bad news from Dr. Sheridan. From a woman he was romantically interested in, of all people. Switching his attention back to the doctor, he saw something was bothering her. Something about his questions? Something about Marshall?

"What else do you want to tell me about?" he asked gently.

She sucked in a breath of air and let it out. "Can we talk off the record?"

"Yeah," he answered, knowing he'd decide when he heard it whether to press her.

"Okay. There was a break-in at the lab yesterday morning."

Marshall's head swung toward her. Apparently this was the first he'd heard of it.

"My boss told me in confidence that someone had been harassing him. A former client who claimed that he'd gotten incorrect test results from us. He said he thought the man had run him off the road a couple of days before that."

"So that's why you wanted me to know it wasn't one of your, uh"— he flipped back through his notes—"macular degeneration patients who came after you."

"Yes."

"Is the information about the former client on record with the officers who investigated the break-in?"

"I don't think so. Walter said he didn't want bad publicity for the lab, so it was better to keep that aspect of it quiet."

Beside her Marshall made an explosive noise. "So he didn't say anything—and tonight something happens to you!"

"It might not be connected," she said in a shaky voice.

"And it might!"

Jack watched the exchange, sure now that whatever else was true, Marshall cared a lot about this woman. And from the way she was glued to his side, it looked like the feeling was mutual.

She raised her eyes to Jack's. "Please, don't tell Walter that I said anything to you."

"This is bullshit!" Marshall spat out. "You could have been raped because your jerk of a boss is trying to protect the lab's reputation."

"Your boss—Walter what?"

"Walter Galveston."

Jack wrote it down, then asked, "Did he tell you the name of the client?"

"He said some of our records were missing."

"Oh, great," Marshall said, his voice sarcastic.

"Ross—" she murmured.

"Okay, I'll shut up." He stood, paced to the far wall, then came back to the couch, leaving several inches between himself and Dr. Sheridan. She immediately closed the distance separating them.

Marshall gave Jack a direct look. "Do you need anything else from her tonight? Or can she go home?"

"I . . . I don't want to go home alone," she said in a small voice.

Marshall hesitated for a beat before saying, "I'll follow you in my Jeep."

"Will you stay with me?"

Jack saw him swallow, saw his features tighten. He wanted her, but he didn't want to be alone with her? Because of what he'd found out from the tests? Was he lying about not having gotten the results? Or was he just anticipating bad news?

Marshall dipped his head toward her. "I'll stay with you."

Her fingers knit with his, clung. "I'm sorry I'm acting like a wuss."

"You've been through a bad experience," Jack answered. "And Ross will make sure nothing happens to you."

He saw the flash of surprise in Marshall's eyes, then turned his attention back to Dr. Sheridan.

"I've just got a couple more questions. Is the door normally locked after hours?"

She thought about that for a moment. "I assume so."

"And there's no alarm?"

"There is. But it wasn't set, because I was waiting for Ross."

Marshall's jaw muscles tightened. "Which means the guy could have come in here and gotten you—and I wouldn't have known about it."

She acknowledged the observation with a quick nod.

Jack stood, wishing the perp had gotten into the building. Instead he'd caught her outside in the rain—which was going to make the crime scene a nightmare for the techs. "Can you show me the place where the attack occurred?"

She stood, glanced at Marshall, then grabbed his hand as she moved toward the door. In the darkness, she pointed to a spot that was partially protected by an overhang. Which was better than nothing. Maybe there was still some evidence that hadn't been washed away.

"Okay. Thanks. I'll wait for the lab technicians," Jack said.

"Thanks," she answered, sounding grateful that she was being allowed to leave. Then, "Do you think you can catch him?"

"I hope so."

She nodded. "I have to get my purse."

Marshall stayed with her as she retreated down the hallway, then returned. "Who else works here?" Jack asked.

"Our receptionist, Betty Daniels." Sheridan stopped and pressed a hand against her lips. "What if she came in here tomorrow morning and got raped? And Hank—Henry—Lancaster. Dr. Lancaster. He's the other researcher on our team."

"Write down their names and numbers, so I can interview them. And Dr. . . . Galveston's."

She opened a Rolodex in the receptionist's desk and copied down the information, which she handed to him.

When they'd concluded their business, he watched Marshall checking out the parking lot before allowing Dr. Sheridan outside and escorting her to her car.

Over the three years they'd been working together, Jack had made a lot of assumptions about the PI. All week he'd been rethinking those conclusions. And tonight had given him a lot more to consider.

ROSS followed Megan home, sticking close behind her as she headed toward Gaithersburg. She turned on to a road called Walnut Lane and drove through an older neighborhood with mature trees and enormous lots by today's standards. When she pulled into the driveway of a small, redbrick ranch, he parked several feet behind her.

By the time he joined her in the kitchen, she'd taken off her coat and hung it on a rack near the back door.

Looking at the wide moldings and real plaster walls, he judged the house to be about sixty years old. Somebody had remodeled the kitchen, a bare minimum job, with dark green Formica counters, white appliances, inexpensive white cabinets, and a white tile floor that was probably hell to keep clean.

She'd relieved the monotony with pot holders and tea towels decorated with black-and-white cows. The cow motif was repeated on the salt and pepper shakers and the teakettle. And the wallpaper between the cabinets and the countertop was of a green meadow.

A lot of men probably wouldn't have given the room much notice. But with his remodeling experience, he found the effect both whimsical and charming.

However, he didn't bother to say so as he carefully kept his distance from her. The way she looked—disoriented, bedraggled, haunted—tore at him. He wanted to reach for her, hold her, comfort her, as much to ease the tight feeling in his chest as anything else. But now they were alone, and it wasn't safe to touch her. Especially after last night's phone call. So he kept his arms stiffly at his sides.

"You want some coffee?" Megan asked in a voice that was barely above a whisper.

"I don't drink coffee."

"Right. I forgot. I've got some herbal tea." She turned toward a cabinet near the stove, opened it, and stood staring blindly at boxes of tea. Tonight had been the most terrible of her life, and here she was preparing to make tea, while the man who could help her get through till morning was standing a few feet away.

He had put his arms around her. Soothed her. She needed more than that from him. More than he was willing to give?

The flood of emotions sweeping through her was dangerous. But she disregarded the danger. With a small sound, she swung back around and faced him, unashamed of the naked need on her face.

"Ross. Please. Hold me."

Only a few feet separated them.

She saw the stiff way he stood, as though powerful forces warred inside him. She had come to understand what they were. His need for her—and his silent vow to resist that need.

Last night, when she had been safely out of his reach, he had allowed himself to give rein to his feelings. She understood that. Distance had made him feel safe.

Now . . . the buried fire in his eyes made her bold enough to take a step closer.

When she moved, so did he, step by step, until she could feel his warm breath, then his flesh. At the moment his lips touched hers, the world contracted to the feel of his mouth, his hands on her body.

Last night she had touched her own lips, imagined his kiss—and come alive with wanting him.

But tonight the reality of the flesh and blood man was more potent than the game they'd been playing.

She opened her mouth under his, drinking in the taste of him—the taste of woodlands and dark shadows where magic lurked. Magic she could only dimly imagine. She'd sensed hidden powers within him. Now she knew they came from the earth and the forest.

She made a small, wanting sound, captivated by the feel of his hands on her shoulders, her back, her ribs. When she said his name again, the syllable was lost in the pressure of her lips against his. He shifted her in his arms, eased back against the countertop, splaying his legs to equalize their heights. A strangled exclamation rose in his throat as he pulled her to him so that his chest pressed against her breasts.

Her tongue met his, retreated, came back again to stroke and slide, the contact sending alternately hot and cold shivers over her skin.

She wanted him. Wanted him to drive everything from her mind but what was happening between the two of them.

Her heart raced at a feverish pace, the beat frantic—as frantic as her need to get close to him and closer still.

She wrapped her arms around him, sealed his body to hers, only half aware of the their surroundings. The only thing of importance was the man whose physical presence had imprinted itself on her.

She felt all of him. Hard muscles. Corded arms. Long legs. And the rigid pressure of his erection against her thigh. That wasn't where she wanted him. Squirming against him, she eased into a more intimate position so that his sex was pressed to hers, with only scant layers of fabric separating their heated flesh.

"God, Megan," he groaned, his hips moving rhythmically against hers, his body like a furnace, heating her.

He shifted her in his arms, found her breast with his hand, stroking and pressing through the fabric. Her nipples were already stiff and aching. The touch of his hand sent a quivering wave of need surging downward through her body, and she arched against him.

The clothing had become an intolerable barrier. Her fingers tangled with his as she reached for the buttons on the front of her lab coat.

Her fingers stopped. She caught her breath as a shaft of reality stabbed through her, and she suddenly remembered why she was wearing her lab clothes at home.

Perhaps he felt the change in her. Perhaps he was struck by the same realization, because he moved her away, putting inches of space between them.

She grabbed for his arm, but he was already turning her so that she was standing next to him, pressed to the countertop.

She stared at him, saw his breath coming hard and fast as he stood with his head thrown back and his hands thrust behind him, gripping the counter.

"Ross—"

"No," he said between gasps of air.

"Why not?"

"Because this is the wrong thing for you."

"Ross, let me decide what I want."

"No. You're vulnerable. I'd be taking advantage of you."

Maybe he was right, but she'd wanted him with a desperation that bordered on madness. She stretched out her hand, then let it fall back, keeping her eyes on his face. His features were contorted, and she saw him struggle to relax them.

"Fix the tea," he said in a raw voice.

The strangled sound and the tight look on his face were enough to make her obey. That and her own embarrassment.

She'd started something he wasn't prepared to finish, and she wanted to duck out of the kitchen and flee down the hall. Instead she mechanically filled the kettle, got two tea bags from the box, and put them into black-and-white mugs.

"Sugar?"

"No thanks." He looked like he wished he were anywhere else as he pulled out the chair farthest from her and sat.

The kettle whistled and she busied herself getting their tea.

Then she scraped out a chair on the other side of the table and sat down, cupping her hands around the mug but not drinking.

"Are you angry with me for asking you to hold me?" she asked, her breath frozen inside her as she waited for the answer.

"No."

"Then what?"

"I'm trying to keep my hands off you," he answered, clamping his fingers around his own mug.

"I thought I made it clear you don't have to do that."

"You've been through a terrible experience tonight. You're not in any shape to make sexual decisions."

"Sexual decisions," she repeated, struggling to keep her voice steady. "That sounds so cold."

When he said nothing, she shifted in her seat. "You and I . . . want each other." That was only a shadow of what she was feeling.

Wanting. Not just sexual wanting. So much more. Needs she was powerless to articulate because she'd never imagined them before.

She saw her own needs mirrored in his eyes. But he kept his hands firmly on the mug of tea.

"I told you that getting mixed up with me was a bad idea. Didn't you call me this afternoon because you had some results of the, uh, karyotyping?"

She sighed, recognizing that he was determined to change the subject—to shift the two of them away from the out-of-control passion of a few moments ago. "Yes, I called about the tests."

He'd been slumped in his seat. He sat up straighter, leaned toward her. "And you found something abnormal?"

"Something strange."

When he sat there, still as a statue, waiting, she went on. "You probably know that the correct number of human chromosomes is twenty-three pairs?"

"Yes."

"You have a twenty-fourth chromosome."

"What the hell does that mean?"

"There are two kinds of chromosome abnormalities, and each can cause major problems," she began, striving for detachment. "There can be defects in the structure of the chromosomes. Or there can be an incorrect number. Each kind of abnormality can result in spontaneous abortions, children who die shortly after birth, mental retardation, abnormalities of sexual development. Down's syndrome is caused by an extra twenty-first chromosome."

"What does a twenty-fourth chromosome do?"

"There are no documented cases of a twenty-fourth chromosome like yours. It simply doesn't happen."

"Except in my family."

"It would seem so."

"And it kills the girl babies."

"Apparently. But the males have some kind of protection against the effects. Which must mean there's some interaction between the protein from the Y chromosome and this twenty-fourth one."

When he nodded, she went on. "But with some males, the protection only holds until sexual development begins."

His eyes were alert, and she could see that he was taking it all in.

"Can you do something about it?" he asked.

"I don't know. I'd love to have a fertilized egg to work with, see what happens if we remove that extra chromosome."

When she realized what she'd said, she pressed her fingers to her lips, looked away.

ON the way home Jack thought about discussing the events of the evening with Laura. Then he remembered Laura wasn't waiting for him on the couch in the living room. Two years, and he still felt like a limb had been amputated. She'd been his wife, his partner. She was the mother of his children, and she would never be waiting for him at home again because some damn drunk driver on I-270 had crossed the median and slammed into her car with enough force to ram the engine block into the front seat.

He gritted his teeth, pushed the awful image out of his mind. There was no point in thinking about it, because it wasn't going to do him any good.

Instead of Laura, his housekeeper, Emily Anderson, was in the living room watching a classic movie channel when he came through the front door. But she switched off the set when he walked in.

Thank God for Mrs. Anderson. She was a sixty-year-old widow with steel gray hair, warm brown eyes, and more energy than a lot of women half her age. For the past eighteen months, she'd occupied the spare bedroom at the end of the hall. She was wonderful with the kids, eight-year-old Craig and his six-year-old sister, Lily.

Jack tried to spend as much time as he could with his children. But sometimes the job interfered. Having Mrs. Anderson made him feel less guilty.

"Another long day," she said, as she bustled into the kitchen and lifted the lid on the pot that sat on a back burner of the stove.

"Yeah." He sniffed appreciatively. "Your Hungarian goulash?"

"Yes. The rice is in the oven."

It was the kind of meal she could serve herself and the kids early in the evening and keep warm for him. The woman would have made a damn good cop's wife if she hadn't been married to an electrician for thirty years.

He opened the fridge, took out the salad she'd set there, and also pulled out a beer. Popping the cap, he took a long swallow.

A place was set at the kitchen table for him. He dropped into a chair, watching her move about the kitchen, getting his dinner. At sixty, she still kept herself trim. If he squinted through half-closed lids and mentally changed her hair color, he could almost make himself believe it was Laura.

"Do you want some company?" she asked, breaking the spell.

"I'd like that."

She set a mug in the microwave, waited for the water to heat, then added a tea bag and joined him at the table.

"So did Craig get into any more trouble with that Dawson kid he was fighting with at school?" he asked after gulping a couple of mouthfuls of stew.

"Not that I know of."

"And what about the math test?"

"He got a B."

"Great."

"He's really working at his grades this semester."

"I know."

They exchanged a meaningful glance. Last semester Craig had been in trouble almost every week—both for academic and social problems. This semester, he seemed to be settling down.

"Lily was picked as one of the painters on the new mural in the school lobby," Mrs. Anderson said.

"I'll bet she's pleased."

"Pleased as punch."

She gave him more information about the kids' day, then he gradually slipped into the old routine of talking about his work—because he still needed an outlet, and Mrs. Anderson was willing to listen.

"I had lunch today with Ross Marshall."

"The guy you call the Lone Wolf? The PI who feeds you information?"

He was surprised she remembered, because he hadn't mentioned Marshall in a couple of months.

"Right. He wanted to talk about a guy he thinks murdered several women in the county."

"And you're going to follow up on it?"

"When he gives me a lead, it's usually solid."

She studied him over the rim of her mug. "But this time you're wondering about it?"

"No." He shifted in his seat. "I went out to take a report from a woman who was almost raped at the biotech lab where she works. Marshall was there."

Her eyes widened. "You mean he attacked her?"

Jack shook his head quickly. "No, he chased the perp away. And it was pretty obvious he and the victim have a relationship."

"You told me he was a loner."

"That's what I thought. But I could see he cares about this woman—and she returns his feelings."

"So why are you still looking so grim?"

There were a lot of reasons. All of them should remain confidential.

But he was sure that Mrs. Anderson never talked about his cases, unless the information was already splashed across the front page of the *Washington Post* metro section.

Still, he had to say, "This can't go any further."

"I'm not going to blab to my bridge group—or anybody else."

"I know. The woman's a doctor who does genetic testing. It seems Marshall came to her because he's got some sort of disease or condition. I don't know what."

"Does he seem healthy?"

"Yes. So maybe he's just a carrier." He cleared his throat. "I was doing a background check on his family. Apparently he had a lot of sisters who died at birth. And some brothers who only lived into their teens."

The lines in Mrs. Anderson's face deepened. "That's sad. It would make a man think twice about starting a family."

Jack nodded.

"How did you happen to be looking into his background?"

"His name came up in another context."

"And you're not going to tell me about it."

He wanted to talk about it. He wanted to lay it all out for her and see what she thought because she sometimes came up with surprising insights. But this time there were simply too many factors, too many variables. More than that, it wasn't ethical to tell his housekeeper that Ross was a suspect in a five-year-old murder. So what he said was "No."

She took another sip of her tea, stared at him assessingly.

"You know I hate it when you give me that look," he said, smiling.

"Well, you've piqued my curiosity. But I suppose that if it's anything significant, I'll end up reading about it in the papers," she said primly.

"Yeah, you will."

17

MAYBE he had slept sometime during the night, Ross thought as he heaved himself off the couch and folded up the blanket Megan had given him.

He'd lain on the narrow sofa, his body radiating heat and tension.

But at least he'd kept himself from going down the hall and opening Megan's door and crawling into bed with her. That had to be some kind of moral victory.

He padded past her door to the bathroom, looked at his hollow-eyed face in the mirror, and rubbed a hand over the stubble on his chin. Although he could see a disposable razor and a can of shaving cream sitting on the edge of the bathtub, he decided it would be presumptuous to use them. Not to mention too intimate, he thought, imagining dragging a razor across his face that had swept up and down the soft, feminine skin of her legs.

But the lure of the shower was too great to ignore. So he found the linen closet, grabbed a towel, and turned on the taps.

The hot water made him feel marginally better. Pulling on jeans and a shirt that were definitely worse for wear canceled out the effect.

Back in the kitchen, he leaned over the sink and peered out the window. It looked onto the street, but he couldn't see much because fog blanketed the area.

Picking up his mug from the table, he used the microwave to warm up the tea he hadn't drunk the night before.

He could hear Megan moving around in the back of the house as he sat at the kitchen table, sipping from the mug.

When the phone rang, she answered in the bedroom. A few minutes later she came into the kitchen, dressed for work and looking upset.

He wanted to hold her again, slide his lips across her hair again. Somehow he managed to keep sitting there at the table as he asked, "How are you?"

"Not great."

He hoped it was because of the phone call—not the attack. "Was that your boss on the line?"

She nodded. "He was in a hideous mood."

"Yeah. Another incident at the lab would do it."

"That. And what I said to the detective. Jack Thornton."

"You mean because you told Thornton somebody had a grudge against the lab?"

She looked down at her hands clasped in front of her. "Walter said he'd talked to me in confidence—that I had no right to bring it up with the police."

"Did you tell him Thornton asked if you could think of any reason for the attack?"

Her hands clenched until the knuckles were white. "I tried to explain what happened. He didn't want to listen."

Her obvious distress tore at him. "The hell with Walter, then."

"Ross, I work for him. It's a small office. It's going to be impossible to do my job if we're having another conflict."

"What other conflict are you having?"

She sighed. "About the way he's distributing the workload. He wants us to concentrate on jobs that will bring in fees. I want to devote more time to my research project."

"You mean the macular degeneration study? Myer's disease?"

"You remembered the name of it?"

"I'm good at details."

"So am I. I don't have any steak in the freezer. But I can give you eggs."

"Eggs would be good."

"Scrambled."

"Fine. Tell me about your project," he requested, partly because he was interested in anything about her and partly because he wanted to keep the conversation impersonal.

For the next five minutes, as she made the scrambled eggs, she filled him in on her progress so far. He sat at the table, enjoying listening to her enthusiasm when she talked about her research, enjoying the efficient way she worked.

"It sounds like you're close to a breakthrough," he said.

"Yes. Are you keeping me talking because the subject is interesting or so we don't have to deal with anything personal?"

He shifted in his chair, sorry she was so perceptive. "Both."

A little smile flickered around her lips, a smile he couldn't read.

She set down the eggs, several pieces of toast, and a jar of blackberry preserves.

He noted that she'd picked his favorite jam without even asking, then cautioned himself not to make anything of it.

They both reached for a piece of toast at the same time, both snatched their hands back, but not before he felt a jolt like an electric shock where his flesh touched hers.

She glanced quickly at him, then back at her plate. In the next few minutes of silence, they both managed to eat some of the food she'd prepared.

"Walter asked me if I was going to stay home today."

"Are you?"

"I'm better off keeping busy." Standing, she scraped the rest of her breakfast into the trash, then put the plate in the dishwasher.

He watched the rigid set of her shoulders, knew she was going to say something he didn't want to hear.

"So when I walk out the door, am I ever going to see you again?" she asked.

"I don't know."

"I want to." She moved to his side, laid her hand over his. No pressure, just a gentle touch, but it was enough to make him instantly hard.

She fixed her blue gaze on him, the color seeming to deepen and intensify.

"I've never felt anything like this," she said in a husky voice.

"Like what?"

"Are you going to pretend you don't know what I'm talking about?"

"I guess that would be a waste of time."

"Yes."

"Why are you interested in a man you know has a genetic defect?" he asked.

"Maybe I can cure him."

"It's too late for me. You can't send a virus to the backs of my eyes and make any significant changes."

"No. But the answer could be just as obvious."

"I doubt it. Besides, I can't change what I am."

Her hand pressed his more firmly. "Ross—"

"Why are you interested in a man who frightens you?"

Her chin jutted up. "You don't."

"That's a lie."

"Okay. Maybe I'm tired of playing it safe."

"Don't be in a hurry to sacrifice yourself to the wolves."

He saw a shiver travel over her skin, but she managed to keep her voice steady. "Don't be in a hurry to throw away something that you know is going to be spectacularly good."

He felt his nostrils flare. Somehow he managed to keep from pulling her body tight against his.

She lifted her hand away, took a step back. "If you're not going to communicate with me, I might as well go."

He ignored the editorial comment and said, "I should leave, too."

She shook her head. "You don't have to clear out because I'm going to work. Just make sure the door's locked."

"You shouldn't trust a stranger alone in your house."

"You're not a stranger." She paused, then said, "There's a package of disposable razors in the medicine cabinet and some toothbrushes I got from a drug company, if you want to use them."

"Okay. Thanks." Although he sat back and stared down at his plate, he was aware of her every move as she gathered up her purse and exited.

When she'd left, he felt more relaxed and at the same time more restless now that she was no longer with him.

He was rinsing off his mug when he heard a car slow down in front of the house.

Had she forgotten something and come back? Anticipation leaped inside him as he leaned toward the window and looked out. It was still foggy, but down by the street, twenty-five yards away, he could see a car had pulled to a stop.

Too big and solid-looking to be Megan's, he decided, and the color was wrong—although it was hard to tell exactly what the color was due to the fog and due to the distance.

The mist also made it impossible for him to see who was behind the wheel. The reverse was apparently not true. Almost as soon as he leaned forward to look out the lighted window, the car started up and sped away.

Had the driver been going to knock on Megan's front door—and changed his mind when he saw a man inside?

Or was the explanation something more sinister? Had someone been waiting for Megan to leave the house, waited until she'd driven away, and then planned to come inside—until he'd seen someone at the window?

All this could be a big coincidence, of course, except that Ross had learned to discount coincidences a long time ago.

His eyes narrowed. He didn't like the implications. Yet there was nothing he could do except turn off the light and sit in the darkened kitchen for a half hour longer, hoping whoever was out there would come back. But no cars pulled up in front of the house. So he went to the bathroom and used the toothbrush and razor Megan had offered him.

DRESSED in his gray uniform, Donald Arnott strolled down the marble walkway at Montgomery Mall. He knew he looked good in the outfit—not like some guys who let their muscles go and their guts hang out. There was even one bozo so pudgy that fat oozed over the top of his belt all the way around his considerable circumference. The jerk needed a new uniform. Or, more likely, a new job. But the mall, like every other public place in Montgomery County, had increased its security staff since September eleventh and the D.C.-area sniper case. And it needed every guy it could get.

Really, it was easy work. And the threat of a terrorist attack gave him the excuse to come down hard on anybody he wanted. Still, the most action he'd seen all week was a couple of girls shoplifting and a woman nursing her baby on a bench. The mother had pulled her blouse up, exposing her big boob for everyone walking by to see. He'd glared at her, letting her know that nursing babies in public was disgusting.

The incident had made him feel energized enough to volunteer for an extra shift when another guard called in sick at the last minute.

He didn't need the money, of course. He'd lucked out on that score six years ago when Arden Mitchner had tried to buy her freedom with money stolen from her drug dealer boyfriend. While Donald waited in the car Arden had hoisted $500,000 of the guy's lean green. Then Donald had taken her home and killed her.

He'd also cleared out of the Fair Hills area and bought his place near Paoli.

When he'd moved to Maryland, he'd made enough profit on the Paoli house sale for a nice down payment on his present property. So he was sitting pretty. Or he had been, until the bastard with the big dog had showed up to try to ruin his life.

He knew the strong emotions churning through him were showing on his face, but he didn't glance around at the mall's lunchtime crowd. Instead he pulled out his walkie-talkie and pretended that he'd gotten an urgent call while he brought himself under control. Then he moved rapidly down to the second-level balcony. When he reached Indulge Yourself, he slowed, feeling his mood lighten. Sandy Knight worked here, and the thought of what he was going to do to her did wonders for him.

Indulge Yourself. What a wimpy name, he thought as he walked through the door. It sounded like a beauty shop or a cosmetics store. But since this was Montgomery County, where the income was one of the highest in the nation, the shop sold expensive toys for adults.

Choice items like three-hundred-dollar leather carry-on bags, brief-cases, key rings with real gold golf tees. Miniature electronics.

There were three or four saleswomen who worked there on a regular basis and a couple of part-timers. Sandy Knight was full time. She came out of the back room when she saw him and smiled warmly at him. She was a bleached blonde who'd probably had her boobs surgically augmented. But the effect wasn't bad, if you liked your women stacked. She was twenty pounds overweight, but her ass was tight. Sandy had told him she worked out a few nights a week at a local gym.

Which made her a challenge. He wanted her. But he'd never taken a weight lifter before. Would she turn out to be so strong that he would have trouble restraining her?

He thought not. But he'd get the cuffs on her right away, just to make sure.

He favored her with an ironic grin. "Sold any ridiculously expensive stuff this morning?" he asked.

She laughed conspiratorially. "One of those overprivileged housewives from Potomac came in looking for something to get her CEO husband for his birthday. I sold her a battery-operated mug that reheats the coffee every fifteen minutes and gives stock market quotations."

He rolled his eyes, shook his head.

"And yesterday evening I showed a guy that five-hundred-dollar watch that does everything but pilot your car. He snapped it up. And he also bought one of those phones where you can download music to a little disk and listen all day. Really, people around here have more money than they know what to do with."

"That's the truth," Donald agreed.

When a customer came in, he moved to the side, then out the doorway, sorry to cut his visit with Sandy short. He was going to take her. But not until he solved his problem.

AS Megan drove to work, breathing in the moldy smell from the rain, she felt sweat pooling in her armpits.

When she'd been a little girl and her father had driven her to school on foggy mornings, she'd sat in the car imagining that the school building might have disappeared into the mist. She played the same game now—imagining that the lab might have disappeared. Because she didn't want to go there.

Last night and this morning with Ross, she'd succeeded in blocking out memories of the attack. But the closer she got to work, the more on edge she became.

By the time she pulled into the parking lot, the freshly dry-cleaned blouse she was wearing felt damp and sticky under her coat.

After shutting off the engine, she sat for a long time, unwanted details coming back to her.

It had been dark and wet. The actual physical encounter had caused a rush of confused sensations. Although she hadn't been able to see her assailant's face or take in many details, there had been something familiar about him. Something. She couldn't say what. Yet she had the feeling she knew him.

Was he the angry client who had come in for genetic testing? Had he been waiting for someone—anyone—to come outside? Or was Walter wrong? Had *she* been the one who'd done the interview, handled the test? And was he now out to get revenge on her as well as the lab?

She tried to tell herself that couldn't possibly be true. Still, doubt tore at her as she sat behind the wheel, swallowing to moisten her dry mouth.

It was too much to cope with—that and the wolf that had haunted her since the last night at Ross's house, she finally admitted with a little inward shiver.

The wolf that had come back to haunt her last night.

When an image of the animal leaped into her mind, she lowered her head into her hands and pressed hard against her eyes, trying to wipe away the picture of the animal. But it stayed firmly in her consciousness.

Ripples of cold traveled over her skin, and she rubbed her hands up and down her arms.

The wolf. The symbol that she was coming unglued.

At Ross's house, the wolf had threatened her. And she'd let herself be convinced that the confrontation had taken place in a dream.

But last night had been different. She'd been attacked. And she'd told that cop, Jack Thornton, that Ross had rescued her, although the image in her mind was of the wolf. Snarling, teeth snapping, chasing away the attacker.

In unguarded moments since the assault, memories of the wolf had nipped at *her* heels. So she'd carefully constructed a cage in her mind to keep him trapped. But she couldn't always keep the door closed. And when it sprang open, the way it had just now, the wild animal leaped out, ready to dig his claws into her mind.

Although she struggled to keep him from prowling through her thoughts, his will was stronger than hers.

The wolf had saved her. Then the animal had disappeared into the darkness of the storm. There was a strange, unreal quality to the way he had appeared and the way he had disappeared that left her dizzy—and terrified.

The rational part of her mind wanted to understand what had happened. But the rational part wasn't in control. Because every time she thought about the lithe gray animal with the bright yellow eyes, she had no choice but to make him go away.

Teeth gritted and eyes squeezed tightly closed, she finally succeeded. Briskly she opened the car door and got out. But she knew the simple act of walking from her vehicle to the lab was never going to feel the same. Her body was strung as tight as a wire by the time she reached the roof overhang. She wanted to rush past. But her legs stopped moving, and she stood stock-still—stared at the place where the man had thrown her to the ground.

Her breath caught. Then she moved on, feeling as if she'd passed some kind of invisible barrier.

Stepping through the door was a relief—until she saw that Betty was staring at her, wide eyed.

She stopped in her tracks, fighting the impulse to back away.

"Oh, God, Megan, the police called last night. Are you okay?"

"Yes," she answered, knowing the high, thin tone of her voice made it sound like a lie.

The receptionist continued to study her as if she were trying to determine the truth of the statement for herself. "I'm so sorry."

"I'm fine."

"You stayed late to work?"

"Yes," she clipped out, hoping to cut the conversation short. She'd never liked being the center of attention, and in this context she liked it even less.

"Do you want to talk about it?"

"I had to talk to the police. I don't want to go over it again," she answered, hoping Betty would drop the subject.

"Is there anything I can do?"

"Let's just get things back to normal."

Betty glanced over her shoulder, lowered her voice to a whisper. "With all the bad stuff happening lately, I'm thinking about looking for a new job."

Megan nodded but didn't say she'd been having the same thoughts.

The receptionist prolonged her agony a moment longer by repeating one of her previous statements. "If there's anything I can do, let me know."

"I will," Megan promised, moving past, wishing she could turn the clock back a day and live the last twenty-four hours differently.

Steeling herself for an even more painful confrontation, she made her way down the hall. To her vast relief, Walter's door was closed. Apparently he was inside licking his wounds. Or he'd gotten his wrath out of the way over the phone this morning.

Like Betty, Hank gave her a long look as she came into their office. But after their conversation the previous day, he didn't press for details she didn't want to give. Thankfully, he went into the lab and left her alone.

Which didn't mean she could concentrate on what she was supposed to be doing. Because she couldn't get her mind off Ross, she got out her notebook and wrote down some of the details of yesterday's test.

Then a kind of numbing lethargy blanketed her. Realizing that she'd never had a cup of coffee that morning, she went to the coffee room and poured a mug.

When she returned to her desk, Walter was standing beside her chair, her notebook in his hand, as he thumbed through the notations she'd been keeping on Ross.

Her little gasp of dismay made him turn and look up.

"What are you doing?" she asked.

"I wanted to have a chat with you about last night's incident," he said, his voice cold and hard and his eyes focused directly on her. He sounded angry. Or was he afraid of something?

She swallowed as he continued to stare, as if trying to pick up some hidden cue.

He didn't say, "I'm sorry you were attacked." He didn't ask how she was feeling. God, was he worried that she was going to sue the lab or something?

After several seconds of nerve-racking scrutiny, he continued. "Then I saw this."

Her eyes flicked back to the notebook. "That's confidential. . . ."

"It's not confidential. It's information about the guy from Lisbon—Ross Marshall. Pretty interesting."

"I wasn't prepared to share it with you yet."

"So I gather."

She set the mug down on her desk, sloshing coffee onto the fake wood surface. Reaching for a tissue, she dabbed at the brown liquid.

"It looks like this guy is pretty amazing," Walter went on. "An undocumented extra chromosome. And he's in good physical and mental health? Why the hell didn't you tell me about it?"

"I haven't exactly had time," she hedged.

"Well, you've got the time now. Give me your impressions. If he's got something that other people might want, like accelerated healing, that could mean big money for the lab."

"He's a private citizen. In the first place, you can't appropriate genetic material from him. And in the second place, it's not something people would want. It causes female offspring in his family to die at birth. And only about half the boys survive puberty."

"But if you could alter the unfortunate aspects, you might have something salable."

"He's not a commodity."

"He came to us. The genetic material we tested is our property."

She had no idea if that was true, legally, but she pretended to know what she was talking about. "I don't think so."

He gave her a hard stare. "I want to see the full report on the cytogenetic analysis you did."

"And if I don't want to give it to you?"

"You don't have a choice. You work for me, and anything you do in this lab is my property."

She wanted to protest, but she knew she was already in trouble over what she'd said last night to the police detective. So she silently cursed her stupidity for leaving the notebook where Walter could see it.

Apparently he considered the matter settled. Turning on his heel, he exited the office, leaving her feeling a mixture of relief, anger, and guilt.

When Walter had seen her notes, he'd gotten off track. He hadn't blasted her for the information she'd given Thornton. But now his interest was focused on Ross, and it was her damn stupid fault.

18

JACK waited until almost noon before bugging Stan Murray, one of the technicians who had showed up last night. Stan worked for an independent lab that handled a lot of the Montgomery County workload. Which made for quicker results than going through the government bureaucracy.

He'd cultivated a friendly relationship with Stan. Still, he knew he was pushing when he asked, "You got anything for me on that attack outside Bio Gen Labs yet?"

"Jesus, it was raining pretty hard out there, you know. If there was any fiber, saliva, skin cells, or hairs from the perp, they're probably in a storm drain on their way to the Chesapeake Bay by now."

"What about the bag of her clothing I gave you?"

"I was waiting for you to ask me that. If I had to guess, I'd say the perp was wearing a raincoat. I do have a little bit of wool fiber."

"From his ski mask."

"There was one thing we picked up from the spot where he threw her to the ground. Dog hairs over near the edge of the building, where the overhang kept some of the rain off. Maybe she was attacked by a German shepherd."

"She said it was a guy."

"Yeah, I guess it would be hard to mistake a dog for a guy. Maybe she was rescued by a Saint Bernard."

"Or she owns a dog."

"The hairs weren't on her clothing. They were on the ground."

"There's a wooded area near the lab. Maybe the dog's a stray, and it was sleeping next to the building sometime in the near past. Or maybe someone who came to the lab for testing left his dog outside. Are you kidding about German shepherds? Saint Bernards? Or do you know what kind of dog hairs?"

"Well, it is something like a shepherd, or a shepherd mix. They're dark gray with light tips. Want me to send them to the FBI?"

"No. Thanks for getting right on this. Let me know if you come up with anything else."

After hanging up, he sat drumming his fingers on the desk, thinking about the attack on Dr. Sheridan. There was something at the edge of his mind. Something that he couldn't quite pull into focus.

Shrugging, he went back to the paperwork on some other cases, sure that if he let the Sheridan thing roll around in his mind for a while, he'd make the connection he was looking for.

HOME again, Ross changed his clothes and fixed himself another rare steak. As he ate, he decided that his leg was almost back to normal. Good news. In contrast to his worries about Megan.

He couldn't stop thinking about the car that had pulled up in front of her house after she'd left for work. Couldn't stop wondering if the attack the night before wasn't what it had appeared to be—a rapist picking a random victim, a woman working late at a lab in an industrial park. What if it had been personal?

He tried to shake that notion. Tried to shake all thoughts of her completely out of his head. After going down the hall to his gym, he picked up a couple of forty-pound dumbbells and started doing arm curls.

When he finished with them, he set the universal gym for leg presses and started on those. Then he went on to push-ups, working until a sheen of perspiration covered his body and his arms were too shaky to lift his weight one more time.

After an hour workout, he showered, then flopped into his office chair, thinking that he was going to catch up on the paperwork he'd promised himself he'd do. After half an hour of staring into space, he decided he might as well go back to Bethesda because it was clear he wasn't going to accomplish anything at home.

JACK pulled out his cell phone and dialed.

"Dr. Sheridan?" he asked when a woman came on the line.

"Speaking."

"This is Detective Thornton. I interviewed you last night after the attack."

"Yes."

"I'm about a mile from your office at the moment, and I was hoping to catch you in."

He heard her voice hitch. "Why?"

"I'd like to ask you a few more questions."

"I wasn't expecting to see you again—I mean, unless you had some information for me."

"Well, what I've found in the past is that when I interview a victim of a violent crime right after it's happened, he or she is usually confused, upset, and running on pure adrenaline."

She gave a nervous laugh. "I guess that's a good description of me last night."

"So I'd like to go over a few details with you now that you've had time to get a little distance. Is there somewhere at the office we can talk?"

She hesitated a minute before answering. "I don't want to talk about it in front of the people here. They've been asking questions, and I just don't want to get into it. Plus . . ."

When she didn't finish the sentence, he said, "Plus your boss said something to you this morning about our previous conversation."

"How do you know?"

"From his attitude last night."

He heard her suck in a breath, then let it out. "Well, I'm not getting any work done." She paused for another moment. "I might as well stop and have some lunch."

He looked at his watch. One-thirty. He hadn't eaten either.

"Do you know the Two Brothers Deli on Rockville Pike?" she asked.

"Yes."

"Could we meet there? In about fifteen minutes?"

He thought about it. A restaurant had its good and bad points for interviewing victims. There were a lot of distractions, although it was past the lunchtime crunch. On the other hand, the setting might help put her at ease.

"Fine." Hanging up, he turned right at the next intersection and started in the opposite direction down the pike, thinking this was his second luncheon meeting in as many days.

As with Ross Marshall, he got there first, found a table in an out-of-the-way spot, and waited for Dr. Sheridan to arrive.

She was prompt. As she came toward him, he noted that she was neatly dressed but frazzled looking. And she hadn't bothered to put on much makeup that morning.

"How are you?" he asked as she took the seat across from him.

"Not great," she answered, picking up the menu and scanning the offerings.

He let her hide behind the lunch selections. "How's the corned beef here?" he asked.

"Good. Lean."

The waitress came to take their orders, and he decided to indulge in a Reuben sandwich. When Dr. Sheridan ordered a bowl of matzo ball soup, he got a cup for himself, as well.

"You like matzo balls?" she asked as the waitress poured them each a cup of coffee.

"They remind me of Mom's dumplings. Where did you acquire the taste?"

"From some of the guys in medical school. I figured today I needed the curative powers of chicken soup." She took a swallow of coffee, as if she also needed fortification before she could talk to him about anything substantive.

"You should watch the caffeine."

"I missed my first cup of the day. Ross doesn't drink it."

"He stayed at your house last night?"

Her color deepened. "On the couch," she said quickly.

He wondered by whose choice. His? Hers? Or were they not as close as they'd looked to be last night? What he said was "I'm not trying to pry into your personal life."

"I hope not."

He'd give a lot to know about her relationship with Ross Marshall.

He reached in his pocket for a notebook, wondering exactly how to play this. Not Spenser for Hire. Maybe he could pull off Detective Marcus Welby.

"If you don't mind, I'd like to go back over the questions I asked you last night and see if you remember any additional details."

"I wish we didn't have to. I'd like to forget about it."

"I understand. But the more you tell me, the more likely we are to catch the guy."

She nodded, looked embarrassed. "There's something I forgot to tell you the other night. You were asking if anyone had a grudge against me or something. Well, it's not a grudge. But there's a doctor from NIH who's been coming on pretty strong to me. He started out acting as if he could help get my project past the roadblock on patient trials of gene therapy. Then I began thinking that his interest was more personal."

"He's threatened you?"

"Not exactly. But he said it would be a mistake to keep avoiding him."

Jack picked up his pen. "What's his name?"

"Dr. Carter Stillwell." She pulled a piece of paper out of her purse and handed it across the table. "I feel bad about making him a suspect."

"Do you think it could have been him?"

"I don't know. I told you the guy wore a mask."

"Could Stillwell have been sitting in his car outside, waiting for you?"

"I guess he could have been. He came to the lab the other day."

"Oh?"

"He'd been trying to get me on the phone—and I hadn't returned his calls."

"He sounds persistent. Thanks for filling me in."

"Please, could you be discreet in your investigation of him? I'd feel terrible if I got him into trouble," she emphasized again.

"You'd feel worse if he turned out to be the perp and he got away with it."

The food came, and they paused for a few minutes to eat.

"Do you remember anything else about the guy last night?" he asked.

She hesitated for a moment. "Nothing specific. But I keep having the feeling that I know him." She shifted in her seat.

"Something that makes you think it's Stillwell?"

She deliberately took another bite of matzo ball before answering, and he was sorry that she could use the food as an excuse for staring down into her plate. "Not specifically Stillwell." She looked uncomfortable, then said in a tentative voice, "Um . . . there's something else I keep thinking about. When Walter said there had been some kind of mistake in a test. I started wondering if it was a mistake I'd made. If it was one of *my* clients."

"Do you often make mistakes?"

"No. But I almost grabbed the wrong tube of blood when I started working on Ross's test," she said as though making a confession.

"So you care about him, and it flustered you."

"I didn't come here to talk about me and Ross."

This time he was the one who flushed. "Sorry."

He thought she was going to switch topics until she cleared her throat and said, "You know each other."

"He and I have worked together on a number of cases. He comes to me with useful information."

She might not have come here to talk about Ross, but she was hanging on his words, so he went on. "We had a meeting about a case yesterday at lunch. He'd called me. So I was surprised to see him again the same evening—in a completely different context."

"A meeting about the killer?"

"What do you know about that?"

"Ross dropped his phone near the killer's place and had to go back for it."

"How did he happen to tell you that?"

"He said that if the guy found the phone, I was in danger, being at his house."

"You mean when you were taking care of him—after he got shot," he said, without missing a beat.

"How did you know that?"

"A lucky guess, actually."

She squeezed her eyes closed. "Damn."

"I'm not going to tell anyone. At lunch he didn't look his usual robust self. I asked what was wrong, and he said he'd picked up something when he was scoping out . . . the killer's place. I got to wondering if he'd picked up a bullet. Did you remove it?"

"He did."

"Ouch."

"The wound got infected."

"And . . ."

"I shouldn't be telling you all this."

"He won't know you did."

"That doesn't make me feel any better about it."

"Do you want to tell me why he came to the lab?"

"No. That's confidential." She spread her hands in front of her. "Please, I'd rather talk about getting attacked—strange as that might seem."

He shifted in his seat, shifted back to the topic that should be the focus of the conversation.

"Okay, let's go over the sequence of events."

She nodded, thought for a moment, and began to speak in a mechanical voice, as if trying to keep her distance from the events of the night before. "I was waiting for Ross after hours at the lab. I heard rain on the roof and realized I needed to close my car window. I grabbed an umbrella and went out. A man attacked me. Ross was outside in his car, waiting for the rain to stop, saw what was happening, and got the guy off of me. I . . . I guess the man escaped because Ross came back to me instead of giving chase."

"That's all of it?"

"Yes."

The response was a little tentative. "What else did you want to add?" he asked.

She hesitated for a second. "I was thinking about the motivation for the attack. At first, it didn't seem sexual. It only got that way after I tried to hurt him. Does that make sense?"

"Can you explain a little more?"

"First he was just hitting me. When I fought back, he threw me to the ground and started pulling at my clothing."

Suddenly she looked as if a lightbulb had gone off in her head. "I scratched him on the neck! I forgot about that part."

"That's a good detail. Something I can look for when I interview Stillwell. Anything else?"

She thought about it—shook her head.

"Okay, after Ross got him off you, then what happened?"

Her gaze turned inward. "I heard a car start. Then Ross was there beside me."

There was something else, something she wasn't telling him. "And Ross couldn't have been the one who attacked you?" he suddenly asked.

Shock and anger flared in her eyes. "My God. No! Why would you even ask that?"

"Some guys like to play hero."

"Ross doesn't play hero. He *is* a hero. As far as I can see, he's risking his life going after a killer. When he went back there the other night to get the phone he'd dropped, he got shot at again."

"He told you that?"

"Yes. And he's had incidents like that before. With some guy named Crawford."

Jack leaned forward. "He told you about Crawford, too?"

"Not much."

"What did he say—exactly?"

"When I got to his house, he was passed out on the floor. He came to and started talking about someone named Crawford. Asking if he'd come back to kill him. He was delirious. I think for a few moments he thought Crawford was there with him in the room."

He'd come back to that astonishing revelation later. For the moment, he asked, "So you're sure Ross wouldn't pretend to ward off an attack to impress you?"

"Are you crazy? Ross doesn't want to impress me. He wishes he'd never met me."

"Why?"

She looked down at her hands. When she spoke, her voice was low and strained. "Because it's obvious we're attracted to each other, and he's fighting the attraction because he's worried about his genetic heritage. And you're taking advantage of my vulnerability to ask me a bunch of questions that are none of your business."

"Yeah."

"So do you have what you need? Because I don't think I can take much more of this."

"I have what I need for the moment."

"Good. Then let me know if you figure out who came after me." She took some bills out of her wallet, dropped them on the table, and walked away—leaving him sitting there flat-footed. There was a lot more he'd wanted to cover. Like asking her about the dog hairs, for example. But now he'd missed the chance.

19

THE fog had burned off, giving Ross an excellent view of the Bio Gen lab as he sat in the Jeep Grand Cherokee. The Sig Sauer .40 that he rarely wore was in a shoulder holster under his arm. When he saw Megan's car come past him, he raised his hand to shield his features under the baseball cap jammed on his head.

He caught only a glimpse of her face as she hurried into the building, but he could tell that she was upset about something.

A deep protective surge of energy flowed through him. He wanted to leap out of his vehicle and go to her, find out what was wrong, and make it right for her But he forced himself to stay where he was, his eyes glued to the door of the lab.

No one else came in or out until forty-five minutes later, when he was surprised to see her emerge again. As she drove out of the parking lot, he followed her back to Old Georgetown Road, then felt his chest tighten when she turned into the parking lot at Montgomery Mall.

Montgomery Mall—where Donold Arnott worked as a security guard.

Megan found a parking spot near Hecht's. He thought about pulling up behind her and yelling at her not to go in. Then a space opened up in the next aisle, and he took it.

When he strode inside, he didn't see her at first, and his heart started to pound. Then he spotted her approaching the fountain.

Quickening his pace, he came up behind her. She must have heard his rapid footsteps, because she stopped short and snapped her head around, her face registering alarm. Then she focused on him, and her features lit up in a smile that burned away whatever resolve he still possessed not to let her get any closer to him.

As he closed the distance between them, he forgot utterly that he'd wanted to tell her a murder suspect was working at the mall. Instead an inane question tumbled from his lips. "Hey. What are you doing here?"

Her smile was still in place. But it had become mixed with an underlying tension. "Ross! I was too . . . . restless to stay at work. I decided some recreational shopping might lift my spirits."

"What's recreational shopping?"

"What women do when they want to give themselves a treat."

He continued to watch her face. "Your boss get on you about your conversation with Thornton?"

"That and some other stuff," she said, her eyes telling him she didn't want to talk about it. "What are you doing here?"

He scrambled for an answer. "I . . . uh . . . lost a pair of binoculars. They're from a store called Indulge Yourself. I thought I'd try to replace them."

"Indulge Yourself. That's out of my price range."

"Yeah. Out of mine, too. Most of the time. But in this case, I'm going for a tax deduction."

He could see her mind working, making connections. "You lost them the night you"—she lowered her voice—"got shot."

He nodded, realizing he had the perfect opening to warn her about

Arnott. After making sure that nobody was close enough to hear what he was saying, he took a step nearer to her. "Something I should tell you. The guy . . . uh . . . the guy you're referring to works here. He's a security guard."

Alarm contorted her face and she looked around quickly before focusing on him again. "Here? You mean he might recognize you?"

Ross managed to hold back a grim laugh. "He won't recognize me. He never saw my face," he said, knowing that Arnott had only encountered him as a wolf. "I was thinking about you coming here alone."

"Should . . . should I leave?"

He thought about that, thought about the women Arnott had killed. They were all similar to each other—and not Megan's type.

"I think you're safe with me. But maybe after this you should, you know, stay away until the case is closed."

She nodded.

"You could come with me to get the binoculars. Then we can have an early dinner," he heard himself saying, because the thought of breaking the contact with her now was simply beyond his power.

Her answer was immediate. "Yes. I'd like that."

They walked along, not touching, but he was very conscious of his hand swinging near hers. He would only have to reach out a few inches to wrap his fingers around hers. Simply thinking about the brush of his flesh on hers sent a bolt of heat surging through him. He kept his eyes directed into the distance so that he would have walked right past the shop if she hadn't stopped.

"Isn't this it?"

He looked at the window. "Yeah."

He let Megan precede him through the doorway. Over her shoulder he saw that the small, dark-haired saleswoman who'd sold him the original pair of lightweight, variable magnification binoculars was behind the counter.

She seemed to know the store's stock, and she'd been helpful with the original selection.

Today her gaze slid from him to Megan and back again, as though she were disappointed that he'd brought another woman into her territory.

Still, her smile was friendly as she asked, "What can I do for you?"

Megan had gone off to examine some of the merchandise featured on Lucite display shelves around the store. While she looked at a phone that was also a portable computer, he turned his attention back to the saleswoman. "Remember those binoculars you sold me a few months ago?"

"The Bausch and Lomb ones? They're top quality. Don't tell me you're having a problem with them."

He felt a sheepish expression creep onto his face. "They were fine. Unfortunately, I lost them."

She gave a small shake of her head. "You lost a five-hundred-dollar pair of binoculars?"

"Yeah. And I want a replacement. Do you still have the same model?"

"We certainly do."

She brought out a pair; he picked them up, turning to look through the lenses at the hand-knit sweaters in the store window across the way. As he adjusted the focus, the knit stitches leaped toward him like they were only a few feet away.

"Yes, these are the ones."

He handed over his credit card and waited while she ran it through the machine.

Five minutes later, he and Megan walked out of the store.

"Did you know they sell a thousand-dollar toilet seat?" she asked in a whisper.

"What's it made out of—gold?"

"Plastic. But the seat's heated. And there are a couple of special . . . attachments. Two different water sprays and something like one of those blow-dryers they have for your hands in some rest rooms."

He laughed. "You're kidding. Right?"

"I couldn't have made it up. My mind isn't that inventive."

"If you say so."

They walked along the second-floor corridor. "We could go to the food court," she said. "That way you can have meat, and I can have a baked potato with cheddar cheese and broccoli."

"Sure."

It was early for dinner, so there were plenty of tables. They each went off to buy food. Megan finished first and was standing by a table partially screened by a bank of greenery, waving her hand, when he stepped away from the counter with his own tray.

He sat, eyed her potato.

"I should buy you dinner."

"Why?"

"You stocked my refrigerator."

A shadow passed across her face. She chewed and swallowed before saying, "You don't owe me anything."

He kept his eyes focused on her until she dropped her gaze.

"Are you worrying about the security guard?"

"No."

"Then what's wrong?" he asked.

She dragged in a breath and let it out in a rush. "I guess you can read me pretty well."

"Reading people is part of the job description."

"Okay," she sighed. "Two things happened today before we met up here. Both of them are my fault. First there was Walter. I was making some notes about your tests. When I came back from getting coffee this morning, he was reading them."

"And?"

"He got excited about writing you up."

Anger flashed through him. "Shit."

Her face contorted. "It's worse than that. He can't decide the best way to exploit the situation. The alternative to fame and glory is keeping you secret and bottling your extra chromosome."

"For what?"

"An extra chromosome usually causes some sort of defect. He could see from my notes that I was impressed with your physique. So he's wondering if there's any advantage to your genetic makeup."

"You told him it kills three-fourths of the children?" he asked.

"I tried to tell him that. He thinks he can work around the problem."

Ross swore again.

"I'm sorry."

"You didn't know."

"I should have been more careful, but I was pretty shaken up this morning." She cleared her throat. "Walter is going through a bad spell because of the break-ins—and because he's looking for ways to bring in more money. When I was out at your house, I had to promise to charge you for private duty nursing. Thank God he seems to have forgotten about that." Looking down at her plate, she picked up her fork and poked at her potato.

"He's likely to be going through a worse spell."

She raised her eyes to his. "What do you mean?"

"I mean, I'm going to have a talk with him and make sure he understands there will be no write-up about my chromosomes. And no exploitation of them, either."

"He—"

"Will follow my advice. I can be pretty effective," he said, his voice low but very firm.

She breathed out a little sigh. "Yes."

He cut off a piece of his cooling steak, chewed, and swallowed. "How the hell did you get mixed up with a bastard like him, anyway?"

"For one thing, I thought he was offering me a good job. And I guess I was looking for a boss who seemed like the complete opposite of my father. I already told you about him."

"Yeah."

"Walter seemed pretty nonthreatening. But since I got to Bio Gen, I've found out there are all sorts of ways to dominate people. I guess Walter uses passive-aggressive techniques. Or he used to. Lately he's skipped the passive mode."

"You could get another job."

"I've thought about it. But there's a catch-22. I don't know whether I can take my research with me. I mean, I've used his equipment. In a way, the lab's been sponsoring me. He told me that work I've done there is his lab's property."

"Was that in your contract?"

"I didn't sign a contract."

"Maybe you need to see a lawyer. Maybe we both do."

SO far it had been a good day for Donald. He'd hassled some kids who were obviously hooking school and made a black guy conform to the no-smoking regulation. The highlight of the afternoon had been hauling a dim-witted fifteen-year-old cunt accused of shoplifting to the mall office and keeping her in custody until the cops arrived— crowding her so that he could feel her breast tremble against his arm as she stood there shaking, waiting for the Montgomery County Police.

He'd gone into a little fantasy, imagining taking her to his secret room, making her confess all the dumb things she'd done, then telling her that what he was going to do to her was punishment for her sins.

Then the police had taken her away. After that he'd amused himself by picking out women and thinking about whether he wanted them.

Now it was his dinner break, which he'd timed to coincide with Sandy's. From a distance she looked so much like his mother that he felt his stomach muscles clench.

Brassy blonde. Too heavy because she loved to stuff her face. He concentrated on arranging his features into a delighted smile as she came out the door of Indulge Yourself.

"You on your dinner break?" he asked.

She looked pleased to see him. "Yes. Cathy is holding down the fort," she said, referring to the little brunette behind the counter.

"It's my break, too. Want to join me?"

"Sure."

They made their way toward the food court, where he got a couple of burgers and she ordered rabbit food—a salad with a few shreds of meat on top. When she caught him staring at her meal with distaste, she hurried to explain. "I'm on a diet."

"Aw, you don't look like you need to be."

"I've been a bad girl."

"You mean in the eating department? Or do you have other vices?"

She flushed. "I was referring to eating."

He tore into his burger. "I like a woman with a few vices."

"Oh?"

He deliberately took another bite of his burger before answering. "I've been wanting to get together with you for a while."

"I'd like that," she answered, making her voice low and sexy before taking a few bites of her salad.

MEGAN leaned toward Ross. "There's something else I should tell you," she said in a resigned voice.

He waited for more bad news.

"Detective Thornton called to ask me some more questions. I didn't want to meet with him in the lab, so I suggested a deli on the pike."

"He'd want to get back to you for details you might not have given him right after the attack."

"He got me talking about you. I probably said too much."

He sat up straighter. "Like what?"

"Like that you'd been shot."

"Shit!"

"He tricked me into it. I'm sorry."

"Tricked you how?"

"Acted like he knew about it."

He nodded tightly. "He's a smart guy. Maybe I underestimated him."

"I'm sorry," she repeated.

"It's his job to get information out of people—any way he can."

Megan still looked so miserable, and he couldn't stand being the cause of the distress. Not when she was already going through a pretty bad time. Reaching across the table, he touched her hand. He should have been prepared for the effect. Or perhaps nothing could have prepared him for the heat that leaped between them.

"Ross," she breathed, turning her palm up, stroking her hand against his. Just his hand on hers, and he was so hard he didn't know whether he was experiencing pleasure or pain.

For long moments, speech was impossible. Whatever he might have been going to ask her about Thornton totally went out of his head. When his brain finally engaged again, he said, "I need to know something else."

She lifted questioning eyes to his, her expression dreamy; he wondered if she was as aroused as he.

With an effort, he managed to ask, "Were you expecting anyone this morning?"

"Expecting anyone? Where?"

"At your house."

"No. What are you getting at?"

"After you left, a car stopped at the curb. When I looked out the kitchen window, it sped away."

She sucked in a breath. "Who was it?"

"I couldn't tell in the fog."

He saw a little shiver go over her shoulders.

"I'm sorry. I wouldn't have mentioned it, but I didn't want to keep you in the dark."

"I appreciate that." Her fingers clamped themselves onto his. "But it doesn't make me want to go home alone tonight."

"Do you want me to come back with you?"

"Yes."

The way she said it, just that one syllable, tightened his body again. He'd stopped kidding himself. Both of them knew what going back to her house would mean.

It was an effort to pull his hand away. They ate in silence then, but he felt the need to hear her voice, to learn everything he could about her. "You said you have a sister?"

"Yes. Dory. She's a couple years younger than I am, and she's still in Boston, where we grew up."

"Is she a doctor, too?"

Megan laughed. "No. She's had a succession of jobs, cocktail waitress being the latest." Her expression sobered again. "And she's gotten mixed up with a succession of men who remind me of our father. I guess the difference between her and my mother is that Dory's prepared to leave them when things get really bad."

"And what kind of men have you gotten mixed up with?"

She flushed. "Not too many. I never had a relationship that went very far. I've always looked for nonthreatening guys. Then it turns out there's not enough substance to make them interesting." She said it forcefully, as if offering him a challenge.

"So I'm not exactly your type," he heard himself saying.

"I told myself you weren't." She raised her eyes to him. "You know how far that got me."

About as far as he'd gotten warning himself away from her.

"Do you want to leave?" he asked, giving her another chance to back away.

She didn't take it. "Yes. Where are you parked?"

"Near Hecht's."

"That's convenient. I'm over there, too."

DONALD took a sip of his Coke.

"Speaking of vices, it's amazing what people come into the shop to spend their money on," Sandy chirped.

He gave her an indulgent smile. "Yeah, you've told me about some of them."

"The guy this afternoon takes the cake. Cathy was waiting on him, but I was in the stock room, and I could see him and his girlfriend. After they left, Cathy told me all about him.

"She said a couple of months ago he bought an expensive pair of Bausch and Lomb binoculars. Top of the line. Five hundred dollars. Then this afternoon, he comes back and tells her he lost them. So he pulls out his credit card and buys a replacement pair. Just like that."

He felt the hairs on the back of his neck prickle. The binoculars he'd found in the knapsack outside the fence were Bausch & Lomb. And he knew they were a damn expensive pair.

Sandy broke into his thoughts. "In fact, there he is over there eating dinner. Him and the girlfriend."

Donald went rigid. "Where?"

"Over there. Behind that bank of plants. It looks like they're getting ready to leave." She inclined her head.

He swiveled around in his seat and saw a good-looking couple—a dark-haired guy and a little blonde.

They got up and walked through the court, their total attention focused on each other. Still, he bent over his hamburger, hiding his face under his cap. Then he looked at his watch. "Hey, sorry, I just remembered, I've got to check on a car that broke down in the parking lot this afternoon. I'll be back in a few minutes."

"No, that's okay. I'll see you later."

He stood, turned, and started down the aisle after the couple, keeping far enough behind them so that they didn't know they were being followed.

They walked through Hecht's and into the parking lot, where they separated.

Pulse pounding, he followed the guy, who headed up a lane and opened the door of an SUV. A Jeep Grand Cherokee.

The license number was DEK 782.

DE—the same fucking first two letters as the SUV that had driven away from his house two nights ago. The same fucking binoculars.

Christ! He felt his heart literally stop—then start up again in double time. He had the bastard—if he could just get a little more information out of Sandy. And if he couldn't, there was always the DMV. Somehow he'd figure out how to get the guy's name out of them.

He went back into the mall and sprinted toward the food court. When he found that Sandy had already left, he bolted up the escalator to Indulge Yourself. She was behind the counter.

"Sorry about that," he said. "I figured I'd better take care of it before the mall closed."

She nodded, looking like she believed him.

He leaned toward her across the counter. "I've been wanting a pair of binoculars like the ones you were talking about. For bird watching."

"They're pretty pricey for bird watching." She reached into the case and brought them out.

He took them from her and turned to look at a sign in the store across the aisle, not really paying much attention to the focus. "Nothing's too good for my hobby."

"I know what you mean. I try not to spend too much on jewelry. But it's such a temptation when you see a piece you want. There's this diamond and ruby pin in Katz's that's just calling to me," she said, like she thought he might jump at the chance to buy it for her.

He managed a noncommittal response, then put the binoculars back and looked around the shop and asked, "Where's, uh, Cathy?"

"She went home when I got back from dinner. Why?"

He gestured toward the binoculars. "These seem okay. But I'd like to ask that guy if he thinks they're worth it. Can you look at the credit slip and give me his name?"

She glanced toward the door, then back at him. "Oh, I couldn't do that. It's confidential information."

He gave her his most boyish smile. "It would be a big help—before I spend that kind of money. I mean, I'm not some fat cat. I have to live on my salary."

When her expression softened, he added, "Please." Jesus, he hated to beg, but he'd make her pay for that later. "I'd really appreciate it."

She hesitated a beat, making him sweat. "Okay. You can stop by tomorrow morning and look."

"Why not right now?" he asked, somehow managing not to shout.

She shot another glance toward the door. "Because my boss comes in sometimes in the evenings, and if he caught me letting someone look at the charge slips, I'd be in big trouble."

He gave her a conspiratorial wink. "I'm mall security," he reminded her. "There's been some credit fraud in the mall, and I need to look at your records."

She managed a nervous smile. "Tomorrow."

He could see that pressing her would be a bad idea. But he was sure of her now. Sure he could get the name. Feeling expansive, he said, "What are you doing after you get off?"

Her face brightened. "I don't have any particular plans."

"What about if we go down to Brennan's? There's a nice crowd there. Music."

"I'd like that. But I'd like to go home and change first. Why don't I meet you around ten-thirty?"

"Great!" He looked at his watch. "I'll see you later, then."

"Yes."

He exited the shop, feeling better than he had in days.

20

ROSS parked in the same spot as the night before, then walked through the darkness to Megan's kitchen door. If someone had leaped out of the bushes and assaulted him, he would have had no warning. The scenery around him was a blur—just the way the mall had been. There was a buzzing inside his head, and his vision had narrowed to the dim triangle of light beyond the doorway.

He stepped inside and saw that she'd turned on the fluorescent light over the sink, so that most of the room was in shadow.

Somehow he remembered to slam the door closed with his foot before reaching for her.

She came into his arms with a sound that was a cross between a sigh and a sob.

"Ross."

He folded her close, held on, trying to bring himself back to sanity. Apparently there was still enough blood in his brain for some of the cells to function.

"I've got to check the house," he managed to say.

Her face was flushed as she lifted it toward him. "Check for what?"

"To make sure nobody's broken in. I think you asked me back here because you were worried about that."

"Partly. And partly it was an excuse." Her voice was high and thick.

He made himself turn her loose, forced his mind to focus on his surroundings as he pulled the Sig .40 from the holster under his arm.

Her eyes widened when she saw the automatic. "Why do you have that?"

"Because I'm supposed to be prepared for trouble."

When he moved toward the dining room, she followed.

"Stay here."

She stopped in her tracks, swaying slightly, and he exited the kitchen, checking rooms and closets before coming back to her.

"Everything's okay." He brushed past her, turned the lock on the back door.

The trip through the house had given him a chance to cool down. "Megan—"

She didn't allow him to finish. "I'm in perfect shape to make sexual decisions."

The buzz was back in his head. Sexual decisions.

"Could you put down the gun?"

"Yeah." He laid it on the kitchen table as if it were a piece of crockery, and she came back to him, holding out her arms.

He walked into her embrace, and everything became sharp, vivid. The scent of her in his nostrils, the scent he remembered from the morning. The feel of her in his arms. The taste of her as he lowered his mouth to hers.

Their lips touched, fused, sealed with heat.

With a small sound she opened for him, and he swept into the warmth of her mouth, his tongue investigating the inside of her lips, the serrated edges of her teeth, the sensitive tissue beyond.

She moaned into his mouth, her tongue no less bold as it found his, then stroked the inner surface of his lips.

A whirlwind coalesced around him, pressing him more tightly to her as his hands swept up and down her back, cupped her bottom, lifting her against his erection.

His mouth never left her. But, finally, like a diver too long below the surface, he was forced to come up for air, his breath rasping in and out of his lungs.

"Come to my bedroom."

He nodded, took a step toward the doorway. The gun registered in his peripheral vision. "Wait a minute."

Her eyes were wide as he snatched it up.

"Can't leave it here," he said, his throat so constricted he could hardly get the words out.

He didn't know whether she was following his logic, whether she understood that anyone looking in the window could see the weapon— use it on them.

PI and lover shot with his own gun.

He abandoned that thought as they stepped into the bedroom. Again the weapon clunked onto a flat surface, this time the dresser, and then he reached for her, clasped her to him, the length of her body pressed to his.

The roaring in his head increased to hurricane force, sweeping away everything in its path but the woman in his arms.

He wanted to see her, wanted everything. Reaching toward the lamp on the dresser, he pressed the switch, sending golden light over her hair, her face, her shoulders.

Mad to feel her satin skin against his, he yanked his shirt over his head, fumbled with the buttons on her blouse. She seemed to be caught in the same wild surge of need as she dispatched the hook at the back of her bra and pulled it out of the way. He tore away the button at her waistband, hearing it ping against the floor.

"Sorry."

She shook her head, helped him shuck off the skirt, her panty hose, and panties.

Naked, she came back to him with a strangled cry that rose to a kind of desperate moan as he clasped her by the shoulders, moving her body so that her breasts swept back and forth across his chest.

He felt the softness of the mounds, the twin points of her nipples. His hands trailed down her back, over her rounded bottom, touching her everywhere he could reach.

Needing to taste as well as feel, he shifted her away from him. Her little exclamation of protest turned into a gasp of pleasure as his mouth closed over one distended nipple.

He drew on her, his body responding to the taste, the texture, the pleasure of her response.

"Ross. Ross. Oh, God, Ross." She chanted his name as she fumbled to open his belt buckle, opened the metal snap at the top of his jeans, lowered the zipper so she could push the jeans away along with his shorts.

When her hand closed around his taut, aching flesh, his brain momentarily shut down. He wasn't conscious of moving. All he knew was that one minute they were standing near the dresser. The next, they were stretched the wrong way across the bed, touching, kissing, exploring each other with a freedom and a passion that overwhelmed him.

He had never needed a woman more than he needed this one. And at the same time, it had never been more important to please his lover as well as himself.

He worshiped her breasts with his hands, his mouth, his teeth, the taste of her driving him close to madness. As his fingers stroked the hot, slick folds of her sex, he watched the tautness of her face, listened to the breath rasp in and out of her lungs.

"Ross . . . now . . . please." She reached for him, her hand firm on his penis as she guided him to her.

His body sank into hers, and he felt completed.

"Oh, Ross," she breathed, her hand lifting to touch his face, her head angling so that her lips could capture his at the moment they became one flesh.

He knew in that instant that he had been alone all his life, and now he had found his mate.

A kind of fierce joy rose in his breast as he lifted his head and gazed down at her.

Her face was radiant, glowing, suffused by passion as he began to thrust himself into her.

She matched his rhythm, clung to his shoulders, climbed toward orgasm with him. The pleasure of it was almost unbearable as he held himself back, waiting for her to reach her climax. And when he felt her start to contract around him, the all-consuming tension exploded into a release that rocked his body, rocked him to his soul.

He didn't have to ask how it had been for her. He had felt it. Sensed it.

He had been made for this woman—and she for him.

She moved her lips against his cheek, clasped him tightly when he tried to shift his weight away from her.

"Stay," she whispered, her hands settling into the place where his spine met his hips as she nibbled her lips against his face. And he felt himself responding to her touch, growing hard again while his body was still joined to hers.

When he raised his head and stared down at her, she grinned, then cupped the back of his head and brought his mouth back to hers, kissed him deeply.

It was incredibly erotic to feel her arousal building again, to feel the small tremors that contracted her inner muscles around him. Incredibly erotic to move his hips just enough to feed the tension building in his own body. Slowly, sweetly until the languid pace suddenly accelerated, and they were racing toward another shattering climax.

Afterward, when he shifted to his side, she let him leave her, but she didn't break their contact completely. Her hand stroked the damp hair back from his forehead.

"You're exhausted," she murmured. "I should have my head examined, taking that much from a man who got shot a few days ago."

"You weren't taking anything. You were giving."

"And taking." She squeezed his shoulder, then slipped out of bed. "Come on, we need to swing around and get under the covers."

The room came back into focus, and he realized they were lying the wrong way across the bed.

While she pulled the bedspread down, he maneuvered his head toward the pillows, then let her cover him. She turned off the light on the dresser but left on the one in the hall.

He listened to sounds from the bathroom, then watched her come back into the room and open a drawer. When she took out a T-shirt, he roused himself enough to say, "Don't. I want to feel your skin next to me."

Silently she put down the shirt, then came back to the warmth of the bed. He pulled her close, needing to feel the length of her body tight against his.

She rolled to her side, her breast pressed against his arm, and he reached out in the darkness, stroking her, feeling her respond to his touch once more. He grew hard again. Wanting her even now.

But he had enough sanity left not to do more than hold her in the darkness as he drifted off to sleep.

21

IT was late. Mrs. Anderson had long since gone to bed, giving Jack a look that said she thought he was working too hard.

He'd told her he'd come upstairs shortly. Instead he'd sunk into the worn leather chair in his office. His thinking chair.

It was the place where he settled when he needed to put together the pieces of a puzzle. Usually that meant he was mulling over a case, trying to fit together motive, means, and opportunity. Tonight he was working on the puzzle of Ross Marshall.

Until the beginning of this week, he'd thought he had a handle on Marshall.

Christ, had it really been only Monday when he'd picked up Ken Winston's old case file from his desk?

It seemed incredible. But there it was.

Purely as a ploy, he'd told Dr. Sheridan that some guys might attack a woman and pretend to rescue her to make themselves look like a hero.

She'd been outraged by that suggestion and had told him heatedly that Ross *was* a hero.

He hadn't exactly thought about Marshall in those terms. Now he leaned back, closed his eyes, and mentally catalogued the kinds of individuals who fed information to the cops.

The reasons varied. Sometimes guilt was the motivating factor. Those were the men and women who came to him on the assumption that providing information in some way atoned for their own sins against society.

Then there were the ones who were greedy for money—who would sell you pieces of other people's lives on a cash and carry basis.

Others were driven by vengeance. They were smarting from some real or perceived wrong, and they wanted to "get even" by ratting out their enemies.

The hardest to deal with were the nuts with a cloak and dagger fantasy who saw themselves as supersleuths fighting crime, corruption, and terrorists, making the world safe for women and small children all by themselves.

They were dangerous—not just to the bad guys but to the public—because there was no telling what they might do to feed their inflated egos.

Another big category consisted of informers he thought of as John Q. Citizen. They wanted to do the right thing, but they were scared to get involved. So when they heard screams outside their window, they were likely to run in the other direction instead of coming to the rescue.

The good news was that they might come forward if pressed—or if their anonymity could be guaranteed.

Ross Marshall was none of the above. Jack pursed his lips, wondering if he'd describe the man as a hero.

One thing was for sure: Marshall believed in what he was doing. He believed in truth, justice, and that "the system" did actually work.

He was every detective's dream source. Knowledgeable, intelligent, professional, completely trustworthy—at least in the dealings they'd had. Although Jack was pretty sure Ken Winston wouldn't agree.

Ross would have probably been a great cop. But there was something that had kept him from taking that route. Something in his background that made him choose to work alone, unless he determined that the only way to clear a case was to give information to the police.

So what had turned him into a loner? His deprived family background? The violent father? His relationship with the long-suffering mother?

Or some defect he saw in his own personality? Something that had caused him to take the law into his own hands five years ago and kill Edward Crawford.

Jack sighed. He was about ready to officially label the Crawford file as a Stone Who Done It—a case that couldn't be solved. Nobody would fault him for that. The evidence suggested that Crawford had been abducting and killing young women. Now he was dead. And there was no proof leading to Ross Marshall as the man who'd put him in the ground—other than that he'd tried to get Ken Winston to take a closer look at the guy.

But what about the current situation? Ross Marshall and Megan Sheridan cared about each other. She'd been attacked.

What would Marshall do if the police—if Jack Thornton—couldn't find the guy who had done it?

Take the law into his own hands again?

He hoped not.

Then there was the tip Ross had given him on Donald Arnott that he'd barely had time to pursue yet. His mind switched gears, and he started thinking about the process he needed to start in the morning. The first thing he'd do was talk with the police in Paoli, Pennsylvania, and find out if the series of abductions and killings up there had stopped when Arnott had moved to the D.C. suburbs.

He was just making a note about that on the pad he carried in his pocket when a noise in the doorway made him look up.

A small figure in a white nightgown stood with one hand clutching the doorjamb. "Daddy."

Lily's face was pale. Tears streaked her cheek.

"Honey, are you sick? What's wrong?"

Her lower lip trembled. "I had a bad dream."

"Come here."

She scurried across the room toward him; he scooped her up, cradling her in his lap.

Her head rested against his chest, and he stroked the soft blond hair that he loved so much. Her mother's hair.

"Can you tell me about it?" he murmured.

"A bad man was chasing me," she whispered, the last word breaking on a sob.

He stroked his hands through her hair, over her shoulders, rocking her. "It's okay. Daddy has you."

She pressed her face against his shirt, turning the fabric damp with her tears. When the flood subsided, he murmured, "Do you want to tell me any more about it?"

"I was running through the hallways at school, trying to get away from him; and every time I thought I got away, there he was again—in front of me." She gulped. "Then I woke up, and I was scared to be in my bed alone. I looked for you in your bed, but you weren't there."

"I'm sorry. I was working late. I'm glad you came downstairs and found me," he answered, continuing to rock her.

"I miss Mommy," she said in a small voice that stabbed at him.

"I do, too, honey."

"If Mommy were still here, you would have been upstairs in bed with her. And I could have gotten in the middle, the way I used to do."

His throat clogged. "Yeah," he answered.

"Can I get in bed with you now?"

He ran a hand through his hair. Christ, was it okay to let a six-year-old girl get in bed with her daddy? Some psychology book would probably give him the answer. Or the family counselor they'd all seen after Laura had been killed.

The answer was probably no. But right now he knew that his daughter needed to know he was there for her.

"I'll come up and lie in your bed with you for a while," he said, standing and shifting her weight so he could carry her up the stairs.

She pressed her face into his neck. "You won't ever go away," she whispered. "The way Mommy did."

"No, I'll never go away," he said, clutching her to him as he climbed the stairs. "Tell me about that painting you're doing in the school hallway."

She snuggled against him. "It's really neat. One thing I get to paint is a cat. Any cat I want. I want to do a gray one—like Mrs. Williams has."

DONALD Arnott leaned against the bar, pretending not to watch the door. But he knew the moment Sandy walked in. Once again it struck him: she could be a carbon copy of his mother, the whore who would spread her legs for any guy, as long as he had the money to pay. When he was a kid, there'd been too many nights when he'd lain on the sofa in the living room, listening to her with some john in the bedroom, both of them so loud it was a wonder the neighbors didn't start banging on the walls.

That had ended abruptly when he was eleven, when one of her low-life fucks had climbed out of her bed and come after him in the morning, thinking he was going to have a little dessert—of the kiddy variety.

Donald had brained the bastard with a lamp. And good old Mom had turned him over to the juvenile authorities. He'd gotten even with her by blabbing about her lifestyle to anyone who would listen. That had kept him out of the detention center—and put him in the foster care program. Which wasn't great. But it was better than life with his slut of a mother.

They'd told him she died of cancer of the liver. He hadn't given a shit about it.

Sandy crossed the floor. In the dim light he could see that she'd frizzed out her hair, put on too much makeup, and wiggled into a red dress that looked like a second skin.

Jesus. What a sight. The first thing he was going to do when he strapped her to the wooden table in his secret room was wash the makeup off her face with paint thinner.

But he wasn't going to get a chance to do that tonight. Tonight he was going to have to be on his best behavior.

So he gave her a wide smile. "You look sensational."

She smiled back, patted that Day-Glo hair. "Why, thank you."

"So what can I get you to drink?" he asked expansively.

"White wine."

Woman's wimp drink. He signaled the bartender and inquired about the house wines. She picked a chablis. When it arrived, he suggested that they repair to a table in the corner.

"So are you from around here?" he asked.

"No. I'm from Michigan."

"What brings you to the D.C. area?"

"There was nothing to hold me in Kalamazoo."

"No boyfriend?"

Her face contorted. "I was married to a real jerk. But that's all in the past."

"Well, I'm glad you're free, white, and over twenty-one."

She took a sip of her wine. "You're the most interesting man I've met in a long time."

"Oh, yeah? How come?"

"You're not what you seem."

That brought a little spurt of alarm. "What do you mean?"

"You've got hidden depths. I know there are things below the surface that you don't show to everyone."

"Good things?"

"Of course."

He relaxed a little.

"You told me about your bird watching."

"Yeah," he improvised. "I have lots of different types of feeders—to attract the different species."

"Oh—which kinds?"

"Uh, robins, cardinals, sparrows."

"I didn't think robins came to feeders."

"Well, I've got special stuff for them. From the Wild Bird Center." He dredged up the name from an ad he'd seen in the local paper. What a waste of time, spending money on birdseed. But Sandy seemed enthralled. "But I'd rather talk about you."

"I'm not that interesting."

"Oh, don't be modest. You're a very charming woman." He lifted her arm, played with the gold and diamond bracelet around her wrist. "This is so pretty," he gushed, trying not to throw up as he said it. "I love your taste in jewelry. Where did you get it?"

He got her talking about clothes and jewelry while his hand dropped to her knee under the table. Smiling at her, he caressed the knee, her leg, working upward to her thigh. That wasn't difficult under the short tight skirt. The problem was the damn panty hose. He hated panty hose.

He would have liked to rip them off. Instead he smiled and made appropriate responses to her inane chatter.

"Let's go back to your apartment," he finally said in a husky whisper.

Her eyes turned cautious. "I don't know you well enough for that."

"Yeah. I guess you're right," he said immediately. "Come sit with me in my car for a little while before we both have to go home."

She hesitated for a moment, then agreed.

He led her to the Land Rover he'd parked in a dark corner of the lot, opened the back door so they could sit on one of the bench seats.

He reached for her, kissed her, turning himself on by thinking about the metal ring riveted to the back of the seat—and what he was going to do to her after he got her where he really wanted her.

He amused himself by seeing how far he could get with the slut, pawing her breasts, reaching under her skirt. Getting her to shuck off the panty hose so he could stroke her cunt.

Because he still needed that credit slip, he made her come with his fingers, gritting his teeth at the disgusting sounds of pleasure she was making, keeping himself hard by focusing on his power over her. Then he told her that if she cared anything for him the way he cared for her, she wouldn't leave him hot and bothered.

When he opened his fly and took out his swollen cock, she reached for him, probably thinking she was going to get away with a hand job. But he took her head between his palms, pulled her mouth down to his rod, and got her to suck him off. Then he watched in amusement as she fumbled in her purse for a wad of tissue so she could spit out the cum.

When he got her back to his underground room, she was going to swallow it. For now he was satisfied that he'd gotten her to suck him off in the backseat of a car in the parking lot of a bar—proving what he'd known about her all the time. She was a slut. Just like all the women he'd punished.

But he kept a sincere look in his face as he thanked her. Acted tender and appreciative. Told her how much he wanted to see her again.

And when they went their separate ways that evening, he was feeling better than he had since he'd shot the dog.

22

IN the morning, reaction set in. Ross knew what he had done. Knew that at least some of what his father had told him had been right—about the selfish greed of the mature werewolf.

He had come to Megan's house with no other thought in his head besides fucking her. He had done the deed—twice. And the thought hadn't even entered his mind that protecting her from pregnancy would be a smart idea.

Jesus—what if he'd started a baby growing in her last night when he'd been thinking about nothing but his own pleasure? What if she were carrying a girl child?

He felt as if a raw, hollow place had opened up in the center of his chest, the pain seeping outward to every part of his body. Megan could soothe the terrible ache. Only Megan.

Last night . . .

Last night had been incredible. Thinking about it made him long to reach for her and see that smoldering look in her eyes again. But instead of letting his own needs take control, he eased away, made it down the hall to the bathroom and stood staring at himself in the bathroom mirror.

The face that looked back sickened him. He'd been kidding himself for the past five years—following some kind of half-baked moral code to make himself feel better about Crawford. But he had no right to think of himself as a moral person.

A werewolf had no morality. He was an animal—who followed his own selfish impulses. And maybe phases of the moon. Or maybe he could shift the responsibility to his genes, he thought with a snort. Maybe the things he did were only what his genes commanded him to do.

He turned on the water, stepped under spray hot enough to sting his skin. But a shower couldn't wash away the feeling of disgust, although he stood under the hot water for a long time.

Then he dressed and quietly slipped back into the bedroom to retrieve his gun and jam it back into his shoulder holster.

The blinds were closed, and the room was still dark. Standing a few feet from the bed, he looked at Megan, feeling his heart turn over in his chest. She looked so peaceful, so trusting. But what if someone had come into the house last night and attacked her?

He wouldn't have been able to do a damn thing about it because he'd been too focused on what they were doing in bed.

His nerves strung as tight as piano wire, he backed out of the room and walked to the sliding glass door in the living room. The need to escape building in his chest like a bomb about to explode, he shed the clothing he'd just put on, leaving everything in a heap on the floor as he unlocked the door and stepped into the gray light.

He was a wolf. That was his true nature.

He had the presence of mind to glance around, note that the houses on either side of Megan's were screened by tall trees and that the back of her property bordered a wide stretch of greenery—perhaps a park.

But checking to see that he wasn't being observed was only perfunctory as the words of transformation sprang to his lips. This morning he welcomed the pain of bones crunching, muscles jerking, cells transforming from one shape to another.

Dropping to all fours, he streaked away, heading toward the trees that bordered the backyard.

* * *

MEGAN woke, then smiled as she remembered the incredible night with Ross. Sleepily she reached out to touch the man who had transported her to another plane of existence.

Until last night, he had resisted her. Resisted the sense of connection growing between them. But when they'd finally come together, their union had been glorious. Not just sex. Something more that she'd never believed could exist. Her essence merging with his while they danced together in a magic world where only the very lucky were admitted.

A small pang gripped her when she found the bed empty. Her eyes blinking fully open, she turned to stare at the impression his head had left in the pillow. He had been here. It wasn't a dream. He was gone now.

Gone away? Impossible. Not after last night. He must be somewhere else in the house.

Struggling to contain the feeling of uneasiness that tugged at her as she slung her legs over the side of the bed, she crossed to the closet and slid into the bathrobe hanging on the back of the door.

In the bathroom, she saw that he'd taken a shower not very long ago. "Ross?" she called.

When he didn't answer, she headed down the hall toward the living room.

The drapes were still closed, but she could see them blowing back and forth, telling her the window must be open. She never left the sliding glass door unlocked. So he must have stepped outside.

In the dim light she saw something on the floor by the window. A pile of clothing. The clothing Ross had worn the night before. And his gun.

Her brow wrinkled. He'd gotten dressed this morning, then taken off his clothing by the back door. And gone outside.

Against her will, her mind streaked back to another time when she'd found an open window, an empty room. His white shorts on the floor of his bedroom.

And outside . . .

Her body went stock-still, and a terrible wave of cold swept through her, all the way to the marrow of her bones. She didn't want to discover what was out there. But an invisible force had grabbed hold of her and was pulling her toward the window. On legs that felt like wood, she stumbled forward, her movements jerky as she pushed aside the drapes and stepped onto the patio.

For a brief moment, she saw nothing but her backyard looking just the way it had looked the day before, and some of the terrible tension eased out of her. It was all in her imagination. All the smoldering anxiety that she was terrified to put into words.

In the next instant the feeling of relief was ripped apart. She saw a flicker of movement at the edge of the trees. Against her will, her gaze riveted to the spot. And as if she'd stumbled from sleep into a nightmare, she saw the gray wolf emerging from the woods, his silvery pelt catching the first rays of the sun, his ears alert and pricked toward her.

The wolf was *here*, her mind screamed.

Immobilized by a soul-deep fear, she watched the animal move toward her. Eyes fixed on her, he closed the distance between them until he was standing less than six feet away.

Her heart was pounding so hard in her chest that she could barely breathe as she stared into his brilliant yellow eyes—eyes that she'd thought held intelligence beyond that of a mere animal.

Human intelligence.

And in that one shattering moment, she knew what her mind had shut away—what her intellect had refused to believe when reality was too terrible to contemplate.

The wolf was Ross!

Even as the thought grabbed her by the throat, she rejected it.

Impossible.

But it came slamming back with a force that physically knocked the breath from her lungs.

Ross was the wolf.

The man who had made incredible love with her last night.

Ross. The wolf.

The first time she had seen the animal, he had threatened her, his muzzle smeared with blood from the kill. He didn't threaten her now. Not physically. He only threatened her sanity.

A sob rose in her throat as she turned and stumbled back through the door.

Shaken, feeling as if she'd been torn into shreds, she backed away from the door, crashed into a low table, and cried out as pain shot through her leg.

Making it no farther than the couch, she collapsed and huddled into herself, her thoughts scattered, fragmented.

She wanted to look away, but her eyes were drawn to the curtains.

Maybe she had been mistaken. Maybe she had somehow made it up.

Just the way she'd made up the other two encounters. Then the curtains moved, and a shaft of sunlight pierced the darkness of the room.

He was coming in. But who? The wolf or the man?

Her breath heaving in jagged gasps, her arms wrapped around her shoulders, she waited.

Then Ross, the man, walked back inside. Naked.

A kind of frozen calm came over her as she stared at him. She should be frightened. She should be angry. But all she could feel was a thousand-pound block of ice compressing her lungs.

The terrible cold held her fast, froze her emotions, leaving her rigid as a statue carved from snow.

Ross stared at her with the same rigid calm, and she sensed that he was working to contain emotions as searing as the ones she felt.

Mechanically he pulled his clothes on. Strapped on his shoulder holster. Afraid that he might come closer, she watched him warily. But he stayed where he was by the wall, regarding her with his dark eyes. Eyes so like the yellow eyes of the wolf.

Why hadn't she seen that before?

Because she hadn't wanted to. Perhaps that was her fault. But he was the one who had hidden the truth.

"You lied to me," she whispered, feeling as if the two of them were confronting each other in the eye of a hurricane. In a little while, the storm would rage again. For the moment, the air around them was clear and calm.

"I never lied. I told you there was a genetic problem in my heritage. You told me I have an extra chromosome. Now you know what it does."

"You let me think that I was going crazy. You let me think I imagined the wolf."

"Are you better off now that you know?" he asked with maddening calm, then continued in the same flat voice. "I was trying to save you. My father told me that by the time I was thirty, I'd start looking for a mate—that I'd bond with a woman, and neither one of us would be able to resist the other—because the werewolf is programed to perpetuate his genes. I told myself that wasn't going to happen to me. To make sure it didn't happen, I started keeping to myself. Then you found me naked and wounded. And I had no control over the situation. You touched me, took care of me, and you're seeing the results." His Adam's apple bobbed. "But maybe it's not too late for you. Maybe if I just walk away now, you can go on with your life and forget about last night."

She tried to take in what he was saying, even as he gave her one last regretful look. Then he turned and exited through the door where he'd come in.

In that moment, the ice that held her fast shattered. She fought for breath, felt the searing pain in her chest—in the very depths of her soul. A cry welled in her throat, a cry of loss and rage. Curling into herself, she raised her arms and cupped them over her head, trying to protect something inside herself that was weak and vulnerable. Yet deep within her she knew that it was already too late.

HER cry of anguish pursued Ross as he staggered toward his car, wrenched open the door, slid inside, then fumbled with the key, his hands so numb he could barely push it into the ignition. He had held himself together long enough to say a few words to her. Then he'd fled, trying to escape pain greater than any he could have imagined.

Finally he succeeded in starting the car. Yanking the vehicle into reverse, he lurched backward down the driveway, almost plowing into a tree near the street.

Hardly knowing what he was doing, he whipped into first gear and roared down the road.

The blacktop in front of him was a blur, overshadowed by the picture in his mind of the horror on Megan's face when she'd finally figured it out. Figured out that the man she had made love with last night was a monster.

A monster who felt as if his heart had been ripped from his body. Because until he had seen that look on her face, he hadn't truly understood what it was to suffer the tortures of the damned.

His hands fused to the wheel, he drove on. He was several miles from Megan's house when he realized he was driving home. To his refuge. Díthreabh. Where he could lick his wounds.

What had happened was for the best. She'd stumbled upon the wolf when she'd been unprepared and vulnerable. And now she was in shock. But in some deep, unselfish part of himself, he knew she would come to understand what she had escaped. She had saved herself. The woman he loved.

The woman he loved. The phrase played over and over in his mind, and he understood what had eluded him until this moment.

If a man like him could love—then he loved her. But it didn't change anything. His love was tainted by his nature—by the genetic heritage he could never escape. He was a werewolf, helpless to stop himself from repeating the cruel behavior patterns of his kind. To keep his mate pregnant, bearing a succession of children who were doomed to die—or doomed to live the savage life they could never escape.

Rationally he knew that Megan was infinitely better off without him. In his heart he was sick unto death.

MEGAN tried to stand, found her legs were still too wobbly, and simply collapsed back against the cushions.

Lowering her head, she buried her face in her hands, her brain too stunned to cope with reality.

Last night, making love with Ross had been the most wondrous experience of her life. This morning, he had shattered her world.

"Ross." Megan spoke his name, not knowing if it was a plea or a prayer or perhaps a curse.

She wanted to cry. She wanted to scream. She wanted to pound the walls with her fists. She did none of those things, only huddled on the sofa, her mind in turmoil as bits and pieces of the past few days came back in flashes.

The books on his shelves. Fairy tales. Myths of night stalkers—vampires and werewolves.

His love of the woods.

His extraordinary recuperative powers.

His secrecy. The way he'd warned her to leave. The way he'd struggled to distance himself from her.

She should have been smart enough to listen to him.

A sound bubbled in her throat—something between a sob and a hysterical laugh.

She'd thought she was going crazy. Seeing the wolf. Having no explanation besides the phantoms of her own mind.

There had been no rational interpretation. Nothing she could have accepted until she'd seen it for herself.

FROM a doorway down the aisle, Donald watched Sandy open the shop. She was dressed for business again, in one of her outfits that looked only slightly less trashy than what she'd worn the night before.

On the drive home, he conceded that he'd made a mistake. He shouldn't have had any sexual contact with her until he'd resolved the problem with the binoculars guy. Now he was going to have to tread carefully.

So he did a couple of circuits of the mall before coming back to the shop.

She was alone in the store and behind the counter when he stepped through the door. Her head shot up when she saw him, and he could see her expression was guarded.

"Hi," he said. "I've been thinking about you since we parted. Wishing we hadn't been in a car, wishing I could have cuddled more and showed my feelings better."

She gave a little nod, and her features relaxed somewhat.

"I want to see a lot more of you."

"I don't exactly feel great about last night."

"I know, baby. And I'm trying to apologize for rushing you into stuff you weren't ready for."

"I wasn't."

Sure, he thought. *Wait till I rush you into something you're really not expecting.*

"So I was hoping you'd let me buy you lunch," he said. That hadn't been on his mind at all, but he figured it couldn't hurt.

"Okay."

He cleared his throat. "Do you have that credit slip for me to look at?"

She looked toward the door. "No."

He struggled to keep the anger out of his voice. "What do you mean, no?"

"I can't let you see the slip. That's against company policy."

Before he could reach across the counter and shake her, she said, "But I can tell you his name. It's Ross Marshall."

He felt the awful tightness ease in his chest. "Ross Marshall. There probably aren't a lot of guys with that name."

"Yeah."

"Sandy, I really appreciate this. I really appreciate you," he added for good measure.

"I just hope my boss doesn't find out."

"How could he—unless you tell him."

"You're right." She pressed her hands against the counter. "I'm off at eleven-thirty for lunch."

He made his features register disappointment. "I'm working until one. So that's not gonna work. We'll have to do it another day."

"Yes. Okay."

"I'd better get back to work, before I lose my job."

She nodded, and he left—then headed straight for the hallway with the telephones and the rest rooms. Choked with excitement, he looked up Ross Marshall in the phone book.

He wasn't listed in the white pages, and Donald's heart plummeted. Shit!

Ordering himself to calm down, he tried information. This part was tricky, now that the system was more automated. So he told the recorded message that he was from out of the area and looking up an old school friend. In the middle of the explanation, a real live operator came on the line; he told her that he wanted to make sure he'd located the right Ross Marshall.

"I have a listing for a Ross Marshall, private detective."

A private detective! Jesus. It was several seconds before he could drag in breath enough to speak. "Could you just read me the address so I can see if it's familiar?"

"Eighty-five seventy-two Stony Brook Lane," she told him.

"Yeah. That sounds right. Thanks." He wrote it down and hung up, feeling light-headed.

A private detective. With a dog. Investigating him!

Well, so fucking what? He didn't have any proof of anything. The dog hadn't come back with a report about the grave.

It was his word against the bastard's. Now.

Soon the bastard was going to be dead.

His next stop was the bookstore, where he consulted one of those detailed street maps. Stony Brook Lane wasn't in Montgomery County. It turned out to be in Howard County, off Route 99.

Was it really him? It had to be. He'd seen the guy's SUV last night, with the same first two license-plate letters as on the SUV from the second time the bastard had come visiting with his damn dog.

He made another circuit of the mall, his mind whirling. When he passed a guy lighting up a cigarette, he didn't even stop to chew him out.

He couldn't keep his thoughts off Ross Marshall. Couldn't suppress the excitement surging through him with the hum of an electric current. It was almost like the way he felt when he got a woman in his car, handcuffed and scared shitless. Almost sexual.

He was breathing hard. His face was flushed. And he knew he couldn't spend the next five hours prowling the walkways of this stupid mall.

Changing directions, he went down to the office, told the dippy little secretary he must have picked up a stomach virus and that he was taking sick leave. Then he went to his locker, got out his coat, and started for his car.

MEGAN sat on the sofa for a long time, unable to rouse herself. Finally, to escape the pain and misery, she pushed herself up and staggered down the hall and got dressed. But once she'd slipped into the car, she wasn't sure where she was going.

Work?

A sound of denial bubbled in her throat. Betty would see she was still upset and try to get her to talk about it.

Another hysterical laugh bubbled up. She couldn't talk about this with Betty. Or anyone else.

Hank would still be wondering what was wrong. He'd slide her questioning looks, but he wouldn't say anything. Walter would still be angry. And God knows where that would lead.

Because if she told any of them what had happened this morning, they would think she had lost her mind. Funny, that's what she'd been thinking herself. Now she knew she was completely sane. As sane as she could be after last night and this morning.

At first she drove aimlessly. But when she found herself near an entrance to Montgomery Mall, she pulled into the parking lot.

She wasn't sure what she was doing there. But she didn't have any better ideas, so she found a parking space and started toward the main entrance.

She was marching up the aisle toward the door when she stopped in her tracks, suddenly remembering what Ross had told her yesterday.

Yesterday, before he'd shattered her life.

She shook her head, refocusing her thoughts. Ross had told her the killer worked here. That he was a security guard. Which meant that hanging around the mall was probably a bad idea.

BECAUSE he couldn't bear the four walls of the house pressing in upon him, Ross fled into the woods. Not as a wolf. Not after the encounter with Megan that morning.

Stopping beside an oak tree, he ran his fingers over the rich brown bark of the trunk, pressing his flesh against the narrow ridges.

Even in his human body, this place always had the power to calm him. But today the pain was simply too great.

Once again he saw the look on Megan's face—the look when she understood that he was the wolf. His whole body ached from the horror he had seen in her eyes. Suddenly unable to stand erect, he folded in the middle, wrapping his arms across his stomach to hold back the pain.

He stayed that way for a long time—unable to do more than fight the sense of loss. He didn't know how he would get through the next few minutes, let alone all the long lonely years that stretched ahead of him.

Jaw clenched, he forced his mind away from his own misery. At least there was one good thing that had come out of the meeting of wolf and woman this morning. It had saved her from a future of sorrow. A future with a man who would take out his savage nature on his family as surely as he would on his enemies.

But there was still the present to deal with. He had managed to save her when she'd been attacked. Yet she might still be in danger—and that possibility twisted like a dull blade into his guts.

Infused with a sense of purpose, he began to think about the car that had stopped in front of her house the other morning. What if the bastard was coming back?

But why had he been there in the first place?

Because he was planning to search for something? Or because he'd found out her address and was stalking her?

He looked at his watch. She should be at work—if she'd managed to make it to work after the scene in her backyard this morning.

Trotting back to the house, he changed into fresh jeans and a T-shirt and made a few quick preparations. Then he jumped into the SUV and headed back toward Megan's house.

DONALD was about to push open the door when he stopped short.

It was *her*. Coming toward the mall. The little blonde who'd been having dinner with the Ross Marshall guy in the food court the night before.

About twenty yards from the doorway, she abruptly stopped walking. Jesus, had she seen him? Did she know who he was? The questions swirled in his head as she turned and rushed back through the parking lot.

It wasn't because of him, his mind screamed, even as he felt sweat break out on his forehead.

Should he go after her? Get back inside? What?

Opting for action, he bolted through the door, then hung back as she got into her car, a cheap little green Toyota.

Because he couldn't risk her spotting him, he couldn't get close enough to read her license plate. Too bad his Land Rover was half a block away. He jogged over to it, and by the time he made it back to the area where she'd parked, she was nowhere in sight.

Shit!

Making a split-second decision, he took a guess at what exit she was using and roared up a row of cars.

At the Democracy Boulevard light, he spied her stuck in a line of cars.

Dodging around a Volkswagen, he joined the line, slipping past a dumb as mud woman who was trying to make a left turn. By the time the woman in the Toyota was a quarter mile down Democracy, he'd caught up.

Yes! This was his day. Nothing could go wrong.

Being careful to hang well back, he followed her toward Bethesda. Before she reached the downtown area, she turned onto Conway Street, and then into an industrial park. He stayed several car lengths behind, waiting for her to get out of her car. But the bitch was just sitting there. What the hell was she doing anyway? Eyes narrowed, he pulled into a parking slot a dozen yards down the row.

23

JACK hung up the phone, made some notations on a lined pad, and put them in the new folder that he'd started.

He'd already ascertained that a Donald Arnott had worked at King of Prussia Mall in Pennsylvania for four years and that he'd resigned eighteen months ago.

According to his performance evaluations, his work had been satisfactory but not outstanding.

Then, pretending to be doing a credit check, Jack verified that Arnott had joined the security force at Montgomery Mall twelve months ago.

With the man's employment established, he put in a call to the Paoli police department. After identifying himself as a Montgomery County, Maryland, detective working on a local murder investigation that might dovetail with women missing from the Paoli–Valley Forge area, he was put through to one of the guys in the squad room, a detective named Paul Carmichael. Carmichael confirmed that a number of women had disappeared from the area without a trace, at three- or four-month intervals. Luckily, the abductions seemed to have stopped—indicating that the perp was either dead or had moved away or had been jailed for another crime. The detective couldn't, however, give Jack an exact time frame without checking back through old case files. But he promised to call back after he had a chance to check.

Jack added Carmichael's name and number to the file.

There was still nothing concrete to link Arnott to the Pennsylvania disappearances or to any in Maryland, for that matter. But the local problem had started after he'd moved here.

His next step was to check out the case files of the women whose names Ross had given him.

Penny Delano. Charlotte Lawrence. Lisa Patterson. Cindy Hamilton. Mary Beth Nixon.

Apparently nobody had studied the cases with an eye toward determining whether one man had abducted and murdered them all. But as soon as Jack saw their pictures, he started getting excited. They were all blondes with flashy clothes. All a little overweight. All between the ages of twenty-five and thirty-five. All from working-class backgrounds. And their addresses made it likely that they had frequented Montgomery Mall.

He had just closed the Arnott folder when his mind made a leap to another subject and served up a connection he'd been unable to make the day before. Reaching for the stack of case files on his desk, he shuffled to the bottom and found the Crawford file. Inside, he turned to the crime scene report from Frederick County.

He found what he was looking for near the bottom of the text. There hadn't been much physical evidence found with the body. But the technician had noted the presence of dog hairs. From a shepherd or a shepherd mix—dark gray hairs with light tips.

Like the dog hairs that had turned up where Megan Sheridan had been attacked.

When he'd first looked through this folder, he'd felt an unaccustomed sensation of cold travel across his skin. He felt it again. Christ, maybe he should have Stan send the dog hairs to the FBI after all. And see if he could get Frederick County to do the same.

And what did he expect to find? That the hairs were from the same animal?

Which would mean what—exactly?

ROSS slowed as he approached Megan's house. There was no car in the driveway.

Good. She'd gone to work after their confrontation this morning. And if there was any way in hell he could help Thornton find out who had gone after her, he was going to do it. Including invading her privacy, searching her house.

He drove at a moderate pace down the street, taking a look at the neighborhood. The houses were wildly spaced, and judging from the lack of cars, it appeared that most people were at work. Anybody taking note of him would see a man delivering a package. He pulled in front of her house and set a brown-visored hat on his head that matched the bomber jacket he was wearing.

Retrieving a cardboard box wrapped in brown craft paper from the passenger seat, he pretended to check her address, then walked up the driveway to the side door. Pulling a set of burglary picks from his pack, he went to work on the lock.

It took almost no effort to get inside.

Christ, he'd have to talk to Megan about getting a new lock, he thought, until he remembered he'd committed himself to not communicating with her again.

With a grimace, he brought in the box, set it on the counter, then stood looking around the darkened kitchen, thinking about how he'd stood there last night holding Megan.

JACK got into his unmarked car behind the station house. He had a lot of checking to do, of course. But so far it looked like Marshall had done his homework.

His first impulse was to scope out Donald Arnott's property, at least from the road. Was it secluded? The kind of place where he could keep a victim captive, and then dispose of the body? But Jack didn't want to go there unless he was sure Arnott was at work.

So he headed toward Montgomery Mall, thinking that there were several advantages to that approach. He might be able to get a look at the guy.

As he pulled into the vast parking lot, he thought about his quarry, tried to see the job of a mall security officer from Arnott's point of view. The man probably liked exercising authority over other people. Plus the mall was a wonderful place to watch women and decide which ones he wanted to cull from the herd—which was doubtless the way he thought about it.

At this stage in the investigation, Jack didn't want it to get back to Arnott that the police were interested in him. So he pulled out one of the fake Provident Credit business cards that he'd had printed up with his name and a phone number that was out of service.

He found the hallway with the mall office and pushed open the door. When the secretary looked up inquiringly, he showed her the Provident card and asked if Donald Arnott was on duty.

"I'm sorry," the receptionist told him. "He went home sick today."

"He did?" *Lucky I didn't go out to his house.* "Hmm. Can I see his work schedule?"

"What's this about?" the young woman asked.

"He's applied for a loan. It's our policy to personally verify his employment."

The girl nodded and handed over the schedule. When he asked if he could have a photocopy so he'd be more likely to catch Arnott at the mall, she willingly obliged.

The look on her face suggested that she didn't much care for Mr. Arnott.

"So what can you tell me about him?" Jack asked conversationally.

"When he came in here a little while ago and said he was going home sick, he didn't look like he felt bad. He seemed excited—like he was going somewhere fun, not home."

"You're very observant," Jack remarked.

She shrugged. "He gives me the creeps. So I kind of started paying attention to him. Yesterday, there was this girl who got caught shoplifting at the drugstore. He brought her in here to wait for the police, and you could see how much he was enjoying himself."

"Like how?"

"Like giving her this mean look that made her cry. Like standing real close to her so his arm was against her breast." The receptionist made a face. "I mean, maybe she deserved to be scared 'cause of what she did. But he was overdoing it; you know what I mean?"

"Yeah."

"I guess I shouldn't have said all that," she murmured, but he could tell that now that she'd gotten started, there was more she wanted to say.

So he stood there looking receptive, giving her a chance to spill it. After another thirty seconds she came out with "I don't know what that woman from Indulge Yourself sees in him."

Jack had passed the store. It was full of gadgets that were way out of his price range. "You mean one of the sales clerks?" he asked.

"Yeah. She's got big blond hair. Wears flashy clothes. I saw them having dinner in the food court last night. She looked like she thought he was pretty special. Yuck. She must be desperate for a guy."

Christ. The receptionist had practically described the other women on Marshall's list of victims. "Well, you've been very helpful," he said. "But I would appreciate it if you don't mention to Mr. Arnott that I stopped by. We like to make our visits a surprise."

Apparently she bought it, because she nodded in agreement.

Jack left the mall office, wondering where Arnott had gone. From the receptionist's description of his behavior, it sounded like he was up to something. But what?

Hell, maybe he was just going to pick up a new television set or a hunting rifle, and he'd decided to call it sick leave.

Still thinking about that, Jack headed for Indulge Yourself.

ROSS'S chest tightened painfully, and he closed his eyes. But it was impossible to wipe out all the potent memories assaulting him as he stood in Megan's kitchen. Maybe it was a mistake to have come here. Maybe he couldn't handle it.

Then he gave himself a mental shake. He was in her house, and he was going to do what he could to ensure her safety.

There was a spare bedroom that she used as a den or a home office. He'd check that out—after he looked through the bedroom.

It wasn't the most logical place to start, but he didn't seem to be operating on logic as he made his way down the hall.

Her scent filled his nostrils, filled his entire head like a cloud of perfumed fog. He stood there, breathing hard. Trying to keep his body from shaking.

When he could manage some measure of control, he stepped through the bedroom door.

He'd conducted searches before. But never when he could barely think.

He raked his nails across the back of his hand, the pain bringing his mind back into focus. Standing very still, he studied the room, taking in details that he hadn't noticed the night before. There were books and magazines on her bed stand. But little clutter in the room.

Bitterly conscious that he was violating her privacy, he turned to the bureau, poking through the drawers, the silky fabric of her undergarments abrading his nerve endings. But he found nothing hidden under the intimate apparel, and nothing of significance in the drawer where she obviously tossed things that she didn't know what to do with.

His next stop was the home office, where he started going through the papers on the desk.

In addition to the usual bills and bank statements, he found a family photo album. Leaning back in the chair, he smiled as he studied pictures of Megan as a baby, a toddler. A kindergartner. Megan with her sister, Dory. He could have spent the day wallowing in the images.

He had no family snapshots from his own childhood. Apart from the portraits taken every year at school, there were no cute little pictures of the Marshalls because Vic hadn't wanted any reminders of the children he'd lost.

His mother had saved the school pictures in the bottom of a bedroom drawer. He knew because one day he'd come home unexpectedly and found her looking at them. Michael. Himself. Adam. Jonathan. Troy. Only two of them were still alive. Himself and Adam. And he hadn't seen his brother in years.

Her eyes had been red, and she'd tried to hide the pictures. But he'd seen—and he'd backed away from the terrible look of sadness on her face.

He sat staring into space for several moments. Then gently laying the album back where he'd found it, he turned to the papers in the desk. When he finished searching, he was no closer to knowing who had attacked Megan than when he'd picked the lock on the door.

AS he stepped through the door of the upscale shop, Jack worked to keep his features neutral.

He'd just been looking at pictures of Penny Delano, Charlotte Lawrence, Lisa Patterson, Cindy Hamilton, and Mary Beth Nixon.

And this woman could have been one of their sisters. Probably at the upper end of the age limit, but definitely a candidate.

"Hi," he said, checking out her name tag. "I'm from Provident Credit, Miss Knight."

As soon as he said the word *credit*, a look of alarm crossed her face.

"I wanted to talk to you," he said, waiting a beat to see if she'd reveal anything more.

"About what?" she asked cautiously, her eyes flicking to what must be a drawer behind the counter.

"Credit," he said again, watching her knit her hands together. She stood there, her skin pale, her eyes guilty.

He gave her a little smile, let her worry for a few more seconds, then said, "One of our customers gave you for a reference."

She let out a shaky breath. "A reference."

"Is that a problem?"

"Oh, no. Of course not."

"Donald . . ." He paused, watching her expression grow expectant. "Samperson."

The punch line left her looking disoriented. "Donald Samperson?" she repeated.

"Yes. He listed you as a reference."

"He did? Well, I don't know anybody by that name."

"Hmm." He took out his notebook, flipped several pages, pretended to consult a previous notation. "Well, Donald Samperson definitely put your name down. Perhaps he was thinking we wouldn't check his reference."

"Yes. Well, I'm sorry."

He wanted to tell her that getting out of town for a couple of days would be a good idea. But that might send her running to her security guard friend for protection.

He left, wondering if she was into something illegal. Something with Donald Arnott?

He'd like to find out what. And he'd also like to make sure she didn't end up in a grave on the Arnott property.

As soon as he got back to the station house, he was going to run Arnott's license plate and arrange for patrols to keep an eye on his car when it was in the mall lot—and on Ms. Knight as well.

24

SHE was a creature of habit. Or maybe she just didn't have any imagination after all, Megan thought as she sat in the parking lot outside the Bio Gen office.

She'd told herself that she didn't want to go back to work this morning. Now here she was. Back at the scene of the crime. The spot where she'd been assaulted two days ago.

And as she sat again in the car, a few feet from where the man had grabbed her, her mind went back to the details of those terrifying few minutes.

The wolf. Ross. He'd known damn well who had rescued her. But he'd let her think it was some kind of fantasy.

She couldn't deal with that part, with his implicit lies and her own complicity. The evidence had been there. She just hadn't wanted to believe her own senses. Deliberately, she turned her thoughts back to the man who had jumped her. He hadn't spoken. He'd been wearing a ski mask. He'd given her very few clues to his identity. But she'd managed to scratch her nails across the skin of his neck. For all the good it was going to do her.

She made a muffled sound in her throat. She couldn't deal with that either. She would go crazy if she kept thinking about that night. Or about Ross.

Opening the car door, she marched into the lab, snatched up the assignment sheet, and silently dared Betty to engage her in conversation as she looked at the next test on the schedule.

In the lab, she started the procedure, working slowly and carefully, focusing on each detail so she wouldn't make any mistakes and she wouldn't have to think about anything else.

DONALD waited several minutes to make sure the little blonde wasn't coming back. Then he eased into gear again and drove past the door where she'd entered the building. A sign attached to the brick wall said BIO GEN LABORATORIES.

Did she work there? Was she going for lab tests or something?

He wasn't going to sit here all day wondering.

Knowing he was taking a chance, he slipped out of his car and walked back to the office.

There was a window in front with venetian blinds cranked partway open. He could see a plump secretary inside sitting at a desk, typing at a computer. Taking a twenty-dollar bill out of his pocket, he folded it into his hand, then opened the door.

The secretary looked up.

"Pardon me, I thought I saw a blond woman come in here a few minutes ago."

"Dr. Sheridan?"

"I don't know her name. But she dropped this in the parking lot." He held up the twenty.

"Oh, my."

Now that he'd established himself as a Good Samaritan, he figured he could ask a question. "Does she work here?"

"Why, yes, she does. Do you want to tell her you found the money?"

"Oh, no. I don't want to bother her at work. Just return it to her."

He stepped back out the door, hurried to the Land Rover, and slipped behind the wheel. There was a smile on his face as he pulled out of the parking lot. Jesus, what a day. He'd gotten the name of the guy—and his girlfriend, too. And he could feel an exquisite tension building in his chest. Things were coming together. He was making them come together. Because now he'd turned the tables on the guy.

Ross Marshall had been stalking him. Now he was stalking Ross Marshall.

ROSS wandered into Megan's living room, sank into one of the chairs, and closed his eyes. He should leave. Now that he'd searched the place and found nothing significant, he had no excuse for being in Megan's house.

The temptation to simply sit here for a few minutes was overwhelming.

He took a deep breath of her scent into his lungs, held it inside himself, exhaled and drew in again, his fingers stroking the fabric of the chair arms.

She had touched that fabric, sat here, he thought, sinking deeper into the cushions.

His eyes blinked open, and he looked around.

Lord, this was crazy. What was he planning to do, sit in her house until she came home? Explain why he'd broken in?

He ordered himself to stand up. Ordered himself back to the kitchen door.

He had just opened it when he saw a car pull away from the curb.

The bulk. The shape. The metallic color. He hadn't been able to see the details in the fog. But he thought this was the same vehicle that had been here the morning after the attack.

Leaving the door open, the box inside, he pelted back to the Grand Cherokee, jumped behind the wheel. But it was already too late. The bastard had gotten away.

Cursing under his breath, he returned to Megan's house, slipped inside, and checked to make sure nobody had come through the open door. Then he picked up the box and locked the door behind him.

DONALD took a ride in the country, to western Howard County to be exact. He could see that it had once been rural, much like the area where he lived. Now there were mansions and small developments sprouting among the cornfields and patches of woodland that still remained. Stony Brook Lane was off Route 99. The mailbox at 8572 said MARSHALL. It was at the head of a long drive that wound upward through a largely wooded plot. He slowed, seeing a rutted track where a number of the trees were posted with No Trespassing signs.

Apparently Ross Marshall didn't like visitors any better than he did. His detective job was probably just a cover for something else, the way Donald used his security guard job at Montgomery Mall.

That made sense. He imagined Marshall was a man much like himself. A man who had his solitary pursuits, who had discovered a rival in the area, and who was bent on eliminating that rival.

Donald's mouth cracked into a parody of a grin. He knew where Marshall lived now. And the more he could find out about the man, the better off he'd be.

He wanted to take the road into the woods and see what was at the end of that driveway. But he had no way of knowing whether Marshall was home.

Considering his strategy, he decided that the best thing to do was hang around for a while. Maybe his luck would hold, and the bastard would leave. If not, he'd come back after dark with a nightscope.

He continued up Stony Brook for several hundred yards, looking for a sheltered place to pull off the road. Finally he backed into a neighboring driveway and cut the engine. Opening the map, he laid it on the seat beside him so he could pretend he was lost if someone came down the drive behind him.

Christ, he was burning to go up and poke around Marshall's place. The dog must be up there. If he was in a pen, it would be like shooting fish in a barrel. But it was too dangerous to do it now.

Maybe the best way to get rid of Marshall was to plant a bomb with a pressure trigger up there. He'd studied up on stuff like that. And although he'd never used one, he had every confidence that he could master the simple techniques.

He smiled as he pictured the man and the dog being blown into such minute pieces that the police would have to scrape the two of them off the trees and nobody could tell which was which. The scenario warmed his heart. But a bomb would raise questions with the police. Why had someone picked such a dramatic way to get rid of Ross Marshall?

Better to come up with something more subtle. Some kind of poetic justice. But what?

He was about to start the engine and pull away when he saw a blue Grand Cherokee come sailing up the road. It braked, turned in at the drive. And he saw Marshall behind the wheel—big as life.

Jesus. Scrunching down in his seat, he watched the SUV disappear into the woods.

As he sat and stared after the vehicle, an elegant but simple plan started coming together for him. A way to get rid of Marshall. Using the woman.

MEGAN found she could work through the day's tests if she concentrated on each step, keeping everything else out of her mind.

By late in the afternoon, she was feeling numb and hoping that when she got home she could fall into bed and sleep.

God. Not into bed. She and Ross had been in her bed. And there was no way she'd get to sleep there. Not now. Not after what she knew about him.

A wave of emotion ripped through her. She wasn't exactly sure which emotion. Fear? Was she afraid of him? Afraid of a man who could turn himself into a wolf? She should be.

But that wasn't what she was feeling.

It was more like longing. Did she still want him? Or was she aching for what she knew could never be?

That was probably it.

As she stood in front of the lab table, she squeezed her eyes shut, trying to block out last night and everything after that. When she opened them, she found Walter standing in the doorway, watching her with unnerving intensity. She'd been so preoccupied with her own problems that she hadn't taken a good look at him in days. Now she saw that he'd lost weight. His face was thinner and his collar gaped away from his pale flesh.

"How are you doing?" he asked, watching her carefully.

The scrutiny made her skin prickle. But she answered "Fine" automatically.

"You're sure? You don't look so good," he pressed.

"Boyfriend trouble," she replied.

He stared at her for another few seconds as if trying to ascertain whether she was telling the truth, then turned away. And it was then that she saw what she hadn't noticed before, because his collar had been tighter. Now, where it gaped away from his flesh, she could see a narrow bandage on the back of his neck.

A gasp rose in her throat. But she managed to choke it back, managed to keep standing there as if the world hadn't turned upside down. Once again she remembered being thrown to the wet pavement, remembered raking her nails across a man's neck.

Frozen in place, she watched her boss stride down the hall and vanish into his office.

Stunned, her head spinning, she grasped the edge of the desk, reliving the attack. She'd thought there was something familiar about the man who'd knocked her to the ground, ripped at her clothing.

Until now she hadn't figured out who he was.

Now here were the scratches on Walter's neck. Scratches she'd put there.

Could it really be true? Walter?

She glanced in the direction in which he'd disappeared, feeling the walls of the lab pressing in around her. It was hard to draw a full breath as she tiptoed down the hall to her office and closed the door.

Fumbling in her purse, she found the number of the police detective who had interviewed her, Jack Thornton.

With shaky fingers, keeping one eye on the office door in case Walter came back, she dialed his number.

The phone rang three times, four, five. Finally a woman said, "Montgomery County Police, Detective Division."

"I'd like to speak to Detective Jack Thornton, please."

"I'm sorry, ma'am. Could you speak up? I can't hear you."

"Is Detective Thornton there?"

"I'm sorry, he's left for the day. Do you want me to page him and have him call you back?"

Megan felt her throat clog. "Okay." She gave her home number because there was no way she was staying at the lab.

But leaving a message wasn't enough. She wanted to talk to him now. She wanted *help* now.

Grabbing her coat, she ran down the hall, past Walter's office, seeing him in the corner of her vision. He was at his desk. Looking normal. Looking like everything was okay, when everything was all wrong.

The reception area was empty. Betty must have left for the day. Thank God. Because Megan wasn't planning to blurt anything to her.

Stepping into the twilight, she crossed the blacktop at a run. Reaching the safety of her car, she pulled the phone from the cradle and dialed the only other person she could think of who could help her.

Ross.

Oh, God, Ross. Please. Please answer your damn phone. Please be there.

One ring. Two. Three. She waited with the blood roaring in her ears, silently begging him to be there.

But he didn't pick up. And when she got his answering machine, she wanted to scream.

When she'd called the police and hadn't gotten Thornton, she'd left her number. Now that wasn't good enough. She had to tell *somebody* what she knew. "Ross, I figured it out," she gasped. "I tried to call Detective Thornton, but he wasn't in. It was Walter. The man who attacked me was Walter. He was just in my lab and I saw a bandage on his neck. And I—"

She gasped as somebody flung the car door open.

"No," she screamed, the phone dropping from her fingers as she was yanked from the car. "No—"

His hand clamped over her mouth as he wrestled her to a big white

SUV parked a few cars away. He opened the door, and she tried to brace her arms, clawing at the opening with her fingernails to keep him from shoving her inside. But he was too strong.

"No, you don't," he panted, tearing her nails as he flung her into the back. The seats had been folded down, making a flat cargo area.

Breathing hard, he hovered over her, blocking the view of anyone who might walk by.

He took his hand away from her mouth, pulled off a piece of duct tape that had been dangling from the far door, and slapped it into place.

Next she heard metal clink, felt cold bracelets circle her wrists. Handcuffs.

He pulled her arms up and attached the cuffs to a metal ring that was fixed to the flat surface of the seat back.

Terrified, arms stretched above her head, she stared up at him as he loomed over her, a frightening look of satisfaction playing over his thin lips.

"Well, now I've got you," he said with a smirk. "I've rescued you from that Ross Marshall guy. I know what he is. I know what he's up to. Stalking me. Him and his damn trained dog. Only I've got you now. And you've got the honor of helping me get him. They'll find your grave on his property and they'll think he's the one who did it. But first we're going to have a good time together. Well, at least I am."

He reached out, covered one breast with his hand. She tried to shrink away, tried to kick at him. But he only slapped her hard across the face, then brought his hand back to her breast, finding her nipple through the fabric of her blouse and twisting so hard that she screamed, the sound a choked gurgle behind the gag.

His muddy brown eyes bored into hers. "Don't worry," he said. "When I get you to my place, I'll pull the tape off. Then you can make all the noise you want. I like to hear my women scream. And you'll scream plenty. Because that's just a little taste of what you're going to get from me. And this."

Pulling out a penknife, he opened the blade and pressed it against her cheek, pressed into her flesh, drawing the blade up along her skin, not deeply but enough to leave a trail of fire that brought tears to her eyes.

He looked at the blood on the blade, pulled out a tissue, and smiled as he wiped it off. "That's just skimming the surface. Before

I've finished with you, there won't be any part of your body I haven't invaded."

Slamming the back door shut, he moved to the front and climbed in behind the wheel. Moments later the vehicle lurched forward, twisting Megan's arms as the man drove out of the parking lot.

25

THE car rocked, and pain jolted through Megan's arms. If she stayed in this position, her bones were going to snap.

Using her feet, she pushed herself up so there was less pressure on her arms. Then, carefully, she maneuvered to the side, working her wrists in the cuffs so that her hands were in front of her. It wasn't an ideal way to travel, but it was less agonizing.

Cautiously she twisted her head and looked at the man behind the wheel, trying to contain the bolt of fear that shot through her. She could feel her mind shutting down as she stared at him. All she wanted was to disappear into some deep, dark, buried part of her brain where he couldn't reach her.

Hide.

But he was probably counting on that. He wanted her scared, powerless, unable to fight him.

So he could get her in his house and kill her.

Kill her slowly, she thought, feeling the sting on her cheek where he'd cut her.

Fear clawed inside her belly. Behind the gag, she felt her breath choking off, felt her brain filling with fog. He didn't need to kill her. She would suffocate in the back of his car if she didn't control her panic.

Deliberately she bit down on her lower lip, the self-inflicted pain jolting through her, bringing the danger into sharp focus.

Don't lose control. Don't hide. Keep functioning, she ordered herself as she tried to breathe slowly and evenly through her nose.

When she had some control of the fear, she went to the next step—

thinking. What did she know already? she asked herself, forcing her mind to focus.

Ross had told her a security guard from the mall was the killer who had shot him. Somehow the killer had figured out who Ross was—who she was. He was going to kill her and pin it on Ross, she realized with a jolt.

God, no.

Again her breath threatened to choke off. Again she kept air moving in and out through her nose.

He'd killed more than one woman. She knew that from Ross. And he was going to kill her, too—unless she could stop him.

But how?

As the car jounced along, she fought a wave of nausea. Ross had said he'd found women's graves on this guy's property. He hadn't told her the man got a thrill from killing.

She squeezed her eyes shut. Not just killing. Terror. Torture.

How long did he keep his victims around? Hours? Days?

A white-hot jolt of terror threatened to overwhelm her. But she managed to contain it.

Nobody was coming to her rescue. Nobody knew where she was. If she was going to escape, she had to do it herself.

She was on her own. She had to get away from him or die trying. Because she had no doubt that a quick bullet in the back was better than what he had planned for her.

ROSS was in his office when he remembered he'd turned off the phone before he'd gone into Megan's house.

Dialing his message number, he leaned back in his chair.

The chair bounced when he heard her voice.

"Ross, I figured it out," she gasped. "I tried to call Detective Thornton, but he wasn't in. It was Walter. The man who attacked me was Walter. He was just in my lab and I saw a bandage on his neck. And I—"

Her voice cut off in a choked gasp. Then she screamed, "No!" as the phone apparently clattered to the floor.

"Jesus! No. Oh, God, Megan," he shouted, even as his mind tried to process what he'd just heard.

It was her boss, Walter. The guy who had attacked her was her boss. And now the bastard had her.

Playing the message back, he listened for details. She'd said he was just in her lab. Praying that they were still there, that the bastard hadn't taken her anywhere else, he jumped back into his car and sped back toward Bethesda.

The trip should have taken an hour. He made it in forty minutes.

Teeth clenched, hands fused to the wheel, he spun into the Bio Gen parking lot.

It was dark when he arrived but he could see Megan's car was still there, thank God. And one other. The Mercedes.

Son of a bitch.

He strode to the door, tried the knob. It was locked. Without bothering to knock and give the bastard any warning, he went back for the picks that were still in his bag, found the right one, and manipulated the lock until he heard it click.

Once inside he sped past the darkened reception room and down the hall, then surged through the door of a plush-looking office where a slender man in a tweed sport coat was taking handfuls of files from a cabinet.

"Walter Galveston?"

The man whirled, goggled at him as he strode forward.

"Galveston! Where the hell is Megan? What have you done with her?"

Utter confusion suffused the man's features. "Megan? I haven't done anything with her."

Ross grabbed the man by the shoulder with one hand. With the other, he yanked the collar away from Galveston's neck, exposing the bandage.

"Stop that! What the hell do you think you're doing?"

Ignoring the protest, Ross pulled the bastard's arms from his sport coat, tossing the garment on the floor before yanking his shirttails from his pants and ripping the fabric up the middle of the back.

As he'd anticipated, Galveston's back was covered with claw marks. "The wolf did that to you," Ross spat. "Now tell me what you've done with Megan or I'll have the wolf rip out your throat." The words were half human, half animal growl.

"Please. I beg you. I don't know where Megan is. She went home."

"Sure."

"That's the truth. I swear."

Ignoring the words, Ross raised a hand, wrapped it around the scrawny throat, squeezed.

The man's eyes bulged; his face turned red.

Ross eased up the pressure. "Where is Megan?"

"I swear I don't know," he gasped.

"You were at her house the other morning. And this afternoon. You saw me at the window."

"I . . . please . . ."

"Convince me you haven't got her now. Tell me why you attacked her in the first place."

A desperate flow of words poured out of the man. "The lab is in financial trouble. I'm going bankrupt. But I've got money stashed in a safe place. Not the bank. I've been making it look like bad things were happening around here. The car accident. The break-in. When Megan was there that night, I got the idea that attacking her would add to the pattern of bad stuff happening at the lab. It would make it look like I didn't have any option besides killing myself when I staged my own death. Please. I went to her house that morning looking for my lapel pin. It's missing. I thought it might have gotten stuck to her clothes or something. You've got to believe that."

Ross peered into the wide, pleading eyes. And he did believe. Oh, Christ, he did believe. But then where was Megan?

"When did you see her last?" he spat out.

"She was here an hour ago. I think that's right. I saw her go past my door. She was in a hurry."

"You bastard." Ross tossed the frightened man against the wall like a sack of trash and ran back the way he'd come.

Reaching her car, he realized that the door wasn't quite shut. And when he pulled it open, he almost choked on a smell that had been burned into his consciousness. Arnott.

Arnott had been in Megan's car.

In the dim light of the overhead bulb he looked wildly around the interior, saw the phone on the floor. Her purse.

One of her shoes.

"God, no!" he roared. *God, no.* Somehow Arnott had found her— and taken her away. Somehow—

A sick dread gathered in the pit of his stomach. Had Arnott seen them together at the mall? And somehow figured out who was stalking him?

But how? How in the hell had he done it? Not because he'd recognized the wolf.

It didn't matter how he'd figured it out. All that mattered was getting Megan out of the bastard's clutches.

He was back in his car, heading into the country as he dialed the police.

"Jack Thornton, please."

"He's gone home for the day. I can have him paged."

"Yes. Tell him to call Ross Marshall at 301-555-9876. Tell him it's urgent. Tell him Arnott has Megan. Tell him I'm on my way out there."

"Spell that name, please."

"A-R-N-O-T-T."

Hanging up, he dialed information and got Jack Thornton's home number.

An older-sounding woman answered. "Hello?"

"Is Thornton there?" he asked, hearing the panic in his own voice.

"He's out. May I take a message?"

"This is Ross Marshall."

"Oh. Yes. Ross Marshall, the PI. He's spoken about you. This is his housekeeper, Mrs. Anderson."

"I've got to reach him. It's a matter of life or death."

"He's at a soccer game with his son. He won't be home for a couple of hours. Did you have him paged?"

"I already did that. But I'll give you the message in case he calls home. Tell him Arnott has Megan. Tell him to meet me there with backup."

He clicked off, concentrating his efforts on driving, praying that he wasn't going to be too late.

MEGAN felt her heart rate speed up as the car came to a stop in front of a gated fence. Arnott got out, unlocked it, drove through, then re-locked it behind the car.

God, they were trapped inside a fence. But she could climb over, she told herself. If she could get away from him. And she had to get away. There were no other options.

He pulled the car to a stop and looked back at her, his expression smug. "Wait right here. I've got to get things ready."

The words sent a sliver of cold piercing through her. After he got out, she started pulling at the handcuffs, trying to slip her hands through the rings. But all she got for her trouble was a pair of chafed wrists.

He returned, looking even more pleased with himself. Opening the back door, he climbed inside and pulled her around so that she was lying on her back again.

Her heart leaped into her throat. Was he going to kill her here in the car?

No, she told herself. He'd mess up the car, and he didn't want to do that, did he?

She could see the bulge at the front of his pants, knew that her helplessness and her terror were turning him on. Good—maybe with some of the blood drained from his brain, he wouldn't be thinking as clearly.

He had done this before. He had been successful. That would make him feel confident. Powerful. And he'd think of her as one of the dumb women he could use and discard as he pleased.

That gave her a tremendous advantage. He'd assume that she was just one more terrified woman he could control.

When his hand shot out to yank off her remaining shoe, her body gave an involuntary jump. He tossed the shoe to the side, then reached under her skirt, grasped the elastic of her panty hose and panties, and pulled them both down and off.

She closed her eyes, turned her head away.

"Look at me."

She swallowed, lay unmoving as she felt his eyes traveling over her body.

"You'll be sorry if you don't do what I say."

She turned her head back, watched the satisfaction spread across his face as he held her gaze with his for a long moment. Then he reached out and ripped the tape from her mouth, making her gasp from the pain.

"You look like a slut with your privates hanging out like that. Like my mom. She was always showing what she had to the guys."

She wanted to say that he'd been the one who'd exposed her. Wanted to ask if that's what this was all about—his mother. But she kept her lips pressed together.

Feeling his fingers stroke the skin of her hips, her belly, she cringed. When he reached down to rake his hand through her pubic hair, thrust his hand between her labia, she couldn't hold back a little moan.

He took out the knife again, and she stared at him wide-eyed, terrified of what he was going to do. He knew she was scared, and he was enjoying it. Bringing the blade down slowly, he cut an almost delicate line in the crease at the top of her right thigh.

She knew he wanted her to cry out. To beg. She didn't know which was worse—giving him what he wanted or keeping silent. So she opted for silence.

When he scooted forward, reached across her, and unlocked the bolt that held the handcuffs to the car, she tried to hold back her sigh of relief. "Time to come into my playroom," he rasped. "We'll cut the rest of your clothes off when I get you on the table."

JACK looked at Craig and grinned. His son grinned back, and Jack felt a surge of love—and gratitude. Last year, after Laura had died, Craig had been eaten up with grief and rage. He'd had problems in school, problems with his friends, problems with the law.

That part was the worst to take. A cop whose son was caught shoplifting.

But the family therapy had helped Craig—helped them all. His kids were doing okay now—except for the occasional times like Lily's nightmare.

"Great game, Dad."

"Yeah." Jack chomped on his hot dog, swallowed a swig of Coke. Before his mouth was entirely clear of food, he started shouting again. "Go for it, Martinez. Go for it."

Craig joined him, jumping to his feet in his excitement.

The moment was spoiled when Jack heard the beeping of his pager. Looking down at the number, he saw that it was his office.

Son of a bitch. Couldn't he even have an evening out with his kid? Was he supposed to be on duty 24/7?

"Craig, I'll be right back."

Trying to ignore his son's look of disappointment, he climbed out of his seat and went to find a quiet spot where he could see what was so urgent.

In the aisle, he almost collided with Emily Anderson. Jesus, what was she doing here?

"What is it? What's wrong? Is it Lily?" he asked, his eyes searching hers.

Emily was quick to reassure him. "No. She's fine. I left her at the Wilsons'."

A sigh of relief rushed out of him. It wasn't his daughter. But then what was wrong?

They huddled against the wall, but it was impossible to block out the noise of the game.

He waited until another round of encouragement from the crowd had subsided before asking again, "What's wrong?"

"Ross Marshall called. He said he paged you."

"Yeah, I just got a page. He called the house, too?"

"Yes. He sounded upset. He told me to tell you that Arnott has Megan."

He stared at her in disbelief. "You're sure that's what he said? Arnott has Megan?"

"Yes."

"Jesus." Dr. Sheridan had paged him earlier and he'd tried to call her back. But he'd only gotten an answering machine.

"He said he was going out to his place. He said for you to come and bring backup."

He looked at his son, who was once again happily immersed in the soccer game, and hated to drag him away.

But Mrs. Anderson had followed the direction of his thoughts. "You go on. I'll stay with Craig. That's why I came here."

His hand gripped her forearm. "Emily, thanks."

"Go on."

"Yeah." He ran down the steps, his phone already in his hand. First he called dispatch and got the same message from Ross. Then he called the station house and asked for patrol cars to meet him at the property of Donald Arnott, 5962 Newcut Road.

MEGAN stumbled, trying to stay on her feet as the killer pulled her after him into a ruined building and then down a flight of rough wooden steps and through a low doorway into a chamber where the air was fetid with the smell of old blood and other things.

It was brightly lit, and she gagged as she saw the racks of knives and other instruments on the wall. In front of it was a wooden table with leather straps. And at the foot of the table was a videocamera on a tripod.

Mouth dry, heart hammering in her chest, Megan knew that if he got her onto that table, she was a dead woman.

She took a few steps forward, then made a terrified sound as she sank to the floor beside the camera, going limp, pretending that the place was too much for her.

"Get up, cunt."

She stayed where she was, limp and unmoving, silently urging him closer.

When she didn't respond, he bent over her.

Bringing up her clasped hands, she smashed the metal handcuffs into his face

He made a grunting sound, and she pushed him aside, slamming the videocamera down on his head, then sprinting up the steps, the rough wood tearing at the bottoms of her feet as she ran.

Behind her she heard him bellow, "Fucking bitch!" The angry exclamation only fueled her sense of purpose as she ran through the building, her cuffed hands making her movements awkward.

DONALD scrambled up, crashed into one of the tripod legs, and went down again. Anger boiling inside him, he pushed himself erect.

"Fucking bitch," he spat out again. She'd gotten the drop on him. And now he was going to even the score. She might have gotten out of the room, but she wasn't going far. Not when the place was fenced and her hands were cuffed.

His guns were in the house. He'd never needed them in this room, never needed them to control the stupid, frightened women he brought here. With a grunt he rubbed his face where she'd clunked him. That bitch was going to be sorry when he caught up with her.

He'd get her, all right. Get her good.

He wasn't going to kill her with the gun, just shoot her in some fleshy part of her body to make sure she was under control. Then he'd bring her back in here for a session she'd never forget.

JACK turned on the radio, listened to the scanner traffic as he headed for Newcut Road.

Satisfied that a patrol car was on the way, he pulled his notebook from his pocket, found Marshall's number, and dialed.

"Hello?"

"Ross, this is Jack. What happened?"

"Are you on your way to Arnott's?"

"Yes."

"Thank . . . G—" the PI breathed, his voice breaking up from interference.

"How do you know he has Megan?"

The transmission was still flaky, but it sounded like Marshall said, "I smelled . . . in her car! All over . . . like rotten . . ."

"What? I don't understand."

"I can smell people. That's how . . . how I . . ."

Doubt shot through Jack. "You're not making any sense."

"Jesus. It doesn't matter . . . how . . . I know he's got . . . I thought it was Walter Galveston. But it wasn't . . . -im. And then I went out to her car and . . ." The transmission choked off. Marshall was probably in a pocket where his cellular service couldn't reach.

"Ross, Ross, can you hear me? Ross."

There was no answer. The line was dead.

Jack set the phone on the seat. The conversation hadn't made a great deal of sense. Was Marshall drunk? Out of his head?

The only thing he knew for sure was that the urgency—the fear—in his voice had been real.

26

THE anger had boiled off, leaving him relaxed, enjoying the hunt on this fine moonlit night—although it was hardly a fair contest. A man with a gun stalking a handcuffed woman. In a big cage.

He knew where she was. He knew there was no possibility of her escaping from this locked compound. So he'd slowed down, letting her think that maybe she had a chance to get away from him before he moved in for the good part.

Now he stood very still in the darkness, imagining he could hear the breath hissing in and out of her tortured lungs as she cowered behind a tree. He'd run her pretty good. She was tired.

Alone, defenseless, and scared shitless.

The bitch had thought she was so smart, whacking him with the cuffs like that. But she was going to learn the consequences of her actions pretty damn soon.

With a grin he started moving forward again, making sure she could hear his booted feet crunching through the dry leaves, playing the flashlight on the foliage, bringing the light closer and closer to the tree where he knew she was hiding.

ROSS eased up on the gas pedal, pulled off Newcut Road, and screeched to a halt in front of the gate, weighing his options.

He could change into wolf form and go under the fence the way he had on the night Arnott had shot him. But he wanted Jack to be able to get inside—if he made it out here in time to do any good.

Snatching the burglary kit from the seat beside him, he leaped out of the SUV and started working on the hasp with a hacksaw. It took effort—and precious minutes—to cut through the steel, but finally he snapped the hasp, tossed the lock to the ground, and pulled the gates wide.

Jumping behind the wheel again, he started up the road—unsure of where he should be going and angry that he hadn't had more time to explore inside the fenced area before Arnott had found him that first time.

The bastard had brought her in here. He knew that. But then what? Was there a room in the house where he took his victims? Or did he take them somewhere else?

That would be the safe bet. Somewhere hard to find. But where the hell was it?

Well, maybe he didn't have a clue where to look, but the wolf would know.

Ahead was a white Land Rover gleaming in the moonlight. Stopping well behind it, he pulled off into the woods, then jumped out and trotted over to the vehicle. When he yanked the door open, he could see that the backseat had been folded down to make a cargo area.

Pushed to the side of the flat surface were a woman's shoe, panty hose, and underpants.

The blood froze in his veins as he stared in horror at the undergarments. The son of a bitch had started undressing her out here. What else had he done?

Keeping the panic at bay, he started tearing off his own clothes even as the words of transformation tumbled from his mouth.

He felt his muscles popping, his shape changing as he kicked his pants away, then he leaped into the vehicle, breathing in Megan's wonderful scent, mixed with the stench of the monster—and blood.

Oh, Lord—blood.

The combination made him gag. Jumping out again, he put his

nose to the ground, finding the trail easily. Megan was wounded. But she'd been on her feet and able to walk. At least he knew that much.

He followed the combination of scents along a dirt path toward a ruined barn, moving cautiously lest the bastard lunge out and pop him again. Because if he got shot this time, he'd be no damn good to Megan.

JACK arrived at the entrance to Arnott's property, knowing backup wasn't coming anytime soon.

Two hotshot rookies had been on their way—but they'd been so excited, they'd crashed into a station wagon at Georgia Avenue and Damascus Road.

He called for another patrol car as he rolled through the open gate. A sawed-off padlock was lying on the ground.

Which must mean Ross was already here—and inside. Jesus, he hoped the two of them were going to be enough.

He spotted a Grand Cherokee pulled off the road and Arnott's Land Rover a couple of dozen yards farther on. He'd run the plate, so he knew the make and model.

Stopping behind Ross's vehicle, he unholstered his Sig P228 and cautiously approached the Grand Cherokee. It was empty.

Proceeding to the second vehicle, he found the door was open, the backseat folded down, and what he assumed was Megan Sheridan's underwear lying in a discarded heap across from the restraining ring that Ross had described.

Beside the car was an untidy pile of men's clothing. Damn—had Arnott already stripped for action? And where the hell had he taken Dr. Sheridan?

Ahead he could see the lighted windows of a house. His best choice was to assume the bastard had taken her there—and that Ross was on the scene.

NOSE to the ground, the wolf sniffed the doorway of the barn. They had definitely come this way, Megan and Arnott—both still on foot.

Cautiously he slipped through the door, his claws scratching across the rough floorboards.

Ahead he could see a bright light coming from somewhere below ground level.

Ears pricked, body tense, he edged toward the illumination and came to a short flight of rough steps.

A shiver traveled over his body. If Arnott was at the bottom of those steps with a gun, anybody coming down was going to be an excellent target—particularly a four-legged animal who would have to negotiate the stairs carefully. But if Arnott was holding Megan down there, then going down was the only way to save her.

He thought about changing back to human form. But then he'd only be a naked man—without a weapon. At least this way he had his teeth and claws, he thought as he set his right forepaw on the steps, listening intently for sounds from below. There were none. But Megan's scent was strong here. So was Arnott's. And other odors overwhelming both their scents. Blood. Tortured flesh. Human waste.

Hugging the wall, he made his way down the stairs. The room was empty but he goggled in horror at the wooden table, racks of instruments, and overturned videocamera. Thank God Megan wasn't here now.

But she *had* been here. Very recently. Now she was gone. So was Arnott. He'd brought her here. And somehow she'd gotten away from the bastard.

A good hypothesis. He prayed that it was true.

But, God, where was she now? She must have gone back up the stairs.

Climbing the steps, he reentered the barn, then stood breathing the night air, trying to catch Megan's scent. He had followed her trail from the Land Rover. He had to figure out where she had gone now.

MEGAN crouched behind a tree, watching the beam of a high-powered lantern play across the foliage, hearing the killer's footsteps crunching on dry leaves. She cowered down, afraid to run, afraid to move, feeling twigs and leaves digging into her bare legs, her bare bottom.

The tree was a barrier between her and the killer. But he was coming closer, relentlessly closer. And if she stayed where she was, he was sure to find her. So she gathered herself together, stood, and ran for a tangle of brambles, her breath burning in her lungs.

When bullets sprayed the ground only yards behind her, she screamed and sprinted faster, the air searing her lungs.

In the distance she could make out the chain links of the fence. But there was no question of climbing it now. She'd be a target perfectly poised for the killing shot.

She dodged to the right, trying to lose herself in the underbrush. Desperately she pressed on, gasping for air, each breath close to a sob as she came to the end of her strength.

Her mind almost paralyzed by terror, she kept moving, her only goal to put distance between herself and the man with the gun.

Then she felt her blood turn to ice in her veins as she realized what she'd done. The fence was directly ahead of her and her only options were to turn and sprint along the barrier, or try to dodge back the way she'd come, making a circle around the killer.

Liking neither choice, she opted to circle back. And then suddenly Arnott was looming in front of her, the gun in his hand and a satisfied expression on his beefy face.

"You bitch. You're going to pay for that little trick," he spat as he pulled the trigger, firing more bullets into the dry leaves before raising the weapon.

Her jaw clenched tight, she braced for the pain of a slug tearing into her flesh.

THE house lights were on, but there were no sounds from inside that Jack could detect. No screams. No pleas for mercy.

He was cautiously peering through a ground-floor window when the sound of a machine gun firing shattered the silence of the night.

Behind him and to the right. In the woods.

Turning, he bolted for the stand of trees, his feet sinking into newly tilled ground, then pounding across the firmer surface of the forest floor.

The sight that greeted him was like a blow to the chest. A man with an Uzi. Arnott.

A woman cowering in front of him, trapped. Dr. Sheridan.

THE sound of machine-gun fire ripped through the air. Digging his paws into the debris on the forest floor, Ross stopped in his tracks.

He was going in the wrong direction. He'd followed Megan's scent into the woods but she must have circled back through the trees, tried to hide in the underbrush. But the killer had tracked her—found her.

Changing direction, he lowered his head and hurtled through a tangle of bramble, the thorns tearing at his fur as he pelted toward the sounds of gunfire, running at top speed but closing the distance with agonizing slowness.

His only thought was *Save Megan.* He had to save Megan. His mate. His woman. That was the one essential idea his brain had room to hold.

A savage snarl tore from his throat as he sprang from a thicket and focused on the man with the gun turning toward Megan, his weapon raised.

With no regard for his own safety, the wolf gave a mighty leap, springing toward the killer.

"Ross, watch out! Ross!"

Dimly, in some part of his mind, he heard Megan scream a warning. But it rolled off him as he hurtled forward, bringing Arnott down in one graceful leap. As they hit the ground, the gun discharged, sending a hail of bullets into the underbrush.

The noise mixed with the scream of terror that welled in the man's throat.

Ignoring the bullets, Ross sank his teeth into Arnott's gun arm, wringing another scream from the man—this time of pain. Frantically Arnott beat at the wolf's head and back with his free hand.

But there was no dislodging the animal. Blind rage made him hold fast, shaking the arm, biting down until the man's fingers went limp and the gun fell to the ground.

Then a knife materialized in the killer's free hand. It arced downward, slicing a gash in the wolf's shoulder.

With a growl deep in his throat, Ross dodged away, then sprang again, straddling the man, pinning the knife arm to his side as he went for the throat, crunching down through flesh and bone with a savage snap of his jaw.

A sound of horror rose from the killer's vocal cords—choked off in a rattling gurgle.

The wolf held on for a moment longer, shaking the limp body, then let it fall backward to the ground.

His muzzle dripping with blood, he lifted his head. As he stared at the woman who cowered away from the scene of carnage, he felt a sharp mixture of triumph and sorrow.

Megan was safe—and he was lost.

A noise penetrated his consciousness, footsteps crunching on dry leaves. Turning, he saw Jack Thornton staring at him wide-eyed.

Throwing back his head, he howled for his victory and his loss, his voice mingling with the man-made wail of approaching sirens. Then he turned and raced away into the darkness.

BESIDE the white Land Rover, Ross changed back to his man form, then bent and pulled on his jeans. His upper arm was stinging from the knife wound, but the cut wasn't deep. Returning to his own vehicle, he pulled his first-aid kit from the glove compartment and tied several gauze pads around the arm before pulling on his shirt and stuffing his feet into his shoes.

After wiping the blood off his mouth, he dashed back to where he'd left Megan and found Thornton on the ground beside her, speaking to her in a low voice.

When he closed the distance between them, she raised her head and stared at him, all the horror of what she'd just seen shimmering in her eyes.

Pain squeezed his heart as he stopped five feet away, because he dared go no closer. "It's okay. I won't touch you," he managed to say in a gritty voice, then demanded urgently, "But you've got to tell me. Are you all right?"

Her lips moved, but no words came out.

He backed up a step. Kneeling on the ground, his face at her level, he focused on her pale, bruised face. But he kept his hands rigidly at his sides to show her he wasn't going to reach for her no matter how much he wanted to fold her into his arms and cling for dear life. "Megan. For God's sake, Megan. Did he hurt you?"

She lifted her hands across her chest, and he saw that she was handcuffed.

Rage and pain welled inside him. "He cuffed you. Oh, Christ. Did he do anything else? Hurt you?"

"He cut me." The words were thin, barely above a whisper, but they slashed through his own flesh.

"Where?"

She raised the cuffed hands toward her cheek. "Here. And at the top of my leg."

"The son of a bitch."

"It's not bad." Her eyes were dazed, and he knew she was in shock. "I got away before he . . . before he . . ."

"Thank God!" Turning to the police detective, he asked, "Can you get her out of those damn cuffs?"

"I don't have the key."

Pushing himself up, Ross went to the ruined body and hunkered down again, his eyes dispassionately assessing the damage the wolf had inflicted. Then, calmly, he searched the pockets and found the key, which he handed to Thornton.

Moments later the restraints clicked open, and Megan rubbed her wrists. "Is he dead?" she whispered.

"Yes," Ross answered.

"Good," she choked out. Then her eyes went to Ross's arm, where blood stained his shirt.

"He cut you, too."

"It's not deep."

He saw Thornton's head swing around, focus on the bloody shirt.

The detective opened his mouth, but before he could comment, uniformed officers came charging through the underbrush, their guns drawn.

Quickly Thornton stood, held out his badge. "I'm Detective Thornton," he called out. "The situation's under control. The suspect's dead."

"What happened?" the lead officer asked. "Did one of you shoot him?" His questioning gaze swung between Ross and the detective.

It was Thornton who answered. "I was too far away to shoot. An animal killed him. A large dog or a . . ." He didn't finish the sentence.

The officer stared at him as if he couldn't believe what he was hearing. "A large dog killed him? A pit bull?"

"I'm not sure."

The other uniform turned to Ross. "Did you see it?"

He hesitated for a minute, then said, "No. I was in the barn—searching his torture chamber."

Ross's gaze caught Thornton's—and held.

"Yeah. He missed the action," the detective said, backing up his story in a strained voice.

Both uniforms went to the body and squatted down, looking at the mangled mess of blood and flesh.

"Jesus," one of them muttered. "His throat's ripped out."

Ross bowed his head, unable to meet anyone's eyes. He'd gone for the carotid artery when he might have simply stopped the man from killing him with the knife. But rage had carried him to the next step.

"Should we put out a bulletin on the animal?" the lead officer asked.
"Sure. Couldn't hurt," Thornton said. Ross was pretty certain the detective didn't think they were going to find anything.

Megan had been sitting with her teeth clamped together. Now she began to speak again, and he could see she was struggling to keep her voice steady.

"He took me to that . . . that torture chamber. I got away, and he came after me with a gun."

"How did you escape?" Thornton asked.

"I pretended to faint. When he came to pick me up, I hit him with the cuffs and ran."

"Good for you," Ross said, his hands clenched at his sides. The need to hold her, press his lips to her pale skin, was an ache inside him. But he could see she didn't want him any closer than he already was.

"I think the room is proof enough of what he's been doing here," he said. "There was a videocamera. Maybe you'll find tapes."

"Can you show us where it is?" Thornton asked.

"Yeah." His gaze swung to Megan. "But she doesn't have to see it again. Call an ambulance for her. She should be checked out in the hospital."

"I'm okay," she insisted in a thin voice.

"Ross is right," Thornton said, backing him up again.

Ross stood, blood roaring in his ears, his eyes focused on Megan. The pain in his heart was almost more than he could bear, because he knew this was the last time he would ever see the woman he loved. He would remember her like this. And remember the look of joy on her face after they'd made love. And all the other moments of the brief time they had spent together.

She had seen him kill Arnott. Seen the savagery of the wolf and cringed away from the man. And now the only thing left for him was to walk away with what dignity he still possessed.

JACK waited until one of the uniforms put in the call, then helped Dr. Sheridan into the backseat of the cruiser. While one of the officers sat with her, he and the other officer followed Marshall through the woods to a ruined barn.

The PI pointed to the opening in the floor, where bright light flowed up a flight of rough steps. "I guess he wanted to make sure he could see every detail of what he was doing."

"Yeah." Jack let Marshall lead the way down the steps into a room that looked like it had been constructed during the Inquisition—except for the modern lighting and the video equipment.

Gagging at the smell, he looked around at the racks of carefully arranged knives and other implements. At one end of the room was a TV with a VCR, next to videocassettes neatly labeled and stacked on shelves.

Penny Delano. Charlotte Lawrence. Lisa Patterson. Cindy Hamilton. Mary Beth Nixon. The murder victims.

If the tapes showed what he thought they showed, then there was no doubt that Arnott had killed the women.

And now he was dead. His throat ripped out. Like Crawford. He'd think about that later. First he needed to get official statements from Marshall and Sheridan.

27

MEGAN heard a car stop in front of the house. Whenever that happened these days, she felt a burst of anticipation—and dread.

Ross. She longed for it to be Ross, and at the same time she didn't know if she could handle seeing him. Not now. Not yet.

Her emotions were still too raw. Her thoughts still in turmoil. Her wounds too fresh.

Crossing to the kitchen window, she looked out and felt a stab of disappointment mixed with relief.

It wasn't Ross, it was the detective—Jack Thornton.

She took a step back, her hands clenching and unclenching as she waited for the doorbell to ring. He'd made her uncomfortable once. Now . . .

Now she was pretty sure the two of them shared a secret that could destroy Ross Marshall.

The bell rang, and she jumped, then tried to will her heart from thumping its way through the wall of her chest as she walked toward the door.

When she opened it, they stood looking at each other for several seconds.

"Can I come in?" he asked.

"Why?"

"I want to make sure you're okay."

"I'm fine," she said without moving.

"Megan, let me come in."

She still had a choice, she thought. But she stepped aside and he followed her into the living room.

"Why are you really here?" she asked.

"To see how you're doing—and to talk about Ross."

She took her bottom lip between her teeth, thinking that they could circle around that latter topic for hours. Instead she decided there was no point in prolonging the uncertainty. "You could have turned him in," she said. "But you didn't. Why not?"

He stared at her, neither of them spelling it out—but both of them knowing exactly what the other meant.

"Can I sit down?" he asked.

She gave a tight nod. He took one of her overstuffed chairs; she sat on the sofa, her fingers closing around the edge of a cushion.

"What purpose would it have served to turn him in?" Thornton asked.

"It depends on whether you think Ross is dangerous."

"Because he killed Arnott?" the detective said.

He was being more direct than she'd expected. If she'd needed proof that he'd lied about the "big dog" that had killed Arnott, he'd just given it to her. Or maybe he was looking for confirmation that *he* hadn't imagined the impossible.

An awkward silence stretched between them.

She was the one who broke it. Ignoring his direct question, she said, "I'm trying to sort through my life, trying to decide what I want to do." She stopped and turned her palm upward. "There are things that are still too hard for me to deal with." She might have been talking about her ordeal at Arnott's. She was pretty sure Detective Thornton knew she was talking about Ross Marshall, werewolf.

"I understand." He cleared his throat. "I'm sorting through stuff, too."

Her heart leaped into her throat. "You aren't going to . . ."

"I'm not going to talk about him to anyone besides you," he said quickly.

"Good."

He shifted in his chair. "I'd like to come back, if you don't mind. Find out how you're getting along."

"Why are you so interested in my welfare?"

"Because I know you're going through a hard time. Because I know there's nobody else you can talk to about . . . . what happened. And there's nobody I can talk to, either," he added.

She hesitated for a moment, torn. Despite his reassurances, she didn't know how far she could trust Police Detective Jack Thornton. But she would find out, because in the weeks ahead she might need a friend.

JACK paused at the entrance to Ross Marshall's property and inspected the NO TRESPASSING signs, then stepped on the accelerator again and nosed the unmarked up the rutted road into the woods.

He negotiated a rickety bridge that crossed a gurgling stream, then emerged into a meadow across which he could see a very nicely proportioned stone and wood house that fit perfectly into the wooded landscape.

The ideal place to live, he thought, for a man like Marshall. Privacy. Woodland. A comfortable home.

It had been a month since Dr. Sheridan had been abducted by Donald Arnott and a gray wolf had leaped out of the darkness to cut the serial killer down.

When Jack turned off the engine and got out of the car, he heard the sound of someone splitting wood—working as if the devil himself were flogging him.

Rounding the side of the building he found Marshall shirtless in the late April sunshine, splitting a log on a chopping block. He stared at the man's tanned skin, seeing his muscles flex. Ordinary skin he told himself. Ordinary muscles.

He waited until the ax had completed its downward swing and the piece of wood had fallen into two chunks before clearing his throat.

The PI turned, looked at him warily as he propped the ax handle against the block. "Did you come to arrest me?" he asked.

"For what?"

Ross shrugged. "You tell me."

"Actually, I came to say that I hope we can keep working together."

Surprise flashed on the other man's face. "Why?"

"You've been a big help to me in the past. It's a good professional relationship. More than that, I think we've gotten to be friends."

Marshall nodded, then asked. "What about that scene at Arnott's?"

Jack had been pretty direct with Megan. This time, he gave a different answer. "I guess you missed it, 'cause you were in the barn."

"Um-hum. And what about Crawford?"

"That's a Stone Who Done It."

Marshall shifted his weight from one foot to the other, still looking uncertain, and Jack understood his reasons. With Marshall, the need for caution must be as ingrained as the habit of looking both ways before crossing the street.

"Why don't you invite me inside? You must be cold now that you've stopped working."

"Okay." The PI picked up a plaid shirt draped across the woodpile and shrugged his arms into the sleeves. As he buttoned the front, he led the way around to the front door. They stepped into a spacious room of gleaming wood and comfortable furniture. Huge windows brought the outdoors inside.

Jack looked around with a touch of envy. "Nice place. I take it you remodeled it yourself."

"How do you know?"

"I did a background check on you when I was investigating the Crawford murder. I know you bought a number of houses and fixed them up. Then put the profits into this place."

"Yeah. It's the American dream—improving your lot in life."

"You seem to have done better than most."

"It depends on the way you look at it."

Jack was wondering how to respond when Marshall spoke again. "I can offer you herbal tea. Water. I don't drink coffee. Or anything stronger." He gave a small laugh. "Caffeine plays hell with my system. And alcohol—forget it."

"Tea is fine."

He followed Marshall into a nicely laid out kitchen with granite countertops that would have made Mrs. Anderson swoon, watched him open a cabinet and gesture toward several boxes of tea.

"I'll have whatever you're having," Jack said.

Marshall filled the kettle and turned on a burner, then pulled down a box of wild blackberry tea.

Propping his hips against a counter, he looked at ease, although the tightness around his eyes betrayed his tension. "So you've decided you don't care how Arnott died or how I get the information I bring you?"

Jack kept his own posture relaxed as he met the other man's gaze. "That's right."

"But you're pretty sure you know."

"Yes."

"And that doesn't . . . make you want to run screaming in the other direction?"

"I believe I'm open-minded enough to handle it."

Neither one of them had said the word *werewolf*, but it hung in the air between them.

"Ross, I liked you from the start. I never understood why you were so closemouthed about your investigative methods. Now I understand better—but it doesn't change my opinion of you. You're a good, solid PI. The information you've given me has always panned out. And I've never had any reason to question your motivation. You're not trying to get even with anybody. Or score points. Or rip anybody off. You're not the Lone Ranger."

Marshall listened, then spoke quietly, almost to himself. "After Crawford, I swore I'd never indulge in vigilante justice again. Never bring myself down to the level of one of the bastards I was tracking."

"But Arnott was pointing a gun at Megan, ready to pull the trigger—you didn't have a choice. Then he went for his knife. Plus you keep forgetting that I would have killed him if I'd been close enough. Now my advice is: stop beating up on yourself."

"Easier said than done."

"Yeah," Jack agreed. After ten years in law enforcement, he had his own burden to lug around.

Marshall got down two mugs, added tea bags and boiling water. "It has to steep awhile."

"Okay."

"Tell me about Walter Galveston. Did you go after him?"

"Megan told him she wouldn't press charges—if he'd agree to psychiatric counseling."

"So you're dead in the water?"

"I'll give you the legal mumbo jumbo on that. The state's attorney could, by law, go ahead with the prosecution, using Megan as a hostile victim. But with the court system so clogged, I'm pretty sure he's decided to nol-pros the case."

"Which means in English?"

"Well, a nol-pros isn't a dismissal. It just means the state's attorney chooses not to prosecute, and the case kind of lies there in legal limbo—unless Walter gets back into criminal activity. Then the state can drag this case out of the archives as an added benefit."

Ross was leaning forward, hanging on the details.

"You haven't talked to Megan about it?" Jack asked, although he was pretty sure he knew the answer to the question. He'd seen her a week ago, and she hadn't mentioned getting in touch with Ross.

"I haven't seen her."

"I'm sorry. I could tell you two care about each other."

He grimaced. "Well, her seeing the wolf take Arnott down had to be a shock even if it was justified. And she'd been treated to a preview of my undesirable qualities."

"It's something genetic? That's why you went to Bio Gen Labs?"

"Yeah. I have a twenty-fourth chromosome. At Arnott's you got a graphic demonstration of the effect it has."

"Your parents had a lot of children who died."

"You *did* dig into my background."

"I interviewed a neighbor, Rosa Lantana."

Ross gave a bark of a laugh. "Is that old bat still alive? I'll bet she gave you an earful."

"Yeah."

Marshall looked down into the mugs, stirred the contents with a spoon. "You want sugar?"

"I'll take it straight."

"Let's go sit where it's comfortable."

They each took a mug and settled themselves into leather chairs in the great room.

When Marshal spoke again, his voice was flat and hard. "To give you the rest of the genetic picture—the girl babies die at birth. The boys hang around until their teens. Then they either turn out like me, or they . . ." He shrugged. "I don't know. Maybe it's a stroke that kills them. It causes a hell of a headache in those who survive, anyway." His hand gripped the mug so tightly that the knuckles whitened.

"I'm glad you trust me enough to talk about it."

"I figure if you tried to tell this to anyone, they'd catch you with a butterfly net and cart you off."

It was Jack's turn to laugh. "Right."

"So you see that any woman who got mixed up with me would be in for a lot of grief." Marshall spoke matter-of-factly, but it was obvious the subject was painful—and one that had been on his mind for a long time.

Jack wanted to tell him that he'd talked to Megan—that she might not make the right decision on her own. He wanted to say that if Ross loved her, he should go after her. Then he reminded himself that things weren't so simple for the man he'd always thought of as the Lone Wolf.

Ross shrugged. "I've been keeping tabs on her, though. I had a chat with Galveston. He's selling her the lab equipment at a very reasonable price. I know she's got financing for her own company and is moving to another location, and that Galveston isn't exercising any claim over research she did while working for him."

Jack already knew those details. He said only, "She deserves that victory—after what she went through."

"Yeah."

When the silence stretched again, Marshall asked, "So what are you working on?"

"Mostly routine stuff. But a few cases you'll appreciate." Over the mugs of berry tea, Jack gave him the details. "Well, call me if you have anything I can use," he finally said, rising from his chair.

Marshall stood, too, facing him.

Jack held out his hand, and they shook, their clasps warm and firm. "Take care of yourself."

"You, too."

He wanted to say more. But he was in danger of embarrassing himself or Marshall with half-baked philosophy about friendship and loyalty. So he turned and left.

THE next time Megan braved the road to Ross Marshall's house was almost three months after she had first come here. It was late in the day, as the last fading rays of the sun kissed the landscape.

Once more, she cut the engine and stepped nervously out of her car. The trees had leafed out, the canopy of their foliage luxurious against the navy blue of the sky.

She looked at the flower beds near the house, making out the shapes of ferns and hostas interspersed with brightly colored impatiens, the arrangement as natural as if it had simply sprung up. But she knew that an artful gardener had placed the plants to suit his own aesthetic sense.

She took several steps closer, breathing in clean country air—then stopped short when she saw a gray shape moving toward her.

The wolf.

Her heart skipped a beat, then started hammering so hard her chest hurt. But she'd done a lot of thinking since they'd parted, and now she stood her ground as he approached, his head up, his gait majestic.

This was the first time she'd gotten a good look at him when fear wasn't slashing through her.

She looked her fill now, feeling her heart turn over. He was beautiful, a wild creature—totally uncaged, totally at home in the forest. Yet his yellow eyes glowed with the intelligence she'd seen that first time—intelligence far beyond that of a mere animal.

Tangled emotions surged through her as he came forward across the meadow, a challenge in his gaze and his posture. The first night she'd seen the gray wolf, she'd turned and run. Now she went down on her knees in the springy grass, bringing herself to his eye level as he stopped within a few feet of her.

"I missed you," she said, holding out her arms. "Come here."

For several heartbeats, she wasn't sure he was going to accept the invitation. Then he moved toward her with maddening slowness, as if he were giving her a final chance to change her mind.

She stayed where she was. And finally, finally he was close enough so that she could reach out, circling his neck with her arms and laying her cheek against his thick coat.

The contact sent a surge of relief flowing through her. She drank in his woodsy scent. Turning her face, she rubbed her lips against the side of his muzzle.

His tongue flicked out, and delicately licked her cheek, and she felt a shiver go through him.

"Mmm. I'm glad to see you, too." She stroked the silky fur behind his ears, pressed herself more tightly to his side.

"What do you think it means when a woman is turned on by a wolf?" she asked. "Well—not just any wolf. Her mate, actually."

He eased away so that the bright yellow eyes could meet hers.

"I guess you're wondering where I've been. I've had some stuff to straighten out. About the lab and my project. And other things." She swallowed, her fingers playing with the fabric of her cloak. "My research on Myer's disease is going to bring in quite a bit of money. Enough to finance my new project."

The wolf cocked his head questioningly to one side.

"Saving girl babies with the twenty-fourth chromosome. And figuring out what to do for the boys when they get old enough to change."

The turbulent look on his face made her shake her head. "You're not going to frighten me away this time."

The wolf stepped back twenty feet, stood looking at her, and she knew what he was going to do. Despite her bold words, a bolt of fear shot through her. But she stayed where she was, her breath fast and shallow.

She had known she must face this. Known it was the ultimate test—for both of them. Wide-eyed, she watched the shape of his body begin to flow the way it had that first night when fever had almost driven him to change. Then he had stopped himself in time. Tonight, he didn't. Seeing the transformation froze the breath in her lungs, and she felt her face contort.

ROSS stood in front of her, a naked man, watching the horror that twisted her perfect features into something that shattered his heart. The sorrow of it was almost too much for any living being to bear.

He had lain awake at night aching for her, yet he hadn't dared to hope for his heart's desire. Then he had seen her get out of the car— and all the longing had coalesced into one terrible driving need to claim his mate.

He had held back his joy when she put her arms around his neck, telling him she accepted the wolf, because he knew there was one crucial test that the wolf's mate must pass.

And now—

Now he felt as if his body and his soul had been torn to shreds and scattered to the winds.

"No. Please. No." She pushed herself off the ground, and he braced himself for unbearable pain. She had come here and given him hope. Then snatched it away.

But she didn't turn her back. Incredibly, she was coming toward him, her loose cloak flowing around her in the wind.

"Ross. Oh, God, Ross," she cried as she hurtled forward, wrapped her arms around him, holding him as though she never meant to let him go. "It's all right. It's all right," she added, the tears in her voice burning his skin.

"Your face. I saw the look of horror on your face," he managed to get out before his clogged throat made speech impossible.

"No. Not horror," she gasped, tipping her head back so that her eyes could meet his. "I watched you, and I thought how much it must hurt—muscle and bone contorting, internal organs changing shape. And I remembered how you'd done it twice—to save me. From Walter and from Arnott. That's what you saw."

It took several charged moments before the words sank in. Yet he still couldn't quite accept that happiness was within his grasp. "Don't you have the sense to be afraid of me? Of us?"

"I'm not afraid. I love you. That makes all the difference."

He sucked in a breath and let it out before it scalded his lungs. "You saw me kill a man."

"To save my life." She repeated what Jack Thornton had said.

"Arnott never would have come after you, if it wasn't for me. He probably saw us together at the mall."

"Ross, stop! That wasn't your fault. And if I were afraid of you, I wouldn't be here. Don't you know that every man and woman struggles with doubts? Regrets? Fears? You don't have to be a werewolf to doubt yourself."

He stared down into her eyes, trying to absorb the words. "God, what am I going to do with you?"

"Love me, I hope."

His head dropped to her shoulder. For long moments he stood listening to the sound of his own labored breathing as her fingers tangled in his hair, stroked across his broad back, drifted downward to caress his naked hips. Somehow it was that contact—the possessive way her fingers glided over his body—that allowed the miracle of their reunion to sink in.

Lifting his head, he looked down at her in wonder. She gave him a brilliant smile. "We had one unforgettable night together. I want a lot more."

Slinging her arms around his neck, she breached the distance between her mouth and his.

His response came in a flood of physical sensation and emotion, like a dam bursting. His mouth opened, devoured hers with all the hunger that had built inside him over the past lonely days and nights.

She tasted wonderful, and he feasted on her. She felt wonderful, and he gathered her close. Her scent was richer, fuller than he remembered. He might have puzzled over that, but she didn't give him time to think.

She spoke against his lips, nibbling the words, "It's a little too cold to make love out here. At least it is for me. Can we go inside?"

Too overwhelmed to voice an answer, he turned and led her to the house. He'd pictured her there, with him. But he'd thought it was simply a fantasy built from his own aching loneliness.

Now she had come to him, and the reality humbled him.

They made it through the front door, but not much farther. The sight of her eyes bright with need and her lips red and moist from his kiss made his knees go weak.

He laid her down on the rug in front of the fireplace, gathered her to him, rocking with her as they kissed and stroked each other, each touch, each kiss fueling the astonishing sensual pleasure building between them.

"I'm overdressed, I think," she murmured.

"Yes." His hands shook as they worked to pull off her cloak and open the buttons on the simple shift she wore. As they had that first time in her kitchen, two sets of hands tangled.

This time, she laughed, the sound pure joy in his ears.

"We could rip it off," she suggested.

"I'm trying to show you I can be civilized," he answered, his voice rough with barely leashed passion.

Finally, after an eternity, she was as naked as he. On a sigh of gratitude, he bent to press his face against her breasts.

She combed her fingers through his hair, holding him to her. He turned his head to find a hardened nipple with his mouth, teasing her with his tongue and teeth, wringing one glad cry from her and then another as his thumb and finger tightened on her other nipple.

In the dark hours of the night, he'd wondered if he'd made it up, if anything could have been as good as the memory of making love with her.

Incredibly, this was better. The taste of her was exquisite, the feel of her overwhelming.

His free hand slid along the curve of her hip, then traveled inward to the thatch of blond hair at the vee of her legs. His fingers dipped lower, finding her hot and wet and ready for him.

A low hum of pleasure vibrated in her throat as her body arched into the caress. Then he felt her hand close around the hard, distended shaft of his penis, and a jolt of incredible animal sensation surged through him.

"I want this inside me again."

Her words and enticing clasp drove him to the edge of madness. Now. It had to be now! He covered her body with his, his eyes never leaving hers as he plunged inside her, feeling some dark, hidden core deep within him shatter.

"Oh, Ross," she breathed, her arms circling his shoulders, and he sensed that she had felt it, too.

She was his mate.

More than his mate. His love. The other half of his being. And he understood now that his soul would have died if she hadn't come back to him.

He began to move inside her, feeling her match his rhythm. He wanted the incredible pleasure to last an eternity, but nothing so intense could endure for more than moments. He felt her inner muscles contract, heard her call out his name once more. And then he was shaking with the force of his own release, his head thrown back as ecstasy washed over him.

Afterward he held her in his arms, watching the satisfied expression on her face, gently touching the faint scar that ran down her cheek.

She turned her face, closed her eyes as she kissed his fingers.

His hand moved lower, stroking possessively over her flushed skin. When his fingers skimmed over the slight swell of her abdomen, he stopped a tremor going through him.

"Megan?" he asked, his voice hoarse.

She opened her eyes, met his questioning gaze, and gave him a small nod.

"Oh, Christ."

When he tried to wrench away from her, she circled his shoulders, held him beside her. "It's okay."

"You don't know that!"

"Yes, I do. It's a boy. I found out this morning. There's a new technique that gives you the sex early. That's why I waited so long to come back here. I wanted to find out before I saw you."

"And if it had been a girl?"

Her face turned very serious. "I . . . would have tried to save her, although I'm not sure I could do anything at this point. With in vitro fertilization, there's a much better chance. If it's a girl, you can remove the extra chromosome before implanting the fertilized egg."

"And with a boy?"

Her features lightened again. "We've got fifteen years to figure out what happens at puberty. I need to do some tests on you. And on your brother, if he'll let me. I'm betting that the key to survival is hormonal."

He stared down at her in wonder. "You'd do all that for me?"

"For us. I'd do anything for us. The question is: Can you accept the idea of 'us'?"

He bent, pressed his forehead to hers. "God, I want to." His voice turned low and urgent as he went on rapidly. "But . . . you didn't choose me, the way any other woman would choose a man. The extra genes I have forced me to find a mate. You came here and touched me, took care of me. That was how the bond formed between us. Neither one of us could control what was happening."

She let him talk, waited until he was finished. "I don't think it's so different from the way other women choose a man," she murmured. "They meet. Maybe by chance, the way we met. And some mysterious chemistry draws them together. But they know they've found the one person for them—in all the sea of humanity."

He hadn't thought about it in those terms. Never. The revelation shook him.

She lifted her face, looked into his eyes. "The important thing is, do you love me?"

"You know I do."

"Then stop worrying about the rest of it. Just let yourself take the leap off the cliff. I'll be leaping with you."

She made it sound so easy. And maybe with her beside him it could be. Maybe she was what he needed to rise above the genes that ruled his life. Perhaps he had found the anchor to his humanity in her—this woman who had come back to him against all odds.

"I love you," he whispered. Then said it again louder.

"Did it hurt to say it?" she asked, a smile flickering at the corners of her lips.

"Only a little. It will probably get easier with practice." He pulled the quilt off the sofa, tucked it around them, and nuzzled his face against hers, trailing his lips up her cheek.

Her arms came up to circle his shoulders, pull his body more tightly against hers. "I can't promise everything is going to work out perfectly. We may have some . . . sadness . . . in our life."

"You mean, we may lose some children?"

"I hope that's not going to be true. But there are no guarantees. There never are."

He sucked in a breath, let it out in a rush. "I think I got the closest thing to a guarantee I could get when they sent a doctor out from Bio Gen Labs—and it turned out to be you."

She snuggled in his arms. "You know what Jack started calling you a long time ago? The Lone Wolf. Ironic, isn't it?"

"You talked to Jack?"

"He came over to find out how I was doing. He kept coming back, and I could open up with him a little more each time. He ended up telling me how much you needed me. That was after he'd been out here and talked to you."

"The sneaky bastard."

"I told him why I was waiting before I came back here."

He thought about that for a moment. "So he found out we're going to have a baby before I did."

Her color deepened. "Do you mind? I had to talk to someone. And he . . . he let me know that he's our friend." She watched his face anxiously.

"I think he is."

He saw the tension ease out of her. Then she gave him a sly smile. "I think if you asked him, he'd be your best man at the wedding."

His face must have told her how unprepared he was for the suggestion.

"That is if you're interested in making an honest woman of me," she added.

"God, yes. I just wasn't thinking that far ahead."

"I'd like to do it soon—before I start showing. I think the ceremony will be a little more decorous that way."

Once the idea took hold, he realized how much he wanted the world to know she was his wife. "As soon as we can," he answered thickly.

She pressed against him, then raised her head. "So now that I know you're not going to send me away, I think you're going to have to feed me. I was too nervous to eat anything before I came here. But now I'm ravenous. I've discovered pregnancy will do that to you."

"You want some chicken soup?" he offered. "I have a bunch of it left."

"Steak, I think. This child I'm carrying is demanding meat."

"Well, then, that's what he'll get." He climbed out of their makeshift bed, hurried down the hall to his bedroom, and pulled on a T-shirt and jeans.

When he returned he saw that she'd dressed in her shift and run her hands through her hair.

He stopped at the entrance to the great room, just staring at the woman who had changed his life, still hardly able to believe she was really in his house—really his. For the rest of his life.

She must have read the expression on his face.

"Believe it," she murmured. Then, *"Go gcumhdaí is dtreoraí na déithe thú."*

He gazed at her in wonder. "You know what that means?"

"Yes. 'May the gods guard and guide you.' I got myself a Gaelic dictionary. I used one of yours when I was here before. I know why you named this place Díthreabh. It's your refuge. Ours, now."

She glided toward him, kissed his lips, his cheeks, his brows as her fingertips stroked lovingly over his back and shoulders.

He gave himself over to her embrace, and in that moment, he finally understood the Lone Wolf would never be alone again.

EDGE OF THE

MOON

PROLOGUE

HIS name was Ayindral, and he lived somewhere between the realm of earth and ageless emptiness. In a plane of existence not of this universe.

Some might have called him a demon, a chimera, an imp, a spirit, or a jinni. Others might see him as a dark god and prostrate themselves before him.

But he was none of those. He was a being of energy. Of light and shadow. Of mental power. A being that humankind would never understand, even in a nightmare.

He had lived since before the planet Earth formed from cosmic dust. He would live on into eternity—if left to himself.

But there were channels of power between his world and the world of humankind, channels that could spell his destruction.

Like a rift in the fabric of time, one of those passageways had begun to open. In his incorporeal fashion, he raised his head and sniffed the air—catching the scent of danger the way an animal of the forest might sense the presence of a hunter.

There was no choice. He must act to save himself. And quickly, before it was too late. Delicately, desperately he cast his mind outward, searching for human beings he could bend to his will—use as his defensive shield.

1

KATHRYN Reynolds swept a lock of fiery red hair away from her forehead and rocked back in her chair.

Rolling the tension out of her shoulders, she stared critically at the computer screen. Two days ago she'd been happy with the brochure she was designing for Sunrise Realty.

Now . . .

Now she had the nagging feeling there was something wrong. Was the text readable enough against the background of rising suns? Should she use a bolder font?

She had just clicked on the color chart when she heard footsteps on the front porch of the white Victorian she'd inherited from Grandma O'Shea.

Heather! Thank God. She hadn't realized until that moment how worried she was. But her sigh of relief evaporated with the sound of the doorbell. Heather wouldn't ring the bell. Unless she'd lost her key—and forgotten about the one she'd hidden under a rock in the bushes. Which, actually, she wouldn't put past her friend and downstairs tenant. Heather had a lot of excellent qualities, but she was also a bit of a flake.

Speaking of which—

The bell sounded a second time, and a male voice called out, "Anybody home?" Kathryn looked down at the long, bare legs protruding from beneath her Redskins T-shirt. Damn! She'd done it again—gotten up and started working, then lost track of the time.

Now it was afternoon, and she wasn't exactly dressed for company. Sprinting into the bedroom, she grabbed the pair of knit shorts she'd left on the chair, pulling them on as she crossed the worn Oriental rug.

After unlocking the door to her apartment, she hurried barefoot down the stairs to the sound of pounding on the front door, then looked through the beveled glass window.

A dark-haired man in a blue uniform stood on the porch, and her mouth went dry.

It was him!

No. She canceled the spurt of panic. It wasn't him. He was too young. Too heavy. It wasn't the guy with the white van she'd seen off and on around the neighborhood for the past week—acting busy. He'd given her a creepy feeling, and she'd asked a couple of neighbors if they knew what he was doing. Nobody had been sure. She hadn't seen him for a few days; and, for a moment, she'd thought . . . But it wasn't him.

Slipping the door on the chain, she opened it and asked, "Can I help you?"

"Heather DeYoung?"

"She's not home right now."

The man looked annoyed. "She's supposed to be here between three and six."

"I'm sorry. Can I help you?" she asked again.

"Mr. Fisher asked me to bring over these carpet samples she wanted to see."

Heather had complained about the carpet in the bedroom, and Kathryn had said she'd go in with her on replacing it. But obviously she couldn't make the selection by herself.

"I'm sorry, you'll have to come back when she gets home."

He jutted out his jaw. "And when will that be?"

"I don't know."

"Yeah, well, I'm late for an installation job because of her, so tell her to get back to Mr. Fisher."

"I'll give her the message."

He picked up a vinyl case he'd set down and stamped back across the porch, leaving Kathryn standing in the vestibule that led to both apartments. Turning to her right, she stared at her friend's door.

When had she last seen Heather? Saturday night? She wasn't sure, because she'd been working on a couple of jobs, and she hadn't been paying attention. It wasn't unusual for Heather to take off for the weekend. And it wasn't even unusual for her to extend a minivacation into the next week—since she worked as a substitute teacher and could turn down assignments if she wanted. But usually she was back by Monday afternoon. Now it was Tuesday. And she still wasn't home.

Kathryn pressed her hand against the wall, running her fingers over the raised strips in the wallpaper, staring at Heather's door. She owned the apartment. She could go in if she wanted and look around, but her own sense of privacy was very strong. So she wasn't going to invade Heather's space just because she was feeling jumpy.

And what would she be looking for if she did go inside? A body? Signs of a struggle?

She grimaced, knowing she was letting her imagination run away with her now.

Slowly she climbed back up the stairs, stepped into her apartment, and locked the door—looking around at the cozy space where her graphic design business shared her living quarters. After Gran had died, she could have moved down to the first floor. But she liked being up here, liked the extra light and the view of the garden—and not having anyone walking around above her. She loved the high ceilings and the old wooden floors and the carefully crafted woodwork that made her home so different from the tract housing developers were slapping up these days. More than that, she was comfortable here. Maybe too comfortable. Sometimes she knew she had a tendency to close herself off like a hermit crab ducking into its shell.

Which was why her friendship with Heather DeYoung, who rented the apartment downstairs, had been so good for her.

The woman could be maddening. Exasperating. A total flake. And at the same time a really good friend. In the year and a half that Heather had lived downstairs, they'd gotten into the habit of hanging out together—taking power walks in the afternoons, going on shopping expeditions. Talked long into the evening about movies and books and the guys in their lives. Shared their problems.

So did her friend have a problem now? Something she hadn't felt comfortable bringing up? Like that little episode last year?

She crossed to the window, ducked under The Spider Plant That Took over the World, and stared down at the bright pink and red azaleas in full bloom, then flicked her gaze back to the empty space in the driveway where her tenant's burgundy Honda was usually parked.

"Dammit, Heather," she muttered. "Where are you? Atlantic City, cleaning up at the slot machines? Why don't you take a minute to give me a call and let me know you're okay?"

Like magic, the phone rang, and she blinked—then sprinted back to the desk and snatched up the receiver.

"Hello?"

There was no answer.

"Hello?"

The silence stretched, and she carefully replaced the receiver in the cradle as she looked at the caller ID.

It said "Unavailable." So it was probably just one of those automated telemarketing calls. Not Heather trying to check in. Or calling to say her car had broken down because she'd forgotten to change the oil.

Like she'd forgotten to charge the battery on her cell phone. Which was probably why there was no answer when Kathryn had called that number.

She grimaced. Maybe it was time to check in with Heather's boyfriend, Gary Swinton. He was a strange guy. Secretive. Always acting superior, like he knew something Kathryn didn't. Privately she called him The Swine, and she'd told Heather she could do better; but Gary was still in and out of her bed on a semiregular basis.

After looking up his number in her Rolodex and dialing, she counted five rings before an answering machine picked up.

"Hey, this is Gary. I really want to talk to you. So leave a message."

Yeah, sure, she thought. Probably she was the last person he wanted to talk to, because she'd made her feelings about him pretty clear.

She almost hung up. Then she took a breath and said in an upbeat voice, "Hi. This is Kathryn Reynolds. I'm trying to reach Heather. She needs to set up an appointment to look at the bedroom carpet samples. If she's with you, could you ask her to give me a call?" She finished by leaving her number, all the time picturing Gary sitting by the machine, listening to her talk.

She considered driving down to his place. But he lived in D.C., in Adams Morgan—not a neighborhood she liked to walk through alone at night. And it would be dark by the time she got there.

With a sigh, she picked up the magic wand sitting on the desk. Too bad she couldn't wave it, say "abracadabra," and command her tenant to appear. Unfortunately, the wand was just a hollow plastic tube about a foot long, one of the toys she liked to play with while she was thinking. It was filled with shiny stars and moons floating in a viscous blue liquid. Turning it on end, she watched the heavenly bodies shoot upward in a swirl of blue, but they didn't give her any insights into Heather's whereabouts.

Her hand tightened on the plastic as she seesawed the cylinder back and forth, watching the moving shapes, trying to banish the feeling of uneasiness that had been hanging over her since she'd opened her eyes that morning. Well, longer than that—if she were honest.

With a small *thunk*, she set down the wand.

What was wrong with her? She was usually rock steady. In charge of her life. She'd been on her own since Gran died five years ago. She'd paid for her own college education with work-study and student loans. After apprenticing for a couple years at one of the big ad agencies downtown, she'd gone out on her own. Her graphic design business was doing really well, and her client list was growing as satisfied customers recommended her to their friends. She'd worked hard to get where she was. And she was proud of her achievements.

But for the past few days, a kind of free-floating anxiety had been hanging over her. Not just because of Heather. It was something else—something she couldn't identify. Like a storm gathering, its low, dark clouds hanging directly over her.

"Really, that's a pretty over-the-top image," she muttered. With a quick shake of her head, she crossed to the window, staring down again at the empty space in the driveway. Heather would be home tomorrow morning, she told herself firmly. But if she wasn't, it was time to get in touch with the Montgomery County Police.

JACK Thornton pulled his unmarked into the driveway of his gray colonial, cut the engine, and sat with his hands wrapped around the wheel for several moments.

All day he'd felt something hovering over him, something that grated on his nerves. And now that he was home, he felt as though he'd made a miraculous escape.

From what?

He didn't know. But he did know he'd had a hell of a day. He'd walked into the middle of a domestic case. The kind that made him wonder if he was a police detective or a mental health worker.

It started out when he'd been driving down Democracy Boulevard and seen a woman dressed in a nightgown and robe, sobbing and running in and out of the traffic. No one else was on the scene, so he'd called in a report, then stopped and identified himself.

By the time a couple of uniformed officers had arrived, Mrs. Westborn had apparently bonded with him.

But seeing the uniforms got her sobbing again, begging him to stay with her, and he'd ended up taking her to Montgomery County Hospital, where he'd interviewed her in an emergency room cubicle.

He'd sensed from the first that she was holding back information—which was one of the reasons he'd stuck with her.

With a good deal of patience and reassurance, he'd finally gotten Mrs. Westborn to admit that her husband was at home—dead. He'd slit his own throat, and the wife had freaked out.

Slit his throat! That had riveted Jack's attention. Slitting a throat wasn't so easy to do, despite its popularity with producers of slasher movies. It took a bit of effort to cut through tough muscles, cords, and rubbery tendons, unless you had a rather large and exceptionally sharp surgical scalpel. Besides, throat-cutting was a kind of slow and painful death, one that normally didn't appeal to suicidal folks.

Jack had sent a couple of uniforms to check out the story while he'd waited with the woman until psychiatric services arrived.

Then he'd gone over to the house to investigate the scene—and found the guy was dressed in a woman's lacy gown and robe.

So much for domestic tranquillity in Montgomery County, Maryland, one of the richest counties in the nation. But he'd learned that more money sometimes meant more problems. Like the bored teenager who had hacked up his friend a few years ago, or the group of boys who'd raped a mentally retarded girl in the woods.

Now he was thinking that murder was as likely as suicide in the Westborn case. Tomorrow he'd start questioning the neighbors, to find out how the couple had been getting along. But he wasn't going to dismiss the possibility of suicide out of hand. Suppose, for example, that Westborn was in serious financial trouble, and he'd seen only one way out?

Six months ago, Jack might have started checking up on Westborn from his home computer. But he'd been smart enough to recognize the signs of burnout. He'd pulled back, vowed to leave the job at the office.

As he stepped inside the door, he was enveloped by the smell of baking chocolate chip cookies. For a heart-stopping moment, he thought that Laura was in the kitchen with the kids. Then reality came slamming back. Almost three years ago, a drunk driver on I-270 had crossed the median and crashed into his wife's car with enough force to ram the engine block into the front seat.

He closed his eyes, banishing the terrible image. He didn't need it. Not now.

He took several measured steps down the hall, focusing on the conversation coming from the kitchen. Craig was talking to their housekeeper, Emily Anderson, and he remembered that seven-year-old Lily was at a friend's for dinner. Emily was going to pick her up later.

Nine-year-old Craig was enthusiastically helping with the cookies.

"You promised I could lick the bowl. If you keep on scraping like that, there won't be anything left," Craig complained.

"I think you like cookie dough better than cookies."

"Yeah. And you got those eggs that come in a carton so I could eat the dough."

"Mm-hmm." The housekeeper chuckled. "I suppose I liked the dough better, too, when I was your age," she admitted.

"Not you, Mrs. A."

"Oh, yes."

Jack set down his briefcase and leaned his shoulder against the wall, enjoying the domestic eavesdropping. His children had gone through a pretty rough patch, and it was gratifying to hear Craig having a normal good time, thanks to Mrs. Anderson. A plumber's widow, she was the perfect grandmother substitute for two kids who needed as much stability in their lives as they could get. And she ran the house with quiet, unobtrusive efficiency.

The timer rang. From the hallway, Jack watched the housekeeper bend to open the oven and take out a cookie sheet. Deftly she used a metal spatula to transfer the cookies to wire racks.

"When can I have one?" Craig asked.

"Well, we both know it's supposed to be dinner first and then dessert."

"Aw . . ."

Emily lowered her voice to a conspiratorial whisper. "You can have a cookie first, if you have it with a glass of milk. Just be sure to eat your dinner—so your dad won't think I'm a bad influence."

"You're a good influence! I've heard him say that."

She made a *tsking* sound as she set the boy up at the table with his before-dinner treat, then popped the last sheet of cookies into the oven.

Jack was about to join them when Craig stopped him in his tracks with a question. "Does a girl have to be married to have a baby?"

He saw Mrs. Anderson set down her pot holder and turn slowly, saw his son watching her intently.

"Uh, why do you want to know?" she asked.

Craig scuffed his foot against the chrome leg of his chair. "Dad tries to be real cool, but he'd probably get uptight if I asked him."

"What made you think of the question?" the housekeeper asked carefully.

"On the playground today, this kid, Billy Patterson, was talking about his sister. He says she's going to have a baby and that her and her boyfriend are probably going to get married."

"She and her boyfriend," Mrs. Anderson corrected. "Craig, this is the kind of thing you *should* talk to your dad about."

"Oh, he got me and Lily this book that explains all about . . . you know . . . about how the mom and dad . . . you know. But I can't imagine anyone doing something that yucky unless they were married and . . . you know . . . had to have a baby."

"Well, some people . . . uh . . . try it out before they get married."

Jack felt a stab of guilt, because he was glad Emily was handling this for him. One of the things he dreaded about single fatherhood was coping with the sensitive stuff.

"Oh." Craig thought about that. "Do you think my mom and dad did it before they got married?"

"I don't know."

"But they did it after. Twice."

Jack took a step back, his stomach knotting. God, what he wouldn't give to do it with Laura again!

Closing his eyes, he took a quick emotional inventory. His wife's loss was no longer a raw wound. Maybe he was even ready to think about a relationship with another woman—although he hadn't met anyone that interested him.

With an inaudible sigh, he returned to the front door, opening it silently, then closing it loudly to announce his arrival before striding down the hall.

Both occupants of the kitchen looked toward the door, embarrassment painted across their faces. Mrs. Anderson bent and checked the oven again. Craig took a gulp of milk.

"What a great surprise. Cookies," Jack said, grabbing one and taking a bite.

HE was slender and of medium height, with pale gray eyes that darkened when he was excited or when he wore his special contact lenses. His hair was fine and blond as corn silk. When he combed it carefully, the medallion-sized bald spot on his crown was invisible.

He called himself many names. Simon Gwynn was his alias today, although that wasn't his real name, of course. He was careful to keep his real identity hidden, because to have possession of a name was to have power over that thing or person.

No one had questioned the legitimacy of Simon Gwynn or any of his other names. They gave him protection—from the police, from those few men who still knew and practiced the ancient magic arts. And from other more powerful forces.

But names weren't his only safeguard. He had many homes, so that he could switch his residence if need be. And there were many disguises that he put on when he ventured forth into the world of ordinary men and women. Not just the clothing—the whole persona, he thought with a self-satisfied laugh. He could look and sound like an old man in a dirty button-down shirt, baggy pants, and a white Albert Einstein wig. He could play a plumber in a visor cap and blue coveralls with the name Jerry embroidered on the breast pocket. A fast-talking salesman in a crisp blue suit, horn-rimmed glasses, and a mustache. He had a wardrobe that filled an enormous closet. And the theater courses he'd taken had taught him the art of makeup. Once or twice, he'd even passed as a woman, although that certainly wasn't his preferred mode of disguise.

Alone at home, he dressed quite simply and all in black. This afternoon he was clad only in loose-fitting silk trousers that slid sensuously against the skin of his legs as he climbed the stairs from the basement.

He'd been down there to check on the prisoner in the soundproof cell behind the locked door in the laundry room. She had been spaced out when he'd scooped her up. Spaced out and all too trusting. Stupid, actually. Too caught up in a relationship to pay attention to little warning signs. But most people were like that. You simply had to understand how to manipulate them. How to assert your will over theirs.

She was still sleeping from the drugs he'd put in her food. If she figured out what he'd done, she wouldn't eat the next time he fed her. But that was okay. If she didn't eat, she'd get weak. And that would only make it easier to handle her when he brought her into the black chamber and used her in the most important ceremony of his career.

As he ascended the stairs, he stroked his fingers gently over the skin of his narrow chest. It was pale, except where it was crisscrossed with a network of fine, raised red lines. He stroked those faint lines, loving the way they felt under his sensitive fingertips. The scars were the product of the lash he'd taken to his own flesh. The lash that was part of the discipline of his studies.

The lines that remained were symbols of his acquisition of knowledge, and he was justifiably proud of them.

When he reached the second floor, he walked with measured paces to the library. The walls were lined with volumes, old and new. *The Golden Dawn* as revealed by Israel Regardie; *The Black Arts*, the brilliant biography of Aleister Crowley; *The Great Beast*, Hopper's *Mediaeval Number Symbols; The Kabbalah*, Butler's *Ritual Magic*. Most of the standard works in his field. He was still looking for *Portal to Another World* on the off chance that it still existed somewhere. But he didn't need it; he'd learned enough on his own from the books he had hunted down in private libraries and dusty shops. Along with the ancient texts and the histories of magic rituals were the other branches of knowledge he had explored. Psychology, pharmacology, economics, social history, anthropology, physics.

He had studied long and hard, delved into mysteries that few understood. He had practiced the rituals he needed, memorized the words of power. And soon he would be ready to put all his hard work to the test.

A tingle of excitement rippled over his skin, and he struggled to regain his composure. There was no room in his life for euphoria. Not yet. Not until he had achieved his goal.

2

IN his dreamless realm, Ayindral felt a ripple in the current of time, a moment in which he could catch the leading edge of the wave and change the course of events.

The woman was the key. The woman who had captured the magician's interest.

But he needed to be sure of the man as well. Delicately his mind probed the world of humans. Sight and sound were alien to Ayindral. Yet he could simulate the tools that humans used.

Through the shrouded fog of his own universe, he opened a window into the world of men. It was only a narrow slit in the time–space continuum, and yet there was an immediate rush of mental energy from one state to another, like a rush of wind, a pulling sensation that turned the core of his being cold.

A soundless scream rose within him. Soundless because he had no mouth, no vocal cords. He was a being of pure energy, and pain was alien to him. Yet he felt it.

Ruthlessly, he ignored the frightening sensation. The danger would come, yet the time of greatest risk had not arrived.

Now he entered the mind of Police Captain James Granger and sent the man a new idea—reinforcing it with a clenching cramp in the gut.

JACK looked up to see Captain Granger standing beside the blotter. "What are you working on?" his supervisor asked.

Jack gestured toward the papers spread across his desk. "I'm doing a background check on Harold Westborn, the guy whose wife says he slit his throat."

"Yeah. I think we can turn that one over to the medical examiner."

Jack blinked. "We're not going to investigate it as a possible murder?"

"Let's see what the M.E. says. If he confirms suicide, then we can cross it off our caseload."

"Okay." That wasn't the way Granger usually worked. Usually he assumed a suspicious death was murder, until the facts showed otherwise. But he figured the captain must have his reasons this time.

Granger's next words confirmed the speculation. "I've got something more important for you. Come into my office."

Jack pushed back his chair, then followed his supervisor to the private enclosure in the corner of the squad room.

When they were both seated, Granger said, "I'd like you to interview a woman named Kathryn Reynolds." He consulted a file on his desk. "She turned in a missing person report two days ago on her tenant, Heather DeYoung. One of the uniforms at the Rockville station, Chris Kendall, took the initial report."

"Uh-huh."

"We have several other missing person reports in the county. Another woman named Brenda Quinlin. A young man named Stewart Talber. And an eight-year-old boy, Kip Bradley."

Jack felt his chest tighten. A kid. About the age of his own children. He remembered reading about it. There was some evidence that the boy had been abducted by his noncustodial father, but neither the man nor the boy had turned up in a month of beating the bushes for them. Jack was still hoping it was the father, because the alternative hit too close to home.

"The missing guy is a mentally-ill man," Granger was saying. "On the surface these incidents don't seem related to each other—or to Heather DeYoung. But you're good at digging information out of witnesses and making correlations. DeYoung was just reported missing. I want your impressions, and then I want you to see if you can find any patterns."

Basically, there was nothing strange about Granger's request. Jack knew he was good at connecting the dots on crimes that might not seem related. Still, Granger's manner put him on the alert. There was something else in play here. Had a bigwig with an interest in one of the cases leaned on the captain?

Jack knew he might never find out. So he simply said, "Okay," took the offered case files, and went back to his own desk to study them.

AN hour later, he pulled up in front of Kathryn Reynolds's nicely pre-served Victorian on Davenport Street. Out of habit, his appraising eye took in details. It was early in the season, but the flower beds were dressed with a fresh layer of mulch. Pink and red azaleas and a variety of daffodils were in bloom, along with white dogwoods.

The plantings were mature, like the house. They might say nothing about Reynolds's tastes. On the other hand, she hadn't ripped out the bushes and paved the yard with antique brick, the way he'd seen with homeowners who didn't want to be bothered with the great outdoors.

His gaze flicked back to the structure. The white siding looked like it had been painted recently. And the paving in the driveway was fresh, which suggested that the owner was doing well financially. The house and garden definitely looked better than some of the other prop-erties in this older Rockville neighborhood of mature trees and wide lawns.

Rockville had once been a sleepy rural community about forty min-utes north of D.C. Years ago, its chief claim to fame was that F. Scott Fitzgerald was buried on the outskirts of town. Now the country church and its graveyard were surrounded by a tangle of highways—a symbol that suburban sprawl had moved out to envelop the area. But there were still neighborhoods, like this one, that looked pretty much the way they had seventy-five years ago.

He sat for several more minutes, still grappling with the odd, disqui-eting feeling that had settled over him in Granger's office. He might have ignored it, but long ago he'd learned to trust his spider senses.

He'd worked with Chris Kendall, the officer who had taken Reynolds's report, back when they were both at the Bethesda station, and he would have liked to talk to him before coming out here. But the patrolman had left the building for a doctor's appointment before Jack had gotten the assignment. Too bad, because the initial police contact was a good source of additional information. The uniforms put down what was required in writing. But there was usually a whole lot they didn't get onto paper. Jack liked to do a little probing into their casual observations, stuff they didn't think was important enough to go in the report, or stuff they didn't even know they'd noticed, until he asked about it. He also paid attention to their opinions, which gave them a chance to express "gut feelings" that were often useful later.

Of course, Jack suspected Granger was probably planning to do the same thing with him. More than once, the captain had sent him out on an interview that hardly seemed top priority, then quizzed him on his impressions.

After climbing out of the unmarked and locking the door, he glanced toward the second floor of the house and caught a flash of red. Red hair, he realized—as fiery as flames flickering behind the windowpanes.

Was that Reynolds? Or someone else? Whoever it was had pulled back the moment he'd looked up. So she was nervous about getting caught peering out or curious about who had pulled up in front of her house?

He hadn't called ahead. She'd said she worked at home, so he'd taken a chance on catching her in—catching her off-balance if there was something going on that she hadn't shared with Officer Kendall.

He tucked the folder unobtrusively under one arm and started toward the front door. According to the initial report, Ms. Reynolds owned the house and lived on the upper story. The missing woman had an apartment on the ground floor.

Jack rang the bell and listened to footsteps coming down an inner stairway. He prepared to confirm the name of the female who opened the door; but the moment the door opened, the breath froze in his lungs so that it was impossible to speak.

He was caught and held by a pair of emerald green eyes, a sweep of wild red hair, and skin like rich dairy cream.

His muscles went rigid. His arm clamped on the folder tucked against his body.

Time seemed to stop, like a scene from a videotape frozen on a TV screen. Unable to move forward or back away, he stared into her eyes, seeing her pupils dilate and then contract.

Everything around him was out of focus, with the exception of the slender young woman standing in the doorway. She remained sharp and clear. Details came to him: the way her breasts filled out the front of her wildflower-printed T-shirt. The smell of strawberries wafting toward him. The startled look in those green eyes.

Along with the physical awareness came a jolt of pure sexual energy, like nothing he had ever experienced in his life. Lust at first sight. It was almost palpable—arching between them like electricity between two contact points. Dangerous and at the same time so compelling that he would have leaped through a wall of fire to reach this woman if she had been on the other side.

The whole out-of-kilter experience lasted only seconds. Then the world as he knew it clicked back into real time. The moment had passed so quickly that it was easy to tell himself that it had all been in his imagination.

He clung to that theory, because if it wasn't imagination, he was hardly equipped to deal with what had happened.

The woman in the doorway took a quick step back, as if trying to escape from the same emotions bolting through him.

For several heartbeats, neither of them spoke.

Finally, Jack dragged air into his lungs and let it out before asking, "Kathryn Reynolds?" He was surprised that his voice sounded normal.

"Yes. And you are?"

"Detective Jack Thornton, Montgomery County P.D."

Reynolds's hands clenched in front of her. "The police? Have you come to tell me something about Heather? Is it bad news?"

"Are you expecting bad news?" he asked, slipping back into his professional mode, carefully watching her reaction.

"No . . . I mean, I don't know. I hope not. I don't know what to expect."

"Can I come in? Then you can tell me what brought you to the station house."

"Can I see some identification?" she countered, as if she'd just realized she should have asked.

"Of course." While he pulled out his ID and shield, he was still mentally shaking his head at his out-of-character reaction in those first few seconds after she'd opened the door.

She studied his ID, then said, "I already filed a report with Officer . . ." She stopped and fumbled for the name. "Officer Kendall."

"Yes." Jack put away his credentials, then pulled the folder from under his arm, opened it, and showed her the forms. "I have the report right here. So can we talk?"

This time she nodded and stepped back to let him into a vestibule. He followed her through a second doorway, then up a flight of steps, watching the unconscious sway of her hips in faded jeans.

He was accustomed to making assumptions about people based on their personal spaces. Seconds after stepping into her apartment, he was thinking that Kathryn Reynolds was a study in contradictions.

In one corner of the room was an antique desk with a computer under a set of mahogany wall shelves. Catty-corner to the desk area were more shelves piled with neatly labeled folders and plastic boxes. The office atmosphere was broken by all manner of whimsical objects that adorned the work area. He saw ceramic cats, a papier-mâché rooster, at least ten fancy glass paperweights, a white unicorn. On her computer screen was an underwater scene with swimming fish and coral. When the computer made a belching, bubbling noise like a toilet flushing, she crossed the room and cranked the sound down.

He turned to hide his grin and saw that the opposite side of the room showed even more of her personality.

Intrigued, he walked closer. She had a flowered humpback sofa, several overstuffed chairs, and a coffee table that looked like it might have started life as a packing case. A ceramic pitcher of dried flowers shared the marble top of a low chest with several Mexican carved and painted animals. A Victorian whatnot held paperback books and antique toys. The pictures on the walls reflected the same eclectic mix.

Looking from the decor to her tense face, he strove to put her at ease. Or perhaps he just wanted her to know he wasn't a total ignoramus when it came to culture.

"You're a fan of Sir Lawrence Alma-Tadema?" he asked, peering at a picture of some very handsome young men and women dressed in classical Greek outfits relaxing around a circular marble structure.

"You like his work?"

He laughed. "Actually, yes. I once caught a burglary case where a whole bunch of his prints were stolen. I started off rolling my eyes at his stuff, but he grows on you."

"Yes. He was out of style for years. But I always did like his combination of realism and romanticism."

He nodded, not sure exactly what she meant, and thinking it was time to get back to business.

He cleared his throat. "So when did you first notice that Heather DeYoung was missing?"

She walked toward one of the easy chairs, picked up a paisley pillow, and clutched it to her middle as she sat down. "It kind of crept up on me. Two days ago I realized she hadn't come home since Sunday night."

"She was missing for five days before you reported it?"

Her fingers clamped on the pillow. "You're making it sound like an accusation."

"I didn't mean to. I'm just trying to get the full picture," he said, still watching her reactions, thinking that facts were never the whole story.

"Sometimes she stays away for several days. It suddenly dawned on me that I hadn't seen her in a while."

"Okay," he answered, noting her discomfort. He still didn't know if it was because of her friend or because of him.

For a split second he thought about what had happened when she'd opened the door. Should he say something to clear the air? Or to find out if she'd experienced the same thing that he had?

The latter would be his primary motive, he silently admitted. A very unprofessional motive.

Usually he had an excellent sense of what questions to ask a witness or a suspect. Today he fumbled for the right approach.

"Let's see. Ms. DeYoung works for the Montgomery County school system as a substitute teacher. That pays enough to support her?"

"She says it does."

"But she could have some other source of income?"

"I don't know."

He set finances aside for the moment. He had other ways of poking into the woman's fiscal solvency. Instead, he quickly switched topics. "So Ms. DeYoung is unreliable?"

She tipped her head to one side. "Where did you get that impression?"

"It isn't unusual for her to take off for several days—on a whim?" He waited for her to answer the question.

"Yes, but she pays her rent on time. She doesn't give me any problems."

"What kind of problems are you referring to?"

"She doesn't play loud music. She doesn't have wild parties. She doesn't wake me up at two in the morning if the toilet's stopped up. She gets out a plunger."

He nodded, thinking about what she was saying and what she was leaving out. "Does she have any bad habits? Drugs, alcohol? Something that could get her into trouble."

"No," she said, but could have sounded more sure.

"But?"

Reynolds swallowed. "I don't like to make judgments. And I don't like to talk about people."

"I understand. But if it will help us find Heather, I'd appreciate your insights."

She hesitated, then answered. "Okay, I don't like her boyfriend."

"Because?"

"He takes advantage. She loves him, but he doesn't love her."

"How do you mean, 'takes advantage'?"

"He's borrowed money from her." She stopped, played with the fringe of the pillow. "I wouldn't tell you this if it weren't important. He told her he'd stop dating her if she didn't have an abortion last year, but she was the one who had to pay for it."

The guy sounded like a real winner, but Jack still didn't know whether or not Reynolds was exaggerating her assessment. "She discussed all that with you?"

"Yes. We've gotten to be good friends."

"What's his name?"

"Gary Swinton."

"Could she be at his house?"

"His apartment," she corrected. "I thought of that. I called and left a couple of messages on his answering machine."

"Do you have a phone number for him, an address?"

"In my Rolodex." She stood, set the pillow down on the chair, and crossed to the desk, where she flipped through cards, then gave him the requested information.

"What about a work address?"

She thought about that. "I know he works at Circuit City. The one in Bethesda. I think he's in small electronics—because he got a good deal for her on a floor model tabletop stereo. But I don't have the address."

"I know where it is. Can you give me a description? Some way I'll recognize him?"

Her hand skimmed across the desk, settled over a footlong clear plastic rod with colored liquid and shiny stars and moons inside. When she tipped it on end, the liquid and the glitter began to flow up and down the tube.

She stared at the bobbing glitter, her brow wrinkling. "He's about thirty years old. Blond hair. Light eyes. They're set close together. His hair is usually just one beat too long—maybe to hide his bald spot. He's average height. Not too heavy. He's got a small scar on the left side of his chin. I guess that would be the most identifying mark."

"Okay. That's great," he said, writing it down. "You're good at detail."

"My art background."

"Yeah."

She was still playing with the plastic tube. He watched the swirl of colors. "What's that?"

She gave a small, embarrassed laugh. "A magic wand."

"Where did you get it?"

"Don't tell me you need one."

"Sometimes I'd like to have one. But I was thinking my daughter would like it."

"Oh, you're married."

"I was. . . ." He let the sentence trail off. Probably she thought he was divorced, and he didn't want her thinking that he couldn't make a marriage work. Then he reminded himself that it didn't matter what she thought about him. He was interviewing her about a missing person—that was all.

"Oh," she said again, twirling the plastic rod in her hand.

His eyes were drawn to the bits of glitter and the swirling blue liquid. For a moment they both watched the shifting motion inside the beveled plastic.

"What would you do with a magic wand if you had one?" she asked.

"Solve Stone Who Done Its."

"What's a Stone Who Done It?"

"A case where there are no solid suspects and no leads."

"Um."

He watched her lips form the syllable, then roused himself from his study of her—a very unprofessional study. "Would it be possible for me to see Ms. DeYoung's apartment?"

She hesitated. "I'd feel like you were invading her privacy."

"Maybe I'd see something that would give me a clue."

"I went down there before I filed the missing person report. I didn't see anything."

"You're not a trained police detective."

She thought that over, then gave a small nod. After putting down the wand, she opened a desk drawer and extracted a key with a pink ribbon threaded through the key chain hole.

She went back down the stairs to the vestibule.

"Did you have the house converted into a duplex?" he asked, already knowing the answer, since he could tell that the work was more than twenty years old.

"No. Grandma O'Shea did it after my grandfather died. She didn't need such a big place, and she needed the income."

"So how did you end up with the property?"

"My parents got divorced. Dad took off for parts unknown. Mom and I moved into the downstairs apartment. I was just starting college when she got a pulmonary embolism. She died."

"I'm sorry."

"It could have been worse. Grandma O'Shea and I were always close, and I moved in with her."

"She died, too?"

"In her sleep. Five years ago. A heart attack. She was ninety-two and able to take care of herself until the end. I guess that's the way to live— and the way to go."

"Yes," he answered, wondering what his own chances were of dying in bed.

They were still standing in the hallway. "I took the upstairs flat and rented out this one," she said, unlocking the door. She stepped into an apartment that was similar to her own in layout. But the similarity ended there.

Her abode had been quirky but orderly. DeYoung was—to put it politely—a slob. There were stacks of mail, newspapers, and other paper on every flat surface, including the floor. When he walked farther into the room and looked toward the kitchen, he saw dirty dishes in the sink and on the counter.

"You say she didn't give you any trouble. It looks like you're going to have to blast this place out when she moves."

"Okay, she's not so neat. But she's a good person. She likes children and animals."

"Mm hmm," he said, thinking it was probably lucky she didn't have custody of either.

He scanned the apartment. To his practiced eye, the owner had stepped out and intended to come back.

He started with the answering machine, pressed the rewind button and listened to the messages. There were several—two from Ms. Reynolds, both asking DeYoung to call.

And a message from the boyfriend, Swinton, two days ago. Which proved nothing. If he'd done something to her, he might have left the message to establish his innocence.

The rest of the messages were at least four days old. One was apparently from the office that handled substitute teachers, asking if she was available to take a biology class at Wootton High School on Monday.

Another was from her mother with some chatty news about various friends and relatives.

"Did she go to work on Monday?" Jack asked.

"I don't know."

He nodded, then strode down the hall to the bedroom and opened the closet. The hanging rack was full of blouses and jackets, packed so tightly together that they had to come out wrinkled.

"I'd ask if you thought anything was missing, but I imagine it's hard to tell," he said over his shoulder.

"I looked in her storage closet. Her suitcases are there."

"Did you check her dresser drawers?"

She swiped back a lock of fiery hair. "I opened some, yes. But I felt like a sneak, so I gave it up."

He opened a drawer and found sweaters in a messy pile. Reaching underneath, he discovered nothing hidden. The next drawer held panty hose and nothing else. The third was a mass of women's underpants and bras. This time, when he slid his hand underneath, he felt several magazines and a book. When he pulled them out, he saw that they were pornography—S and M oriented. One magazine cover showed an almost naked woman chained to a crossbar. A man was standing over her with a whip. The other magazines were similar. And the book looked like a dominance and submission how-to manual. He made a snorting sound. It seemed that a routine case had just gotten more interesting.

Before he lost the chance to catch Reynolds's unvarnished reaction, he glanced up. She was standing stock-still, staring at the literature as if he'd pulled a box of rattlesnakes out of the drawer.

3

KATHRYN managed to draw in a breath.

She felt Detective Thornton's gaze on her.

"You said you and Ms. DeYoung are friends. Did you know she was interested in . . . unusual . . . sexual practices?" he asked.

"No!"

He continued to stare at her like he didn't believe her, like he thought maybe she and Heather were into some kind of dirty little games together. She shifted her weight from one foot to the other, resisting the impulse to flee the room. "Honestly, I wouldn't have thought . . ." Her voice trailed off.

"Do you mind if I take this stuff?" he asked, waggling the book and magazines in his hand. "And a piece of her clothing."

"Do what you want!" Turning, she fled the room, fled from the apartment and up the stairs. It was several moments before she realized that Detective Thornton had followed her. He'd put the magazines into a paper grocery bag, which he must have found in Heather's kitchen. She assumed there was also a piece of Heather's clothing in there.

His eyes stayed fixed on her, and she made an effort to calm down, although her pulse was pounding.

"Why are you so upset?" he asked.

"I'm not."

He continued to stare at her, letting that obvious lie hang in the air between them.

She sighed. It was none of his business, yet she felt compelled to say, "Apparently my . . . my father was interested in that kind of stuff. That's why my mom divorced him."

It was his turn to say "Oh."

She focused on the fish swimming across her computer monitor, thinking that her parents' screwed-up relationship was none of this man's business. Mom was dead. Her father was, too, for all she knew. What had happened between him and Mom was a long time ago, so long ago that Kathryn had locked the knowledge in some deep, hidden corner of her mind. Maybe she'd actually forgotten about it.

Then the door to the memories had blasted open—when she'd seen the "literature" from the bottom of Heather's underwear drawer. She remembered her mother standing in the bedroom, holding a magazine that looked remarkably similar to the one Thornton had found. She remembered the mixture of anger and sadness on her mother's face.

A few months later, Mom had moved them out of the house and into Grandma's. And she and Mom had never talked about why they'd cleared out. It had stayed buried—a family secret that had finally sunk into the swamp of bad memories.

Until a few minutes ago when Thornton had pulled those magazines from the drawer.

Lord, did other families have similar stuff they didn't talk about?

Probably, she told herself. Maybe even Jack Thornton. His marriage had ended. There must have been reasons.

Well, that was none of *her* business, she thought as she watched a sea horse bob up and disappear again, aware that Thornton was watching her, hoping that she'd divulge something he could sink his teeth into. But there wasn't anything—at least with regard to Heather. And she wasn't going to share more about her background than she'd already blurted out.

"Do you have any additional questions for me?" she asked, hearing the hard edge in her voice. She wanted Jack Thornton out of her apartment.

He cleared his throat. "Do you have a picture of Ms. DeYoung? And could you give me the phone number of her next of kin?"

Next of kin. In case Heather was dead. "Her mother is Margaret DeYoung. She lives in Philadelphia." Once again she opened her Rolodex and found the number.

"Are they on good terms?"

"She doesn't see her often. But I think they get along."

"Would she go there if she were in trouble?"

"Maybe."

"Okay. Thanks. If you can just give me a picture, I'll get out of your hair."

In fact, she was easily able to accommodate the detective. A couple of weeks ago, she and Heather had been out in the yard enjoying the azaleas, and they'd decided that the bright masses of flowers would make a nice backdrop for some pictures. She'd gone back inside for her camera, then ordered double prints when she had the roll processed. Shuffling through the shots, she handed one to Thornton.

"Thanks. I appreciate it," he said, slipping it into the folder with the missing person report.

Now that he was leaving, she was able to raise her eyes to his and asked the question that had been gathering in her mind. "Do you think you're going to find her? I mean—find her alive."

"I hope so."

"But you're not counting on it."

"We've barely gotten into the investigation. I should ask, is there anyone besides the boyfriend that you think might want to do her harm?"

"I didn't exactly put it that way!"

"Noted." He stared at her, making it impossible for her not to speak.

She took a calming breath before answering. "Okay, there is one other thing I should tell you. Some things have happened around here. Vandalism, I guess you'd call it."

"Such as what?"

"Little things. Trash from my trash cans spread around the driveway. Some black spray paint on the white lattice at the bottom of the porch. Stuff like that."

"Did you report it to the police?"

"It didn't seem worth it."

"So—are you having a fight with any of the neighbors?"

"Not that I know of. I don't know if it has to do with me—or Heather."

"Thanks for telling me," he said, but she had the feeling he was reproaching her for holding back until the last minute. She swallowed. "Okay, there's one more thing—since you're asking. There was a workman in a white van hanging around the neighborhood last week. I never found out what he was doing. But he gave me a . . . creepy feeling."

"Did you get his license number?"

"It was smeared with dirt," she said, suddenly feeling as if she should have tried harder.

He wrote that down, then said, "I may get back to you with more questions. Here's my card, in case you think of anything."

She accepted the small white rectangle, flexing it in her hand as he walked toward the door.

He hesitated for a moment, as though he wanted to say something more, and she felt her nerves jangle as she waited to find out what he was thinking. Was he going to mention that first charged moment when they'd faced each other at the door?

To her relief, he remained silent, then left.

She closed and locked the door behind him, then moved to the window, standing back where she thought he couldn't see her, since he'd already caught her watching him when he arrived. But he didn't look back as he climbed into his car and drove away. When the vehicle was out of sight, she let out the breath she hadn't known she was holding. She'd wanted him to leave, but now that he was gone, she felt strangely let down. Backing away from that part, she went over the rest of the encounter. After those first few moments, she'd kept herself together while he was here, until she'd seen that magazine he'd pulled from Heather's drawer.

Before that, she hadn't known that Heather had any interest in sadomasochism. If she'd had a clue, she would have told her to run—not walk—away from that sick bastard Gary as fast as she could.

Unfortunately, Heather hadn't said anything. Or asked for help. And now Kathryn was left with a clenched feeling in her gut. And the sneaking suspicion that she didn't know Heather DeYoung as well as she'd thought. Or Gary Swinton. She'd had bad feelings about the guy. What else was he hiding?

Stiff-legged, she crossed to the kitchen and filled the kettle at the sink. While she waited for the water to boil, her mind flashed back to Detective Thornton.

Something had happened when she'd first opened the door to him and they'd stood facing each other across four feet of charged space, something she couldn't explain—a sudden awareness of the man that had taken her breath away.

So many impressions had assaulted her at once—with no time to sort them out. Now she took a mental step back and tried to analyze why the encounter had been so arresting.

He'd been wearing a tweed sports jacket over a light blue shirt and dark slacks. She wasn't the kind of woman who went around mentally undressing men. But she sensed that there were taut muscles under the conventional outfit.

She stopped thinking about his body and called up his head and face. His hair was dark and thick and probably a little too long for a police detective. His eyes were dark, too. Dark hazel, almost black. And she'd have to describe his features as chiseled.

With her art training, she was interested in faces, in what they told about people. She'd guess he was in his early thirties. Yet there were lines fanning out at the corners of his eyes. Laugh lines, although she had the feeling he didn't laugh often. Along with the deep creases carved between his nose and mouth—they told her he'd done some hard living.

Everything about him—small and large details—had riveted her attention in the few seconds he'd stood there in the doorway. Not just visual impressions. She'd caught the scent of his body, too, a mixture of soap and man and subtle aftershave. She'd heard his indrawn breath. And for a moment out of time, she'd thought she sensed the beating of his heart.

She shook her head. Now *that* was going a little far.

Yet she'd felt a connection that went far beyond a conventional first meeting. An emotional connection. A sexual connection. Oh, yes, sexual. That had been a strong component.

She could remember no other incident like that in her life. It was like being caught in a sudden cyclone, wind whirling around them, cutting them off from everything but the taut, sharp awareness of each other.

And it wasn't just her. Detective Thornton had stared at her as if she were the focus of every need he'd ever felt—every longing that had ever made his chest clench.

He wasn't married. He'd told her that while they were talking about the magic wand. She knew his marital status shouldn't matter. But it did. More than she wanted to admit.

She sighed, picked up the mug of tea, and cupped her hands around the smooth porcelain, feeling the warmth seep into her bones. Then she lifted the mug to her lips, taking small sips, focusing on the soothing flavor of the tea.

As she started back toward her desk, the Alma-Tadema painting caught her attention. She knew the title. It was called *Under the Roof of Blue Ionian Weather*. She also knew it had been called one of the artist's finest paintings of sunny indolence.

The description made her grin. She'd always liked the picture. Now she focused on details that she'd simply skimmed over in the past. Taking up most of the picture was a circular, tiered white marble structure called a lounge. Sir Lawrence had so meticulously rendered the marble that she could imagine running her fingers over the smooth surface. The sea was in the background. And, as in many of the artist's works, a flowering bush softened the hard lines of the marble. In this case, she saw it was a pink oleander, rising from behind a low marble wall. Six handsome young men and women lounged in various comfortable poses. Some wore flower garlands in their hair. All were dressed in flowing classical raiment.

Her eye went to the two women at the center of the painting. One was dark. The other had curly red hair and creamy skin—similar to Kathryn's own. Nobody in ancient Greece would have had that coloring. But Alma-Tadema had been famous for mixing women from his own Victorian England with darker Mediterranean types.

It had been a long time since she'd studied a painting with such attention to detail. She leaned forward, admiring the exacting depiction of the scene. It was so very real that she suddenly had the odd feeling that she could step right into the sunny afternoon scene and mingle with the men and women there.

What an idea!

And all because Thornton had drawn her attention to the picture that she'd walked past dozens of times every day.

She made a small sound. Determined to get her mind off Thornton, reminding herself that she didn't particularly like the man—even if she wanted to make wild, primitive love with him.

PERHAPS money couldn't buy happiness, but it could buy all the creature comforts of the twenty-first century, Simon thought as he climbed the wide stairs to the second floor of his primary residence, running his hand along the smooth wooden banister.

He loved the polished wood. Loved everything about his house. It was full of little details that made life here so fulfilling.

The place was a mansion, really. The most opulent of his houses and apartments. He used the others at his convenience, but this was his real home—on five prime acres in eastern Montgomery County, in a development where every edifice was custom built. There was a wide green lawn in front and natural woods in back, and the house was set in the center of the property. Far enough from his neighbors for the privacy he needed, the mansion had been built for a guy who was flush with success in the dot-com boom of the late nineties. He'd sold drugstore products online. But he'd had to give big discounts and free shipping to get sales. When his financial structure collapsed, he sold off his estate to pay his debts.

Mr. Dot-Com's financial crisis had been Simon's windfall. He'd scooped up the house for a fraction of its value.

The exterior was classic redbrick Georgian, with graceful white Ionic columns supporting a triangular portico.

Entering the library, he stood for a moment, breathing in the scent of old books—a mixture of leather, paper, and mold. A pleasing combination to his senses.

After absorbing the atmosphere of the room, he crossed to the sculpted leather chair where he liked to read and practice the rituals he used in his ceremonies. Propping his feet on the footstool, he leaned back and closed his eyes, chanting the words of power that he had memorized, making sure he had the difficult syllables and the intonation right.

"*Sotou ar athorebalo mriodom arogogorua-brao aeoou ooo photeth ma gaia.*"

His voice was sonorous, the words beating and swelling and rever-berating in the room as he gave them a life of their own. He knew how to perform an effective ritual. The words themselves must have importance—they must flow like an epic poem from the mouth of the master magician. They must roll from his lips like water coursing down a mountain channel.

He knew the meaning of each word, knew their derivation from his study of the ancient texts. *Sotou*. Thou, the Savior! From the Greek *soter*. *Athorebalo*. Thou Goddess of Beauty and Love, whom Satan beholding, desireth!

The ritual was called *Liber Samekh*. He was only practicing now, only making preparations for the real event. Yet he felt his own excite-ment. Reaching down to the soft silk of his pants, he stroked his fingers along the hard shaft of his cock. Only a light, teasing stroke. Because he was a man of discipline. Because this was only foreplay. Only a rehearsal for the real thing—the ritual in the basement ceremonial chamber that would end with a blood sacrifice and his own shattering sexual climax—releasing the energy that would bring him unimagined power. Power kings and dictators had only dreamed of. Because he would command the obedience of a demon. The creature would be forced to steal for him. Spy for him. Terrorize his enemies. Kill them if he asked. Do *anything* if he wished it.

From Ayindral. He had spoken the other words of power in a strong, clear voice. But he only whispered the demon's name.

As always, when he uttered the syllables, he felt the hairs on the back of his neck stir. The reaction sent a surge of anger coursing through him. Anger at himself, because he was never less than honest—on his own terms.

A tiny kernel of fear still lodged within the strong fortress he had built around his negative emotions. Fear he should have conquered long ago, through the hard work and discipline that had been the focus of his life for the past ten years.

He had studied long hours to divine the demon's name. He knew that the name was the key to enslaving the supernatural being—to har-nessing his incredible power. Yet each time he thought about the cap-turing ceremony, a small prickle of doubt scratched at his will.

His hands balled into fists at his sides, and he willed himself to be calm. Willed himself to that place where he knew that victory would be his—very soon.

Despite his efforts at self-control, the unsettled feeling hung over him like a cloud of poison gas.

He knew how to make it go away. Rising from the chair, he crossed the room and switched on the monitor that gave him a view of the basement cell.

The woman was huddled on the narrow bunk, dressed in the white cotton gown he'd left in the cell for her. While she'd been asleep from the drug in her food, he'd taken away all her clothing and her jewelry, stripping the rings from her fingers and removing her ankle bracelet. When she'd awakened, she'd had a choice. She could stay down there naked and exposed. Or she could put on the gown he'd left for her. She'd chosen the latter. It wasn't a sexually provocative garment. It was like a gown a child might wear for a baptism. Modest, long, embroidered with lace. It would be her shroud.

Watching her lying on her side with her head bent and her arms clasped around her knees soothed him. She was helpless. She was his to use as he desired.

And he would—when he was ready.

Of course, she hadn't been the one he'd really wanted, not in the beginning. The object of his desire had been her good friend. The redhead. The moment he'd seen her, she'd reminded him of the girl in school he'd . . . liked.

"Patience Hampton." He whispered her name aloud.

He'd never forgotten her. Never. They'd both been lonely, and they'd studied together in the school library, where they'd shared some of their secrets. He'd thought she liked him, but then an older guy had showed an interest in her, and she'd shut her friend Simon off. Well, not Simon. That wasn't his name back then. He'd been . . .

He clenched his teeth and bit off the memory. He wasn't that pitiful boy.

Today he was Simon Gwynn, self-made man.

But no matter how far he'd come, he'd never forgotten Patience Hampton. His first victim had looked a lot like Patience. Red hair. Creamy skin. Green eyes. Every time he saw a woman who reminded him of her, he felt that tug in his chest, that tug to use her in a ceremony. But it was too dangerous to repeat a pattern. He never repeated himself.

So he'd done the next best thing—switched his focus to the redhead's friend. Because he knew it would hurt her. Disturb her. Frighten her.

*   *   *

JACK figured there were probably two hundred Starbucks in the Washington, D.C., area, all with the same moss green and beige interior appointments and the map and compass stuff printed on the rounded platform where you picked up your order.

How many of them were there around the world? Five thousand? There must be a whole factory set up in Mexico or some other cheap labor country where they produced Starbucks furniture twenty-four, seven.

On the way back to police headquarters, he stopped at one of the coffee shops and indulged in the blend of the day—laced with a good shot of half-and-half. A little rich for his blood—but he figured he could use it this morning instead of the crankcase sludge in the squad room.

He took the steaming paper cup out to the unmarked and sat with his eyes unfocused, still trying to understand what had happened between himself and Kathryn Reynolds. Something weird. Something he might have explained away as a delusion sixteen months ago.

Back then, he'd been the kind of guy who didn't believe in anything beyond his own experience in the rock-solid natural world. Then he'd started investigating a private detective named Ross Marshall, who often brought him information on hard-to-solve cases. Missing person cases and murders, usually.

Jack took a small sip of the hot coffee, thinking back to the events of the spring evening that had changed his perceptions of the universe.

When Dr. Megan Sheridan, the woman Ross loved, had been kidnapped by a serial killer, he and Jack had sped to her rescue. And he'd discovered a startling fact about his friend. Ross Marshall was a werewolf.

If he hadn't seen the wolf in action, he wouldn't have believed it possible. That night, he'd become a believer. The knowledge might have sent him running as fast as he could in the other direction. But he'd known that Ross was governed by his humanity, not his werewolf heritage. They were still good friends and still working together, the two of them solving cases where the enhanced faculties of a wolf made the difference between success and failure.

In fact, the shirt he'd taken from DeYoung's closet was for Ross, who used his wolf sense of smell to track people who seemed to have disappeared off the face of the earth.

Now his knowledge of Ross Marshall's double life made it possible for him to wonder if there was something extraordinary about Kathryn Reynolds.

Like—was she a witch? Did she have some sort of supernatural powers, different from those of Ross Marshall but no less potent?

Was there a quirk in her genetic makeup that set her apart from other human beings? Something besides that wild red hair that his fingers itched to stroke? Simply standing in front of her, meeting her for the first time, he'd wanted her with a strength that rocked him to the core.

Had she snared him in a net? Was she a temptress making the first move on another victim? He snorted and almost spilled the coffee. Carefully he set the cup down on the console as he thought back over that astonishing first encounter.

Maybe her feelings hadn't exactly matched his. But she'd looked startled and confused, as if she'd been caught up in an encounter completely beyond her previous experience. Something strange. Like an obscuring cloud of smoke from a peyote fire that had enveloped the two of them—then just as quickly blown away.

So where did that leave him with Kathryn Reynolds? He didn't know. Part of him wanted to run as fast as he could in the other direction. And part of him wanted to explore what had happened between them in those strange, out of reality moments—and go beyond them, to something more substantial.

His face contorted. Whatever personal connection the two of them had felt was hardly the point of their meeting. She'd called the police because her tenant, Heather DeYoung, was missing.

His mind jumped to the cache of porn in DeYoung's drawer. Reynolds had reacted strongly. She'd given him a plausible reason for her response. She'd seemed surprised. And he was a pretty good judge of people's reactions. But she still might have known about DeYoung's interest in S and M. And been shocked that the woman was keeping such literature in a dresser drawer.

He'd like to find out what Reynolds really knew. Was she telling him the truth—or was she an accomplished liar?

He was still mulling that over when his cell phone beeped. He saw from the number that it was Granger calling.

"Where are you? I want to know what you've dug up on that suicide," the captain said as soon as Jack identified himself.

"The suicide. Isn't the coroner's office handling that?"

There was a small pause on the other end of the line. "Yeah, that's right. You were interviewing that woman who reported her tenant missing."

"I'll start doing a background check as soon as I get to my desk."

"Right. And you're going to look for a connection to those other cases."

"Yeah."

The captain clicked off, and Jack lowered the phone, staring at the speaker, his brow wrinkled. It sounded like Granger had had some kind of memory lapse. Was the guy just working too hard, or was he due for some medical leave?

AFTER Starbucks, the coffee in the squad room tasted as bad as he'd expected. Still, Jack was used to having the stuff available on his desk. So he poured himself a mug and got down to work, putting in requests for information on Heather DeYoung.

He might have done some more poking around DeYoung's apartment, but he'd had the feeling that finding any coherent records would take hours.

And then there had been Kathryn. She'd watched him as though he were committing burglary, not conducting an official police investigation.

Kathryn. He brought himself up short. A half-hour ago she'd been Reynolds. And she'd better stay Reynolds.

His mouth set in a firm line, he got to work. First he made requests to utility companies, phone companies, credit card companies.

Next he pulled up DeYoung's motor vehicle records. She seemed to get pulled over for a moving violation at regular intervals—just far enough apart to keep from getting enough points to suspend her license.

There was also a notation that she'd received a second request to bring her car in for an emissions test. But he already knew she wasn't the most responsible person in the world.

While he was checking DeYoung's background, his mind kept straying back to Kathryn Reynolds.

He'd be justified in investigating her, too, he told himself. In some cases, the individual who reported a person missing was the person responsible for that disappearance. He didn't want that to be true of Kathryn, but he couldn't dismiss it out of hand.

The phone on his desk rang, and he picked up the receiver.

"Thornton."

"Jack, I'm sorry to bother you."

It was Emily Anderson, his housekeeper, who made a point of not interrupting him at work, except in an emergency.

Instantly on the alert, he asked, "What's wrong?"

"Jack, it might not be anything."

"Tell me why you called."

"Lily's missing."

4

IT was hard to speak when his heart had leaped into his throat, blocking his windpipe. But Jack managed to croak out a request for more information.

"You know she was supposed to go to a friend's after school. Jessica Barrett."

He didn't remember, but he managed a small affirmative sound.

Emily rushed on. "She was supposed to call me when she got there. Sometimes she forgets, so I finally called the Barrett house. Mrs. Barrett said that she thought the girls had changed their minds and come here."

Jack cursed under his breath, thinking that the woman's irresponsibility was beyond comprehension. He'd naturally assumed she was picking the girls up from school.

"So Lily and her friend still aren't at the Barretts'. And they're not at our house, either?"

"Yes."

"And when should they have gotten home?"

"School was out at three. They should have been there by a quarter after three."

"Okay. I'm going to look for them. What's the address?"

Emily gave him the street and number, which he wrote on a sheet of notepaper and shoved in his pocket.

"Call me on my cell phone if they show up," he said. "And I'll keep in touch with you, too."

He saved his work, turned off his computer, and made a rapid escape from the building, glad he had a job where he could come and go without having to sign in and out.

As he climbed into the unmarked, he was thinking how much things had changed in a few hours. He'd gone to interview Kathryn because her tenant was missing. Heather DeYoung had been purely a professional concern. Now his daughter was missing, and his pulse was pounding so loudly in his ears that that was all he could hear.

WELL, she hadn't been missing for days. Only a little over an hour. Not long in the grand scheme of things. But he was a cop, and he knew what could happen to a child in a very short time. A mom could turn her head away for a few seconds, and some bastard could scoop up her kid at the mall.

He tried not to think about all the terrible possibilities. But he couldn't stop his mind from flashing back over old cases. Cases that made his stomach tie itself in knots when he thought about them in terms of Lily.

He forced himself not to drive more than ten miles above the speed limit. The elementary schools were out. And the middle schools would be dismissed soon—which meant lots of kids on the streets, kids who weren't so careful about watching where they were going.

As he headed toward his neighborhood, he phoned Emily again.

"Have you heard from her?"

"No, Jack, I'm sorry."

"Not your fault," he answered, then focused on getting more information. "Jessica Barrett—what kind of kid is she? Has Lily gotten into trouble with her before?"

"She's a nice child. I wouldn't have let Lily go there after school if I was worried about her."

"Right. I wasn't questioning your judgment."

"Jack, I know you're worried. We both are."

"Yeah. Don't let me take it out on you," he answered, thinking that if he stayed on the line much longer, that was exactly what would happen.

At the school, he made himself take several deep breaths before jogging around the redbrick, one-story structure.

On the playground at the back and side of the building, he scanned the blacktop, the climbing equipment, the soccer field. His heart stopped when he thought he caught a glimpse of Lily's light brown hair. But when he sprinted closer, it turned out to be another girl.

"Shit!" The reflexive expletive drew stares from the children and a mother who happened to be on the scene. He flushed as she pulled out a cell phone. Probably the cops were about to get a call about a suspicious guy hanging out around the school.

Hurrying back to the unmarked, he climbed inside and pressed his palms against his eyes, picturing the likely route that Lily and Jessica would have taken.

By the time he reached the Barretts' place, frustration and fear bubbled inside him. Jumping out of the unmarked, he strode to the door and banged on it loudly.

After half a minute, a scrawny teenage boy with shaggy hair and a torn Grateful Dead T-shirt came to the door. Jack sniffed, pretty sure he detected the aura of pot clinging to the kid's clothing.

"Where's your mother?" he demanded, looking into the boy's muddy brown eyes. When the kid shrugged, Jack pulled open the screen door, resisting the urge to grab the boy by the shoulders and shake him till his eyeballs fell out of his head.

He settled for taking one menacing step forward. "Listen, son, your sister is missing. Along with my daughter. Why aren't you out looking for them?"

The kid blinked, taking a good look at Jack for the first time. "Sally was supposed to walk them home. But she didn't. M . . . Mom told me to stay here, in case they showed up. I'm supposed to phone her if I see them."

"Yeah. If they *do* show up, call me first." He pulled out one of his cards, wrote the cell phone number on the back, and tossed the card into the hallway.

He wasn't proud of taking out his impotent anger on the boy, but his nerves were too raw for control. He wanted to scream out his frustration. He wanted to speed along the street, but he forced himself to creep along, his eyes scanning first to the left and then to the right.

A block and a half from the Barrett house, he heard a dog barking furiously. It was a large dog; he could tell that from the deep, barrel-chested sound. Not normal barking like a dog warning off someone walking past the back fence. This sounded more furious and dangerous.

* * *

KATHRYN stared at the old photograph. Gran as a young woman standing tall and proud beside her new house. This house. Only the azalea bushes were tiny, and the car in the driveway, which was gravel instead of macadam, had headlights like bugs' eyes, a square top, and high fenders.

A wave of longing for what had been and would probably never be again swept through her. "Oh, Gran," she whispered, "I wish I could talk to you now. About so many things. My work. Jack Thornton. Heather."

The woman in the photograph didn't answer, of course. Kathryn rubbed her hands over her arms, staring at the material possessions she'd pulled out of the storage closet. Old photo albums. Gran's sterling silver dresser set, carefully wrapped in plastic. Her button box. Her postcard collection. So many precious things that Kathryn hadn't been able to throw away—because they were the last links to her past. Today she'd felt the need to touch them, look at them once more.

Somewhere outside, the loud barking of a dog drifted toward her. The sound was far away, yet she tipped her head to the side, listening for a moment, feeling a small spurt of uneasiness. The sound faded, and she turned back to the collection of memories.

"I got my values from you, Gran, didn't I?" she murmured. "Work hard. Love your family. Keep your private business private. Stay productive."

Which was why she was sorting through this stuff *now*, she told herself firmly, since she needed a rational explanation for her behavior. She hadn't been able to keep her mind on her job since Detective Thornton had left. And if she couldn't work, then she needed to do something else useful—like figure out what should finally go to consignment shops. Or Goodwill.

"So what about the love part?" she asked, still speaking aloud, as though her grandmother were sitting in the easy chair in the corner. "You were so warm and generous and loving. That's how I know something important is missing from my life. Is that why I've fixated on the first man who knocks on my door?"

Gran didn't answer. If she had, her words would have been drowned out by the sudden sharp noise outside. The dog was barking again. Only now it was louder. Closer. More frantic. It sounded like an animal in trouble. Or an animal about to attack someone.

Jumping up, she ran to the window, craning her neck. Although she saw nothing unusual, the uneasy feeling wouldn't go away.

Stepping over a box of old tablecloths, she hurried to the door, opened it, and pounded down the stairs.

JACK craned his neck, seeing nothing. The noise was coming from off the street. A backyard? Or a wooded area along a stream? An isolated location?

He was out here because he was looking for his daughter, but he'd just encountered another situation. It sounded a lot like the animal had someone cornered, and as a cop—as a good citizen, for that matter—he couldn't simply drive away from obvious trouble.

Pulling to the curb, he cut the engine and started up the blacktop path between two houses. Wind rustled the dry leaves still clinging to the oak trees overhead. Through a screen of tree trunks, he saw a large backyard with a wooden playhouse a handyman father must have lovingly built for his kids. It had wood siding and flower boxes with artificial flowers under the windows. A solid wooden door was closed. The windows had mullions but no glass panes, as far as he could see.

A dog charged around the corner of the house—a Doberman. It was jumping and barking and snapping its teeth, directing its fury toward the little building. When it threw its body against the side, the house rocked.

One of the mullions cracked under the assault. The animal stuck its head inside, and he heard a child's terrified shrieking from within. If the dog got in there, it was obvious he was going to tear the kid to shreds.

If Jack had been able to assess the situation from the street, he would have called for backup. Now he was on his own. And the first thing he had to do was get the dog away from the child cowering in the playhouse.

If he called the dog, would it leave the kid alone? Would it calm down? Or attack him?

He had never been in a situation where it had looked like he might have to shoot a dog. But he drew his Sig before giving a loud shout, "Come on, boy. Come away from there. Good dog. Good dog."

The animal whirled in his direction, teeth snapping in the face of this new enemy. In those first few seconds of confrontation, it was apparent that the animal wasn't going to calm down. A deep growl rose in its throat as it leaped away from its previous target. Focused on Jack, it picked up speed, its teeth snapping as it headed straight toward the new target.

Jack held his gun in a two-handed grip, pointed at the charging streak of black and brown as he took careful aim.

"Daddy! Watch out, Daddy!"

The child's cry riveted his attention just as the dog leaped.

God! It was Lily in there!

Thrown off his stride, he scrambled to find the dog again, knowing he couldn't risk a wild, random shot in the middle of a residential neighborhood—with his daughter somewhere in front of him.

It was already too late to get the dog before it reached him. He braced for the deep, tearing sensation of canine teeth sinking into his flesh.

But it never happened. Once more that day, the normal course of time seemed to stop. It was like someone had thrown a switch, making everything around him freeze. The leaves on the trees went still in place. The wind stopped blowing. The dog seemed to hang in midair—three yards from him.

Jack Thornton was the only moving, breathing thing in the freeze-frame universe. He had time to bring the gun into firing position, time to pull the trigger before the dog reached him. As he fired, time snapped back into its normal forward course.

The dog yelped once, dropped to the ground. And Jack knew by the way it lay still and the lack of blood on the wood chips that he'd shot it in the heart.

KATHRYN stood transfixed. Moments ago, the angry barking had enveloped her, solidified the breath in her lungs.

Now . . . there was utter silence. Feeling unsteady on her feet, she leaned back against the door frame, staring into the afternoon sunshine, struggling to catch her breath.

She had the strange conviction that disaster had been averted. Yet she had no idea what had happened.

For several minutes, she stood in the doorway, all her senses on alert. But she saw nothing unusual. Heard nothing. With a shake of her head, she stepped back inside, made her way up the steps, clutching the banister. Back into the living room—she blinked, staring at Gran's things still spread over the floor. .

Lord, she'd been sorting through this stuff, trying to decide what to keep and what finally to let go of. But she'd forgotten all about what she'd been doing when the dog had claimed her attention.

*   *   *

JACK stepped around the dog, holstering his gun as he rushed toward the playhouse. Pulling open the door, he looked inside and found two little girls. Lily and her friend. They were both white-faced, both sobbing.

He went down on his knees. Reaching inside, he drew them both into his arms, feeling their small trembling bodies press against him as he stroked his hands over their backs.

"It's okay. It's okay," he murmured.

Lily hiccuped, struggled to speak. "Jessica wanted to show me this house on the way home. We . . . we were only going to stay a few minutes. Then . . . then the dog came. He was trying to bite us."

"I know, honey. I know."

She tried to look over his shoulder, but he kept her head down so she couldn't see the dead animal.

Still, her voice quavered as she said, "You shot him with your gun."

"Yes."

He calmed the two girls down, then moved back so he could make eye contact.

"Did the dog bite you?"

"No," both girls answered, although he had to reassure himself by checking their exposed skin. He couldn't find any tooth marks.

"How did you get away from him?" he asked.

"We were playing in the little house when we heard him barking. Then he was running toward us, and we shut the door and pushed that wooden piece down," Lily answered.

"That was exactly right."

"But then he kept jumping at the door and the window, and shaking the whole house. He was going to get in—until you got here," Jessica said. "How did you find us?"

"Well, I was looking for you, and I heard him," he answered, adding a heartfelt but silent "Thank God."

DELIBERATELY, Kathryn focused on the boxes she'd pulled out of the closet, determined to bring order out of chaos. If not her disordered thoughts, then these things.

She'd never use the linen and damask tablecloths, she told herself

firmly. Or the box of old fabric. They could go to one of those upscale
consignment shops. And the same with the postcards and the little animals that had come packaged in boxes of tea.

She stopped, suddenly picturing herself sitting on the floor,
watching a small girl playing with the ceramic lions, monkeys, and
giraffes.

Jack's child. She'd just met the man today, under emotionally trying
circumstances. But she was back to daydreaming about him—and his
daughter.

She dragged in a breath, held it for a moment, and let it out before
carefully gathering up the animals and setting them back in the cardboard box. She would save the animals. But was she doing it for the
wrong reasons?

JACK glanced at the dog lying on the wood chips, thinking that Animal Services would take hours to arrive.

His alternative was to find a patrol car in the area. Leaving the
girls for a moment, he knelt beside the dog, feeling guilty as he
stared down at the still form. He'd never shot a dog. And it gave him
a queasy feeling now. But there had been no alternative. The animal
had been crazed, out of control. After getting the girls into the backseat of the unmarked, he picked up the radio and called for a uniformed officer.

Next he called Emily on his cell phone and told her that he'd found
Lily and Jessica. She wanted a full report on what had happened, but he
kept it to a minimum, then called the Barrett house.

He got the teenage boy again and said he was on the way back with
Jessica, and to tell his mother, if he could get in touch with her.

By the time he had hung up, a patrol car was rolling to a stop in
back of the unmarked. Climbing out, he talked to the officer, a guy
named Jacobs, telling him what had happened.

Jacobs could have asked him to stay at the scene, since he was the
one responsible for the dead dog, but when he explained the situation,
and the officer saw the strained faces of the girls in the backseat, he told
Jack to take them home.

He drove straight to the Barretts' house. By the time he got there,
Mrs. Barrett had just pulled into the driveway. Her face a mixture of
fear and relief, she rushed to his car, pulled the back door open, and
gathered Jessica to her, hugging her close.

As he climbed out and walked around to the other side of the car, she said, "Mrs. Anderson got me on the phone. She told me about the dog." She raised her face to Jack. "Thank you. Thank you for rescuing the girls. I had a hairdresser appointment, and my neighbor's daughter was supposed to walk them home. But she must have forgotten. I'm so sorry. I should have reminded her in the morning."

Jack gave a tight nod. He wasn't going to say he understood. He only knew Lily wasn't going to the Barnett's again after school.

"Do you know who the animal belonged to?" he asked. "It was a Doberman. There was a license tag, but no name."

"I'm sorry, I haven't seen a dog like that around here."

"Okay. We'll try to find the owner—and see if the dog's rabies vaccination is current."

Alarm contorted her face. "Did he bite Jessica—or Lily?"

"They said he didn't. And I checked for bite marks. They both seem to be okay, just shaken up. If it will make you feel more secure, you can take Jessica to the emergency room."

Mrs. Barrett nodded. "Do . . . do you want to come in?"

He thought about that for a moment. He had one more thing to say. But he could say it here. He looked from Lily to Jessica and back again. "Don't leave school and walk home on your own." His gaze focused on Lily. "You can always go in the office and call Mrs. A to pick you up. She was worried. So was Jessica's mother."

Lily's face crumpled. "I'm sorry." She gave a gulping sob. "We just thought it would be okay to walk home. And we only stopped for a minute. And . . . and . . . somehow it was more than a minute," she added.

"I know, honey. But I think you see now that it can be dangerous not to be where you're supposed to be."

His daughter was crying in earnest. He returned to her side of the car, opened the door, and hunkered down. She didn't move, and he gathered her close.

"It's okay."

"You're mad at me."

"No. I was worried about you. I'm glad you're safe." He hugged her for long moments, until he felt her calming. Then he looked toward Mrs. Barrett. "I'd like to take Lily home."

"Yes. I understand completely," Mrs. Barrett answered.

He made sure Lily was buckled in, then closed the door and got behind the wheel.

As he started for home, he glanced in the rearview mirror and saw his daughter huddled in a corner of the backseat.

She saw him watching her. "I'm sorry, Daddy. I won't do it again."

"I know."

"I was scared."

"I was, too."

"Is it all right to shoot a dog?"

He dragged in a breath and let it out before answering. "If he looks like he's about to attack someone."

He saw her digesting that. He hadn't liked resorting to his weapon, but he hadn't seen any other alternative—not when the animal was charging him with a murderous look in its eyes.

He took Lily home, where Emily doctored her with chocolate chip cookies. After making sure everything was okay, and filling in the housekeeper on more of the details, he went back to police headquarters. First he called Animal Services and made sure that the dog had been removed. Then he wrote up a report on the incident. Finally, he gathered together the papers he'd started on the DeYoung case and put them in a folder.

He'd kept himself busy. Kept his mind busy. It wasn't until he climbed back into his car that he allowed himself to think about what had happened outside the playhouse.

Not the part about the girls and the dog. He'd been scared, but he'd dealt with that. It was the other part—*The Twilight Zone* part.

He sat for a moment, his hands wrapped around the wheel, his eyes staring toward the redbrick wall of the headquarters building but not really seeing it.

Instead, his vision was turned inward, to the moments when the Doberman had charged him. He'd been ready to fire. Then Lily had called out, and the shock of hearing her voice had totally blown his concentration. He'd thought he was dead meat. Or at least mangled meat.

Before the dog could sink its teeth into his body, something had happened, something so strange that he could hardly believe it—even though he'd experienced it. The world around him had frozen in place. The dog had seemed to stop in midair—hanging there like an inflated toy filled with helium.

He shook his head. That little space of suspended time had given him the chance to get his gun back into firing position.

And it wasn't the only instance when he'd stepped into *The Twilight Zone* today. The first time had been at Kathryn Reynolds's house. Then he'd felt encapsulated in a moment of time with her, felt a connection to her and a jolt of sexual energy.

The sensation had been intense, yet it had made him feel vulnerable—vulnerable to Kathryn Reynolds and vulnerable to his own needs and weaknesses.

He blinked, realizing that he'd been driving without paying attention to where he was going, and he'd missed his turnoff on Falls Road.

He went down to the next development, then circled back to his street.

Ten minutes later he was pulling into his own driveway. As he had at the station house, he sat staring into space.

He'd always had a strong sense of himself. Always believed that he was responsible for his own actions. Twice today, he'd felt as though free choice had been rudely yanked away from him.

He couldn't explain either experience, let alone both of them. Was he going crazy? Becoming delusional? The thought sent a chill skittering up his spine.

It wasn't that! He knew who he was. He knew what he was doing. He was still functioning the way he always had. Yet he couldn't turn off the disturbing thought that some outside force had entered his life.

The very idea was absurd. He tried to shake it from his mind. But it stayed lodged there, like a bullet in soft tissue—festering.

5

THERE was nothing like fearing for your child's life to put things into perspective. Lily was shy with him at dinner, but Jack had drawn her out, made sure all over again that she knew how glad he was that she was safe. And after dinner he, Lily, and Craig played the kids' favorite game, Sorry.

Some evenings he knew he neglected his fatherly duties. Tonight he supervised bath time, then read to both kids, holding Lily tight against his side as he sat with her on her bed, still thanking God that everything had turned out all right.

At times over the past three years, he'd felt damn sorry for himself. Now he counted his blessings.

The next morning, he was in a philosophical mood as he drove toward Research Boulevard. So he'd had a couple of really weird experiences. This was another day, and as far as he was concerned, nothing strange was going to happen, if he had anything to say about it.

Nevertheless, when traffic ground to a halt on Gude Drive, his mind went into a little fantasy that his car could fly over the stopped vehicles and land on the other side of the mess.

Of course, he stayed on the road, trapped like everyone else, creeping past a three-car smashup and arriving at work half an hour late.

First he pulled out the number he'd copied from the dog's tag and checked the database at Animal Services.

Some of the terrible weight lifted from his shoulders when he found out that the dog had a history of violence. There were several complaints from neighbors about the owner, Clark Spencer, who had apparently trained the dog to guard and attack. It had bitten two men—both seriously.

Spencer had been warned to keep the animal in his fenced yard. But apparently the dog had gotten away—and gotten into trouble again.

Jack told himself he'd performed a public service by taking a dangerous animal off the streets, yet he couldn't totally let go of his guilt. He was thinking that officers who shot and killed a criminal suspect got counseling from a department shrink. He could probably make an appointment now if he wanted.

Maybe he needed it. But he couldn't quite picture himself talking about his present mental state. What was he going to say—that he'd been experiencing time distortions?

Yeah, right. That would probably be enough to get him pulled off active duty.

With a sigh, he went to his E-mail and started checking the information that had come in overnight on Heather DeYoung. She had four credit cards, all with heavy balances. Her phone was in danger of being disconnected unless she paid the bill. And a collection company was after her to pay up on the large-screen television she'd bought on sale in January. About the only monetary responsibility she took seriously was her rent, probably because she knew that staying on good terms with Kathryn was important.

Make that *Reynolds*, he told himself firmly. *Not Kathryn.*

He leaned back in his desk chair, contemplating his next move. He needed to find out if, by some chance, DeYoung was with her mother. But he didn't want to alarm the woman, since her daughter was an adult who apparently often went off on unexpected trips. And he wasn't bound by law to discuss Kathryn's suspicions with her.

Picking up the phone, he dialed the number that Reynolds had given him.

"Mrs. DeYoung?" he asked.

"Yes," a woman answered. Her voice was thin and weak. She sounded like she was in her eighties. He hated to run a con on an old lady, but in this case he was willing to take any advantage he could.

"This is Jake Thorn at the USA Redemption Center," he said.

"The what? Speak up."

Oh, good, she was hard of hearing. "I'm trying to get in touch with Heather DeYoung," he shouted into the phone, seeing heads turn in his direction in the squad room. Everybody within twenty miles was going to hear his pitch. "She's the grand prize winner in the Win America contest. I'm trying to deliver her prize."

"Why are you calling me? I'm her mother. She doesn't live here. She lives in Maryland."

"I've checked at her residence. Ms. DeYoung isn't at home. We have a forty-eight-hour deadline to deliver her Pontiac Grand Am. After that, we go to the runner-up."

"A car! Oh, my. I'm sure she'd like a new car. She's always complaining about the one she has."

"Well, we'd like her to have the grand prize. So I'm hoping you can help. Her landlady says that she's out of town for a few days, but she doesn't know where she's gone. Could you tell me how to get in touch with her?"

"I . . . I'm sorry. I don't know where she is. Did you check with that fellow she goes around with?"

"Her boyfriend?"

"Yes."

"You don't like him?" Jack asked, catching the woman's tone of voice and figuring he couldn't lose anything by slipping in the personal question now.

"He's beneath her. I think she can do better."

"Well, I'd appreciate your calling me if you hear from your daughter. That's Jake Thorn." He gave her the number of an answering machine that didn't tie into the police switchboard, then urged her to let her daughter know about her good luck, if she phoned. By the time he hung up, he figured he'd done what he could to win the mom's cooperation. She'd put Heather in touch with him—if it was humanly possible. And if she hadn't called back in forty-eight hours, he'd contact her as himself and fill her in on the missing person report.

Next up was the boyfriend, who worked at the Circuit City in Bethesda. Of course, it was possible he wasn't there today. Like he and DeYoung had decided to take off together. But he wasn't counting on it. He'd bet Swinton was in town, and he wanted to interview him before he had time to make up a story.

He took Montrose to Rockville Pike. The traffic was moving well, and he arrived at the shopping center not long after the store opened.

Inside, he found the small electronics section. There were two salesmen in the area. When one of them turned around, he immediately recognized Swinton from Kathryn's description. He confirmed the identity from his white tag with his name in blue letters.

"Gary Swinton?" he asked, walking forward.

"Yes."

"Could I talk to you for a few minutes?"

"What do you want?"

"Montgomery County Police. I want to ask you some questions."

Jack gave him credit for showing very little reaction. "About what?"

"Heather DeYoung."

"What about her?" Swinton looked around and found that the other guy in the department was listening with interest. "Why don't we go outside?" he said. Unlike Reynolds, he didn't ask to see Jack's credentials. Because he'd been expecting this interview?

As they walked through the stockroom and then onto the loading dock, Jack was thinking that for the time being, he might as well play Mr. Nice Guy. Easygoing. Relaxed. Just here to get some facts about a woman who might have skipped town to avoid a bunch of credit card bills.

Swinton reached into his pocket and pulled out a crumpled pack of cigarettes. He didn't ask if Jack minded; he simply lit up.

Jack took a step back. Before the kids had been born, he'd been a smoker himself. But Laura had shown him some articles on the effects of passive smoking, and he'd managed to stop. Usually he didn't crave tobacco. But times like this, when someone was standing a few feet away, puffing like a chimney, it was hard not to bum a smoke. He shoved his hands into his pockets, noticing that Swinton was watching him.

"What about Heather?" he asked again.

"When was the last time you saw her?"

"Last week. Why?"

"Her landlady hasn't seen her in a few days; she's worried."

Swinton shifted his weight from one foot to the other. "That bitch! Did she sic you on me?"

"She said you were DeYoung's boyfriend. What have you got against her?"

"She's self-righteous. Thinks she's better than everybody else."

"She seemed to have a pretty high opinion of Ms. DeYoung."

"Yeah, well, she talks to her against me."

"About what?"

"About stuff that's none of her business."

Jack waited to hear something specific. When nothing was forth-coming, he figured he could come back to the subject later. "So you saw Ms. DeYoung last week. What day?"

Swinton took a drag on his cigarette and expelled the smoke, look-ing thoughtful. "I was out at her place last Wednesday. We had dinner. Watched some TV. And"—he made a waggling gesture with his hand—"we went to bed."

"You didn't spend the night?"

"No."

Jack filed that away. Sex implied a certain intimacy. Spending the night implied another level to the relationship—unless it was a one-night stand. Or unless one of the participants had young children at home—and wanted to make sure he was there in the morning.

Well, that was certainly an inappropriate thought! He knew damn well it had nothing to do with Swinton and everything to do with his personal interest in Kathryn Reynolds.

"How long have you been going together?"

"A couple of years."

"Do you know where she might have gone? Or why?"

There was a momentary flickering in Swinton's eyes. "No."

Either he was lying, or he was thinking about something incrimi-nating.

"You parted on good terms?"

"Yeah. Why are you asking prying questions?"

"Because she's missing. And I'm trying to establish when she was last seen, and what her state of mind was. Did she seem worried about anything?"

"Her credit card balances were creeping up. She wasn't happy about that."

"Would that make her skip town?"

"I don't know."

"So you don't know where she is?"

"No. I already told you that. Sometimes she goes away on trips."

"By herself?"

"If she feels like it."

"Where does she go?"

"Atlantic City. New York."

"Do you know of anyone who would have reason to harm her?"

Again there was the slight flash in Swinton's eyes. "No," he said, making his voice firm. Then he took another drag on the cigarette.

Well, there was something going on with Swinton, but he wasn't going to find out what it was while they were standing here, and he didn't think that hauling him down to headquarters would be productive at this point.

"Thanks for your time," he said.

"No problem."

Jack walked down a flight of stairs on the loading dock, then around the building to the unmarked.

He would come back to Swinton again. But right now, he was going to attack the case from a different angle. It was time to contact the detectives working on the other three missing person cases and see if he could find anything that would connect them.

KATHRYN reached for the magic wand on her desk and turned it first one way and then the other, watching the stars and moons rise and fall in the blue liquid.

The random patterns usually helped set her mind free, so that she might get a sudden insight into her work that had eluded her as she focused intently on the computer screen.

Today her thoughts jumped back to Jack Thornton—the way they did every time she let down her guard.

She'd never been obsessed with a man. She'd always been slow to get into a relationship—for all the good that had done her with Sam Hastings, her last serious boyfriend. They'd gotten close, and after eight months, she'd thought they were heading toward something permanent. Then he'd been offered a promotion and a big raise if he'd transfer to the Chicago branch of his company immediately. And he hadn't hesitated a heartbeat.

Kathryn had convinced herself that she was in love with him. She'd thought that the job offer might be the event that would tip the balance in the relationship. She'd thought he might ask her to marry him and move with him to Chicago. She'd been nervous about leaving everything familiar and going halfway across the country. But at the same time, she'd been excited.

It had turned out she didn't have to worry about moving. Sam had promised to keep in close touch. After a few weeks, she knew that either he'd found someone else in the Windy City, or he hadn't really been as interested in marriage as she'd thought he was. Or he'd been a damn coward. He'd wanted to break off with her, but he'd been too chicken to say the words. Moving away had given him an easy option.

She'd been sad and hurt. The unceremonious ending of the relationship had been a blow to her self-esteem. But she'd come out of it stronger, she told herself. More self-reliant. More cautious about men. More realistic. She'd let Heather talk her into going to a bar a time or two. She'd dated some of the guys she'd met. But she hadn't connected with anyone who rang her chimes.

Until Jack Thornton. She'd gone to bed fixated on the man. And from the moment she'd opened her eyes, thoughts of him had begun worming themselves into her mind. And not just her mind. She'd awakened aroused, wanting him. And disgusted with herself for the reaction.

She looked at the wand she was having so much fun manipulating, and gave a short bark of a laugh. It was a hard plastic rod about twelve inches long, and it felt good in her hand. A penis substitute?

Was that why she'd been playing with the thing so consistently since he'd been here?

There was no one else around to see her blush, but that didn't stop her cheeks from growing warm. With a shake of her head, she put the thing down. But when she picked up her Koosh Ball, her former favorite toy, and started bouncing it in her hand, the tactile experience was much less satisfying.

Before she could cancel the idea, she moved the ball to one end of the wand and added a similar sized rounded glass paperweight next to it.

Giggling, she stared at her handiwork. A penis and testicles! It had been a long time since she'd indulged in anything so silly. She felt like a little kid drawing dirty pictures on the sidewalk with chalk.

With kids, it was just a naughty impulse. On an adult level, she was able to think in more concrete terms. Like, the wand would make a pretty good dildo. With stimulating ridges spiraling up the side. Of course, it wasn't all that big in diameter. Probably Jack's penis was a lot thicker. At least she hoped it was a lot thicker.

Because that would feel so good when it was inside her.

She sucked in a sharp breath, then pressed her palms over her face. Good God, what was wrong with her?

The direction of her thoughts was so out of character that she was almost unable to believe she was behaving this way.

Since when was sex the only thing she could think about? Since she'd met Jack Thornton.

She sat very still, lowering her hands to grip the arms of her chair, because the notion had leaped into her mind that reaching up and cupping her breasts would feel very good right now. Not just cupping them, playing with her nipples that had suddenly gotten hard. Her eyes drifted closed as she imagined Jack Thornton's hands on her. They were large hands, strong hands. But she decided they might be gentle when he caressed a woman. She let herself slip further into the fantasy, one hand lifting to brush back and forth across a taut nipple.

A small moan escaped her lips.

With a grimace she snapped her eyes open, then pushed her chair away from the desk and stood up, knowing that it would be a very good idea to stop thinking about Detective Thornton touching her, making love to her.

Trying to be as objective as possible, she examined that thought, too. It wasn't just sex she wanted. Not just temporary gratification— although sexual arousal had certainly been heating up her body since yesterday. She was also picturing herself waking up next to the man every morning. Sitting across the breakfast table. Stepping into the role of mother to his daughter.

The fantasy had crept up on her when she'd looked at the ceramic animals. Now she was adding to it, and she knew the daydream was totally unrealistic. Not least because she was sure that she and Jack Thornton had rubbed each other the wrong way during their one meeting. He'd acted like she was a suspect, and that had made her feel defensive. Or was she reading more into the interview than she should?

She gave a mental shrug. What she needed was something else to occupy her mind, now that she'd sorted through the storage closet. Like maybe going down to Heather's apartment and searching for clues.

As soon as she thought about Heather, she felt guilty. She'd met Detective Thornton because she was worried about her friend. She was still worried. And she wasn't going to let her fantasies wipe out her sense of responsibility.

Grabbing the key, she unlocked the door to the inside stairway, then walked rapidly down to Heather's apartment. Once inside, she stood in the dim light, seeing the place the way Jack had seen it. It was pretty messy, and she knew that had prejudiced him against Heather.

She brought herself up short. She hadn't come here to reflect on how Heather's lifestyle struck Jack Thornton. She'd come here to try and find something that would help the police.

Systematically, she began moving her hands through drawers, feeling clothing that had been thrown inside without being folded. Jack had found the porn magazines and the book in one of Heather's underwear drawers. Kathryn found something else stuffed in between a couple of T-shirts. Something that felt weird.

Gingerly she drew out a plastic bag containing a rectangle of what looked like off-white construction paper. As she turned it in the light, she saw that one side was covered with a series of small yellow squares, each with a picture of a cartoon character in the middle. Each colored picture was about a quarter of an inch in diameter. There were thirty of them on the sheet. And places where she could see that several more had been torn off.

She'd never seen anything like it before, and she didn't know what it was. But she was pretty sure it was something that Heather didn't want anyone to find.

She sniffed at the stuff. It didn't have any odor. She used her fingernail to scratch at a picture, and some of the paper fibers came off. She thought about lifting her finger toward her mouth, then checked herself.

No. Better not taste it. She slipped it back into the plastic bag.

So was this something that she should report to Jack Thornton? Something that had to do with Heather's disappearance?

Or was she looking for an excuse to hear the detective's voice?

She didn't know the answer to that. But she did think she had an obligation to tell him what she'd found.

Back in her apartment, she shoved the plastic bag into her middle desk drawer, retrieved the business card from yesterday, and dialed his number.

"This is Jack Thornton," his deep voice began, and she felt her heart leap inside her chest.

"I'm out of the office right now, but if you'll leave a message, I'll get right back to you. If you need immediate assistance, you can press one to have this call transferred."

She hung up, reluctant to leave a message and wondering if his absence was a sign that she wasn't supposed to tell him about this stuff—whatever it was.

A sign?

It wasn't like her to look for signs and portents. But then, a lot of things she'd done recently weren't like her. Particularly spending a lot of time thinking about a man she barely knew and one she hadn't exactly met under friendly circumstances. And then looking for excuses to talk to him.

6

THE danger grew, like a large black hole opening wider and wider in the fabric of his universe. He could feel it with a sickening pull that brought primal fear bubbling within him. He had never endured this kind of assault. Never feared for his very existence. And he had miscalculated—expended too much of his energy on manipulating the physical world. Stopping time.

The second instance had been justified. He had done it to save Jack Thornton from the dog's fangs. He needed Thornton. It was too late to find another man.

But the first manifestation—when the man and woman had stood in the doorway facing each other—that had been a mere trick. A way of making a point. And now he regretted the effort it had taken.

He was weakened. He needed to regenerate. But he felt wings of fear beating . . . beating . . .

He must act—soon. And the woman was the key. She had always been the key.

WITH a sense of momentous purpose, Simon stepped into the ceremonial chamber.

The time was close, so close, and he was ready. He stood for a moment, enjoying the feeling of power surging within his body. Through the silk of his black pants, he slid his hand along the hard shaft of his penis, allowing the arousal to build as he gazed admiringly at the details of the chamber he had created. Simply coming here made him pulse with power, but there was more than mere pleasure involved. Much more.

When he'd bought the house, the chamber had been an ordinary basement recreation room. Now it was completely transformed. From floor to ceiling, along the walls and over the small windows, hung yards of gathered fabric. It was black, as was the slate tile on the floor. The room was designed to insulate him from the world. Yet he could still cast his own destructive power outward. And he would soon, very soon. After the sun had set.

Deliberately he let his hand drop to his side, exercising the discipline that was such an important part of his demeanor. Without discipline he had nothing. Sexual satisfaction was a poor goal in itself. It must be nurtured, rationed, used to achieve his ultimate objective.

He stood for a moment, moving his shoulders and arms, loosening the muscles; enjoying the feeling of strength that had already begun to build inside him.

The universe was like a vast ocean. An ocean with great invisible tides. Most people were simply swept along helter-skelter by forces they could never hope to control. Forces they didn't even comprehend.

But some were brave and clever enough to master the cold, black currents that rose from the depths of the universal ocean. He was such a man. A man who could make others bend to the strength of his will.

He walked to the long wooden table, checking the leather ankle and wrist straps attached to the sides.

Beside the long table was a smaller surface, bare except for a folded rectangle of purest white silk. With reverence he slipped his hand inside and gently removed a small dagger. It was very old and very rare, the handle beautifully worked with old Celtic signs. He had found it at an antique shop in Dublin, and from his research, he had known at once what it was—a ceremonial dagger from the time of the Golden Dawn.

It was expensive. But he had gladly paid the price the dealer was asking.

As he turned the weapon in his hand, he admired the balance, the workmanship, the long, tapered line of the blade. It was narrow and delicate, like a woman's finger turned to silver. He pressed his thumb against the point until it pierced the flesh, welcoming the sharp pain as a red drop welled up.

Raising his finger to his mouth, he sucked the sweet, thick blood. His own essence. A small sacrifice.

A prelude.

KATHRYN stretched her arms above her head, then reached to massage the tension in the back of her neck. It was almost midnight, and she'd been at the computer most of today and yesterday, feeling like she was getting very little done. But as she brought up the text and graphics on the monitor, she conceded that the Sunrise Realty brochure had worked out better than she'd expected. She wasn't claiming that the design was her best work. But it was the best she was going to do in any kind of reasonable time frame. She'd already put in about five extra hours that she wasn't going to charge to Sunrise.

Now she was exhausted. It wasn't simply a physical weariness. It was emotional as well.

Three days had passed since she'd reported Heather as a missing person—and her friend hadn't shown up, hadn't called.

With a sigh, she pushed back her chair and stood. But once she was on her feet, it was all she could do to drag herself down the hall to the bathroom, use the toilet, wash her hands and face, and brush her teeth. She left her jeans in a heap on the braided rug, then tottered across the floor and fell into bed.

Sleep seemed to tug at her with an unnatural eagerness. It claimed her moments after her head hit the pillow.

Her slumber was instantly deep. And only minutes passed before a dream sank its needle-sharp claws into her.

She cried out in her sleep. One moment she was warm and safe in her bed. In the next, she was somewhere else entirely.

Nowhere familiar. Not at all.

Her eyes blinked open. She was in some strange land of swirling, gray mist that obscured her vision and made her feel like she was breathing in water when she tried to drag air into her lungs.

It was cold in this place, cold as a cavern deep inside an iceberg. Perhaps that image came to her because she felt immense weight pressing against her, weight that made it impossible for her to stand erect.

Terror gripped her by the throat, muffling the scream that rose within her soul.

There was no color here. No sound. No solid ground below her feet or sky above her head. And she knew with a terrible jolt of insight that if she stayed here, she would lose her sense of self.

Lord, she had to get away. Had to escape.

Desperately, she forced herself to stumble forward with no idea where she was going. It was hard to walk, let alone run. Her bare feet sank into a thick, spongy surface that shifted dangerously each time she took a step. But fear kept her moving—not simply fear of the environment. Somewhere off to the side, she sensed a presence beside her, keeping pace with her, a presence so terrifying that it robbed her of what breath she had left.

The thing had no body. No form. It was just a huge, indefinite bulk that might swallow her whole if she allowed it to catch her.

She gasped, choked, turned her head away like a child afraid of monsters in the dark, trying to pretend that the thing in the mist was simply a construct of her imagination. But she knew she could never have conjured up the monster or this place on her own.

Her eyes stung as though someone had thrown acid in her face. Squeezing her lids tightly shut, she staggered blindly forward, each labored breath more choking than the one before. Her lungs burned like fire. Her heart drummed in her chest. And the pulse pounding in her head was like the roar of giant waves crashing on a rocky shore.

Confused, disoriented, she knew only one thing for sure. This land was not meant for human beings. It would kill her—soon. She understood that much as she doggedly put one foot in front of the other, sinking farther into the stuff below her feet with every step she took.

Then her toe hit something hard, something that felt alien in this place of bog and mist.

She yelped in pain and surprise—and also relief—as she staggered forward onto a blessedly flat surface that held her weight.

After the place of cold, swirling nothingness, the feel of solid ground and the warmth around her were gifts almost beyond bearing.

Her eyes snapped open. Reaching out a shaky hand, she found and gripped a low, solid wall as she dragged in a breath of clear, pure air. Sunlight streamed around her with the clarity of a bright summer day.

A deep sigh of relief flowed from her throat. Bending her head, she slid her fingers over the wall, caressing smooth marble, seeing the slight variation in the polished stone and the joints where the large blocks butted against each other.

The stone was warm from the sun. Smiling, she raised her gaze, and saw the pink blossoms of an oleander bush several yards away. The lower half of the bush was partially hidden by the backrest of a wide, circular bench, at the top of a structure that looked rather like a small stadium. No, not a stadium—a lounge; she suddenly remembered the name.

As she looked around at the silent scene, she thought vaguely that there should be two young women seated on the bench. One dark-haired and the other with red hair much like her own. But they were absent.

Beyond the bench and the bush, she saw the sparkling blue of the sea and the lighter blue of the sky.

This place was not in Rockville, Maryland. Not in the United States, she was pretty sure. And yet it was so achingly familiar that she wanted to weep with gladness.

"Under the roof of blue Ionian weather," she murmured. As she mouthed the words, she suddenly realized where she had gazed on this scene before.

The painting.

It was as if she had stepped into the picture that she and Detective Thornton had looked at together.

The sun was hot, and she ran her hand along her arm. It was bare, and she looked down to see she was wearing a sheer, sleeveless gown that cupped her breasts and draped gracefully around her legs.

Part of her knew that she was dreaming. Yet no dream had ever seemed this real, this vivid.

Because her fair skin had always burned easily, she stepped into a shaded marble walkway leading to a part of the lounge that was hidden from the viewer of the painting. Moving forward, she peeked around the corner and saw another long marble walkway. Every few feet, slender columns were topped with vertical wooden pieces covered with gracefully trailing vines.

A flash of movement caught her eye. Far down the outdoor corridor she saw a man striding toward her. He was dressed like a Roman general, in a short, belted tunic and leather sandals. His hair was dark; his bare legs, muscular. His face was in shadow, but she didn't need to see his features to know it was Jack Thornton.

She hadn't seen him since he'd come to her house to ask about Heather. Yet he'd invaded her thoughts so often that it felt like almost no time had passed since she'd been with him.

"Kathryn!" he shouted, breaking into a run, then stopping abruptly in front of her, his breath coming hard and fast.

From running? Or from the same reaction she was feeling?

She sighed his name, and it was the most natural thing in the world for her to open her arms to him. He reached for her at the same time, gathered her in; and she felt as if she'd finally come home to her long-lost lover, after wandering for centuries in the wilderness.

She was swamped by a raft of sensations. The feel of his hard muscles. The subtle scent of his body. And then his mouth came down on hers, the contact with his lips exquisite and erotic. Waves of heat seemed to come off of him, heat that made her own temperature rise in response.

In that moment, she knew that she was his, now and until the moon and stars dropped from the skies and the seas boiled away.

He was good at kissing. She found that out at once. He nibbled at her mouth, gauging her response before increasing the pressure, taking her lower lip between his teeth, then easing up so that she made a small sound of protest, begging for more.

He drew back, his eyes meeting hers, silently asking how much she wanted.

"All of you," she breathed, knowing it was the truth.

He held her gaze for a long, charged moment, then dipped his head again, his arms tightening around her as he took the level from erotic to mind-blowing in the space of heartbeats. He tangled his fingers in her hair, angling her mouth, making demands that she was happy to grant, swirling his tongue over the sensitive inner tissue of her lips, then probing more deeply, claiming possession as though she were an ancient princess captured by his Roman legions—and his for the taking.

He was the conqueror. But he was no enemy.

They were two halves of one whole, each incomplete without the other. Anchoring her hands over his shoulders, she pressed her body against his to keep from swaying on her feet. She felt as if she had been caught unawares in a strong wind whipping off the ocean, so that staying upright depended on clinging to him. He seemed to have the same problem, because he braced his legs, leaning back against the marble wall. The effect equalized their heights as he slid his hands down her body and brought her aching center against the hard shaft of his erection.

The contact felt exquisite, right.

She had always been a sedate lover—afraid to reveal too much of herself. Now she slid her hips against him, reveling in the wonderful sensations the friction generated. But it wasn't enough. She needed more, needed to feel his hands on her.

His thoughts seemed to follow hers, because he moved her upper body back a few inches, then gently cupped his big hand around one breast the way she'd imagined as she sat at her desk, wanting him.

The scene in her office seemed like a dream now, and this was her new reality.

"Oh!" Through the sheer fabric of her gown, the warmth and pressure of his hand felt wonderful. And when he found the tight bud of her nipple and began to play with it, she felt an arrow of pleasure shoot downward through her body, piercing her center.

He slipped the narrow shoulders of her gown onto her upper arms, lowering the bodice. Pushing the fabric out of the way, he pressed his face against her breasts, turning his head first one way and then the other before finding one distended nipple with his tongue and then his mouth.

She cried out, cupping her hands around his head, holding him to her, swaying slightly on her feet, pressing her sex against his erection.

Nothing in her life had ever felt so good, yet she needed more. She needed him inside her, needed that with a desperation that took her breath away. And she could tell from his harsh breathing that his passion matched hers.

A wayward thought skittered through her mind. What was he wearing under that Roman soldier's tunic? Was it like a Scottish kilt? If she pulled the fabric out of the way, would she find him bare, find his hot, distended penis?

She was naked under her own gown. All she had to do was pull it up and out of the way. Then he could lift her, fit her body to his.

SIMON stepped into the ceremonial chamber. His eyes skimmed over the woman, still dressed in her demure white gown, lying on the long wooden table. Earlier, he had brought her here from the cell next door. She was fixed to the table by leather straps that pulled her hands above her head and secured her feet.

She was also drugged—sleeping. In this important ceremony, her terror would only be an interference. It might break his concentration, and concentration was essential for success tonight.

The room had the feel of a sheltered, secret cave. Around the perimeter, set on pedestals, were seven candelabras. Each had seven arms holding seven slender, scented tapers. Walking to the closest one, he murmured an incantation as he touched a glowing light to each of the seven tapers before proceeding to the next pedestal.

When all the candles were lit, he crossed to the serving table and discarded his only garment, his black silk pants, hanging them neatly on a bar at the end of the table.

Then, picking up a crystal pitcher, he raised it high and poured the water into a silver bowl, listening intently to the gurgle of the liquid, like a mountain brook flowing over smooth, moonlit stones.

Cleaning his body was a simple ritual, but nonetheless important for his success. Everything must be done in order; everything must be done correctly.

First he wet his hands and wrists. Next he poured the water up his arms, across the network of scars on his smooth white chest, and onto the taut column of his neck. Then he splashed water downward, feeling his excitement grow as the cool water dripped onto his penis.

He was aroused, primed for action, excitement pulsing through his veins.

When he had dried himself with a towel, he picked up the white stick of chalk and stooped. With swift, sure strokes, he drew the magic circle on the slate floor, enclosing himself, keeping him safe from harm.

His eyes smoky now, he stood for several heartbeats, filling his lungs with deep drafts of the thick perfume from the candles while he stroked his penis, building his power, enjoying the mixture of arousal and anticipation.

The room blurred, and his head jerked up sharply. For just a moment, he felt the touch of another presence.

Impossible. Not within the protective circle. Yet his eyes searched the shadows beyond the glow of the candles. For one terrifying moment, he sensed an entity crouching in the corner, a mass of darkness darker than the floor and curtains.

It was the demon. Waiting for him to make some mistake.

But there would be no mistake tonight. He was in control—of himself, of the ceremony. And the demon couldn't really be here. Not yet. Could he?

Carefully he checked the circle. It was intact. Then, ruthlessly, he shut out everything besides the steps he must take to establish his domination over the demon.

First he crossed to the serving table, unfolded the silk cloth, and pulled out the silver knife. Then he walked to the long table. Delicately he inserted the tip of the knife into the white fabric of the dress, cutting a line down the middle of the bodice. With the flat side of the blade, he moved the fabric apart, exposing the woman's creamy breasts.

Nice breasts, he thought, enjoying the view, pretending for a moment that it was Kathryn Reynolds stretched out on the table.

It would have been nice to have her here. But he didn't need it to be her. Any man or woman would do. His victims were not for his physical enjoyment. They were only an instrument to complete the ceremony.

Taking a step back, he began to chant the words he had memorized. The words that would bind the demon to his will at the climax of the ceremony.

His voice was loud and precise. He spoke the first part of the ceremony in Greek, in accordance with ancient ritual, then switched to English.

I have captured your name.
Ayindral.
I will capture your essence.
I will capture your power.
Ayindral.
I call you to my will.
Ayindral.
Ayindral.
I command you to obey.

One hand stroked his throbbing erection as it stood out like a staff from his body; the other hand raised the silver knife.

Once more he stepped to the table. One hand still pleasured himself, the other raised the knife for the killing stroke—aiming for the heart of his sacrificial victim.

But as he brought the knife down, an unexpected image flashed into his head. An image that was none of his doing.

It was a man and a woman standing at the edge of a small marble amphitheater. From their dress and the setting, it looked like a scene that could only have taken place hundreds of years ago.

Yet there was an immediacy to the tableau that riveted him. He focused on the woman's red hair.

Patience. Patience all grown up and with her lover.

He couldn't see her features clearly. The man's head was in the way. But he saw the passionate kiss. Saw hands stroking. Heard moans of pleasure as they aroused each other to a fever pitch.

He strove to dislodge the vagrant scene from his mind. It had nothing to do with him. No place in this room. No place in the ceremony.

Yet the vison compelled him, broke his concentration. And he knew the demon had thrust it into his mind. The words of the chant faltered, even as he realized that it was too late to fight off his own orgasm. He tried desperately to pull himself back from the brink, but the inevitable happened.

Sexual climax overtook him, made his body jerk with the familiar ecstasy of release, yet he knew at the moment when his hot seed spurted onto the table and onto the white dress that he had failed.

The knife had missed its mark, missed the woman's heart. But she was wounded. And his only alternative was to finish her off.

A howl of rage rose in his throat, reverberating off the curtained walls of the ceremonial chamber.

He had been so sure of victory. But in that terrible moment, he knew to the depths of his soul that the demon had outsmarted him.

7

JACK felt Kathryn sliding her hand up his inner thigh. One minute he was waiting with quivering anticipation for her fingers to clasp his aching cock. In the next, he was clamping his hand on top of hers, stopping her upward progress. "Don't."

Her eyes blinked open. The pupils were dark and dilated, the effect sexy and arousing.

But he could see confusion warring with sensuality—mirroring the emotions that clashed within himself.

He shook his head, striving to clear the sexual fog from his brain. "Something. Something's happening," he managed, speaking between panting breaths.

His gaze focused on her breasts. They were beautiful, the coral-colored nipples tight, the skin flushed. It took all his self-control to gently pull the bodice of her dress back into place.

She didn't move as he took a step to the side, pressing his shoulders against the smooth marble behind him, staring at her across three feet of charged space.

"Jack?" she whispered again. "What was that? What just happened?"

"I don't know! Didn't you feel something? A vibration? A change in the air?" When he said it aloud, it sounded insubstantial.

He saw her swallow. "Yes."

With part of his mind, he ached to close the space between himself and the beautiful woman staring at him with large, worried eyes, pull her back into his arms, and finish what they'd started. But he thought that if he did what he wanted, he would be falling into a trap.

Set by whom? Kathryn? Or some outside force that had been poking its busy fingers into his life for the past few days?

Frustration made him run a shaky hand through his hair.

Her face seemed to echo his own uncertainty.

"This is a dream," she said in a halting voice looking from him to their surroundings and back again. "We can do anything we want. Things we both want. Can't we?"

He blinked, reached down to press his palm against the marble, warmed by the sun but cooling now. It felt so real, so solid. More detailed and real than any dream he could remember in his life.

Then he looked down at the costume he was wearing. It was like something out of a Roman epic. Kathryn, too, was dressed like she'd recently come from central casting.

"Why are we dressed like this? Why are we in this place?" he pressed.

Slowly she shook her head. Her voice grew stronger as she asked, "Do you know where we are?"

"No."

"Come here." She beckoned, and he followed. He would have followed her anywhere.

She led him around the corner, into a small marble amphitheater. It looked vaguely familiar, but he couldn't figure out the context. Behind the last rounded wall he saw a bush with feathery leaves and pink flowers. Beyond that was a jewel-blue sea sparkling in the sunshine.

"California?" he asked uncertainly, trying to put the scene into some familiar context.

She laughed. "I don't think so. Remember the Alma-Tadema painting you admired at my house?"

He did remember, and suddenly realization dawned. "We're in the painting!"

"Yes."

"Both of us," he said.

"So whose dream is this?"

"Mine," she said. "I'm thinking and feeling this."

"So am I. And I'm thinking this is edging into *The Twilight Zone*. Do you remember going to bed—falling asleep?"

"Yes."

He watched her carefully, feeling his chest tighten. This was a dream, yet they shared the reality. And he realized that there was one big advantage in this fantasy world. He could ask questions that wouldn't pass his lips in Montgomery County, Maryland. "Are you a witch?" he blurted. "Did you draw me here with some kind of magic spell?"

She gave a small laugh. "I told you, I'm a graphic artist and a publicist."

"You could still be a witch."

"What, exactly, do you mean by that? Do you think I use that little magic wand to work spells?"

"Do you?" he pressed.

"Of course not."

"Do you have special powers? Can you do things that other people can't? Manipulate the physical world?"

She tipped her head to one side, looking like she was giving his question careful consideration. "I don't think so. I never have. At least as far as I know."

"Should I believe you?" He was desperate to get at the truth.

She had taken her lower lip between her teeth, then eased up the pressure. "Why shouldn't you?"

"Because"—he gestured toward his tunic—"despite this outlandish getup, I'm a red-blooded American cop. Early twenty-first century. And I don't have any other way to explain what's happening to me."

"To us!"

He tried to read her tense features. Her eyes told him she was telling the truth. If he could believe his own observations. Maybe he couldn't. Maybe he was too off-balance.

He dragged in a breath, let it out slowly. "I'm sorry. I'm a little tense here."

"Make that two of us."

The broken sound of her voice and the pain in her eyes tore at him. His own anxiety was making him push her—press her for answers she didn't have.

He reached for her then, folding her into his arms, wanting to hold on to her even as he restrained the impulse to take up where they'd left off.

She moved her head against his shoulder. "Okay—if you want honesty, when I saw you here, all I could think of was making love with you. The way I've been thinking about it since I first laid eyes on you. Then you stopped us, and my mind kicked back into gear. Now I'm scared."

"Me, too," he heard himself admitting. So much for his solid macho image.

"What's happening to us? And what do we do about it?"

"I don't know," he answered. Then an idea struck him. He set her a little away from himself, then took the top of his left hand between the thumb and finger of the right hand. When he squeezed, it hurt.

"What are you doing?"

"Seeing if I can feel pain."

"Didn't you feel pleasure? When we were kissing and touching?"

"Yeah."

"Then why not pain?"

He shrugged, already thinking about another experiment. Jack Thornton, boy scientist! "If one of us gets hurt here, will the injury exist in the real world?"

She gave a little shudder. "What a thought."

He surveyed the scene, looking around for something to use. When he peered over the wall, he saw several sharp stones lying on the dark soil. There was about a yard of ground between the wall and the edge of the cliff. He vaulted over, staying away from the edge.

Kathryn was leaning over the wall, her eyes large with alarm. "Be careful."

"I am." Stooping, he picked up one of the stones and pressed it against the outside of his arm three inches below the elbow.

"Don't!"

Ignoring her, he made a small scratch. "Let's see if I have it when I wake up."

"How could you?"

"Why not? Everything else here is—different from a normal dream." He squeezed the rock in his hand, feeling the solid mass and the sharp edges. He tossed it into the air, watched it plummet downward, then disappear into the water far below. Straining his ears, he thought he heard the small splash.

As he turned back to the marble lounge, he found Kathryn's eyes fixed on him. He looked from her to the top of the wall. The ground was lower on this side, and he decided he couldn't make it over gracefully. So he walked around the end and stepped back into the marble structure.

Kathryn swept her skirt under her and arranged herself gracefully on the curved bench, looking at him with a challenge in her eyes. "Now what?" she asked.

He sat down on the hard surface and leaned back, careful to keep several feet of space between them. He'd been out of his mind with lust for her a few minutes ago. Now he thought he had some objectivity back.

"Now we exchange some information," he said, hoping his voice conveyed that they were back to business.

"Like what?"

"Like you tell me something I don't know about you. And I tell you something about me. And tomorrow, we see if we were both really here."

She lifted her head and looked at him. "So—are you divorced?"

His chest tightened. "My wife was killed in an automobile accident."

Her face registered surprise and compassion. "I'm so sorry."

"I'm coping. It's been almost three years."

"You said you have a daughter."

"Lily. And a son, Craig. Lily is seven and Craig is nine."

"Yesterday you only mentioned your daughter. That must be tough, taking care of two children."

"I have a housekeeper. She's a godsend."

She studied his face. "You look . . . upset. Did something bad happen?"

"Lily went missing yesterday afternoon."

"Oh! Is she all right?"

"It was only for an hour. I found her."

"I'm glad."

He nodded, remembering his panic, suddenly wondering what it would have been like if Kathryn had been by his side, sharing the worry. He could have leaned on her strength, because if there was anything he sensed about her, it was strength.

He caught himself up short. He'd just met this woman. He didn't know if she was involved in the disappearance of her tenant. He certainly couldn't trust her. Not on any level.

Especially since the two of them were sitting here in this fantasy setting, having a conversation that would go over just fine during social hour in a mental institution.

Hi. I'm Jack. I think I'm a Roman general. And you? Are you a vestal virgin? Or something else?

"You've got a strange expression on your face," she commented.

"I'll bet. I was thinking that this dialogue would be perfect for *One Flew over the Cuckoo's Nest.*"

She laughed, and he liked the sound.

They shared a grin, probably the first relaxed moments of their short relationship. He wanted to slide toward her, reach for her hand. Trust her. Although he stayed where he was, he asked the question that had been hovering in his mind since their first meeting.

"When I came to your house, and you opened the door, I felt like time stopped. Like we were caught together in some kind of time bubble. Did you experience that?"

"Yes," she whispered. "That's part of what scares me."

"Yeah." Her shaky voice and her admission made it possible for him to add, "It happened again later that day. When I was looking for Lily. I found her and a friend hiding inside a little playhouse. A mad dog was trying to get at them."

"The dog!"

He felt a shiver travel up his spine. "What do you know about it?"

She shook her head. "Yesterday, I kept hearing a dog barking. I felt like something bad had happened. But I couldn't see anything. And then suddenly it stopped."

"You heard it? It was miles from your house."

She could only stare at him, shrug. "Maybe it was some other dog."

"Sure."

"Jack—don't make it sound like I did something wrong. I don't even know what happened. Please tell me."

He sighed, watched her closely. "The dog turned on me, and I thought it was going to snap me in half."

Her exclamation sounded genuine. Like she truly was finding out about this for the first time. Still, he kept his gaze fixed on her as he added, "Then that time thing happened again. The extra seconds let me get my gun into position and fire."

She opened her mouth, and to his surprise, the first thing she said was "You must have hated shooting a dog."

His chest went tight. "Yeah."

"I guess you had to do it. Thank God you're all right. And Lily."

He nodded, caught up in remembered emotions. He jerked himself back with another question. "With you—was the time-stopping experience only once, when I came to the door?"

"Yes."

"So for you it was just when we met. And for me it happened again—when I was in danger."

She had clasped her hands together in her lap, and he saw that her fingers were locked so tightly that they looked bloodless. "What does that mean?"

He shrugged. "My best guess, the first time—somebody wanted to make sure we noticed each other. Then they wanted to make sure I didn't buy the farm."

"Somebody? Who would have the power to do that?"

"Someone with psychic powers."

She gave a nervous laugh. "I thought cops were too down-to-earth to worry about stuff like that. Just the facts, ma'am."

He shrugged. "I used to be like that—until I found out that one of my best friends is a—" He stopped abruptly.

"A what?"

"It's better if I don't go around discussing his situation. He's got enough problems without my blabbing his secret. The important point is that he's made me look at the world a little differently."

"Okay," she agreed—too quickly—and he knew she wanted to ask about Ross. But she didn't, which immediately boosted her in his estimation. He relaxed his guard a little, thinking that there wasn't anything wrong with some personal questions. Once the idea had taken hold, he heard himself asking, "So if this is a dream—is that what you wore to bed?"

"No. A T-shirt. Don't tell me you went to bed dressed like Mark Antony."

"Hardly."

"Then what?"

Trapped by his own line of questioning, he answered, "Briefs."

He had made a mistake, getting personal. His body was starting to respond, and he knew the conversation could get out of hand very quickly. Yet he was unable to resist another intimate querry. "Are you in a relationship?"

"No."

While he was still wallowing in a wave of relief, she said, "I was managing my life just fine—until you knocked on my door. I haven't gotten in any trouble with the law. I support myself. I keep in shape. I'm a volunteer art teacher at the local elementary school."

There was no reason he needed to know any of that. But he was glad to hear those facts and he wanted more.

Inwardly, he cursed himself. He should be sticking to business. Deliberately making his voice hard, he asked, "Did you have something to do with Heather's disappearance?"

Her reaction was swift and angry. "How dare you! I reported her missing."

"That's the way it works sometimes. The person responsible calls the police—to deflect suspicion."

"Thanks for the heads up," she answered, her voice thick with sarcasm.

Before she could marshal more defenses, he shot her another question. "Why were you so on edge when I found that porn material in her dresser? Are the two of you into something together?"

"Of course not!" Anger flashed in her voice—and in her eyes.

"So you're not into whips and chains when you make love," he pressed.

"I'm not like my father, if that's what you're getting at. I think you have a pretty good idea of what I like when I'm with a man."

His throat constricted, but he stood his ground. Still watching her closely, he switched subjects quickly. "I talked to Swinton yesterday. He told me you talked to Heather about him—about stuff that was none of your business."

"Like her abortion?"

"He wasn't specific."

He had more questions he wanted to ask her, but she cut him off with a brusque "I've had enough of your interrogation."

As she spoke, she got up and walked away, out of the lounge and into the corridor of columns.

"Wait," he called out, then started after her. But when she was about thirty feet away, she vanished into thin air. And he was left standing in an empty fantasy landscape.

8

THE scene wavered. He wasn't sure why he tried to hang on to it, his hands clawing at empty air. But the effort was wasted.

Less than a minute after Kathryn disappeared, Jack was back in his bed, the sheets twisted around his sweat-drenched flesh. His body felt strangely heavy. His mind felt like it might fly right out of his skull.

He glanced at the glowing numbers on the clock radio. It was four in the morning. He knew he wasn't going back to sleep anytime soon.

Heaving himself out of bed, he stood for a moment in the briefs he'd told Kathryn he was wearing, the night air cooling his damp skin. Once he'd slept in the buff, but now that the kids might come bursting into his room at all hours of the night, he'd opted to cover up just a bit.

He reached for his robe, then stopped, remembering something he'd deliberately done in the dream. In the bathroom, he turned on the light and held up his left arm. Below his elbow was a small red line. He knew for damn sure it hadn't been there when he'd gone to bed. It was the mark he'd scratched with the rock—unless he'd somehow scraped himself on the sheets.

He stared at the injured skin, feeling a prickle at the back of his neck.

A dream. But not a dream!

After pulling on his robe, he padded down the hall toward his home office. Before he got there, he stopped outside Craig's room, pushed open the door, and stepped into his son's world.

Stooping, he picked up a T-shirt and a pair of jeans from the carpet and carried them to the hamper in the corner, under a poster of Cal Ripken. There were other posters on the wall. All sports figures. His favorite players from baseball, hockey, football. He was really into sports. Which was great. Better than pot or sex.

Lord, it made his chest tighten to think of those things in the same breath with his son. Yet he knew damn well how young a kid could be and still get into serious trouble.

He crossed to the bed, looking down at the sweet, innocent face, wanting to reach out and make physical contact with his son. Not with a dream, with something real and important.

But he kept his hand at his side, afraid to wake the boy. Long seconds passed before he turned toward the door again.

The warm, fatherly glow was punctured on the way back across the room when he stepped squarely on a Lego piece and had to bite back a curse. Craig might be growing up, but he still played with some of the toys he'd enjoyed as a little boy.

Hobbling into the hall, Jack leaned against the wall and lifted his foot, inspecting the damage. They were overdue for a chat about room cleaning. He'd let that slide, but he had to focus on discipline—as well as the fun stuff.

Until a few days ago, Craig and Lily had been the center of his emotional life. Suddenly, Kathryn Reynolds was taking up a lot of his attention.

He didn't want to think about her now. Not while he was focused on his son—on his children. But he found it impossible to get the red-headed siren out of his mind. And as he stood in the hall, leaning against the wall, he felt his breathing accelerate once more.

Although he barely knew Kathryn Reynolds, there was no way to kid himself about wanting her. He burned to possess her body. And he would have made love with her a little while ago, if something hadn't stopped him. He didn't even know what that was.

A vibration in the air? A sense of some evil presence? He shook his head. He only knew that he'd stopped on the brink of making a bad mistake.

His hands squeezed into fists. He was treating this like it had been real, when it had only been a dream.

A dream. No, much more than a dream, he admitted. An experience with the sharpness and vivid flavor of the most intense reality.

Deliberately he backed away from the sunlit landscape where he'd almost ravished Kathryn and reached back into his own past—trying to recapture the feel of his late teens and his early twenties. Actually, there had been some pretty memorable sexual escapades. Before Laura, he hadn't been into commitment, just getting what he could. But the drive to score had changed with Laura. He'd still wanted to make love. But he'd kept that desire in check, because he sensed that she could mean so much more to him than all the other women who'd passed through his life.

He'd been horny. But he'd been in control.

Now he felt like he was in a speeding truck, heading toward an inevitable crash. Somehow he had stopped. In the dream. In real life, would he have the same control?

He cursed softly under his breath. He should have fucked her a little while ago. In Never-Never Land where there were no real consequences. Instead, he'd pulled away and made it harder—yeah, harder—to maintain his self-control.

Jack Thornton, you're a jerk, he told himself as he strode down the hall to his office, where he firmly closed the door and booted up his computer.

Grim-faced, he accessed AltaVista, then asked the search engine to find web sites that included Lawrence Alma-Tadema.

Some had only essays about the artist. But others belonged to art dealers who offered prints and posters of the artist's work.

Jack paged through them, then came to the scene that was now burned into his memory. The painting was called *Under the Roof of Blue Ionian Weather*. With a strange sense of uneasiness, he studied the details: the marble structure, the bush behind the low wall, the sea, the sky. It was exactly what he remembered from the dream—except that the people were missing. He and Kathryn had been the only two figures in the scene. They hadn't been dressed exactly like the models in the picture. The people had been wearing a bit more. Draped, flowing dresses for the women. And a cloak covering the man's tunic.

But when he paged through other works by the artist, he found women in various stages of undress and Roman soldiers wearing outfits similar to what he'd been wearing in the dream.

He brought back *Under the Roof of Blue Ionian Weather* and stared at the scene. It was the place, all right. And he knew more about it than what was in the picture. He'd climbed over that low wall, used a stone to scratch his skin, then tossed the stone into the sea and heard it splash far below.

Weird.

So how had he and Kathryn gotten there? Had some outside force directed his dream? The same outside force that had stopped time twice?

He tapped his knuckles against his lips. The speculation was absurd, yet he'd learned not to dismiss facts simply because they were inconvenient. Two very strange things had already happened to him. Then the dream tonight.

He glanced at the clock again. It was four-thirty. An obscene hour for a social call. Or even a business call.

Yet he was pretty sure that Kathryn would be as wide awake as he was now. Edgy. Sexually aroused, the way he was, even though he was still trying to ignore the persistent sensations.

Should he call her? Part of him said no. But another part screamed yes.

His hand rested on the receiver, and he was thinking he should go ahead and pick it up.

He had valid reasons. Professional reasons. She was involved in a case, and he couldn't let go of the feeling that she was holding back information. But he knew damn well that professional concerns weren't motivating him now. So he pulled his hand back, then got up from the chair and headed for the bathroom and a cold shower.

SIMON'S jaw was clenched as he drove toward Sugarloaf Mountain. When he'd discovered the place, he'd liked the juxtaposition of the name with his private graveyard.

Sugarloaf Mountain. A confection of a private park. And a great place to get rid of the bodies that tended to pile up from his rituals.

The dead woman from tonight's debacle was in the trunk, sealed in plastic, so there was no worry about bodily fluids or trace evidence contaminating the carpeting.

He drove carefully, not taking any chances of some cop finding his latest victim.

Rolling his shoulders, he tried to relax, but it was impossible to let go of the tight feeling of his muscles. He was angry—with himself most of all.

He'd had few setbacks in his life since he'd clawed his way out of his miserable early years.

He had been born in Dundalk, a poor neighborhood at the northeastern edge of Baltimore. He'd lived in a cramped row house with Mom and Dad and eight brothers and sisters. It had been like living in a chicken coop. He hadn't even had his own bed until he'd pulled off his first job and moved out.

While the rest of the family was gathered around the television set, eating their junk food and watching their mindless sitcoms, he'd withdrawn into the books he got from the public library. Mostly he stayed in the reading room. When it was closed, he hung out on the back stoop of his house, unless it was so cold that his hands began to freeze as he turned the pages.

His interests were far-reaching. He read about theater, magic, far-away places, the finer things in life. Books showed him there was an-other kind of life besides the dysfunctional family into which he'd been born. The dysfunctional family that laughed at his books and teased the shit out of him.

Ignoring them, he sucked up information like an industrial vac-uum cleaner. The magic, particularly, drew him. Not parlor tricks. Real magic. Dark rituals that brought power. But he knew there was danger as well as potency in the ceremonies. He understood that the potential for disaster was greater than the potential for gain. He'd seen that cartoon with Mickey Mouse. *The Sorcerer's Apprentice*. Most people watched it and laughed. He knew it was based on an impor-tant truth: a little bit of knowledge was a dangerous thing.

So he studied and bided his time. And the older he got, the more he looked for excuses to stay away from home. He worked in the stock-room and did odd jobs for an antique dealer downtown. And he kept track of the owner's money flow. After a major antique show, he was likely to have a lot of cash around.

Even back then, Simon had been patient. During three years as a trusted employee, he had carefully worked out how to acquire that cash—all the time planning his disappearance into another identity.

It was only a first step, of course. But he'd gotten away with twenty thousand dollars—a small fortune, back then. Seed money he'd used to pull off other jobs, steadily improving his living standard and giving himself the leisure he needed for his most important research—into the rituals of the Golden Dawn.

It was a discipline that fascinated him. A discipline that few had mastered. He'd put in years of hard work and watched his success grow. But everything he'd done so far was only a prelude.

So many magicians down through the ages had tried to enslave a demon and failed. He'd thought he knew why. He'd done everything right. Using the sexual energy of orgasm and releasing the life force of a living sacrifice weren't some half-baked ideas he'd come up with on his own. He'd studied the nineteenth-century rituals. And the ancient texts before them. He'd known what he was doing. But he'd thought that following everything to the letter would neutralize the demon's defenses.

He'd been overconfident, and he'd been wrong.

At the turnoff for the park, he switched off his headlights, then stopped to open the chain. After fastening it again, he drove toward the East View parking lot.

When he reached the far end of the lot, he cut the engine and sat in the darkness, fighting a tinge of uneasiness.

His eyes probed the shadows under the trees, and he wondered what he was looking for. Nothing! He was just overwrought from the fiasco of the ceremony.

After releasing the trunk latch, he climbed out of the car. It was no problem to heave the body over his shoulder and pick up the shovel he'd brought along.

The ground here was broken by rock outcroppings. But there were open places where the soil was easy to turn. He found one and set down his burden.

A few minutes after he started to dig, he felt the hairs on the back of his neck stir, and he looked up sharply, his eyes and ears probing the darkness once more.

He saw nothing. Heard nothing. Yet his heart was pounding in his chest.

To his right, the moonlight shimmered on—

On nothing but a place where the tree branches were thick, he decided as he took a step closer.

Still, he couldn't completely let go of his fear.

Could the demon be here?

Impossible, he told himself. The demon couldn't live in the world of men. Not yet. Not until the two of them had established the link of master and slave. And it couldn't come to him of its own will. It had to wait until *he* was focused on *it*.

It couldn't be the demon, he told himself firmly. Yet it was long moments before he felt comfortable enough to return to his business.

Quickly he began to dig. It didn't have to be a deep grave. Just a few feet deeper than the body. If somebody found it a couple of years from now, what would it matter? Simon Gwynn would have a new name and all the power and wealth he needed to maintain his safety.

The shovel bit into the dirt, which he lifted and set in a pile. The motion was automatic, a nice workout. His anger still simmered below the surface, but he had it under control. Anger never did any good. It was a waste of energy.

He had better things to do with his mind while he dug the grave. As he shoveled up dirt, he brought back the image of the couple who had broken his concentration and spoiled the ceremony.

They were dressed for a play or a movie. Like a costume drama set in ancient Greece or Rome. He wasn't exactly sure, because the history of costume wasn't his major field. But he would do some research and figure out the era.

So had he really been viewing an ancient scene? One that the demon had dragged from the past?

Or what?

Something more recent? A man and a woman in costume.

Patience Hamilton and her lover?

Jesus, did the demon know about her?

Or was this something else entirely?

KATHRYN lay in the darkness, her body rigid, her mind churning, her hand clutching Jack's card. She wanted to call him, needed to hear his voice—needed that connection she'd felt to him. But she wasn't going to be the one to pick up the phone.

He should do it. Damn him! Because if she made the call, she was going to look like she was pursuing him. She'd spoken to him candidly in the dream. Too candidly. Now she refused to give him more reason to think she was chasing after him.

Maybe he hadn't phoned because it was only her dream. The abashed, embarrassed part of her wanted that to be true. The needy part wanted him to tell her that they'd connected emotionally in the dream—that what happened between them was all right. So she lay in bed, wide awake, all her senses on alert, which was probably why she heard a noise outside that might not have reached her ears under ordinary circumstances. A quick rattling, as if someone had stumbled over the trowel that she'd left near the back door.

A *zing* went through her nerve endings. Without turning on the light, she slipped out of bed and padded to the window, lifted a slat in the blinds, and peered out into the darkness. Below her she could see a cat streaking across the lawn.

A cat! That was all.

She went back to bed and pulled the covers up to her chin, but she was much too tense to sleep.

Finally, when she heard the newspaper hit the front porch, she pulled on sweatpants under her T-shirt and padded down the inside stairway.

Opening the front door, she took a step outside. Before she cleared the doorway, her ankle hit something taut and invisible.

A scream tore from her throat as she pitched forward, putting out her hands to break her fall as the porch floor came up to meet her.

For long moments she simply lay there on the cold boards, too stunned to move. Then she pushed herself up to a sitting position. First she inspected her hands where she'd hit the painted wood surface. They were scraped, but the damage wasn't serious.

Carefully, she flexed her arms and legs. Then with narrowed eyes, she turned to the door frame. At first she could see nothing. Then she spotted a piece of plastic fishing line stretched across the opening, about eight inches from the sill. On one side it was secured to the door hinge. On the other side, it was wound around a nail head that protruded slightly from the door frame. Not a nail that anybody had hammered into place recently, she knew. The darn thing had been sticking out for months, but she'd never gotten around to fixing it. Too bad!

Who would have done this? Someone who wanted to hurt her? Or someone who had a beef with Heather? That would mean it was someone who didn't know her tenant was missing, since the front door led to both apartments.

And what was the motive?

She had no answer. Back inside, she debated what to do. She'd been ignoring little things. Like the spray paint and the tire tracks over the flower bed. Maybe that had been a mistake. It certainly would be a mistake now, because she wanted this incident on record with the police.

So she dialed 911. When the operator came on, she explained what had happened and that she was in the upstairs apartment.

"We'll have a patrol car out there as soon as possible, ma'am," the woman told her.

How soon was that, Kathryn wondered as she quickly washed, changed her T-shirt, and pulled on clean sweatpants.

She was pacing back and forth, stopping periodically to lift one of the slats in the blinds, when she saw a cruiser roll to a stop in front of the house.

Hurrying downstairs, she made sure that the officer, whose name was Lorton, didn't trip over the fishing line. After examining it and taking photographs, he unhooked it and put it in a plastic bag. Then he dusted for fingerprints—and found none.

Straightening, he asked, "Has there been any other trouble here?"

"Some vandalism. I didn't think it was all that serious, but this is another matter. I could have broken my neck."

"Yes," he agreed, which didn't make her feel any better. "Anything else unusual going on?"

She sighed. "My downstairs tenant has been missing for almost a week."

"You filed a report?"

"Yes. And a Detective Thornton has been out here to talk to me," she said, keeping her hands at her sides so she wouldn't twist them into a knot.

The officer wrote it down.

"Anything else?" he asked, giving her an opportunity to tell him about the strange stuff that had happened between her and Jack. She kept that to herself.

Lorton departed, leaving her with the same unfinished business that had kept her up since she'd awakened from the dream. She wanted to talk to Jack. Now more than ever. She wanted him to tell her what to do.

Finally, swallowing her pride, she picked up the phone and called him. But after all that, once again he wasn't even in the office.

Damn him!

9

JACK had been planning to go to Kathryn's in the morning. But as he was shaving, he changed his mind. Maybe he was too chicken to confront her. He preferred to think he should get another perspective. So he decided to exercise another option.

After breakfast with the kids and Emily, he went upstairs to his office and called Ross Marshall.

"Would it be inconvenient if I came over this morning?" he asked.

"You've got some business to discuss?"

"Yeah. I've got to stop by the office and take care of a few things. Then I'll drive over."

He put down the phone, his gaze fixed on the bookshelves in back of the desk. He was still sitting there, staring into space, when he heard a light tap at the door.

"Yes?"

Lily pushed the door open and peeked in. "I came to kiss you good-bye."

He opened his arms, and she scurried into them, holding tight to him. Turning his face, he kissed her cheek. "I love you, honey."

"I love you, too, Daddy." She pressed closer to him.

"What?"

In a barely audible voice, she asked, "Are you mad at me, Daddy?"

"No, sweetheart."

"You seem mad."

"Do I? I think I'm just preoccupied."

"What does that mean?"

"I'm thinking hard about a case."

"Oh."

"Thanks for saying something."

"You don't mind?"

He gave her another hug. "Of course not. The only way you can know what somebody is feeling is for them to tell you."

She thought about that and nodded.

"You don't want to be late for school. I'll see you after work."

"I love you, Daddy," she said again, then turned quickly and headed for the stairs, leaving him feeling overwhelmed.

You bring a baby home from the hospital, he thought, *and you don't have a clue about what you're getting into*. Babies turned into children with distinct personalities and a whole bunch of needs. Here he was lusting after Kathryn Reynolds, and he had no idea how she was going to interact with his children.

He snorted. Kathryn again. Invading his thoughts in every conceivable context. So was he thinking about fucking her? Or bringing her home to meet the family? It was a little premature for the latter, he decided as he headed to the office.

He'd been collecting information on the other three missing persons, and he needed to look at the new material coming in. After sorting through the various bits of information, he picked up the bag with DeYoung's T-shirt. He hadn't logged it in as evidence. Not when he knew he was collecting it to give his werewolf detective friend a whiff of her scent.

The thought brought a grim smile to his face. Ross Marshall had an uncanny sense of smell. And he was better than a tracking dog, because he had a wolf's senses combined with a man's brain. A very potent combination.

Ross lived in the western part of Howard County in a still rural area. He'd bought a large piece of property several years ago, with a stream and woods where he could wander as a wolf at night.

The house was at the top of a hill, up a rough road paved with loose gravel and across a wooden bridge that looked like it wouldn't hold the weight of his car. But he'd been over it often enough, and he knew that Ross and Megan regularly crossed it in their SUVs.

He cleared the woods and stopped for a moment, studying the sign that said DÍTHREABA. It meant refuge in the old Gaelic language, the language of Ross Marshall's ancestors.

Taking his foot off the brake, Jack drove up the hill, impressed as always with the setting and with the house that Ross had remodeled by himself. It was a modern structure of wood and stone, with massive windows that faced the meadow on one side and the woods on the other three. Ross had designed the house to bring the outside in—so that he had the best of both worlds, a comfortable interior environment with natural vistas that fed his soul.

After cutting the engine, Jack walked toward the front door. Movement behind the large living room window caught his attention, and he stopped in his tracks.

Through the glass he could see Ross and Megan Marshall. Apparently, they weren't expecting him so soon, and it was very clear that Ross's acute senses were not turned toward the outside of the house.

He and Megan were standing in the middle of the rug, holding each other close, swaying slightly—their mouths fused.

It was a very private moment. Jack knew he shouldn't intrude. But in his hypersensitive state, he couldn't turn away. The waves of sexual energy coming off the couple behind the window caught and held him—and set his own nerve endings quivering.

He'd suspected that there was a high degree of sensuality in the bond between a werewolf and his mate. It appeared to be true. In a moment he expected to see steam coming off the man and woman in the living room.

Ross slid his hands down Megan's back, cupped her bottom, and rocked her body against his.

Jack's breath caught. He was struggling to take a step back when a noise intruded on the scene. It took him seconds to realize it was a baby crying. By that time, Megan was already out of the room and rushing down the hall.

Released from his new role as a voyeur, Jack walked rapidly back to the unmarked, where he dragged in several deep breaths and wiped his damp palms down the sides of his trousers. After taking half a minute to collect himself, he opened the car door and slammed it loudly.

Ross was standing with his back to the window. He didn't turn as Jack came up the sidewalk. And he waited several seconds before opening the door.

His face was slightly flushed.

"I appreciate your seeing me," Jack said.

"You're always welcome here," Ross answered.

They stood awkwardly facing each other until Megan came down the hall, holding the baby.

Jack and Megan had become good friends during the time before her marriage, when she'd been estranged from Ross and wondering if she dared contemplate a future with such a man.

In the end, there had been no way she could turn away from him. Their marriage was strong, he knew. Not just physically, but emotionally as well.

This morning, she seemed to have regained her equanimity more quickly than her husband—but she'd been forced to focus on her son.

When she smiled at Jack, he smiled back.

Joshua had stopped crying, and from the way Megan was cradling him against her chest, Jack could see that the baby was nursing.

Husband and wife exchanged a long, lingering look. Then Megan's gaze came back to Jack again. "Good to see you."

"Yes. How are you doing?" he asked, still feeling like an intruder.

"Well, the son and heir is teething—which is making our life a little difficult," she answered.

"Hang on, and he'll be in a new phase before you know it."

"I hope so." As she spoke, she settled herself in the rocking chair. Ross crossed to the mother and child, standing behind the chair, reaching down to cup his son's head and stroke the fine black hair.

Megan tipped her face up, and they exchanged a look of unconscious sensuality—reminding Jack of years ago when his own children had been babies. Nursing could be a turn-on, Laura had told him. And there had been times when he'd sat beside her on the bed, his hand lightly stroking her shoulder as he waited for her to finish feeding Craig or Lily so they could get back to some rudely interrupted quality adult time.

The eye contact broke, and Ross raised his head. Aware that he had been staring, Jack looked down, watching Megan's knees as she began to rock gently.

"Get Jack a mug of tea," she said to her husband.

"Uh-huh. Tea."

Jack followed him into the well-equipped kitchen, another dividend of Ross's remodeling skills. He'd supported himself while he was in college with two very different jobs. He already had a reputation as a private investigator—using his wolf senses to solve robberies and nail adulterous spouses. At the same time, he was working as a carpenter's apprentice. Both careers built from those fledgling beginnings. Ross continued solving crimes, earning substantial fees. And he used some of the money to start buying and rehabbing fixer-upper houses.

His comfortable home in the woods was the culmination of his real estate ventures. Jack knew Ross had expected to live here by himself in this refuge from the world. Then he'd met Megan, and his life had changed.

Ross swept his hand toward the shelf of tea boxes. "What's your pleasure?"

Jack focused on a box. "Ginger-flavored green tea."

"I didn't know you were into green tea."

"A sudden impulse," Jack answered, wondering at his choice, then remembering he'd seen a similar box on Kathryn's counter.

He must have made a face, because Ross paused in the act of extracting a tea bag. "Changed your mind?"

"No."

Ross studied him, then turned to the sink. Apparently he'd added one of those instant hot water faucets, because instead of reaching for the kettle, he simply put the tea bags into two mugs and filled them with steaming water. All the modern conveniences for the descendant of ancient werewolves.

While the tea steeped, Ross asked, "So what kind of case did you come to discuss?"

"Missing person. A woman. I brought along one of her T-shirts. I was hoping you could figure out what's happened to her."

"I can give it a try. But I need more to go on. Like, if she left in a car, there won't be any trail to follow."

"I know. And it won't do any good to check her boyfriend's car. I'm sure she's been in it for legitimate purposes." Jack sighed and looked back toward the great room where Megan still rocked and nursed the baby. "Can we go outside?"

"Sure."

They each picked up a mug and walked to the front door.

"Back soon," Ross told his wife.

About six months ago, Ross had built a fieldstone patio at the side of the house. Jack suspected that Megan might sit there when her husband was in wolf form, roaming the nearby woods, since she couldn't join him physically.

But he didn't mention his speculation as they settled themselves in Adirondack chairs, facing the forest. Ross sucked in a breath of the early spring air, his expression appreciative, and Jack wondered what scents the werewolf caught that were undetectable to a normal man.

"So what are the details of the case that you don't want Megan to hear?" he asked.

Jack set his mug on the table between the chairs and knit his fingers together. The details of the case weren't exactly the problem. It was his personal involvement, but he knew he was going to ease into that part.

"A young woman disappeared late last week. Her landlady made the report. The missing woman, Heather DeYoung, works as a substitute teacher for the Montgomery County school system. She's got a lot of debts. The landlady doesn't like the boyfriend, and I share the opinion."

As they both took sips of tea, he quickly filled in other facts—leaving out the personal stuff like the time distortions and the dream. But as he felt Ross's keen eyes on him, he knew that his friend was reading between the lines.

"So what do you think?" Jack asked when he'd finished.

"I think you're attracted to the landlady. But you're worried she's mixed up in the case somehow."

Jack let out a breath. "Something like that, yeah. You always were perceptive."

They sat in silence for several moments.

Jack scuffed his shoe against a flagstone, staring intently at the polished brown leather, steeling himself to take the next step. "I need to talk about an aspect of this I haven't touched on yet. Probably anybody else would think I'm crazy. I figure with your particular background, you're going to be open-minded."

"Just spit it out. You'll feel better."

"Easy for you to say!"

"Well, I was the loner who kept his background secret for years. Until I found out I could trust Megan—and you."

Jack deliberately unclenched his jaw and began to speak, describing in stark terms his meeting with Kathryn, the incident with the dog, the dream, leaving out some of the embarrassing details.

"So are you going to send for the guys with the butterfly nets to take me away?" he asked when he'd finished.

Ross's hesitation had his heart pounding.

"I never met a man who had his feet planted more firmly on the ground than you," he finally said.

Jack exhaled the breath he'd been holding. "So—you've got all those books on paranormal stuff. Myths. Vampires. Werewolves. Did you ever run across anything like this?"

"There's always Einstein's theory of relativity."

Jack laughed. "Maybe I should study physics."

"Time distortion isn't so strange. When people are under stress, their sense of time can speed up—or stretch out. Megan told me it happened to her when she took care of me after I got shot. She was sitting on the bed, and I was delirious. I started to change into a wolf. Thank God, I didn't get very far. But she told me later she felt like she was living in slow motion."

Jack hung on his friend's words. "So it was associated with something paranormal. I mean, with your shape-shifting."

"Yeah." It was Ross's turn to laugh. "Let's hope the FBI isn't recording this conversation. They'd haul us both in."

"You and Megan have straightened out your problems."

"That's relative. We've still got some stuff to face. Like, how many of our children the wolf gene is going to kill."

Jack winced. "Yeah. Sorry."

"Megan's doing more genetic studies down at the lab. After hours, when her staff's gone home."

Again they were silent.

Finally, Ross asked, "Did you talk to Kathryn about the dream?"

"Not yet. I was going to rush over there this morning. I came here instead."

"Talk to her."

"I was hoping you could offer some insights. You're the one with the special talents. Do you think Kathryn is a witch—that she's doing this?"

"What's her motivation?"

"Hell, I don't know. Maybe she likes to play with men. Drive them crazy with lust—then suck the life out of them."

Ross laughed, but his hands were rigid on the mug of tea. "Crazy with lust. That's a good description of the werewolf when he meets his mate."

"Are you trying to make me feel better?"

"I'm trying to tell you I understand. At least the sexual part. The rest of it—I don't know. I've never read about anything like what you're describing. And I've read a lot—trying to relate my problems to the literature of the occult and to the literature of human experience."

"Yeah."

"One comment I can make. You're uncomfortable, and you're trying to pin it on her."

Jack nodded, acknowledging it was true.

"I don't think I've been much help."

"Actually you have." Jack heaved himself out of the chair. "I'll leave the T-shirt with you. Her address is in the bag. And the boyfriend's address, if you have time to do some snooping around for me."

"Do you want to borrow some books? General stuff on the occult and witchcraft might give you some ideas."

"Yeah. Thanks."

They went back in and found that Megan had returned the baby to his bed and was warming some homemade cranberry-nut muffins in the oven. Ross and Jack both polished off two while they inspected the bookcase.

He left with an armload of volumes including *Visions of the Occult, The Golden Dawn, The Black Arts, Creatures of the Night, The Ways of the Sacred,* and several volumes from the *Time-Life* series, Mysteries of the Unknown.

Time-Life! Maybe he should call the Psychic Hotline, too.

After locking the books in the trunk of the car, he started down the long driveway, then paused at the bottom, checked his messages—and found that Kathryn had called him twice.

Well, he'd been deliberately ignoring her—although there was no way to stop thinking about her. Now he knew that putting off a confrontation any longer only spoke of his own cowardice. And nobody had ever accused him of that. So he checked in with headquarters, then drove back to Davenport Street in Rockville.

AFTER the exercise in the woods, Simon slept for a few hours and woke refreshed.

He'd made a mistake. He'd been too confident. Now he must go back to his textbooks and study the rituals—as soon as he conditioned his body.

He spent an hour in his home gym, splitting his time between the StairMaster and the weight machines. After that, he showered and carefully combed his hair, checking with two mirrors to make sure his bald spot didn't show.

Next came a simple but nourishing breakfast. Blueberry yogurt with a quarter-cup of granola. Half a grapefruit. And a cup of orange spice tea sweetened with a teaspoon of honey—no more.

After rinsing the dishes and stacking them in the dishwasher, he repaired to the library, feeling a serenity descend over him as he pulled out one of the old volumes.

The Golden Dawn, as revealed by Israel Regardie. Complete with a comprehensive index. He didn't need a road map. He'd read and reread the volume so many times that he knew it by heart.

Going back to the basic rituals always soothed him. Just for the pleasure of it, he went through the Banishing ritual of the Pentagram, focusing on eliminating any negative energy that still clung to him.

He was calling up the positive aspects of the Astral Light when a shudder went through his body as the woman's image came to him again. The woman in the ancient setting.

He hadn't seen her face, but it wasn't Patience, he realized, as he focused again on the wild red hair. Of course. That hair was the giveaway. It was Kathryn Reynolds—the one he'd wanted in the first place. He didn't know much about her except that she owned the house where DeYoung had rented an apartment, lived alone, and didn't have a lot of friends.

He'd made it a rule to vary his victims. An older woman. A child. A teenage boy. A younger woman—but a completely different type from his last female victim.

He'd told himself he couldn't have another redhead. Not yet. But now . . .

Now she was involved. She was dangerous. The demon had dragged her into it. He'd turn that back on the creature—and use her in the next ceremony.

He felt excitement coursing through his veins as he began making plans. He'd drive out to Davenport Street this morning. Maybe he'd even be able to scoop Ms. Reynolds up and ask her what the hell was going on. Of course, maybe she didn't understand that the demon had its hooks into her and the man. But that didn't matter. Simon was sure she could give him some information before he sacrificed her.

He stared across the room at the floor-to-ceiling bookcases, but his vision was focused inward. When he'd been in her neighborhood before, he'd been posing as a workman. He'd driven his white van and been dressed in blue coveralls. It would be dangerous to go back in the same persona. He was as careful with locations as with his victims. He never repeated a disguise in the same place. And this was a rule he had no need to break.

The white van was still in the five-car garage. It sat beside the Saab, the Dodge SUV, the Mustang, and the old navy-colored Crown Victoria with the dent in the front bumper and the scratch on the driver's door. Yes, that was the one he'd drive, dressed in a gray wig and a blue striped suit. If anybody asked, he'd be an old guy looking for his nephew's house. But he didn't quite have the address right. Yeah, that would do. Trying to suppress a feeling that bordered on glee, he hurried toward the dressing room where he kept his costume wardrobe and his makeup table.

10

AYINDRAL blinked awake. He had averted the ultimate disaster, but after the ordeal of the ceremony, he had been too weak to do more than drift. Now he knew he must reach out again. Slowly, tentatively, he cast his consciousness into the world of mankind, and a jot of fear dug its talons into the soft, vulnerable part of him, the hidden core that held his essence. He was spent from the terrible effort he had exerted to break the magician's spell. It was vital that he renew his life force now in the way of his kind. Yet his enemy was on the move again. The human—who called himself Simon Gwynn—was even now making plans.

He was strong. And he was determined. And he was preparing for renewed conflict.

A tremor seized Ayindral, sending currents through the thickened cloud that made up his being. He felt that cloud dissipating, drifting apart into the ether. He wouldn't let that happen. And he would never allow Gwynn to enslave him. If he knew there was no way to avoid defeat, he would gather all his remaining power and send his life force out in a great destructive wave, wiping away a large chunk of Gwynn's universe.

But that would be his last resort. The thought of his own death was fearful;

he had always been. He had expected that he always would be. He would try to prevent the end of his existence.

He must resist Gwynn. But for now, he must gather his strength. For this space of time, Jack Thornton and Kathryn Reynolds must cope with the magician on their own.

GRIPPING the handles of the wheelbarrow, Kathryn trundled a forty-pound bag of topsoil out of the old garage at the end of the driveway. The structure had probably been built for a Model T. It wouldn't hold a modern car, so she'd turned it into a storage shed.

She let down the legs of the wheelbarrow with a thump. So far this morning, that bastard Jack Thornton hadn't called her back. Her cell phone was in her back pocket, just in case he deigned to communicate with her.

She'd been pacing back and forth across the living room, her nerves screaming, when she'd finally decided she had to get out of the house. So she'd called the school and asked if any classes might be interested in some art instruction. The secretary had been sorry. She'd love for Kathryn to come over—but not this week or the next, since the kids were prepping for standardized tests.

So she drove to Frank's Garden Center and bought a couple of flats of pansies, one of the few annuals that could withstand the chill of a Maryland spring. By June, the summer heat would fry them. But right now, they were lovely.

She'd picked light blue and yellow, a combination she loved. Still silently cursing Jack Thornton, she set the flats on the edge of the patio while she brought fresh dirt to fill the pots.

She'd learned the rhythms of planting from her grandmother. In the fall, you emptied clay pots so they wouldn't crack from the soil inside freezing and thawing. In the spring, you filled them with fresh dirt and started planting.

She dug the sharp point of her shovel into the plastic bag of dirt, then spaded the dark soil into the pot. A tingly feeling at the back of her neck made her look up quickly. Across the street she could see Marge Blanco raking leaves that had collected on her lawn during the winter.

Marge waved to her, and she waved back. Then the view was cut off by a navy boat of a car driving slowly down the block. The driver was an old geezer with silver hair and a lined face. He had a slip of paper in his hand, and he was peering at house numbers, then back at the paper.

He slowed to a crawl, staring at her, then rolled down his window. She was sure he was getting ready to speak to her, and she took a step toward him. Then he turned his head in the other direction, and speeded up.

What was that all about? Had Marge spooked him?

With a shrug, she went back to her work. Picking up one of the pansy flats, she began considering where she'd place each plant in the pot. The deliberations were interrupted by the sound of a car door closing. The old guy again?

She looked up and saw Jack standing on the sidewalk, watching her with unnerving intensity. Her hands turned numb. Unable to hold on to the flat of flowers, she felt it tumble to the ground at her feet.

He came toward her, walking slowly.

She'd spent the morning cursing him for leaving her twisting in the wind. Now she was helpless to do anything but speed across the lawn toward him, reach for him the way she had the night before.

Her need for him was beyond her understanding, beyond anything she had experienced in the past. Yet it existed on some deep, instinctive level.

He reached for her at the same time, and she sighed as he folded her into his arms.

"Jack." She had time to gasp his name before his lips came down on hers. Time to clasp his shoulders as his mouth ravaged hers. He tasted of need and passion and some dark seductive ambrosia, sweeter than any wine. The kiss was as potent as it had been in the dream—primal and intense—as if the two of them were caught in an earthquake, clinging to each other lest they lose their footing and tumble to the center of the earth.

When he silently demanded that she open her lips, she did his bidding—then made a low sound of pleasure when his tongue took possession of her mouth, like the Roman warrior from the dream, seizing the spoils of victory.

There was no safety with this man. No way to go slowly. Without conscious thought, she was carried into some dark, erotic realm where nothing but passion existed. In the space of heartbeats, she was lost to everything but Jack Thornton.

He angled his head, his mouth hungry and demanding, demanding more than she had ever given to any man.

Unsteady on her feet, she clung to his shoulders, pressed her body into the heat of his, borrowing his strength to stay erect.

The world contracted around her, walling them off in some private place of their own.

She sensed his toughness and his vulnerability. Tasted his masculine essence. Felt his hard muscles beneath her hands. She forgot they were standing on her lawn, forgot everything but the man who held her in his embrace.

But it filtered into her consciousness that somebody was speaking. Not Jack. Somebody with a high, annoyed voice. An old man, she realized dimly.

"Hey, lady, you too busy to help me out?"

Her head jerked up as she struggled to focus her eyes, then saw the dark blue car that had come down the street before. The old geezer at the wheel was scowling at them, and she felt her face heat.

Jack stiffened, looking as disoriented as she felt. He sucked in a draft of air and waited several seconds before turning. But he didn't break the contact with her. Instead, he slung an arm around her shoulder as he faced the street.

She saw his eyes narrow as he asked, "Can I help you?"

"I hope so. You know this address?" The old guy slammed the gear lever into Park, then slid across the seat, waving a small square of paper at them.

Jack strode forward and took the paper from the man's gloved hand. *Gloves,* she thought, with one corner of her mind. It was too warm for gloves—unless maybe you were an old guy with thin blood.

Embarrassed at getting caught in public in the grip of a passionate embrace, she hung back, watching Jack shake his head.

"You're a cop, right?" the old man was saying. "A big shot detective."

"I'm a detective, yes. How do you know?"

"Your government license plate is a clue. Plus, you look like a dick. So you should know this area."

Kathryn folded her arms across her chest, listening and watching the exchange, sure that the old guy was enjoying himself. He'd liked interrupting their kiss. He liked being rude to a cop—without doing anything illegal.

"That address isn't in this neighborhood."

"Some help you are!" The old guy gave him a caustic look. "What's your name?"

"Detective Jack Thornton."

The man gave him a satisfied smile, then slid back behind the wheel, slammed the gear lever into Drive, and eased away from the curb. In seconds he had disappeared.

Kathryn stared after him, wondering what kind of guy took such pleasure in deliberately interrupting a very personal encounter. At least he hadn't asked Jack if he was on duty—which she suspected he was.

She glanced across the street, relieved that her neighbor was no longer outside. If she and Jack were lucky, maybe Marge had departed the scene before they'd started kissing.

She turned her face toward him. "Maybe we should go inside."

He slipped his hands into his pockets, regarding her with nar-rowed eyes. "If we go inside, we're going to end up in bed," he said, his voice flat and hard, as though he wasn't very happy about that prospect.

She shouldn't be happy about it either. She didn't know him well enough to make love. That hadn't stopped her in the dream. It was Jack who had stopped then. Jack who had stopped now, and that knowledge was embarrassing. The moment she'd seen him, she'd been out of control. So had he. But he'd pulled himself back.

"I'm sorry," she murmured.

"About what?"

"Getting you in trouble. Do you think that guy is going to call the police department and report you?"

Jack shrugged, but she could see from his face that he wasn't happy about the prospect.

Figuring she had nothing left to lose, she said, "About the other part—ending up in your arms. I'm not sorry about that. I liked it. Are you going to pretend you didn't?"

Instead of answering the question, he said, in a voice that was less harsh, "We need to talk." He walked around the house toward the gazebo, and she followed.

Stepping inside, he leaned his shoulder against one of the posts that held up the roof, looking at her, his hands in the pockets of his dark pants once more.

She leaned against a post opposite him, returning his gaze, thinking again how good he looked to her—whatever he was wearing. He'd been devastating dressed as a Roman general. He was still devastating in his detective's clothing. Above and beyond the sexual compulsion, he had a basic appeal that drew her to him.

Realizing she was too shaky to stand, she sat on one of the benches, drawing her legs up under her, suddenly aware that was how she had sat on the marble seat in the dream. From the expression on his face, she suspected that his thoughts were paralleling hers.

She could dance around the subject. Instead, she said, "You're thinking about the painting."

"Yeah."

"So we both agree that we were there?"

"Tell me something you didn't know before then. I mean something I told you when theoretically we were both sleeping in our own beds."

She looked down at her hands. "You have two children—Craig and Lily. Craig is nine and Lily is seven." Trying for a light note, she added, "And you look very sexy dressed like a Roman general."

"Thanks," he said, his tone sardonic.

Instead of spouting more information, she asked one of the questions that had been deviling her since the night before. "Do you have that scratch you put on your arm?"

"Yeah. I'd show you, but taking off my jacket and rolling up my shirtsleeve out here is only going to raise more eyebrows."

"I'll take your word for it."

Neither one of them spoke for several seconds.

"What are you thinking now?" she asked.

"I'm trained in investigative techniques. I'm trying to apply my police detective skills. Unfortunately, this is like a case where you find a dead body. But nobody saw anything. There's no physical evidence. There's nobody with an obvious motive. So I'm still trying to figure out—why us?"

She shrugged. "I don't know." Deliberately looking him in the eye, she said, "Contrary to what you may think, a wild, irresponsible sexual escapade with a guy I barely know isn't my normal behavior."

She was pleased to see him struggling to bite back a grin. "An interesting way to put it," he said, keeping his voice neutral. Then, "Not my style, either."

She kept her eyes on his. "After I woke up from the dream, I waited for you to call me. Why didn't you phone me last night? Or this morning?"

"I wanted to get some distance."

"I don't think either one of us is going to have much success with that."

"Oh, yeah? What do you know that I don't?" he asked, the challenge obvious in his voice.

"The same thing you know! Stop looking for hidden meanings in everything I say. Are you still accusing me of being a witch?"

"If you're not a witch, then we're back to the other theory—that it's some outside influence."

"You prefer witchcraft?"

"Christ, what a choice!"

In the dream she'd told him she was scared. Pride kept her from saying it again, but she wrapped her arms around her shoulders, rocking slightly as she fought to hold herself together. There was nothing she could say about their shared experiences that would make either one of them feel better. But she did have something to offer him. "Well, I do have some information to give you."

She watched him stiffen. "Like what?"

She dragged in a breath. "Like somebody tried to hurt me this morning."

She had the satisfaction of seeing his face whiten. Maybe— No, she wouldn't let herself hope for any genuine concern on his part. He wanted to take her to bed. But the impulse wasn't his choice. This morning he was just a cop doing his job.

"What happened?" he asked.

She kept her voice steady. "When I came out to get the paper, I tripped over a piece of plastic fishing line strung across the door frame."

"Were you hurt?"

"I scraped my hands—that's all."

"Let's see." He reached for her hands, turned them over, cradling them in his large palms as he looked at the scrape marks. Gently, he ran his thumb over the one where her hand had hit with less force. It was just a light touch. Still, she felt it all the way to her toes.

For long moments, neither one of them moved, until he must have realized that he was holding on to her. He was simply examining the scrapes. But after the wild, erotic kisses they'd exchanged, just his touch had the power to make heat pool in her center.

Perhaps his reaction was as strong, because she heard his breath quicken.

He cleared his throat, turned her hands loose. "Where's the fishing line?"

She snapped herself out of her trance. "An Officer Lorton took it away. It was across the bottom of the front door frame."

"You made a report?"

She raised her chin. "I wanted it on the record."

He strode around the house, bent down to look at the scene of the crime.

"The line was strung between the hinge and that nail," she said, pointing.

"Do you have any idea who did it?"

"Not at all. After the dream—I thought I heard someone outside. Then I saw a cat, and I figured that was what I'd heard. I guess I was wrong."

"Fingerprints?"

"Lorton didn't find any."

"Who wants to hurt you?"

"I don't know! It could be someone who wants to hurt Heather. The front door leads to her apartment, too."

Mentioning Heather made her remember what she'd originally intended to tell him, before events had gotten away from her. "There's something else. Yesterday, I went back to Heather's apartment and did some more looking around. I found something. . . ."

"What?" he demanded.

"I'm not sure. I'm thinking the best thing is to show it to you."

"Is this a ploy to get me inside?"

"You certainly are a trusting bastard."

He heaved a sigh. "Sorry. As I said last night, I'm on edge. Let's go in."

TWO streets away, Simon sat in his car, grinning like Ronald McDonald—only he had a gray wig instead of a bright red one.

With a sharp laugh, he bounced his palms against the steering wheel, pleased with the way things had worked out this morning.

"Hey, lady, you too busy to help me out?" he said, repeating his opening line with an exaggeration of his old man voice.

He'd been going to scoop up Reynolds—until he'd seen that nosy neighbor watching him.

So he'd sped up and turned the corner, thinking he'd try again in a few minutes. Then he'd come down the street the second time and hit the jackpot.

Confrontation wasn't his style. He had always been cautious— stealthy. But when he'd seen the guy get out of his car, he'd known that the last time he'd seen the man, he'd been dressed like a Roman general.

Jesus! He could hardly believe it. The guy who had been with Reynolds in that vision. The vision that had broken his concentration.

Goose bumps had risen on his arms, and he'd known he had to get the hell out of there.

Then reason prevailed. He was in disguise. They had no way of knowing who he was, either dressed like this or dressed like Simon Gwynn, for that matter, and if he played his cards right, he'd come out on top of the situation.

So he'd eased the car forward. The government plate had instantly registered. The guy could have been a county building inspector, of course. Or from the tax department. But Simon had studied cops—and this guy looked like one.

Two seconds of conversation had confirmed that hypothesis. And the stupid bastard had given up his name—just like that. Of course, he probably didn't have a choice. He was a public servant; he couldn't hide his identity.

He was still grinning over the turn of events when the full implications of this couple struck him, and his features turned sharp. They had been in the vision. They had destroyed his concentration.

Which must mean the demon was the one who had brought them together—forged the bond of sexual energy that had destroyed his ceremony.

Once the idea took hold, it began to resonate. Of course the demon was using them! What else could explain last night?

A low sound rose in his throat. They both had to be eliminated—and quickly.

But his original plan to simply kidnap Reynolds was too dangerous. Now that he knew someone would be looking for her—her lover boy police detective. And the cop would be a dangerous opponent.

What he had to do was get rid of Jack Thornton. Which meant making some other quick arrangements.

He started the car again, in a hurry now. As he drove, his mind was busy, already making plans for the ceremony he would perform.

JACK let Kathryn walk past him, then followed her up the stairs to her apartment. Again, he stood aside as she opened the door. He felt the stiffness of his body. The determination that he wasn't going to reach for her again.

Inside, he folded his arms in what he knew must look like an uptight gesture as he stood in the middle of the living room, waiting to
find out if she really had something to show him or if she was making
an excuse to get him in here.

She opened a desk drawer, took out a letter-size envelope, and held
it out to him. He saw she had clamped her bottom lip between her
teeth—the way she'd done in the dream, he suddenly remembered. He
didn't want to think about the dream. Or anything strange. He
wanted to focus on a real case he might have a chance of solving.

He dragged his gaze away from her and lifted the flap on the envelope, pulling out a piece of paper impregnated with colored dots, each
one stamped with a picture of a cartoon character in the middle.

"Jesus!"

His exclamation had her gaze drilling into his.

"What?"

"Were you using this stuff with her?"

She looked confused. "What stuff? What is it?"

"You're saying you don't know?"

Her face turned stormy. "Jesus is right. Every time you have a
chance to think the worst of me, you do it. Whatever that paper is, I
don't have a clue about it."

"Acid," he said, hearing the anger in his own voice.

"Acid?"

Either she was naive as hell or she was a wonderful actress. "LSD,"
he clarified. "Did you and she trip together? And now you're feeling
guilty about it?"

"Of course not! I didn't even know what it was." Her posture
changed as she took in the implications. "You're saying Heather took
LSD? People still use that stuff?"

"It's certainly not as big as it was in the sixties. But people fool
around with it. Didn't they teach you about it in health class? Didn't
people in college do it?"

She sighed. "I guess I was in the wrong crowd in college. And as for
health class . . ." She shrugged. "Maybe I was absent when they covered it."

"The cat ate my homework," he muttered.

"What?"

"Forget it."

He saw that Kathryn had picked up the magic wand and was flipping it back and forth in her hand. His gaze was drawn to the damn thing. For several moments, he watched the blue liquid and the suspended sparkly stuff swirl back and forth.

The wand was just a toy. A novelty. It couldn't really have any magic powers, could it?

He strove to wipe that dumb notion from his mind as he slipped the envelope into an evidence bag. Too bad that his prints and Kathryn's were on the paper. He hoped they hadn't obscured some that might be more pertinent. Like maybe those of the boyfriend, Gary Swinton. Was that what the guy had been hiding? That he and Heather had been doing illegal drugs together? Or was there something more?

"Okay, if you aren't worried about my connecting you with Heather's drug use—what are you worried about?"

He saw her face pale. "What, exactly, do you mean?"

"Since the first time I came here, you've acted like you had something to hide. What is it?"

He watched her face harden, watched her struggle to relax. Long moments passed when he thought she wasn't going to answer the question.

Finally she gave a small shrug. "Family tradition, I guess. My mom had some bad experiences with the police."

"Like what?"

"I told you she found that porn stuff that belonged to my dad. After that, they had some pretty violent fights. Mom called the police a time or two before she threw Dad out. Let's just say the cops weren't very helpful," she said, speaking quickly, as though she were trying to get it over with. "Mom was left with a basic . . . dislike for the boys in blue, which she passed on to me. Which made it hard for me to make a report on Heather in the first place. But I did it. And I've continued to cooperate with you." By the time she was finished, she was standing with her hands on her hips and her jaw thrust forward.

She'd made him understand her basic attitude better. "I'm sorry about your mother," he said.

"It was a long time ago."

"But it still influences your thinking."

"Yes."

More gently than he'd spoken before, he said, "Thanks for the information. On Heather."

She nodded.

He half-turned toward the door.

"You're leaving?"

"Yeah."

"Jack—" She took a step toward him, reached out a hand. All it took was that simple gesture for a jolt of sexual need to zing through him.

He stiffened, anticipating her touch, fighting the unwanted reaction. "What?" he asked, his voice and his posture rigid again.

She dropped her hand. "We have to talk about us."

"There is no us!" he said as firmly as he could, willing it to be true. He had children who needed him. He had cases he was working on. He had no time for some kind of crazy sexual compulsion. Before she could engage him in a conversation, he pulled the door open and escaped.

Somewhere in his mind, he knew he was deep in denial. But he couldn't cope with her, couldn't cope with his need. Couldn't cope with what he saw as failure. He was a disciplined man. Yet discipline broke down every time he was with this woman. Rather than take what he wanted—what she was silently offering—he fled.

It wasn't until he was in the car that he remembered somebody had tried to injure her this morning. And, as a cop, he had a responsibility to do something about it.

11

AS soon as he got back to work, Jack checked with Lorton and found out the officer could add nothing to what Kathryn had already told him. Next he looked at reports from the neighborhood, trying to determine whether the fishing line stretched across Kathryn's doorway was an isolated incident.

He found that over the past few days, there had been several break-ins within a five-block radius. Nothing too big. Someone had jimmied a sliding glass door, gone in, and boosted a television set and stereo equipment. A lawn mower had disappeared from a nearby garage. The older daughter in a Moslem family had been harassed. Kids had stolen several cars. But none of the crimes seemed to have any connection to a fishing line stretched across a door frame.

He had to go on the assumption that someone had specifically wanted to hurt Kathryn—or DeYoung.

He wanted to see Gary Swinton's expression when he asked him about the line. And he was about to leave for Circuit City when Captain Granger asked for an update on the missing person cases.

Not now, he thought with exasperation. What he said was, "I'd be happy to update you."

Glad that he could give a coherent account of the investigations, he spent an hour going over what he knew about each of the three cases that Granger had asked him to try and tie together—feeling uncomfortable at the way the captain was looking at him. He kept waiting for Granger to reveal what was on his mind, but his boss remained silent. So Jack plowed ahead with the facts he'd uncovered when he hadn't been tied in knots by Kathryn Reynolds.

There was still no word on the missing child, Kip Bradley, or his father, Henry Bradley. But Jack had discovered some deep-seated hostility between Bradley and his ex-wife. She said he had taken off for Montana, where he had relatives who were willing to hide him. Jack had contacted the relatives, who claimed not to have seen him. He'd also contacted the Montana State Police, who had gone out to the ranch and failed to find Bradley.

The young mental patient, Stewart Talber, was another matter. Now in his early twenties, Talber had been in and out of mental hospitals and various outpatient programs since he'd been diagnosed as paranoid schizophrenic at the age of fifteen. Most recently, he'd been living in his mother's house out in the country. The mother had died two months ago, and his relatives were worried about him. But when they'd come out to the house with two county mental health workers, Talber had disappeared. Jack had talked to some of his relatives and determined that Talber had a history of disappearing—so there was no proof that anything sinister had happened to him. Jack had intended to check out homeless shelters in D.C. and Baltimore, but he hadn't gotten to it yet.

The case of the young woman, Brenda Quinlin, did bear some similarities to Heather DeYoung. She was single and lived alone. She'd failed to come in to work after a week's vacation. But there still wasn't enough information to link the two cases—except that the two victims were young women who had disappeared when they weren't necessarily expected home. Which could imply that they might have been stalked.

"So that's all you've got?" Granger asked when he finished. "Nothing that would show a connection?"

"I've just started."

"You usually work faster than this."

Jack shrugged. Granger was right, but he couldn't dredge up any excuse that he liked the sound of. "I was just going to interview De-Young's boyfriend again."

"Okay. Go on."

Jack grabbed some peanut butter crackers from the machine, then drove to Circuit City.

Walking into the small appliance department, he looked around for Swinton. He wasn't there, and Jack's next stop was the manager's office.

"Where can I find Gary Swinton?" he asked.

The secretary stopped chewing her gum and rolled her eyes. "Gary? He was here this morning. Then he said he was sick, and left. He's been out a lot lately. Mr. Victor is probably going to fire him. Only I don't think he really cares. He's been acting like he's got more important things to do."

"Uh-huh. How long ago did he leave?"

"A couple of hours."

"Thanks," he answered. His next stop would be the D.C. apartment where Swinton lived.

He checked the address that Kathryn had given him—it was in the Adams Morgan area, which spread out from the intersection of Eighteenth Street and Columbia Road.

Once it had been a white-bread, upscale D.C. neighborhood. Now it was one of those melting pots where African Americans, Hispanics, Asians, and whites lived together in tolerable proximity. A colorful mix of ethnic restaurants and shops, secondhand stores, older apartment buildings, and row houses lined the main arteries.

Swinton's address turned out to be a small redbrick apartment house off Columbia Road. Jack found a place to park down the block, then walked up the cracked sidewalk to the building. It wasn't exactly a slum. But some of the hall tiles needed replacing, and the wall could use a new coat of paint.

Swinton lived in 3B. Since there was no elevator, Jack walked up two flights. When he got no answer, he walked down to the basement, where the super lived.

Inside the man's apartment, he could hear a television blaring. His first knock yielded no results. He attacked the door with a noisy fusillade—finally attracting the attention of a wizened old man who opened the door a crack, blocking access with a safety chain.

"You seen Gary Swinton recently?" he asked.

"Who wants to know?" the old man asked.

"The police," Jack answered, showing his badge and ID through the crack in the door.

The super peered at the credentials through thick glasses. "You're from Montgomery County. You don't got no jurisdiction here."

"Actually I do. I'm pursuing a lead in a missing person case. Can I have your name, sir?"

The old guy blinked. "I'm Barry Wagner. Who's missing?"

"Heather DeYoung," Jack answered, showing a copy of the photograph Kathryn had given him. "Have you seen her around here?"

"I seen her here with him."

"Recently?"

Wagner thought about it. "A couple weeks ago, maybe. I don't keep track of stuff like that."

"Swinton left work early, saying he was sick. But he doesn't answer his door. I'd like to get in there."

The super thought that over, then decided to cooperate.

As they walked slowly upstairs, Jack asked, "How big is the apartment?"

"Living room, bedroom, kitchen, bathroom. You want me to come in with you?"

"No. Just open the door. I'll lock up when I'm finished."

The door yielded easily to Wagner's key. "Swinton?" Jack called out as he entered. "Gary?"

There was no answer. As he stepped into the living room, he saw immediately that there was one trait the occupant and DeYoung had in common. They were both slobs. But Swinton outdid her by a factor of ten. The cheap, faux wood coffee table and end tables were littered with discarded fast-food containers.

The kitchen was similar. Food splatters had dried on the counters. The sink was loaded with dirty dishes.

He made a quick stop at the bathroom, wrinkling his nose. Apparently Swinton couldn't aim straight when he peed.

He had trouble picturing a nice young woman in this environment. Someone who lived downstairs from Kathryn. Without warning, his thoughts switched from DeYoung to her landlady. He'd banished Kathryn from his consciousness for the past few hours. Now awareness of her came rolling back like water pouring from an earthquake-damaged dam.

His whole body went rigid, and he squeezed his eyes closed, struggling to wipe her image from his mind. It did no good. He saw her as she had looked in the dream—when they'd been making love. Her red hair a cloud of flames around her head. Her green eyes heavy-lidded. Her lips swollen from his kisses.

He remembered pulling down her bodice and exposing her gorgeous breasts. Creamy breasts with coral tips. He was instantly hard. Instantly angry with himself for allowing the reaction to sneak up on him.

Like a drowning man snatching at a lifeline, he focused on the anger, inch by inch dragging himself under control.

"Fuck!" The expletive tore from his lips. In the next moment he was laughing. Fuck. Yeah, that was what he wanted to do. With Kathryn Reynolds.

He pictured himself leaving Swinton's squalid apartment, driving to her house. Pounding on the door. She would see him and come into his arms. Ten seconds after that, they would be tangled together on her Oriental rug.

With a low sound of denial, he cut off the fantasy, thinking that he'd gone through so many emotional changes in the past few minutes that his head was spinning—and his cock was twanging like the neck of a banjo.

For several moments, he stood in the hallway, assuring himself that he was in control of his mind and body. He knew he was just telling himself what he wanted to hear. Never in his life had he been more out of control—more surprised by what he found himself thinking and doing.

When he felt as if he could attend to his job, he stepped into the bedroom, wondering if he was going to find a dead man.

The room was empty. He found a rumpled bed, open dresser drawers. A mixture of more or less clean and dirty clothing littered the floor. It looked like the place had been searched. Or like Swinton had cleared out in a hurry. Jack cursed. If Granger hadn't held him up, would he have gotten here in time to catch Swinton? Or somebody else still here?

On the other side of the bed, Jack stopped short. He'd almost stepped into a vinyl suitcase that lay open on the floor. He could see knit shirts, jeans, underwear thrown inside. More evidence that Swinton had been packing. It looked like he'd abandoned the effort. Or somebody had interrupted him. Stooping down, he saw dark spatters on some of the fabric. Blood?

What the hell had happened here? Reaching for his cell phone, he began to dial the D.C. police.

*   *   *

AFTER the morning's exertions, Simon had changed into his black silk pants and a comfortable black shirt. Stroking his fingers over the smooth fabric, he walked with his characteristic measured steps to the butler's pantry, where he contemplated the rows of wine bottles, each one stored at the proper angle to keep the cork moist.

In cultivating his comfortable lifestyle, he'd introduced himself to the finer things in life. One of those was wine. Over the past few years he'd attended wine tastings so that he had the proper appreciation for the output of the world's wineries. On the whole, he preferred European vintages. But there were some decent products from South Africa—and even some from the Napa Valley.

He'd already considered several bottles and settled on the Georges Duboeuf. Beaujolais-Villages Nouveau.

He'd allowed the wine to breathe for half an hour. Now, from one of the cherrywood upper cabinets, he brought out a long-stemmed red wineglass. After pouring some of the wine into the glass, he held it up to admire the ruby color. Next he swirled the red liquid gently in the glass, then inhaled the bouquet. Finally he took a small, appreciative sip.

There was nothing like a good glass of new Beaujolais, he thought as he took the glass with him into the library and settled into his favorite chair.

Things were shaping up very nicely. Tomorrow he'd call the police department and report Thornton's indiscretion with Reynolds. That should do wonders for the cop's reputation.

Then there were the plans for the upcoming ceremony. It was something he hadn't tried before, but he had worked out the basics. Now he had to settle on some of the protocols he was going to use. This ritual must be perfect. Did he need a protective circle, for example? On the face of it, he thought not. But omitting it might be a mistake—if the demon was hovering nearby, ready to interfere.

For just a moment, a shiver slithered over his skin. He sat up straighter, firmed his jaw. He was in the fight of his life. But there were ways to defeat the demon. And in the end, Ayindral would be the slave of a great magician named Simon Gwynn.

He had no doubt of that. And no doubt about using his skills to kill the cop—Jack Thornton—now that he had the essential ingredient for such an important ceremony.

Tomorrow evening, he would send his psychic power outward in a dark, destructive wave that would catch Jack Thornton by surprise, sweeping him along and drowning him in its awesome force.

The time frame was short, since he must work quickly to remove the cop before he could go after Reynolds—and use her to enslave Ayindral.

Usually he would have taken at least a week to purify himself. There were many roads to purification. Fasting or restricting food. Abstaining from sexual gratification. Even the old Native American technique of a sweat bath. Some modern magicians might even have denied themselves the wine. But wine was a common ingredient in many rituals. Rituals of the church. And rituals of black magic as well.

More important, he had found that one glass helped relax him.

Taking a sip, he began reading through the section on astral projection in the *The Golden Dawn*.

KATHRYN spent the afternoon working on a brochure for a group medical practice in Bethesda, a team of women doctors and other professionals who provided a variety of services to female patients. There were several gynecologists and internists in the group, along with an acupuncturist, a doctor of homeopathic medicine, a chiropractor, a plastic surgeon, and a specialist in laser skin treatments.

They'd gotten a glowing report on her from another client and had asked her to design a brochure that gave a comprehensive overview of their practice, along with selected details of each specialty. She'd been enthusiastic about the commission, so she'd done some preliminary layouts before finishing up the assignment for Sunrise Realty.

The previous work gave her something to start with, thank God. Because most of what she'd done today was sit at the computer and move sentences and phrases around on the screen while she went over every word—every touch—she and Jack Thornton had exchanged.

When she caught herself thinking about driving past his house to see where he lived, she felt the air solidify in her lungs.

What was wrong with her? Was she planning to stalk the man if he wouldn't agree to make love with her? The idea that she would do something so . . . outrageous repelled her. And frightened her.

Pushing her chair away from the computer, she stood up, clenching and unclenching her hands. Finally, she found her walking shoes, put them on, and pounded down the steps. An hourlong walk around the neighborhood would help settle her down.

It was getting dark when she arrived back home. Although she wasn't very hungry, she did fix a little dinner, some cottage cheese plopped onto salad greens and topped with a little bottled blue cheese dressing.

After that she took a shower. Then there was no excuse to stay up. Rummaging in her dresser drawer, she found one of her favorite T-shirts and pulled it on. It was light green, with a mountain meadow of bright wildflowers spread across the front.

Climbing into bed, she looked at the collection of literature on her nightstand. She was in the middle of a romance novel that she'd been enjoying. But she hadn't picked it up in days. Instead, she reached for a gardening book with plenty of pictures.

Ten minutes later, when she felt her attention wandering, she turned off the light and eased down under the covers. For a time she enjoyed some blessed oblivion. Then, like the night before, a dream seized her by the throat. She tried to scream. But no sound made it past her lips. Once again, she was in a strange, gray, formless place where no human being could live.

It was as bad as the first time. Instantly she was cold as death. And engulfed by swirling gray mist that clouded her vision and turned to water in her lungs when she tried to take a breath.

There was no color in the gray mist. No sound. No solid ground beneath her feet. She'd escaped from this place once. Or maybe she'd been allowed to escape. Now she stumbled forward again, her feet sinking into the spongy goop.

Was Jack here, too? Was he waiting for her again?

When she tried to call his name, only a wheezing sound came out. *Jack. Jack. Please help me*, her mind screamed.

He didn't answer. Yet words seemed to form in her head.

He isn't here. He isn't here. He isn't here. The statement echoed and reverberated directly in her brain. *You must bring him something. Bring him something. Bring him something.*

No one had spoken aloud. Yet she knew the commands came from the huge, indefinite bulk she'd sensed before. Not a person. Not an animal. Some otherworldly being she didn't understand.

But one thing she knew: It could grab her anytime it wanted. Shake the life out of her body. Still, determination kept her stumbling forward, trying to escape.

Ahead of her, through the gray fog, she saw a tall clear column filled with swirling blue liquid with shiny stars and moons shooting upward, then falling back through the hollow tube.

It was the magic wand, she realized with a spurt of astonishment. Only a hundred times bigger, the action inside more violent. And it was standing there like a guidepost—glowing in the fog.

She staggered toward it, stretching out her hands. For less than a second she thought she felt the smooth plastic surface. Then it was gone. And all at once, she was free. One moment she was in the gray, terrifying place. In the next, she was standing in a dark woods.

She stood with her heart pounding, dragging in gulps of pure, clean air. Her shoulder brushed a tree trunk, and she reached out to press her palm against the rough bark, anchoring herself to something solid.

Last time, when she'd escaped from the place of terror, she'd stumbled into an Alma-Tadema painting. This time was different. She was in a nighttime woods—dark and shadowy but visible in the silver radiance of the moonlight filtering down through the branches above her.

A light wind riffled the foliage overhead, and when she dragged in a breath, she caught forest scents. Heard an owl hooting far away. Closer by, she caught the scurrying of tiny feet in the underbrush.

Now what? Was Jack here? Was he looking for her?

Her heart leaped at the prospect of seeing him again. Then she dismissed the sense of anticipation with a wry laugh. She'd bet he wasn't looking for her. If he was here, he'd probably be running in the opposite direction.

Trying to put him out of her mind, she cast her gaze down to see what she was wearing. She was dressed in the light green flowered T-shirt she'd worn to bed. Now the shirt topped brown stretch pants and the walking shoes she'd worn this afternoon.

It was chilly, and she wrapped her arms around her shoulders, rubbing the goose bumps that had risen on her skin.

This was just a dream, she reminded herself. Yet she knew it was like the last time—more than a dream.

Firming her lips, she began to move through the woods. Dry leaves scrunched under her feet as she made her way forward. In some places she had to detour around large outcroppings of rock. In other spots, brambles tore at her pants.

After tromping through the underbrush for several minutes, she came to a wide trail where the ground was covered with wood chips. It led upward for several yards, then changed to a short flight of stone steps.

She stared at the pathway, thinking how different this scene was from the last dream. It was less static. More like a real place—like the real world. But where? Beyond the steps was a rustic sign, SUMMIT 1,282 FEET.

Well, she was on some mountain, obviously. She could take the path upward. Instead, she kept moving through the trees, avoiding the worst patches of underbrush and the huge rocks. Ahead of her she saw a flicker of movement and went very still. Someone else was here—coming through the trees.

Jack?

Her pulse started to pound. She'd met him in the picture dream. She longed to meet him again—in another dream—where all the controls of the real world were removed. This time . . . This time they would make love.

His name hovered on her lips. But something stopped her from calling out to him. Moving from tree to tree, she made her way closer. When she finally saw her dream companion clearly, she struggled to hold back a gasp. He was a ghostly form, almost transparent, so that when she stared straight at him, she saw right through his body.

His head whirled around, and he looked toward the tree trunk that partially hid her.

She froze in place, wishing she could turn invisible. Or was that almost true? When he looked at her, was she like him—ghostly and transparent?

For long moments, he seemed to be staring directly at her hiding place, and she was afraid to move, afraid to breathe.

Finally, he gave a little shrug and turned back to what he was doing—digging a hole in the ground, working fast, the dirt flying. Then he picked up a plastic-wrapped bundle from the ground, a bundle that looked about five and a half feet long and perhaps a couple of feet wide.

She made a low sound of distress as she saw the shape. It looked like a body! Or some misshapen rug.

As she watched, he dumped the bundle unceremoniously into the hole he'd dug, then began to shovel the earth back in place. He was working fast, breathing hard.

He finished by smoothing out the dirt, then gathering up armloads of dry leaves and scattering them over the fresh-turned ground. For a moment he stood looking at his handiwork. Then he turned and started rapidly down the hill, paralleling the path.

She stayed in back of him, running to keep up. But he had a head start, and he was fast. Beyond the trees, she saw an open area that resolved itself into a blacktop parking lot. By the time she arrived, he was already pulling away—in a car that appeared to her as indistinct and ghostly as the man who was driving it.

She had never paid much attention to the make and model of cars. Now she was too far away to see any of the ghostly insignia. There was no light over the license plate, so she couldn't see that either. Three red taillights mocked her as the car braked, after pulling out of its parking space, and sped away.

She stifled a sob, frustrated that she had no way of knowing who he was. She tried to tell herself that it didn't matter. That he was just some construct of her imagination. That he hadn't really been there at all. But she couldn't fool herself.

She didn't know why he was transparent as mist. But she knew this dream had something important in common with the last one. It wasn't random. She had been brought here for a purpose.

Squeezing her eyes shut, she tried to figure out what she should do. Then she remembered the voice she'd heard at the start of the dream. *You must bring him something. Bring him something. Bring him something.*

Bring him something!

In the darkness, she stumbled down the hill to the parking lot. At this hour of the night, it was empty. But at the far end, she could see another sign.

Quickly, she strode across the blacktop and walked around to the far side, so that she could see the legend. She had only moments to read the words. Then, the scene around her began to fade.

With an almost physical desperation she tried to hold on to the dream. But it slipped through her fingers. And she was alone in the dark. In her own bed.

12

EAST view parking lot.

Kathryn's eyes blinked open as she pressed her head against the pillows, bearing down to assure herself that she was back at home and not in the woods.

"Jack," she murmured aloud. She hadn't met him in the dream. Had he been there? In some other part of the woods? Had he missed the main event? Or, this time, had it been only *her* dream?

Pushing herself up in bed, she bent her knees and then circled them with her arms, holding tight.

Lord, now what? What, exactly, had she seen?

She still wasn't sure. But she knew she had to discuss it with Jack. She'd been given a clue. A piece of evidence.

Her sense of purpose deflated somewhat when she swung her head to the right and looked at the clock. The green numbers on the display said three fifty-six.

He wouldn't want her to call him now. Probably he'd be annoyed. And what could she tell him? That she'd seen a transparent man bury a transparent body, and she didn't even know where.

But could she figure it out? What did she know about the place? As she often did when she was thinking about a project, she walked to the window, pulled up some slats in the blind, and stared out. At first she saw nothing of the actual view. Then something outside caught her attention. There was a car parked across from her house.

It wasn't a car she recognized from the neighborhood. Standing in the darkened room, she stared at it, wondering if someone could be inside.

What a notion! Who would be sitting in a car at night on the street?

She tried to dismiss the idea. But it stayed wedged in her mind. With jerky steps she crossed the room and switched on the nightstand lamp. Seconds later, she heard an engine start. By the time she returned to the window, the vehicle was gliding away into the night.

She watched until the taillights disappeared into the distance. It was so much like the dream that goose bumps bloomed on her skin. Yet it wasn't the same car. The shape had been different. At least she thought so. The one outside had been smaller—sportier.

More important, it hadn't been a ghost image. It had been real and solid. And it was impossible for her to dismiss the idea that someone had been out there watching her. Or watching for Heather to come home.

She hated to grasp at that explanation. But it was the one she preferred, under the circumstances.

With a sigh, she turned away from the window and hurried down the hall to the living room. More than ever, she needed to talk to Jack. But she wasn't going to use the car as an excuse. She was going to come to him with something.

During the time it took for the computer to boot up, she paced back and forth across the floor, stopping to pull aside the curtains to look out. The car had not returned, but that didn't give her the expected sense of relief.

After establishing a link to the Internet, she went directly to one of her favorite search engines, then hesitated as she considered what to ask for.

The woods hadn't been a specific place she recognized. But they'd had the look of the local area. Either Maryland or perhaps nearby Virginia or Pennsylvania. Somewhere rural with mountains and rocky soil. The path and the parking lot made her think she'd been in a state park. Or maybe a national park?

Making a decision, she typed in "Maryland" and "parks." A long list of references appeared on the screen. But as she scrolled down through the entries and tried some of the web sites, nothing seemed right.

Over the next half-hour, she looked through more information on parks, seeing nothing that struck a chord with her.

Leaning back in her chair, she contemplated the nighttime scene. She'd seen two signs. One had been near a path and referred to a mountain summit over a thousand feet high. The number had been in her mind when she'd awakened. Now she knew she should have written it down.

Well, what about the other sign? It had said EAST VIEW PARKING LOT.

Trying another combination of key words, she typed in "Maryland," "mountain," "East View." Again, she spent a frustrating half-hour and found nothing.

Damn!

She looked at her watch. It was now seven in the morning. Early. But she couldn't make herself wait any longer.

She'd wanted to come to Jack with something concrete. But she wasn't going to get it. So she might as well call, she decided, as she went into the kitchen to find his card, then reached for the phone and dialed.

"Hello."

The person who answered was a woman, and Kathryn felt her throat constrict—until she remembered that he had a live-in housekeeper.

"Hello?" the woman asked again.

She cleared her throat. "This . . . this is Kathryn Reynolds. Detective Thornton came to my house to ask me some questions about a missing person case."

At that moment a thought leaped into her mind—a thought she hadn't considered before. She'd seen a man burying a body. Oh, Lord, could it have been Heather? She tried to reject that idea. But now it had lodged in her brain.

"Just one moment. I'll see if he's available."

"Thank you."

She waited with her pulse pounding in her ears, wondering if calling him at home had been a good idea.

Then she heard his voice, and she sighed out his name. "Jack."

"What is it? What's wrong?" he asked, sounding like he might care about what happened to her.

"Something's happened. There . . . there was a car outside my house last night," she heard herself blurt, when that wasn't what she'd called about at all. "I turned on the light, and he went away," she added quickly. "But . . . but there's something else. Another dream."

"Oh?"

"I . . . I don't want to talk about it over the phone. Can you come over?"

"Yes. Give me a few minutes to make sure the kids are all set."

She let out the breath she'd been holding. She'd thought he might protest. But he was coming over.

"I'll be there as soon as I can."

"Thank you." As she hung up, she swept her hand through her hair. She'd been up half the night. She probably looked like hell.

The good news was that she didn't have to sit around stewing, waiting for him. She had time to change her clothes, brush her teeth, and wash her face. She was just putting on a little bit of lip gloss when she heard the doorbell and rushed to answer it.

She almost threw the door open, but she had enough sense to check the peephole and see that it was him.

When she opened the door, he was standing with his arms stiffly at his sides. The look on his face made her throat thicken. The last time they'd been together, he'd pulled her into his arms. This time she could see he was determined not to lose control of the situation.

"Come in." She stepped aside, and he followed.

"Do you want some coffee?"

"Do you have some made?"

"No, but I could use a cup."

There was an unacknowledged intimacy to the encounter. He'd come over to talk about the case. But there was no way to deny the undercurrent of sexuality vibrating in the air. Or to dispel the feeling of familiarity that came from his standing in her living room.

She hurried into the kitchen and filled the automatic coffeepot with water.

"I've got several kinds of coffee," she said over her shoulder. "Kenya. Kona. Jamaica Blue Mountain."

He laughed. "Are you trying to put Starbucks out of business?"

"No. I figure coffee is safer than a lot of other vices."

"Me, too," he answered, and they were both silent as they noted they had something in common besides wanting to jump each other's bones.

She made herself busy, then turned to get the sugar and found him leaning comfortably against the counter, watching her.

Their gazes locked, and she knew how easy it would be to end up in each other's arms again. But she was pretty sure he wasn't going to start anything. And if he could manage it, so could she.

"You're lucky you have someone to take care of your kids," she said.

"Mm hmm."

"Do they take their lunch to school?"

"The school sends out a menu for the week. It depends on what they're having. They love pizza. Macaroni and cheese is another matter."

"Oh," she said, wondering if the conversation could get any more inane.

Finally, the coffee was ready. She took hers with milk and sugar. He took just milk.

When they'd carried their mugs to the table and sat down, he leaned back in his chair and stretched his legs, crossing them at the ankles.

He looked relaxed, but in the time they'd spent together, she'd learned to read him—perhaps because she was so focused on him—and she could see the tension simmering below his calm surface. She wanted to reach out and cover his hand with hers. Just to make contact with him, she told herself, knowing it was only part of the truth. Since the moment she'd met this man, she'd wanted . . . everything he could give her. But she wasn't going to beg. Instead, she kept her hands to herself by clamping them around her mug.

"Someone was watching your house?" he asked.

She gave a small nod. "At least I think so. I can't be sure. All I know is that he was out there. He left when I turned on a light."

"He? You saw him?"

"No. I was just making an assumption."

"I'll arrange to have a patrol car drive by periodically."

"Thanks." She cleared her throat. "You think it has something to do with Heather? . . . Or that fishing line across the door frame?"

"I don't know. But I'll find out."

She clung to the reassurance in his voice.

"Thanks," she repeated. Then added, "I wouldn't have seen him— except that I woke up after another dream."

"Was I there?"

She laughed. "I wish you had been."

The comment generated another moment of silence during which they sipped their coffee.

"Tell me what happened," he said.

"It started like the last one. I was in that gray place where you can't breathe."

"What gray place?"

"It doesn't start that way for you?"

"No."

"Oh, goody. It's just me. I come awake in . . ." She stopped, swallowed. "An awful place. It's like a land of fog." She shuddered as she remembered it. "Not a land where people can live. I can't catch my breath. I feel like I'm drowning, but I'm not underwater." She gave an involuntary gasp. When he reached across the table and laid his hand over hers, she turned her palm up and knit her fingers with his. They sat that way, his hand anchoring her to him.

"It's cold," she whispered. "And creepy. And . . . and there's . . . something watching me." She heard her voice rise at the end.

"Something?"

"A . . . a . . ." She clamped his hand more tightly, unable to speak above a whisper. "I don't know what. But it spoke to me this time."

His eyes widened. "What did it say?"

She gulped, suddenly fighting back tears. "That I should bring you something."

His eyes never left her. "It . . . this thing referred to me? By name?"

She thought back, trying to reconstruct what had happened. Unable to meet his gaze, she whispered, "I was scared. Terrified. I was . . . I called out to you. He . . . it . . . told me you weren't there. But I should bring you something."

Despite her best efforts, the tears leaked out now. She clutched his hand, clutched at her emotions, struggling to rein them in as she heard him swear under his breath.

"I . . . I'm sorry . . . ," she managed.

He let go of her hand, came around the table, and pulled her out of the chair. Cradling her in his arms, he crossed the room and settled on the

EDGE OF THE MOON

sofa, holding her and rocking her while she tried to get control of herself.

His hand smoothed her hair as he murmured soft, indistinct words, and she imagined that he might comfort his daughter this way.

She let herself melt against him, letting his strong arms and the masculine scent of his body envelop her. The feeling of safety and closeness helped. By slow degrees she got control of herself. Pushing away from him, she stood, swaying slightly on rubbery legs. When he reached to steady her, she moved to the desk and pulled a tissue from the box.

Feeling more in control, she came back to the living room area. But she didn't trust herself to sit by him again—not without reaching for him. So she settled in one of the easy chairs.

"I didn't even get to the good part," she said.

"Which is?"

"In this dream, I saw a man bury a body. At least, that's what I think I saw. And I think that's what I'm supposed to bring you. Information."

"Okay."

"Only I don't know where I saw this scene. It's in the woods. Somewhere in Maryland—or maybe a nearby state. But I can't figure out where."

"Okay," he said again. "Let's start from the beginning. You were in a place where you couldn't see, and you couldn't breathe. And something spoke to you?"

"Yes." She remembered another detail and added, "Then . . . then I saw the magic wand." His narrow-eyed look had her hurrying on. "It was like the wand on my desk." She stood and crossed the room again, picking up the object in question from beside the computer.

When she held it out, he took it, turned it upside down, and watched the shapes and the blue liquid swirl. "It's just a toy. Isn't it?"

"I always thought so. But it was in the dream. Much bigger. A guidepost—showing me the way out of that terrible place."

"And then?"

"Then I was in the woods. At a mountain. I saw a trail and stone steps and a sign that said SUMMIT. There was a number, over a thousand feet." She watched him write that down.

"It was a park. I'm sure of that. Only I did a web search of parks. And I can't find anything about it," she said in frustration.

"Tell me what else you know."

She gulped. "The man. He . . . he wasn't solid. He was like a ghost. It's hard to describe. I saw him in the woods. Saw what he was doing. But I could see through him. He had something wrapped up—

something that looked like a body. He dug a hole, put it in. Covered it over, spread leaves around over the fresh soil. Oak leaves."

He kept writing. "Have you seen him before?"

"I . . . I'm not sure. Maybe there was something familiar about him."

He hesitated for a moment, then asked, "Could it have been Gary Swinton?"

She considered the question. "I don't know. But I don't think so."

"What happened after he buried the body?"

"He started down the hill. To a parking lot. His was the only car; I guess because it was at night. I don't know what kind of car. Something with an odd-looking shape."

"A car you've seen before?" he asked, apparently still trying to tie the incident to present reality. "The car that was outside your house?"

"I don't know!" Helplessly, she shook her head. "In the dream, the car was like a ghost, too. Hard to see. The license plate wasn't lighted. I ran after him. But he got away." She stopped, took a breath, then let it out. "What do you think it means that he was like a ghost?"

He shrugged. "I don't know. Maybe that what you were seeing wasn't real?"

"It was real!"

"Okay." He thought for a moment. "Then maybe it happened at a different time. You were seeing something that had already happened. Or was going to happen."

She considered that. "I didn't think of that! Where did you get that idea?"

He shrugged. "I don't know. I'm just trying to come up with an explanation. What happened next?"

"I walked across the parking lot, and I saw a sign. It said EAST VIEW PARKING LOT."

She watched his eyes brighten.

"Yeah?"

"Do you know where it was?"

"Maybe. Can I use your computer?"

"Of course. Do you want me to get on-line?"

"Yes."

After she'd brought back the connection to the web, he typed in the URL of a search engine. Not the one she'd used, she noted. He didn't start with the information she'd given him. Instead, he typed in the name of a place: Sugarloaf Mountain. There were hundreds of references—some to places in Maryland, others, farther north.

But he zeroed in on a site that included Sugarloaf Mountain, Frederick County, Maryland. The text said the summit was 1282 feet high. When she saw the number, she was pretty sure it was right.

"Why couldn't I find it?" she asked, her fists clenched.

"It's privately owned," Jack said, pointing to the screen. "That's why it wasn't under 'parks.'"

"But how did you know?"

"I've taken my kids there. It's not a bad hike to the summit. Have you been there before?"

"No. Never."

"But you went there in your dream. Apparently you didn't make the place up. How far were you from the path leading up from the parking lot, do you think?"

She cast her mind back. "I wasn't keeping track. It could have been fifty feet. A hundred. But I know it was to the left as you face the parking lot. Through the woods."

She watched him write that down. "So you think what happened to me was 'real.' I mean—that I saw something important?"

"I'm going on that assumption."

She felt goose bumps pepper her arms, and rubbed them vigorously with her palms. "And some strange being who lives in a place of gray mist wanted me to see it—and to tell you about it?"

His face was hard now. "That's one explanation. There are others I can think of."

"Like what?"

"I'd rather not start spouting theories."

He'd spouted theories earlier. Now he was uptight again. She sighed. "Okay, then. Why me? Why us? And what is that thing I sense in the mist?"

"Damned if I know!"

"Are you giving up the theory that I'm a witch?"

"I'll hold that in reserve."

"Is that supposed to be a joke?"

He ran a hand through his dark hair. "I wish I knew. Have you ever had a . . . uh . . . mystical experience before?"

"Never!"

He studied her as if he were trying to decide whether she was telling the truth.

Breaking into his thoughts, she asked, "So now what? Do we go out there, and I try to find the place?"

"No."

"But . . ."

"Think about it! How would I write it up? You reported Heather DeYoung missing. Now you're saying you know where she's buried."

"Heather!" she gasped. She'd been half-thinking that the body was Heather, but she hadn't allowed the speculation to get very far. "You think it's her?"

"Unless this is totally unconnected. Don't you think it's more reasonable to assume that it's all tied up together?"

"Yes," she managed.

"I have a P.I. friend who has fantastic . . . tracking abilities."

"The man you mentioned before?"

"Yes. I already brought him that sample of Heather's clothing. He can probably locate the grave. I'll go out there with him. If he finds something, I can use him as my source—and keep you out of it. As long as I can testify to a judge that I've used him before, that the information gleaned from him has proven truthful and productive in the past, and that he's credible, I'm in good shape." He explained, then continued as though he were giving a lecture to a new recruit in the detective squad. "I've also got to make a case that revealing his identity would endanger his life or his effectiveness or his credibility.

"Then I've got to come up with corroborating evidence to support the information. It doesn't have to be that much, just enough to show the judge that I've done some background. If Ross says he traced the killer to a wooded area at Sugarloaf Mountain, I can check the vicinity for footprints, fresh-turned earth."

"You think it's worth investigating," she said carefully. "But you'd go to all that trouble to keep me out of it?"

"Yeah."

"Why?"

"A lot of reasons. The best one is that I think paranormal evidence is going to get the case laughed out of court. And I want to get a conviction on this case."

He got up, and she knew that she didn't want him to leave. But there was no use trying to give him her reasons. If she told him she thought they'd connected on a more meaningful level this morning, he probably wouldn't want to hear it. But there was another issue, too. A nagging fear that tugged at her.

She found herself trying to prolong the conversation. "You're going out there today?"

"Late this afternoon."

"Why not earlier?"

"My P.I. friend works best at night."

She might have asked him to explain that. Instead she said, "Sugarloaf Mountain must be a big place. You don't need my help?"

"You gave me some good landmarks. It's above the East View parking area. Not far to the left of the trail."

"Yes. But . . ."

"If I need more from you, I'll get back to you."

"Promise you'll call me and tell me what you find."

"I will."

He took two long steps toward the door, then turned. "One more thing. I'm going up there with Ross Marshall. Let me give you his number, just in case."

She felt another flicker of unease that she couldn't explain. "Jack, be careful!"

His face contorted. "I was going to say the same thing to you. I don't like hearing that you saw a car sitting outside last night. Or that somebody tripped you up yesterday morning. Is there somewhere you can go for a few days?"

She felt her chest tighten. "You think I need to?"

"I don't know. It would make me feel better."

She wanted to ask if that meant he cared about her beyond the fact that she was a witness in a case he wanted to solve. But she didn't press her luck. Instead, she said, "I'll keep the doors locked. I won't go out after dark. And you said you'd have patrol cars watching out for me."

"Yeah. You have an alarm system, right?"

"Yes. My grandmother had it. I don't use it much. I'm on the second floor."

He sighed. "Then it's probably not state of the art. Is it connected to a service that will call the police if somebody breaks in?"

"No. It just rings an alarm here."

"Well, turn it on when you're inside. And when you go out."

"All right."

She wanted to go to him, cling to him. She was afraid—not for herself, but for him, although she couldn't explain why. So she stayed where she was, feeling helpless and worried.

After he left, she turned the bolt on the door, then hurried to the window to watch him get into his car, still struggling with fears she couldn't name.

13

A year ago, Jack would have turned himself in to the department shrink if he'd contemplated digging up a grave in the woods based on the kind of evidence Kathryn had given him. She'd seen a ghostly figure in a dream. On the face of it, he should dismiss her story out of hand. Yet he'd traveled far enough into the unknown that he took her report at face value. He'd even come up with a reason why the figure had looked like a ghost.

He snorted.

Then there was the nice authentic touch that she hadn't been able to dredge up the location, although she'd obviously wanted to tell him where she'd been.

Sugarloaf Mountain wasn't a sure thing. But if he had to bet on it, he'd bet he was going to find something when he went out there.

In the parking lot at police headquarters, he called Ross from his cell phone.

"I've got a new development in the missing person case," he began. "And I could use your help."

"With?"

"My contact gave me the approximate location of a grave. It's up at Sugarloaf Mountain."

"A nice ride in the country. You want me to do some . . . uh . . . sniffing around up there?"

"Right. I was thinking, we could get there around four. That way, we could do some looking around before dark. Then you could do your thing," Jack said, aware that they weren't on a secure line.

"Yeah. You know the Park and Ride on this side of Frederick?"

"Yeah."

"I'll meet you there."

After hanging up, Jack told Emily he'd be out on an investigation that evening. Granger had started the ball rolling with a request to tie the Heather DeYoung case into several previous missing person cases.

Now, as Jack collected more information on all of them, in the back of his mind he was thinking that if there was one grave up at Sugarloaf Mountain, there might be more. And he wanted to be prepared to do identifications.

Why Sugarloaf, he wondered as he looked up the phone number of the office there, then called to say he would arrive around-four in the afternoon on police business and wanted access after hours.

They wanted a fax with the information, so he typed that up and sent it.

His mind was only partly on the work. He kept thinking about the details of the interview with Kathryn.

He hadn't realized her dream experience had been different from his. He'd simply appeared in the Alma-Tadema picture—although he hadn't recognized it at the time. She'd been drawn to a strange, airless world, where an indistinct but massive creature was watching her. He grimaced. A supernatural being?

What did it want with her—and him?

Something.

As he thought on that for a moment, a ready explanation leaped into his mind. He and Kathryn had met because he was assigned to the missing person case. What if the damn thing *wanted* the two of them to solve that case?

But why?

Maybe it was a ghost. One of the victims. And it was in purgatory until the murder was solved. Was that misty, airless world she'd described purgatory?

He pursed his lips, marveling that he was thinking along those lines. If a ghost broke the case, he'd better have a lot more evidence to back it up.

Inevitably, his mind went back to Kathryn. Her magic wand had been the guidepost to her exit. An interesting touch.

The image of something familiar. Something from her world—in that hostile place she'd described.

But why the wand?

He'd spent several hours each evening with the books he'd borrowed from Ross. And he'd learned some pretty amazing stuff—which he hadn't been prepared to share with her, because he could hardly believe he was considering such oddball scenarios.

Of course, some of it was pure twaddle. Like the myth of Atlantis, which he'd read about in several books. But he'd definitely been interested in an essay on hypnosis as a possible explanation of what had happened to himself and Kathryn. Suppose some agency was beaming suggestions to both their subconscious minds? That might account for their apparently sharing a dream, although it didn't explain how it had been done when they'd started out in completely different locations.

He could even fit Kathryn's latest dream into that script. Forget the ghost. Suppose someone had knowledge of the disappearances—now probably murders. And that individual wanted to feed information to the police without getting caught.

Clairvoyance was another mechanism he found himself considering. He'd read an account of the famous mystic Emanuel Swedenborg interrupting a dinner party in the summer of 1759 to go outside. When he came back, he was pale and shaken—insisting that a fire had already burned several houses near his own and that his residence was in danger. The dinner guests were startled by the report, since Swedenborg lived in a city three hundred miles away, an enormous distance in those times. The next evening, a messenger confirmed the mystic's account of the fire.

Something similar could have happened to Kathryn in this latest dream, although she claimed she'd never had any mystical experiences before.

Of course, if he was honest, he couldn't rule out drugs, although he couldn't figure out how someone had slipped the same hallucinogen to both Kathryn and himself. But LSD had turned up as part of the case. Kathryn said she'd found it in a drawer of Heather's bureau. Was she telling the truth?

He grimaced. He was still considering her as a suspect. Probably because he wanted to distance himself from the growing relationship developing between them.

Relationship? No way! This had started off as pure, unadulterated lust. Yet a relationship was what it had felt like this morning at her apartment.

He pulled his thoughts away from Kathryn and back to the investigation of the four missing person cases.

By three, it was time to leave for his meeting with Ross. Just as he was packing up, Granger sought him out again.

"You making any more progress on those cases?" he asked.

"Uh . . ."

"Jack, what's going on with you?" the captain asked.

He shrugged. "I've been a little distracted lately. Lily went missing. I found her, but it was kind of traumatic."

The captain pinned him with a look. "I got a complaint about you this afternoon. From a guy named William Strong. He says you were engaged in public lewdness yesterday morning."

Jack swore. "Oh, yeah? I'd hardly call it that! A kiss isn't lewdness."

"You were with Kathryn Reynolds. Were you on your own time?"

"No."

"I'm going to have to write this up."

Jack felt his chest tighten painfully, until several thoughts occurred to him. He struggled to drag in a breath before he said, "You say a man named William Strong reported me and Reynolds? He claimed he was looking for an address in the neighborhood. So he didn't live there. I gave him my name. How did he know Reynolds's name?"

Granger shrugged.

"Do me a favor. See if his name and address check out before you write it up."

"You think he's not legit?"

"Yeah, that's what I think," Jack said. He didn't have any solid facts—just a hunch and the hope he was right. "Maybe something else is going on," he added. "Reynolds has been having some problems with vandalism. And someone was watching her house last night."

"Did she report it?"

"Yes."

"I'll check that out."

"Fine."

Since he'd joined the Violent Crimes unit, Jack had gotten along with Granger. Now he wasn't so sure. And the captain's next words made him blink.

"I let you drop the Westborn investigation to focus on the missing person cases. Was that because you wanted to spend more time with Reynolds?"

Jack studied his superior. "Wait a minute. *You* asked *me* to try and come up with connections on the missing persons. And if you remember, I didn't even know Reynolds then. You sent me to her house."

Granger ignored the last part, meeting his gaze head-on. "No. It was your idea."

Jack stood there, wondering if he was going crazy—or was it Granger? The captain had told him to drop Westborn, but this was the second instance where he seemed to have forgotten about it.

Jesus, he wished he had some proof of how he'd gotten the assignment. He swallowed. "Can we talk about this later? I have a meeting set up with an important contact."

"Okay," the captain agreed, looking just as reluctant as Jack to continue the conversation. Maybe until he got a line on William Strong.

"I think I'm going to have a breakthrough in the missing person case," he said, hoping to hell it was true.

"I'll be waiting for your report."

Jack nodded, gathering up some papers and shoving them into his briefcase.

He left the building, his pulse pounding.

What was going on?

The old man who styled himself William Strong had called in a complaint. He'd like to check him out. But he didn't have time to do it now.

And Granger was acting like he had early Alzheimer's. Great!

He could come to no conclusions about that, and he tried to bring his thoughts back to the upcoming task as he approached the Park and Ride. Ross was waiting for him, his hips propped comfortably against his Jeep Grand Cherokee.

He waved to Jack, then grabbed his knapsack and loped forward with the easy stride of a predator. A wolf. He looked relaxed and ready for an adventure. Probably he and Megan had gotten the baby to sleep so they could have some quality time together.

The speculation made Jack flash back to his own situation. Why was he resisting the pull of Kathryn Reynolds? They were both consenting adults. Making love with her wasn't going to hurt anybody else.

He recognized the rationalization for what it was as soon as it surfaced. He wasn't free. He had his family to consider.

"I appreciate your meeting me on short notice," he said as Ross slipped into the passenger seat of the unmarked.

"Well, it's a chance to get out in the woods—for a good cause."

"Yeah."

Ross gave him a long look.

"You appear . . . disturbed," he said.

"As in crazy?"

Ross laughed. "As in worried. Want to talk about it?"

Jack sighed, wondering where to start. "Granger got a report that Kathryn and I were engaged in public lewdness."

"Chasing each other naked around the Rockshire parking lot?"

Jack laughed. "No. Kissing outside her house. Unfortunately, I was on duty at the time."

Ross whistled through his teeth. "Not good."

"The really interesting part is that the guy who reported us claimed to be looking for an address in the neighborhood. He asked my name. But not Kathryn's. Then he included her name in his complaint."

"You're right. Interesting."

"I asked Granger not to write it up until he checked the man's name and address. I'm thinking he'll find they won't exist."

"Which should let you off the hook."

"Yeah. But that's not my only problem." Quickly he filled in Ross on Granger's memory loss.

"Nothing like that's happened before?" Ross asked.

"No."

"So—what do you think?"

"I wish to hell I knew." Jack sighed. "As long as I'm spilling my guts, maybe I can ease into the rest of it."

Ross remained silent. Jack shifted in his seat and said, "I keep running into more paranormal stuff. That's why we're taking this ride in the country. This time Kathryn had her own dream. I mean, I wasn't there. It wasn't a fantasy setting. She was up at Sugarloaf, a location she'd never been to before, but she described it pretty well to me. She saw a guy burying a body a little way up the hill from the East View parking lot. And I'm betting that you'll be able to find the spot."

"I'll do my best."

"There's a strange element," Jack added.

Ross shook his head. "You mean stranger than what you've already told me?"

Jack laughed. "Unfortunately, yes. The guy she saw looked like a ghost."

"So maybe it's a hundred-year-old body."

"That occurred to me when she first started describing what she'd seen. But after the guy finished burying the evidence, he drove away in a late-model car."

"Did she recognize him?"

"Not so she could pick him out of a lineup. But she said there was something familiar about him."

"Mm hmm." Ross took in more details. "Have you been reading the books I lent you?" he finally asked.

"Avidly—when I can snatch the time. I never knew there was so much weird stuff floating around."

"You've led a sheltered life."

Jack laughed again. "There are few people who could say that to a detective who works in Violent Crimes."

"Yeah. It probably takes a werewolf. Or a vampire."

Jack's head snapped toward his friend for a moment, then he brought his gaze back to the road. "You believe in vampires?"

"Why not? The ancient myths must come from somewhere."

Jack felt a wave of cold sweep over his skin. Vampires. And what else?

"I get the feeling you've had a bunch of frightening thoughts over the past few days."

"Unfortunately, yes."

"Like what?"

"Nothing that makes perfect sense. But maybe you can comment." Jack began summarizing his reading. "So, what do you think?" he asked, trying to breathe around the tightness in his chest.

"None of it seems quite right."

"That's what I was thinking."

Ross was studying him again. "You're in a unique position, you know. For centuries, humankind tried to figure out the secrets of the universe. We had all sorts of mechanisms for explaining the unexplainable—for warding off the devils and the darkness. Modern man, pardon the non-PC designation, feels more secure because he's got science to explain his world. Now you're thrust back into the dark pit of the unknown."

"Gee, thanks for pointing that out. What should I do, have an exorcism ceremony?"

"I wouldn't recommend it. Unless you believe in devils."

"I don't!" Jack insisted, wondering if he meant he didn't want to believe in them. He cut his friend another look. "When you talk about being thrust into the dark pit of the unknown, I take it you're speaking from experience."

"Yeah."

"What did you do?"

"I found Megan. And she helped me make peace with the furies nipping at my heels."

"Don't suggest that I put my trust in Kathryn. She's part of the problem."

"So was Megan, if you remember. But I figured out I needed her."

Ross made a low sound. "Okay, that's not quite accurate. She forced me to admit that I could trust her."

Jack nodded, wishing he were free to take his friend's advice. Clearing his throat, he asked, "So, uh, what do you think about beings we can't see, beings we can't imagine? Beings who live in a place that isn't our world. Another dimension. Or another universe. Another—" He stopped, unable to finish the thought.

"Why do you bring up another universe?"

"The dreams start differently for Kathryn than they do for me. She describes a gray place where she can hardly see, hardly feel the ground under her feet, hardly breathe. She knows she'll die if she stays there. And to put the icing on the cake, there's something there—watching her." He shuddered.

"Something?"

"She calls it a presence. Too bad neither one of us has the terminology to describe it."

"So, are you thinking the two of you are being stalked by a creature from another dimension? Actually, it's as workable a theory as anything else. Maybe angels are creatures from another dimension. Maybe devils. Things men admire or fear. Things they can't express any other way."

"So why would a being from this other place be screwing with people from this world?"

Ross shrugged. "Hell if I know. If that's what it is, then I guess you have to figure it out."

Jack grimaced. "Yeah. The easy part. I guess we have to leave that for later. Let's start with dead bodies in the woods."

14

THEY checked in at the park gate and got a combination that would unlock the chain across the road after hours. Then Jack drove to the East View parking area, where there were still a few cars.

After climbing out and stretching, he looked toward the hill above the parking lot. It was broader than he'd pictured. "More ground to cover than I remembered."

"Let's walk around up there a little," Ross suggested. "I don't think someone would bury a body within fifty yards of the parking area. So we can start above that level."

"Yeah. Kathryn entered the scene near the path," he said. "She wasn't sure how far she walked. But she knew it was to the left."

They started walking back and forth, their eyes on the ground. After half an hour, Jack began to think that he'd been overoptimistic about discovering anything. But he kept going, because he'd brought Ross all the way out here—and he wasn't going to give up until his friend called it quits.

Another fifteen minutes passed, and the sun began to set. Jack's hopes were almost extinguished. Talk about looking for a needle in a haystack.

When he opened his mouth to speak, he saw that Ross had stopped and was sniffing the air. Then he moved toward a patch of ground that didn't look much different from the rest of the area. "Here," he said.

"A body?"

"Something dead. Underground. I can tell you better after it gets dark."

"You're going to change?"

"Yeah. But I prefer to do it in private." He hesitated a beat. "You're not going to freak out on me, are you?"

"I think I can keep it together," Jack answered, with more bravado than he was feeling.

"We won't be able to talk, of course."

Jack nodded. Of course the wolf couldn't talk.

He thrust his hands into his pockets, feeling a chill travel over his skin as he watched his friend disappear into the woods. He'd established a bond of trust with Ross, a bond that went deeper than he'd realized.

He wasn't sure how long he waited. He only knew that the light was almost gone when a gray wolf stepped carefully from behind a tree.

He was a magnificent animal. Large and proud and beautifully marked. Still, Jack felt the hairs on the back of his neck tingle as keen yellow eyes regarded him. It was one thing to know that Ross Marshall was a werewolf. It was quite another thing to stand face to face in the woods with an animal that could tear him to shreds.

"So, let's go hunting," he said.

It was eerie to see the wolf nod, then move forward to sniff the ground where Ross had said a grave was located.

Jack switched on the large flashlight he'd brought, watching the animal paw up some of the leaves.

Picking up a stick in his mouth, he turned his head and jabbed it at the dirt.

Jack came forward to anchor the marker more firmly in the soil— which was loose and easy to probe, as though it had been turned recently.

When he finished, he looked toward the wolf again. The animal had lifted his head and was sniffing the air once more, before moving to another location not far from the grave. Again he pawed up leaves, then turned his head toward Jack, who moved forward to meet him.

"Another grave?" he asked.

The wolf nodded, as Jack found a second stick and probed the dirt. Again, it was not packed down.

The wolf was already moving in a rough circle around the general area. Once more, he stopped and pawed.

"More?"

The animal confirmed the question with a nod. By the time he was finished, he had indicated five separate locations, and Jack had marked them all with sticks.

The wolf stopped, making eye contact once more.

"You think that's all?" Jack asked.

The animal nodded, then trotted away in the direction from which he'd come. Minutes later, Ross Marshall emerged from the woods, tucking his shirt into his jeans. "I make five graves," he said.

"That's more than I expected. The captain sent me off to investigate three previous missing person cases. Plus the recent one."

"Somebody's been busy."

"And he likes this burial ground. Which is one of the few patterns I've picked up. Before this, there was almost nothing to connect the cases. A woman who looked nothing like DeYoung. A boy. And a young man. I can't even be sure these are all his victims."

"But you can be sure Heather DeYoung is here."

Jack's head snapped around. "You're sure?"

"You gave me that T-shirt. Her scent is here."

"Okay. Good. Well, not good. I'm sorry she's dead. But at least I've got something to run with."

He gave Ross a direct look. "Thanks for helping me."

"You looked a little spooked, at first. But it worked out."

Jack laughed. "Well, think how you'd feel if I opened a door to another universe and a fallen angel came riding through on a fire-breathing dragon."

"When you put it that way, I can see your point. But you've got to admit that one little wolf doesn't equal a fallen angel and a fire-breathing dragon."

"Some people would think so."

They started back to the parking lot. "So, now I need to notify the Frederick County cops that I think I've got a graveyard from a serial killer in Montgomery County. Although, as I said, we can't be sure who else is buried here. And we can't be sure if the perp lives near his victims or is traveling down to our area from up here." He thought for a moment. "On top of that, I've got to think of a good reason why I came up here. The best solution would be if we could have found something of DeYoung's up there in the woods."

Ross gave him a penetrating look. "You're thinking of planting evidence?"

Jack sighed. "Yeah, listen to me! But that would give me something concrete to start with—rather than a psychic dream from Kathryn Reynolds. And we know the damn bodies are here."

"Do it any way you want. Remember, before that killer scooped up Megan, I refused to tell you *how* I got my information. You were willing to work with me. Some detectives weren't quite so happy about it."

Jack nodded, remembering his conversation with one of Ross's former police contacts. The man had been sure he was guilty of murder, but he hadn't been able to prove it.

Thinking about that made him feel edgy. He'd given Kathryn a rationale for using Ross as a source of information on this. But he knew he needed more than his friend's testimony.

His mood hadn't improved forty-five minutes later as he turned in at the Park and Ride and thanked Ross again.

Ross had stopped asking questions, electing to remain silent during most of the ride. Now he said, "Are you okay?"

Jack cut the engine and sat with his hands wrapped around the steering wheel, feeling that he needed to anchor himself down—although he wasn't quite sure what that meant. "Not exactly," he said slowly.

"You want me to ride back home with you?"

"You think I need baby-sitting?" Jack asked, more sharply than he'd intended.

"I wouldn't put it that way," Ross answered easily.

Jack made an effort to relax. "Sorry, I'm sort of preoccupied. I'm not very good company right now. I'll call you tomorrow and let you know what happened."

"Yeah, I understand." Ross studied him for a moment, as if debating whether to let him drive himself home. "Just be sure to call."

"Of course."

Jack watched Ross climb out of the unmarked and return to his SUV, feeling relieved to be alone. The relief lasted only a few minutes. Once he was back on the road, the tension gripped him again. He couldn't stop thinking about ancient myths and creatures of the night, and what you did to escape when you thought some supernatural force had you in its talons.

SIMON stood in the hallway, breathing deeply. He felt the blood pumping in his veins, felt his excitement building. Excitement he would turn into destructive energy. But along with the power, he felt raw nerves poking through his skin like a mass of small spikes.

He hated to admit the last part. There was no reason to worry, he told himself. He had prepared carefully. He knew he was in control of the ceremony. Still, he felt those sharp little wounds in his skin. Self-inflicted wounds, he told himself.

Mentally, he went over the preparations he'd made. The protective circle was in place—except for the break in the line where he would enter it.

And his victim was ready, too. Laid out on the table. Lightly sedated. But the guy wasn't going to stay that way. For this ceremony, Simon wanted him awake. Wanted him to know what was happening to him, and what *would* happen. This time, the victim's pain and fear were an important part of the process.

A tall candelabra stood on a table beside the door. It was an antique that he'd bought at an auction of furnishings from a Catholic church. The irony had always warmed him when he thought about how the priests would react if they knew what he was doing with their precious artifact.

Sitting beside the candelabra was a box of old-fashioned matches. Simon struck one, then touched it to the wick of a taper, watching the small flame flicker to life. Swiftly he lit the rest of the candles, then drew in a deep breath and let it out before opening the door and stepping into the ceremonial chamber.

It was a sacred place. Sacred to him. Not a church, but a space he had created where his purposes could be achieved.

The candles flickered, and he felt a cold wind moving his hair and the fabric of his pants.

A curse sprang to his lips.

Ayindral was here. Watching. Somehow, he was here, in this world.

Well, there was nothing the bastard could do, he assured himself as he stepped into the room and set down the candelabra. With a hand that shook slightly, he picked up the strips of tanned animal skin that would complete the circle. Stepping inside the protective line, he knelt and swiftly completed the defensive perimeter. Then he stood, and walked to the man strapped down on the table.

JACK kept his gaze focused on the road as he headed back toward Montgomery County. He tried to give all his attention to simply driving himself back home, but the need to escape clawed inside his chest like a wild animal desperate for freedom. Escape from what? He didn't even know.

He told himself to calm down. And as they had so many times during the past few days, he found his thoughts turning to Kathryn. He knew he'd made a decision. He was going to stop by her house and get a piece of Heather's jewelry. It was a good solution to the problem—a piece of evidence that he could say he'd found at a burial ground—but it also made him feel slightly queasy. He'd always been a straight-arrow cop. Now he was getting ready to turn himself into Mark Furman.

He thought about calling Emily and telling her he was going to be later than he'd expected. But how late? He didn't want to think about how long he might stay at Kathryn's and what he might do there.

He grimaced. No matter where his thoughts strayed, they kept coming back to her. To making love with her.

KATHRYN stood in her kitchen, her heart thumping in her chest. Hardly knowing what she was doing, she grabbed a mug from the shelf, filled it with water, and dropped in a bag of green tea. With shaking hands, she set the mug in the microwave. The turntable began to move, and a spark arced off the rim of the cup.

"Oh, shit!" she exclaimed, pushing the Off button. She'd grabbed a mug with a gold rim, and the metallic paint had set off a reaction inside the microwave.

The machine stopped, and with shaking hands, she opened the door and pulled out the mug, cradling it in her palms as she looked down, unseeing, at the cold water and wet tea bag.

She felt a terrible tightness in her chest, and an almost palpable vibration in the air around her.

"Jack?" she whispered. "Jack?"

He didn't answer, of course. He wasn't here. Yet she felt connected to him—as though an invisible wire were tugging at her, pulling her closer.

This was like the dreams. Only she was awake, the way she had been when she'd heard the dog barking. Then she hadn't understood what was happening. Now she knew she was waiting for some dire event.

With eyes squeezed tightly shut, she stood very still, barely breathing, trying desperately to make the connection with Jack stronger. So she could warn him? Be with him?

She didn't know her specific goal. She only knew that she had to get closer to him.

All at once, she could see him. He was in his car. Driving down a narrow road, coming to her.

Or was it all her imagination? Was she seeing him in his car because she ached for him to be with her?

She stood in the middle of the kitchen, gripping the mug, telling herself that everything was going to be all right—even when she knew it was a lie.

THE traffic on Route 270 was heavy, and Jack decided to turn off onto a secondary road.

As he negotiated a turn, he heard a man scream.

What? It sounded like the guy was in the car with him. His gaze bounced to the passenger seat. Nobody was there, of course.

But he couldn't stop himself from craning his neck to look in the back of the car.

The scream of pain was followed by a plea. *"Jesus Christ, don't do that!"*

"Ah, you're awake," another man said, his voice crackling with excitement. *"I want you conscious for the ceremony."*

Jack blinked, shifted lanes rapidly as the honk of a car horn brought his attention back to the road. The other driver shook his fist at him as he sped past—then shot into his lane and hit the brakes.

Jack hit his own brakes, narrowly avoiding rear-ending the son of a bitch.

The other car sped away. He thought about pulling out his flasher and giving chase, then forgot about the idea as another high-pitched scream of pain filled the car.

"No! Stop! For God's sake, stop."

This time, he thought he recognized the voice. Jesus! It was Gary Swinton!

"Swinton?" he called out, knowing in some part of his mind that the man wasn't in the car.

All he heard now was the chanting of words—smoothly flowing words in some language he didn't understand. They rolled on, filling his head.

The road in front of him dimmed, and he saw a room—a room draped in black, lit by flickering candles.

The scene was sharp and clear. As sharp as the dream with Kathryn. Sharper than reality. Swinton lay naked, strapped to a wooden table, his body slick with sweat, his face contorted with pain and fear. Another man leaned over him—naked to the waist, wearing black trousers in some thin, slinky material. His back was crisscrossed by scars. One hand gripped the edge of the table where Swinton lay. The other hovered over the naked man, holding a candle in an elaborate candlestick, tipping it to the side so that hot wax dropped on the man's midsection. Overlaying the scene was the sound of a voice, chanting smoothly, relentlessly.

Jack had the sensation of standing in back of the chanting man, staring at his blond hair, carefully combed over a bald spot. Though he strained to change the angle of the picture, he couldn't see the man's face.

He forgot where he was, what he was doing. All his attention was focused on the scene in the dark chamber as the hand slowly brought the candle lower. The strangeness and the horror of the scene riveted him.

"Jack! Jack!" Kathryn's voice pierced the bubble around him, and the danger to himself came back in a sharp zing of awareness. Abruptly, his attention snapped back to his own reality—to the car he was driving. He felt his right front tire bite into gravel. He was on the shoulder, and he yanked desperately at the wheel.

But it was already too late. The road curved in the wrong direction, and he shot off the highway. He whipped across a patch of weeds, then down a sharp incline.

There was no question of steering. He rode the vehicle down the hill like a runaway locomotive. The car struck an obstruction he couldn't see, then skidded and rolled over, so that his head hit the column at the edge of the windshield.

That was the last thing he remembered.

15

THE mug in Kathryn's hand crashed to the kitchen floor, the shattering of crockery mingling with the scream that tore from her throat.

"Oh, God, Jack! No!"

She saw the wild plunge of the car, saw the vehicle turn over. But she couldn't see inside, didn't know what had happened to Jack.

For long moments she couldn't move. Then, carefully, she stepped around the broken crockery and headed for the phone.

She didn't even know whom she was going to call until she had picked up the phone number Jack had left her. With wooden fingers, she punched in the numbers.

After several rings, a woman answered.

"Hello." In the background, a baby was crying.

"I . . . I'm sorry," she stammered. "I must have the wrong number."

"What number were you calling?"

"Ross . . . Ross Marshall."

"This is his wife, Megan Sheridan. Can I help you?"

Kathryn dragged in a breath, then let it out in a rush. "There's been an accident."

The woman gasped.

"No, no—not Ross," Kathryn managed. "It's Jack. His car went off the road and crashed. He went out with . . . with your husband. Does Mr. Marshall know where he is?"

"You say there's been an accident. But you don't know where?" the woman asked carefully.

Kathryn made an effort not to start shouting. "I'm in my living room. I . . . I saw his car go off the road. I saw it turn over. I don't know how I saw it. But I know it's true. It's what happened."

There was only a moment's hesitation on the other end of the line. "Okay. Ross was stopping on the way home to pick up some groceries. Let me give you his cell phone number."

"Thank you!" Kathryn gripped the pen so hard that she felt the plastic giving as she scribbled down the number. To make sure she'd gotten it right, she repeated it back. When Megan Sheridan had confirmed it, Kathryn hung up and then immediately called the private detective.

She waited with her hand clamped on the phone as it rang once, twice, three times. Finally a man answered.

"Mr. Marshall?"

"Yes."

"This is Kathryn Reynolds."

"What's wrong?" he asked immediately.

Again she had to drag in a breath and let it out before she could speak. "Jack's car has gone off the road. It's turned over. Do you know where he is?"

He didn't question her source of information. Instead, he said, "I think he was going to your house. That would put him on 1-270."

"No. He's on a secondary road."

"Okay, he must have turned off. Which is the best route to your house?"

"West Montgomery Avenue."

She had snatched up her purse when Marshall said, "Don't go there. You'll never get through in the traffic." He paused for a moment. "I'll report the accident, if somebody hasn't done it already. They'll take him to Montgomery County General Hospital. I'll meet you there."

"Yes. Thank you." Kathryn hung up, then stood for a moment, telling herself she had to get a grip. If she crashed her car, she wasn't going to do Jack any good.

As she charged out the door, her mind went back over the conversations. Megan Sheridan had been surprised to hear from her, but she'd been cooperative. Ross Marshall hadn't questioned her story or her need to get to Jack. What had Jack told them about her? Specifically— what had he told Marshall?

She couldn't answer the questions. She could only pray silently as she drove to Montgomery General Hospital.

The emergency room was full of people. Some looking sick. Others were obviously injured. Still others were waiting for word about loved ones. As she stepped through the door, she scanned the crowd and found a tall, dark-haired man standing with his shoulder propped against the wall, watching the entrance.

The moment she walked in, he came toward her. "Kathryn?"

"Yes. How did you know?"

"Your hair. Jack told me you have wild red hair."

He held out his hand, and she shook it. "Ross Marshall."

"I'm glad to meet Jack's friend. I'm just sorry——" She broke off before she could finish the platitude, and began again. "Is he here? How is he?"

"He's here. I don't know his condition." He reached to clasp her shoulder. "Take it easy. Jack said you're a strong woman."

"He did?"

"Well, that was the implication."

She gave a tight nod. "Have you seen him?"

"He's in the back. They're working on him. I'm going to tell the nurse that you'll be here waiting for information." He stopped, ran a hand through his hair. "I'm going over to his house—to tell Mrs. Anderson. She'll have to tell the kids."

"Craig and Lily." She pressed her fingers against her lips. "Oh!"

He nodded. "They lost their mother in an automobile accident. This is going to be tough on them."

"He's going to be okay!" she said.

"Yeah. Jack's tough."

He cleared his throat. "I gave the receptionist your name and told her that you're Jack's fiancée. That way they'll give you any information available."

She caught her breath, feeling her face go tight.

Again, he clasped her shoulder. "I know the two of you have gotten close."

"Not because Jack is comfortable with that."

"Are you?"

"Well, if you know the circumstances, you know it's hard to be exactly comfortable. But I'm a woman; I think in terms of relationships. Jack's a man; he thinks in terms of avoiding entrapment."

Marshall laughed.

She gave him a considering look. "I get the feeling you've been there yourself."

"Yeah, but I got over my male reluctance. Now I'm happily married." His expression grew serious again. "As I said, I know you're close. No matter how it started."

"What did Jack tell you about us?"

He swallowed. "Let's not get into that now. What's important at the moment is that I think you're entitled to the latest information about his condition."

She sighed, told herself he was right. "Yes. Thank you. But maybe you'd better go get his family. I'll stay here and wait."

"Okay. And I'll tell Mrs. Anderson that you're a good friend."

"She already knows I'm involved in a missing person case. I talked to her this morning," she murmured.

An expression flashed across his face, an expression she read all too well. Gasping, she reached out to grab his sleeve. "What did you find at Sugarloaf Mountain?" she demanded.

He kept his gaze steady on her. "I'm sorry."

"You found Heather up there?"

"I can't tell you with one hundred percent certainty. But I'm pretty sure that's true."

As she swayed on her feet, he caught her and led her to a plastic chair, easing her down. She was aware that people were staring at her, but she didn't care.

"I'm sorry," he said again.

"I was . . . afraid of that," she whispered. "I guess I've already started coming to terms with it."

He nodded. "I'll be back as soon as I can."

She watched him disappear into the parking lot, then turned her attention toward the door where patients were called for treatment.

When she'd first set eyes on Jack, she'd felt like time was standing still. Now, each second seemed to stretch into a century.

She leaned her head against the wall, closed her eyes. Maybe some protective mechanism helped her doze off, because she felt herself jerking awake. Someone was calling her name.

She jumped up, hurried toward the voice, which belonged to a rumpled-looking man in a white coat.

"Ms. Reynolds?"

"Yes. Can you tell me about Jack?"

"I'm Dr. Hammersmith. Detective Thornton has a concussion and a dislocated shoulder."

"A concussion!"

"He's awake. We'd like to keep him for a day or two, to observe the head injury. Under the circumstances, I'd say he escaped with a minimal amount of damage."

She nodded, trying to take that in. "Can I see him?"

"Yes. For a few minutes. We're going to admit him to the neurological floor. That's the second floor."

"But he's out of danger?"

"Things look pretty favorable. But we need to keep him under observation."

"Okay. Thank you," she answered, thinking that the doctor was expecting Jack to recover, but he wasn't willing to say that for sure.

He led her into a busy open area where personnel were rushing off on various emergency errands. They stopped at the entrance to a treatment cubicle, secluded from the main area by curtains. Jack was lying in a hospital bed, low rails raised on either side of the mattress. Her gaze shot to his face. One of his eyes was swollen closed. His complexion was deathly pale, except where it was discolored by bruises turning purple. His arm was in a sling, strapping across his chest.

She must have made a noise when she saw him, because his good eye flickered open and focused on her.

His lips moved, and she thought she heard him whisper her name. Seeing him like this made her insides clench. And, at the same time, it made her realize that her feelings for him ran strong and deep.

"Jack." Swiftly she crossed the room. She wanted to gather him into her arms, but she was afraid to hurt him. So she restrained herself, leaning over him, reaching for his good hand and squeezing it gently.

This time when he whispered her name, she heard him clearly.

She bent to brush her lips against his cheek. "Just rest."

He sighed, closed his eye again.

"Ross went to get Mrs. Anderson."

He made an effort to rouse himself. "Better if the kids don't see me this way."

"I'll tell them you're mending."

The brief exchange seemed to have exhausted him. His good eye closed again, and she felt his fingers loosen.

Once more, she brushed his cheek with her lips, then stepped back. She wanted to stay, but she knew that he needed to rest.

Out in the waiting room, she spotted Ross again. He was standing with an older woman and two children, a boy and a girl. The boy looked achingly like Jack. The girl had more delicate features. Probably her mother's.

The trio must be Craig, Lily, and Mrs. Anderson.

Her heart turned over when she studied the children's pale, pinched faces. They'd lost their mother a few years ago in an automobile accident. Now their father was in the hospital for the same reason, and they had to be scared—no matter how much their housekeeper had contributed to their stable home.

Kathryn wanted to rush to them and offer what comfort she could. But when Ross waved his hand to usher her over, she saw the older woman's expression turn disapproving.

The negative reaction made her throat tighten. But she understood it. Mrs. Anderson had talked to her about a case Jack was working on. Now she was suddenly being billed as a close friend of his. And she'd been allowed to go in and see him—while his family was still in the waiting room.

Instead of hurrying over, she came slowly toward the little group. "Hello, I'm Kathryn Reynolds, Jack's friend. We talked this morning, Mrs. Anderson."

The woman gave a tight nod.

"And this must be Craig and Lily."

"Yes," the boy answered.

She started to offer her hand to the housekeeper, then thought better of it when she saw the woman's unfriendly expression had hardened.

"Is my daddy going to be okay?" a trembly voice asked.

Kathryn lowered her gaze toward Lily. "Yes, I just saw him. He said he's feeling pretty good," she said.

"I want to see him."

"I'm sorry. They don't let children into the emergency room, and I think your daddy's taking a nap now," she said, remembering that Jack hadn't wanted his children to see his battered face.

The little girl's lower lip trembled. She looked so miserable that Kathryn bent down and folded her close, feeling the little girl cling to her. "It's going to be okay. Your daddy told me to tell you not to worry."

"He's not going to die," Craig said emphatically. Then turned it into a question. "Right?"

"That's right," Kathryn answered, praying that it was true.

The housekeeper's hard voice interrupted. "I can take care of Craig and Lily."

Knowing she'd been put in her place, Kathryn stood up again, her eyes going to Ross. "I think I should go home now," she said.

"There's no reason you can't stay," he answered, but he sounded uncertain.

"No. I know when it's time to leave," she said, her voice barely above a whisper because she was afraid she was going to burst into tears if she tried to manage more volume. "You stay here with Mrs. Anderson and the children. They need you. I'll be okay."

Quickly she turned away, blinking to clear her vision. Without waiting for a reply, she started for the door—then saw that a broad-shouldered man had come in and was looking around. Ross spotted him, too, and rapidly crossed the tile floor. The man looked grim, and Ross drew him aside, away from the family that was now seated on a plastic couch.

She couldn't hear what they were saying. But when Ross glanced in her direction, she made her way over to the alcove where the two men were talking.

"This is Captain Granger, Detective Thornton's superior," Ross said. "Kathryn Reynolds."

The captain studied her, his expression not exactly friendly. "Aren't you the woman who filed the missing person report in the DeYoung case?"

"Yes."

"What are you doing here?"

"Detective Thornton and I . . ." She spread her hands, not knowing exactly what to say, particularly since Ross had introduced the man in very formal terms.

"How did you know Jack was here?" he asked.

It was Ross who answered the question. "I have a police scanner in my car. I heard what had happened, and I called Ms. Reynolds because she was waiting for word on what Jack and I had discovered."

Kathryn struggled to keep her expression steady. That wasn't exactly the truth. But she knew why Ross had to give the answer he did.

Granger looked like he was having a bad day. "So my detective runs off the road in a one-car accident—in his company car," he muttered. "Which is always fun to explain to Internal Affairs—and the press."

Kathryn opened her mouth, then thought better of protesting.

Granger was already speaking to Ross again. "How did you two end up at Sugarloaf Mountain?"

"I had some information pertinent to the case."

"Yeah, you come up with some pretty amazing leads," Granger said in a voice that didn't make it sound like a compliment. "So you and Thornton spend the afternoon up at Sugarloaf. Then he comes back and crashes his car. What were you doing up there? Having a party?"

"Of course not," Ross snapped. "You can have his blood alcohol checked. And you can have a drug screen done, too."

"I will. And how, exactly, did this particular expedition come about, if you don't mind my asking?" Granger pressed.

"I found a piece of Ms. DeYoung's jewelry up at the mountain location."

Kathryn blinked.

Granger issued an immediate challenge. "Jack didn't say anything about that."

"I guess he was planning to put it in his report." Ross slipped his hand into his pocket and pulled out a small plastic bag. In it was a circle pin that Kathryn recognized.

Lord, had he really found it up there? Or what? She could only stare at the piece of jewelry. "That's Heather's," she managed as he handed the bag to the captain.

Granger's head swung toward her. "So you can conveniently corroborate the information."

"Yes. I've seen her wear it. Is that bad?"

Granger scowled. "Convenient, as I said. There's something going on here that I'm not picking up, isn't there? Are the three of you in some kind of conspiracy or something?"

Ross cocked his head to one side. "Like what?" he asked, keeping his voice mild. In the face of Granger's accusations, Kathryn might have shouted the question.

"You tell me," Granger muttered. "What's your story—that you were hiking up at Sugarloaf and found this jewelry? That you knew it was related to a case Jack happened to be working on?"

"That sounds right."

Granger snorted. "Okay. We'll get back to that later."

"The important point is that both Jack and I believe you'll find DeYoung's grave up there. As well as several other graves—all related to the missing person cases Jack has been investigating."

Granger's gaze swung toward Kathryn. "You don't seem surprised."

"I was starting to feel like Heather wasn't coming back," she murmured. "Then, before you got here, Ross told me he was almost sure she was dead."

"Convenient," Granger muttered again.

"Are you accusing her of something?" Ross asked, his voice low and level.

Granger gave him a hard look. "What are you, her lawyer?"

"No. I'm just trying to figure out why you're coming on so strong," he said, sounding deliberately controlled.

"Because Thornton hasn't been himself since he asked to get into the missing persons investigation. And then, this afternoon, I got a complaint about him—and Ms. Reynolds."

Kathryn sucked in a sharp breath.

"And you checked out William Strong?" Ross asked.

Granger stared at him. "Thornton told you about that?"

"Yeah, he did. And he told me he thought the guy was going to turn out to be bogus. Was he?"

A slight flush spread across the captain's cheeks. "As a matter of fact, the name and address don't check out."

"So it looks like somebody who wanted to make trouble for Jack or Kathryn."

"That doesn't excuse the behavior."

"Pretty innocent behavior, the way I heard it."

Again Granger looked at her. "Is that right?"

"Yes," she managed, feeling her cheeks flame. Bending the truth had never been her strong suit, yet in the face of this man's attack, she felt like it was her best choice—if she wanted to help Jack.

"Maybe we should get back to your missing person case." Ross's voice cut through her discomfort. "You need to identify the site, so I'll be glad to go up there with a crime scene team and show them where we marked the graves."

Granger was looking at him thoughtfully. "I'll contact Frederick County and apprise them of the situation. When we get a court order, I'll let you know."

"Fine," Ross answered.

Kathryn stood there, taking it in, thinking that there was a subtext to the conversation that she couldn't quite read.

Ross turned to her. "I appreciate your meeting me over here. But you might as well go on home." He sounded impersonal—like she'd merely come out of duty or something. But the look in his eyes as he met her gaze was intense. And she was pretty sure he was trying to get her out of there without any more questions. "Probably the captain will want to express his sympathy to the family."

Granger scowled at him.

"Okay. Thanks," she said.

"I expect you to make yourself available if we have any more questions," the captain said.

"Of course."

Granger strode off to see Mrs. Anderson and the children. Kathryn couldn't hear what he was saying, but his voice sounded milder.

"Is there anything else I can do for you?" Ross asked.

She thought about that. With his unqualified defense of Jack and his kindness toward her, this man had earned her trust in a very short time—unlike Captain Granger, who had earned her instant dislike. Keeping her voice low, she said, "Jack told you what's been happening to us? That we've . . . shared a dream? That I dreamed about going up to Sugarloaf and seeing the man burying the bodies? Only I guess it wasn't happening at the same time that I was there. It was something that was going to happen. Or had happened."

"Had happened," Ross supplied.

"You don't have any trouble with any of this weird stuff?"

"What did Jack tell you about me?"

"Not much. You're his good friend. You have extraordinary detective skills. And I guess you have some secret that you don't talk about much."

"Yeah." He hesitated for a moment, then lowered his voice so that she had to lean forward to hear him. "The ER waiting room isn't the place to talk about my background. Let's just say that my mind is open to stuff that other people might consider over the top. So when Jack talked about the two of you having the same dream, I didn't dismiss it as paranoid psychotic ravings."

"I'm glad to hear that. Did you have any insights for Jack?"

"Nothing of any immediate help."

She glanced toward the group at the other end of the room and saw Mrs. Anderson looking at her as she spoke to Granger. She would have liked to know what the woman was saying. It couldn't be anything good.

"I'd better go," she said to Ross.

"I'll meet you here in the morning."

"Yes. Thanks." Turning, she started for the door, keeping her gaze focused straight ahead. She'd been on the verge of tears before the captain had walked in. And she'd kept herself together in the face of his interrogation.

Now she was close to breaking down again. She wanted to talk to Jack. And if not Jack, Ross. He had some things to explain to her. Like how he'd gotten Heather's circle pin. But she couldn't ask him now.

The cold reality of the conversation with Ross and Granger began to sink in as she stepped into the parking lot. Heather was dead. And Jack—

Jack was beyond her reach. By the time she got to her car, tears were streaking down her cheeks. She wiped them away with the back of her hand, then made an effort to get control of herself so she could see to drive.

All the way home, she kept thinking about her relationship with Jack. She'd come rushing down to the hospital like she had a right to be there. But seeing his family had made her realize how badly she was kidding herself. He had a son and a daughter who were his first responsibility. What part could she play in that life? She and Jack had been drawn together by circumstances neither of them understood. From the first moment they'd laid eyes on each other, there had been a wild, out-of-control sexual pull between them.

Jack didn't think that meant anything beyond the physical—because some outside force had pushed them together. She could understand his point of view, although it wasn't true for her. What she felt for Jack went a lot deeper then sexual compulsion, but she couldn't expect—or demand—the same from him.

Telling herself the truth only deepened her misery. By the time she turned onto her street, she was sobbing. She pulled into the driveway, cut the engine, and hunched over the wheel, struggling to calm herself.

Kathryn! Someone called her name. Not aloud. The voice resounded inside her skull.

Raising her head, she looked around, not knowing what to expect—until a noise behind her had her whirling in her seat and craning her neck so she could see in back of her.

She stared in confusion when she saw that a car had pulled in front of her driveway, blocking her in.

She gasped when she recognized the angular shape. She still didn't know the make and model, but she was almost certain it was the car she had seen up at Sugarloaf Mountain. The car that had been driven by the man who'd buried Heather's body.

16

IN the light from the streetlamp, she saw the car door open. A man climbed out and jogged toward her.

Something was in his hand. As he drew closer, she saw it was a gun pointed toward her.

Her heart blocking her windpipe, she acted instinctively, twisting the key in the ignition.

When the engine roared to life, she threw the car into Drive, spinning the wheel as she came around in a tight circle across the grass. The vehicle clipped an azalea as she crossed the lawn, sank into the grass, then mowed down a flower bed. But she didn't slow down. Crossing the sidewalk, she bumped down the curb onto the street, not bothering to turn on the headlights.

When she risked a quick glance in the rearview mirror, she saw the man was running toward his car. Seconds later, his vehicle lurched after her.

Desperate to escape, she took the corner on two wheels, driving through the night with her headlights off.

Twin beams came toward her out of the darkness. When the driver spotted her, he honked, but she ignored him.

Her eyes flicked to the rearview mirror, and she saw lights behind her. Was it the guy? Or somebody else? In the darkness, she couldn't tell.

Teeth clenched, she made a quick turn at the next block, then another turn, and another, weaving through the neighborhood like a drunken snake, thankful that she knew the twists and turns so well.

She kept glancing back. The lights had disappeared, and as far as she could tell, there was nobody following. But she didn't allow herself to relax. He could have turned off his headlights, too. And he could be coming up on her fast. A sob welled in her throat. As long as she was in the neighborhood, she wasn't safe.

When she reached Route 28, she was forced to turn on her lights or risk an accident. Hands gripping the wheel, she eased into the stream of traffic, watching the rearview mirror as closely as the road in front of her.

She didn't see the familiar shape of the car. But she still didn't feel safe. She headed for Rockville Pike, driving toward Bethesda. After several miles, she turned in at one of the well-lit, busy shopping centers that lined the Pike, then used the off-road exit connecting it to the next strip mall.

In the second parking lot, she pulled up to the curb and sat with the engine running in case she had to make a quick getaway.

To stop herself from shaking, she wrapped her hands around the wheel. Reality was finally sinking in. The man who had buried Heather had been parked on the street, waiting for her to come home. And he'd probably been there last night, too, in a different car.

She tried to figure out what to do, but after everything that had happened, her brain felt almost too numb to function. First she'd seen Jack's car crash. Then she'd rushed to the hospital. After a few minutes with him, she'd had to deal with both Mrs. Anderson and Captain Granger. Then she'd gone home, and the man who had killed Heather had almost gotten her.

The logical thing was to call the police. But she couldn't bring herself to do that, not after her interview with the captain. He hadn't bothered to hide his anger with Jack—and her, too, she was pretty sure.

If she started talking to the cops, there was no way to keep Jack out of it. And when she started trying to explain all the weird stuff that had happened to the two of them, she was going to sound demented. Which wasn't going to do Jack any good—or her, either. So the best thing was not to get started.

Did her reasoning make sense? She couldn't be sure. She only knew she couldn't go to the police. Not now. Not until she could consult Jack. And there was no chance of that until he was better.

Then what?

Ross's face swam before her. Ross would help her, but his phone number was at home, and she couldn't risk going back there.

A sob welled in her throat, and she knew that she was on the edge of hysteria. Pressing back against the headrest, she took several shallow breaths, ordering herself not to come apart.

When she was feeling a little calmer, she exited onto the Pike once more and drove toward D.C.—until she spotted the low profile of a motel on her side of the road.

After pulling under the lobby entrance canopy, she looked in back of her again. The guy wasn't there.

She knew if the killer had followed her, getting a room would be a dangerous idea. But she was almost certain she'd lost him. Since he didn't know where she was, spending the night here would be a lot safer than going back home. In the morning she'd figure out what to do. Right now, all she wanted was to feel safe.

She was deciding which credit card to use, when her mind canceled the decision. You could trace people through their credit card transactions. Which meant that she should pay in cash.

Luckily, she was prepared for that eventuality. Long ago, after Gran's purse had been stolen, she'd tucked emergency money—three fifty-dollar bills—under the floor mat of her car. Before getting out, she found the money, then went inside and rented a room for the night. The place was one of those two-story motels where you registered, then drove to your room. So she didn't have to explain why she was arriving without any luggage.

After locking the door, setting the chain, and tipping a chair back under the doorknob, she looked around the room. It wasn't anything fancy, but it wasn't too bad. At least the blue spread, curtains, and carpeting looked clean.

But the air was cold, and she suddenly felt chilled to the bone. Shivering violently, she crossed to the bathroom, and turned on the shower with a shaky hand.

She stayed under the hot water for a long time, using the soap and shampoo provided by the management. Finally, feeling better, she got out and dried herself, then put her T-shirt back on. After using the hair dryer mounted above the light switch, she washed out her underwear and hung it on a towel rack.

By the time she was finished, she was so worn out that she could barely move. She'd been going to see if she could get Ross's number from information. But now it didn't seem worth the effort. If she'd been thinking clearly, she might have decided she was being compelled to go to bed. But coherent thought had been washed away with the hot water. She could only stagger across the room, turn off the lights, and crawl into bed, pulling the covers up to her chin like an animal seeking refuge in its burrow.

She was asleep almost as soon as her head hit the pillow. And there was almost no opportunity to rest. Almost at once, she was in the strange, airless land where humans had no place.

The fear was still there, nipping at her heels. But this time it was less, because she knew where safety lay. The huge incarnation of the

magic wand was shining in the distance. She staggered toward it, gasping as she reached the milestone, then broke free of the thick fog.

As soon as she stepped into untainted air, she knew where she was.
Not Sugarloaf Mountain, thank the Lord. Instead, she was back in the
Alma-Tadema painting. Well, not exactly. It was the landscape of the
painting. Only now the brilliant midday sunlight was gone—replaced
by the softer light of early evening.

And she wasn't alone.

A man dressed in faded jeans and a dark T-shirt was standing at the
edge of the marble structure, staring out to sea, his hands stuffed into
his front pockets. She saw him only from the back, but she knew who
it was.

"Jack!"

He turned, and a smile of welcome broke out on his face. A relaxed,
open smile that was achingly new to her.

"Kathryn. I was hoping you'd come."

She walked swiftly toward him, stopping a few feet away, thinking
that she was going to show him she wasn't controlled by passion—that
the two of them could have a conversation without grabbing each
other.

Hours ago, when she'd seen him in the hospital, his face had been
bruised, one eye swollen closed. His arm in a sling.

That image faded as she stared at him. He looked as he had before
he'd left for Sugarloaf. Well, not exactly the same. He looked happier,
more relaxed than she'd ever seen him. He wasn't in his persona of Jack
Thornton, police detective. He was off duty. At ease.

As she took him in, she saw him doing the same with her. For the
first time, her focus shifted away from him. She looked down at her
own garb and saw that she was wearing only the T-shirt that she'd put
on in the motel. It was a long T-shirt, skimming her hips, but much
too revealing to be wearing out here in the open.

His warm look told her that keeping their hands off each other
might not be so easy.

"I was going to say 'We have to stop meeting this way,'" she managed.

"You mean just when I've decided it's a good idea?"

"A good idea," she breathed, trying to keep her tone light, but he
must have seen something on her face that disturbed him. And she recalled that he was excellent at reading people.

"What's wrong?" he asked. "I mean, beyond the usual problems?"

"What . . . uh . . . do you remember before this?"

She watched his thoughts turn inward, watched his features cloud, knew the moment when comprehension dawned. "Oh, Christ!" he exclaimed. "I went off the road." He gripped her arm. "What happened to me? Am I dead? Is this heaven?"

Her throat clogged. "Heaven? I hope not. If this is heaven, then we're both here. And I didn't think he got me."

His hand tightened on her flesh. "You don't think *who* got you?"

"I . . . I shouldn't have said that."

"Yeah, but you did. What happened to you?"

"The man I saw in my last dream. He was waiting for me when I got home from the hospital. When I pulled into the driveway, he blocked me in. At least I'm pretty sure it was him."

"Shit!"

"It's okay. I drove around him. I . . . I got away. Then I went to a motel on the Pike."

"You're sure he didn't follow you?" he demanded. "You checked?"

"Yes. I'm fine."

"Thank God for that." His face contorted. "But when you wake up, I don't think I'm in any kind of shape to protect you." His expression clouded. "My car turned over. What happened to me?"

"You have a concussion. And a dislocated shoulder."

"Oh, shit."

"You're going to be okay."

"Yeah, well, I've screwed things up pretty good. I'm not going to be on active duty anytime soon. Damn! I was driving to your house. To get something of DeYoung's—to salt up there at the grave site." He stopped, cursed again, his expression contrite. "Sorry, that's a wonderful way to tell you that your friend is dead."

She reached for his hand, knit her fingers with his. "Ross told me. He . . . he already got something of Heather's. A pin. He showed it to Captain Granger."

"Granger! You talked to Granger?"

"He came to the hospital. He was . . . pretty hostile."

"I'll bet." He shook his head. "Something's going on with him. I can't figure it out. He asked me to try and connect the missing person cases. Then somehow he decided it was *my* idea."

She stared at him. "That's. . . . weird."

"My thoughts exactly."

It was a strange discussion. They were both talking quickly, exchanging information as though it were perfectly normal to be meeting in a dream. But then, for them, it was!

"There *is* some good news," she told him. "You were right about William Strong. He doesn't exist, so . . . uh . . . Granger couldn't write you up."

"That's something, anyway."

They discussed the captain for a few more minutes, coming to no real conclusions. Yet she felt the tightness inside her chest easing. All too often, she had felt she and Jack were antagonists. Now, they were trying to figure things out together.

"How did you hook up with Ross?" he asked.

"I called him and asked him to meet me at the hospital."

"*You* called *him*?"

She gave a small nod. "I . . . I saw the accident. Like a . . . a vision. I saw you go off the road."

His reaction was more matter-of-fact than she might have expected. "Just like I saw the ceremony."

"What ceremony?"

He grimaced. "I saw two men in a room hung with black curtains, and one of them . . ." He stopped. "You don't want to hear about this."

"I think I have to." Her fingers clamped on his. "Jack, we're in this together. We're tied together by this thing. You understand that, don't you?"

"Yeah. I understand it." His grip tightened on hers. "I was just trying to skip the gory details. But, okay. One man was wearing black trousers and standing over another man, strapped naked to a table. The one in the trousers was torturing the one who was strapped down."

She felt her throat close, understanding why Jack had wanted to hold the information back. He gathered her to him, cupping the back of her head and pulling her face against his shoulder.

When a shudder went through her, he pulled her closer, then leaned back against the wall and took her with him.

She stayed in his arms for only a few moments. Then, struggling to show him that she wasn't going to go to pieces, she eased away and pressed her shoulders against the opposite wall. "Did you see his face?" she asked.

"Which one?"

"Either."

"The man with the black pants had his back to me. All I saw was a network of scars on his skin and a bald spot at the back of his blond hair. The man on the table was Gary Swinton."

. "Oh, my God! Swinton? You're sure?"

"I interviewed him a couple of days ago. He was hiding something, but I didn't know what. I went to talk to him again after you gave me that paper with the acid, but he'd left work. When I got to his apartment in D.C., it looked like he'd been packing—then gotten interrupted. There was blood in his suitcase."

"Oh, Lord!"

"What I'm thinking is that he helped Black Trousers capture your friend."

"Black Trousers?"

"That's what I'm calling the guy whose face I couldn't see. My guess now is that Swinton drugged her. Probably he got her used to doing drugs with him, so she wasn't worried about what was happening."

She sucked in a sharp breath.

"Swinton must have worked out some deal with the other guy to be paid for his services. Then it turned sour. Maybe Black Trousers was angry that I was investigating Swinton."

The thought of The Swine handing over Heather for money turned her stomach. "Unfortunately, that sounds like something he might do."

"It looks like he paid for it. I wouldn't want to bet he survived the session in that room."

She nodded tightly. "I should have called the police sooner. I mean, when Heather first disappeared."

"Jesus! Don't blame yourself! You had every reason to think she was just off somewhere having a good time."

She didn't want him to make excuses for her. "Maybe you would have found her."

"Probably not in time. This guy has been hiding his activities for months—maybe years." ·

Quickly, he stepped forward, reached for her, and she came back into his arms, relief flooding through her as he folded her close.

In some corner of her mind, she warned herself that this wasn't real, that maybe nothing between them was real. But reality had never been more achingly immediate.

His deep sigh matched hers as he pressed her to him. His hand swept down her back, encountered the edge of the T-shirt, and continued downward, stroking her bare bottom.

The passion she'd struggled to contain, flared. Terrible things had happened today. Too much to take in. She didn't want to think about the real world. She only wanted to be with this man—to take comfort from him and give him comfort in return.

"Jack?"

For a long, charged moment their gazes locked, and she saw the smoldering heat in his dark eyes.

17

HE lowered his head, brought his mouth down to hers, his lips moving urgently, potently in a passionate kiss that swamped her senses.

She had wanted this from the moment she had set eyes on Jack Thornton. Now she wanted so much more. Everything.

But she would take what she could get.

His fingers stroked up and down her arms, then found the sides of her breasts. She couldn't hold back a small sob of gratification and surrender. She heard wind roaring in her ears and understood that it was her blood rushing in her veins.

He raised his head, and her eyes snapped open.

"I think we need to find somewhere more comfortable than a marble bench," he muttered.

"Yes." Kathryn smiled at him. She had never been in this place before the first dream encounter. Hardly ventured beyond the boundaries of the painting. But she was confident as she took him by the hand and led him down the marble colonnade, stopping to grab a sprig of the fragrant vine that trailed from the horizontal beams above them.

She twined the stem around her wrist and Jack's, binding them together.

"Handcuffs?" he asked with a smile in his voice.

"Uh-huh. I'm not going to let you get away this time."

"Not a chance."

For now, she thought. *At least for now.*

Her heart squeezed, and her fingers tightened on his. He returned the pressure, and she wanted to pull him to a stop—make him promise that they could turn dreams into reality. But she kept moving—hurrying lest he come to what he considered his senses.

Halfway along the walk, she turned between the columns, leading him through a field of pale white flowers swaying gently in the shimmering moonlight, then up a small hill toward a round marble pavilion. They were both in a hurry now, taking the flight of three steps at a run and ducking under gauzy hangings into a rich, private enclosure—a bedroom fit for one of the Greek gods. A bedroom dominated by an opulent round bed covered with plum-colored silk.

"Clever of you to bring me here," he murmured.

She nodded wordlessly, unable to explain how she'd known this place would be waiting for them.

He turned her toward him. One of his strong hands tangled gently in her hair, playing with the strands as he angled her head so that he could ravage her mouth.

"God, I love your sweet mouth and your red hair. It's so wild and sexy, and thick," he said, teasing her lips with his as he spoke the words.

"And I love everything about you. Not just your body. All of you. The better I get to know you, the more I understand how extraordinary you are, Jack Thornton. You're a hero to me."

He grimaced. "I'm no hero. I'm full of very human flaws."

"Everyone has human flaws. You have fewer than most people."

When he opened his mouth to protest, she went on quickly, "I don't think we came to this nice bedroom to argue, did we?" She had never thought of herself as a bold lover. Now she slid her hand slowly, seductively down his body, stopping when she found his erection. Cupping her palm over the hard shaft, she rocked her hand against him.

"Ah, Kathryn, are you trying to drive me crazy?" he growled.

"I'm trying to . . . get what I've wanted since I first set eyes on you."

"Oh, yeah." ·

His eyes locked with hers, and for wild heartbeats she thought she might drown in the scorching intensity of his gaze.

Then he swept her into his arms and took her down to the horizontal surface of the bed, and she sighed out her triumph and her relief. This time . . . this time there would be no turning back.

She felt her body tune itself to the wordless vibrations rumbling deep within him. Vibrations that touched every part of her—physical and spiritual. And she knew he felt her response as he rolled to his side, clasping her against his heat and hardness as he devoured her mouth with kisses.

He tugged at the T-shirt, breaking the kiss only long enough to pull the garment over her head and toss it away, leaving her naked on the bed.

"Lord, you are so beautiful," he said, his voice husky, his hand tracing the curve of her hip, then drifting upward as he reached to circle her hardened nipple with his forefinger.

"Oh!"

He smiled, leaning forward to repeat the caress with his tongue. The sensations were exquisite, and even more exquisite when he sucked the nipple into his mouth.

She clasped his head in her hands, her breath coming broken and fast as he built her pleasure—with his hands, with his mouth.

She had thrilled to his kisses. Now she thrilled to his knowing touch. She had thought that when they made love, it would be sharp and fast—out of control. But the pace slowed to a long, sweet exchange of pleasure.

Together they took off his jeans and shirt, touching and kissing all the while. When she had him naked, she stroked her hands greedily over his body, loving the texture of his skin, the thatch of dark hair spread across his chest, his narrow hips, the jutting shaft of his penis.

He was beautiful and hard. Aroused—for her. And she gloried in his reaction. Whatever happened later, she would have this moment in time to remember.

His hand slid down her body, finding the moist, swollen flesh of her sex, and she arched into his caress, rocking against his fingers, increasing the wonderful sensations.

Her blood had turned molten, but her physical response was only part of what she felt. She was with him—soul and body—as they drove each other higher and then higher, until the urgency was beyond bearing, and she knew that she would die if she didn't feel him inside her.

"Jack, now. Please, now," she begged, reaching to clasp him, guiding him to her.

He entered her, and her breath caught.

For a long moment, he stared down at her, his eyes dark with passion. Then he began to move inside her, and she climaxed almost at once, calling out with the wonder of it.

Waves of pleasure took her, but it wasn't enough. Not nearly enough. Just a taste of paradise. Eagerly, she surged against him, with him, asking for more.

His hand moved between them, stroking and pressing as he kept up the rhythm—taking her up, up beyond the sun.

The second climax tore through her, carrying her away on a wave of ecstasy so intense that she dug her nails into his shoulders.

Her joy was complete when she heard his shout of release and felt him go rigid above her.

She clung to him, tears gathering at the backs of her eyes. Making love had been wonderful. Beyond anything she had ever experienced. Beyond anything she could have imagined. Now she could only anchor herself to him, vibrating with the aftershocks of pleasure that still quivered through her.

Clasping her to him, he rolled to his side. The physical storm had left her limp. The emotional storm was even more intense. There was so much that she wanted to say; but, for the moment, the words remained locked in her throat.

He held her, stroking his hand over her damp shoulder.

"That was incredible," she said, hearing the thickness in her voice.

She felt him nod, and knew that he still couldn't acknowledge the glory of it. So she simply cuddled against him, floating in the aftermath of exquisite pleasure.

She dozed. A dream within a dream. Peaceful at last after the past few days of tension.

Sometime later, her eyes drifted open.

Jack had drawn away from her and was lying with his hands behind his head, his gaze focused on the gauzy canopy above them.

"Jack?"

He turned his head toward her, and she saw that the barrier he'd let down a little while ago had snapped back into place.

Her disappointment was like a physical blow. But she was determined not to let him know how much he'd hurt her by closing himself off again.

Tangling her fingers in the sheet, she murmured, "Relax. It's only a dream. You don't have to feel guilty about making love with me."

He stared at her, trying to read the expression that she was struggling so hard to keep unreadable. "It's a dream. But it's more. We both know that."

She gave a small nod.

"A reality dream," he muttered. "An altered reality—that we're able to share."

"Okay. Yes."

"But the sixty-four-thousand-dollar question is—How did we get here?"

She didn't want to say what she was thinking, but she had told herself that she was going to be honest with him—whatever the cost. "I guess someone brought us here."

"Right. Like maybe Black Trousers. I mean the guy who was torturing Swinton."

She winced, wishing he hadn't brought that up *now*.

Jack got up, pulling on his jeans as he plowed on. "We have to find out who he is. He was . . . intoning . . . words I couldn't understand. It sounded like he was working a magic ceremony."

"To have some effect on us?"

"On me. To make me crash the damn car. Apparently it worked. I heard him, saw him; and I forgot where I was and what I was doing. Like now. We've both forgotten the real world, haven't we?"

She didn't quite understand the analogy, and quickly dipped her head so he couldn't see the hurt in her eyes.

"What are we supposed to do?" she whispered.

"I don't know! I don't like being manipulated."

She saw the frustration and anger bubbling inside him and said quickly, "We were brought here. But once we got here—we acted of our own free will."

"Did we?"

The two words were the cruelest he'd ever spoken to her. Still unable to speak above a whisper, she managed to say, "I don't know how we got here. But I know how I felt when I saw you. I was so happy to be with you. And I won't let you take away the joy of our making love." She swallowed. "Only the two of us were in bed together. Giving each other pleasure—showing each other how much we cared. At least that's how it was for me. I didn't feel like I was with a man operating under some outside influence. I was with a man who was totally focused on me—on making love."

She couldn't meet his gaze, didn't want to see the expression on his face.

Feeling very vulnerable and very naked, she climbed out of bed, pulling the sheet with her. There were low chests of drawers at one side of the enclosure. In one, she found a pair of silky white slacks and a matching top, which she quickly donned.

When she turned back to Jack, he was gripping one of the marble pillars.

"Did you see my children? Did they come to the hospital?" he asked.

His children. Of course he would want to know about Craig and Lily.

"Mrs. Anderson brought them." She looked down at her hands.

"What? Are they all right? What happened?"

Ashamed that she'd let her own emotions intrude, she said quickly, "They're fine. I was thinking that Mrs. Anderson wasn't too pleased to see me."

He nodded.

She was still looking at him when she caught a subtle vibration in the air. A wrinkle in the texture of the dream.

"You feel that?" he asked, his voice low and urgent.

"Yes," she answered. Then her eyes went wide as a shape loomed beyond the gauzy curtains that formed the walls of the pavilion near her. They parted, and a figure stepped into the room.

It was a man of medium build, medium height. The lower half of his body was clad in the black trousers Jack had described. His chest was bare, the pale skin covered by a network of scars. And his face was a horror mask, distorted by a stocking or something similar pulled over his head.

His right arm was bent across his chest, and she saw he was holding a silver knife. He moved the weapon in front of himself, swinging his gaze from her to Jack and back again.

"Get away from him," Jack shouted at her, but her feet were rooted to the spot.

The man shifted his weight from one foot to the other, then lunged at her, the knife flashing.

Finally released from her trance, she ducked away, grabbing a pillow and throwing it at the attacker's face as Jack charged forward. The man swung to the right, and Jack was too far away to stop the knife from slashing at her, slicing through the fabric of her gauzy shirt, cutting into her skin.

She screamed, screamed again as the weapon flailed toward her a second time.

Before the blade reached her, Jack caught the man by the shoulders and pulled him away from her.

The two of them rolled across the floor. With her foot, Kathryn reached out and stamped down on the arm with the knife, sending the weapon clattering across the marble floor.

Black Trousers cried out in pain. "You bitch."

Jack grabbed his hands, pulled them above his head. "What do you want with us?" he shouted. "Did you bring us here?"

Kathryn didn't expect an answer, but he gave a high-pitched laugh. "Me? Me? Don't you have a clue what's going on?"

"No. Enlighten us."

"Not a chance," he spat out.

And then the dream began to dissolve around her.

"No! Oh, God, no!" she screamed, unable to hear the sound of her own voice.

"No!"

One moment she and Jack were grappling with the invader. In the next, she was gone from the frantic scene—lying in bed, panting, crying out in terror and frustration.

In bed.

Not her own bed.

Where was she? Some new dream? Alone.

New panic seized her by the throat.

God, where was Jack? Was he all right?

She leaped from the bed, then remembered where she was. A motel room, where she'd gone after Black Trousers had tried to grab her.

Black Trousers. Oh, Lord! He was the man with the knife. Somehow he had gotten into the dream with them.

As the reality of his presence flooded through her, she felt pain slice across her midsection. Looking down, she saw a dark stain had soaked into the fabric of her T-shirt. She gasped, then rushed into the bathroom and turned on the light. Blinking in the brightness, she examined the stain.

It was blood. And when she pulled up the shirt, she found what she expected to see—a slash across her midsection.

Jack had scratched himself with a rock. But she'd never seen the injury. Now she had her own proof of what would happen if she was injured in one of what he'd called their reality dreams. She turned on the water, grabbed a washcloth, and washed away the blood. The wound wasn't deep, thank the Lord, since she had no way at the moment of treating it beyond cleaning it with soap and water.

She hurried through the first aid, then stared at her bloody T-shirt. It was the only thing she had to wear, but it looked like she'd been in a street fight.

Her stomach clenched. She couldn't stay here. She had to get to the hospital and make sure Jack was all right.

Quickly she reached for the underwear she'd washed the night before. It was still damp and clammy, and the feel of it made her cringe. With a grimace, she tossed it onto the edge of the tub, then pulled on her jeans and shirt again.

Was she going to keep this room? She didn't know. But she'd paid for it until eleven this morning. So she stuffed the key card in her purse as she headed for the door. Minutes later, she was driving up Rockville Pike toward the hospital.

The lights of an all-night drugstore shone from one of the shopping centers. After a quick debate, she pulled into a parking space and entered the store—speeding down the aisle toward the clothing section, where she snatched a black T-shirt and a package of underpants off the rack. The clerk didn't even glance at her bloody shirt when she paid for her purchase. Back in the car, in the darkness of the parking lot, she scrunched down below the dashboard, dragged on underwear, and changed her shirt.

Minutes later, she was pulling into the hospital parking lot. The doctor had told her where to find Jack. Acting like she had every right to be there, she marched through the emergency room, then took the elevator to the second floor.

18

AS the elevator started upward, Kathryn was torn between wanting the car to go faster and dreading what she'd find when she arrived on the second floor.

Nobody was at the nurse's station, so she went behind the counter and found Jack's chart—with his room number.

In the movies, they put guards outside of a cop's room when he was in danger. But this wasn't the movies. And nobody besides the two of them knew what had really happened to him.

Her heart was pounding as she stepped inside the private room and crossed rapidly to the bed. When she looked down at him, her chest tightened. She was still shocked by the sight of his bruised face and the sling strapping one arm to his chest. He was sleeping, an IV line attached to the other arm. Was he still in the dream? Was he in danger? Should she wake him? Or was that the wrong thing to do? Anxiously, she studied his face. He looked peaceful, but what did that prove?

She'd been cut, and a dart of fear stabbed at her. Pulling back the sheet, she raised his gown, examining his chest and stomach—looking for slash marks.

His good hand caught her wrist, scaring the spit out of her.

Her gasp of alarm was met by his curse. "Jesus! I thought it was him." Then, "What are you doing?" he demanded in a voice that sounded stronger than it had the day before.

Lifting her gaze to his face, she found he was staring at her—a mixture of emotions on his face. Relief. Surprise. Uncertainty.

Her own voice wasn't quite steady as she pulled his gown back into place and said, "I was looking for knife wounds."

"I'm fine." His gaze went to her midsection, and she noted that the swelling had gone down on the eye that had been closed the day before. "But I think *you* got cut. At least, I remember him slashing at you."

"Yes."

His expression turned stormy. "How bad was it?"

"Not bad, just a slash across my stomach. I washed the blood off."

"That bastard!"

A sound at the door made them both look up. It was a nurse, and Kathryn waited to be told she had to leave. But apparently the unit was pretty relaxed. The nurse only said, to Jack, "You're awake. Good. Let me check your pupils and your vital signs."

Kathryn stepped out of the way, waiting tensely while the woman went efficiently through her routine. She relaxed a bit when it looked like everything was okay. Finally, they were alone again, and she said, "Tell me what happened after I left."

"I was trying to get some information out of him. Then—there was a . . ." He trailed off. "I don't know what. Something else was there. Something I couldn't see. But I sensed it, like a huge storm cloud hovering over both of us. Some kind of . . . being." He stopped, swallowed, looked angry. "Black Trousers sensed it, too. I could tell he was scared. He . . . he disappeared and the dream disappeared, too. And I was back here."

She nodded. "The thing you described. It . . . it sounded like what I told you about—in that place where I can't breathe." She went very still, her mind taking another leap. "It's there every time I have one of the dreams. And this time you were aware of it, too. Do . . . do you think it could be what's dragging us in there?"

His face contorted. "We're talking about something you can't see except as a large, dark shape? If it's causing the dreams—and the other stuff we've been experiencing—how the hell do we fight it?"

"I don't know how—but we will."

He studied her closely. "Lord, you look so fierce. If you can fight this thing, so can I."

"You had the stuffing knocked out of you—I'm still on my feet."

"Okay, I'll accept that excuse."

"It's not an excuse!"

"Then let's get some work done. Can you describe the thing any better?" he asked.

She thought about it. "I can't describe it physically. I can't really see it. Like I said, it's got no shape. No features. But I feel like it's watching me. And it's spoken to me. Spoken in my mind."

"What else?"

"It lives in that place where I start the dreams, I think. Or maybe a place that's even less hospitable to humans—but the thing changed the conditions a little so I can be there, at least for a little while."

She saw he was listening intently, also saw that the short discussion was taking a lot out of him. Pressing her hand over his, she said, "We can talk about it later."

"No. This is important. We need to talk about it now. While it's fresh in our minds."

"Jack, I can see you're worn out. If you don't get some sleep, you won't be in shape to discuss anything."

He considered the advice, then gave a tight nod. "Maybe you're right."

"I'll stay here." She looked around, saw the bulky plastic easy chair in the corner. "I'll get some rest, too. And when you wake up, we'll talk again."

She could see he didn't like it, but she also saw that his energy was draining away.

Settling down in the chair, she watched him slip into sleep and knew he must have been making a tremendous effort to stay conscious. Her own energy level was pretty low.

As her eyes started to drift closed, a voice whispered in her head. The voice she had heard before. *Stay awake. You must stay awake.*

She sat up straighter, gripped the arms of the chair. It was the thing she had encountered in the dream—the thing they had just been talking about—speaking to her again. Only this was no dream. It was reality.

"Why?" she said aloud.

If you both sleep at the same time, he will find you.

There was no doubt in her mind about whom the voice was referring to. It was Black Trousers.

Somehow, he had found them together in their last dream. He could do it again.

She shuddered, pressed her spine against the chair back. There was no reason to believe a voice whispering in her head. Yet she believed.

"What does he want?" she asked.

To kill both of you.

"Why? What did we do to him?"

There was no answer. "Why?" she repeated. Then, "Are you trying to help us? Hurt us?"

Again, there was only silence. She could choose to dismiss the warning, but she elected to keep herself awake. So she sat in the chair, watching Jack, telling herself she must keep him safe.

Twice a nurse came in and roused him, checking his pupils and taking his vital signs. Each time, he went right back to sleep, and she was thankful for that. And thankful the nurses didn't ask her to leave.

Sleep tugged at her, and she dug her nails into the palms of her hands, then stood up and crossed to the small bathroom, where she splashed water on her face.

Around six, she was standing with her hips propped against the window ledge when Jack opened his eyes again.

He looked toward the chair, and the disappointment on his face gave her a small jolt of hope. Then he found her, and his features smoothed out again. So he felt something! But he wasn't going to tell her about it. At least that was how she decided to interpret his behavior.

"Did you sleep?" he asked.

"No."

"Yeah, sleeping in a chair isn't all that great."

"It's not that. It's . . ." She trailed off, then started again. "I might as well tell you straight out. The thing spoke to me again. Here."

His expression sharpened. "Oh, yeah? What did it say?"

"That if we both sleep at the same time, he can find us again."

"Oh, shit! You believe that?"

"Yes."

He swore again. "Crank up my bed, will you?" He looked around. "Better yet, help me get to the bathroom."

She eyed the IV line. "Is it all right for you to get out of bed?"

"It better be." He pushed himself up, swung his legs to the side of the bed, and she hurried to move the stand with the IV line so it wouldn't pull out of his arm. On his feet, he swayed slightly, and she reached to steady him.

He grimaced as he looked at the tubing. "I feel like an old guy in a nursing home."

"No, you feel like a guy who was in a car that rolled over," she corrected him, thinking he was probably uncomfortable with her helping him. Slowly, they crossed to the bathroom, her arm around him. After easing the IV stand inside, she closed the door and waited outside. The toilet flushed, then she heard water running. When he came out, his face was damp, and she assumed he'd splashed it with water—and probably also taken a drink.

They reversed the trip, and he sat down heavily on the side of the bed. "I could use some civilized clothing," he said, gesturing toward the hospital gown. "It's disconcerting to have a breeze blowing on your butt."

She laughed.

"Maybe I should call Mrs. Anderson. She can bring me some pajamas—and some clothing to wear home." He looked at the clock on the wall. "And I can talk to the kids before they go to school."

He lay back down, and she cranked up the head of the bed so that he was sitting comfortably. Then she moved the phone to the long table that swung across the bed.

After dialing the number, he leaned back and closed his eyes. "Emily," he said when the housekeeper answered.

Kathryn watched him, torn between drifting out of the room and listening to the conversation. When he didn't tell her to give him some privacy, she decided to stay.

"Yes, I'm much better," he said, then was silent, apparently listening to a long monologue.

"Kathryn and I have gotten close," he said, and she knew he must be responding to some complaint about the night before.

Close. That was a bland description of what she felt, but she had no right to argue the point—not when he had other people in his life to consider.

Again there was a lengthy comment that she couldn't hear. Instead of responding, he said, "Why don't you put Craig on?"

In a moment he was speaking to his son, his voice steady and reassuring, and she felt her heart squeeze.

When she volunteered at school, she got to see lots of kids—and lots of parents. So she knew Jack was a good father—as good as any child could hope for.

"Yes, I'm fine. Yes, I miss you, too," he was saying. "I'll be home as soon as I can. Craig, I love you. You don't have to worry about me, I'm fine. Well, my arm's in a sling, and my face is kind of bruised. But I'm going to be as good as new." After a bit more conversation with his son, he said, "Let me talk to Lily now."

He repeated what he'd said to Craig, reassuring his daughter in a warm, deep voice that made Kathryn feel good just listening to it.

Then he asked to speak to Mrs. A. again, and requested the pajamas he rarely wore and some trousers and a button-down shirt that he could wear home.

When he was finished with the phone call, he flopped back, his eyes closed.

"You're a great father," she murmured.

"I try my best. Sometimes I worry it's not good enough."

"Just from meeting them here, I can tell they're good kids."

"That's as much Emily's doing as mine."

"She was upset that I got to see you, and she didn't."

"Yeah."

She waited for him to tell her what the housekeeper had said. Instead, he asked, "How did you manage to see me, by the way?"

"Ross told them I was your fiancée."

"Oh." He looked down at his hands, and she wanted to assure him he could put an announcement in the paper saying it wasn't true.

It was almost a relief when he changed the subject. "You were telling me about the thing watching you. The thing with no body. No shape. What else do you know about it?"

He had come right back to where they'd left off.

"It's intelligent. Not like an animal. Not like a person. Not anything we can understand. It doesn't have senses in the way we think of them. It doesn't want to be here." As she struggled for some other way to describe the creature, another voice chimed in.

"It sounds like something that doesn't belong in this universe." The observation came from Ross, who was standing in the doorway.

"How long have you been eavesdropping?" Jack demanded.

"Long enough to know that you need some distance from the present subject. So why don't you tell me what happened when you went off the road?"

Jack sighed. "Okay, maybe you're right. But I'm counting on your not thinking I've plunged off the deep end."

"We've gone past that, don't you think?"

"Yeah," Jack answered, then told Ross about the ceremony that had captured his attention while he was driving.

When he finished, Ross looked thoughtful. "It seems like you're up against a guy who knows how to use magic to alter reality."

"You think that's possible?"

"You're telling me it is."

Jack sighed. "Yeah. I was working my way toward something like that."

"I don't know much about black magic. But from what you describe, it sounds like he sacrifices a victim as part of his ceremony."

Kathryn sucked in a sharp breath. "You think that's why . . . how he killed Heather."

"I'm afraid so."

"Heather and Swinton. And at least four other victims. There were five graves up at Sugarloaf," Jack muttered, then leaned back and closed his eyes. "Apparently Black Trousers has been practicing his craft for a while."

Kathryn studied his face and posture. He was looking exhausted again. "I think you need to sleep some more."

"I'm fine," he said automatically.

"We'll go get some breakfast," Ross said. "And you get some rest. Then we'll continue the conversation."

Before Jack could object, Ross gestured toward Kathryn. "Let's get some food."

She hesitated. She knew Jack needed to sleep, but all at once the idea of leaving him alone made her chest tighten.

She told herself she was being ridiculous. Nothing was going to happen while she and Ross were downstairs for a little while.

Still, her steps were slow as she exited the room. She wasn't sure she could eat, but she dutifully let Ross lead the way to the cafeteria.

"You don't look so great yourself," he said, as they stepped out of the elevator.

"I didn't get much sleep." She stopped, realizing that Ross didn't know what had happened after she'd gotten home. Quickly she filled him in on the man who had tried to block her car in the driveway. "I'm pretty sure it's the same guy I saw digging Heather's grave. The magician."

He whistled. "He's been busy. You can't go back to your house. At least alone. After breakfast, I can take you back there to get some clothing. Then you can stay in our spare room."

"I can't."

"Why not?"

She swallowed. "God, I keep forgetting that I've lived a thousand lifetimes since I saw you last night. After I checked into that motel, I went to bed—and Jack and I met in a dream again. This time, the magician showed up. He attacked both of us with a knife."

"Jesus!" Ross exclaimed.

"The bad part is that if we get hurt in one of those reality dreams, the injury is real. He gave me a slash across the stomach. It's not bad," she added quickly. "But I was pulled out of the dream before Jack. That's why I rushed here so early—to make sure he was all right."

Ross nodded.

"Then when I sat down in the chair beside Jack's bed, the . . . the thing we were talking about when you came in spoke to me. It said that if Jack and I slept at the same time, the magician would find us again. So I have to stay near Jack—so we can figure out whose turn it is to sleep." She grimaced. Then asked the next logical question. "What does the otherworldly creature have to do with the magician?"

"I don't know. But we'll find out."

He sounded so sure that Kathryn felt some of the hopeless feeling lift.

"The two of you need to come to our house—so Megan and I can torture you to keep you awake." He laughed. "Actually, if you come home with me, Joshua may not let either one of you sleep."

"Joshua is your little boy?"

"Yes. He's seven months old."

She smiled at him. "You sound like you have such a normal life. I can't get over how you accept all these nutball explanations without acting like I'm crazy. I tell you a creature from another universe talked to me while I was in Jack's hospital room, and you don't even blink."

They had reached the entrance to the cafeteria. Over to one side was a small walled courtyard filled with tables. It was probably more appealing in the noontime sun, so none of the tables was occupied at the moment.

"Let's go outside for a minute," Ross said, holding the door open.

When the door had closed behind them, he turned to face her, his gaze appraising. "Well, the reason I don't have any trouble accepting your wild story is that I've got my own wild story." She saw him shift his weight from one foot to the other, watching her.

"You don't have to tell me anything you don't want to," she said quickly. "It's enough that I know you're on our side."

"What did Jack say about me?"

"That you could find Heather—if anybody could. That you'd be able to find the body I saw him bury. He didn't say it in so many words, but I know he trusts you implicitly." She swallowed. "And I gather from what he said that you have . . . something in your background that you'd rather not talk about."

"Yeah. That's right." He scuffed his foot against the concrete.

"Ross, I don't need to know what it is."

He sucked in a breath and let it out. "Under the circumstances, I think you do. The reason I'm good at sniffing out graves is that I'm a werewolf."

Kathryn stared at him, wondering if she'd heard him correctly. But the tight expression on his face told her that he'd just given up a deeply hidden secret. Still, she heard herself saying, "You're not making that up?"

"Sometimes I wish I were. It can be a difficult burden. So maybe you want to reconsider my invitation to come home with me."

She shook her head, still trying to wrap her mind around his admission. Probably she should be more shocked. But she knew she'd been prepared to hear something extraordinary about Ross—prepared by the aura of the man and by what Jack had hinted at.

But more than that, she'd changed over the past few days. When she'd first met Jack in that painting, she'd literally stepped out of the ordinary world and into a universe where anything was possible. "You've been a good friend to me. I thought from the first that you were someone I could trust," she said.

"So you can deal with a friend who's a werewolf?" he pressed.

She saw the tension in his face and reached to clasp his hand. It was a large hand but, aside from that, totally ordinary. She didn't allow herself to imagine it as anything else—a wolf's paw, for example. "You've shown me what you're like. And I know that Jack trusts you with his life."

"Thank you."

She couldn't hold back a small laugh. "Jack said you'd be good at investigating the grave up at Sugarloaf. I guess I understand why. You've . . . uh . . . probably got a sense of smell that's way beyond anything . . ." She had started to say a sense of smell that was way beyond human capacities, but realized at the last moment how that would sound.

He breathed out a small sigh. "Yeah."

"Thank you for telling me. I'm sure you don't broadcast the information."

"No. But I wanted you to understand why I'm open to strange scenarios. Jack came to me, worried about what was happening. I listened and told him that anything is possible." He reached for the door. "Come on, you need to eat something."

Allowing him to change the subject, she followed him back into the cafeteria. When she would have settled for picking up a cup of coffee in the cafeteria line, he ordered her bacon, eggs, and toast, then made sure she ate some of the breakfast.

"Heather's circle pin. How did you get it?" she asked after she'd chewed a bite of toast.

"Before I picked up Mrs. Anderson and the children I stopped at your house and found the key under a rock near the door." He lowered his voice. "I know Jack was planning something similar—to keep you out of his report. So I went ahead and did it for him." He gave her a direct look. "He's a good cop. He's never done anything like that before."

She nodded, then tried to eat a little more of her eggs. But the longer they sat there, the more anxious she got. She'd thought it was all right to leave Jack; now she was regretting that decision.

"I have to go back upstairs," she finally said.

"Okay. I'll meet you in Jack's room."

They both left the cafeteria. Ross stepped into the men's room, and she hurried to the elevator, then waited impatiently for it to reach the first floor. Back on the neurological floor, she practically ran down the hall. Ahead of her, a man in a white coat was checking the numbers on the doors. He looked like he was one of the hospital staffers, a doctor or an orderly. Or a male nurse.

She couldn't see his face, but from a distance, he looked vaguely familiar. He was brown haired, about medium height and medium weight. Had she seen him when she was in the emergency room last night?

The man stopped in front of Jack's room. Stiffly, he reached for the door handle and walked inside.

She felt her breath catch. Then she was running toward the room.

19

JACK was dozing when he heard someone running down the hall, then come bursting into his hospital room.

He saw two things simultaneously. Kathryn pelting into the room, her breath coming in jagged gasps, a look of terror on her face—and a brown-haired man in a white coat and black slacks standing calmly beside his bed.

He took it all in with one swift glance. With one hand, the man was reaching for the IV line attached to Jack's arm. In the other he held a hypodermic.

The man's serene expression changed in response to Kathryn's noisy entry.

"No," she screamed.

Instinctively, Jack lurched up in the bed, lunging at the intruder, knocking the hypodermic into the air—and sending a jolt of pain through his recently dislocated shoulder.

The hypodermic flew up in an arc, drops of liquid flying into the air.

Striking that one blow used up all his reserve of strength. He put up his arm as the man came toward him. But it was like trying to stop a tidal wave with a paper boat. The man flung him back onto the bed, and he gasped as the violent landing jolted his shoulder again.

He saw Kathryn dart to the bedside, pick up a water pitcher, and fling it at the intruder, scoring a direct hit on his forehead.

The man howled in pain, cursing as he lunged around the bed and shot toward her.

Without many options, Jack pressed the call button, hoping that for once, the nurse would arrive and take the guy's attention away from Kathryn.

He watched her jump backward with the agility of a gymnast. She pulled on the wheeled table that extended over the bed, putting it between them, then savagely pushing it forward.

It struck the intruder in the midsection, and he howled again, then pushed the table out of the way before turning and leaping for the door.

Before he could make a clean escape, he crashed into a nurse coming into the room.

Flinging her out of the way, he dodged past as she fell to the floor, screaming.

Kathryn was trying to get out the door and follow the guy, but the nurse grabbed her and hung on.

"Let me go! He tried to kill Jack. We have to get him," she gasped.

But it was already too late.

She freed herself and made it into the hallway, but came back moments later with her shoulders sagging. She was followed by Ross.

"What happened?" the P.I. demanded.

"Someone was here," she gasped out. "He tried to kill Jack."

"Which way did he go?"

"I don't know."

"Probably the stairs."

The nurse had recovered her composure and was leaning over Jack. Grabbing his wrist, she started to take his pulse. He couldn't hold back a sharp laugh. When in doubt, fall back on basic medical procedures.

Kathryn came up behind the nurse. "Is he all right?" she demanded, her voice urgent.

"As far as I can tell. I'll call Dr. Samenow."

"We need to test that hypodermic and find out what's in it," Jack said.

"Yes." Kathryn moved to the far side of the bed and started to stoop down.

Fear leaped through him. "Don't," he shouted.

When her head swung toward him, he said in a calmer voice, "We don't know what's in that thing. I don't want you anywhere near it."

He looked at the nurse. "Get some gloves to pick it up, and bring a box to put it into. Something where the needle can't stick through."

"A container for biohazards?"

"Yes. I don't want anyone getting a dose of poison on my account."

Wide-eyed, the nurse scurried off.

Kathryn leaned toward him as he held out his good arm toward her. Well, "good" was a relative term. It wasn't the arm in a sling. But it was still tangled up with the IV line. He wanted to pull the damn thing out, but he didn't want to cause any more damage. So he left it in place as he folded her into his embrace.

He was overwhelmed by her courage. Overwhelmed that she'd put her own life on the line for him.

But he would have done the same for her. And that knowledge, too, was overwhelming.

He couldn't tell her what he was feeling. He could only hold her tightly. For long moments, neither of them moved—or spoke.

Finally, he said, "It looks like you saved my life."

She kept her face buried against his neck. "Lord, what if I hadn't come back in time?"

He swallowed with some difficulty. "You did."

She turned her face so she could press her lips to his unshaven cheek, and he turned his head so that his lips met hers.

The kiss wasn't passionate. It was more an acknowledgment of words he couldn't speak.

A throat-clearing noise from the doorway made Kathryn look up. Emily Anderson was staring at them as though they'd just been photographed nude in bed together. Neither one of them was nude, and he was the only one in bed—although he wouldn't want to get up in front of her, with his butt hanging out of his hospital gown.

Kathryn stepped away from him, turning to confront Emily.

The housekeeper gave them a long look before making a *tsking* noise. "I . . . I'm sorry if I interrupted something," she said, sounding like she was actually glad that she'd arrived in the nick of time to prevent Kathryn from climbing into bed with him. "You asked me to bring you some clothing." She held up a small bag.

"Someone . . . someone just tried to kill Jack," Kathryn said. "I . . . I'm grateful that he's all right."

Jack saw Emily's expression change as she tried to work her way through the statement. "Oh, my," she said, dropping the bag onto the tile floor.

Jack gave her a direct look. "Kathryn risked her life to save mine."

"Oh!" His housekeeper's gaze swiveled from him to Kathryn and back again.

Jack sighed. "Emily, you're an important part of my family. I'm sorry that I haven't had a chance to talk to you about Kathryn, but a lot has been happening quickly. I was investigating a missing person case. It's turned into a serial murder case. One of the victims is Kathryn's tenant. That's how we met." He paused, considering what to say next. "We've been working together, and we've . . . realized that we care about each other."

As he watched his housekeeper absorb that information, he continued, "It looks like the murderer tracked me down here. And she chased him off a few minutes ago."

He saw Kathryn staring at him, probably wondering what he meant by "care about each other." He wasn't sure he knew the definition himself, but he did know that denial was becoming more and more difficult.

At that moment, the nurse walked back into the room, carrying a plastic box. A doctor was right behind her, presumably Dr. Samenow. Behind him was Ross. It was suddenly very crowded in the small room.

His hand covered by a surgical glove, the doctor bent down and carefully picked up the hypodermic. Just as he'd set it in the plastic box, a uniformed police officer walked into the room. It was Carl Boswell, and Jack gave silent thanks that he'd worked with the guy before and they'd gotten along well.

"I'm responding to a call about a murder attempt on the patient in room 231," he said. His eyes widened when he saw Jack. "You're the intended victim?"

"Yeah. It's a long story. I was working on a kidnapping case that's turned into a serial murder." He repeated what he'd told Emily. "At least, it will be when somebody digs up the graveyard at Sugarloaf Mountain. I was on my way back from there when the murderer tried a little vehicular homicide."

"He caused your accident?" Boswell asked, obviously struggling to assimilate new information.

"Yeah. I'll get back to that in a minute. Right now, the important point is that the murderer tracked me down here and decided to make a second attempt to get me off his back. At least I, have to assume it was him."

He was aware that everybody in the room was staring at him.

Kathryn and Ross were both waiting quietly for his story. He wasn't going to talk about magic ceremonies. But he wasn't going to let the connection go, either. Putting the experience in terms anybody could understand, he said, "Last night, he ran me off the road near Damascus." As he uttered the statement, he silently told himself that in a way it was true.

He also noted that Ross was struggling to hold back a grin at the way he'd put it. Lord, was he doing it again—twisting facts to suit his purposes? But he couldn't think of any other way to connect the two incidents.

At the same time, he was thanking God that there hadn't been any other cars in sight when the accident had happened. So there was nobody to dispute his version of events.

"His car hit yours?" Boswell asked.

"No, he edged me over to the side. I was trying to stay on the pavement, but I lost control of the vehicle when the road took a sharp turn."

Boswell wrote that down, along with a few more imaginary details. When he'd finished, Jack went on to what had happened after he'd opened his eyes and found the guy standing over him, ready to inject something into the IV line. He raised his head toward the doctor, who still held the hypodermic ensconced in its plastic box. "You can turn that over to Officer Boswell. The sooner he gets that stuff to the police lab, the sooner we'll know what it is."

Samenow looked reluctant, but he handed over the evidence.

"Did you tell the officer who arrived on the scene of the first attempt?" Boswell asked.

"I wasn't thinking too straight right after the accident. I had a concussion, and the details eluded me. Dr. Samenow can confirm my medical condition last night. After I was admitted, some of it came back to me."

"What kind of car was he driving?"

"A 1985 Ford Crown Victoria," Jack answered, naming the car driven by the guy who had called himself William Strong.

Kathryn gasped. "You . . . you think it's the same person as the old man who drove by my house?"

"Yeah, I do," he answered, the conclusion taking on more weight as he continued to speak. "I think he alters his appearance, which is one reason we haven't caught him yet."

He saw her vision had turned inward. "You have something to add?"

She swallowed. "I'm pretty sure I saw him in my neighborhood before Heather disappeared. He . . . he was dressed like a workman. He had a white van, but there was no name on the side. I think he must have a closet full of disguises."

Jack gave her his full attention. "What else have you been processing while I was lying here in bed?"

"Nothing," she said in a thin voice, and he was sure she wasn't telling the truth. Well, there was plenty of stuff *he* didn't want to talk about in front of the people crowded into his hospital room. She probably felt the same way.

"We both saw him a few minutes ago, although he was doubtless in some sort of disguise, probably a wig and a mustache."

Kathryn nodded tightly.

Jack turned back to the doctor. "I'd like to get out of here."

"If you're well enough to leave," Kathryn jumped into the discussion.

"I'd better be. Because it's obvious I'm not safe when someone can walk in wearing a white coat and try to inject something into my IV line." He gave her a direct look. "And you aren't safe, either."

He saw her complexion go a shade paler, felt his own blood run cold as several terrifying thoughts struck him. This guy not only knew a lot about both of them—but he also had means beyond normal human capacity. He'd slashed Kathryn in a dream, and she had the mark to prove it. And there was no doubt he'd caused the accident on the road—even if he hadn't physically been there.

Jack swung toward Ross, ready to beg an urgent favor. But he stopped short as he looked around the crowded room.

"I need to speak to Ross alone. It's important. But first I hope we can get this thing out of my arm," he said, gesturing toward the IV line.

Kathryn turned and walked out the door. He knew she was hurt, knew she was wondering why he didn't trust her. But he couldn't talk about his motives now.

The rest of the crowd followed Kathryn out, except Ross and Dr. Samenow, who walked to the side of the bed and detached the IV drip before removing the needle from his arm.

"How long do I have to wear this sling?" Jack asked.

"Three weeks."

"Shit! That's just what I need."

"You can remove the sling to take a shower, if you hold your arm in that position," Samenow offered.

"Yeah, thanks. That's something. But it's not going to help my accuracy with a gun," he said, thinking that if he was going to be facing Black Trousers with his right arm tied to his chest, he'd better get some practice on his left-handed shooting skills.

"I want to check your eyes and your reflexes," the doctor said, "before I sign you out."

Jack sighed. He'd conveniently forgotten why they'd kept him in the hospital overnight. Not because of his arm—but because he'd suffered a concussion.

Samenow glanced at Ross, then went through a routine examination.

"I can clear you to leave," he said.

"Good."

"And I'll write you a prescription for pain medication." He scribbled on a prescription form and left the slip of paper on the bedside table.

After the doctor had departed, Ross closed the door. "What do you need?" he asked.

"Kathryn and I have to disappear until this guy is caught. I've already asked a lot of you, but could you go with Emily and get my kids out of school? Then . . ."

"Then they can stay at my place," he said quickly. "After I pick them up, we'll stop by your house and get some clothing. And I'll make damn sure nobody is following us."

Jack let out the breath he'd been holding. There was nobody he trusted more than Ross Marshall to keep his children safe, but he understood that having houseguests wasn't easy for a man who prowled the woods at night as a wolf. "Are you sure we won't be cramping your style?" he asked.

"No," his friend answered, his tone unequivocal.

"There's the supernatural angle," Jack said, wanting to make sure he touched all the bases. "That's how he got to me on the road. That's how he got into our dream."

"I'm better equipped to handle the supernatural element than most."

"Yeah. Right. I can't thank you enough for this. I owe you one."

"It will be a long time before we even that score," Ross answered. "Do you need some cash?"

Jack thought about that. "I can raid an ATM on the way out of town."

"Do you know where you're going?"

"I'd rather not decide yet. And I think it's better if you don't know. The fewer links my kids have to that guy, the better."

"Right."

"I'll think of some way to thank you," Jack said again. Then, "Could you ask Kathryn to come in here?"

"Will do."

Kathryn walked slowly into the room, her head lowered. "I was starting to think you might trust me. I guess I was wrong," she said.

"I trust you."

"But you wanted me out of the room when you talked to Ross."

"I needed everybody out. I didn't want to waste time making selections."

"Okay."

"I asked him if he'd take Emily to pick up the kids at school. I want as few people as possible to know where they are. Not even the cops."

Her expression turned contrite as she took several steps toward him, then stopped. "Oh, Jack. I'm sorry. I thought . . ."

He cut her off ruthlessly, because he'd dealt with as many emotions as he could handle this morning. "You and I have to get out of here, too."

"Where are we going?"

"Let's hold off talking about it."

She nodded tightly.

"So, could you help me get dressed?"

"Yes."

He kept his directions brisk. "Take the sling off, so I can get my shirt on."

"Is it all right to take it off?"

"Not for long. The doc said I could take a shower, if I kept the arm across my chest. But I'll wait on that. I want to get us out of here." He stopped, and gave her a direct look. "You asked if I trusted you. It goes both ways. We need each other to get Black Trousers off our backs. And his friend," Jack added, his eyes seeking hers.

He could see from her pinched features that she knew what he meant. The being she'd tried to describe.

"YES," Kathryn murmured, tacitly agreeing. They needed each other at the moment. But he wasn't making any plans for the future. Well, they were together now. With a killer and an otherworldly being after them. She was scared, yet at the same time, she felt as if she'd been handed a chance to be with Jack—in the real world.

She struggled to keep her expression neutral as she carefully worked his sleeve up his arm. She could see that moving his shoulder hurt, but he was struggling not to show the pain. At the nurse's station, they reclaimed his property, then got his Sig from a safe downstairs. He stuffed the shoulder holster into the bag that his housekeeper had brought, then tucked the gun into his belt—on the right side—and pulled his shirt over it.

"Can you shoot left-handed?" she asked.

"I need some practice. Can you shoot at all?"

She laughed. "Grandma believed in self-protection, so she dragged me to a target range every few months."

"Good for her!"

When they reached the car, he said, "I'd like to get out of town right away, but I need to stop by police headquarters. I want to check out a laptop computer, so I can get into the databases I use."

She unlocked the door, then waited while he cursed as he buckled the seat belt.

"Make sure nobody's following us," he said as they pulled out of the hospital parking lot.

She looked in the rearview mirror, then looked again as she pulled out into traffic. As far as she could see, no car was sticking behind them.

"Nobody I can see, unless he's using a magic spell to track us," she murmured.

"Let's hope to hell not."

SIMON was still seething with anger. Things weren't working out the way he'd been sure they would. The cop hadn't died when he'd driven off the road.

But he was right there in the hospital—hurt and helpless. With his closet full of disguises and fake ID's, it had seemed like an easy matter to finish Thornton off. And he'd been so close to breaking the demon's unholy alliance. Then the woman had come charging into the room, stopping him from injecting the insulin into the IV line. It wasn't a poison; it had legitimate medical purposes, which was the beauty of it. The authorities could think that someone had made a mistake. Except that Miss Bitch, Kathryn Reynolds, had come in and fucked up his plan. He'd sprinted for the stairs and gotten out of the building. Then some dark-haired dude had come charging after him, but he'd escaped and driven home, wanting to speed but staying under the limit.

Jesus! That had been close. He'd thought he'd had the perfect solution. Now . . .

Well, he wasn't exactly back to square one. He was aware of Kathryn and the cop even now. The demon had established a connection among the three of them—a connection that went more than one way. Simon had used it to find them in that sexual fantasy of a dream last night. They'd had sex. And they'd dropped their guard. He smiled as he remembered the expression on their faces when he'd joined them in their wet dream. And he would do it again, the next time they both slept. Meanwhile, they were in his mind, like a background buzz. They were both awake, so he couldn't go to them now. But he was working on it.

He thought about Sugarloaf Mountain, and anger flared again. He'd had a bad feeling about the place since he'd buried Heather DeYoung's body. He wouldn't go back—ever again. But there was still the matter of Gary Swinton. Well, there were plenty of other places besides Sugar-loaf. He'd used some before. He'd get rid of Swinton's body somewhere else tonight. Most of his body.

KATHRYN turned right, toward police headquarters.

Ten minutes later, Jack directed her to a parking space in the detectives' lot, saying, "It would be better if I had the unmarked."

"Do you want me to wait for you?"

His answer was sharp and instantaneous. "Not out here! Come up to the waiting area. I'll be as quick as I can."

She could see his energy was seeping away, see that he was in pain. He left her on a bench in a wide hallway and was back in twenty minutes, carrying a black case that she presumed held the computer. He still looked like he should be in bed—which was where she was going to put him as soon as they got where they were going.

Before they could make their escape, the door he'd come through opened again, and Captain Granger stepped into the hallway.

"Where are you going with that computer?" he asked.

Jack turned to face him. "I need it for research."

"But you're on medical leave."

"That doesn't mean I'm going to stop looking for the serial killer."

"I've assigned Dave Culligan to the case."

Jack leaned back against the wall and took several quick breaths. She wanted to turn and scream at Captain Granger to leave him alone. But she managed to keep silent.

"Good," Jack said. "But I want to do some research on my own. I've been in direct contact with the perp. Culligan hasn't. You should be getting a report from Carl Boswell. The guy who told you his name was

William Strong came into my hospital room this morning and tried to eliminate me. There are several witnesses. The lab will give you a report on the stuff he tried to inject into my IV line. And, FYI, he was the cause of last night's accident."

"Did you put that into the accident report?"

"Like I told Boswell, I was concussed last night. My brain's functioning better now. The perp has found me twice. Once on the road and once in the hospital. Apparently he's been stalking Kathryn, too. So we're going to disappear for a while. Maybe when you dig up those bodies, you'll get some clues to his identity. If I hear you've arrested him, I'll get back into contact with you."

"How will you hear?"

"On the evening news. In the newspaper."

"I can't just have one of my detectives disappear."

She saw Jack's mouth tighten. "If I don't—if we don't—he'll get us. Because it looks like he's made this personal. You want to be responsible for our deaths?"

20

KATHRYN watched Captain Granger shift from one foot to the other as he pondered how to respond. "I can put a twenty-four-hour guard on you," he finally said.

"In this case, that's not going to work," Jack answered.

"Why not?"

Jack looked like he wished he'd kept his mouth shut. He shrugged. "Okay, if you want to know, it's because this guy is psychic," he said, punching out the answer. "And he's using his powers to fight us."

The captain goggled at him. "You got hit on the head last night. Did the doctor discharge you, or did you leave against medical advice?"

Kathryn's gaze swung between the two men.

"My brain is working fine. I'm not delusional," Jack growled. "The guy used his psychic powers to find me on the road last night. He didn't follow me. He just came out of nowhere."

"More like you didn't know he was on your tail," Granger countered.

Jack didn't bother to argue. Instead, in a quiet voice, he said, "When you catch up with him, you'll find that he's using the victims he murders as a part of magic ceremonies."

"Jesus!"

Jack sighed. "I guess I can't blame you for thinking I've gone off the deep end."

Kathryn had held her tongue because this was between Jack and his boss. Now she couldn't stop herself from jumping into the conversation. "If he's gone off the deep end, so have I. Because we've both experienced the same weird phenomena since this guy came after us."

Granger pivoted toward her, looking her up and down. "Oh, yeah? Such as what?"

"Such as sharing the same dreams," Jack answered. "And when we wake up, we've exchanged verifiable information. Stuff we couldn't have known before we discussed it in the dream."

Granger looked like he'd swallowed a bottle of vinegar. "You expect me to believe that?"

"No," Jack answered. "Because I think he's messing with your mind, too."

Granger's face darkened. "You'd better explain that."

"Okay. You remember that *I* wanted to compare the various missing person cases and see if I could find any link between them. The way I remember it, *you* asked *me* to drop the Westborn suicide investigation and look into the missing person cases."

"You're still on that kick?"

"Yes. I was busy with my own stuff. I didn't even know we had that many missing person cases until you brought them to my attention. Until you pulled the files and gave them to me. What would be my motive for launching an investigation? You know I'm not a glory hound. I'm just a working stiff detective who already had enough on his plate."

Kathryn took in shallow breaths as she watched the captain consider that. Instead of responding directly to Jack, he said, "You signed out the computer?"

"Yeah."

"Then take it. And get out of here before I change my mind about your sanity."

Jack followed his advice. Pushing away from the wall, he picked up the black case and headed for the exit.

Neither Kathryn nor Jack spoke until they were back in the car.

"What if he comes out here and asks what the guy's motive was for getting into his mind?" she asked as she started the engine.

"I guess he hasn't gotten that far yet. Good thing, because then we'd have to tell him it wasn't the killer—it was the being from the other universe who did that!"

It struck them both funny, and they started chuckling. She sat with her hands gripping the wheel, laughing hysterically.

Jack stopped first.

"I suppose you're going to tell me it only hurts when you laugh," she said.

That set them off again. Jack leaned his head back. "Actually, it does hurt," he finally said between puffs of breath.

She immediately turned serious again. "You need something for the pain."

"I need to keep my head clear."

"Do you have a prescription?"

"Yeah."

"Let's fill it, then go pick up some of my clothes, if you're planning for the two of us to get out of Dodge."

"That's what I'm planning. But I wasn't including a stop at your house."

She swung her head toward him. "We have to stop there."

"Why? You can pick up what you need at a cheap department store."

She didn't want to answer the question out loud. Just hearing the words in her own head made her chest constrict. But she felt like she had no choice. "I need my magic wand," she said in a low voice, watching his eyes narrow.

"You're kidding, right?"

"Unfortunately, no."

"You need it for—what? Casting spells?"

"Are we back to thinking I'm a witch?" she asked, hearing her voice go high and thin.

"You said it—not me."

She dragged in a breath. "I said it because I knew it would be a serious mistake to leave it behind. I don't know why I need the damn thing. I just do. I'm sorry, but I have the terrible feeling that if I leave it at home, we're both going to be sorry."

She watched him consider that. Lifting one hand off the wheel, she pressed it over his. "This is like your discussion with Granger," she said. "We're talking about something that can only be taken on faith."

He sighed. "Okay. You can get the damn thing. I just hope Black Trousers isn't waiting at your house—the way he was last night."

"You want to skip it?"

"No!" He sounded angry. Probably he was in pain. As she drove away, he closed his eyes.

She was torn. She hadn't been home since her frantic drive across the grass. But she knew with gut-tightening certainty that the wand was important.

So she drove home, casting frequent glances at Jack, seeing the tension in his jaw. The jaw relaxed, and he looked like he could be sleeping, but his eyes blinked open when the car slowed. Sitting up, he looked around.

"Drive around the block," he said, "I want to check out the neighborhood."

"Okay." She followed directions, her eyes scanning the streets, the houses, the cars, looking for one of the vehicles she remembered. The strangely angular car, the old Ford, or the white van. None of them was on the street. Everything looked peaceful and normal. But she had learned that looks could be deceiving.

The last time she'd been in the driveway, she'd almost been killed—or kidnapped. The thought of being trapped made her throat close. After a quick glance at Jack, she pulled to a stop at the curb and cut the engine.

He opened his door and stepped out, swayed slightly, and reached to steady himself against the car.

She was almost to the door when something lying on the porch caught her eye. At first, all she saw was a ring. The ostentatious gold ring with the round diamond that Gary Swinton always wore on his right hand. She'd asked him about it once, and he'd told her with considerable pride that he'd won it in a poker game.

She'd never seen it off his hand. Now it was wrapped around something pale and white that lay slightly curled on the porch like a bleached slug. She stared at it, trying to comprehend what she was seeing. At first her brain refused to take it in. When she finally did, she let out a high, bloodcurdling scream and backed away, bumping into the wall of the house and lurching to a stop.

Jack was instantly at her side, his gun in his left hand as he turned in a circle, checking the area for invaders.

When he saw nothing, he came back to her. "What is it? What's wrong?"

She pointed to the porch floor.

"Jesus!" Stooping, he examined the object—which she had recognized as a human finger—circled by the gaudy ring.

She tried to speak, heard her voice crack, and tried again. "That's Swinton's ring. I . . . I guess . . . that he must be . . ." She couldn't say it.

"You're sure it's his?" Jack asked, his eyes fixed on the grisly object.

She pressed back against the wall. "Yes. He was really proud of it. He always wore it."

"Okay. This should help Granger focus his mind on the case."

Jack ushered her inside, away from the porch. When she started up the stairs, he called out, "Wait! I want to check the apartment first."

"Okay." She eyed the gun in one hand and the other arm strapped to his chest. "I guess I'd better unlock the door for you."

"Details!"

They made their way up the stairs, where she opened the door, then stood back with her heart pounding while he entered the apartment and checked out the interior. The door had been locked—but that didn't prove Black Trousers wasn't inside.

Her breath was fast and shallow as she waited for him to deliver his verdict.

"All clear," he said when he returned.

She felt like a great weight had been lifted off her shoulders as he tucked his gun back into his waistband. "You've got ten minutes to grab what you need. Then we're out of here."

While she hurried into the bedroom, he pulled out his cell phone and began punching in numbers. She could hear him saying that he and Kathryn Reynolds had found a human finger wearing a ring belonging to Gary Swinton outside her house, then asking for a crime scene team.

The unnerving conversation continued in the background while she threw shirts, pants, and underwear into a small bag, then grabbed the magic wand off her desk. She was going to shove it right in with the other things, but the feel of the hard rod in her hand stopped her. It was only a plastic toy, but it felt almost alive in her grasp.

Jack had finished his phone call, and was watching her. "You sure you don't work spells with that thing?"

She flushed. "Not so far."

"But you're planning to."

"I don't know *what* I'm planning," she insisted, her voice coming out more strident than she'd intended. "I just know that this thing is important. Remember, I told you I saw it as a guidepost when I was in that . . . that place . . . where we think the creature lives."

"Speaking of which—I notice he hasn't put in an appearance lately."

"Actually, in the hospital, he told me I shouldn't sleep at the same time you do."

"Why not?"

"He said if we do, the magician will find us."

Jack grimaced. "You're sure it was him? And not the magician trying to trick us?"

She slumped against the wall. "No! I'm not sure of anything. We could assume it was my imagination," she offered, even though she was pretty sure that wasn't the case.

"I guess I'm beyond that point," he replied, his voice gritty. "It was one of them. I'd just like to know which one."

She studied him, hardly able to believe the conversation.

"You mean you've gone from a true doubter to a true believer?"

"Christ, if I could walk away from this mess, I would. But it feels like I don't have any choice. Neither of us does!"

She swallowed. "I guess not."

"So tell me—where's the fantasy creature now?"

"I don't know. Sometimes he goes away."

"You keep track?"

"I've started thinking about it. I guess he was the one who . . ." She stopped, sucked in air. "Who stopped time so you could escape from that dog."

He gave a tight nod.

"But he wasn't here when the old man came by my house and lit into us," she said without making any reference to what had actually happened on that occasion.

"I guess not."

She felt a strange tingling on her skin, like small electric prickles. At the same time a thought popped into her head. "You said Ross lent you a bunch of books. Maybe . . . maybe we should ask him for some more. Maybe we'll find something . . . that will explain this."

She could see he was considering the suggestion. "Yeah. We need to understand what's going on. And like Ross said, we don't seem to be getting very far by ourselves." His brow wrinkled. "When we went up to Sugarloaf, I asked him to meet me at the Park and Ride on this side of Frederick. . . ."

A sound outside made them both start. Jack drew his gun and moved to the window, staying next to the wall as he looked out.

When she saw him put the weapon away, she let out the breath she'd been holding.

"It's the cops. Unless the perp has a patrol car," he added. Then, "No, I recognize the officer. It's Dick Hamilton."

Several long moments passed before the officer came up the stairs. After he and Jack greeted each other, he said, "I saw the finger. Nice calling card."

"For a serial killer. You know that the guy is after me and Ms. Reynolds?" Jack asked.

Hamilton nodded. "Yeah, it's gotten around the department pretty fast."

"Okay. That's why we don't want to stick around. Can I leave this crime scene to you? It's just the porch. He hasn't been in here. The door was locked, and there were no signs that anything had been disturbed. Captain Granger said Dave Culligan has been assigned to the case—since I'm officially out on sick leave. So you'll want to inform him."

"You've got it. I'll secure the scene."

"Thanks."

Hamilton started for the door.

"We'll be right with you," Jack said. When the officer had left, he used her phone to call Ross. The P.I. had already arrived home with Mrs. Anderson and the kids, which was obviously a relief to Jack. They arranged to meet at the Park and Ride in about an hour.

Kathryn locked the front door behind them, thinking that Black Trousers could probably get inside if he wanted to.

Hurrying across the porch, she studiously directed her gaze away from the . . . ring.

After sliding behind the wheel, she waited while Jack spent several more minutes talking to the officer. By the time he climbed back into the passenger seat, she saw that his skin was flushed.

"You need to rest," she murmured.

She expected him to offer a macho protest, but he only gave a tight nod.

"Are we going to pick up clothing at your house?"

"No, we're getting out of town. Where's the closest ATM?"

"The shopping center a couple of blocks away."

When she pulled up near the machine, he got some money, then started to protest when she did the same.

"Consider this enforced vacation a Dutch treat," she told him. "I'm from the generation where the women pay their own way."

"The Montgomery County P.D. should be treating us," he growled.

"Maybe we can collect later. Right now, where to?"

"A cheap department store—Target, maybe."

"Can you tell me where we're heading after we meet Ross?"

"I've been thinking about that. Somewhere near Harper's Ferry or maybe Shepherdstown. Somewhere rural—but where we can get back to the city pretty easily."

"Do you care which?"

"Take your pick. Just check the rearview mirror—to make sure we've made a clean getaway."

In a few minutes she looked over, and was glad to see that he was dozing. She wanted to get him into a bed, where he could get some real sleep. But she settled for his nodding off in the car while she drove. It looked like they'd made a clean getaway, yet she kept having the feeling they were being followed. Every few minutes, she glanced in the rearview mirror, watching for a car she recognized or a car that stuck with them. When she saw nothing, she ordered herself to relax. By the time she pulled into a shopping plaza about twenty minutes later, she had damped down her fears, but they were glimmering below the surface—small internal prickles like the little electric shocks she'd felt on her skin earlier.

SIMON was calmer now, in complete control. Anger had no real purpose in his life. It only got in the way of effective action.

He had made a mistake going to the hospital. He'd pictured the detective alone and helpless. Too bad that hadn't been the case.

But no harm done. He had learned an important lesson. Overconfidence was dangerous. He must stay calm and steady. Then he would get what he wanted.

He sat in his favorite chair, sipping a glass of Jekel Vineyards chardonnay. Usually one long-stemmed crystal wineglass was his limit. This afternoon he'd allowed himself two, in celebration. He would defeat the demon soon. He knew it. The creature was weakening, expending too much energy fighting him. Soon it would exhaust its resources, and he would bend it to his will.

Meanwhile, he had to deal with Kathryn and Thornton. He closed his eyes, projecting his mind outward, searching for them. It was getting easier now, easier with every passing hour.

They were in a car. In a parking lot. At least that's what he thought he' saw. He couldn't be absolutely sure. Not until they dreamed together. Then he would come for them again.

KATHRYN was aware of the moment when Jack's eyes snapped open, and he looked around. "Where are we?"

"The Target in Sykesville."

"As good as any place." He reached for the door handle.

"You just got out of the hospital. Tell me what sizes to buy, and I'll pick up some basic clothing for you."

She saw him hesitate, torn between machismo and fatigue. Fatigue won.

"Okay. Get stuff that's easy to get in and out of. Sweatpants would be good." As he spoke, he dug his wallet out of his pocket.

She wanted to refuse the money, but she'd told him they were going Dutch. So she went inside with a list of items and headed for the men's department. If the circumstances had been different, she would have enjoyed the shopping expedition. It was a pleasure to pick out shirts that she knew would look good on him. She couldn't stop herself from savoring the intimacy of buying items like underwear, shaving cream, and disposable razors. Picturing him in tight, white briefs gave her a sexual jolt. Immediately she told herself to cool it. They weren't going on their honeymoon; they were hiding out from a serial killer. And, as she'd pointed out to him, he was just out of the hospital. He needed rest, not sex.

Before leaving, she made a quick pass through the grocery department, where she stocked up on canned soup, cheese, salsa, corn chips, nuts, pretzels, peanut butter, and jelly. Bread. Mayonnaise, tuna fish. And a selection of drinks—from instant coffee and tea bags to sodas. For fun, she threw in some candy bars and cookies.

In less than half an hour, she was back at the car—stopping short as she saw Jack slumped in the front seat. He looked so vulnerable that she felt her heart squeeze.

She tried to tell herself they had escaped from Black Trousers. But had they? He'd reached out and found them in a dream. What would stop him from finding them again?

Jack sat up with a start when she slipped back into the driver's seat, then blinked. "Finished already?"

"And ready to meet Ross."

"You know the Park and Ride?"

"Yes."

The assurance was all he needed to let himself doze off again. He didn't wake until they pulled into the parking area.

Ross was waiting for them. A large cardboard box sat on the hood of his SUV. He hoisted it up and brought it to the car, where he stowed it in the trunk alongside their clothing.

"The kids are okay?" Jack asked.

"Yes." But he didn't look entirely sure.

"What's wrong?" Jack asked anxiously.

"Nothing. Lily wants to play down by the creek. I told her she has to stay inside."

"Yeah, she's been a handful lately."

"We'll try some tempting indoor activities."

"Tell her I said for her to mind you."

"Will do."

Jack looked torn.

"We could stop and see them before we leave," Kathryn offered.

"No. That's too dangerous," Jack answered immediately. "I don't want them anywhere near us until the bastard is in custody."

She gave a tight nod, knowing how hard this was for him.

Minutes later, they were on the road again.

While he slept beside her, she headed toward Harper's Ferry, then on the spur of the moment veered off to Charles Town, West Virginia.

"Where do you want to stay?" she asked Jack when she saw his eyes had blinked open again.

"A motel on a secondary road. Nothing fancy. The best would be a place with individual cabins—where half the units are empty."

She laughed. "I'll try."

She came close to his requirement about twenty miles outside of town, in a rural, wooded area. A faded sign advertised cabins, and she pulled up a short, rutted driveway to a rustic office.

"I'm kind of conspicuous with this arm in a sling."

"Then I'll register."

"As whom?"

She'd been going to use her real name. Now she stopped and reconsidered.

"As Mr. and Mrs. James Taylor?"

He laughed. "That will do."

Leaving him in the car, she stepped into the office. A heavy woman wearing black stretch pants and a pink sweater with multiple pulls in the weave said they could rent a very nice cabin with a kitchen unit. The price was so low that Kathryn expected to see cockroaches scurrying across the floor. But the one-room cabin was clean and neat, with a charming old quilt covering the double bed, and a small kitchen area where she stowed the groceries.

The place had a warm, country appeal, and she liked the way she and Jack fit into the picture. She looked up to see him setting his bag down near a battered old dresser, and was struck with a mixture of emotions.

She'd dared to daydream about going off with him to a cabin in the woods—just the two of them. In her imagination, she'd made it a sexy little adventure. She'd gotten her wish—with a twist. They were here to fight for their lives. Against Black Trousers. And . . . something else, a being from another world who was somehow tangled up with the magician.

Jack looked up and found her watching him. "Your turn to sleep."

"I . . ."

"Don't argue. I've been sleeping off and on half the day. I'll get you up in a few hours. While you're sleeping, I'll do a little light reading. And eat some of this nice nourishing food you've thoughtfully provided."

"You like my taste in junk food?"

"It's perfect."

He crossed to the kitchen, opened the freezer compartment at the top of the refrigerator, dropped ice cubes into a glass, then added Dr. Pepper. After carrying the drink and a bag of onion and sour cream chips to a table in the corner, he settled into the Morris-style easy chair and started sorting through the box of books Ross had brought.

Kathryn wanted to cross the room, lean over the chair, and wrap her arms around him. Instead, she closed the curtains across the windows, used the bathroom, then pulled off her jeans and crawled into the double bed, wearing just her T-shirt and panties.

She knew Jack was watching her, and she liked that, liked the fact that her legs were long and sleek below the T-shirt.

The lamp behind his chair cast a warm pool of light. She watched him pretend he hadn't been very aware of her, watched him settle back and open the bag of chips. Then reach for a book.

He looked up, saw her regarding him, and smiled. "Sleep."

"I like watching you."

"An old broken-down cop?"

"Stop fishing for compliments. You're not old. And you're not broken-down."

He gestured toward the white sling. "I wouldn't be much good in hand-to-hand combat."

"If you came over here, I'd show you how wrong you are."

"Oh, yeah?"

"Yeah."

A grin flickered on his lips, and she thought for a moment that he might actually come to her. Instead, he said, "Grab some sleep while you have the chance."

She wanted to ask what could happen later. But she tucked that thought away and snuggled down under the sheet and quilt.

When she closed her eyes again, exhaustion took over. She'd been operating on nerves for hours, and letting go was suddenly a luxury. Quickly she left the world behind and slipped into oblivion.

JACK watched her, wanting to join her in the bed and strip the T-shirt off her. Sure! One-handed would be a little awkward. Resolutely he turned back to the pile of books. There were so many volumes. What should he read?

As he shuffled through them, one felt hot when his fingers touched the cover.

He blinked, pulled his hand away, then gingerly touched the cracked and faded blue leather again. It felt like a stove burner. Only it looked perfectly normal.

The title was *Portal to Another Universe*. By Jonathan Zacarias, written in 1787. With clumsy fingers, he flipped through the pages. They fell open in his lap to page 28, and he stared down at the old print, his pulse starting to pound.

FOR a short time, rejuvenating slumber cradled Kathryn.

Then she awoke. Well, not awoke, literally. She was *there* again—in that place of dim light and unbreathable air. The place of fear. The place where a huge, dark presence hovered over her like low, storm clouds bringing the fury of a tempest.

"No," she gasped, struggling to pull herself back to the world. But the land and the being held her captive as surely as if she'd stepped into a steel trap.

Relief flooded through her when she saw the magic wand. Eagerly, she staggered toward the beacon shining in the gloom. But this time when she reached it, there was no sense of relief.

She was on a grassy hill. Under a blue sky. But still her lungs burned.

Then suddenly ropes captured her hands, pulled her backward, bound her to the plastic post that till now had been a symbol of safety.

She saw that faggots of wood were piled around her. And as she watched in terror, flames sprang up, leaping at her, reaching for her flesh.

A tongue of fire licked at her, and she screamed at the burning pain. "No! Please stop! Why are you doing this to me?"

You ran away.

"No."

Go back where you came from.

"No. We can't. He'll find us."

You think he won't find you here? He wants to enslave me! You must stop him.

The fire receded, and images came to her then—hazy, ghostly. Like at Sugarloaf Mountain. Only now she was seeing the chamber Jack had described. A ceremonial chamber, hung with black. But it wasn't Swinton tied down on the table in the specteral scene. She gasped when she saw it was Heather—unconscious. Wearing a white dress slit down the middle to bare her breasts.

Black Trousers stood over her, chanting, a knife in one hand, his other hand . . .

She gagged. His other hand was on his erect penis, stroking in time to the words he was chanting.

In a corner of the room, the dark presence hovered. And then interspersed with the scene was another—herself and Jack that first time, he in Roman military garb. She in a sheer white gown.

They were kissing, touching, totally absorbed in each other. And all at once she knew that the scene had flashed into Black Trousers's mind, making the downward stroke of his knife falter.

He climaxed then, his seed spewing onto the table—even as he cried out in rage. And she understood the ceremony had failed.

Then the flames leaped around her once more. And she screamed in pain and terror, screamed again, then struggled against the force clamping her in place.

21

"KATHRYN! Kathryn!"

"No! Don't! Please don't! Oh, God, please stop," she gasped, trying to wrench away from the force that held her.

"Kathryn, it's just a dream. You're all right. You're with me. With Jack."

Finally, the words penetrated the horror and the terror. Her lids blinked open, and she found herself staring up into his worried eyes. It was his hand on her shoulder, holding her down.

As soon as he saw that she recognized him, he eased up the pressure. She blinked, her eyes filling with tears, and she clutched at his shoulders. When he grimaced, she realized she must be hurting him, and relaxed her grasp. "I'm sorry," she whispered. "I didn't mean to hurt you."

"I'm okay. What happened? One minute you looked like you were sleeping peacefully. Then you were flailing around, moaning. It was another one of the dreams, wasn't it? Another one by yourself," he said between gritted teeth.

She nodded, her mind spinning back to the dream. There were so many things she needed to say.

"A magic ceremony," she gasped out. "I saw a magic ceremony. Like you did when you were driving. Only it wasn't Swinton strapped down to the table. It was Heather. It was like up at Sugarloaf. I could see them. But they were ghostly." A sob escaped her lips as she recalled that picture.

Jack reached for her, folded her close. "I'm so sorry."

She nodded against his shoulder, wanting to wipe the terrifying image from her mind, yet knowing that it was important. All of the dream was important.

"You don't have to tell me any more."

"Yes, I do. I have to tell you the rest. It's the key to what's been happening, I think. It wasn't just the ceremony. And I saw us, too."

"Us? In his clutches? He's going to get us?"

"Oh, Lord, I hope not. No. That's not what I mean. I saw us . . . from that first dream in the painting. Remember, you stopped kissing me because you thought something was happening?"

"Yes."

"Well, I think I know what it was. I . . . I . . . think the magician saw us while we were there. And seeing us messed up the ceremony for him." She knew she was babbling, knew she must barely be making sense, but she couldn't stop. "But that wasn't all of the dream. He was punishing me. That's how I know. . . ."

Jack interrupted her, his voice urgent. "Who was punishing you? Black Trousers? Or was it the demon?"

Her eyes widened. "What demon? What are you talking about?"

"The creature. That's what it is. Well, not one of Satan's minions, if that's what you mean by a demon. It's what you've been telling me—a being from another universe."

She gasped. "How . . . how do you know? I thought I was alone in the dream. Except for that thing."

He turned and gestured toward a book that lay splayed open on the floor. "While you were dreaming, I was reading about it in *A Portal to Another Universe*, by Jonathan Zacarias. One of the books from Ross. I was shuffling through them, trying to decide what to read, and that one felt like a hot brick."

She sucked in a sharp breath before telling him the rest of it. "Hot. Right. I was hot, too. In the dream. I was tied up at a stake—burning. And the stake was the magic wand."

"Jesus! That bastard!"

Fearfully, she held up her hand, inspecting the flesh. It was whole, unburned. "At least it didn't carry over into the real world this time. I guess he just wanted to give me a warning."

"A warning about what?" Jack asked, his voice grim.

"He . . ." She stopped, readjusted her thinking. "The demon thing was angry. He told me to go back home. He wants us to save him from Black Trousers."

She waited for Jack to make some objection.

Instead, he looked toward the book he'd dropped on the floor.

"Yeah. I was reading about it."

"You were?"

"It's hard to make sense of the text. The writing is pretty convoluted. But it was talking about a magician trying to enslave a demon with a magic ceremony."

She took a gulping breath as the pieces of the puzzle fell into place in her mind. "I think it's what I told you. I saw him *doing* the ceremony. Black Trousers. He had Heather strapped down on a table. He was going to kill her, and at the same time he was . . ." She stopped, gulped again. "He was masturbating."

"Jesus!" Jack said again, making no attempt to hide his revulsion.

"But we stopped him. He saw us, and he lost his train of thought. So maybe that's what's going on. The demon brought us into it. And now he wants us to go back and stop Black Trousers again."

"Okay, after reading the book, I can buy that. But why us?" He gestured in frustration with his good hand. "Why is he giving us all this information *now*? And why the hell doesn't he just give us the guy's name, so I can arrest him?"

She shared his frustration. "Maybe he's finally telling us stuff he didn't want to reveal because he's gotten desperate. And . . . maybe there's a magic spell that keeps him from telling us Black Trousers's name."

"That's just great." Jack muttered. "The problem is, we're screwed either way. If we don't stop Black Trousers, the demon keeps torturing you."

"Not just me. Us," she corrected.

"Yeah, well, right now it looks like you're taking the brunt of it. But that's nothing compared to what happens if Black Trousers does get it right. If he succeeds with his damn ceremony, we don't want to be anywhere around."

Kathryn took in the ominous tone of his voice. "What happens?"

He gestured in anger toward the book. "Jonathan Zacarias wrote *Portal to Another Universe* as a warning. His friend succeeded in the ceremony, but the demon wasn't willing to let himself be enslaved. You've heard of the Nemes explosion when they thought a big chunk of southern France was incinerated by a meteor. Well, that was the demon avoiding capture. And there's no reason to assume this one won't take the same route. Which means the explosion is going to be like a nuclear weapon landing on Rockville."

Kathryn gasped. "That's what you read in the book?"

"As near as I can figure it out—yes."

"You've got to call Granger."

"And tell him what—that a demon is going to blow up Rockville? He'll put us in the loony bin for sure, and then we *won't* be able to do a damn thing."

She looked around the warm, cozy room, feeling trapped. "What are we going to do?"

He ran his good hand through his hair. "I wish to hell I knew."

The anger in his voice made her raise her head. "Jack, I'm so sorry."

"For what?"

"I got us into this."

He smoothed her damp hair back from her face. "How do you figure that?"

"I reported Heather missing. Then you came to my house. That's how all this started."

His jaw muscles tightened. "You had to make the report. It was the right thing to do."

She breathed out a small sigh. "But look at the consequences."

"You mean, I got to meet you?" he said, his voice low and husky.

She felt her heart stop, then start up again in double time. Somehow, she managed to say, "You made it pretty clear you wished you hadn't."

"That was when I was freaked out by the . . . bond forming between us. It was too fast. I couldn't deal with it."

"The bond, yes," she said softly. "Are you saying you can deal with it now?"

"Not completely. I don't like knowing that outside forces are operating on me—on us. But there are compensations. I've found out what kind of woman you are."

"What kind?"

He grinned. "Are you fishing for compliments?"

"Maybe I need some."

"You're the bravest woman I've ever met."

"How?"

"What you go through every time you step into one of those dreams would have driven a lot of people crazy. And then there was the way you threw yourself at Black Trousers in my hospital room."

"I had to!"

"Why?"

"You were in danger. And, Jack, I care very much what happens to you."

"Kathryn." His hand stroked gently down her cheek. She turned her head so that her lips brushed his fingers. He went very still. Watching him intently, she opened her mouth, using her teeth, then her tongue, to play with his flesh.

Desire flared between them——desire and something so much more profound that her breath caught. "Jack, please. I don't want to think about magicians and demons and terrible explosions right now," she whispered.

"Neither do I."

"Oh, Jack." She clasped her arms around him and found his lips with hers.

When the kiss broke, he said her name, his voice thick with emotion. Yet in the next moment, she heard him make a rough noise.

"Oh, Lord, Jack, is your arm hurting?" she asked, abashed that she'd been thinking about making love when he had just gotten out of the hospital that morning.

"It's not that. I was sitting across the room, watching you sleep, thinking about how much I wanted to make love with you. But I can't help comparing myself to how I was in the dream—when I didn't have my damn arm strapped to my chest. I'm afraid I'm not going to be much good to you, sweetheart."

She gave him a slow smile. "If that's your only problem, then lie back and relax, and we'll see if we can work something out."

His gaze locked with hers, he did as she asked, easing to his back, giving her control of the situation. Feeling powerful and alive, she bent over him—kissing his mouth, his cheek, his hair, gentle kisses that were as full of warmth as they were filled with desire.

She ached to tell him she'd fallen in love with him. But she kept the words locked inside her, trying instead to show him how she felt.

Carefully she reached down to unbutton his shirt, spreading the fabric apart so she could slide her hand over his chest, under the sling, playing with the thick hair covering his warm skin, and finding his nipples with her fingers.

Each time she touched those dark nubs, he sucked in a quick breath, and she grew more confident in her power to please him.

When she moved away from him, he made a sharp sound of protest, but she only smiled at him as she pulled her shirt over her head and tossed it onto the floor. Nerves stopped her for a few seconds. Ignoring them, she reached around to do the same with her bra.

His heated gaze made her nipples harden as if he'd touched them.

"Sweetheart, you are so sexy. So beautiful."

She felt beautiful. She felt like a sex goddess. Holding his gaze, she reared up on her knees and skimmed her panties down her legs.

Naked, she bent over him, sweeping her breasts back and forth across the part of his chest that she could reach and the fingers trapped in his sling.

"Kathryn, dear Lord," he gasped out, then gasped again as her hand slid down his body to find the rigid shaft of flesh behind the fly of his jeans.

He arched into her touch, and she heard his breath catch as she rocked her hand against his erection.

She had never held a man more firmly in her power, and she took complete advantage of him, slowly lowering his zipper.

She gave him a lazy, provocative smile as she reached inside his pants, her touch going from light to firm and back again, her whole being caught up in the excitement of giving him pleasure. She had never been so bold with a man, never felt her own excitement grow as she teased and aroused and pushed him toward the edge.

"Kathryn, please," he moaned.

Quickly she skimmed his jeans and his briefs down his body, and he helped her kick them away. He was still wearing his shirt, but she wasn't going to take the time to get rid of it.

She had much better things to do, she decided, as she lowered her head to his erection, caressing him with her face, then using her lips and tongue and finally taking him fully into her mouth.

He made low, incoherent sounds as he used his good hand to play with the silky flesh of her bottom, then reached between her legs to find her most sensitive flesh, stroking and caressing and turning her molten while she indulged her appetite for him.

"Kathryn, stop. I want to be inside you when I come," he grated.

"God, yes."

Raising her head, she looked into his smoldering eyes, her gaze locked with his as she straddled him, using her hands for balance as she lowered her body onto his.

He cried out—half curse, half thanks—as she brought him inside of her.

Going very still, she stayed where she was, her eyes drifting closed, as she focused on the wonderful feeling of his penis filling her so completely.

"Look at me," he demanded, his voice husky.

She opened her lids to see that his eyes had darkened with passion. He gave her a slow smile as he took a visual tour of her body, starting with her face and slowly moving downward.

She might have felt vulnerable and exposed. But his words were too warm for that. "Lord, what a beautiful view," he whispered.

"Of you, too. You are so beautifully made. So masculine."

Slowly she began to move, building her own pleasure and his. With his good hand, he reached up to caress first one breast and then the other, his touch inciting her to quicken the pace.

His eyes held hers as she climbed the high peaks, knowing he was taking the journey with her.

She felt his body go rigid below her, heard his shout of pleasure. Then she was driving for her own climax, her movements frantic now until release seized her. Her whole body seemed to vibrate in a series of strong contractions that shook her to her very core, then left her limp and panting.

She would have collapsed on top of him, but she remembered his injured shoulder and shifted to his left side, sliding down onto the bed beside him.

His arm came up to clasp her close. Her eyes drifted closed, and she dozed, warm and relaxed in the aftermath of passion.

SIMON sat in his easy chair, reading more on astral projection. But his mind was only half on the book. He was open, alert, waiting for the opportunity he knew would come. This morning he'd felt the need for action. Now he knew he only had to wait for the next time the redheaded bitch and the cop dreamed together.

The minutes ticked by as he crouched like a spider in the center of its web, waiting for a hapless insect to come along.

Finally, it happened. The delicate strands of the web sent out a vibration. His body jerked, and he knew the time had come. They were both sleeping. Their guard was down.

His face contorted. They'd been having sex again. He could feel that, too, feel the satiety and the lazy relaxation of their minds and bodies. And feel their vulnerability.

They had fled Montgomery County. He had felt them moving farther from him—in distance. But they could never get far enough away.

They were his.

He closed his eyes, watching them. They were in a rustic-looking room. Snuggled together in a pine bed covered with a much-washed quilt.

They thought they were safe. Let them dream on—for a few more minutes—until he got there. This time he sensed that they were sleeping in the dream world, too. He could sneak up on them, plunge his knife into the woman, and be gone before the cop could do anything about it. And then the triangle would be broken—and he would be free to go after the demon.

Quickly he left the library and hurried down to the ceremonial chamber, ready to say the spell that would bring him into their dream.

JACK stirred. He had been lying snug and warm, his arms around Kathryn. Both arms, which meant this must be a dream, because in some corner of his mind he remembered that he'd been in an automobile accident, and his right arm was in a sling.

But when he reached for her, she wasn't there.

He heard her scream—a bloodcurdling sound that he felt from the roots of his hair to his toes.

He was out of bed in an instant. Not the bed in the cabin. The bed in the Greek pavilion where they'd first made love.

He dashed outside, looking wildly around—seeing a wall of flame shoot up to his right. And through the flames, he could see Kathryn, tied to a stake, the fire licking at her white skin, searing her flesh even as he watched.

"No," he cried out, running at full speed toward her, determined to snatch her from the inferno. Before he reached her, the dream dissolved around him, and he shouted out again in renewed panic.

Then his eyes blinked open, and he found himself in the bed again. Kathryn was lying beside him, tears leaking from her eyes.

"Oh, God, sweetheart, sweetheart," he crooned, holding her against himself as best he could, cursing the damn injury that kept him from pulling her fully into his arms.

He felt her trying to rein in her tears and finally bring herself under control.

"It's okay," she finally murmured.

"What do you mean, okay? How the hell is that okay? You were in the middle of a fire—tied to a stake."

She gulped in air. "It saved us. Black Trousers was coming, like he did the last time we dreamed together, and the thing woke us up in time."

Jack stared down at her. "You saw him?"

"I felt him. At the end, I felt him. He had to wake one of us. He seems to pick on me."

Jack let loose with a string of curses. "And he's getting more violent. What the hell does he want from us?"

"You know what he wants! We have to find Black Trousers. Because either he's going to get us—or the demon is going to push us beyond what we can take."

"Yeah. Great." Jack heaved himself up and reached for the jeans that had ended up draped over the foot of the bed.

Kathryn pulled on the T-shirt and panties she'd been wearing. She was covered up before he'd finished struggling into his jeans.

"Find Black Trousers. Sure," he spat out as he paced back and forth across the cabin. "He's been killing people for months, maybe years, and nobody's found him. He's a clever bastard. He makes sure his victims don't fit any particular pattern. He uses a bunch of disguises. He has different cars and vans. Which probably means he has plenty of money." He stopped, and dragged his good hand through his hair. "And I can't protect you from him. I can't protect my family. I had to leave them with Ross Marshall."

She crossed to him, took him in her arms.

"Do you know how it makes me feel that I can't protect you?" he asked.

"Yes."

"How do you know?"

"You said you'd discovered what kind of woman I am. I always knew what kind of man you are. Steady. Responsible. Strong. And beating himself up for not cracking this case. Jack, you're the one who figured out he's a serial murderer."

"With your help."

"Okay, then. We make a good team. So let's get to work."

Easing away from him, she walked to the kitchen, where she began opening bags of snack foods. Willing her hands to steadiness, she poured pretzels, cookies, corn chips, and salsa into bowls she found in the cabinets.

By the time she'd carried it all to the table, she was feeling more grounded. "Something to drink?"

"Dr. Pepper. It's perfect for this place."

She poured the drinks while he brought his laptop computer to the table.

"Come sit over here, so you can look at the screen with me."

"What are we going to do?"

"See if two brilliant minds can come up with his picture."

"But he's always been disguised."

"Let's see if we can work around that."

She pulled over a chair, drawing close to Jack. He turned and kissed her ear, and she snuggled closer. "I like working with you, Detective," she said.

"But I'd better keep my mind on business." He brought up a program that let victims of crimes build a picture of the perpetrator. Pulling the computer close to his body, he typed with his left hand and used the fingers protruding from his sling to press the shift and control keys.

"Want me to type?" she asked.

"I can do it."

"Okay. Then I'll be right back."

Probably, he thought, she was going to the bathroom. Instead, she opened her overnight bag and got out the magic wand. Jack watched her carry it back to her chair, then turn it slowly in her hand as they began to work.

"You think that will help?"

"It can't hurt."

He turned back to the computer, starting with a general face shape.

"Long but not too narrow," she said, pointing with the wand to one that looked right.

They progressed from that to hair—dark and long.

She and Jack both had excellent visual memories—she because of her art background, he because he'd trained himself to observe people. And they had no trouble building a picture of the man who'd come to the hospital room.

As his face emerged, Kathryn felt goose bumps raise themselves on her arms. They were finally getting somewhere! Doing something constructive.

Unless he'd worn contacts, he had gray eyes. Narrow lips. An average sort of nose. Slightly hollow cheeks. A face that looked smooth— except for a big mustache.

"Take the mustache off," she murmured. "It doesn't look right."

Jack followed directions.

"That's him," she whispered.

Jack didn't seem so certain.

"What?" she asked.

"The hair is wrong," he mused. "It was long and dark in the hospital. But remember, I saw him doing that ceremony in the privacy of his own torture chamber. He's got short blond hair." With a few keystrokes, he changed the hair. "Yeah. That's better."

Jack copied the face into another file, then added other details—

coming up with the old man who had stopped to ask directions, then reported them to the police department.

Again, Kathryn felt spooked. "He changes his looks, but when you've got the eyes and mouth, you can see it's the same guy."

Jack nodded and saved the files. "You want to go on and do the workman you saw around your neighborhood? The man in coveralls?"

"I don't think we have to bother. He looked like a cross between the young image and the older one."

"Okay. Then bring me the phone," he instructed.

Kathryn watched him unhook the instrument, then plug the computer into the connection.

"A modem?"

"Yes." He wrote Granger a memo, explaining that these were two composite pictures of the guy who had tried to murder him—one as he usually looked and one in his old man persona.

Almost as soon as he'd sent them, he was surprised to receive a reply, thanking him for the pictures and adding, "The lab identified the drug from the hospital as insulin. In sufficient quantity, it would be lethal. We're not sure how much he was intending to inject into your IV line because some of it spilled on the floor."

After returning the captain's thanks, Jack rocked back in his chair. "Sounds like he's joined the team."

Kathryn seesawed the wand in her hand. "Want to tell him about the demon?"

Jack laughed. "Sure! Just when he's acting like we're not insane. Let's see if we can feed him some more information." He switched to a web site with various makes and models of automobiles.

"We already know he's got a Crown Victoria."

"How did you know that?"

"I'm a cop. I know cars. So let's figure out the one you saw at Sugarloaf and across your driveway. What was the shape?"

"Angular. With a strange kind of projection at the rear window. Something unusual."

"Speaking of the rear—how many taillights? Three—or just two?"

She answered quickly. "Three."

"Then it's a newer model—after the upper taillight law came into effect."

He brought up another web page with premium models, and they began paging through the pictures.

*   *   *

SIMON clenched and unclenched his fists. He had missed his chance to kill the woman while she was in the dream. The demon had woken her up. With fire.

He'd felt the heat. Heard her gasps of pain. That was something, anyway. The demon didn't mind hurting her. The damn thing was getting desperate. Driving Reynolds and Thornton to the limit. Maybe the creature would make a mistake and kill them.

Simon chuckled. That would be a nice irony. The demon was flailing around in its death gasp—and it didn't care whom it hurt. Even the man and woman it had chosen to save its miserable hide.

He felt a tug on his consciousness, and the focus of his thoughts quickly changed.

For a moment, a picture of his own face floated in his mind. Not a photograph. A drawing—that looked like it could have come from a computer.

Reynolds and Thornton had worked up his image. And not just one drawing—two. Himself as he looked now. And himself as the old man.

As he stared at the two images in his mind's eye—so real, so accurate—he felt his heart blocking his windpipe.

He'd been careful with his disguises. But he'd made a mistake at the hospital. He'd figured nobody was going to identify him. So he'd only relied on the mustache and the wig.

Christ! They'd nailed him.

The walls of the library seemed to close in around him, and he took several breaths, then crossed to the window and flung it open.

He stood staring out at the woods in back of his house. He'd thought he had time to plan his attack.

And now he was going to have to move fast. Very fast. Not just with magic ceremonies. With modern technology.

22

HE sat for a long time, sending his thoughts toward the man and woman in the small, rustic bedroom.

A cabin in the woods. About an hour away, he guessed.

He smiled, thinking that the connection was growing stronger— thanks to the demon. The creature had thought it was so clever, sending their image to screw up his concentration the night he'd used Heather DeYoung in the ceremony.

But it worked both ways. He could watch them easily now. They had finished with the composite drawing. And they were looking at pictures of cars.

He cursed again. They had looked at the Ford the old man had driven. They had the make and model.

He gritted his teeth, ordering himself to think this through. He was so close to success. One more ceremony, that was all he needed. The demon was weak. It couldn't hold out against another direct attack.

He looked around the library. He loved this room. Loved the house he had decorated to his own specifications.

Was it time to leave? Yes, he'd better go to one of his other residences. For now. When he had all the power a man might need, he would come back and reclaim his rightful place.

But first he had some things to do.

JACK brought up some pictures of Acuras.

"Any of those look familiar?"

She peered at the shapes. "I don't think so."

They went on to Mercedes-Benzes.

She leaned forward, peering at the screen. "Not that."

When he brought up Saabs from the early '90s, she gasped. "Yes!"

"It's got the strange projection over the back window, all right. And there's nothing else quite like it. I should have thought of it myself."

He was typing in another web address. It turned out to be the Department of Motor Vehicles. After giving his police authorization, he waited for a menu to appear.

First he went into the database of vehicle registrations. In the state of Maryland, there were only eight men who owned all of the cars in question—an early '90s Saab, an '88 Ford Crown Victoria, and a van.

Jack marked their names, then went to the register of licensed drivers.

Kathryn watched, her heart pounding, as he brought up the driver's license of the first guy, James Butterworth.

They stared at the picture. Butterworth was a sixty-year-old black man. Definitely the wrong guy.

They went on to Timothy Folger. He was white. But he had close-cropped red hair and had gotten his license only two years earlier—as soon as he was of legal age.

"Simon Gwynn." Jack read the next name on the list, then brought up the picture on his driver's license.

Kathryn gasped as she stared at the color picture. "That's him. Without the wig and the mustache or the old-man makeup."

Jack let out the breath he must have been holding. "One and the same."

They looked at each other, and she felt the sense of triumph bubbling between them. He jumped up, picked up his cell phone from the table, and pressed the activation button.

"You're calling Granger?"

"Yes." He punched in the number, then waited, tapping his foot. When the captain came on the line, he said, "I've identified the bastard through his car registration and driver's license." He walked back to the computer screen. "His name is Simon Gwynn. He lives at 2935 Tilbury Way. A pretty swanky address."

In response to something Granger said, he answered, "Then bring him in for questioning. Kathryn and I will come down there and identify him as the guy who tried to inject the insulin into my IV line."

He hung up, turned to her. "Granger is sending Culligan and two uniformed officers to bring him in."

"So we're going back to Rockville?"

"Let's wait until we hear from the captain." He looked at the phone in his hand. "I want to stay out here where Black—uh—Gwynn won't be looking for us, and I want to see how the kids are doing at Ross's."

He punched in another number, and the phone was answered almost immediately.

"So how is everything going?" Jack asked.

She saw him grin, then listen some more. "We may be able to pick them up tomorrow. But don't say anything yet. I'd like to talk to Craig and Lily, if they're not too busy."

She smiled as he spoke to each of his children in turn. It was obvious that the kids still needed reassuring. And Jack told them that he'd be seeing them soon.

When he had completed the call, he looked better than she'd ever seen him. More at ease. "When Granger picks up Gwynn, he'll call us." He looked at his cell phone. "There's no reason why we can't go out for something to eat."

"Okay," she agreed, when what she really wanted to do was stay here, holed up with him. "Do you want to shower first?" she asked.

"Yeah. But you're going to have to help me in and out of my shirt—and sling."

"I don't mind."

In fact, she enjoyed the intimacy of being close to him, helping him with simple, everyday tasks.

Then she took her own quick shower. They stopped at the office, where the manager recommended an old inn up the road, where they could go dressed in the casual clothes they'd brought.

The restaurant was charming, with log walls that contrasted nicely with crisp white linen. The waitress found them a table in the corner by a fireplace.

The crisis was over, and she wanted to talk about what might happen between them now. But they were both worn out, and she didn't want to put any pressure on him. So they were mostly silent, except when she asked about his shoulder. Or when they discussed what food to order.

They had finished an excellent bruschetta appetizer when his cell phone rang.

With a look of anticipation, he answered. She watched his expression quickly change—heard his low curse.

"Shit!"

Every muscle in her body tensed. From what she could hear of the conversation, she gathered that Gwynn hadn't been home when the cops had arrived.

Jack hung up and took a swallow of the red wine they'd splurged on. "I guess the celebration was a little premature," he said.

"What happened?"

"Gwynn skipped out on us."

"Because we chased him out of the hospital?"

"Maybe. All the cars we identified were in the garage. Granger went back to his DMV record. It turns out that he also owns a Dodge SUV and a Mustang. He's in the SUV."

"Strange he didn't take it to Sugarloaf," she mused.

"I guess he wanted to travel in style when he was going up there to bury bodies."

"Have they dug up the graves?"

"The Frederick County cops have excavated two of the sites that Ross and I marked. There are three more."

Their meal came, and Kathryn was sorry she'd asked about the burial ground. The chicken cacciatore that had sounded so wonderful tasted like paste.

Silently they picked at their food. Then Jack pushed back his chair. "I can't eat any more. But you go ahead."

"That's okay. I can't either."

Outside, they paused in the garden, and she looked around. The feeling of being watched was strong, and she drew closer to Jack.

"What?"

"I just feel . . . spooked."

They drove slowly around the parking lot. There was no Dodge SUV. And no person who looked remotely like the old man or the real Simon Gwynn—which proved nothing, of course.

Still, it was hard to wipe away the dread hanging over her.

"You think he's looking for us?"

"That would be a logical assumption."

"Do you feel like we're being watched?" she whispered.

"Yeah. But not necessarily by Gwynn."

She felt the hairs on her arms prickle. "The demon?"

"I was hoping that if the police picked up Gwynn, he'd leave us alone. Now I have to assume he's still around."

"We haven't seen him recently."

Jack shrugged. "You mean since he set you on fire in that last dream?"

She made a low sound. "Right, since then. I've felt like he wasn't in this world. Maybe he can't stay here for long periods of time."

"Maybe."

They rode silently back to the cabin, where she watched Jack set his gun and his phone on the table, then settle down in front of the computer. "You sleep for a couple of hours," he said. "I'm going to see what else I can find out about Simon Gwynn."

He was right; they had to take turns sleeping. So she crawled under the covers, conscious of the scent of lovemaking. She glanced over at him. For almost an hour he'd been happy and relaxed. Now his face was as grim as she'd ever seen it. It hurt to look at him, so she rolled onto her side and pulled the covers up to her chin.

This time, there was no interference with her sleep. As she drifted off, her last thought was that she was being given a precious gift.

It was dark, with the only light coming from the cracked bathroom door when Jack gently shook her shoulder. She sat up and rubbed her eyes.

"I hate to wake you."

"It's okay." She turned her face, kissed his cheek.

His hand came up to stroke through her hair. "I was going to let you sleep all night. Then I figured I'd better get some rest."

"Yes. You need to sleep, too." She wanted to lie beside him. Just hold him while he slept. But she knew that was too dangerous.

So she climbed out of bed and forced the conversation back to business. "What else did you find out about Gwynn?"

He eased under the covers. "As far as I can figure out, the name is an alias he adopted six years ago."

"Oh."

"I have no idea what his real name is. Probably he's used other names, too."

She nodded, still standing beside the bed, looking down at the man she loved.

His next words were hardly romantic. "The gun and the phone are on the table."

"Yes. Thanks."

He lay back and closed his eyes. She carried the weapon into the bathroom while she used the facilities. By the time she came back to the bedroom, it looked like Jack was already asleep.

After switching on the lamp, she picked up the book that he'd been reading earlier, *Portal to Another Universe*.

It was hard going—full of convoluted sentences. The best she could do was thumb through it, picking up various bits of information.

"The magic circle was a bastion, its protection paramount, a girdle of tutelage against the cosmic forces which waited in the ether to overwhelm him and tear him asunder. There were yet forces which might leap the moat and challenge him."

She shook her head as she tried to work her way through that. Was it English? Sort of. But she could translate it into clearer terms: The magician protects himself within a magic circle, yet the circle doesn't offer absolute protection.

She set the book on the table, got up, and walked restlessly around the room. But she was drawn back to the volume. Opening it to another section, she read:

"The magician must make his bargain with the forces of the universe in a bubble of utter and serene calm. He must subjugate all external abstractedness to his will. Distraction from his purpose is the fatal flaw in the attainment of his goal through magic agency, and may lead to the disharmony of all he strives to achieve."

Okay—so that seemed to be saying that the magician had to concentrate fully to make his ceremony work.

She wanted to get up and pace again. Instead, she stayed with the book. Despite the convoluted language, she was gaining some understanding by reading it.

A passage caught her eye, and she felt her breath go shallow. "The sacrificial victims are of two discrete modes. One is passive—rendered unconscious by the magician. That is the way of safety. But the victim's consciousness is the bolder stroke, for the terror of the one to be sacrificed is a powerful enhancement to the working of the spell."

She shuddered. That was pretty clear. You could have your sacrifice unconscious—or awake. Awake was better, because then you could use her fear as part of the ceremony. The downside was that you'd have trouble controlling her.

She felt nausea rise in her throat, trying to picture what kind of person would want to follow this advice. She huddled in the chair, fighting the feeling that someone was watching her. Her and Jack.

Around the edges of the curtains, gray dawn was filtering into the room. But there were still dark shadows gathered in the corners. She kept turning her head quickly, her gaze probing those corners and the line where the ceiling met the wall. The notion came into her head that the demon was here—that it had been reading over her shoulder. Or, even more spooky, that it had been picking the passages it wanted her to know about.

She struggled to release the claws of fear jabbing at her. All along Jack had felt some outside force was using him—them. And he'd been right. The thing had burned her. Terrified her. But it had also saved Jack from the dog. And she had to thank it for that. If the truth be told, she had to thank it for bringing them together.

She looked over at the man sleeping on the bed, one arm strapped to his chest. So many of her relationships with men had turned out to be disappointments. This one might turn out the same, yet what she'd found during the short time with Jack was precious to her.

"So, why did you pick us?" she asked, her breath stilling as she waited for an answer. "Why did you throw us together?"

If the thing was here, it didn't choose to answer the question.

Dawn had broken outside the window, and she lowered her voice, thinking that it would be a shame not to give Jack a few more hours of sleep—if he could get them.

"Why couldn't you just tell us Gwynn's name?" she asked.

A jumble of images flooded her mind then. She saw Gywnn, standing inside a circle, a circle she knew gave him some kind of protection—from humankind and from the demon's kind as well.

So what could you do to the circle to make it less effective?

She was pondering that when the cell phone on the table suddenly rang, making her jump.

Jack instantly sat up, and she brought him the instrument.

Pressing the Transmit button, he said, "Hello."

She saw his face drain of color. "You lying bastard!" he shouted, but he kept the phone pressed to his ear.

23

JACK'S vision blurred as he listened to the gloating voice on the other end of the line.

"I have your daughter."

"I don't believe you, you scum," he answered, because he didn't want it to be true.

"Well, I'd let you talk to her, but she's sleeping at the moment."

He couldn't hold back a strangled protest.

"Call your friend, Ross Marshall. I'll be back in touch with you in fifteen minutes. And don't call the cops. The second you call in your cop buddies, she's dead."

The phone clicked off, and he was left with the feeling that he would never draw another full breath.

Kathryn came into focus.

"Please—tell me what's happened," she breathed.

"The bastard says he has Lily."

"Oh, God," she gasped, and moved to his side, wrapping her arm around his shoulder even as he began punching numbers again. He felt the tension in her arm. When he finished, he pressed his hand over hers.

Ross came on the line almost immediately.

"Is Lily there?" Jack asked in a voice that was barely under control.

He heard his friend make a sharp, anguished sound. "Jack, she's not in her bed."

"You're supposed to be watching her!"

"Jesus, you don't have to remind me of that."

Jack struggled to get control of his anger as he listened to Ross's explanation.

"Yesterday, she wanted to go down and play at the creek, and I told her she had to stay up here. She was . . . upset about that. We've gone down there before, but I told her it wasn't a good idea this time, and that she needed to stay in the house unless Megan or I went out with her. I thought she was okay with that."

He dragged in a breath. "Then, a few minutes ago, Craig came into our room to say that she was missing. We've torn the house apart. I was just going down to the creek to check."

Jack closed his eyes, imagining it. Lily had promised she wouldn't get into trouble again. But now she was under a lot of stress. She'd lost her mother three years ago, and she was worried about her father. It seemed the combination was too much for her.

"Maybe she's down at the creek," Ross was saying.

"Yeah. Let's hope so. Unfortunately, I got a call from the killer. He says he's got her."

"Jesus." Ross stayed on the line, and Jack could hear his friend breathing hard as he sprinted outside. There was the sound of an engine turning over, then tires squealing on gravel. He waited centuries for the car to skid to a halt again, then pictured the bridge across the creek and the shallow water running over rocks underneath.

When he heard Ross curse, he felt his heart stop. "What! What is it?"

"I smell him. He was here, all right."

"Oh, Christ."

"Jack, I'm so sorry."

"I know. It's not your fault." He forced himself to say the words that must be said. "You told her to stay in the house, and she went out. She's . . . she's in a phase . . . where she makes her own decisions."

"I should have kept better watch on her."

"I should have told you that she hasn't exactly been a model of obedience lately, but I thought we'd worked it out. A few days ago, she and a friend were going to the other girl's house after school. They took a detour—and got into some trouble." While he spoke, he heard noises on the line and knew that Ross was already back in his SUV.

"Jack, I don't think she's been gone long. I'll go out on the road. See if I can spot him. Do you know what he's driving?"

"A Dodge SUV. He's going to call me back"—he looked at his watch—"in three minutes. I'll let you know what he says."

"Okay."

Kathryn had been standing stone still. Now she turned and wrapped him in her arms.

"Oh, Jack. I'm so sorry."

He let himself lean into her, laying his head against her shoulder, trying to hang on to the tattered shreds of his emotions.

When the phone rang, he almost jumped out of his skin, then glanced at his watch. Not three minutes.

He eased away from Kathryn, needing the space. Should he answer? What if it was Granger? If it was, he couldn't answer the call.

He debated in an agony of indecision, then pressed the button. "Hello."

"I see you talked to your friend."

"What are you doing, monitoring my calls?" he asked, already knowing the answer to the question. The curse of the cell phone, he thought. But he hadn't figured the guy could get to him that way.

"You can probably work out how I'm doing it. If you have the time. But I think you're going to be too busy."

"I want my daughter back."

"She would make a good sacrifice. Youth and innocence count for a lot."

"No!"

"The thought of my killing your little girl distresses you?"

"You bastard!"

"Keep a civil tongue in your head when you talk to me."

Jack swallowed, struggled to stay calm and clearheaded—and to remember everything he knew about hostage negotiation. Not enough. "Okay," he answered.

"I'll use your beautiful little daughter if I have to. But she's not the one I want. You can get her back."

"How?"

"By trading her for Kathryn Reynolds."

A curse sprang to his lips. "No."

"It's your decision. You know, like that movie *Sophie's Choice.* Um—didn't Sophie end up killing herself?" Gwynn continued in a silky voice. "I'll give you a few more minutes to think about it. Meanwhile, if you call the cops, I'll kill her. And if you call Ross Marshall back, I'll kill her for that."

The phone went dead, and Jack was left listening to empty air, feeling like a wrecking ball had hit him in the chest. He struggled to catch his breath, struggled not to scream out his anger and his anguish.

"What does he want?" Kathryn asked, her arm moving toward him, then falling back, as though she weren't sure what to do—how to help him.

There was nobody who could help him now. He didn't want to tell her, but he understood that keeping silent was not an option. Slowly, he raised his eyes to hers. "He said he was willing to trade Lily for you."

He saw the blood drain from her face, felt his own spirit shrivel. He had to drag in a breath before he could manage to say, "God, I can't lose her. And I can't lose you."

"Oh, Jack." She moved swiftly then, reached for him, clung with a terrible strength. "It's all right. I can do it."

He felt too numb to answer. Lord, had he heard her right? Without a moment's thought, she was volunteering to trade herself for Lily. A sound of anguish welled from deep inside him as he used his good arm to pull her closer. He wanted to tell her not to do it. But he couldn't say that. "Kathryn," he managed. "Why?"

She drew back so she could meet his eyes. "Jack, I met her at the hospital. She's such a good kid. She doesn't deserve to be dragged into this."

"She went out of the house when Ross told her to stay inside!"

"I know, but she's just a little girl."

"Oh, God, Kathryn, what am I going to do?"

"Let me get her back for you."

"She could already be dead," he said in a choked voice. "That would be just his style."

"Don't think that way!"

He could only stand there, despairing.

"Jack, she can't fight him off. But I can."

He found himself arguing with her when he still felt so numb that he knew his brain hadn't caught up with his mouth. "How? Nobody's fought him off. Heather is dead. Swinton is dead. And a bunch of others. We don't even know how many."

She stroked her hands gently over his back. "Jack, I won't lie to you. I'm scared. But *there is no alternative.* Is there?"

He fought the sick feeling threatening to surge up his throat. Defeated, he whispered, "No."

"I know more than Heather. More than Swinton. We've been into this thing for days. And I . . . I was reading that book Ross gave us. It's got a lot of information."

He pulled away from her. "Information! Christ, if this were about information, we'd have him in custody," he shouted. Then, more quietly he said, "I can't ask you to do it."

"I know you can't. But I will."

"God, no. I can't lose her—and I can't lose you," he said again, because it was the only thing he *could* say.

"Which is why you can't be the one to make the decision. Jack, I love you," she whispered. "I wasn't going to say that. But I want to say it now. Maybe it sounds crazy, but I saw your family, and I loved them, too."

Before he could answer, the phone rang again, and he felt dizzy. "Hello," he said.

"What's your answer?" Gwynn said.

"Kathryn is willing to come to you."

"Excellent."

"How do I know you'll keep your end of the bargain?"

"You don't. You'll have to take my word for it."

He bit back another oath.

"We'll have an exchange. When I have Reynolds, I'll tell you where to find your beautiful little daughter. But don't make any calls."

"All right."

"Bring Reynolds to the old Caldwell farm. It's on Route 97. After Logan Road. When you're coming from the Frederick area, start looking for a mailbox with the number 9507. It's about a quarter-mile farther on. Then an eighth of a mile up a gravel lane to the farmhouse. The front door is unlocked. Put Reynolds in the living room and leave. I want her tied up, by the way. You'll find rope there. Leave as soon as you drop her off—and start driving toward Damascus. After I have Reynolds, I'll tell you where Lily is. And remember, no phone calls—or I kill the kid. You have all that?"

"Yes."

"Repeat it back to me," Gwynn ordered.

In a low, gritty voice Jack repeated the instructions, watching Kathryn. She looked so beautiful. So calm. Yet he saw the tightness around her eyes.

"Leave Charles Town right away."

"You know we're in Charles Town?"

Gwynn laughed. "I know everything. That's why I always get what I want."

The phone went dead, and Jack was left feeling as though he'd stepped into a frozen arctic wasteland, the cold wind burning his skin to the bone.

He saw Kathryn watching him.

"We have to go," she said.

He closed his eyes, clenched his fists, fighting not to scream. He felt her cross to him, felt her brush her lips against his. He pulled her close, crushing her mouth to his, devouring her, drinking in the taste of her.

She was the one who pulled away first. Crossing to the luggage, she opened her bag and took out the magic wand.

"If you take that with you, he'll find it."

"I'm giving it to you."

"Why?"

"I don't know. I think you'll need it." She held the wand toward him.

He took the other end, and for a moment they stood there, each holding one end of the hard plastic. It should feel cool, but somehow heat seemed to pulse in the depths of the blue liquid.

He felt like he was in one of their dreams as he shoved his gun into his waistband, then left the cabin and walked toward the car.

Dark clouds had gathered in the sky, the gloom hanging over him like a shroud.

When Kathryn started to climb into the driver's seat, as she'd been doing since he'd left the hospital, he stopped her. "No. I'd better drive."

"Why?"

"Because I have to drive away from the damn farmhouse. I'd better start doing it now. Thank God you've got an automatic."

He was grateful that he had something to focus on. After dropping the wand on the seat beside his hip, he leaned forward, shifting into reverse with his left hand, then let go and turned the wheel, thinking he'd better be careful and not crash the car.

Then he pulled around and down the narrow lane that led to the highway.

Kathryn was sitting beside him, her hands folded in her lap.

"I love you," he said. "I never thought I'd say that to any woman again."

She turned toward him, her eyes shimmering with tears. "Thank you for telling me that. I know it makes this harder for you."

His voice was steel as he said, "I'll get you out of this. I promise."

"I know."

"Did you see *The Last of the Mohicans*?"

"Yes."

"Do you remember what he said to her when he had to let the Indians take her captive? He said, 'Stay alive. Stay alive, and I will find you.'"

"Yes."

"Do it!"

"I will."

"I'll beat the crap out of you if you don't," he said, knowing he was speaking nonsense.

She laughed, moved closer, and laid her head on his shoulder.

"There's stuff I want to tell you. Stuff I'm thinking about how I'm going to get you back. But I can't tell you any of it. If I do, he might get it out of you."

"I understand." Closing her eyes, she murmured, "Let's talk about something else. Tell me what I have to look forward to."

He swallowed hard. "Will you marry me?"

"Oh, yes."

"You're not afraid to be a stepmother?"

"I'll have Mrs. Anderson to help me—if she lets me in the house."

"Oh, she will!"

She nodded against his shoulder. Then whispered, "Well, since I've got you in the position where you can't say no to me, tell me we can have a baby together. You have two wonderful kids. I want one of your children."

"Wonderful! A couple years ago it was Craig who was acting out. Now it's Lily. I want to strangle her," he grated, his hand clamping on the wheel as he struggled to keep his anger from breaking through.

"Just hug her when you get her back. Hug her for me."

He nodded, because he knew if he tried to speak, he would start to sob.

He wanted to scream. He wanted to drive the car into a tree so he wouldn't have to drive to that farmhouse. Then the choice would be taken away from him. Instead, he kept the vehicle pointed toward the cliff at the end of the world, while they kept talking about the future—each clinging to what hope the other could give.

All too soon, he was turning onto the rutted drive. He kept hoping against hope that the farmhouse wouldn't be there. But it was where Gwynn had said it would be.

SIMON watched them from the dark shadows of the woods, his excitement growing to almost overwhelming proportions. They were here! He hadn't been absolutely sure they would show up. But they were here, and he had won. In a little while, he would go get the woman, and then he would complete the ceremony.

He'd thought about whether he was going to give back the little girl. He'd decided to do it for now. She'd keep Thornton busy.

Later, when he had the demon in his power, he would finish off Thornton—and his family.

But not yet.

He watched them get out of the car, watched their jerky movements. They were scared. Good.

He stayed where he was, watching from a distance. He wasn't going to take a chance on Thornton pulling something tricky. He'd acted like a man who knew he was defeated, but his cop instincts could still kick in.

So Simon would wait until Thornton left, then wait twenty more minutes before going down to the house to get the woman.

Still, it was hard to stay where he was. Hard to contain his excitement.

STIFFLY, Jack got out of the car, the magic wand stuffed into one side of his waistband and the gun into the other. His footsteps rang hollowly as he climbed the sagging wooden steps, vividly aware of Kathryn right behind him.

The door opened, and he stepped into a bare room, then cursed.

"What?"

"I should have brought a blanket for you to sit on."

"I'm sure I won't be here long."

She looked at the rope lying on the floor. "He wants you to tie me up."

"Yes."

Her face blank, she sat down, took the cord, and used it to tie her ankles. He was hardly able to watch her, hardly able to believe she was preparing herself for her own kidnapping. Then they both worked at tying her hands, since the sling would have made the maneuver impossible for him to do it alone.

When he was finished, he could barely breathe as he stared at the bonds. He reached toward her, but she shook her head.

"You have to go," she whispered. "You have to go to Lily."

"Oh, God, Kathryn. I *will* get you back."

"I know."

He prayed he wasn't lying. Quickly he kissed her and walked out of the room, because if he didn't do it quickly, he would never do it.

The tears in his eyes made it almost impossible to see as he staggered outside. It had started to rain, the cold drops pelting him as he walked woodenly to the car and lurched it down the road. It took several moments before he realized he'd forgotten to turn on the windshield wipers.

He switched them on, and the windshield cleared, but his vision was still blurred by tears as he drove toward Damascus—his heart pounding as he waited for the phone to ring.

24

HE screamed curses he would never have used in front of Kathryn, pounded his good hand against the steering wheel. Cursed the bastard who had put him into the fires of hell.

He didn't know what made him pull the magic wand from the waistband of his jeans.

As soon as his hand closed around it, it felt burning hot. He held it up, looking at the swirl of blue and the flecks of shiny stars and moons. The damn thing looked as cool as it ever had. But it felt like a white-hot poker.

He shoved it into the sling so it rested along his arm, grasping the hard plastic with his right hand.

Then he started driving through the rain again, the burning wand giving him a strange kind of comfort.

He came to a crossroad, sped past, then gasped as the rod turned from furnace to ice in his hand.

"Jesus!"

When he screeched to a stop on the wet pavement, it warmed again. When he made a U-turn, the temperature increased. It grew even hotter when he turned right on the crossroad.

His heart leaped into his throat. Daring to give himself a sliver of hope, he kept driving through the pounding rain, braking again when the rod turned freezer cold.

It was telling him which way to go. He knew that in his gut. Like the child's game. "You're getting warmer." Only this was no game.

"You're showing me where to find Lily?"

There was no answer—just the burning plastic against his hand.

He hadn't thought beyond Gwynn's phone call. Now he knew there was something else he could do. Turning in at a gas station, he leaped out and fumbled the correct change into a pay phone, rain pelting his back as he called Ross.

"Where the hell have you been?" his friend demanded.

"Gwynn told me he'd kill Lily if I called anybody. I figured he's got a line on the cell phone. I hope to God he's not using magic to monitor every pay phone in the area. I'm at a gas station on Woodfield Road." Quickly he told his friend what had happened. "The magic wand is leading me to Lily. Meet me out here. When I know she's safe, I'll go back for Kathryn. He won't be expecting me back so soon. He thinks I'm going to be driving miles out of my way. But I'm close to her. Very close."

"I'm on my way. I called Granger. Where's Kathryn?"

Jack gave the address. "For God's sake, tell him to be careful."

"He understands."

Jack splashed back to the car, then sped down the road again, his tires throwing up curtains of water as he let the hot and cold temperature of the wand guide him. To his daughter—he hoped.

While he drove, he muttered out loud. Talking to the demon, he supposed. "You bastard, what do you want from me?"

If you let him get me, you and your family are all dead. The words were very faint, only an echo in his mind. Maybe he'd made them up, but he didn't think so.

"Why did you let him get her? You could have stopped him," he shouted.

No. Too weak. You must do it.

Jack cursed, then braked as the rod clamped in his fingers turned to ice.

KATHRYN sat with her head pressed against the wall, the hard surface anchoring her to sanity. Her bound hands were crossed in her lap; her heart was pounding.

She'd gone from calm acceptance to pulsing fear and back again. She'd helped Jack tie her up. She'd volunteered for this. Now she was covered with ice-cold perspiration and wondering about her own sanity.

Except that she saw no alternative. She couldn't let Gwynn use Lily in his ceremony.

But, oh God, now what?

She had to think. But her brain felt like a big bowl of rice pudding. Closing her eyes, she listened to the sound of rain drumming on the roof as she ordered herself to take shallow, even breaths.

Stay alive, Jack had said, *stay alive.*

If her hands and feet hadn't been tied, she might have jumped up and run like hell.

But that wasn't an option. She had volunteered to come here, and she couldn't leave.

So how was she going to keep this bastard from killing her? By being docile? By fighting him? By talking back? Stroking his ego? She didn't know what approach was best.

Above the roaring in her ears, she thought she heard footsteps splashing through the rain outside, and her eyes snapped open.

She was looking into the gray eyes of Simon Gwynn, and down the barrel of a gun.

Except for the wig and mustache, he was the man she had seen at the hospital. Instead of a white coat, he was wearing a black silk shirt and black trousers.

She wanted to tell him that black was the wrong color for blonds, but she decided to keep that observation to herself.

Somehow she held her gaze level, somehow she kept from clenching her bound hands as every rational thought fled from her brain.

He studied her for painful heartbeats, the silence making her skin crawl. "So good of you to sacrifice yourself for the child," he finally said. "But then I thought you would. Gary told me so much about you—how nicey nice you were, how you were always so concerned for Heather DeYoung. You know, the irony is that it was you I wanted all along. But I had to be careful. I couldn't take another redhead so soon, so I decided Heather would do. And Swinton made it easy for me. All I had to do was offer him a lot of money, and he drugged her and brought her right to me. And he kept you distracted by those nasty pranks of his, like the trick with the fishing line." He laughed. "Of course, he did it because he hated your guts. He told me all that when he was trying to get me to let him go—instead of using him in that nasty little ceremony where I drove Detective Thornton off the road.

"And now you're here because you think your detective is going to come back and rescue you? Well, you'll be long gone from this place before he gets back."

She couldn't stop her throat from closing, and she knew he sensed her fear.

He stared at her, and she tried to read the expression in his cold gray eyes. Should she keep him talking? Flatter him? Beg? She canceled that. One thing she knew—begging wouldn't work.

"Jack thinks I'm on his side. I could ... you know ... change sides ..." she heard herself saying. "I want a strong man. You're stronger than Jack."

He laughed. "That's right. But I don't believe you. You're like Patience."

"Who?"

"The girl who tricked me so long ago. You look a lot like her with that pretty red mane."

She struggled to hold back a moan as he hunkered over her and wound his fingers in her hair, holding it up and letting it fall back into place, before he slapped a piece of duct tape over her mouth. Next he pulled a hood over her head, and she was thrown into terrifying darkness.

*   *   *

JACK went back to the crossroad and howled in agony when the damn thing stayed icy. Then he figured out he'd turned the wrong way.

Five minutes later, he was driving up another rutted lane—his tires sinking into puddles as he skidded to a halt. Throwing his door open, he dashed through the cold rain and charged into another abandoned farmhouse.

His wet shoes almost sent him sprawling on the wooden floor as he sped through the house. He found Lily in one of the bedrooms, curled on her side, sleeping. She whimpered when he picked her up and gathered her close with his good arm, crying out his relief as he rocked the precious bundle against him.

He had her. Thank the Lord, he had her. He slid down to the floor, cradling her in his lap as he took a colossal risk and called Ross, praying that the magician was too busy now to be monitoring phone calls.

Jack gave Ross his location and asked him to come get Lily. Hanging up, he leaned against the wall, holding his daughter in his lap, trying not to weep. He was stroking her silky hair, listening to the sound of her breathing, when Ross charged through the door.

Lily stirred against him, and Jack tensed. But she didn't wake. He was torn. He wanted to talk to her, assure himself that she was all right. And he knew she would want him there when she woke. But he couldn't have everything.

"Take her to the hospital. Make sure she's all right. And call Emily, get her to meet you there," Jack said, stroking his lips against Lily's soft cheek, then lifting his head, his gaze burning into Ross's. "I'm going back for Gwynn."

His friend gave him a critical look. "You're in no shape to go after him on your own."

"Granger's on the way. You take Lily."

"Okay."

Ross picked up the child, cradling her in his arms. Jack stood with his shoulders pressed to the wall, trying to catch his breath, taking one last look at his sleeping daughter before trotting back to the car.

For a time, the magic wand shoved into the wet fabric of his sling had been just a hard rod of plastic. Now it burned his flesh again.

He started the car, heading back toward Logan Road.

When the phone rang, he pulled onto the shoulder and answered as quickly as he could.

"Hello."

"Your daughter is at 9037 Carter Drive."

Pretending he didn't already have Lily, he shouted, "You're not lying to me?"

"Go pick her up."

I already did, you bastard. And now I'm coming to get you, if Granger isn't already turning in to the drive.

Jack drove as fast as he could through the pounding rain—one hand on the wheel and the other wrapped around the magic wand. It was hot again, and this time it was directing him toward Kathryn.

Only he didn't need magic. He knew where he was going to find Gwynn.

Just a few more miles, he kept chanting in his mind. Gwynn wasn't expecting him to have picked up Lily and come back so soon.

The phone rang again, and he cursed as he pulled to the shoulder so he could answer.

It was Granger. "Jack, I'm sorry. The house your friend sent us to is empty."

"Empty!"

"He's cleared out."

"God, no!" he shouted into the phone. He had been so sure that, with his head start, he could get back to Kathryn before Gwynn took her out of there. He'd been counting on that advantage. He'd been wrong.

Granger was speaking, and he realized that he'd missed part of the conversation. Then the phone went dead.

"Fuck!" He stared at the instrument—pressed buttons. Nothing happened, yet the battery showed enough of a charge to receive a message. If he'd been in his unmarked, he would have put in the spare battery, but he was in Kathryn's car. He opened the glove compartment, rummaged through gas station slips and her owner's manual, but found nothing useful.

"Fuck!" he said again, because there was no other way to deal with his frustration.

Then he forgot about the phone as the magic wand flared hot, then went ice cold, then hot again.

"What the hell?"

You must go to her. Hurry.

"Did you turn off my phone?"

Yes.

"Jesus, what are you thinking? You think I don't need Granger's help?"

You must do it by yourself.
"Why?"
No others may see.

He shouted out another oath, then pulled back onto the road and pressed his foot on the accelerator—following the heat of the wand.

HE was strong. Kathryn had found that out when he'd picked her up, slung her over his shoulder, and carried her to a car.

She lay there on the backseat in her damp clothing, forcing herself not to scream when he tightened the knots on her bonds.

Cold and shivering, she heard him talking to Jack—telling him where to pick up his daughter.

A scream bubbled in her throat.

Jack had to go get Lily now. Then he'd come back to the farmhouse, and it would be too late for her.

Jack. Oh God. Jack, find me. Please, find me.

The phone call was over quickly. He clicked off, drove on. All too soon they were slowing down again. Cutting the engine, he climbed out and opened the back door, and she steeled herself to feel his hands on her again.

If she could have screamed, she would have. But the duct tape kept her terror locked in her throat.

He picked her up, carried her through the cold rain, then under some kind of shelter.

A porch? She heard a key turning in a lock. A door opened, then slammed behind them as he walked across a hard floor that magnified the sound of his footsteps.

Then they were going down a flight of steps.

Her heart pounded. The spit in her mouth had turned to stone.

Another door opened. Seconds later, he laid her on a hard surface. She felt him cutting the cord that bound her legs, and kicked out at him.

"Is that how you plan to help me?" he growled as his fist pounded into her stomach. The pain made her gasp. By the time she could breathe again, he'd secured her legs to rings at the end of the table.

It was all happening too fast, and there was no way to fight the terror.

He fingered the cord on her hands, then pulled them above her head and secured them to a metal ring.

When she was immobile, he pulled the hood off her head, a smile flickering on his lips as his gaze swept over her.

The breath froze in her lungs as she stared up at him. When she'd told Jack she would change places with Lily, she had never in her imagination thought that she would end up strapped to a table.

She was going to die here. She knew that now. Unless . . .

Please, she silently begged. *Please take the gag off my mouth.*

"You just relax," he said. "I must purify myself for the ceremony. I'm sorry you can't see the chamber in my primary residence. This is just a poor substitute—a room I fixed up in case I needed a cozy place to work away from home." He stopped and laughed, reaching out to stroke his fingers against her hair.

"Such beautiful hair," he murmured. "I love red hair—like Patience. Since we broke up, I've had a thing for redheads. I was going to take you that morning—before I caught you and Thornton on the lawn. But now everything's worked out the way I wanted."

His hand moved down to her cheek, and she struggled not to cringe.

"Heather had a pure white ceremonial gown. I don't want to take a chance changing your clothes. Not when I already have you tied down. But that wet shirt and sweatpants certainly don't look appropriate for an important ceremony."

He turned from her, and when he pivoted back, he had a knife in his hand, the knife she'd seen in the dream.

She gasped behind the gag and tried to twist away, but her bonds kept her in place.

He inserted the knife tip in the damp fabric of her shirt, ripping a line down her side, parting the material and pulling it away. He cut other slashes in the knit, cut the shirt away from her body, then severed her bra straps. In moments, she was naked to the waist.

"Nice," he murmured, looking down at her, tracing the curve of her breasts with his finger.

Unable to stand the look of satisfaction on his face, she squeezed her eyes shut.

When the knife blade touched her thigh, she couldn't hold back a whimpering sound. But he was only cutting away her sweatpants and panties, leaving her naked on the table.

His hand skimmed the triangle of hair at the base of her legs. "It's a shame we don't have more time," he murmured. "But since time is of the essence and you came to me of your own free will, I'll make it easy on you. We'll do it as soon as possible. You won't have to wait too long for me to plunge my knife into your heart."

As she listened to him, every muscle of her body felt like it was fighting an electric current. Then he was gone, and she flopped back against the table.

Jack had told her to stay alive. It didn't look like she was going to manage that. She felt tears stinging the backs of her eyes, but she was too proud to let them leak out.

25

JACK pulled back onto the road, relying on the same method he'd used to find Lily. In the back of his mind, he knew it was the demon controlling the magic wand. But he didn't let himself dwell on that. If he let himself think about what he was doing, he would start to scream. He had started out hating and fearing the creature that had interfered in his life. He still felt those emotions. Yet he knew that he and the creature must work together now, if he was going to save Kathryn's life.

Obscene images rose in his mind. Ruthlessly, he shut them out because they could only drive him mad. With a single-minded purpose, he concentrated on the feel of the hard plastic rod where it nestled inside the sling.

He was learning how to use the damn wand. When the plastic was hot, he sped forward, slowing down when he reached a crossroad, feeling for a subtle change that would tell him whether he should go straight or turn.

He wasn't even paying much attention to the route—just driving like an automaton, through the driving rain, following the directions of the wand. The directions of the creature.

Somewhere in the western end of the county, he blinked, came out of his dreamlike state as the wand pulsed in his right hand, stinging his skin, shocking him into full awareness.

He was on a narrow gravel lane, much like the lane he'd traveled less than an hour earlier, only longer and wetter.

Coming around a curve, he caught his breath. The SUV was parked in front of a redbrick rancher. A house about forty or fifty years old, he judged. Nothing remarkable.

He looked down at the wand, wondering if it had led him to the wrong place. This couldn't be Gwynn's house. It wasn't grand enough. Yet the wand had told him he was going to find the guy here.

He started to hit the brake hard, then checked himself, slowing gradually so as not to give himself away with a' squeal of tires and a shower of water and gravel.

A new thought struck him, then. Maybe Gwynn wasn't even in the house with Kathryn. Maybe he had planted the car here and gone somewhere else.

He craned his neck, saw that the road ended here. But was there another structure hidden back in the woods?

He didn't have time to make mistakes. He had to act. And the wand was burning so hotly that he could barely stand to keep it inside the sling. But he left it where it was, because the pain helped focus him. Stepping out of the car, he moved quickly toward the house, splashing through a puddle and onto the floor of the porch.

His heart speeded up as he saw a trail of wet footsteps. When he looked through the window, he saw they continued across the floor of the empty living room.

The door was unlocked. Stepping inside, he followed the wet trail across the floor and down a hallway to another door.

KATHRYN lay on the hard table, her skin covered with goose bumps, her nipples tight from the damp and cold. She was alone, but somewhere nearby she could hear Gwynn moving around. Could hear water splashing. Was there still something she could do? Some way to save herself?

It took every scrap of will she possessed not to weep in terror. Holding on to her self-control, she turned her head, looking around for some source of help.

She was in a room like the one she'd seen in the dream. It must be in the basement, judging from the flight of steps he'd carried her down. Black curtains hid the sharp angles of the walls, and candlesticks stood on tables around the room. But none of the candles were lighted. The illumination was low and came from a small lamp on a table in one corner.

This was where she was going to die, she thought with a kind of strange detachment.

Jack, I love you, she murmured inwardly, trying to send the thoughts out to him. *It could have been so good. No. I mean it was good. It just didn't last long enough. I'm so sorry we couldn't have had more together.*

It seemed like only moments later that Gwynn was back. He was naked to the waist, his only garment a pair of silky black trousers.

The trousers were thin, and she saw that he was aroused.

She swallowed, tried to look somewhere else besides that thick rod at the front of his pants. But she couldn't take her eyes off his erection.

When he lowered his hand to stroke himself, she felt the breath solidified in her lungs. Reaching out, he touched one of her tightened nipples with a fingertip. "You want me?" he asked.

The obscenity of the question clogged her throat. She longed to cringe away, but there was nowhere to go, nowhere to hide.

Summoning every scrap of courage that remained, she raised her eyes to his face, seeing the tension and the triumph in his expression.

Please, take off the gag, she silently begged. *You think you know what's going to happen. But let me tell you the truth. You're not going to like it.*

Her hopes crashed as Gwynn turned away. She heard him chanting in a language she didn't recognize, watched as he finished inscribing a white circle on the black floor.

When he was finished, he walked back to the table, still chanting.

Her eyes riveted on the silver knife in his hand. He had used it to cut away her clothing.

Now there was nothing between her flesh and that knife. Not even a thin scrap of fabric.

But he wouldn't just kill her—would he? He'd make it part of his ceremony.

She clutched at that as he bent over her.

With his free hand, he ripped the tape off her mouth, and she bit back a scream of pain.

Dragging in a steadying breath, she let it out in a rush and began to speak—quickly, urgently, knowing that keeping Gwynn's attention was her only chance to do what Jack had asked her to do—to stay alive. "You can hold your ceremony. You can kill me, but you won't get what you want. The demon will kill himself—kill everyone within miles of here—before he lets you capture him."

She saw at once that she'd scored a point. He'd been looking like a man in total control of events. Now a flicker of uncertainty invaded his features.

"What do you think you know about it?" he demanded.

She forced herself to meet his gray eyes. "More than you want me to know. Have you read a book called *Portal to Another Universe?*"

"No."

"Pity," she said, hardly able to believe that she could talk coherently. She was naked, totally vulnerable, totally under this man's control. But she wasn't going to give up. *Stay alive. Stay alive.*

"I've heard of the work. It's been lost for centuries."

"You're wrong. My werewolf friend lent me a copy," she tossed off. "I was reading it last night."

"No. You're lying. What do you mean—your werewolf friend?"

"He's Jack's friend. He found your graveyard at Sugarloaf Mountain. And if you get out of this room alive, he'll find you and tear you to pieces."

JACK stood rigid on the other side of the door, his teeth clamped together to keep himself from screaming.

He'd silently turned the knob and pushed the barrier open a crack—then held back a curse as he took in the scene before his eyes. Neither of the people in the room knew he was there. They were too focused on each other.

Kathryn was naked, secured to a table. Gwynn was dressed in his black trousers, leaning over her.

It was all he could do to stop himself from bursting into the chamber and drilling the fucker. But not when he was holding his gun in his left hand. And not when Gwynn was standing over Kathryn with a knife.

Instead he strained his ears. They were talking, and he felt a surge of pride and gratitude. She was doing what he'd asked her to do. Keeping herself alive. Gwynn hadn't started the main part of the ceremony, but he could kill her if he thought he was cornered.

He saw Gwynn's hand move, and he almost leaped through the door, but he forced himself to hold back.

With a snarl of rage, the magician slapped her across the face.

She cried out, then, incredibly, started talking again.

"It won't do you any good to get angry with me. You should have read the book before you got into something too big for any man to handle. It tells about a magician who was trying to do what you're attempting.

"He died. So did a lot of other people. When the demon knew he would lose the struggle, he blew himself up. The description makes it sound rather like a thermonuclear explosion."

"No!"

KATHRYN kept her eyes focused on the magician's twisted face—knowing that some part of him believed her. "You don't have to take my word for it. Go ahead with what you're doing, and you'll find out."

"You can't stop me with your lies," he flung at her.

"I'm not lying. You're welcome to try it—if you think you know more than the last stupid bastard who made the attempt."

"Shut up. Just shut up," he shouted. Whirling away from her, he stood stiffly, chanting again, his voice rising, the tone no longer under his control.

The room seemed to shimmer with a blue light—everywhere except a large area near the top of the far wall, where it looked like a gray cloud had gathered.

She felt breathless, felt a terrible pressure against her chest. It was one of the sensations she had experienced in that place where the creature lived. The demon.

And something else was happening. In the air above her she saw dancing shapes, floating like motes of dust, only larger and shiny.

She stared at them, seeing moons and stars—like the moons and stars from her wand.

Despite everything, an exclamation of wonder welled in her throat, just as the door burst open, and she saw Jack step into the room. He had a gun in his hand.

"POLICE, freeze," Jack shouted.

Gwynn whirled toward him—his arms outstretched—and a tongue of fire that looked like it came from a flamethrower shot from his fingertips, hitting the gun, making it fly out of Jack's hands. The weapon landed on the floor, melted into a twisted shape.

Jack stared at the ruined weapon as he screamed out a curse and staggered back.

The magician whirled away from him, began a louder chant that filled the room, and Jack knew he had launched into the ceremony—hurrying through the preliminaries so he could reach the ending more quickly.

"No! You fool, you'll die with us," Jack shouted.

Gwynn ignored him, his words coming faster and louder as he stepped toward Kathryn, raising the knife above his head.

The air in the room pulsed and thickened, holding Jack in place. Making a tremendous effort, he shook himself free and charged toward Gwynn. Before he reached the magician, he hit the circle on the floor, hit an invisible barrier, and was flung back against the wall—sliding to the cold cement as searing pain reverberated through his shoulder and down his arm.

On the table, Kathryn screamed and struggled, desperate to escape. But she couldn't break free of her bonds.

Jack pushed himself up and somehow staggered to his feet, the clawing pain in his shoulder almost more than he could bear.

The rational part of his mind howled in despair. The magic circle had stopped him, flung him back. But some core of him refused to give up even in the face of what seemed like certain defeat.

Let me in! The words echoed in his head. Low and urgent, the creature's power flared in one last desperate command.

Jack went very still, his eyes fixed on the terrible scene unfolding before him. Gwynn was rapidly building to the climax of his ceremony. And there wasn't a damn thing Jack Thornton could do about it.

He had reached the point of desperation. There was no way he could save Kathryn, nothing left besides surrender to a force that had terrified him from the first moment he had considered the idea that he was no longer in control of his own destiny.

He had battled against that fear. And at the same time, he had fought for his free will with every fiber of his soul, of his body, of his intellect. Yet in this terrible moment of defeat, everything changed. With no other way to save Kathryn, he didn't hesitate to surrender his soul.

"Yes," he screamed, throwing aside his carefully marshaled defenses, inviting the one thing he had fought with strength born of primal dread.

For one moment of unimaginable fear, he was open and vulnerable to powers beyond human imagining. In the next, he felt as though shards of glass had lodged themselves in the tissues of his brain, filled the inside of his head, tearing at each cell with steel claws.

The shock of slicing pain was too great for any human to withstand, and he blacked out for several seconds, standing with his shoulders braced against the wall. Then his eyes blinked open, and he found that somehow he could endure the knives stabbing into his mind.

He saw the scene through a grainy, gray haze that wrapped itself around him. He felt his skin turn icy cold and, at the same time, hot as the fires of hell. Words came to his lips. Words in some ancient language he had never heard and didn't understand. His own magic chant giving him power that no human being had ever possessed or would ever possess again.

His voice rose in strength, filling the room. Gwynn whirled to face him, his features contorted in a mask of shock and rage, his lips moving in a frantic stream of words. But Jack could no longer hear the syllables above the screeching in his ears.

He was almost blind. Almost unable to stand against the tremendous force pressing down against his shoulders. When he tried to draw in a breath, he felt as though his lungs were filling with water. And he knew this was what Kathryn had endured every time she entered one of the dreams.

But she had stood it. And so could he. It took a tremendous effort to raise his arm. Still, he managed it—pain tearing through his injured shoulder as he brought the wand into position. Into firing position.

He had no idea what would happen next. In amazement he watched a stream of molten flames flare from the tip of the plastic tube—like the flames that had come from the magician—only hotter, a mixture of blue and gold like the interior of the wand. As though there had never been a barrier, the flames arrowed past the protective circle, striking Gwynn in the chest.

The magician screamed in agony, his face a mask of rage and shock. For heartbeats, he stayed on his feet. Then he swayed sideways and toppled to the floor, his body lying in a crumpled heap.

The darkness in the room swelled and swirled, like a living, writhing presence. Jack gasped for breath, struggling to pull air into his lungs. Then a shock wave threw him to the ground, followed by a thunderclap that sounded as though the very fabric of time and space had been torn open.

The dark, swirling substance in the room rushed toward a jagged, gaping hole that opened in the air, tugging and pulling at him, so that he thought he would be swept along with it into a dark, airless place where no man could live.

He tried to call Kathryn's name. But once more he lost consciousness.

For long moments, there was only blessed nothingness. When he came back to himself, Kathryn was calling his name.

He opened his eyes, turned his head toward her, blinking as he took in the scene.

"Jack, oh God, Jack. Are you all right? Jack, answer me!"

He pushed himself to a sitting position, staring across at her. She was naked, her cheeks streaked with tears. "Kathryn."

He got to his feet, teetered unsteadily as he crossed the room—crossed the circle that had stopped him moments earlier. First he knelt to check Gwynn, finding no pulse in his neck. Then he staggered to Kathryn.

Leaning over, he delicately touched her hair, pressed his cheek to hers, then turned his head and kissed her on the lips, relief and gratitude surging through him.

"Jack. Thank you for saving me."

"It wasn't just me," he said in a low voice. "The demon led me here. The demon worked that trick with the wand."

"And now he's gone," she said.

"Yes," he answered, realizing as he said the word that it was true. They'd been entwined with the creature for days. Now there was a void where the presence had been.

He let that knowledge sink in as he worked awkwardly to free Kathryn from her bonds, "Did Gwynn . . . hurt you?"

"No," she murmured. "I'm fine—now."

When he'd freed one of her hands, she helped him with the other side.

Once he'd freed her, he kissed her again, then pulled down some of the black drapery and spread it over her naked body, hugging her to him.

Finally, he turned to look around the room. The first thing he saw was the gun. He'd seen it melt. Now it was intact again. And when he picked it up and checked the clip, he found that one round had been fired.

"Jesus!"

Kathryn sat up, clutching the curtain around her. "What?"

"Did you see my gun lying in a melted heap on the floor?"

"Yes."

Quickly he crossed to Gwynn and rolled the magician over. Instead of a burn mark on his front, there was a bullet hole in his chest. A perfect shot to the heart.

"It looks like I shot him," he muttered as he came back to Kathryn. "Is that what you saw?"

"I . . . I saw fire shoot out of the wand."

"Yeah," he answered, picking up the gun and shoving it back into his waistband. He pulled out the wand and looked at it. It was unblemished, the beveled plastic clear and bright, the stars and moons swirling in their blue liquid.

"You said the demon did that?" she asked. "How?"

"I let him into my mind, and he killed Gwynn."

She stared at him. "You let him in? Lord—that must have been . . ." She fumbled for the right word.

"Scary," he supplied. "But it was the only way I could save you—save us."

"Oh, Jack!" She pressed her cheek against his middle, and he stroked his fingers through her hair.

In the distance he heard sirens. He hadn't told Granger where he was going. He hadn't even known. But it sounded like somebody had called the police.

Kathryn pushed herself off the table, swaying on her feet as she pulled the curtain around her like a toga. He steadied her, held her to him.

"We'd better get our stories straight," he said quickly. "I mean—you saw me shoot Gwynn. Because that's the only way anybody's going to believe us."

"Yes." She turned her head. "And how did you find me?"

He ran a hand through his hair, at a complete loss. "Jesus. I don't know."

"You'd looked through records to see what other property Gwynn owns?"

"Yeah. Right. Let's hope he owns this place."

His arm slung around her, they climbed the steps. "We'd better go out," he said. "Before they come in here with guns blazing."

The rain had stopped, and the sun was fighting its way past the clouds as they staggered together onto the porch. Jack slung his good arm around Kathryn as two police cruisers roared into the yard.

Granger jumped out of the unmarked, looking them both over. "I see I missed the excitement," he said.

"Gwynn's down in his ceremonial chamber—dead. I shot him." He pulled out his Sig. "You want this, I assume."

"Yeah."

Granger bagged the gun, and two uniforms entered the house.

"He shot him to save my life," Kathryn said. "He was going to kill me in one of his ceremonies. Like he killed Heather. He cut off my clothing and he was going to stab me in the heart."

Granger nodded, then turned to Jack. "Why didn't you tell me where the hell you were?"

"The phone went dead! I guess you found this place the same way I did—by checking other properties he owned."

"Right," Granger agreed, then looked toward Kathryn. "Do you need medical attention?"

"No." She looked down with distaste at the black curtain. "Do you have anything I can put on?"

"I'd give you my shirt, but getting out of it is a major effort," Jack said.

"I've got some clean gym clothes in the back of my unmarked. If you don't mind a guy's sweats," Granger offered.

"No. That would be fine."

He brought her the clothing, and she disappeared into the bathroom.

While she was gone, the two uniforms emerged, their eyes wide as they reported on the ceremonial chamber and the table where Kathryn had been tied down naked.

Staying on his feet had become too much effort for Jack. He sat down heavily on the damp steps. When Kathryn returned, she sat down beside him, locking her fingers with his good hand.

"He should be back in the hospital," she said, raising her eyes to Granger.

"An ambulance is on the way." The captain scuffed his foot against the gravel of the driveway. "I'm sorry," he said in a low voice. "You were right about this case. I was wrong."

Jack gave a tight nod.

Kathryn raised her chin. "We figured out it was Gwynn who turned in that complaint on us. He was driving past my house, getting ready to kidnap me. But he saw Jack there, and he took an opportunity to try and get Jack off his back."

Granger muttered his agreement with her scenario.

Afraid that Kathryn was going to push the captain harder, Jack tightened his grip on her hand.

She picked up on the signal, looked toward him, then pressed her lips together. And he thought she was going to make a very good cop's wife.

"BEDTIME," Jack said.

"I want to stay up with Kathryn," Lily protested

"I know. But we're practicing listening to what adults tell us."

Lily gave a little nod, her gaze fixed on Kathryn. "But she'll still be here in the morning."

"Yes," Jack said, feeling the thickness in his throat. He'd been torn. He'd never thought that a man with children should move his fiancée into the house. But the thought of her alone in her duplex had made his stomach knot. Intellectually, he knew the danger was over from Swinton, from Gwynn, and from the dreams. Yet he simply couldn't allow her out of his sight. So he'd insisted she move in with the family.

Things were working out pretty well. Emily had volunteered to find a new position. He'd convinced her that the family needed her. And Kathryn had added her voice to the warm assurances, telling the housekeeper how wonderful it was to move into a smoothly running home. But Emily could have some more time to herself now. So the women were working out their relationship. As were the kids and their soon-to-be stepmom.

Craig was a little prickly. Probably because he felt he had to keep the memory of his real mother alive. But Kathryn was dealing with that, too.

"Let's go up, and you can tell me what story you want me to read," Kathryn said to Lily.

"The King's Stilts."

"Okay. And tomorrow after school, we can get some more books out of the library. I'll pick you up, and we'll go right there."

Lily's eyes sparkled. She was sucking up the attention that this new woman in her life seemed to love lavishing on her.

"We can call you when we're ready," Kathryn said to Jack.

"I'll come up with you," he answered, heaving himself off the sofa. He'd reinjured the shoulder in the fight with Gwynn and set back his recovery. But he'd also learned what was important in life.

He wasn't going to miss the moments with his family. So while Kathryn supervised Lily's bath, he stepped into Craig's room and made sure his son's homework was finished, then talked about the Orioles game they were going to attend.

He was coming back down the hall when the conversation in his daughter's room stopped him in his tracks.

"And the same bad man that kidnapped me, kidnapped you," Lily was saying.

"Yes."

"Were you scared?"

"Yes. But I kept thinking your daddy would come rescue me."

"Me, too."

Jack's chest was so tight he could barely breathe. They'd agreed it was better not to tell Lily why Kathryn had ended up in Gwynn's clutches. Maybe when his daughter was older, he'd explain that her stepmom had saved her life. Right now, that was too much of a burden for her slender shoulders to bear.

He stepped through the door, and they both turned to face him. "Sit with us while Kathryn reads," Lily demanded.

"I'd like that," he said, thinking that they'd have to be a little stricter with his daughter. But not now.

A half-hour later, they'd finally turned off the lights, gone into the master bedroom, and closed the door.

It was a masculine room. He'd swept away any feminine overtones a year ago. And he was glad that no traces of his previous relationship lingered here. He'd already told Kathryn she could redecorate any way she wanted.

"Things are going pretty well," he said.

She nodded.

"You're good for Lily."

"I love her. And Craig. And you. And I feel like Emily and I have come to an understanding. She knows she'll always be the kids' grandma, which is wonderful, since neither one of us has any parents left."

He reached for her with his good arm, holding her close as best he could. "I love you so much. When I first saw you, all I could think about was getting you into bed. Now there's so much more I want with you. Lord, I was lucky to find you."

"It's the same for me."

For long moments, they simply clung to each other, caught up in the joy of being alone.

"So—how soon do you think we can manage a wedding?" he asked in a voice that wasn't quite steady.

"Oh, pretty quickly. If we just have Emily and the kids. And Ross and Megan."

"I want you to have a wedding you'll remember. Something fancy."

"Fancy. Right. Just your style." She thought for a moment. "Well, I've heard about a fancy wedding pavilion down at Disney World. Would that do?"

"You're kidding?"

"No. I think it would be fun. And easy. I'm sure they provide all the trimmings—except that I want to splurge on a dress." She warmed to the idea, adding details. "And if Emily will take the kids off for tours of the theme parks after the ceremony, I think we'll all have a wonderful time. We can rent one of those—what are they called?—tree houses. So we end up with a bedroom door that locks."

"Yeah, a door that locks. That better be in the contract."

She snuggled against him, then raised her head and laughed.

"What?"

"Maybe we should film it, so we show it on a Valentine's Day segment of *Oprah*. You know—couples telling how they met."

He chuckled. "Yeah, right. A demon brought us together."

"We never did find out his name." The name was important, they had discovered from reading *Portal to Another Universe*. It was kind of a compulsion, learning all the gory details. The book explained that the magician had to know the demon's name to capture him.

"I just think of him as the SOB," Jack muttered. "He put us through hell."

"Which makes heaven all the sweeter," Kathryn whispered, raising her mouth to his for a long, eager kiss that quickly turned passionate.

Jack looked toward the bed, then back to Kathryn. "I'm sorry you're leaping into the reality of parenthood. But it will be safer if we let the kids settle down for a half-hour first."

"I found that out last night, when Lily stood outside the door, twisting the knob," she answered. "They're curious about us—alone together."

"I know, but things will settle down."

They kicked off their shoes and stretched out on the bed in their clothing—touching and talking and making plans for the future until the heat building between them was too great. Kathryn got up and wove her way on shaky legs to the door, where she checked the lock—then returned to Jack.

As he lay on his back, watching her standing over him, slowly starting to unbutton her blouse, he thought that he was the luckiest man in the world.